THE
ALTERNATE

John Martel

A SIGNET BOOK

SIGNET
Published by New American Library, a division of
Penguin Putnam Inc., 375 Hudson Street,
New York, New York 10014, U.S.A.
Penguin Books Ltd, 27 Wrights Lane,
London W8 5TZ, England
Penguin Books Australia Ltd,
Ringwood, Victoria, Australia
Penguin Books Canada Ltd, 10 Alcorn Avenue,
Toronto, Ontario, Canada M4V 3B2
Penguin Books (N.Z.) Ltd, 182–190 Wairau Road,
Auckland 10, New Zealand

Penguin Books Ltd, Registered Offices:
Harmondsworth, Middlesex, England

Published by Signet, an imprint of New American Library,
a division of Penguin Putnam Inc.
Previously published in a Dutton edition.

First Signet Printing, April 2000
10 9 8 7 6 5 4 3 2 1

ACKNOWLEDGMENTS
"If I Were a Carpenter," by Tim Hardin. Words and music by Tim Hardin.
  Copyright © 1966 (Renewed) Allen Stanton Productions. International
  copyright secured. All rights reserved. Used by permission.
"Star Dust," by Hoagy Carmichael and Mitchell Parrish. © 1929 (Renewed) EMI
  Mills Music, Inc., and Hoagy Publishing Company in USA. All rights
  outside USA controlled by EMI Mills Music, Inc., All rights reserved. Used by
  permission. Warner Bros. Publications U.S. Inc., Miami, FL 33014.
"Thin Line Between Love and Hate," by Robert Poindexter, Richard Poindexter,
  Jackie Members. © 1971 (Renewed) Cotillion Music, Inc. & Win Or Lose
  Music. All rights administered by Cotillion Music, Inc. All rights reserved.
  Warner Bros. Publications U.S. Inc., Miami, FL 33014.

REGISTERED TRADEMARK—MARCA REGISTRADA

Printed in the United States of America

PUBLISHER'S NOTE
This is a work of fiction. Names, characters, places, and incidents are either the
product of the author's imagination or are used fictitiously, and any
resemblance to actual persons, living or dead, business establishments, events, or
locales is entirely coincidental.

I think that what makes life worth all the trouble are the people around you; in the end, little else really matters. This book is for two of those people, whose very existence has perhaps justified my own:

My son, Jay, a lovable soul whose brillance and wit as a writer often move me to boast that I'm a block off the young chip;

My daughter, Melissa, whose beauty, strength, and indomitable spirit have constantly nourished my own.

ACKNOWLEDGMENTS

Special thanks to my agent, Fred Hill, who refused to let me off easy, and to my loving and indispensable wife, Bonnie, who refused to let me drive her crazy. Thanks also to my editor, Brian Tart, and to Dutton president Clare Ferraro, for their wisdom and unsparing support.

I am grateful for the help and encouragement of several good friends with generous hearts and perceptive eyes, especially George Beckwith, Jon Beckman, Barbara McHugh, Bonnie Nadell, Irene Moore, Patsy Smith, Diane McEwan, Mary Eggleston, and to Eileen Cruz, who never said no to frantic late-night pleas for typing help.

I am again indebted to the mysterious and reclusive singer-songwriter Joe Silverhound for permitting me to use words from his songs, this time a blues ballad called, appropriately, "It Kills Me."

Finally, thanks to all my buddies at Farella Braun & Martel, especially Jim Haydel, Randy Wulff, and Doug Young, whose enthusiastic reaction to an early draft provided sustenance for the long trip that lay ahead.

There is something every woman wears around her neck on a thin chain of fear—an amulet of madness. For each of us, there exists somewhere a moment of insult so intense that she will reach up and rip the amulet off, even if the chain tears at the flesh of her neck.

—R. Morgan ("Goodbye to All That," in *Going Too Far,* quoted by Dworkin 1981:101)

PROLOGUE

Lara Ashford, 1974 Miss Nebraska, third runner-up Miss America, and now the occasionally faithful wife of ex-congressman Elliot Ashford, steps out of the bath, wraps herself in a towel, and examines herself in the large mirror over the counter. To "view the wreckage," she muses with an ironic smile.

She turns suddenly, startled by the sound of a door closing downstairs. The maid? No, she left an hour ago for the weekend, on the bus by now. A shudder passes through her, but then music breaks out below and through the upstairs master bedroom speakers. It's Annie Lennox singing "Thin Line Between Love and Hate" good and loud, the way she likes it. The way he knows she likes it.

She relaxes, shouts down for him to make himself a drink.

But her visitor is already charging toward her through the doorway of the bathroom, and Lara Ashford's incipient mock scolding mutates into a scream of terror as her face is slammed hard into the mirror in front of her.

It's a thin line, the music blares, *between love and hate . . .*

As her fingernails tear at the hand that is yanking her head back, the towel slips to the floor and her sudden nudity adds to a sense of hopeless vulnerability. Her face in the mirror is now as white as the Italian marble under her feet but for the blood already spilling down her cheeks.

Come on, baby baby, the music persists, though she isn't hearing it now, *you don't give a damn about me . . .*

For one horrible instant, Lara sees them posed side by side in a blurred macabre portrait, but then the reflected images come speeding toward her again and the mirror collides with her face with shattering force.

She tries to scream but gags on her own blood. She tries

to fight back, but it's the futile struggle of an insect on the end of a pin. The room is growing dark now, her mind succumbing to the merciful paralysis of shock. She is only vaguely aware that the hand still locked onto her neck is again propelling her head toward the splintered mirror, and she knows it now, oh God yes, she knows she's going to die. Maybe she even deserves to die, she thinks, but Jesus, not like this!

It's a thin line, between love and hate . . .

The hand jerks her head back yet again, but it doesn't matter anymore. She looks at herself for the last time, her image fragmented now in the shattered glass as if viewed through a kaleidoscope.

Wreckage.

She hears a voice shouting something, but she can't make out the words as her head is shoved into a final collision with the mirror, fusing what is left of her face with its ghastly reflected image. Spicules of glass merge with splinters of bone, cartilage, and flesh, setting off a blast of exploding light inside her head. Ribbons of blood course down her left breast, spreading across a small black cross tattooed there.

Finally, she is allowed to collapse to her knees, but her head is jerked back once more, exposing her white throat. A towel is wrapped around a gleaming shard of glass and its stiletto tip is thrust into her throat.

As life drains out of Lara Ashford, she is finally blessed with unconsciousness. Blessed because as the end approaches, the point of the glass lance is only beginning its grisly work.

PART ONE

THE INVESTIGATION

Neither the sun nor death can be looked at steadily.

—La Rochefoucauld

I

The various and arcane means by which one human being sometimes ended the life of another had always fascinated Grace Harris, head of the district attorney's homicide trials team, but this one, she thought, took the cake.

"A shard of glass?" she said, as Chief Investigator Sam Quon fished the object from a canvas pouch. Quon, graying hair, medium height, and an unlined, expressionless face that gave no hint of his nearly sixty years, had moved from the police department to the D.A.'s office nearly twenty-eight years earlier.

"Yeah," he said, "this is it." He then offered the eighteen-inch exhibit to Grace Harris with outstretched arms, as an acolyte might hand his bishop a scepter. She gingerly touched the point, then rocked the glass blade in both hands, gauging the heft of it.

"One would think," she said softly, "that a man as wealthy as Elliot Ashford could have used something more elegant."

Quon nodded.

They stood in the center of District Attorney Earl Field's spacious office on the third floor of San Francisco's Hall of Justice, waiting to brief him, knowing he would want to be involved in the press conference soon to begin. They were flanked by luxurious—some said garish—textured silk coverings on which were hung abstract paintings by unknown African-American artists, a form of decor favored by Field over the more traditional service plaques and professional certificates his predecessor had displayed. The district attorney had made a good deal of money in private practice before entering public service and didn't mind showing it off—a practice that both antagonized his detractors and delighted his supporters.

"What broke the mirror?" Grace asked.

"Her face," said Quon.

Grace shuddered as she handed the shard back to the older man. She then picked up the coroner's report and began turning the pages with fingers uncommonly long and graceful for a petite woman. Grace had always been shorter than her friends when growing up and had hated it. Now, at five feet three, though she still sometimes envied those pencil-thin models that would have towered above her, she was grateful at the age of forty-two to still be petite in the right places. Her ankles were trim and shapely, and her flat, firm stomach betrayed no evidence of a pregnancy now sixteen years in her past. Time, and a rigorous regimen of work and exercise, had treated her body kindly, and her facial features were similarly delicate but for eyes that were large and warm and the color of chestnuts.

"Ever meet her, Sam?"

"Once, back when her husband was on the Police Commission. Not too bright, but a real beauty. Long black hair like yours. Same height as you, too. In fact, she looked a lot like you."

"Why, Sam Quon, I think you just complimented me."

"So sue me," said Sam. "Anyway, she was a bit weird, but always smiling, looking much younger than she was. Ashford made life easy for her."

"Not so her death," said Grace softly, still thumbing through the coroner's report. She turned back to page one.

Case number 97-5597, Lara Ashford: The body is that of a forty-four-year-old Caucasian female with brown eyes and black hair, 64 inches in length and weighing 108 pounds.

Grace unconsciously pursed her lips as she skipped down to "time of death," estimated at 8:00 P.M. based on "early nonfixed lividity" and incipient signs of rigor mortis in her neck and jaw. The body was just beginning to cool to the touch when they found her.

Without looking up, she said, "The maid heard Lara arguing with her husband at around seven?"

"Yeah," said Quon, "on the way out for her weekend off. Heard quite a commotion. Five hours later, Ashford claims he 'discovered' his wife's body when he got home.

She'd been dead at least three hours at that point according to forensics."

"Home from what?"

"A movie."

"Of course."

Quon anticipated the assistant D.A.'s next question and added, "Alone. The movie was a rerelease of *A Man for All Seasons* and in its third week. Slow night, only three people on duty and nobody saw him. Ashford couldn't even remember who played the part of Sir Thomas More. Great movie. Bad choice."

Grace arched an eyebrow. "The old 'phantom alibi' routine?"

Quon nodded. "It's strange, isn't it? A rich, smart politician with Mafia connections does his wife, walks off leaving his own blood on her fingertips, and can't come up with a decent alibi in more than three hours?"

Grace nodded. "What else do we have on him?"

"More than you'll ever need," said the chief investigator. "She's murdered not long after the maid hears Ashford screaming at her. Ex-lover's name mentioned. No sign of a break-in. Outer doors locked. Lights out. No rape. Nothing stolen. Crime lab also finds jealous husband's blood type in the bathroom sink near her body and on a towel. Throw in the fake alibi when apprehended and it's verdict for the People."

She nodded again, handed the file back to him.

"High-profile," he continued, "has all the elements. Celebrity suspect. Beautiful victim. Big bucks and Pacific Heights venue. Particularly heinous crime. This is the one you've been waiting for, Grace."

"Amazing Grace" Harris had headed the homicide trials team for the past four years, supervising a staff of six top assistant district attorneys and personally trying two or three first-degree murder cases a year. She had earned the highest regard of her opponents at the criminal bar and was current chair of the Bar Association's criminal law committee. She had been honored for helping to organize the association's legal services outreach to the poor and served at the clinic six nights a month.

But she knew Sam was right. This was the case that would provide the public recognition that all her honors and years in the trenches had failed to produce. She hardly dared imagine where it all might lead, but it was no secret that Earl Field had his sights fixed on the governor's mansion and that a determined group of professional women would support her if she chose to run against Chief Assistant Jack Klegg, Field's heir apparent.

She pictured her father back in New York, astonished as he read about her election as district attorney of San Francisco, and the thought sent a pleasant shiver up her back.

"Am I right?" said Sam. "Slam dunk for the good guys? Hello? Earth to Grace. Come in, Grace."

Grace met Sam's intelligent, patient eyes. "Probably, but it just doesn't figure Elliot Ashford would be this foolhardy."

"The *hell* it doesn't," boomed a voice from the doorway.

Grace and Sam turned to see Earl Field strolling toward them, flashing what he called his "ten-dollar smile" and looking fit in one of his tailored $1,500 suits. Grace mused that voters who had paid that kind of money for their automobile or for their first and last month's rent—people to whom Earl Field was justly a hero—seemed to revel in the D.A.'s excess as much as in his attacks on the rich. When a reporter once suggested that his flashy attire seemed out of step with his liberal social agenda, Field had smiled and replied, "You can't bring a dying city to life dressed like an undertaker."

Field greeted each of them warmly, then circled his desk and took a seat in his high-backed swivel chair. "Elliot Ashford *is* foolhardy, Grace," he said, opening the file Sam had put on his desk. "Almost as foolhardy as he is arrogant."

"Arrogant, yes," said Grace, taking a seat across from him, "but nobody took Ashford for a fool when he was the conservatives' fair-haired boy in Congress."

"Oh, he was in Congress all right," said Field with a raucous laugh, exposing teeth that would have looked unnaturally white even without the contrast of his ebony skin. "Which explains why the deficit got so high. Notice how things have improved since he left?"

Grace smiled but persisted. "If Elliot Ashford, with all his rumored mob connections, brains, and money, killed his wife between seven and eight, he'd have had at least three hours to concoct a better alibi than going to a movie alone. The defense will argue that makes him either innocent or too stupid to have even located the congressional men's room."

"Okay, Grace, you win. You've convinced me he's even more arrogant than he is foolish. The man's problem is that he's been getting away with murder in this town so long he thinks he's above the law."

Grace saw the warning spark in the D.A.'s eyes and decided to back off. For now, at least. She was aware of Field's hatred for Ashford and saw no point in deflecting any of it toward herself. The politically conservative Ashford had been using his wealth and media contacts to harass Earl Field since the day Field entered politics as the only black member of the Board of Supervisors, then later as a crusading state assemblyman, and now as the city's chief law enforcement officer.

Some insiders believed that Field was envious of Ashford's fame and immense wealth, but others conjectured that their mutual animosity was grounded as much in their similarities as in their differences. After all, both men were smart, colorful, and dashing, drove fast cars, wore expensive clothes, and had shamelessly frequented Las Vegas. Both loved power and had gained it without yielding to the conventions normally associated with elective office, and both were revered by their constituents in a city known for its eclectic and tolerant nature. Finally, both had married beautiful women, and as of yesterday, they shared the status of eligible bachelors.

But Grace knew their bitter enmity went deeper than politics and was more primal than a matter of clashing political philosophies. She knew that Earl Field had committed the unpardonable sin of dating Lara Lake before she became Lara Ashford, and had then compounded his initial offense years later by asking her to dance one night at an inaugural ball in Sacramento. Lara had risen to his invitation a bit too eagerly, onlookers recalled, then smiled as they slow-danced away from the heat of Elliot Ashford's glare, her white-gloved arms twisting like pipe stems around Field's tux-clad shoulders and licorice neck, drifting across the floor as smoothly as a pair of ice-skaters toward a column behind which a beat photographer for the *Sacramento Bee* was about to have his prayers answered.

Grace felt Field's eyes on her, reading her thoughts.

"He's been a crook, Grace, now he's a wife killer. Sure, he's also been a burr under my saddle and people will talk. Let 'em talk. I've got his ass planted on a steel bunk on the sixth floor, and it's going to stay there until it's time for him to be strapped down and dance the funky chicken flat on his back."

"You'll ask for the death penalty?" said Sam.

"Hell yes, Sam. The guy tortured her. 'Special circumstances'!"

Sam looked unconvinced. "Sure, she was tortured, Chief, but going for the needle on Ashford on a domestic-violence killing will make it tougher to get a murder one conviction."

Field looked up, his eyes smiling. "Nearly thirty years a D.A. investigator and it just now comes out you're opposed to the death penalty?"

"Earl's right," said Grace. "We can't make exceptions."

Sam shrugged. "I'm just saying the guy's got fans out there."

He might have been President, some San Franciscans said of Elliot Ashford. He had made all the right moves since his election to Congress in 1978, had once even given the keynote at the Republican national convention and, thanks in part to his populous home state, had even been considered a front-runner as a vice presidential candidate. But a tabloid piece picked up by the *Washington Post* revealing lurid details of Lara's fling with U.S. Senator Dwight Clifton—the name overheard by the maid during the argument just before Lara's murder—combined with sudden cash-flow problems, had forced the publicly cuckolded Ashford back to private life in San Francisco.

Despite his expulsion in shame from the nation's capital, Elliot Ashford remained in the national limelight, for no city, not even San Francisco with its colorful, chaotic history, could boast a man with more notorious and contradictory credentials than Elliot Ashford. Although the SFPD organized crime and drug units suspected that his construction company now fronted a mob money-laundering operation, he had once sat on the mayor's Police Commission.

Known as a fiscal conservative during his service in Washington, he had personally provided seed financing for the city's second-largest homeless shelter. And although friends said he had forgiven his gorgeous wife's indiscretions, he now sat in the city jail charged with her murder.

The newspapers and tabloids were in ecstasy, for the celebrity couple had been dogged for years by rumors of adultery and other consensual sins unbefitting their high social station. Ashford's list included reckless gambling and womanizing; even Lara's older sister Shannon was rumored to have succumbed to his charm, causing a bitter rift between the sisters. And Lara's association with cult figures in San Francisco, together with the graphic exposé of her affair with Senator Clifton in Washington, had helped relegate her husband to a political boneyard from which not even his ambition and wealth could deliver him.

The jealous-spouse motive made spicy tabloid reading, thought Grace, but the media's interest in the Lara-Clifton affair had died out with the famous couple's return to San Francisco, and they'd have to find a better motive.

"How long will it take to get a DNA blood match on Ashford?"

"They're working up a PCA analysis as we speak," said Sam. "It'll confirm the type AB match we've already got."

"Sounds like a slam dunk," Field murmured.

Grace watched her steepled fingers tapping against one another as they did sometimes when something was troubling her.

"Something bothering you, Grace?" asked Field. "You're uncharacteristically quiet today."

"It seems almost too perfect," said Grace. "I guess I'm looking for the grinch."

"Say again?"

"The grinch," said Grace. "For starters, it's August now. I suppose they'll stall long enough to try for a Christmas mercy verdict."

Field stirred impatiently. "No grinch. We won't let them stall. No mercy verdict. It's airtight, Grace. Clear jealousy motive. Ashford's blood everywhere. Lied about where he was."

"Then he'll try to plea-bargain."

"We won't let him."

"All the way?"

"To the death," said Field, grinning. "Hell, Grace, you're supposed to be the by-the-book hard-ass in this office. What the hell more do you want?"

"What do I want?" said Grace, trying to control a growing impatience with Field's macho optimism. "I want an analysis of the victim's fingernail scrapings for starters. Then I want PCA DNA confirmation on the blood, a thorough investigation of all other suspects—ex-lovers, rivals, cult associations, whatever. Then I want statements from all the neighbors and relatives as well as confirmation of Ashford's reputed mob connections. That's what I want. For *starters*."

"You heard the woman," said Field to Sam. "She wants the perfect case."

"The perfect case?" said Grace, shaking her head. "There's no such thing."

"Well, this is as close to one as I've ever seen, and with your help, Grace, I'm going to nail the bastard."

Grace's head snapped around. "With my *help?*"

"It will be terrific," said Field, his head buried in the police report. "We've never tried a case together."

"Together," she murmured as the realization sunk in. She glanced at Sam. He looked away.

Grace had found the grinch.

2

The next day, Grace Harris, Earl Field, and Sam Quon ducked under the yellow tape at the doorway of Ashford's Pacific Heights mansion and walked into the entry rotunda. Six flying buttresses arched thirty feet above them and met at the top in a spectacular crown of gold-leaf detail. Between each support, the late morning sun slanted through a web of leaded and stained glass, tinting the walls and marble flooring with a rose hue that seemed a harbinger of what lay ahead.

"Impressive," said Grace.

"If you like an architectural soufflé of Frank Lloyd Wright and nineteenth-century Gothic," sniffed Field.

"I could adjust," she said.

"I hope you have a lot of friends," said Quon. "The place has sixteen rooms."

"With this house," she said, "I'd have friends."

He then led them into the living room, centered on a fireplace the size of a station wagon. They glanced to the right at an indoor swimming pool covered with a sliding roof. Fine art hung everywhere: a Sisley and a Caillebotte in the living room, a pair of Calders in the dining room, and a Poussin in the upper hallway. The view of the Bay from the upstairs master bedroom was interrupted only by a grand circular garden with a Henry Moore at the nucleus. A golden sheen on the leaves of the surrounding trees hinted of autumn, and the sky looked freshly washed, clear but for some puffs of altocumulus clouds hanging like white cotton candy high and to the northwest.

In surreal contrast, the master bathroom looked like a slaughterhouse. A crude figure-outline drawn in chalk on the dark marble floor marked the spot. A rust brown residue of dried blood spread beyond the chalk lines and covered nearly half the Italian granite countertop as well.

Grace swallowed hard as she imagined the violence of the act, the remnants of its raw ferocity revealed in scarlet stains splattered high across the adjacent south side of the room. Lara Ashford had dressed here, thought Grace, made herself up here, bathed here, died here.

Grace methodically traced the final downward passage of one of the victim's hands—the right one apparently—as it reached out before sliding downward in bold finger-strokes toward a brass fixture that was also caked solid rust-brown. There were five distinct crimson spoors leading to the hand's final resting place on the floor.

She glanced up at Field and saw that he and Sam were studying the missing drainage trap from the red-stained basin on the left.

"It's marked and in the lab, Chief," said Quon. "Ditto the towels."

Glass from the shattered mirror still covered the floor.

"A violent struggle," said Grace, looking around. "My guess is we'll find our verdict under her fingernails."

Sam nodded. "The DNA work on the scrapings will take a while, but that should lock it up for us."

"Tell them to rush it, Sam," said Field gruffly. "I'm going to hang this bastard."

Grace noted his use of the first-person singular and started to say something, then decided to wait until they were alone.

"Are the police looking at other possible suspects?" asked Grace.

"What other possible suspects?" said Field. "We've got everything but a video of Ashford doing the deed!"

"True, but I always like to—"

"There *are* no other suspects, Grace. Not this time. Look at this mess! It screams out domestic violence!"

Sam jumped in. "I think the cops pretty much agree, Grace."

"So when we're accused by the defense and maybe the press of 'rushing to judgment,' " said Grace stiffly, bending down for a closer look at blood traces on the tile floor, "we just say 'Hey, the cops agreed with us'?"

"Lighten up, Grace," said Field, "we've got our—"

"Wasn't Senator Clifton in town on a fund-raiser?" she said, now down on one knee, staring at the floor. "And aren't there rumors that the lady had a local boyfriend? I also remember a bit in an old Herb Caen column years ago suggesting that Lara's own sister—Shannon something—had a fling with Ashford, resulting in a major falling-out between the two women. They hated each other. Have the police talked to her? Have we? And wasn't Lara involved in some weird touchy-feely circles? Come on, Earl, Lara wasn't some shrinking violet or a prim Junior League matron. She was *out* here."

Grace could feel Field staring down at her back, watching her as she rubbed a finger over the stained tile.

"Are you finished, Grace?" he said.

"Almost," she said, rising and studying one of the basins, also blotched with a rust-colored residue. "Until we get a clear DNA match, we'd better show the good citizens that we still consider people—even people you don't like, Earl—innocent until proven guilty. It's in the Constitution. Check it out."

Grace glanced up and saw that Field was giving her a surprised look, a look that said she was being excessively scrupulous and living up to her hard-ass reputation. She was used to Earl always needing to be the smartest guy in the room, but he had irritated her, talking about what *he* was going to do, treating her like a reasonably able subordinate. And now *she* had irritated *him*.

But Field gave Sam Quon a wry smile. "Sam," he said, "is this the same avenging crusader who in her early years prosecuted a pregnant woman for a convenience-store milk heist, sent away a functionally blind man for rape, busted a seventy-year-old street beggar on a battery charge over a failed purse snatch, then, in later years, sent five men—all black—to death row?"

Grace's eyes narrowed. She had accepted the litany as the usual teasing until the racial reference. The trouble with Earl, she thought, was you never really knew for sure. He could be charming you with his perfect smile at the same time his eyes were flashing danger.

"Those five men p-picked their victims, Earl," she said, trying to conceal her vexation, hating her slight stammer. "I didn't pick them as defendants."

"Easy, Grace," said Sam. "The chief is just referring to that tattoo on your forehead that says 'Do the Crime; Do the Time.' "

Everyone laughed, Grace too, though it hurt that everyone thought of her as hard-nosed and rigid, a zero-tolerance prosecutor who'd put you away for just *looking* like you might tear the label off that mattress. It was the way she had seen her father, an ultraorthodox Hasidic Jewish rabbi who thought all that was necessary to achieve Utopia, Arcadia, and the Elysian fields was rigid adherence to the Law. She'd always been critical of her father's rigidity, his legalistic nature, but she had come to see that the apple truly never falls far from the tree.

Field softened his eyes. "Hell, Grace, we've got more than enough evidence right now. Let's take it to a preliminary hearing next week. He'll be held to answer in two hours."

Grace winced inwardly. "That would be dangerous, Earl. We'd be opening up our entire case to the defense long before we have to. Worse, our witnesses would be subjected to cross-examination if we took it to a prelim."

"You'll make sure they're well prepared."

"That won't stop the press from coming out of the woodwork."

"You've got a problem with the First Amendment, Grace?"

"You mean the Fourth Estate?"

"I mean it'll be a walk in the park."

And a very high-profile walk at that, Grace thought. She knew that like many politicians, Earl Field was often caught between ambition and duty. Well, she mused, at least he had begun speaking in the first-person plural.

"Let's take it to the grand jury instead, Earl," she said. "No reporters, but no defense lawyers or cross-examination either."

Field looked at Sam, who offered a barely perceptible nod. Grace could practically hear Field's brain computing the possibilities. Was he so eager for the publicity he would risk jeopardizing the case by giving the defense an advance shot at their witnesses?

"Oh, hell, all right," he said gruffly. "Go ahead and prepare a grand jury application."

"Soon as we get back," she said.

"And work up a witness list too, Grace. Bare minimum."

"Done. Want me to handle the tech people?"

Field said nothing, just stood there staring at the chalk outline. Grace began to think he hadn't heard her.

"That won't be necessary," he said at last. "Without any defense lawyers present, I can handle it alone."

"Alone? But—"

"That way we can keep you in the wings for a while; you know, our secret weapon."

Grace and Sam exchanged a look. Sam's seemed to say, The grand jury was your big idea, kid. Checkmate and game to the smartest guy in the room.

"Let's get the hell out of here," Field added, and walked briskly past them.

"Right," said Grace, no longer able to conceal the frustration in her voice.

A smile brightened Earl Field's face a week later as he sat alone at the head of the conference table in the west wing of his spacious office, studying the morning papers. His name was mentioned eleven times on the front page of the *Chronicle*—a record since his election three years before. He knew that this publicity would confirm Grace's suspicion that he had insinuated himself into the case purely for political reasons. Good, let her think it. Newspapers from L.A., Chicago, and New York littered a flawless twelve-foot slab of glass cantilevered off aluminum cylinders, all heralding the indictment of the ex-congressman. Ashford's former political visibility had combined with the heinous nature of the crime to generate nationwide publicity, and Field had added fuel to the fire by leaking information to a reporter at a local paper. He now had one of the highest profiles of any Democrat in California, and the publicity surrounding this case would keep it that way.

Knowledgeable trial watchers would say the district attorney was already trying his case. Good. He smiled, thinking how right he had been in predicting a walk in the park. Following a two-hour hearing—with brief appearances by the Ashford family's maid, the lead police homicide inspector, the county coroner, and his chief forensic pathologist—Ashford had swiftly been indicted. Delicately brandishing the murder weapon, Field had led the coroner through his testimony, emphasizing the rarity of Ashford's type AB blood found on the fingertips of the victim and on a towel that had apparently served as a makeshift handle for the shard of glass that had delivered the coup de grâce.

The district attorney rose and refilled his cup with a special Colombian blend from a beaker brewed hourly by his confidential secretary. He paused at the sideboard and stared out over the factories and warehouses toward the Bay. He had been lucky no one on the grand jury had asked about the fingernail scrapings, last seen in a sealed plastic bag between the two carved marble washbasins.

Lucky, because no one could account for the whereabouts of that crucial bit of evidence.

He returned to his chair and the comfort of the *Chronicle* article. He turned to the part that described "exclusive new evidence, revealed by a reliable source." He grinned at that—his mother used to call him "reliable" too—then read that Coroner Thomas Yang, one of California's leading authorities in criminal forensics, would testify that the victim had been "tortured by puncture wounds to the breasts and genitalia before a thrust of a glass shard into the throat mercifully ended her pain."

The *Chronicle* article didn't stop there, nor did the chain of proof connecting Ashford to the vicious murder. Dr. Anthony Ferrero would testify at trial that the killing typified the frenzied rage found in cases of domestic violence, corroborated by a previous wife-battering incident called in to Washington, D.C., police by a neighbor. Throw in the maid's testimony, a solid blood-type match, a fake and discredited alibi attempt, and the absence of forcible entry—circumstantial, to be sure, but it all added up.

Earl Field smiled as he tilted back in his chair, but his satisfaction at the agreeable publicity began to fade as he contemplated the challenge before him.

He knew that rusty as he was, he could easily have won this case even without Grace Harris. Anyone could. The trick would be how to lose it, and lose it in a way that didn't blow his chances of being elected governor.

3

The presiding judge's appointment of the Honorable John G. Hernandez as trial judge had come as no surprise. Hernandez was an impeccable choice, a man widely admired for his intelligence and his firm, but evenhanded, judicial temperament. The P.J. wanted no repeat of the Simpson debacle.

Judge Hernandez's first judicial act would be to hear a defense motion to reconsider an earlier judge's denial of bail. A copy of the motion was served on the D.A., and Grace Harris's secretary cheerfully carried the documents into her boss's office.

"Read all about it," said the secretary. "Here's the summons for your debut."

Grace scanned the motion in twenty seconds and said, "Same thing they tried before. John Hernandez will deny the motion from the bench without even wanting to hear from me."

She found Earl Field in his office, hunched over the defendant's moving papers.

"We lucked out," she said.

"John Hernandez? You bet. Liberal, but true-blue, law-and-order. Just like you, Grace. I tried a case before him when I was in private practice. Solid. Won't rattle. See Ashford's motion?"

"It's a farce," said Grace, holding up the three-page motion in her right hand. "Absolutely nothing new. Want me to walk it through alone?"

Field raised an eyebrow, then leaned back, hands locked behind his head as he took in a deep breath and let it out, staring at the ceiling. Then he pitched forward in his chair again and studied the motion papers as if for the first time, his palms planted on either side of the document.

Grace stood watching the performance with increasing curiosity, then moved closer to the desk that separated them.

"Alone," he repeated absently, as if to himself, his eyes still staring blankly at the papers between his hands.

"I just meant we might look overly concerned showing up together."

"My thinking precisely, Grace," said Field, looking up at her across his ebony barricade of a desk. "I'd better go à la carte. Save you for the after-dinner surprise."

Grace bit her lower lip. She should have seen it right away, she told herself. Field wasn't going to share the lime-light this case would generate with her or anyone else. She would be the woman behind the man.

Papa would approve.

"I'm not good at coming out of a cake, Earl," she said, standing in front of his desk, arms folded. "Maybe it's time to talk about whether I'm coming out at all."

Field flashed his perfect smile and slowly rotated his carefully groomed head.

"Grace, Grace, Grace," he said, his tone light and concil-iatory, hands still flat on the top of his desk. "I'm simply off on another fool's errand unworthy of your consummate skill and competence: a 'farce,' as you so aptly put it, a bail request hearing even *I* can't lose."

The phone rang and he picked it up, then offered Grace an apologetic shrug. "Sorry, Grace, I've got a problem in South City."

"You've got a problem right here on the third floor, Earl."

"What?"

"You're about to lose the head of your homicide trials team."

Field rose to his feet. "Grace, don't be—"

"Realistic?" said Grace, taking the phone that was still in his hand and replacing it in the cradle. "I'll *co*chair this case with you, Earl, but I've paid my dues and I won't *second*-chair with anyone, not even you."

Field met her gaze, then looked away. "I never intended for you to function as second chair."

"Nor did I," she said, and headed for the door. "Go ahead and handle this motion alone if you want, but from tomorrow on, it's either a full partnership or you can get Jack Klegg to schlepp your briefcase to court for you."

As Grace walked out the door, she glanced back and saw Earl Field reaching for the phone, gloomily shaking his head.

As Grace expected, the judge made short work of the bail motion, despite the vigorous advocacy of Ashford's lawyer, a stocky pit bull from Los Angeles named Al Menghetti who was known for his string of acquittals in high-profile cases. Grace mused from her seat in the back of the courtroom that Menghetti's appearance, with his double-breasted herringbone suit, massive girth, size eight, square-shaped head, and fleshy, pockmarked face, presented a conspicuous contrast to the handsome, small-boned district attorney. Once the arguments were under way, however, she had to admit that Menghetti made his points efficiently and with just the right touch of passion. He then swung into his conclusion with a review of Good Citizen Ashford's sterling record in support of law-and-order legislation while "serving this district in Congress."

Earl Field yawned for effect.

"No one has done more for our criminal justice system," intoned Menghetti, moving behind his client and dramatically placing both hands on his shoulders, "and no one has asked less of it."

Grace wondered if Earl would open by saying no one has done less and asked more, but Menghetti wasn't finished.

"All he asks now of the system is that he be released on bail, so that he might rejoin his friends in mourning the loss of his cherished wife."

Field started to rise for his reply, but Hernandez waved him back down without looking at him.

Hernandez, youthful-looking for his fifty-five years, without a trace of gray in either his hair or mustache, was known for making decisive rulings based on law and common sense, not glib rhetoric.

"I agree with Judge Lucy McCabe's earlier ruling, Mr. Menghetti," he said, glancing at the reddening face of Elliot Ashford. "This is a capital murder case alleging torture, on top of which your client is known to possess great wealth and useful connections. I consider him a viable flight risk."

A low rumble went up from the gallery in Department 26: reporters, family members, and the usual curious spectators who just wanted a peek at Elliot Ashford.

"One moment, Your Honor," persisted Al Menghetti, planting his stocky frame against the oak lectern. "Mr. Ashford's picture is on the front pages of newspapers all over the world! I ask you: Where's he going to go?"

John Hernandez looked down at Menghetti with a smile that briefly softened his stern face. "Nowhere, Mr. Menghetti," he said quietly. "Your client's going absolutely nowhere."

4

Elliot Ashford was led toward one of the small visitor rooms on the sixth floor of the Thomas J. Cahill Hall of Justice, feeling like one of his horses being guided to the paddock. He had been brought up from the facility at San Bruno early that morning and placed in a small holding cell.

The clang of steel doors, the smell of his own jail sweat, and the clinging chill of an ill-fitting orange jumpsuit would stick in his memory forever, even if he did get out of this mess alive.

What the hell is happening to me? he thought.

"You say somethin', Elliot?" grunted the guard.

"No," said Ashford sullenly, hating the man's easy familiarity, "but I would like to know the identity of my visitor. Is it my lawyer, Mr. Menghetti?"

"Dunno. Some guy from outta state."

Tony! thought Ashford. Bless you, my boy! My salvation, and not a moment too soon!

While he waited in the bleak room—four gray acoustic tile-paneled walls, a gray ceiling, a small wooden table, and two chairs—Elliot Ashford pondered the fate that had involved him with men like Carmine Rizzo and Tony, Carmine's firstborn son; men who took enormous pride in their loyalty to one another, but who until now had left him hanging by his thumbs.

Just as Meyer Lansky had once sent Bugsy Siegel to run the Flamingo, Don Carmine Rizzo had assigned son Tony to manage the Acropolis. Tony and Elliot Ashford soon became casual friends, and ironically, it was Tony's generous extension of credit that proved to be Elliot's undoing.

Elliot's trouble had begun with the rocketing of interest rates to nearly 20 percent during the recession of the early eighties. Resource International, the engineering and construction company that dominated the consolidated financial statement of the family holding company, was already choking on debt when a massive housing and shopping center project in L.A. went sour in 1984 and nearly took the company down. A bad time for Elliot to be serving in the House of Representatives in Washington, D.C. An even worse time for him to lose nearly four million dollars in less than a year playing baccarat at the Acropolis.

"Something can always be worked out," Don Carmine had said to Elliot after Tony had reported the situation, and a deal was struck that would not only excuse Elliot's debt but save the company. And now, here he was in a twelve-by-twelve-foot cell, waiting for the Rizzos to save him again.

The door opened.

"Hello, Elliot," came a raspy voice.

"Julian? Julian Gold?" exclaimed Ashford in disgust. *"Jesus!"*

"The former," said Gold, offering a bony hand. "Sorry to disappoint you."

Elliot turned away to avoid taking the extended hand.

"Where's Tony?" asked Elliot coldly.

"In Chicago, of course," said the Chicago Mafia's master strategist and *consigliere,* the lawyer who had masterminded the deal in which Ashford's debt to the Acropolis was forgiven. Don Rizzo had not just wiped out the debt, but had plowed sixty million dollars into Resource International in return for 34 percent of the Ashford family holding company stock and Elliot Ashford's commitment to leave Congress to resume active management of the company. The stock, though illiquid, was worth much more than sixty million on paper, but Ashford knew enough about the Rizzo family to realize he had no choice.

As the family's anointed Las Vegas *bruglioni,* Tony Rizzo was also charged with keeping an eye on the Chicago family's new investment in Resource International. Tony looked young for his forty-eight years. He was five years younger than Elliot, a little taller than Elliot's six-foot height, and possessed of a low hairline and even lower IQ. Tony was smart enough, however, to see that one of Elliot's greatest gifts was in the management of his burgeoning corporate empire—so long as he was not distracted by politics, gambling, or a cheating wife. Tony's gift, it turned out, was in making sure that Elliot was not distracted.

For Elliot's part, he regarded Tony Rizzo much the same as he viewed his three pet rottweilers: obedient, protective, and undemanding. Though he missed the gambling he had been forced to relinquish as part of the deal with Carmine, he began to embrace and enjoy the notoriety of having people think he was "connected." So what if people thought he was a key figure in some dark empire? He loved it.

"How are they treating you, Elliot?" said Gold, pushing his half-moon glasses higher on his hawklike nose.

Elliot paced, feeling the *consigliere*'s amused eyes on him.

"Something funny, Julian? You think this is *funny*?"

"No," said Gold, his eyes scanning Ashford's jail garb. "It's just that you look quite scholarly with your wire-rimmed spectacles and that austere jumpsuit; more like a celibate in a monk's cell than a prisoner."

"I'm every inch a prisoner, I assure you," said Elliot coldly, looking closely for the first time at the older man. Gold, bent from childhood polio and burdened with a corrective boot on one foot, gazed back at him. A shiver passed through the younger man as he studied the *consigliere*. Gold's pallid face was as expressive as stucco, except that his down-turned mouth, soaring eyebrows, and nose gave him the look of a crippled bird of prey. Elliot wanted to grab his bony shoulders and shake him, but the visitor made no response, just shifted his impassive gaze toward a fly perched above the door of the bleak conference cell.

Gold coughed into a handkerchief, which he carefully folded and restored to his pocket. "Don Carmine is concerned about three things, Elliot. First, this Op-Ed piece from yesterday's Chicago *Tribune*. Listen:

"The murder trial of an ex-congressman from San Francisco is expected to reveal the continuing reach of the Chicago crime syndicate. The Rizzo family is known to be in partnership with defendant Elliot Ashford, conceivably a West Coast Mafia don himself.

But the source of the problem is right here in Chicago,

*and it's time for the FBI and our local authorities to vigor-
ously deal with it!"*

"My God," said Elliot, "that's ridiculous!"

"Agreed," sniffed Gold. "I detest split infinitives. But
the point is that while Carmine knows you did not kill Lara,
the notoriety surrounding this unfortunate incident has already migrated to Chicago, causing him considerable
embarrassment."

Ashford spun around and stared at Gold, his eyes glazed
with anger. "*Unfortunate incident? Considerable embarrassment?* I've lost a *wife* I loved, for God's sake; I'm facing
the death penalty for something I couldn't possibly have
done; and you talk to me about Carmine's *embarrassment*!"

Ashford's outburst seemed to go unnoticed by Gold as
he folded the clipping and put it away. "Second, there is
the little matter of his sixty million dollars."

"Christ, Julian, he should know he needn't be—"

"Please, Elliot," said the *consigliere,* "allow me to
finish."

Although Gold's voice remained calm, Ashford noticed
that a spark had flared again in his normally stony eyes.
"We simply need to know more about your key personnel,
the executives who will be protecting Carmine's investment
while you are detained."

Ashford let out a short, sardonic burst of laughter at
Gold's euphemism and turned away from him.

"Third, and most important," Gold continued, as casually
as if reading from a wine list, "you must understand that
Tony cannot assist you in this matter."

Ashford's head snapped around. He took a quick breath
and fought to remain calm.

"Tony cannot '*assist*' me?" growled Ashford, almost
choking on the words. He ran long fingers through his
straight blond hair, then turned back toward the wall and
slapped it so hard his hands stung. "Hell, Julian, haven't I
'assisted' *him?* Haven't I protected his identity so far? But
now he's *got* to come out here. He's my *alibi,* for God's
sake!"

"Carmine appreciates your silence," said Gold, but then
his expression hardened as he added, "and you'd do well
to maintain it. Use your head, Elliot. Carmine cannot allow

Tony to admit he violated the terms of his parole that night. He'd be looking at a minimum fifteen to thirty years in a federal penitentiary."

Ashford's shoulders sagged as the cold reality of his situation began to set in. He lowered himself into a chair, rubbed thumbs against his red-streaked eyes.

"Okay, then," he gasped at last, "you want to protect your precious investment? Then get me the hell out of here! I was once on the *Police Commission,* for God's sake, and some of the thugs in here can actually read newspapers. They'll kill me before the state can get around to it!"

Gold again made no response to his outburst, and Ashford felt compelled by the silence to turn around, to confront the older man's cold gaze.

"Tony's *got* to come out here and testify, Julian," he whispered, hating the fear seeping into his voice. "He's got to tell the truth!"

Gold hunched his scoliotic shoulders into a shrug. "Come now, Elliot," he began, "try to understand the situation. You're a lightning rod out here. You've shot your mouth off against the D.A. for years and presumably derived satisfaction from doing so. It's no secret you hate his politics and the fact that he was once friends with Lara."

Ashford wanted to scream, to drive Gold's composed face, with its trace of a condescending smile, into the wall. "Don't be absurd!" he said. "Lara dated him once or twice, for God's sake! Before I even knew her."

"I'm just trying to tell you," said Gold, brushing away a fly perched on his shoulder, "that I sympathize. But now Mr. Field has the upper hand and there's too much heat surrounding you. Do you really expect Carmine to put his only son on the sacrificial altar for you? To allow Tony to repeat the mistake he made coming out here that night? Or even admit that he was out here? That would be shameful."

"Shameful," murmured Ashford. He fell into a chair, planted both elbows on the table, and let his face sink into his hands. His skin was cold. He sat like that for a minute, feeling slightly faint, barely hearing Gold's continuing monotone.

"Tony himself now realizes he took a stupid risk breaking the terms of his parole to come out here to work with you that night."

Ashford's head snapped up. "Work with me? Listen, Julian, I didn't ask Tony to break his parole and fly into Napa that night. Indeed, I told him I could answer all his questions about the year-end figures by telephone! Sure, we worked together that night, but the real reason he came out was to see his mistress of the moment—Ruth Sikes or Sipes or something like that—a girl he's put up somewhere in Sonoma."

"Yet another lapse in Tony's judgment that Carmine would not like hearing about. In any event, he won't allow any of it to come out now, so put it out of your mind."

Ashford leapt to his feet. "I'm damned if I will," he said angrily, meeting Gold's eyes. "I'm damned if I'll let Carmine throw me to the wolves!"

Again, Gold's only response was a cold, metallic glare, but Ashford held his gaze this time. He knew he was irritating the powerful *consigliere,* but Gold was in *his* town now, and he was not accustomed to bowing to others, let alone to this walking cadaver.

"You're not hearing me, Elliot," Gold said. "A parole violation would give the feds the excuse they're looking for to nail Tony for good. Carmine will never allow that to happen, even if Tony wanted to help."

"And *you're* not hearing *me,* Julian! Need I remind you that if I cease to function as chairman of the board of the family holding company for a period of one year, the terms of my father's trust require reversion of all stock in Resource back to the Ashford Foundation, including Carmine's?"

"I know that, Elliot, and Don Carmine understood that risk at the time he made his deal with you."

"Well, that's ducky. And does he also understand that if I'm convicted, I can't serve as chairman? And that the insurance policy he took out on my life won't apply if I'm executed for a crime? That his sixty million will die with me?"

Gold nodded. "He understands."

Elliot laughed genuinely for the first time in days. "Then don't you see, old sport? You and Carmine have no choice but to help me out of this mess!"

Gold said nothing for a moment, then swatted absently at the pesky fly, now darting between them. "Another way of looking at it, Elliot, is that you have no choice but to let us. But forget about Tony; he won't be a part of it."

Ashford leaned across the table, succumbing to a growing despair, his contorted face within inches of Gold's.

"You're still not getting it, Julian," he growled. "Field hates me, as you have brilliantly deduced. He's also got a truckload of circumstantial evidence. If this case goes to trial, it could get very messy. *For all of us.*"

Gold shrugged, his eyes cold and unlit. If he had perceived any threat in his words, he gave little indication of it, other than to briefly raise one eyebrow and issue a bored sigh.

"You are innocent, are you not, Elliot?" Gold said finally, in the tone of a lawyer questioning a witness. "Still the benign Brahmin, known for his kind deeds and great contributions to the commonweal? One of nature's noblemen?"

Ashford's features went blank. He knew Gold rarely engaged in sarcasm, and certainly not humor. "Your point?" he murmured.

"Specifically," continued the *consigliere,* "you told the police you cut yourself shaving that night, isn't that so? Some residue in the basin combined with your wife's blood, did it not?"

"Of *course* that's what I told them," shouted Ashford, "because that's precisely what happened! The basin I shave in is right under the mirror the killer pushed her into."

"Excellent, and the towel—with both your blood and hers on it?"

Ashford shook his head impatiently. "I must have wiped blood onto the towel after I shaved. This may not have occurred to you, Julian, but that's precisely what towels are for."

Gold's fierce gaze forced Ashford to drop his eyes. He then sat back down across from the *consigliere,* rubbed his temples with both hands, and tried to subdue his emotions.

"Don't you see, Julian? The killer must have had Lara's blood on his hands or gloves, then wiped them on the towel after I'd used it. Or maybe he used it as a handle for the weapon, which mixed her blood up with mine that was already there!"

Gold sucked in a deep breath, exhaled, and seemed to

will his reluctant features into something close to a smile,
though only his lips participated. Ashford hated that smile,
hated the man behind it, hated having to explain himself
to him.

"So, Elliot," Gold said, "verdict for the defendant! You
see? You have no need for Tony. You need only to relax."

Ashford looked away, feeling it all slipping away.
"You're a lawyer, Julian; you know it's never that easy.
Without Tony, Field will find a way to beat me."

Gold shook his head as if impatient, though Ashford
knew the *consigliere* never yielded to such commonplace
emotions. After a minute of silence, Gold glanced over his
shoulder, then leaned in close and spoke so softly Ashford
had to put his ear against the *consigliere*'s mouth to hear
him.

"There are things you don't know, Elliot; things I cannot
tell you. But when I tell you to relax, you would be well
advised to do so."

Gold's words were both threatening and comforting, and
but for the tone of finality with which they were uttered,
Ashford would have sought clarification.

"Okay, Julian, I'll try," he said at last, hating the sound
of his own voice, the frail murmur of a supplicant, "but
at least get me out of here on bail. I can't bear another
day here."

Gold said nothing, his attention again drawn to the solitary fly that had now landed and was grooming itself on
the table between them. Ashford couldn't stand the silence
and rose to his feet.

"Damn it, you officious bastard, *say* something!"

Gold's hand slammed down on the table. Ashford
jumped. Gold turned his hand over, then flicked the dead
fly from his palm onto the floor with the side of his other
hand.

"Sit down, Elliot, and pay attention. Now."

Ashford looked at the tiny corpse with mingled repugnance and empathy. Then he sat.

"Understand that we want you out of here as much as
you do. To this end, I've instructed your lawyer to file
another bail motion now that Judge Hernandez has the
case."

"If that's meant to reassure me," said Ashford, all hope

now drained from his face, "it's not working. The other judge practically laughed in Menghetti's face."

"I realize that, but we think part of the problem is that Mr. Menghetti is from Los Angeles and lacks political juice with the judges here. Accordingly, we are negotiating with a top Montgomery Street firm to make a special appearance on a bail hearing."

"Which firm?"

"The best in town. Caldwell & Shaw."

"C&S? They're *corporate* lawyers, Julian. What do they know about criminal—"

"Al Menghetti would continue to do the heavy lifting after the bail hearing. We could decide later if we want to keep C&S in the picture."

"Who from Caldwell & Shaw would make the pitch?"

"His name is Barrett Dickson."

"Dickson," murmured Ashford. The name was familiar. "So how many cases has he won, say, in the last three years?"

"His recent record is not the issue here, Elliot. Please don't make me repeat myself. Menghetti will continue on as lead counsel, and *his* record is sixteen acquittals in murder cases in the past three years." Gold paused, as if thinking about what he would say next. "As for Dickson, if you must know, he's tried only one case in eight years and that one didn't work out so well."

Ashford choked out a laugh. "Wonderful," he said. "You'd be handing me over to the one lawyer in town who couldn't defend a parking ticket."

"It's simply not important, Elliot. We get his firm's name on our pleadings."

"Juice."

"Precisely," said Gold. "More important, he was a law school classmate and close friend of the trial judge."

"Was?"

"He's still highly regarded by Judge Hernandez as well as others who knew him when he was at the very top of the trial bar."

"Then won't it be obvious to the judge that Dickson is trading on his friendship?"

"He won't think that. Dickson's reputation for integrity is such that the president of the American College of Trial

Lawyers told me he would shoot craps with him over the telephone."

Ashford smiled at this, but turned serious again. "Then why would Dickson do it?"

Gold shrugged. "A senior partner of the firm is going to float it past Dickson today. He seems to think he will."

Ashford rubbed his temples, exhausted from the confrontation with the *consigliere* and needing desperately to end it.

"He won't get in the way, Elliot. And he's reputed to be highly intelligent."

"He sounds like the kind of 'highly intelligent' person who gets lost on the way to his Mensa examination."

Gold shook his head impatiently. "We need this firm, and the C&S partner I'm dealing with expects that Barrett Dickson will want to meet you before he commits to do anything. So be nice, Elliot. Lose the arrogance for once."

Ashford slumped in his chair. Nobody had talked this way to him since the day his asshole of a father died. *God,* how he'd like to tell the slimy *consigliere* to just bugger off, to look him straight in his ferret-like eyes and remind him that this was *his* city; to remind him that he could put Tony Rizzo back in prison with a single word.

But Gold's icy expression silenced him, for despite his fear and frustration, Elliot Ashford knew that getting crosswise with Carmine Rizzo's right hand could get him into a different kind of trouble, the kind you can't beat in court with a smart lawyer.

There was more than one way to die inside prison walls.

5

Legal observers opening their papers over coffee the next day were stunned to read that Barrett "Bear" Dickson had been invited to join the Ashford defense team as a consultant for the "early phases of the case." Some readers were even more surprised that Caldwell & Shaw, one of America's elite corporate law firms, would involve itself in the defense of a suspect in a vicious murder, especially a suspect with rumored ties to the Mafia.

But a few insiders knew that Caldwell & Shaw, like many large firms that had expanded too quickly and were staggering under the burden of bloated overheads, was in a financial slump, pursuing new clients with the desperation of jackals in a lean winter.

An amusing article in the metro section described Dickson as a "hard-luck, hard-drinking man" who, having lost a major securities fraud case in 1993—only his second loss in over twenty years of trial practice—had been asked by the judge if he wanted the jury polled. Dickson was quoted as having said, "No, Your Honor, I want them bound and whipped." He was arrested on a DWI late that night and never tried another big case.

Page 17 offered a 1965 picture of Dickson outside Saigon in army fatigues. The caption proclaimed that he had been "born into one war—1941—and nearly killed in another."

The photo showed him to be a large man with a generous nose, wide mouth, powerful jaw, and prominent cheekbones. Otherwise, it was an ordinary face, under ordinary-looking, short-cropped hair that lay forward and flat against his huge head. The ring finger of his left hand was missing, shot off in a scrape near Pleiku, apparently justifying the exaggerated "nearly killed" reference. The man's eyes were not plainly visible in the photo, but appeared heavy-lidded and distrustful.

It was hard to tell from the picture whether he was smiling at the photographer or squinting into the sun or just looking for something off in the distance.

Traffic Court at the San Francisco Hall of Justice, known to regular practitioners there as "the Snakepit," was the department where young lawyers cut their teeth on misdemeanors and where unlucky old-timers finished out wasted careers. The gallery in daily attendance in this courtroom often reflected its bleak and frenetic mood: homeless people smelling of booze and unwashed clothes, noisily relishing its warmth and modest entertainment value.

"People versus Vessey!" shouted the clerk, a formidable black woman, and the raucous crowd went silent as a gorgeous young woman in a tailored beige suit with white collar and cuffs approached the rail—she could not have looked more out of place at a longshoreman's bar or in a boxing ring—followed by a giant of a man in a rumpled suit carrying a battered briefcase. The antique bag, yellowed and cracked, with a flap with a catch on it that passed through the handle before it latched, was the only clue that the man might be a lawyer.

A young assistant D.A. was already inside the rail, laying out his files and beaming toward the defendant and her lawyer as they approached. The large man passed through the rail, delayed momentarily when his briefcase was caught in the swinging door. He wrestled it free, then reached down to shake hands with the rosy-faced prosecutor who wore his reddish hair perfectly parted on one side and a navy blue suit the color of his eyes.

"Hello, Mr. Dickson," said the prosecutor. "I'm Bill Hancock."

"I've no doubt of it," said Barrett Dickson, managing a tired smile because he saw the kid was nervous. He's afraid of me, Barrett thought. He doesn't know yet that it never gets easier and that I'm scared, too. Damn sure knows nothing about being fifty and trying a case in traffic court for the first time. Jesus, what a zoo.

"Call case number 164227," shouted the clerk.

"Ready for trial, Your Honor," shouted the prosecutor

with the nerve-jangling enthusiasm of a marine recruit. "William Hancock for the People."

"Barrett Dickson from the firm of Caldwell & Shaw," said Barrett, "representing defendant Monica Vessey."

The judge acknowledged him with a nod that seemed to Barrett both respectful and melancholy, and Barrett sized him up as a kindred spirit—a man who might have a flask in the fold of his robe to help cope with the combination of ennui and anxiety that comes with the territory called the Municipal Court bench. At least there was no jury, thought Barrett; he couldn't have done this in front of a jury.

The appearances were noted and the drunk-driving trial of Monica Vessey, daughter of Sherman Vessey, chairman and CEO of Macro Dynamics, one of C&S's most prized clients, was under way. Hancock rose to give his opening statement, most notable, Barrett thought, for its enthusiasm and brevity.

"The people will prove that on the night of July 18, 1997, Ms. Monica Vessey was driving a motor vehicle in the vicinity of Taylor and Bush with a blood-alcohol content of .08, and that she drove said motor vehicle at said time and place through a red light, entered the intersection illegally, then struck a steel pole to which another red light was attached."

The kid's calming down and gaining momentum, thought Barrett. He's figured out the importance of home-field advantage.

"The traffic light violation and the collision serve as clear corroborative proof of her intoxicated condition, Your Honor, and at the close of the evidence, the People will ask that she be found guilty as charged."

The judge nodded sympathetically toward Barrett, who slowly rose to his feet and, in a gravelly and slightly tremulous voice, began to proclaim his client's innocence.

"Her blood test was right on the line, Your Honor: .079. She never would have been charged had she not hit the pole. The prosecution, therefore, is forced into a syllogism: Because she did B, she must have been guilty of A; because she ran a red light and hit a pole, she must have been drunk. The problem for the prosecution is that there is absolutely no evidence that she ran a red light. If there were, I would concede that one might also surmise there was intoxication.

"But there will be no such evidence, Your Honor, and we will ask for an acquittal on all three charges."

Barrett knew his concession involved risk, but his style when he had been on top had always been to concede realities, not struggle against them. He also had been told that this judge valued candor above all else. Finally, he knew from pretrial discovery that there were no witnesses to the crash other than Monica Vessey. The judge would have to accept her word that she was legally entering the intersection and had been victimized by a speeding scofflaw who had entered the intersection against the red light from her left and forced her to veer into the light pole to avoid being hit by him. In his closing, he would argue this was a simple case of a reputable young woman, dining out, a glass of wine or two; nothing more. A victim, not a criminal.

But why was the goddamn kid smiling?

"Call your first witness, Mr. Hancock," growled the judge, whose manner toward the younger man revealed his disdain for the cruel fate that had consigned him to this Devil's Island of a courtroom. The boy has a future, thought Barrett, at least a shot at one. Not so the judge, whose despair was written in spidery veins that crisscrossed his scarlet face.

"Call Officer Jenkins, Your Honor," said young Hancock, oblivious and smiling up at the bench.

It was all over in five minutes, which is all the time it took for Officer Jenkins to explain that he was liaison officer with the Department of Public Works and that modern stoplights in San Francisco contained a light filament that registered the color at the time the light was disabled.

"And what color was the light when the defendant crashed into it, Officer?"

"It was red, Mr. Hancock."

Barrett felt heat flooding his body, even into his clammy hands. He felt his heart pounding up into a throat suddenly dry as road dust; Vietnam all over again, his mind paralyzed with fear and confusion. Why hadn't he learned that about traffic lights? Why had he believed this girl? What the hell was he doing in a courtroom, anyway?

"Cross-examination, Mr. Dickson?" said the judge, looking even sadder than before.

"One moment, please, Your Honor."

Barrett leaned toward his client, his hand cupped around her ear to shield her from the smell of his breath. "We've got a problem," he said.

"My 'problem,' " snapped Monica Vessey, her eyes burning with anger, "was in allowing Daddy's firm to handle this case. Are you really a lawyer? What in the hell are you going to do now?"

Barrett pulled himself back from her rage, trying hard to conceal his own anger, at least from the judge. He took in a deep breath and let it out, then leaned toward her again.

"I'm going to give you another chance is what I'm going to do," he said. "You're a spoiled brat and a liar and you might kill somebody next time, but even so, you deserve fair representation under this fucked-up system of ours."

"You can't talk to me—"

"Shut up and listen. Do you know what a mistrial is?"

"Of course I do," snapped Monica Vessey.

"Good. Get ready to ask for one."

"*What?*"

But Barrett had already risen unsteadily to his feet, had met the judge's dead eyes, and had cleared his throat to speak.

"Your Honor? I'm going to lunch. Have a nice day."

With that, he walked out the door, hurried to his car, and drove straight to Moose's Bar and Grill in North Beach.

Two hours later, Barrett looked up from his vodka rocks, pretzels, and newspaper to see longtime friend and C&S partner Mike Reasoner taking a stool next to him.

"Nice work, Bear. Your disappearing act cost $3,000 for contempt of court and two calls to the Hall of Justice to squash the warrant for your arrest."

"Thanks," said Barrett, looking straight ahead. "I'll pay the firm back, of course."

Mike said nothing.

"Did she get her mistrial?"

"Of course she got it," Mike snapped impatiently. "What else could the judge do when her lawyer vanished like Amelia Earhart fifteen minutes into the trial."

Silence.

"Did C&S lose papa's business?" asked Barrett.

"Not yet, but Steve Wilmer's knives are sharpened, Bear. You've put your head on the block with this little caper."

Wilmer was the recently elected head of the C&S executive committee. He had run on a platform of cutting costs and downsizing; clearing the firm of "dead wood."

"Who's going to represent the girl?" said Barrett.

"Jesus, Bear," said Mike, turning toward his friend, "are you listening to me? This is strike three!"

"*Who did you send her to?*"

"Doug Young, over in the Mission District."

"Good. He's tops."

"That stuff will kill you someday, Bear," said Mike.

"Okay, I'll stop," said Barrett, making a show of pushing the pretzels away.

Mike rolled his eyes. "Why not give up past regrets while you're at it?"

Barrett felt Mike's eyes on him as he polished off the vodka rocks.

"I mean it," Mike said, "you never used to drink at lunch."

"Not to worry, Rabbi Reasoner. It's been a rough morning. Normally, just a tiddly or two before dinner. I'm fit as a fiddle, and now I'm square with the law as well, all thanks to you, noble friend."

Mike's drink arrived and he touched glasses with Barrett. "So where the hell you keeping yourself lately?" asked Mike. "Your picture's on milk cartons."

"Here and there, Michael. Billing a few hours at what's left of our firm. Handling ragbag duties such as this morning's adventure. Doing some reading. Taking piano lessons."

"Piano lessons?"

"Always wanted to do something in music. Don't sing so good, as you may recall, so I rented an upright. I'm learning 'Stardust.' How did you find me?"

"You weren't at your apartment or on a barstool at Stars or the Washington Square Bar and Grill. The manhunt led here. What's with the white carton? Planning on eating your leftover Chinese from last night here at the bar? Classy."

"That's Ginger II."

"As in Fred and Ginger?" referring to Barrett's only housemates, a pair of goldfish.

"Ginger's gone. Fred's bereft, just stares at his food as it sinks slowly past him. Less than a year old and a widower."

Mike nodded. "Give him my condolences."

"Just came from the pet shop. Got to mate him before he floats on his side like Ginger."

"You might keep an eye out for yourself while you're at it," ventured Mike. "You look tired, Bear."

Barrett gave a little grunt. "Yeah, I know. Seems like one morning I looked in the mirror and found that an old man had moved into my skin during the night."

Mike touched Barrett on the arm. "You're in your prime, Bear, but a man needs hard work and a good woman. It's been years now since you've tried either one."

Barrett felt a muscle twitch in his jaw but didn't think Mike would notice. He shrugged his massive shoulders, pulled the pretzels back, and noisily crunched one between his teeth.

A good woman. He thought he had found one, until Ellen ran off to Provence with a bond salesman in 1985, taking everything of value but their nine-year-old son, Jared. Barrett could still smell the salesman's schlock cologne; picture him hanging around the house, hawking his corporate high-yield bonds, bragging about his world travels.

"What really happened out there this morning, Bear?"

Barrett shrugged. "How was I supposed to know they could tell the light was on red at the time she disabled it. Damn thing was like a watch stopping at time of impact. Like a voice shouting from the grave."

"So you made a mistake. Lawyers make mistakes."

"I made a mistake going back into a courtroom."

"Well, forgive me, old buddy, but you damn sure didn't stay long."

"I did what I had to do. She's got Doug Young now and a fresh start. How's Nancy?"

Mike Reasoner winced and put his glass to his lips. Barrett caught the bartender's eye and pointed an index finger at his empty glass.

Mike had married Nancy Livingston six months after the

marriage of Barrett and Ellen Farr had dashed Mike's secret hopes with Ellen. Barrett knew his best friend had
been infatuated with Ellen, but Mike's love for Barrett
soon swept away his envy, and his own marriage to Nancy
had turned out remarkably well. Indeed, the silver medal
Nancy had represented in Mike's race for conjugal bliss
had turned, with time, into gold, whereas the alchemy had
worked in reverse for Barrett: divorced in 1986, Ellen's
suicide in 1993, and Jared, their only child, now grown and
blaming his father for everything.

"Nancy's holding her own," said Mike. "Still doing the
chemo."

"She's a brave girl, Michael, the best. Any change?"

"They're pulling out the stops at Stanford Medical.
We're optimistic."

Barrett nodded, his mind wandering as he stared past the
huge bronze moose stationed near the sunlit entrance and
through the door toward Washington Square, with the stee-
ples of Saints Peter and Paul Church looming toward the
heavens on the north side.

The bartender arrived with fresh drinks. They clinked
glasses together.

"So," said Barrett, exhaling loudly and taking a sip from
his drink, "what brings you here?"

"You know why I'm here, Bear," said Mike after an
awkward silence. "The firm wants you to represent Elliot
Ashford."

Dickson grinned devilishly into his glass. "Correction,
Mike. The firm wants me to carry Al Menghetti's books
and keep his pencils sharp. They want me to put my arm
around Ashford whenever John Hernandez is looking.
Then they want me to sit quietly and watch *Menghetti* represent Ashford."

"Slow down a minute, Bear. This could be a great opportunity for you; for all of us."

Neither man spoke. Neither drank. Bartender Bobby
McCambridge hummed Cole Porter. Someone yelled for a
cab outside.

Barrett finally broke the silence: "Mike?"

"Yeah?"

"Butt out, okay? Go sue somebody. File a writ. Get laid.
Just let me be."

Mike Reasoner turned and took in his friend's profile: the short but disheveled graying hair, the rumpled suit, and the florid face. Barrett had smiled when he spoke, but could not hide the cynicism that engulfed his features.

"Hear me out, Bear. Then I'll leave you and Ginger II alone. C&S is in trouble. The partners just approved a severe downsizing program that has everyone watching their asses. Nobody is safe, certainly not Your Eminence after the debacle du jour. Steve Wilmer's plan is to—"

"Please don't talk to me about Steve Wilmer," grunted Dickson, rapidly shaking his huge head. "I'll hear you out, Mike. I owe you that much for your unsolicited efforts to salvage my unworthy ass. But don't mention that human pencil to me again."

Barrett and Mike had unsuccessfully argued that electing the shrewd, forty-three-year-old, fiscally conservative corporate partner would deal a fatal blow to the firm's already fading tradition of collegiality and professionalism. Wilmer had not forgotten.

"All right," said Mike, "forget Wilmer. But taking on the Ashford case is a winning strategy for everyone involved."

Barrett laughed again. "It sounds like a strategy that came to Wilmer on radio waves through the fillings in his otherwise perfect teeth."

Mike shrugged, then said in a quiet voice, "Actually, it was my idea. . . ."

"*Your* idea?"

"The publicity you'd get could launch a profitable white-collar crime group. C&S is the only major firm in town not getting fat representing corporate executives charged with securities or tax violations."

"And I'm the only senior partner in the firm without anything important to do."

Mike shrugged. "You're also the only senior partner with criminal defense experience. Have you forgotten the TDA case?"

"I'd like nothing better," said Barrett, crunching another pretzel between his teeth. "My masterpiece."

Barrett had defended the corrupt head of a giant securities and tax scam in 1993, his last major court appearance. The case was lucrative to Caldwell & Shaw, but the client, if he lived, would spend another ten years in federal prison.

"Come off it, Bear. That case was a loser no matter who defended it. Besides, you were pushed into it too soon after Ellen died."

"Ellen didn't just *'die,'* Mike."

"Bear, for God's sake—"

But Barrett silenced him with a look reflected in the giant mirror behind the bar, a look that said we've been through this too many times already: Mike insisting that Barrett was justified in using his skill and influence to regain custody of his only son Jared in 1993; that Ellen would have eventually killed herself anyway. Barrett countering that she just happened to commit suicide the same night her asshole of an ex-husband locked her out of his apartment during a freezing storm, just hours after stripping her of the only thing left in life that was arguably hers.

"Okay, Bear, I'll shut up, but killing herself that night proved she wasn't fit for custody."

Barrett slowly turned his head. "You've still got it backwards, Mike," he said hoarsely. "My proving her unfit for custody led her to kill herself. More accurately, I exploited a vulnerable legal system and used the law to kill her myself. If you don't believe me, ask Jared, who puts me right up there with Son of Sam and Ted Bundy. If you could ever find him, that is."

"Still haven't heard from the kid?"

Barrett shook his head. "Not since Ellen's funeral in '93." He sipped his drink.

Mike took in a deep breath and let it out slowly. "Sorry I brought it up, but the fact remains—"

"The fact remains that even if I bought into your Great Idea, I'm not fit to represent a defendant in a case of this magnitude. I offer this morning as Exhibit A."

"You'd just be consulting, Bear. Lending your illustrious presence to a motion to reconsider bail."

"A *bail* hearing?"

"Sure. Just a special appearance. Some preparation and a presentation to Judge Hernandez. A few hours out of your busy schedule."

"John Hernandez. Were you the one who told Ashford's people we were classmates in law school?"

Mike Reasoner looked away.

"Okay, Mike, let me make sure I've got this right," continued Barrett, a thick index finger jammed against his temple. "All you want me to do is exploit my lifelong friendship with John Hernandez in order to free a closet Mafia don who carved up his wife's privates. Am I close?"

Mike exhaled and gazed at the ceiling.

"And I'm to do this," continued Barrett, "so that C&S can leverage the resulting publicity into attracting big fees from business executives who cheat their stockholders and the U.S. government."

Mike turned toward him then and spoke so quietly Barrett had to turn his head. "Among the myriad of things that have escaped your memory, Bear, is the fact that the U.S. government presumes people innocent until they're proven guilty. You've also apparently forgotten your sworn obligation as a trial lawyer."

"A trial lawyer is also an officer of the court."

"I know. That's the hard part. You're sworn to be both."

Barrett grunted and signaled the waiter for another drink. "Preaching doesn't become you, Mike."

Barrett noticed that Mike started to rise, then sat back down and took a sip of his scotch and squared his shoulders.

"I can't deal with your cynicism about the criminal justice system, but damn it, I can and do remind you that our legal system extends equal justice to rich and poor alike."

Barrett roared with a laugh that attracted the attention of people seated at the far north end of the dining area under the mural of Emperor Norton. "What have you been smoking, Mike? Wrapping the firm's exploitation of the greed of the nineties in an American flag isn't your style."

"Your skepticism is noted for the record, Bear, but let me finish. My proposal would put a third of our profits from your new group into a fund to resume *pro bono publico* work at C&S. Or maybe you've also forgotten how important you used to think that was."

Dear, good-hearted Mike, thought Barrett. Where does he get the stamina? The unflagging optimism? Maybe if I'd been born Jewish. He watched Mike run a hand over his balding head.

"Look, Bear," he said at last. "We're not dealing with a whole lot of choices here."

"Ah, yes," said Barrett, pulling back the pretzels and

fishing one out. "If I reject this generous opportunity, Wilmer will have the excuse he needs to finish me off."

"He controls the executive committee," Mike said, then leaned toward his friend. "He's got everybody on quota. Lawyers are overworking cases to bill more hours to the client. He's firing secretaries, Bear, seniority be damned; laying off associates who have young kids and nowhere to go. People are hurting, walking around on eggshells, hiding behind closed doors. He's even after old Winston Cray."

"Winnie?"

"Winnie, Billy Chase, you, me. Everyone who came out against him last year. Drop around sometime and take a look at the wreckage you seem so eager to abandon."

"So it's my fault."

"I didn't say that. Exactly. What I mean is, you're the one who could still change things if you wanted to."

Barrett smiled wryly.

"What's so funny?" said Mike, plainly irritated.

"I was just thinking about what Cleopatra said to Anthony in Shaw's version. 'The library in Alexandria containing the entire history of the world is burning,' she screams. He tells her, 'Let it burn; it's a shameful history.' "

"Well, the firm's is not and neither is yours," said Mike. "Until TDA, you'd won more major cases than anyone in the city."

Until TDA, thought Barrett. Four years had passed and he still didn't know how it had happened. Beaten by some young pup from Bakersfield, and not just beaten either. Whipped. The case had squeezed the confidence out of him like a boa constrictor; slowly, one day at a time, one breath at a time, until finally, suffocating, he had willingly entered its gaping jaws.

"No," said Dickson quietly. "Go back and tell Wilmer you were Lincoln to my Douglas and Clarence Darrow to my William Jennings Bryan, but I somehow withstood your dogged persistence."

"I haven't even begun to persist. That comes after the begging."

Barrett smiled and stirred his drink and said nothing. After a few minutes of silence, Mike reached into his pocket for a twenty, rose, and turned to face his friend.

"Well, okay then, Bear. Have it your way. What do I tell Wilmer?"

"Tell him you found me dying of malnutrition under a highway overpass. Tell him I've succumbed to opium, visions of gypsy moths, and the wiles of a gorgeous young albino woman from Sumatra."

Barrett stuck Mike's twenty in his friend's top jacket pocket, smiled, and added, "Relax, old buddy. Steve Wilmer is going to find a way to get me sacked no matter what I do. It's for the best."

"Not if you take this case. You've still got friends at the firm."

"Name one—besides yourself."

"I wouldn't want to implicate anyone else. Look, just make a try for Ashford's bail. That'll get the dogs off your ass at the firm. If you find it's working out, then take it another step. Your choice. Al Menghetti would do the stand-up work at trial. You'd deadhead for a month or two, but pick up a fee of three or four hundred thousand for the firm and enough publicity to launch your white-collar crime group. Maybe in the process, we could even turn the firm around. Meanwhile, I'd be a hero for talking you into taking on the case. We'll both get our gold watches at sixty-five and you wouldn't even have to do—"

"Anything important?"

"You've got to survive nearly nine years to retirement, Bear. I know enough about your finances to think *that's* important."

"Important to you, too, Mike?"

Mike glanced at Barrett's enigmatic half smile, then rubbed a hand across his own mouth, bobbed his head from side to side, then sat back down and finished off his drink. The friends lapsed into an embarrassed silence. Mike signaled for another drink.

"Isn't this really about your own finances, Mike?" said Barrett, giving his friend the old Dickson laser-look, a searching glare that had broken many a hostile witness during Barrett's fifteen-year reign as San Francisco's top commercial trial lawyer.

Mike looked away.

"It's a simple question. I know you lost a bundle on GreenLink."

GreenLink, Inc., had been a high-flying C&S client that seemed headed for the stars—until Mike had gambled most of his savings on it and proved once again that what goes up often comes down.

Mike nodded gravely.

"So, Michael, how many years do *you* have to survive at good ol' C&S before you can claim your retirement?"

Mike sipped his drink, then bobbed his head from side to side like a prizefighter trying to evade punches.

"I'd also guess losing the firm's health plan right now would be a little inconvenient for a guy with a sick wife and a badly cracked nest egg."

The color drained from Mike's face. A man next to Mike popped a match into flames and the smell of sulfur clashed with the scent of baked garlic from the kitchen. A busboy dropped a tray of glasses, followed by sympathetic applause.

Mike stared into his drink.

"Why the hell didn't you just say so?" said Barrett.

"You've got enough problems without me playing on your sympathies, Bear. Sure, I'm on Wilmer's hit list, too. Fact is, this conversation—the way it's turning out—may be my last assignment."

The room suddenly went quiet, and Barrett fantasized that everyone in the building had stopped talking just to hear what he would say next. So he didn't say anything.

Mike slid off his seat. "Shit, Bear, forget it. I'm just—"

"Hold on, Mike," said Barrett abruptly. "I'm afraid I might fuck it up, but I'll do what I can."

Mike's head snapped around.

"But I want to meet Ashford first," Barrett added. "Get the ground rules set. A special appearance for the bail hearing only. Nothing more, okay?" He picked up his half-full glass, then put it back down. "Get those dogs off your ass. Then I'm out of law and into real estate."

"You're *what?*"

"You heard me, and don't be such a damned snob. It's an honest living and I'm excited about it."

"I know you'll be honest, which is why you won't make a living."

"In that case I'll move in with you and Nancy."

"Commercial leasing?"

"Hell, no. I'm going to put nice people into nice houses."

Mike let out a sigh, but said nothing for a minute. "The firm was your life, Bear," he said at last.

"Things change. Now I just want to be left the hell alone. So this is it, okay?"

"My word on it," said Mike, offering his hand, "and I'll go a step further: if after talking to the guy you still think he's a liar or Mafia, you've got my blessing to just walk away from the whole thing."

Barrett smiled. "But not if he's just a murderer, right?"

Mike flushed and spun off his seat, but Barrett couldn't tell if he was angry now or just still embarrassed. Then he was walking toward the door, but got as far as the bronze moose before he stopped, turned, and walked back.

"Forget something, Mike?"

"No, but you have."

Yeah, thought Barrett, he's angry.

"Listen, Bear, I can take your cynicism about the system and your distrust of your talents, but that's not what's really eating you and it's time you faced up to it."

Barrett continued to stare up at the large TV screen at the far left end of the bar—some kid on Sports Channel doing a three-sixty on a snowboard—but he felt Mike's eyes on him.

"You've achieved the ultimate conceit, Bear. You think you've become some kind of jurisprudential Dr. Frankenstein with the law as your monster. Use a courtroom, go to prison. Right?"

Barrett turned and stared at Mike as if at a stranger. "Bobby! I think Mr. Reasoner's gotten into the loco weed again. Bring him another drink."

But Mike's clear, challenging eyes remained locked on him. "I'm saying it's not just losing you're afraid of, Bear."

Barrett looked away. Then he caught the bartender's attention again and noisily shook the ice in his empty glass, "Bobby, I'll join Mr. Reasoner."

But Mike was out the door.

6

Like her fellow workers at Ward and Company, Amanda Keller devoured every lurid piece of media coverage she could find on the Ashford murder case. Every weekday, after watching the news over breakfast with her invalid mother, she dressed, then bused to work, where she had installed a small radio at her desk in the file room so she could check for any developments.

She had even begun a journal; a scrapbook actually, with articles and clipped-out news photos of the principal characters in the unfolding drama. Her record of the case began with Ashford's arrest on August 9, two days after the murder, leading to his indictment on August 20. When the trial commenced, she planned to supplement newspaper articles and photos with her own daily impressions.

She had already started thumbnail sketches of Earl Field, Elliot Ashford, Grace Harris, and Al Menghetti. When the trial started, these summaries would be expanded and taped under the subject's corresponding newspaper photo. Field's pictures always excited her; so handsome, confident, powerful. Ashford was good-looking too, but Amanda didn't go for bookish types. Or murderers either.

Anyway, with Rick Frame out of her life now—"Rick the Prick," her mother called him—it was nice to have a project. Rick, the latest in a string of disappointments, would have another think coming if he thought he was going to get back in her good graces.

Leaving the elevator at five o'clock sharp, Amanda nodded to acknowledge the afternoon security guard's lustful grin. She knew her long legs and Monroe-like looks attracted the attention of both men and women, but had always felt slightly uncomfortable under their gaze. Even the most admiring glances reminded her of judges at those child beauty pageants she had hated, even though she always won.

Only during her brief halcyon days in L.A. as a daytime TV star, when the cameras and klieg lights swept away all her inhibitions, had she felt worthy of the adulation she received. Only when she began playing the character of Sharon McPeak in *Hope's People* did she feel like a real person. The more she played Sharon, the more comfortable she had become as Amanda, a woman suddenly in contact with the world outside herself. She smiled now as she remembered how women of all ages would come up to her on the street, telling her how much they liked her as Sharon McPeak, trying to pry secrets from her. Would she marry Henley? Was Evan going to be captured? Even an occasional male would shamelessly admit watching *Hope's People* at 2:00 P.M. every weekday.

But that was nearly a decade ago, before she had ruined everything by ignoring her mother's advice and marrying her agent, a controlling Hollywood veteran whose powerful presence had made her forget she generally preferred tall, good-looking men.

"Don't be a damned fool," her mother had warned her. "Keep business out of your bedroom, child!"

But she had married him anyway, a decision that would eventually end her career in the soaps, and a mistake her mother would never let her forget.

She had tried everything during the first eight years following her exile from Los Angeles to make her way back into the entertainment industry: auditions for the highly competitive TV commercial spots arranged by her modeling agency; local theatre and movie parts, for which she was usually dismissed as being either too tall or too old for the part; even fashion-modeling interviews, where she was told she was "too voluptuous."

Nothing clicked. She was a television actress living in a city without significant television work.

So she took casual jobs—a Safeway checkout clerk, a salesperson, a cocktail waitress—anything to keep the unemployment checks coming between jobs while she tried to resuscitate her career. Though Amanda's mind was quick, the problem was her temper was even quicker. She seldom held a job more than a few months before her growing impatience and resentment would explode in the face of a supervisor or coworker.

Good riddance, she would say after quitting or being fired, then slink back to the Office of State Unemployment.

Most humiliating of all was her current capitulation, which took the form of permanent employment in the file room at Ward and Company, a large commercial real estate leasing company. She had considered it just another temporary job after being pushed into it by her mother ("No health plan comes with those unemployment checks, child!"), but that was two years ago, and now, because she was white and had somehow managed to remain the object of the male office administrator's lustful ambitions without yielding to them, she found herself chief clerk, supervising three green-card Latinos who did all the work.

Today, like every other day, Amanda walked to the elevator at 5:00 P.M. sharp, and was soon on her way to Dave's World Gym, her one extravagance. After a quick workout, Amanda caught the bus to the Noe Valley flat she shared with her mother. Upon entering, she could barely see Lucinda Keller's face in the dark, airless room, nearly opaque with blue smoke.

"You're late, honey," said Lucinda Keller, without turning her head from the TV. "Be a good girl and get your mother a new pack of cigarettes out of the cupboard."

Amanda's vision adjusted to the point where she could make out the ruins of her mother's once beautiful face, on which time and bitterness had now plowed dry furrows. Skin hanging from under the older woman's chin wobbled as she spoke, and her eyes never left the television screen, the only source of light in the musty room. She was dressed in an ankle-length satin housecoat, under which she wore a blouse closed high on the neck, with long sleeves and lace cuffs. An ivory-edged amethyst pendant hung from her neck on a thin gold chain.

"Soon as you've done that, can we eat, sweetheart?" Lucinda added, her Southern accent soft as cotton.

"Yes, Mother," Amanda said. "Just let me take off my coat."

"And don't forget my wine."

"I won't," said Amanda, though it was obvious her

mother didn't really need another glass. "How was your day?"

Amanda shook the August rain out of her coat and hung it on a hook by the door, not expecting an answer. She sniffed at the musty odor and opened a window, quietly so Lucinda wouldn't hear. The sight of a young couple outside walking hand in hand along the sidewalk caught her eye and caused her throat to tighten. She turned away, reached for her inhaler, then took in the cluttered living room as if for the first time: the cracked walnut wainscoting and the threadbare, plaid-covered couch that Lucinda Keller seemed to grow out of like a plant, floating in a bog of embroidered pillows of all shapes and sizes. Amanda's spirits had been buoyed somewhat by her workout, but now sagged as she stared at the framed dime-store art, the fake fireplace no bigger than a shoe box, ceramic figurines everywhere, and a huge oval rug she suspected to be the source of the room's moldy smell.

"You got some mail from the county," said Lucinda in a playful, singsong tone. "Have you been naughty, young lady? Gettin' speedin' tickets?"

"Not likely without a car, Mother," said Amanda, handing her mother a fresh pack of Pall Malls. "Looks to be from the jury commissioner."

For the first time, Lucinda turned her head. "What do *they* want?" she said, removing a cigarette and lighting it with a Zippo lighter. Her smoking was so automatic, the cigarettes seemed to light themselves. Amanda had always marveled at how Lucinda could inhale and speak at the same time. It was like watching a Scottish bagpipe player.

Amanda stared at the envelope, transfixed, remembering her horoscope this morning. *Be prepared for something unexpected and life-altering today,* it had said.

"Well, go ahead and open it, dear."

Amanda obeyed, and her heart quickened as she scanned the contents.

"It's a summons to jury duty, Mama!"

"Well hoopty-doo," said Lucinda, smoke bursting in puffs from her nose as she spoke. "Call 'em in the morning, child. Make some excuse."

But Sharon McPeak had been a juror in a three-week criminal trial on *Hope's People* and Amanda had become fascinated with the process. What would it be like to be a real juror, instead of just playing one? To be able to judge someone else the way everyone had always judged her? And, best of all, to be able to escape from Ward and Company, even for a few days? Maybe it was a *sign!*

Unexpected and life-altering.

"I'd like to do it, Mother. It could be exciting; maybe I'd even do something worthwhile for a change."

"Worthwhile? Is that why they pay the poor fools five bucks a day? Make more than that pickin' artie-chokes down in Salinas." She blew smoke into the greenish glow from the television. "You heard me, child, make up somethin'. Tell 'em you do something important. Now can we eat, honey?"

The smoke hung there, and so did the words. Amanda looked at the lines running from the corners of her mother's eyes and the deeper grooves that spread from either side of her nose, encircling her pinched mouth like open pliers. Amanda hoped the tightening in her throat would not loosen itself into words she'd later regret. She shut her eyes and held it in like she always did.

"Yes, Mother," she said quietly. "I'll lie. I'll tell them I'm important."

"That's my good girl."

Amanda retreated to the kitchen, then prepared and served Lucinda her dinner. She finished hers quickly, then returned to the kitchen with her wine and read the latest on the Elliot Ashford case. She scissored out the lead article for her journal, then glanced at the entertainment section and began working on the Jumble puzzle. The puzzle helped fend off thoughts of what Rick had told her three nights before. Not that she was surprised. He was beautiful, but too young to handle a real woman. Amanda knew he loved her, would always love her, but like all the others who had run away, Rick simply wasn't secure enough for her.

Still, his withdrawal had been painful, coming as it did without warning: a telephone call at the office to break their movie date. She said no problem, but her suggestion of dinner the following night at Rose Pistola in North Beach was greeted by a telling silence.

That was it. Amanda could read silences better than a priest in a confessional. Better than anyone alive.

Now, alone in the kitchen with her puzzle, she tried to think of a seven-letter word illustrated by a cartoon of a smiling rodent-like creature.

The word was "hamster." Of course. Amanda wondered why it had taken her so long to get it. Didn't she run in circles all day, going absolutely nowhere? Then spend another forty minutes on a treadmill at Dave's World Gym? Then race back home on the bus and start the whole damn thing all over again?

"What are you doin' out there, dear?" said Lucinda. "Come out here and watch television with me."

"I'm busy right now, Mother."

Amanda couldn't get the jury summons out of her head. What if it was the Ashford trial?

"Oh, come sit a spell, darlin'. It's Charlton Heston."

Amanda took in a deep breath, then let it out noisily and joined her mother on the couch.

"By the way, Amanda, this wine tastes like coal oil."

"It's a different kind, Mama," said Amanda. "We've got to economize somewhere. I can't keep showing up at work looking like a bag lady on Market Street."

"Well, don't buy it again, hear?"

Oh, shut up! Amanda wanted to scream. As her mother reached for another cigarette, Amanda noticed that though the cuffs on Lucinda's blouse were beginning to fray, the nails extending from her nicotine-stained fingers were perfectly manicured.

"Hard day, sweetheart?" said Lucinda, then turned the volume up and locked her eyes on the credits of the movie just starting.

"Awful. Is it all right if I go to my room?"

Lucinda gave her a hard look, grunted good riddance, and grabbed her wineglass with a liver-spotted hand. The glass clattered against her teeth as she put it to her lips and drained it. Amanda sat back down.

"I'll stay awhile, Mother," Amanda said, touching her mother on the arm as gently as if defusing a bomb.

"Oh, go right ahead," said Lucinda. "Leave your mother here alone all day long, then deny her a few minutes of your precious time in the evenin'!"

"It's not my fault you sit here all day," said Amanda quietly, withdrawing her hand as she stared blankly into the credits scrolling across the screen. "You could go out if you wanted."

Lucinda's head snapped around and she fixed Amanda with a hard gaze, her lips tightened into a white line.

"Go *out*?" said Lucinda as she slowly snuffed out the barely smoked cigarette, then calmly picked up a clean glass ashtray and whacked it twice against her right leg, producing two dull thuds.

Amanda looked away.

"Go *out*?" She hit the leg again, harder this time, her face now red with anger and self-loathing. Feeling anger rising within herself too, Amanda rose and moved a step away.

"I didn't ask you to come home that night, damn it!" said Amanda, words suddenly flying out of her mouth in a staccato rush. "And I didn't get Daddy drunk at that party and I wasn't the one who let him get behind the wheel."

"Well, maybe not," said Lucinda, her eyes alert and penetrating now, "but how about that tantrum you threw when we was headin' out the door. Bad enough you knew I was already worried sick about your fever."

"Particularly," said Amanda, trying to hold her ground, "with the Southeastern Pageant finals coming up?"

"You wanted that as much as I did!" Lucinda snapped.

"I didn't know *what* I wanted! I was only six years old, for God's sake!"

"And do you know how old I was when I lost this leg, Amanda? Younger than you are now! No wonder Paul killed himself! I was thirty years old and my life was over!"

"You were still beautiful; you could have—"

"Could have *what*? You tell me, Amanda, how many women—*women,* I'm saying!—have you known with only one leg at the age of thirty? Then widowed at thirty-four?"

"I suppose that was my fault, too," said Amanda without conviction, for when she was a child, she had indeed blamed herself for the car accident that had crippled her mother. Maybe she still did. She vaguely remembered her petulance and exaggerated whimpering late that afternoon when they were getting ready to leave her for an overnight with a sitter she hated. She also remembered her ill-concealed hatred of her father, particularly after the accident. Four years later, she would see his blood-soaked hair and skull fragments splattered above the headboard of his twin bed, the shotgun sticking out from between his legs, much like the other thing she had seen there so many times. All of it her fault.

Amanda didn't wait for Lucinda's response. She walked out of the room, knowing she had to get away before one of them did something that couldn't be repaired with a prosthesis.

Amanda Keller was ready for something life-altering.

7

"We'd better get cracking, Chief," said Sam Quon, entering Earl Field's office. "I just heard the news. Hi, Grace."

Two weeks had passed, and the news was that Al Menghetti had exercised his client's right to a speedy trial guaranteed by the Constitution and the California penal code. In California, this meant only sixty days from arraignment.

"I suppose he thinks he's being clever," said Field in a bored tone. "It worked for Simpson in L.A., but it won't work here because we'll be ready for him. Right, Grace?"

"I hope so," she said absently.

Field raised his eyebrows.

"Are we boring you, Grace?" he said.

Grace forced a smile. "I'm here," she said, though her head was still reeling from a telephone call ten minutes earlier from an *L.A. Eye* reporter asking what she knew about certain alleged illegal campaign contributions to District Attorney Earl Field. Grace would have to confront him as soon Sam left.

"You say you 'hope' we'll be ready," said Field. "Translation please?"

"I just mean I'm not sure. There are too many things in this case you still haven't had the time or inclination to tell me. Maybe you know what Ashford's defense is going to be, for example, but I don't. I don't even know what happened to the victim's fingernail scrapings. I also don't—"

"The clumsy bastards," Field muttered, and slammed a book down on his desk.

Grace knew Earl Field had been at war with the SFPD for three years. The most publicized part of his swearing-in speech had been a challenge to the Irish-American police chief to start appointing African-Americans to top spots on the force.

"Bigoted sonofabitch," he added. "Main qualification for promotion at SFPD is to get yourself born a white man." He looked at Grace and added, "And I mean white *man*."

Grace nodded.

"So I take it the victim's fingernail scrapings have not turned up?" she asked, directing her question to both men.

Quon looked at Field, whose face tightened in a show of concern. "Still missing," said Field, rising to gaze out the window at the mass of fog slowly yielding to the morning sun. "Dumb mick bastard. Dumb fucking bastard!"

Grace and Sam Quon exchanged a glance. Sam must be seeing it too, she thought. Though hardly a saint, Earl Field never displayed a temper, rarely indulged himself in gratuitous profanity, and could be cool in front of a firing squad. This was not Earl Field.

"I've prepared a tentative witness list," Grace said to break the tension in the room. "It's based on spotty knowledge to be sure, but we've got to start somewhere."

Field rose from his chair, started to pace, then took his seat again. "Okay. Good. Let's talk witnesses."

"I assume you want Sam to do the usual," said Grace. "Follow up the police statements of friends, neighbors, financial people, possible enemies, separating the wheat from the crap."

"Right," said Field. "I want witnesses to the Ashfords' well-publicized fights, Sam. If the maid heard them arguing, others did, too. Then get into the phone records the police have. Find a call from the Ashford residence that Lara might have made to Senator Clifton. Something Ashford might have overheard."

"The police already checked that out," said Sam. "Nothing."

"I'll bet dinner," said Grace, "they only checked Senator Clifton's D.C. and Oklahoma City home and office telephones. Get the senator's travel schedule and lodgings, Sam, then see if you can match up incoming or outgoing calls to the Ashford residence from wherever he was out on the road."

"Well, yes, of course," agreed Field quickly, but Grace sensed his annoyance. "And check Ashford's club and business contacts; anyone who might have observed that our man has a short fuse."

"You've seen the police reports on that, Chief, and—"

"Of *course* I've seen it, Sam, but I want you to take everything Whitey did a step further!"

"Got it," said Sam, but Grace saw a puzzled look on the chief investigator's face.

"Then go and *get* it," said Field. "And while you're at it, check out our forensic-expert stable and begin nailing them down for testimony during the week of October 13."

"I'll give you a hand there, Sam," said Grace.

Field nodded and said, "At trial, Grace, I'd like you to handle all the DNA and other technical witnesses, both the direct examination of our experts and the cross-exam of theirs. I'll make the opening statement."

Grace was not surprised about the experts—Earl had little patience for technical evidence—but she had expected they would at least discuss splitting the opening statement.

"So after you inflame the jurors' passions with rhetoric," she said, forcing a half smile despite her frustration, "I get to put them to sleep with experts. How about Ashford's cross?"

"Just put together a cursory workup for me on the off chance I need it. Ashford won't take the stand."

"Probably not," said Grace, determined to control her growing irritation until they were alone, "but how can you be sure?"

Sam Quon said, "The computer produced a felony on him."

"Tell me it was something nasty," said Grace.

"Couldn't be better," said Field. "Penal code section 245(a)(1)."

"Assault with force likely to produce great bodily injury," Grace murmured.

"He was young," continued Sam, "but it was messy, and if he hadn't been the son of Harlan Ashford, he'd have done hard time. Put some punk in the hospital for looking sideways at his girlfriend."

"Excellent," said Grace. "He didn't happen to use a martini stem did he?"

"Sorry," said Quon, "this was his early, pre-glass period. The chief is right, though: we won't see him on the stand."

Field stroked his mustache. "Tell me about this Al Menghetti, Grace. You've tried a murder case against him. I understand he's both competent and confident, someone we shouldn't underestimate."

"Confident?" said Grace. "My God, Earl, the man doesn't think the laws of physics apply to him."

"Ego problem?"

"He struts while seated," she added. "He also skates close to the ethical line without quite tripping over it and hasn't lost a case in three years."

Field said, "This time he loses."

Grace nodded and said, "Have you decided how we should handle final arguments?"

"Glad you reminded me," said Field, picking up the police report. "Will you draft some rough opening and closing arguments for me by, say, a week from next Wednesday."

Grace made no reply at first, just stared at him through narrowed eyes, noisily tapping a pencil on the armrest of her chair. Field was perusing the police report and didn't seem to notice her.

"No," she said finally. "I won't."

Field noticed her.

"Sam," he said, "give us a few minutes, okay?"

Sam Quon quickly headed for the door. Grace took a deep breath.

"Now, what were you saying, Grace?"

"I said I won't prepare a draft argument for you."

"Would you care to say why?"

"Several reasons come to mind," Grace said, meeting his gaze head-on. "First, if this is your idea of full partnership on a case, I'm glad I'm not just your second chair. Which leads me to a second reason: I don't know enough about this case to draft a letter to my mother.

"Third, we all have our own style of presentation and I'm sure you would not be comfortable with mine."

Field slowly nodded his head. "I see," he said, and a half smile put his handsome features into harmony, a response she knew was intended to make her feel she had been unduly petulant.

"And would there be a fourth reason?" he said.

Grace smiled back. "Yes. It will be hard to find time to

prepare your half of the argument when I'll be working on my own part."

Field issued a tired bark of laughter and held up his hands in mock surrender. "Okay, okay. We'll split final arguments. You start, I'll finish. But at least give me an outline of my part."

"Fair enough. Just one more thing. I'm not sure how to put it, Earl, but at times you seem almost more eager to smear the police than you are to nail Ashford. I think Sam is noticing it, too."

"That's crazy, Grace," he said, bristling.

"Okay, Earl," she said, holding in her frustration when she saw the look of weariness on the D.A.'s face, a face suddenly much older than his fifty-one years. "If you say so."

Field massaged his temples. "Look, Grace, I want to do both, okay? It's just that I've got a lot on my plate right now. Important as it is, this case is just one of my problems."

Unbidden, Grace sat down across from him and leaned against his desk. "Look, Earl, I don't want to be one of them; I'd like to think I could help with solutions. But you've got to let me *in*. I'm not out to steal your thunder in this trial or your job either."

Field said nothing for a minute, but Grace thought she saw the trace of a smile and a slight relaxation in his posture. She crossed her legs and gazed down at her foot, then added, "At least until you move on to the State House."

"Hell, Grace," he said, his smile broadening, "I know you want to be the first female D.A. as much as I want to be the first black governor. But first things first, all right?"

"Of course," she said, steeling herself. "But speaking of politics, I owe a callback to a reporter from L.A., something about campaign contributions from out-of-state?"

Field stared at her as if he hadn't heard her, but she saw his shoulders hunch. Then he rose slowly, like a man with a bad back, and walked back over to his window.

"What did you tell her?"

He knows it's a woman, she thought. So she's called him, too.

"Nothing, of course," said Grace. "I told her I was in a

meeting and would get back to her. Obviously, I had to talk with you first."

"Good. Just forget it, Grace. I'll handle it."

"*Handle* it?" Grace said. "What's to handle?"

Field turned around and Grace was shocked by the change in his expression. He seemed to have aged years in a moment.

"Jesus, Grace," he said, falling into his chair and rubbing his eyes. "Just give it a rest, okay?"

Grace felt a pang of compassion, but couldn't let it go just yet.

"Not if it's affecting a case I'm involved with," she said softly. "A case that you, or someone looking a lot like you, just assured me I was now totally into. Talk to me, Earl, or I'll have to get it from her."

Grace watched Field studying his hands, obviously grappling with a difficult decision. Then he looked up and spoke in a hoarse whisper.

"Okay," he said, then let out a deep sigh, almost a groan. "The tabloid thinks I took some tainted money."

"Do they think they have anything?" she asked, her tone neutral.

"Since when do they really *need* anything?" Then, with a croak of sardonic laughter, he added, "What *I* don't need right now is a pack of yellow journalists raggin' my black ass."

Grace hesitated, cleared her throat. So it might be true, she thought. A shiver passed through her as she wondered for a second or two if she really wanted to know more.

"Tell me, Earl," she said at last. "Do they have anything?"

"Do they have anything?" he echoed. "Shit, Grace, there's not a politician—from the dogcatcher of Delano to President of the United States—who hasn't taken a buck he regretted."

"Including you?"

"Hell, Grace, for God's sake, haven't you read the allegations about our President turning the White House into a bed-and-breakfast for Democratic high rollers and a few alien undesirables?"

"The White House isn't my problem. The courthouse is."

Field turned toward her, fiddled with the knot on his tie,

then spoke in a hushed tone. "I tell you this in confidence, Grace, okay? Consider yourself my lawyer for purposes of this discussion."

Grace started to shake her head, but he held up his hand. "Hear me out. Several months ago, long before this case came up, some guys from Chicago had some wild-ass scheme to turn Alcatraz into a West Coast Atlantic City. They called it their 'bingo project' and engaged me—through Jack Klegg—to give them a legal opinion on whether it was a violation of the equal protection clause of the Constitution to discriminate in favor of Native Americans and against Italian-Americans."

Jack Klegg had been Field's campaign manager and confidant then. As chief assistant now, most observers considered him to be the prime candidate to succeed Field as district attorney when he stepped down. Other observers, including Grace and Sam Quon, considered Klegg to be a prime asshole.

Grace's mouth fell open. "An opinion about gambling? In *w-writing*?"

He shook his head impatiently and said, "The guys told Klegg an oral opinion would suffice, and in answer to your next question: Yes, the 'fee' was in the high five figures."

"And these 'guys' turned out to be '*wise*guys'?"

Field turned around, arms extended in a supplicatory gesture she had never seen him make except during speeches. "We're talking gambling here, Grace, not some wildlife preserve for sea otters."

"Tell me it wasn't the Rizzo family."

"I wish I could."

"Oh my God," Grace murmured.

"Relax, Grace, nothing ever came of it."

Grace felt her stomach tighten. "Until now," she said. "Did the *Eye* reporter mention the Elliot Ashford connection?"

"She didn't have to."

Grace made no reply, other than to fold her arms and stare down at her feet. She saw the case in ruins, torpedoed by scandal. She'd be dragged down with it. An image of her father crowded into her overheated thoughts: an image of him reading the *New York Times*—not a story about his daughter winning a major victory and ascending into high public office, but about an attorney general's investigation into the conduct of the West Coast prosecution team.

"Isn't it obvious what you have to do, Earl?"

"No, Ms. Manners," he said, "it's not at all obvious."

"Then I'll tell you."

"Don't bother. I already know what the infallibly scrupulous Grace Harris would do and what she would say. But what I need from you now is to keep doing what you've been doing here since the day I took office."

"Making you look good," she said, her face reddening.

"Exactly," he said, smiling, as if she had made a joke. "Unless, of course, you want out—after hearing all this."

She stared at him, trying to get beneath the smile, the apparent candor in his eyes. He met her gaze without wavering. He's serious, she thought, suddenly uncertain what to say next. She wanted this case. Did she want it too much? How far would *she* go to stay in the game?

Grace rose to her feet, planted her hands on his desk, and leaned in so close to the district attorney she could smell his expensive cologne.

"I'll think about that," she said, "but first, you've got to send back every dollar to those bozos."

"I did that as soon as the conflict arose, before we even went to the grand jury on Ashford. I'm the city's chief law enforcement officer for God's sake!"

"Good," she said, wondering how far she could push. "Second, you've got to make a preemptive strike with the local press: 'I took the fee in good faith—blah, blah, blah—then returned it when I learned the ex-client was said to be a stockholder in the company of a man I was about to prosecute.' "

"I *did* take the money in good faith, Grace. It was Ashford killing his wife that's made it inconvenient. But going public now would be way too risky."

Grace shook her head hard. "Too risky not to. Experience tells us that most diseases disappear more quickly in sunlight than when covered up. Need I cite examples?"

"In this case," countered Field, rising and walking back to the window, "a disease that remains covered is as good as healed."

"I'm sure that's exactly what Nixon told John Dean."

The D.A.'s head shot up and his eyes were suddenly

alert, as if he had just swallowed a double espresso. "What I mean, Grace, is that I did nothing wrong in taking the money! It wasn't my fault the sonofabitch murdered his wife, and I resent the comparison with Nixon!"

"Resent it all you want, Earl. It's the one the press will make if you don't move first. I'm not saying you did anything wrong, but that's all the more reason to be the first to come forward."

"Don't make a federal case out of this, Grace."

"That would be up to the U.S. Attorney," said Grace. "I'm just a lowly local assistant D.A."

Field got to his feet, walked around, and sat sideways on his desk, close to Grace. Eye level. Intimate.

"Not for long," he said, the infectious smile back in place. "You'll soon be sitting in this office—right there in that chair—but you've got to understand that the straight arrow doesn't always hit the target."

"Is that another way of saying the ends justify the means?"

"Damn it, Grace, they sometimes *do* in politics! You've got to loosen up a little. Hell, if I hadn't done a dozen things you'd characterize as sins against the Torah, I wouldn't be in this office and you wouldn't be head of homicide trials no matter how damn good you were! This place would still be a honky old boys' country club."

He paused, leaned in close to her.

"You don't think the people out there know I've cut a few corners now and again? You think they give a damn? Hell no, because they believe this office is just the start of what I can make happen for the people out there! They *believe* in me!"

"I'm one of those people, Earl," Grace said after a moment of silence. "But if one of those dozen sins includes concealing money you took from a Mafia family that's directly connected to a man we're prosecuting—"

"Okay, hold it right there, Grace! Do you think he's guilty?"

"Of course he's g-guilty, but—"

"Okay. Next question. Do you think we stand a chance of convicting him if I go public right now? The answer is no, so the *first* thing we've got to do is remember that we represent the people of this state, then go out and convict the sonofabitch!"

"No, Earl," said Grace, meeting his powerful gaze without blinking, "the *first* thing we—you—have got to do is get this albatross off your neck!"

Field exhaled, then slid sideways off his desk and into his chair. "Okay, okay," he said, his voice resigned again. "I'll tell her the truth—*if* she calls back. Hell, maybe she was just on a fishing expedition based completely on rumors and won't even follow up."

"But if she does," said Grace, "full disclosure?"

Field thought for a minute, then rose again and put out his hand. "Okay. Full disclosure. My word on it."

Grace left, knowing this crazy case would be a tightrope walk for both of them. This damn *Eye* thing, the missing evidence, having to baby-sit Earl during the trial. Well, she would make the best of it, and thank God, at least one thing was clear in this sea of intrigue and confusion:

Elliot Ashford was dead-bang guilty.

Earl Field dialed Jack Klegg's number.

"Speak," came the voice of the chief assistant district attorney.

"It's Field. The problem is spreading, Jack. You've got to get that *Eye* bitch off my back. She's called Grace Harris."

"Harris knows?"

"She'll be cool. She calmed down when I told her the money had been returned."

Silence. Field's manicured nails drummed his desktop.

"I'll take care of it," said Klegg. "I'll call Chicago pronto and see if they're aware this *Eye* reporter could be trouble."

"Do you think I *should* give the money back?"

"Don't be ridiculous," said Klegg, and hung up.

8

Barrett Dickson had never been on the sixth floor of the city jail. It seemed unreal to him, like being on a movie set. Bright fluorescent tubes lined the ceiling in the windowless visitation area, yet the room seemed dark and desolate, redolent of fear, anger, and resignation. He flashed his state bar card and driver's license to the sheriff's deputy, then waited for the clang of admittance. He stared through steel bars at a row of cheerless people talking into telephones to loved ones on the other side of bulletproof glass. He entered the waiting area and overhead to his right a pregnant, plain-faced girl in her early teens, perched uncomfortably on a hard metal chair, telling another woman how their wedding reception at a Mission Street bar had gotten out of hand. Barrett picked up fragments of her story, how her young husband had "seen some kid makin' a pass at her and ended up hurtin' him worse'n he meant to," then took off in a stolen car. "The kid's still in the hospital," he heard her add.

Barrett shivered despite the suffocating heat, but could not detach himself from the girl's misery. A blanket of makeup failed to warm her washed-out features, and her bright, floral-patterned dress served to dull by contrast any light left in her eyes. Her hands were folded together tightly on her lap. The girl looked toward him, catching his eye before he could turn away. He wanted to tell her that stealing a car was just the beginning; her young man would eventually steal her dreams. But he sat there mute as she turned back to the other woman.

A guard appeared and led Barrett into a private interview room to which Ashford was quickly delivered, clothed in orange pants, socks, and T-shirt, his exquisitely cobbled English shoes replaced by prison thongs. They took seats on either side of a small wood table. Barrett produced a business card, then looked back through the door's chicken-wired Plexiglas window as a pockmarked trustee passed by, operating a noisy floor buffer.

Barrett's eyes drifted back to the prisoner. The overhead fluorescent lighting had turned Ashford's still-tanned face into a verdigris mask. His eyes, black specks rimmed in scarlet, glowed with the fury of a coyote Barrett had once seen caught in a spring trap. The sweep of Ashford's wrath seemed to include his prospective lawyer, and Barrett felt a dampness spread across his back, along with a sudden rush of anger at Mike Reasoner.

Neither man offered his hand.

"Can you or can you not get me out of here?" were the prisoner's first words.

Barrett shrugged and offered a half smile. He had seen men look like this in Vietnam, had probably looked like this himself, and wondered if just below Ashford's veneer of resentful arrogance lay a child's fear of the unknown. Barrett had represented many silver-spoon executives in his day, but never one suddenly uprooted from a sixteen-room mansion, manacled, and thrown into a six-by-eight holding cell.

"And hello to you, Mr. Ashford," said Barrett. "The answer to your question is that even if I sign on, I can't guarantee getting bail set, and even if I get it set, it will be very high."

Light glinted off Ashford's rimless glasses as he briefly considered the disclaimer.

"And so will your fee, I suppose. Well, don't confuse me with someone who concerns himself with such matters. Just get it set, and send me a bill for the bail and $50,000 for your half hour in court, plus expenses. Fair enough?"

"The firm wants $75,000, in advance."

"Highway robbery," said Ashford. "Not that I'm in a position to complain."

"Right on both counts."

"And what if you fail to get bail set?"

"Firm takes the money anyway."

Ashford looked like he was going to break out laughing. "Jesus," he said, managing only a half smile. "Your firm gives greed a bad name."

"You're telling Noah about the flood," said Barrett.

Elliot Ashford's eyes betrayed surprise. "When do you start?"

"I haven't decided to do it yet. I haven't completed my investigation."

Ashford's eyes flickered again behind the glasses, but otherwise concealed the irritation Dickson knew his remark had provoked.

"No commitment either way," snapped Ashford. "I haven't completed mine either. Any other conditions?"

"Only that this would be what's known as a special appearance. In other words, if we proceed in your behalf on the bail hearing, our firm does so without commitments as to future involvement." *Christ,* Barrett thought, *I'm sounding just like one of them.*

"Considering your firm's outlandish rates, I couldn't be happier," said Ashford, though the skin drawn suddenly tight across his jaw and a twitching at his temples told Barrett that Elliot Ashford had rarely been so unhappy. "I'm not quite a billionaire yet, after all."

Barrett smiled as he watched the patrician's left hand reach toward a nonexistent suit-coat breast pocket for an absent silk kerchief with which to clean the small-lens spectacles he had removed from the bridge of his aristocratic nose with his right hand. Frustrated and muttering to himself, Ashford then pulled a corner of his T-shirt through a zipper in his jumpsuit and began cleaning the glasses. Barrett was surprised at his own rush of sympathy for the handsome, arrogant mandarin, looking so pitiably absurd now, so utterly wretched.

Barrett was reminded of how the boys at Saint Anthony's, where he had lived from the age of four to fifteen, would capture moths in a mason jar and watch them beat the protective dust off their own wings against the glass.

"So," said Ashford, making an obvious effort to calm himself, "let's start by you telling me about your criminal defense experience."

Barrett shrugged. "Won't take long. One case. I defended an executive in a securities and tax scam out of the Caicos Islands. He was convicted."

"That's *it?* That's supposed to reassure me?"

"I'm not here to reassure you, Mr. Ashford, though your case should be considerably easier than his."

"How so?"

"He was guilty."

Ashford rolled his head and eyes impatiently. "Is this the place where I fall on my knees, weep genuine tears, and tell you how right you are? That I'm 'absolutely one hundred percent innocent'?"

Barrett smiled. "You could skip the knees part, given the physical circumstances."

"I'll skip the whole thing, thank you. Besides, you're the one who said it would be easy. What makes *you* think I'm innocent?"

"Simple. From all I hear, you're too smart to do something this stupid. You wouldn't have left tracks, and you would have had a real alibi."

"You're right. So what would you plead as my defense?"

"That you're too smart to do something this stupid. You wouldn't have left tracks, and you would have had an alibi."

Ashford raised an imperious but approving eyebrow. Barrett looked around him, then leaned toward him.

"Now let me ask you some questions, Mr. Ashford. Two actually."

"Be my guest."

"Are you able to explain where you were the night of the murder?"

"Why is that germane, if you're just in for a bail hearing?"

"If I were to succeed, you would be free."

Ashford gave him a quizzical look, then said, "All right, the answer—at the risk of sounding like one of you barristers—is 'Yes and no.' You don't want to know the details, but Al Menghetti knows that I was with an important man at the time my wife was killed. A man who happens also to be a convicted felon, currently under indictment. He won't testify or even admit to being in California that night."

"Why not?"

"Leaving the state would be a fatal parole violation if it became known. What's your second question?"

"I'm still on my first," said Barrett. "What's his name?"

"Are you my lawyer?"

"No. Not yet, anyway."

"Then let's hear your second question."

Barrett moved even closer. "Fair enough. Did you, or did anyone at your behest, murder your wife?"

"No," said Ashford dismissively. "What else?"

Barrett studied the prisoner, disappointed by the lack of righteous indignation in Ashford's denial. Menghetti will have to reinvent this cold piece of work if he puts him on the stand, thought Barrett. He knew that most lawyers instruct their clients to just be themselves on the stand, but Barrett knew that with hard work and a video camera, a top trial lawyer could turn Hyde into Jekyll.

"Nothing, for now," he said abruptly, remembering that none of this would be his responsibility.

"So when can you start?"

"I'll give you an answer to that question within forty-eight hours," said Barrett, giving the door a hard double-rap that hurt his knuckles.

"When you complete," Ashford said, his voice soft as cashmere, "your investigation."

To Barrett's relief, the guard opened the door.

"That's right," he said, and hurried out.

As he reentered the main visitors' room, Barrett noticed the pale-faced girl in the floral dress, still waiting. Prisoners on both sides of the walls, he thought. That could be my daughter, if I had one. Or Jared's wife, if he's married now. Keep walking, Dickson.

But he stopped, gave his head a despairing shake, then turned back and handed her his card. "If I can help you," he said, looking into her frightened eyes, "I will."

He watched her study the card, then put it into her purse, taking care not to bend it. She managed a smile and he nodded, then passed through the steel-barred door and into the elevator. Soon he would reach the splendor of the free outdoors and fresh air.

That was smart, he thought. I'm supposed to be selling real estate next year.

He headed for Moose's.

9

Leviticus Heywood looked around in wonder as he got off the elevator at the penthouse suite on the fiftieth floor of the Imperial Building, the offices of Caldwell & Shaw.

The opulence! The exquisite waste of it all! Diverse elements of matter had surely never been bound together with such restrained elegance. Soft lighting from sunken canisters spread downward across flawless koa wood paneling. At his feet in the reception lobby, a border of dark Italian marble circumscribed the perimeter of a carpet he guessed cost more than he made in a year.

His inspection was interrupted by the modulated tone of an elegantly attired receptionist in her mid-fifties, perched like an owl on a chrome and leather chair, elbows resting on a slab of marble that matched the ebony richness of the floor.

"May I help you, sir?" she asked.

"Mr. Heywood to see Mr. Dickson," he said, handing her his card, but instead of looking at it, she merely nodded toward one of the brocade-covered client chairs lined on either side of her.

Lev remained standing, taking in the view of Coit Tower and beyond to the Bay, Alcatraz, Angel Island, and Belvedere. Sailboats bounced on the water like windblown toys playing beneath stratus clouds drifting no more than fifty feet above where he now stood.

He wondered how long this ostentatious display of wealth and achievement could be maintained. He had read that C&S was hurting. This was his first investigation assignment for the "Montgomery Mayflowers," and he was curious as to why they were breaking the color line on this one. He suspected it was his work in the TDA trial in 1993, work that had helped a young lawyer out of Bakersfield whip Barrett Dickson's butt. Or maybe the white-shoe snobs were just looking to take on a house nigger. It wouldn't take long for him to find out.

Either way, he had decided that he'd deliver his report to Dickson and bail out. He didn't feel right lining up with an outfit like this and representing a right-wing defendant with big bucks against one of the top African-Americans in West Coast politics.

And Leviticus Heywood always went with his feel.

Lev was also curious as to why Dickson was being considered for the Ashford case. Dickson had seemed distracted during the TDA case and had ill concealed his dislike for his obviously guilty and morally corrupt client. He had seen Dickson in court only on dog-shit *pro bono publico* cases after that, representing tenants and small-time victims of the system. It made no sense, him popping up again in the highest-profile case in San Francisco's history.

His thoughts were again interrupted by the voice of the receptionist, announcing his arrival to someone at the other end. Her words were civil in substance, but were spoken in a tone that said, There goes the neighborhood.

"Hello, Mr. Heywood," said Barrett, entering the reception area a minute later. "Long time."

"Has been that," said Lev, returning Barrett's uneasy smile. Heywood was almost as tall as Barrett, and though both had played football—Dickson with the Stanford varsity, Heywood with the 49ers—one would never guess it now.

"You've grown a beard since the TDA case," said Dickson as he led Lev down the hall and into a surprisingly small office.

"I've grown older, too," said Lev, fingering the gray flecks covering his chin, "but mainly I've grown around the waist."

As they exchanged pleasantries, Lev's investigator's eye took note of the sparse furniture and decorations. Nothing but a few framed certificates: U.S. Supreme Court, Order of the Coif, American College of Trial Lawyers, American Board of Trial Advocates. A framed picture of a boy rested on a credenza behind Dickson's chair, next to a smaller one of a much younger Dickson with a much older man.

That was it. No files, no litter, just a smattering of correspondence. A shelf held copies of books ranging from Plato's *Republic* to three different biographies of Thomas Jefferson and novels by Mishima, John Banville, Allen Wheelis, and Paul Bowles. Hanging over the credenza were quotes from Sunzi's *Art of War*.

> *The wise man delights in establishing his merit, the brave man likes to show his courage in action, the covetous man is quick at seizing advantages, and the stupid man has no fear of death.*
>   *He will win who knows when to fight and when not to fight.*

"Have a seat, Mr. Heywood. Take a load off that anterior cruciate ligament."

Lev smiled. "Medial cardial ligament," said Lev. "1979, my second season. Same result. Got scissored between a cornerback and a middle linebacker."

"That makes it '78 then when you were Rookie of the Year."

"Runner-up. Earl Campbell got it that year."

"Heisman Trophy in '77?"

"That's true. You know your football, Mr. Dickson. You play?"

"Not the way you did, Mr. Heywood, but it got me out of Kansas and into a university in California. For that I'm grateful."

Leviticus nodded. "I got no complaints, either."

"Well, then," said Barrett, "tell me what other poor miscreants you've bedeviled since the TDA case."

Lev snorted disdainfully. "If your client in TDA was just a 'poor miscreant,' I'd hate to see one of your real bad apples."

"Well, sir, you won't have long to wait if I take on a limited engagement with Elliot Ashford, and your report will have a lot to do with whether I do."

Heywood said nothing. Dickson seemed pleasant enough, but Elliot Ashford was bad news. The whole thing added up to a bad fit. Let some other P.I. go down with this ship. He corrugated his forehead into an expression of skepticism as he glanced around again, taking in the bare walls, the single window, the decanter on a side cabinet, then back to Dickson. This was a man traveling light.

"Your kid?" said Leviticus, indicating the picture on the oak credenza.

"Yeah. He's mine."

"That you and your dad?"

"Sort of. That's Sam Caldwell, a great lawyer and gentleman who co-founded this firm. Can I get you something, Mr. Heywood? Coffee?"

"Naw. One more preliminary question, Mr. Dickson, if you don't mind. I was just wondering, why me?"

Barrett poured himself a cup of coffee and spiked it with something out of an etched-glass decanter. "Why *not* you?" he said. "You and that crazy cowboy kicked my ass in that TDA case. I figured I'd rather have you on *my* side this time. If I take it on, that is."

"*If?* Any lawyer in town would cut off one of his fingers to get a piece of this case."

"I'm not any lawyer, Mr. Heywood; fact is I'm not much of a lawyer at all right now. I'm still picky, however, about what kind of accused murderer I try to put back on the street. Besides," he added, holding up his left hand, revealing the stump of a missing ring finger, "I'm running too low on fingers to give up another one."

Heywood said "Uh-oh," and clenched his teeth in an embarrassed smile.

"Hell, I love that missing finger," said Barrett, laughing. "It got me out of Nam."

"You seem to be a man blessed at gettin' out of places," said Lev.

Barrett paused, took a sip of coffee, and made a face. Then he broke into a smile as if Lev had said something funny and glanced wistfully at the picture of himself with Samuel Caldwell.

"It's a gift," he said softly.

Lev said nothing, mentally rolling up his sleeves, and Barrett seemed to read his mind. "Okay, let's get to work. I've got problems with this case unrelated to the merits. I'm a friend of the judge, which is why they want me. If I can get past that, I'll come on board and try to get bail granted—unless he's one of the bad guys."

"Excuse me, counselor, the man's charged with murder.

I assume you knew that when you considered gettin' mixed up in this case."

"Sure," said Barrett, seemingly undisturbed. "But I'd represent a guy charged with murder if I thought he was basically a decent guy."

"So you want to know if the Mafia rumors are true."

Barrett shook his head. "That's not it, either. Hell, I wouldn't know a wiseguy if he was breaking my own knee-caps. The bad guys I'm fed up with are the three-piece economic animals who run America these days; guys at the top taking eighty, ninety million a year in salary and options while their employees go eight to five plus overtime for thirty K. Those guys hurt the country more than the wiseguys because they operate just inside the law and take more money out of the system than they can possibly spend."

"Ain't Ashford one of 'those guys'?"

"That's what I want to know," said Barrett. "He's loaded all right, but from what I've heard, he spreads his money around like Robin Hood."

"Like a sailor on shore leave," said Lev, scanning his notes. "Spends it like there's no tomorrow."

"With Earl Field on his case," said Barrett, "there may not be."

Lev shrugged. "Don't write Ashford off. He's got good PR."

"PR?"

"Spends all that money out loud, if you know what I mean. The usual white-shoe causes: new city library, modern art museum, big bucks to the ballet and symphony. Makes page two or three every time. But his biggest press since he left Washington comes from sponsoring a homeless shelter on Eighth, plus which he just seeded a project for on-the-job training for street people. He's got a bunch of them working at Resource already, so it can't be said he don't put big money where his big mouth is."

"So he might be one of the good guys, after all," said Barrett, "assuming I can get past his politics."

Lev raised gray-streaked eyebrows. "Never heard a defense lawyer apply a 'good guy/bad guy' test.

Dickson shrugged.

"Interesting," said Heywood. "Maybe I'll take a cup of that coffee."

"Plain?"

"Yeah, plain," said Lev with a wry smile, finding himself drawn to this strange bird. "Black."

Barrett smiled back at him. "So, what else have you found out about our boy Elliot?"

Leviticus summarized his written report and the state's case against Ashford. Other than rumors of some missing evidence, the police had done a thorough job, but he had decided to double-check Ashford's alibi and confirmed that no one working the theatre the night of the murder remembered seeing him.

On the plus side, Heywood hadn't found any 911 domestic-violence calls preceding the murder—other than one from a neighbor back in D.C. that had moss on it. In fact, the people he had interviewed so far expressed the belief that Elliot and Lara coexisted quite peacefully, despite Elliot's apparent view of their relationship as a one-way open marriage. He seemed to have forgiven and forgotten Lara's colorful lifestyle and rumored affair with Senator Dwight Clifton. He even welcomed her occasional appearances at the opera and symphony on the arm of his close friend and business associate, Anthony Rizzo, when he, Elliot, was out of town—before Rizzo got convicted of racketeering and entered a plea bargain that made him a virtual prisoner within Cook County, Illinois.

"So the D.A. can show means and opportunity," Leviticus concluded, "but the routine domestic-rage-killing motive is lame."

"Maybe routine," said Barrett, "but messy."

"I'd say the murderer was considerably beyond cranky."

"What about Ashford's rumored Mafia connection?"

"Another one of the roles he likes to play," said Lev, reaching for his coffee. "I figure the man for a mob groupie, a high-class Jack Ruby, nuzzlin' up to criminals as well as cops, and all the while tryin' to sell himself in Pacific Heights as San Francisco old money."

"San Francisco doesn't have 'old money.' "

Lev shrugged. "Anything stays in my wallet twenty-four hours qualifies."

Barrett nodded.

"Anyway, he failed to convince his neighbors. Overdoes everything. Cars a touch too slick, parties a bit too flashy, sixteen-room house done up a little on the garish side. Bought himself a string of purebred Arabians tryin' to impress the Woodside horsey set, though I gather he'd bet against his own horses if his bookie told him to. Even tried to play polo one season but fell off his horse and now pays someone else to ride the pony. They laugh at him behind his back down there, but nobody turns down an invitation to his house."

Barrett nodded again, an image of the man forming in his mind: the kind of man desperately trying to buy respectability and acceptance, yet pulled irresistibly toward notoriety, and now maybe toward a death sentence. Barrett felt another stirring of sympathy for Elliot Ashford breaking through his repugnance.

"Any other suspects?"

"She had some strange cult-type friends and a sister—Shannon Lake—who is said to be in love with Ashford and is rumored to have hated Lara. Then there's the whole Las Vegas and Chicago crowd and, of course, Senator Clifton, who just happened to be in town that night for a fund-raiser."

Barrett made some notes on a pad. "If Ashford's not Mafia," he asked Heywood, "what's the Rizzo connection?"

Leviticus explained Rizzo's 34 percent stake in Ashford's heavy construction company and its subsidiaries.

Barrett said, "That's it?"

Leviticus said, "That's it."

Dickson hummed a tune Lev thought sounded like a butchered version of "Stardust," then snatched a dusty corporations code from a shelf and took a quick look.

"Somebody in Chicago must have researched California law before they made the investment. Says here a minority stockholder is captive to the majority in this state for all practical purposes unless he owns at least thirty-three and one-third percent of the common stock. Then he's got clout. That's why Rizzo wanted thirty-four percent."

Lev nodded and looked at his notes. "Carmine Rizzo's brains are carried around in the head of a lawyer named Julian Gold. Poor health, worse disposition, but once a

smart and reputable corporate lawyer at a firm called Katz,
Cowan & Van Winkle. Chicago's finest. Gold bolted the
partnership twelve years ago and joined Rizzo as his *consigliere*. Ex-partner at the Katz firm told me they mourned his
departure with a three-day party."

"Yeah," said Barrett. "I've heard about him. What about
Field's feud with Ashford? Could this be a grudge match,
with Field using his office to even a score?"

Heywood shrugged uncomfortably. "You may be asking
the wrong guy on that one, counselor. I voted for Earl
Field. He's my man."

"I see. So I guess I'd also be asking the wrong guy
whether there's any fire in that office under all the smoke
people are smelling?"

"Sorry to disappoint you, counselor, but the SFDA's office is riddled with honesty."

"Okay. How about the woman who's preparing the case
for Field, and why do they call her Amazing Grace?"

"She don't lose, for one thing," said Lev, relieved to be
moving away from Earl Field. "Tougher than Vince Lombardi for another. A ball-bustin' law-and-order type who
doesn't cut deals. She's fair, but don't ever expect her to
cut you any slack."

"How come Field's got her warming the bench?"

Lev shrugged. "My guess is she'll be in uniform when
the game starts."

Barrett nodded again, then shifted gears. "Did Ashford's
lawyer okay a call to Tony Rizzo in Chicago?"

"Yep, and I called him. He was a little coy with me, but
my take is that Rizzo was with him the night of the
murder."

"So you think the alibi is for real?"

"Sure. But no way is Big Daddy gonna let his kid admit
he was out here hangin' with your boy the night of the
murder."

Barrett sweetened his coffee from the decanter, then
said, "So on balance, you don't think Ashford did his
wife?"

Leviticus Heywood scrunched his face and rubbed his
nose with the palm of his huge hand. "If I was you, counselor, I'd quit worryin' about who did it. First place, like

you said, you're a short-timer. You're gonna cut and run, right? No offense intended."

"None taken. Cutting and running is my specialty."

"Second place, Earl Field don't give a rat's ass either way. Everyone knows the D.A. hates Ashford and just been waitin' to catch him spittin' on the sidewalk. They'll pull out all the stops."

"Full-court press."

Lev nodded. "Full-on two-minute drill. He'll be convicted."

"So you do think Ashford did it?"

Lev gave Barrett an amused look and said, "I didn't say that. He might be clean."

"Then why a conviction? What happened to reasonable doubt?"

Leviticus Heywood smiled and said, "My wife would say my doubts regarding the law can't be reasonable because they're so numerous."

Barrett smiled, then looked straight into the investigator's dark eyes. "Are you not telling me something, Mr. Heywood?"

"I'm not tellin' you a lot of things."

"You know what I mean. About Ashford. About Field."

Lev slowly rose to his feet. "My bill's in back of my written report. Good luck, counselor."

"I'll see you out."

"I can find my way."

"Hold on a minute. I'm hearing you say that a guy on defense may have got himself caught in a power play around end; in this case, left end."

"Like I said, you know your football pretty good, counselor, for an ex-Stanford player. And your local politics, too."

Barrett got out of his chair and walked close enough that Lev could smell the pungency of brandy beneath the acid aroma of coffee. "What if I decided not to 'cut and run' after the bail hearing?" he said. "Would the investigative services of Leviticus Heywood be available to me?"

Lev met Barrett's direct gaze, then for reasons he couldn't rationalize—other than going with his "feel"—he held out his hand and said, "Call me, counselor."

10

Grace Harris hurried up the rain-swept steps to the Thomas J. Cahill Hall of Justice with Sam Quon at her side. Flash cameras began flickering in the gloom from the top of the stairs as photographers snapped her picture.

"Uh-oh," said Sam. "Hope the boss doesn't find out someone has leaked your highly classified involvement in the Ashford case."

Grace tried to smile at Sam's rare jab at the district attorney. His loyalty to Earl Field was as steadfast as her own had been. "It won't be a secret after today, Sam," she said without smiling, and ignoring shouted questions from reporters thrusting microphones in her direction. "I'm coming out."

Although the photographers were behind them now, a larger burst of candescence lit up her face, followed seconds later by the sound of thunder crashing in the distance like cannon.

"This weather," she shouted over her shoulder.

Sam nodded and moved up beside her as they hit the top step. "This early in the season, for God's sake!" he shouted back. "El Niño should be booked and charged with assault."

As they gained the safety of the foyer, another blast of light drew their attention back outside to a gaggle of human forms tilted against the wind, some carrying imploded umbrellas, others tugging at hats or chasing them. Vehicles crawled behind headlights still glowing at 8:00 A.M. as they poured off 101 and 280 onto flooded city streets. Water raced down Bryant Street like an ocean surf, and branches of wind-battered sycamores lashed at the sky.

Gaining the quiet confusion of her cluttered office, Grace reopened her umbrella and tossed it upside down in a corner, then hung her coat on a rack and shook water from her hands. Sam appeared with steaming cups from the employees' coffeepot, and Grace used hers to warm her fingers.

"Now, what's this about you 'coming out'?" said Sam.

"Take a look at these," she said, and handed him two new Ashford case filings, one entitled Association of Counsel, the other a renewed motion to set bail.

"Again?" he said.

"I'm opposing the motion in twenty minutes," she said, her tone edged with anger.

"Really. How come the chief is passing this one up? The press will be all over the courthouse."

"Earl is testifying in Sacramento on some new proposed drug legislation."

"Why the long face? Isn't this what you've been waiting for?"

"Jack Klegg notified me at home," Grace said, trying to lighten her tone. "An hour ago. The papers were delivered a half hour later."

"Oops."

"Didn't give me time to get my hair done."

"Or prepare for the hearing," he said. "Is this Klegg's revenge for Earl assigning you to the case instead of him?"

Grace shook her head. "He knew Earl had to have a woman on the case, plus he's as rusty as Earl."

Sam shook his head. "Earl's rusty," he said. "Klegg's corroded."

"Anyway, Klegg said it would be routine and it should be."

Sam looked at the moving papers. Below Al Menghetti's typed name, the motion was signed "Caldwell & Shaw, by Barrett Dickson."

"Barrett Dickson? Caldwell & Shaw?" said Sam. "So it's true."

"Yeah. He's a buddy of the judge, plus he's got some new doctor to testify."

"The usual song and dance?" said Sam. "The poor little defendant is too sick for confinement to a cell."

Grace shrugged. "I suppose."

"As if that ever works," said Quon.

* * *

Grace was surprised to feel her heart beating hard against her rib cage as she and Sam entered Department 26. Sam took a seat in back. Grace saw that Al Menghetti and Barrett Dickson were already there, lounging casually in the jury box.

Seated, Menghetti appeared to be as tall as Dickson, but she knew the Los Angeles lawyer was long-waisted and, when standing, little more than average height. He seemed to be made of squares and rectangles, an unfinished sculpture piece. His breadth, combined with an eighteen-inch neck, square jaw, and thin, unsmiling lips, communicated power and confidence.

Grace mused that she and Field should be grateful the matter was not going to be decided in a tag-team wrestling match.

She went through the rail and shook hands with Menghetti. He grudgingly introduced her to Barrett Dickson, whose damp palm revealed that he would probably be arguing the bail motion himself. Menghetti then walked away, obviously unhappy to be saddled with co-counsel. Maybe she could exploit this apparent tension as the trial progressed.

She took in the rumpled state of the once great lawyer who had so inspired her when she was just starting out. More than ten years ago now, she had heard he was in the courthouse and had slipped into the back of the courtroom just as he was dissecting a hapless CPA on cross-examination. She had been both exhilarated and depressed by what she had seen, wondering if she could ever do what he seemed to be doing with such ease.

But now Barrett Dickson had the look of someone recently awakened from a near-death experience. He smiled awkwardly as he stood up in a clean but wrinkled suit, wearing shoes as dull as his expression. His face was florid and puffy, with tiny veins that spread from his nose to merge into prominent cheekbones, betraying his rumored affection for the grape. Though he looked damaged, there was an appealing gentleness in his face that took her by surprise. His expression was devoid of self-pity, but he had the manner of a man embarrassed by his six-foot-five-inch height, as if he owed smaller people an apology for looking down at them. Only the gritty baritone voice seemed to accord with the brilliance she had seen in that courtroom more than a decade earlier.

Still, he's friends with the judge, she reminded herself, suddenly annoyed, and that might make him the most effective lawyer in the courtroom today. She decided to meet the defense's obvious exploitation head-on.

"Aren't you a bit wide of your specialty today, Mr. Dickson?" she said. "I thought you were a civil practitioner."

Barrett shrugged. "Perhaps I am a bit in foreign waters, Miss Harris, though George Bernard Shaw once claimed the right to speak on medical matters because his uncle was a doctor."

"Speaking is one thing; you've just walked into the operating room, Doctor."

"Well, as Woody Allen says, ninety percent of living—"

"—is just showing up," said Grace. "I know. But I can't think you really wanted to show up in *this* case, Mr. Dickson."

He said nothing to this. Just looked at her in his inscrutable, gentle way. Grace concluded that Dickson's eyes, though red-rimmed and swollen, were his best feature: large and dark green, but curtained-off somehow. He was, she decided, interesting-looking, though not classically handsome. What he had was an inestimable presence, derived mainly, of course, from his size, but also from a dangerous intensity behind those melancholy eyes that Grace knew had broken many a witness. She would have to be careful with this man.

"Call me Barrett, okay?" he said, more alert now, as if awakening from a nap. "Look, I'll give you another parable, this one from the sage lips of Yogi Berra: 'If people don't want to go to the ballpark, nobody's going to keep 'em from going there.' "

"Translation please?"

Dickson glanced over her head as two bailiffs escorted Ashford out of an adjacent holding cell and into the room, dressed in a gray pin-striped suit, white shirt, and conservative tie.

"Watch this," he said simply, then excused himself and walked away.

Barrett Dickson's enigmatic remark sent a chill of uneasiness into her stomach. It came across as a challenge or at least a forewarning. *Watch this?*

She turned and saw that Ashford did not appear ill at all; indeed, he looked to be in decent health under the circumstances. His eyes were clear without hint of illness, and his features and grooming were as precise as Dickson's were haphazard. He even smiled at her. A louder warning signal went off on the instinctive right side of her brain. *Something's not right here.* She wondered if Earl Field had intuited the same thing and decided that testifying before a hostile senate committee in Sacramento might be safer than attending this "routine" hearing. She prayed she would not stammer in front of Dickson.

All rose as the Honorable John Hernandez took the bench. "So, Mr. Dickson," he said, "you'll be joining us in this matter?"

Dickson rose unsteadily and spoke in a deep but slightly tremulous voice.

"For purposes of this motion, at least, Your Honor. I have little to offer a man of Mr. Menghetti's experience, other than perhaps a view of the forest—a product of my distance from the trees—a dubious contribution at best."

"The court values perspective," said the judge, half smiling, "but in view of the clear allegations of murder with special circumstances, a little law would be prized even more."

"Ah, there's the rub, Your Honor, for I must also confess to a general ignorance of criminal law. I hope, however, to persuade the court that the facts underlying this motion might render my ignorance moot."

"The court notes, Mr. Dickson, that in the past whenever you asserted 'ignorance,' opposing counsel reached to protect their wallets."

Laughter erupted among the reporters in attendance, quickly silenced by the bailiff's glare. Grace glared, too, wondering how she might interrupt this love-fest.

"You flatter me, Your Honor, but from the perspective of my admitted ignorance, I recently asked Mr. Menghetti whether he had reminded the court when this motion was argued before—"

"Twice before," said John Hernandez.

"Twice before, Your Honor—that the case should not

be *presumed* to be one of 'special circumstances' until a probability of such circumstances was shown to exist."

Grace decided she had to break this up somehow. She stood and said: "I would not be so impertinent as to suggest that Mr. Dickson was correct in his self-assessment of abysmal ignorance, Your Honor, but—"

"I don't think I used the word 'abysmal,' Ms. Harris," said Barrett, grinning broadly at her.

"You didn't need to, counselor," said Grace, grinning back and noticing, despite her tension, that the man had a marvelous smile. "Your Honor, Mr. Dickson is apparently unaware of the testimony of Dr. Yang concerning torture."

Barrett Dickson turned toward her, but stared off somewhere in the middle distance between them as if he were trying to recall her name. He rubbed his eyes wearily, then shrugged and said, "I thank counsel for lending support to my assertion of ignorance, but feel that in this one regard at least, Your Honor, hers might well humble my own. If it please the court, I would like to call Dr. Stuart Margolin, who is present here in court."

Grace asked herself why she was feeling so uneasy about this ostensibly routine hearing and why she was being so acrimonious. He had probably set her off with that "Watch this" remark. She turned and watched the doctor—a thin man with a shoe clerk's thin mustache. Everything about the man was thin—his hair, his wrist in the air as he took the oath—everything except his voice, which boomed out of his thin lips with an operatic timber and a Cronkite-like authority.

"So, Doctor," said Dickson after qualifying him as an expert, "have you an opinion on whether there was torture in this case?"

My God, thought Grace, realizing she had been set up. She felt she should object, but had no grounds. Her objection was to Jack Klegg's treachery, and that couldn't be dealt with here. Was Earl aware of this?

"I have," said the witness.

Grace forced herself to calm down and make the best of it.

"And what is that opinion?"

"In my opinion, there was no torture."

Grace felt the blood rising in her face. *It'll just be routine,
Grace. Not to worry.*

"Why do you say that?" continued Barrett.

"In my opinion, the killer inflicted the puncture wounds
after he had severed the victim's carotid artery."

"Meaning?"

"She was already dead."

"And how do you know that?"

"It's evident from the photographs; primarily, the relatively minor amount of blood loss from the wounds to the
breasts and labia."

Grace noticed that Judge Hernandez was scribbling like
a secretary taking dictation. She was feeling hot all over
now. *This invitation from Sacramento came to Earl just last
night, Klegg had said. The motion can't amount to anything,
but at least you'll get your name in the papers.*

Jack Klegg would be proven right about that, at least.
There were no less than a dozen reporters on hand to cover
this hearing.

Dickson said, "To oversimplify, Doctor, are you saying
the heart had already stopped pumping at the time the
assailant applied the puncture wounds to the genitalia?"

"Exactly."

Dickson turned to the judge and extended his hands,
palms up, and said, "Ergo, if it please the court, no
torture."

"Cross-examine, Ms. Harris?" said Judge Hernandez.

Grace's heart sank. She could see that the judge was
going for it and that they were—she was—about to lose
Elliot Ashford. She knew she'd get nowhere with the obviously well-prepared doctor. He would be testifying at trial,
however, and she needed to learn as much as she could to
prepare for their next confrontation, when the playing field
would be more level.

She started by asking him if he had read the opinion of
Dr. Yang that there *had* been torture.

"Yes. Reasonable medical minds often differ on these
matters," he admitted, "particularly on the speed and dissi-
pation of blood flow."

"So you concede that Dr. Yang is a 'reasonable medical mind'?"

"I don't know Dr. Yang, but I'm sure he's a fine practitioner. He's just out of his element on this particular matter."

"Are you aware that Dr. Yang had the opportunity to study the body of the victim during the autopsy?"

"Yes, that's what I was told."

"You have never seen the body, have you?"

"No."

"You merely looked at pictures of the body?"

"Pretty much, though I studied the complete reports of the criminalists and medical people as well as the autopsy photographs."

"When did you see this material for the first time?"

"Mr. Dickson provided them to me just last week."

"Just last week," she repeated, shooting a glance at the judge. "Would you agree that participating in the autopsy afforded Dr. Yang a more effective basis for an opinion on this issue than the cold data you were provided and that he m-might, therefore, be more in his 'element' than you are in yours?"

"Your point is well taken, Ms. Harris, but remember that Dr. Yang was merely looking at a cold body on a slab, long after all bleeding had ceased."

She could feel it slipping away. This guy is good, she thought. But I'll be ready for him next time.

"Moreover," Dr. Margolin continued, "Dr. Yang has not had the advantage of spending most of his professional life teaching and testifying on morbidity and blood-loss patterns as I have. I assure you, Ms. Harris, the woman was quite dead at the time the puncture wounds were inflicted."

After another ten minutes of questioning, Grace had learned all she could and the doctor was excused. Dickson rose to address the court, listing Ashford's many ties to the community and the various reasons he could not possibly leave the area. He reminded the judge that as a former member of the city's Police Commission and a militant law-and-order advocate in Congress, Ashford was in imminent danger of physical assault by other inmates. Dickson closed by urging that the court exercise its discretion and, in the interest of fundamental fairness, set bail at $250,000.

When her turn came, Grace pointed out that Ashford was being protected in a separate cell, but Judge Hernandez had indeed been impressed by the doctor's testimony.

Bail was set at $750,000, which Grace argued was chump change to Ashford, but again to no avail.

She glared at Dickson and slammed her briefcase shut even as the judge was leaving the bench.

"Ms. Harris," said Dickson, more relaxed now, daring to flash that damn smile again, "it's not the end of the world. Mr. Ashford is not a flight risk, nor is he a serial killer stalking his next victim. You'll have your day in court with twelve jurors."

"That's right, Mr. Dickson, and unless you went to school with all of them, too, your client will have his day on death row."

Barrett's smile disappeared. "Would you like to put that implication on the record, counsel? I'm sure the judge would accommodate you."

Grace's eyes narrowed defiantly. "The judge has done quite enough accommodating for one day," she said, and strode through the rail, her thin waist, trim ankles, and train of dark hair closely trailed by Dickson's admiring eyes. She motioned Sam Quon to her side with a wave of her hand and strode from the courtroom.

Grace tried to compose herself. She realized that her desire to impress Dickson was compounding her distress now in losing to him.

"Tough break," said Sam. "You got blindsided."

"And not by Dickson," she said, striding faster with each step, trying to control her anger.

"You were pretty rough in there, Grace," said Sam cautiously.

"I shouldn't have said that to him about the judge."

"It won't get back to him. Dickson's not that kind of guy from what I hear. Let me buy you a cup of coffee. It's only round one, Grace."

"We took some heavy punishment, Sam," she said, keeping up her rapid pace. "A wife killer, back on the streets."

"At least he's fresh out of wives."

Grace didn't smile. "What I don't understand, Sam, is why Klegg didn't tell me Dickson was going to make his pitch on the absence of torture."

"If he knew, it means he either wanted Ashford out on bail or just wanted to see you lose."

"Or both."

She felt Sam's questioning eyes on her.

"Do you think Klegg knew what approach Dickson was going to take?" Sam asked.

"I don't know. The papers were cleverly ambiguous. But I intend to find out."

Back in the half-empty courtroom, Elliot Ashford clutched Barrett by the arm.

"That was magic, counselor," he said. "I'm in your debt."

"$75,000 will fully satisfy that debt, Mr. Ashford."

"Of course," said Ashford, tightening his grip on Barrett's arm, "that was our arrangement. But now we've got to persuade you to stay on with us, don't we, Al? I'm serious, Barrett, anything you want. Hourly rates plus a major bonus when we win. Sound fair? That was marvelous, wasn't it, Al? Just from looking at the photos?"

"Well done, Dickson," said Menghetti, extending his hand magnanimously, if not enthusiastically. "I should have caught the blood-flow patterns myself."

"You've had your hands full, Al," said Barrett. "Anyway, it was the doc who persuaded the judge."

"Humble, too," said Ashford, beaming at Barrett. "A regular Abe Lincoln. We insist you stay with the ship, Dickson."

Barrett gave Ashford an amused look. People hate lawyers, he thought, until the minute they need one themselves. Still, for a second, the invitation produced a seductive twinge in his gut, the kind he used to get when he had done well and someone wanted him. It had been a long time since someone had wanted him.

"Well, Barrett?" said the beaming defendant. "Join the crew?

"I only signed on for the short cruise, Mr. Ashford," said Barrett, making his way through the rail and toward the door. "I'll consider it, of course, but I'm inclined to disembark here."

"It will be the trip of a lifetime," said Ashford.

"I've no doubt of it," said Barrett, not looking back. "Bon voyage, gentlemen."

II

The telephone awakened Barrett the next morning in his small apartment on Telegraph Hill near Coit Tower. He fumbled for the phone and squinted at his clock as a woman's voice he couldn't identify came through the receiver. It was almost noon, but he didn't feel like talking to a stranger with his throbbing head propped on one elbow and a mouth that tasted like the inside of a motorman's glove. He had not just disembarked last night, he had walked the gangplank. What he felt like doing was going down the hill to one of his favorite bars, the Washbag or Moose's, and not talking to any strangers there either, particularly strangers like this one who insisted on scheduling a meeting tomorrow with Messrs. Ashford and Gold to discuss the "scope of your participation in the trial."

Now he remembered. Despite his parting "Bon voyage," two cashier's checks had been delivered to his office within two hours of the judge's ruling: one to the order of Caldwell & Shaw for $75,000 and another for $350,000, marked "advance for trial services."

There had been no note.

Now, too hungover to protest or explain, he grunted, "Tell Mr. Ashford I'll call back."

Dickson put his feet on the floor, one at a time. He sat there for a while, then lumbered into the kitchen, where he fished a relatively clean glass out of the crammed sink and swallowed four aspirin. He turned on the gas to heat some coffee, but then couldn't find a match. The smell of the gas sent a wave of nausea through his stomach and awakened memories of a white Mercedes in a dark garage still reeking of an equally noxious odor and the dead weight of Ellen's body in his arms.

Barrett had met Ellen Farr in 1971 at Esalen, near Big

Sur, California, home of the human potential movement. He was thirty, single, and working at C&S as an associate attorney. He had come to Esalen to attend a weekend seminar on nonviolent confrontation led by a Buddhist monk and a gritty female veteran of civil rights demonstrations in Selma, Alabama. Barrett, bruised by his own violent youth, then Vietnam, had hoped that the courtroom might prove the ultimate catharsis for anger; a place where people with a grudge might allow their legal champions to spit verbal bullets and refrain from shooting at each other with real ones. Barrett smiled sadly now at the notion, wondering what had become of that idealistic youth, the kid with the optimistic—if somewhat wary—view of his future.

The lecturers at Esalen were both brilliant and obscure, but the thing he would remember most was Ellen Farr, surely sent by Saint Emilian, patron saint of orphans, to pick his unworthy ass out of the crowd and give his life new meaning.

Ellen had a Phi Beta Kappa key, an advanced degree in differential psychology, and a great pair of legs. She had led Barrett's "trust group" experience on Saturday morning, demonstrating poise, intelligence, and just the right touch of Esalen quirkiness. Barrett had failed the exercise—he kept lifting his blindfold, certain he was being led by his "trust partner" over the edge of some precipice—but had enjoyed watching her later as they stood on a cliff overlooking the Pacific; watching as her carelessly worn blond hair was tossed from her face by an offshore breeze, revealing large, pale blue eyes and a full smile that made everyone feel good just being in the same space with her. Whenever she called him by name or threw him the most trifling compliment, his heart ached with pleasure, and when she treated others with equal warmth, he felt an unreasoning envy.

She had told him he would be happier if he could trust people more. "Take more risks," she said, making him feel ashamed. He had thought of responding with "Really? How's this for taking a risk? Marry me tomorrow." He said no such thing, of course, but returned to his room late that afternoon aware that he had fallen hopelessly, tragically in love with this fascinating woman.

Later that night after dinner, he scrambled to grab a seat

next to her—not easy at 238 pounds even in those days—
in the rear of a dimly lit room for a presentation of Gestalt
dream analysis. She asked him if he had come to have Fritz
Perls raise his level of trust, flashing him a bemused smile
that made him feel like a freshman transfer student.

"I've decided to trust my luck," he had managed to say,
"by asking you out next weekend."

She smiled, but wordlessly settled in to hear the presentation. Barrett fidgeted nervously until Perls was nearly finished, then asked her to go outside, along the cliffs that
overlooked the ocean. She surprised him by agreeing, and
a minute later was standing close to him, her hair the color
of barley in the pale light of the half-moon rising over the
trees, her delicate features exquisite in silhouette as she
stared across the pool toward the rippling neon sea far
below them. He asked her questions about her past,
touched her arm, felt the softness that seemed to melt into
his own skin, sending an electric current down his spine.
Again, she didn't move away from him or remove his hand,
and he became less aware of the voices from within the
building, the smell of smoke from the chimney, the even
rhythm of breakers exploding against the rocks below. He
barely even heard her words, so enthralled was he by the
warmth of her skin under his touch, the sight of her breasts
rising and falling with each breath.

She told him about growing up in Bend, Oregon, on the
Deschutes River; about going to college in Eugene, then
moving to Piedmont, California, when her father was
tapped to head a bank in San Francisco. She spoke of her
rebellion from her parents, running away to L.A. with a
man she had planned to marry but didn't; about a modeling
stint that paid well but didn't lead anywhere; about attending night school to finish her psych degree; and—a jarring note here—about falling in love at first sight from a
distance of a hundred feet or more with a man in a black
T-shirt signing for a deaf group at a rock concert at Fill-
more West in San Francisco. She dreamily described the
easy grace of the man's movements in the dull glow of a
single spotlight as his hips swung in time to the music and
his flowing arms and hands conjured words out of sound
like a sorcerer. Barrett wondered for a moment if she had
forgotten he was there, and found himself suddenly and

painfully jealous of a man long lost in the past of a woman whose last name he didn't even yet know.

The charismatic man had turned out to be a "Rolfer," a deep-tissue massage therapist of the Ida Rolf school, living in Big Sur. He introduced her to Esalen, then disappeared, rumored to be headed for the East Coast.

She told her story without rancor or sadness and then asked him questions, too, which he answered as honestly as he could. He told her about having been abandoned as an infant, then later being sent to a Catholic school for boys in Topeka from which he had been delivered after high school thanks to his size and ability to catch a football. He confessed he hadn't known Stanford from Purdue, but knew which to choose when he was told Stanford was near the Pacific Ocean.

When they had run out of questions and found they both liked red wine, good books, and big-band music, they stood together in silence under the moon, gazing at the sea.

"Have you been out there?" she asked dreamily, looking westward across the ocean. He wasn't sure if she meant deep-sea fishing or travel to the Orient. She had meant had he been across the Pacific—to Asia, Bali, places like that. He had said, sort of, but it wasn't exactly a pleasure trip. A strange look passed over her face then, and she said she hadn't been anywhere, speaking in a tone suddenly edged with resentment. Had Barrett not been in an erotic trance at the moment, he might have detected that the object of his desire was revealing a dark side. Instead he put a protective hand around her waist and told her he'd be happy to spend his life right where he was at that minute. Her smile returned and she put the palm of her hand to his cheek and kissed him full on the mouth. He put his other hand around her thin waist and urged her hips into his hardness and felt the hot tip of her tongue exploring his lips, his teeth, his own tongue.

A sudden burst of laughter from inside caused her to pull back and give him a look that said she was a little surprised by what was happening.

"I never got your last name," he said, to ease the tension.

But she just smiled again, clasped her hands behind his neck, then pulled herself up onto her toes and kissed him again.

"It's Farr," she whispered in his ear.

"To where?" he asked, trying to catch his breath.

"My last name. Ellen Farr."

He laughed at himself and giddily breathed in the clean smell of her hair, luminescent in the moon glow. His body pulsed with new energy and the conviction that whatever he had accomplished in his life and whatever he had become had been to prepare himself for this woman.

Ellen Farr. He mouthed the words to himself as if in prayer and pulled her closer. He dreaded having to leave in the morning, but pictured them driving up to Carmel or nearby Nepenthe next weekend for dinner.

But next weekend suddenly seemed light-years in the future. He considered asking her to join him at the baths right now, but feared she would say no and dash his joyful delirium, or say yes and mar his image of her essential virtue. So he said nothing, a silent sentinel, hardly breathing for fear she might move.

Barrett heard a catch in her breath—an endearing sound Barrett had heard babies make—and eased his hold on her. She looked up at him and gave him a quick kiss on the cheek that pleased him in its casual hint of domestic intimacy, but then she turned and started back toward the conference room. She was going back inside!

"You haven't answered my question," he said quickly, hating the strained sound of his voice. "About seeing me next weekend."

She looked back over her shoulder and extended her hand toward him. "Of course I have," she said, giving him a playful smile that said she was now, and would forever be, a step ahead of him.

And Barrett smiled with relief as he reached for her hand, like a man seizing a life jacket.

It had taken two years of living with Ellen, then another two years of marriage, before Barrett began to trust her fully. He had never trusted anyone or anything in his life. He guessed that trust was something kids learned from their parents.

Then, after twelve more years together, it had taken Ellen only one day to betray and forever destroy that trust. Without warning, she ran off, leaving a note that read:

Forgive me, darling Bear, but I'm suffocating.
   *I beg you not to destroy Jared's view of me when you
try to explain the unexplainable to him.*
   *I love you. Try to believe this really has nothing to do
with you.*

Ellen

It was 1985. Jared was nine and Barrett was indeed as
fair to Ellen as he could be as he tried to explain and
rationalize her sudden departure. He particularly resented
her for sneaking off without talking to Jared. How could
she leave me? he would think; but even more bitterly, he
would ask, How could she abandon Jared without so much
as a word? It was six months before he learned that her
leaving truly had indeed not so much to do with him as
with the handsome young bond salesman who had stunk
up their house with his cologne and who apparently shared
Ellen's yen for travel. At last, Ellen would see the world.

A year later, Barrett dissolved the marriage, maintaining
full custody of Jared, but in 1987 Ellen returned to San
Francisco, now married to multimillionaire Barry Van den
Berg, and won the boy back. Then came 1993 and Barrett's
courtroom custody victory over his divorced and now dis-
graced ex-wife.

Barrett had managed to survive for a few months after
Ellen's suicide that same night and Jared's disappearance
the following day, persevering like the good soldier he had
tried to be, endeavoring to remain the skilled professional
he had become; trying to forget how he had pushed Ellen
over the edge of despair by using his legal skills to wrest
Jared from her arms.

But then he awoke one morning and realized that whatever he had become had come apart. He began to envy
Ellen's desperate courage and the peace she had purchased
with it. Her death had shoved his face, as Lara Ashford's
had been years later, into a harsh and unforgiving mirror.
And what he had seen reflected there had killed his enthusiasm for life as surely as if it had been pierced by a shard
of glass.

Barrett found himself standing in front of his stove, staring at a burning match he had somehow located and struck.
He managed to light the burner just as the match burned

out in his fingers. He shook the pain out of his hand, then opened a can of beer and the blinds of his living room window.

He had moved to the Telegraph Hill apartment in 1988, a year after he lost custody of Jared. It wasn't much of a place, for he had also lost a bundle on the GreenLink investment. It had a small kitchen with flowered paper and the permanent smell of burnt toast, an eight-by-ten living room with a fireplace the size of a microwave oven but with a decent view of the Bay, and two bedrooms, each with a king-size bed. He had still hoped to win Jared back at the time.

His own bed had only twice received an overnight female guest, and only one of those experiences had turned out halfway decently. The other bed had never been used at all. He preferred being alone.

He sat for a minute on the worn couch in front of the fireplace, then strolled back to the counter that separated the kitchen from the living room, and flipped through yesterday's mail—bills, ads, a book of discount coupons, and a note from building security reporting that he had gone off again without fully closing his front door.

He fingered the checks Ashford had sent. $425,000 was a lot of money, and he knew that there would be a sizable bonus in the event of an acquittal. He smiled as he studied the checks, concluded he must have done pretty damn well in court yesterday. The realization set off another twinge in his empty stomach: not quite that old peak-experience-electric-surge up his spine, but a pleasant feeling he had almost forgotten. Was it the rush of knowing he could still do it? he wondered. He had never stopped to analyze the sensation when it was as commonplace as the jolt now delivered by the first drink of the day.

Or was it simply the guilty pleasure of savoring something all the more because he had stolen it. Grace Harris simply hadn't prepared for his no-torture scenario, even though he had called Field two days before to disclose it to him. Too bad in a way, for he liked the woman and didn't like seeing her uncomfortable.

He liked her a lot.

He sat down at his upright piano and opened the sheet music for "Stardust." He began practicing, leadenly striking the keys with two thumbs and seven thick fingers that often caught a black key along with the intended white one, creating a dissonance of the sort that would not have provoked envy in Bartók or Hindemith.

He had mastered the treble staff—at least intellectually—but was still having trouble with the bass notes, scattered as they were all over the damn page, many of them well outside the five lines that constituted his security zone.

He began to sing along in a voice that expressed enthusiasm but had absolutely nothing else going for it.

"Sometimes I wonder why I spend the lonely nights dreaming of a song"

The phone rang. He let it ring.

"The melody, haunts my reverie"

He had made it all the way to *"When our love was new"* when the phone rang again, and this time he snatched it up.

"And each kiss an inspiration," he crooned into the receiver.

"Are you drunk?" Mike Reasoner bellowed from the other end.

"Now there's an idea."

"You're entitled, hero. Again, my congratulations."

"For what? That modest victory barely rose to the level of a parlor trick. Your granddaughter could have won that motion yesterday, Mike. Maybe even you could have."

Mike chuckled. "How's Mr. Ashford taking to his regained freedom?"

"Swimmingly. His secretary called me this morning from his suite at the Ritz. Guess he doesn't want to face his house yet. Wants me to stay on the case, by the way."

"Bravo! This trial could put you back on top, Bear!"

Dickson gave his head an exasperated shake. "I think that's what they told Faye Dunaway when she was offered the role of Joan Crawford."

"Seriously, Bear, this case will—"

"I'm going to say no, Mike."

"Oh."

"You haven't forgotten our deal?"

"No, of course not," Mike said. "You've done all I asked. Thanks to you, I'm safe, for the rest of this year anyway."

"Good," Barrett said, and botched an F major chord.

"But, Bear," Mike added, shouting over the cacophony, "you're not, and if Wilmer finds out Ashford wants you to continue and that you're going to refuse . . ."

"He'll have the final piece in place, like he always intended."

"Exactly," Mike said. "Now admit it felt good to be back in the saddle again."

"Not as good as it feels to be out of it and headed for real estate."

Mike said nothing.

"Unless, of course, you persuade me I should become a professional musician instead."

Mike grunted something, then said, "Okay, Bear, I have to respect your decision. But at least pretend for a minute that you still work at C&S. You and I are on the agenda at today's executive committee meeting regarding the status of the firm's involvement in the case."

Barrett considered. If this was it, at least he'd go out like a man.

"All right. Let's get it behind us. What time?"

"Four o'clock."

"I'll be there."

"Good, but if Wilmer doesn't find out Ashford wants to keep you on, don't tell him, okay? Then I can say you've done all Ashford asked of you. Nancy and I will be home-free and you'll remain a hero, something we could use around C&S right now."

" 'Unhappy the land that needs heroes,' " said Barrett. "Brecht."

Mike was silent.

"But that was long ago," continued Barrett, singing again and wildly striking the keys of the shuddering upright, *"and now my consolation—"*

"—is a vodka martini," interrupted Mike. "I'm hanging up now, but for God's sake, Bear, be nice today. Okay?"

"I'll be sweet as honey, Mike. Mr. Congeniality. Considering the things Steve Wilmer's tried to do to me for the past two years, I think I have been amazingly nice to the sonofabitch."

"*Nice?*" said Mike. "I think you're in denial, Bear."

Dickson said, "The hell I am."

Mike said, "See what I mean?"

12

Grace Harris pulled several strands of gray away from her head with a thumb and forefinger. She wondered if she should start dyeing her hair. She was looking tired lately. Worn. The mirror below her kitchen clock could be cruelly candid in such matters, particularly in the fog-filtered lighting of a typical San Francisco late summer dawn. Forty-two years, a troubled, troublesome sixteen-year-old son, and more than three hundred felony convictions had begun to record themselves on her pale, drawn face. And now she faced the Ashford case, her biggest challenge of all, and the logical next step in an unblemished career that lacked only public recognition for her accomplishments. There would be more silver in her hair by the time the verdict was rendered in this case, she thought, but perhaps there would be a pot of gold as well.

District Attorney Grace Harris.

That would show those white-shoe lawyers on Wall Street who had rejected her as a trial candidate because she suffered an occasional stammer under stress—as in during job interviews. Show her father, too.

But it would have to be seen as her victory as well as Earl's, and she'd be competing for a share of the credit with a man who was the city's media darling and could play the press as well as he played politics. She'd have to grab her own slice of glory, not expect him to give it to her. She would feel no shame in this, for as much as she needed the case, Earl Field needed her on the case even more.

Fact: The majority of the jurors in long trials like this one would be women.

Fact: Her involvement would dilute criticism that Ashford's indictment was politically motivated or the product of a personal vendetta.

Fact: If TV were allowed in the courtroom, she—at five feet four in medium heels—would make Field look taller than his five feet seven.

Fact: If something went wrong, she'd be there to take the fall.

She dropped a bagel in the toaster.

"Morning, Mom," said Aaron, shuffling into the kitchen in his knee-length extrabaggy shorts, his head shaved but for a circle at the top.

America's future, thought Grace, taking a closer look at his black Converse high-tops, a T-shirt that proclaimed "Rasta Power!" and faded purple socks that sagged from his ankles.

"Good morning, Pumpkin," said Grace. "Are you planning to go to work looking like that? I don't think so."

Aaron ignored her. She was his mother.

"Aaron?"

"Geez, Mom, excuse me for living. You sure are bitchy on Thursday mornings."

Grace let the remark pass. She *was* feeling cranky and didn't want to get into a discussion of her late Wednesday nights out: secret, anonymous sessions at an Emeryville piano bar where, for as long as they'd let her, she gave voice to her soul in waves of lighthearted, unstammering song followed sometimes by an hour of lighthearted, uncomplicated sex with a lawyer friend from the East Bay with whom she had broken up four years earlier when he had decided Aaron was more baggage than he wanted to pack. It had been hurtful, but not bitter, and he was a considerate lover. It wasn't much, but it kept her from withering into a dry stalk. Like the way she was feeling today.

"Okay," she said, "so I'm bitchy, but that haircut makes you look like you've had a lobotomy."

Aaron snorted the way he'd been doing lately, a guttural sound from halfway down his throat. She remembered how he had spent the entire year of his sixth grade speaking to her only in a Donald Duck voice, and the grunt, though irritating, was eminently preferable.

"As for your clothes," she continued, "I was under the impression you were still in high school, not the NBA."

"Get used to it, Mom. Everybody's stylin' this way. Everybody's got this cut, too."

" 'Everybody' to your mind, Aaron, includes Skip Hodges and perhaps one other human being in the entire free world. So I won't 'get used to it,' and *you* will be more respectful."

Aaron shrugged. "Anyway, Skip said his dad don't mind." Skip's dad was Aaron's summer employer.

"Doesn't mind." The smell of burnt bagel crinkled Grace's nose.

"Doesn't mind," mocked Aaron, affecting an exaggerated British accent. "Anyway, it's what's cool, Mom."

The bagel finally surrendered itself. Grace shoved in a fresh one and glanced at her son, already engrossed in the auto section of the morning paper. It jarred her again how much he looked like his father, and she flashed on the day in 1979 when she first introduced Abe Harris to her family. With the marriage less than two weeks away, it was time to face the Havan Nagila.

"The man's not Jewish!" the Rabbi Piakowski shouted as soon as Grace was alone with him in the living room of the small Brooklyn flat. Her father paced, hands locked together behind his back. "The man is named Abraham Harris and he's *not Jewish?*"

"Quiet, Papa, he'll hear you."

"So what does it matter he hears me? I assume he is already aware he is not Jewish."

"He was named after Abraham Lincoln, Papa," said Grace, unable to suppress a smile.

Grace's mother, who had sung at Grossinger's in her twenties during the heyday of the borscht belt of the Catskills, was in the kitchen with Abe, trying to get him to eat something.

Her father shook his head. "If you insist on having children with this *goy,* I hope you will at least choose to be a devoted mother."

She frowned, knowing what he meant. The Hasidics—described as "urban Puritans" by her Jewish professor at NYU—were an ingrown, isolated, and deeply spiritual community in which women were expected to be mothers and nothing more. It had been bad enough when she had gone to college, even worse when she insisted on going to law school. Not even a male Hasidic Jew should be exposed to such decadent influences. But a *woman?* Impossible.

"Papa, things are different now," she said, unable to let it go, "and we're in America, not Poland."

She was hurt, but not surprised, when her father refused to attend the wedding. He had lost his daughter to the forces of secularism.

Later, after the vows, as she and Abe stood under the *huppah,* it took Abe three attempts to smash the ceremonial glass with his foot. Sympathetic laughter released the tension, but the more Orthodox observers on the bride's side of the aisle took it as an omen.

They were right, for seven months to the day after Aaron was born, Abe, no longer employed and increasingly prone to violent mood swings, packed his things and headed back to New York. He wrote three months later to say he had caught on with an international trading company and would be sending money soon from Asia. He never wrote again. In her dreams, she saw him dead, buried deep in foreign clay.

The doorbell rang, not once but at least a dozen times in succession. "Enter fart-face!" shouted Aaron, and Skip Hodges, indeed looking just like "everybody" too, skipped into the room.

"Hi, Mrs. Harris."

"Good morning, Skip."

She was gratified to see that Skip had deigned to doff his baseball cap upon entering the kitchen.

"Skip's folks are throwing a little birthday bash for me tomorrow night, Mom."

"You're invited, Mrs. Harris," said Skip, eyeing the burnt bagel.

Grace frowned. "Aaron? I thought you and I were going to the Hard Rock Cafe for your birthday tomorrow night."

Aaron looked puzzled for a minute, then said, "Oh."

Grace said, "Yeah, oh."

"I guess I forgot. Can we do it some other time? We've already invited a bunch of friends over to the Hodges' place."

Some other time. The words had a familiar ring. How many times had she said them to Aaron during her climb to the head of the homicide trials team after leaving the downtown firm?

"Sure, honey," she said, kissing the top of his head, eliciting another snort. "Some other time. Now finish your breakfast while I get ready for work."

After Aaron and Skip had skate-boarded off to Hodges' Hardware Store on Van Ness and Grace had cleared the wreckage left in their wake, she took a last look at herself in the full-length mirror, then grabbed her purse and bounded down the stairs. If she hurried and the traffic cooperated, she could still sneak into the weekly staff meeting, late but unnoticed.

The cold morning breeze off the Bay stung her eyes as she stepped outside the apartment building. After Abe left, she had been lucky to find an affordable apartment in San Francisco's tranquil Russian Hill District, nestled like a demilitarized zone in the center of a triangle formed by prosperous Nob Hill, sleepless North Beach, and the heartless Financial District.

On her way to the office, her thoughts turned to how she would confront Jack Klegg for having set her up the day before. How much had Earl known about Dickson's planned strategy? How much had he told Klegg? Would Earl back her on this? If he didn't, it would mean Earl had ceded even more authority to his chief assistant. Klegg would be as happy as a dog with a bone, and she would be the bone. Worse, with Klegg assuming more control, the case against Ashford would inevitably suffer. To Earl and Jack Klegg, this case had become more about politics than justice.

An hour later, Grace saw Jack Klegg through her open door heading purposefully down the hallway. He was obviously surprised to see her, and quickened his pace, acting as if he hadn't seen her. She followed him down the hall and into his office, then loudly shut the door behind her.

"Grace!" said Klegg, turning with one arm still in his coat. "What can I do for you?"

Chief Assistant Jack Klegg was lean and wiry, medium height, and ramrod straight. His perpetually tanned skin lay tight across prominent cheekbones. A wine-colored birthmark spilled up one side of his neck over the extra-high starched collars he always wore. His eyes were blue, but small and close-set. He had shed his U.S. Marine uniform two decades before, but still looked every bit the part.

"I'll tell you what you can do, Jack," said Grace. "You can quit jerking me around, especially when it puts a murderer back on the street."

Klegg didn't flinch, though he moved casually behind the security of his oak desk. He tilted back in his swivel chair and spoke as if he hadn't heard the accusation. "I heard about the bail hearing going south yesterday. What happened?"

"I thought *you* might tell *me*," said Grace, glaring at him through narrowed eyes. "Were you aware that Dickson's doctor was going to talk about blood-flow patterns and the absence of torture?"

Klegg shrugged. "Well, something like that, sure. At least I think that Al Menghetti or Dickson told Earl something to that effect."

"Is that when you persuaded Earl to go 'testify' in Sacramento?"

Klegg looked surprised. "Don't be ridiculous."

"Why didn't you tell me what the pitch was going to be, Jack? I might have been able to engage in some last-minute damage control."

"I *did* tell you, didn't I?" said Klegg, rubbing one hand across his burr cut. "At least I'm sure Dickson's papers mentioned a doctor, didn't they?"

Grace planted her hands on Klegg's desk and leaned close to him. "Jack, don't play games with me. You knew I would assume Dickson's doctor was going to do the usual song and dance about the prisoner being too ill to remain confined."

"That may have been what you assumed, Grace," Klegg said, offering her a grim smile that revealed a lower row of exceptionally small teeth. "Maybe in this instance you assumed too much. Dangerous to do that in our business."

Grace gave him a hard look but wouldn't be sidetracked. "When did Earl get back from his testimony in Sacramento?"

"It was postponed," said Klegg, swiveling sideways and crossing his legs. "He attended another meeting here instead."

"Postponed," repeated Grace. "So there n-never was a Sacramento trip; the whole thing was bullshit."

Klegg clicked his tongue and said, "Bullshit, Grace? Naughty."

"Yes, Jack, bullshit. Earl's the bull and you're the shit who's trying to turn him into a steer."

Another smile slowly spread across Klegg's clean-shaven face. "That's good, Grace. Earl will love that when I tell him, though he may be shocked at your dock worker's lexicon."

She wished she could smile back, just for one moment be as coolly malicious as the man favored to succeed Earl Field as D.A. But the best response she could manage was to meet his mocking gaze.

"You sandbagged me, Jack, which may work for you politically, but not for the people out there we're supposed to be representing—"

"Oh, spare me the sanctimonious crapola, Grace," he interrupted. "Even Earl laughs at your version of Judge Roy Bean in a Peter Pan collar. He *laughs* at you! Calls you a Vince Lombardi with tits! Did you know that?"

Grace flinched from the cruelty of Klegg's barb, relieved that he had swung further around and could not see her. He put his feet up on the sill of the window to his left, and looked out at the sunlight breaking through the fog as if Grace were no longer there.

But Grace *was* there, composed again, head thrust slightly forward over folded arms, now staring at Klegg's back, at the perfectly pressed white shirt stretched across his shoulders, at the blotched but neatly trimmed neck rising out of the rigid, starched collar.

"Here's what I do know, Jack," she said with quiet intensity. "I know your ambition helped Dickson put a murderer back out on the street. If Ashford kills another woman, it's your fingerprints next to his on the glass."

Jack Klegg spun back around to face her, but then rested his clasped hands on the desk and stared at them for several seconds before speaking. He was no longer smiling.

"I'll let that go, Grace, for now anyway. But if you aren't willing to pay the price of being a team player—even when it means getting roughed up a bit—you're going to be out on the street with Ashford."

"You're going to fire me, Jack?" she said, feeling her heartbeat racing again. "I don't think so. You may n-not have heard, but I'm trying a high-profile murder case right now. You know—the one you expected Earl to put you on instead of me?"

"I had no interest—"

"And you know the real irony, Klegg? I was being kept on the sidelines in this case, but now, thanks to you, I'm finally out of the closet."

"Are we finished here, Grace?"

"Almost," said Grace, leaning in again. "Stay out of my way, Jack. Now that I'm into this case, I'm going to make sure we win it. Then, when Earl moves on to Sacramento, I'm going to run against you and show the city what a manipulative Nazi shit-heel you really are."

Grace realized that Klegg was not looking at her, but over her shoulder at a door that had opened but was already closing. She turned and spotted Earl Field backing quietly into the hallway.

"Earl!" said Grace. "Come in. We were just talking about you."

"Oh, hello, Grace, uh, Jack. Sorry. Heard the bad news, Grace."

"Here's some more, Earl," she said, walking straight up to the district attorney. "Your chief assistant is a dissembling sonofabitch. If he had told me what I hope to God you expected him to tell me, I could have had Dr. Yang in court and maybe even kept Ashford locked up."

"I'm not sure what you're saying, Grace," Field said, already straightening his shoulders and regaining his poise. "But I'll damn sure find—"

"As for you, Earl," she interrupted, "the next time you want me to take a bullet for you, *ask me yourself.*"

13

Another freak storm hit that afternoon, leaving Barrett Dickson and other unprepared San Franciscans soaked through and cursing the local weather forecasters who had predicted "a high-pressure area building off the coast" and a return to the usual "late summer morning fog, clearing by midday."

California had become a state that suffered either too much or too little rain, caught in a cycle between drought and flood tide as it waited for the next earthquake. And now, El Niño.

Still, as Barrett slouched toward his confrontation with Steve Wilmer, his drenched worsted wool suit jacket pulled up over his head like a monk's hood, he mused on how his fellow citizens of the Golden State would remain undeterred in their use of fluorocarbon products, from air conditioners to aerosol whipped cream, all as vital to their lifestyle as melatonin, DHEA, and the other essential California food groups.

He grimaced as he remembered his last argument with Steve Wilmer a year earlier, when Wilmer asked him to represent the firm at a benefit for World Environmental Consciousness to do some client networking. Barrett had refused. He had attended too many of those feel-good save-the-environment galas, been served too much beef grown on what was once South American rain forests, had seen too many aerosol-sprayed heads arriving in eight- and twelve-cylinder gas burners. His refusal to go had initiated Wilmer's campaign to oust him from the partnership, a crusade now broadened to include Mike Reasoner.

Mike watched as Barrett entered the conference room, soaked through and looking like a beached walrus. Mike tried to read his friend's expression, but the veteran trial lawyer was wearing his poker face. Winston Cray, a septuagenarian who had succeeded Sam Caldwell as head of the firm when the founder retired in 1970, rose to offer congratulations on Barrett's bail hearing victory. Cray, a top trial lawyer in his day, had "somewhat democratized" C&S—his term for it—hiring the first Jewish lawyer and pushing the silk stocking firm into a *pro bono publico* outreach program for the poor. Now he sat on the executive committee at Steve Wilmer's sufferance, a sop thrown by Wilmer to the older C&S partners.

Steve Wilmer, now in his mid-forties, had already graced the covers of the *National Law Journal* and the *American Lawyer*. He was brilliant and manipulative, yet capable of charming those who might advance his personal agenda of power and wealth. Although his hair was thinning on top, he looked ten years younger than his forty-four years, which meant he could get away with wearing a goatee, the style au courant.

"My God!" said Wilmer, slowly extending his hand to the newcomer. "If Dickson gets the shakes today, we'll all drown."

Barrett rejected the proffered hand in favor of wringing out his tie as he said, "Not to worry, Wilmer. I read somewhere that sharks never drown."

Bad start. Mike felt heat spreading through his body, but Wilmer seemed unruffled, indicating to Mike that he might have heard of Ashford's offer and knew that Barrett would refuse to accept it. Then, true to Barrett's prediction, Wilmer would have him for lunch.

"I'll gladly suffer that poorly crafted riposte from you today, Barrett," Wilmer said, winking at Todd Jamison, the third and youngest member of the executive committee, "assuming a check for $75,000 comes with it."

Barrett gave Wilmer an ambiguous smile, tugged his wet sport coat into something close to its original configuration, then took a seat at the large conference table next to Mike Reasoner and across from Todd Jamison and old Winston Cray.

Jamison was a business lawyer who shared Wilmer's commitment to minimizing firm expenses—frivolities such as charitable contributions, *pro bono publico* work, and raises for paralegals and secretaries—thus improving the "bottom line." The most noteworthy thing about Todd Jamison—other than his recognized genius in the field of mergers and acquisitions—was that he smiled constantly, a trait Mike decided was a device intended to mask this lack of a sense of humor. He seemed to have decided that if he appeared amused by everything, no one would detect his inability to catch the subtle nuances of a joke. Glancing at him now, Mike suddenly realized that it was the firm's lateral hiring of Jamison and Steve Wilmer into the C&S partnership that had sounded the death knell of the firm's already flagging esprit and professionalism.

"Well, Barrett," continued Wilmer, seating himself, hands folded in front of him on the table, "are we to see the fruits of your good fortune?"

Barrett reached into his inside jacket pocket, removed an envelope, and, with a flourish Mike considered excessive, handed it not to Wilmer but to Winston Cray across from him.

Wilmer stared at the envelope as it made its journey across the table.

"Is that the $75,000 check?" said Wilmer.

Barrett nodded once, as Cray, with an obvious tremor, opened the envelope and extracted the check. He then began fumbling for his glasses.

"Pass the goddamn thing down, Winnie," said Wilmer. "We haven't got all day!"

Mike saw Barrett's eyebrows jump, but was relieved to see his lips remain in repose, his great jaw motionless, his expression relatively serene.

Cray reddened and complied, delivering the check with liver-spotted hands to Todd Jamison, who passed it on to Wilmer as if it were electrically charged. Mike glanced at Cray, who stared down at the table, looking like a man who had lost everything but the capacity to be humiliated.

"Are we finished with item two?" said Wilmer. "If not, we'll skip to item eight, the famous Ashford project."

Winston Cray raised his hand. Wilmer ignored him.

"I think Mr. Cray has something to say, Steve," said Barrett.

"Yes, Winnie," said Wilmer impatiently. "What is it?"

"Regarding item two on the agenda. Can we not find

some other use in our firm for the secretaries you are laying off, at least the ones who have been with us ten years or more?"

Wilmer didn't even look up. "It's not our job to find work within the firm for people we don't need. That's the whole point of getting rid of them. Let's move along now."

Mike saw Barrett bite his lip and stare at the ceiling.

"Couldn't they become pool secretaries?" persisted Cray.

"Christ, Winston," said Wilmer, "come to the party! The whole point is to cut our costs, not just move people around!"

"But, Steve," urged Cray, "we know there is bound to be overflow work now with more lawyers assigned to each secretary."

Mike knew the old man was expressing his convictions only because he knew he had the presence of temporary moral support from Barrett and himself.

"Not so," said Wilmer. "That's what computers are for: to take up the slack."

"Left by people," said Mike suddenly, unable to contain himself.

Wilmer's head snapped up, his eyes narrowed and sparking. "That comment is out of order, Mike. You're here as a guest to aid in our discussion of item eight. We are, I regret to say, still addressing item two."

"I'm also here," snapped Mike, "as a senior partner in this law firm, interested in the welfare of its people."

"For this year, anyway," said Wilmer in a menacing tone that vanished as quickly as it had come. "We'll now move on to item eight and the Ashford case."

Mike sat fuming, wondering where Barrett's new restraint had come from and wishing he had exercised some himself. He was putting himself back on thin ice with Wilmer.

"All right then," said Wilmer, taking up a fountain pen, "the record . . . will show"—he spoke slowly as he scribbled, taking dictation from himself—"that all members . . . of the ExComm are present. In addition . . . partners Michael Reasoner and Barrett Dickson . . . by invitation of the committee . . . stand in attendance."

Barrett smiled blissfully, gazed at the ceiling again, and addressed Wilmer in a tone of mock respect. "That's wonderful," he said. "I've always wanted to . . . *'stand in attendance.'* "

"Physically, anyway," said Wilmer, not missing Barrett's sarcasm. "At least until cessation of your few remaining vital signs and the coroner signs off, which, incidentally, is why I'm trying to hurry this meeting along."

Steve Wilmer, unflappable as always. Nearly as tall as Dickson, with chiseled features and barren of excess body fat, he had lettered in crew and starred as captain of the Dartmouth football team before moving on to Yale Law. He neither drank nor smoked until the day he graduated from Yale, a commitment he had made to his father, Justice Harrison Wilmer of the Fifth Circuit Court of Appeals. This alone, worn like a badge of discipline by Wilmer, sufficed in and of itself to ensure Dickson's enmity from the day they met.

Winston Cray cleared his throat. "Can't we have a little civility here, Steve? Barrett achieved something yesterday the top criminal defense lawyer on the West Coast had twice failed to do."

Wilmer glared at Cray. "Would you like to run the meeting, Winnie?"

Cray looked down at his hands.

"The reality," sneered Wilmer, "is that Barrett managed for the second or third time in nearly four years to go into court for a *paying* client, introduce an articulate blood expert to a judge who happens to be one of Barrett's best friends, then somehow stayed awake for thirty minutes. Christ, Winnie, even you could have pulled that off."

Barrett gave Wilmer a glowering look and Mike realized he'd better cool things down before an eruption.

"Steve," he said, "what Bear did in there had nothing to do with his past friendship with John Hernandez. The client was amazed, as was Al Menghetti."

"Amazed, was he?" said Wilmer, a crafty smile widening his bird's nest of a goatee. "May I assume, therefore, that Mr. Ashford wants you to continue on as a regular team member, Dickson? And at a pretty penny?"

Mike groaned inwardly at his own stupidity. He had done everything but tell the sonofabitch about Ashford's offer.

"That's true," said Barrett.

"And, with the best interests of the firm at heart, I'm

sure you agreed and have received an advance of, say, another $75,000?"

"That's not true."

"Steve," said Mike, surprised by Barrett's answer. "I don't think you appreciate the difficulty of what Barrett was being asked to—"

"Mike," said Wilmer coldly, "I repeat, you are here as a guest. As such, please address your remarks to the committee only when time is yielded to you."

"I agree, Mike," said Barrett. "Don't try to explain our art form to this bean counter. He's far too taxed from 'trimming fat' from this carnivore we used to consider a professional law firm."

Wilmer smiled amiably. "We lost half our fat the day you quit showing up for work, Dickson."

Barrett shrugged. "Point taken, Stevie, but I saw profit-per-partner figures in the *American Lawyer* last month that would bring Chapter 11 to mind if we were a corporation."

"Turnarounds take time, Dickson," said Wilmer, betraying a rare defensiveness. "We've had a temporary slowdown."

Dickson issued a wry smile and said, "Wilmer, that understatement rivals Emperor Hirohito's message to the troops on the eve of his surrender to the Allies when he said, 'The war is proceeding in a less than favorable manner.' "

Wilmer glared at Dickson as he said, "All the more marvelous, Barrett, that the very man whose antics contributed the most to this condition has reappeared atop a gleaming white horse to rescue us. Are you or are you not going to take on the trial?"

Mike watched Barrett take in a deep breath, then noisily let it out again through full cheeks, like a tire springing a leak. Mike was feeling dizzy, convinced now that it was over for both of them and there was nothing he could do about it.

Wilmer waited in the silence, savoring the moment. For once, the King of the Bottom Line would be happy to forgo a significant fee in return for something even more important to him: Dickson's scalp.

"But you've already answered that, haven't you, Barrett?" Wilmer said at last. "Well, then, I think I speak for the executive committee—the majority of the executive committee—when I say that you will be remembered here at Caldwell & Shaw as having once been a significant contributor. Your retirement will be—"

"Delayed," Barrett said. "Hell, Stevie-boy, I wouldn't give up this opportunity for the world."

Mike's head popped up and he saw Wilmer—the Unflappable One—give himself away then, though only in his eyes and only for a split second. Mike doubted that anyone else caught it, other than Barrett of course.

"That's *wonderful,* Dickson," said Wilmer, smiling again as if he had found something momentarily misplaced. "You *do* want to do it. In that case, may I ask if the client is aware of your . . . problem?"

"My only problem right now is you, Stevie-boy, which could quickly become *your* problem if you pursue that theme."

"You hear that, Todd?," said Wilmer in mock fear. "Winnie? You heard him. The man is threatening me!"

"I heard it," said Jamison, "and I suggest this meeting be adjourned. This is getting—"

"Real?" ventured Barrett.

"What is 'real' here, Dickson," said Wilmer, "is that the notion—authored by your cohort Reasoner—of involving you in anything even *potentially* productive was insane from the outset."

Clever, thought Mike, dropping his head back in his hands. Wilmer was ready with a backup plan just in case Barrett agreed to represent Ashford.

"I admit," continued Wilmer, "that when the concept was first advanced I thought it might be professionally feasible—"

"By which you mean," said Dickson, "financially remunerative. M-O-N-E-Y. You and your cold-nosed toadies have ripped the heart out of this firm in deference to the bottom line, then you've voted yourselves the bottom line. *So don't talk to me about what's 'professionally feasible.'* "

Wilmer blinked, then turned to Jamison and said, "Did you want to say something else, Todd?"

"Uh, well yes. Yes I do. Want to say something."

"About the quality of the client we're dealing with here?"

"Yes, precisely," said Jamison quickly, as Wilmer resumed scribbling in his minute book. "In my view—a view I know to be shared by a vast majority of the partners—C&S should not get into bed with a rumored Mafia don, guilty *or* innocent. I herewith change my vote concerning this project."

The bastards were ready all right, thought Mike.

Wilmer nodded and said, "I concur with brother Jamison, but on two additional grounds. First, the past twenty minutes with you, Dickson, has been the longest week I've spent in years. You are belligerent, contentious, and a defective loose cannon. Second, a difficult case like this without a twelve-point recovery program to support you would inevitably embarrass both you *and* the firm."

Mike saw muscles working in Barrett's jaw as his friend began speaking in a quietly menacing tone of voice.

"I suggest," said Barrett, "that you leave issues concerning my health to me."

"Wrong again, sir," said Wilmer through pursed lips. "Your health and reputation may be your business, but the health and reputation of the firm are mine."

Wilmer paused, picked up his pen again, and began writing as he spoke. "For the reasons noted, the ExComm unanimously agrees . . . to recommend to the partnership that C&S withdraw from the case . . . of People versus Elliot Ashford."

"Funny," said Mike, trying to snap out of his despairing funk, "my health as well as my hearing is just fine, but I'll be damned if I heard any motion or observed any unanimous vote."

Wilmer glared at Mike but made a motion, quickly seconded by Jamison. "All in favor, signify by saying 'aye.' Speak up, Winnie!"

"I . . . abstain," Winston Cray said in a barely audible voice. Mike saw everyone in the room turn toward the withered little man, but Wilmer continued to write in his minute book: "Passed by a majority vote," he said, shooting a final hard look at Cray, whose eyes remained fixed on the grain of the conference table in front of him.

"I'm confident, Dickson, that when the full partnership hears my report on your abusive attitude today, they will want nothing further to do with you either. Your presence is no longer in the best interests of the firm."

Barrett rested his elbows on the table, his hands together, fingertips touching his chin, eyes half closed. Mike saw it all slipping away, yet Barrett seemed completely at peace as he began to speak.

"Yes, Stevie-boy, make your report. Just be sure you also tell the full partnership that the real abuse today was dealt by you. You've insulted Mike and me, of course, but hell, we're used to it, so no big deal. But you've also been rude and insulting to one of C&S's most respected leaders. And *that's* unforgivable. Wilmer, you're unworthy to sit at the same table with Winston Cray, let alone be his partner."

Mike saw Cray's thin shoulders straighten and his thin lips hint at a smile as he gave Barrett a small, dignified bow of his head.

"Second, based on what you have said, be advised that I will voluntarily withdraw from the firm, effective immediately."

Now it was Wilmer who allowed himself a smile.

"Third, I will be personally and individually associating with Al Menghetti on the case of People versus Elliot Ashford."

Mike watched Wilmer's eyebrows involuntarily angle themselves under his suddenly furrowed forehead.

"Fourth, I wish the record to reflect that I'm handing another check to Mr. Wilmer, made out to the firm in the sum of $350,000 as a retainer. I'll phone your regrets to Mr. Ashford and tell him you'll be returning the check."

Wilmer pounded a fist onto the table. "*You said you hadn't received an advance—*"

"For $75,000. That's what you asked me, Wilmer. Did I fail to mention they sent me four times that amount?"

"That's four point six times," murmured Jamison out of habit.

Wilmer's eyes widened in a moment of rare confusion as he stared at the check. Barrett noisily rose from his chair, gave his wet and rumpled clothing another tug, then bid Mike and Winston Cray good-bye and headed toward the door. As he reached it, he added, "I'll make my own financial arrangements with Mr. Ashford."

Mike turned to look at the suddenly pale presiding partner as he stared slack-jawed at the certified check, at which Jamison was also now staring over Wilmer's right shoulder, his perpetual smile nowhere in evidence.

But Mike smiled, and doubted if he'd ever stop.

"Fourth," said Barrett, "I'm sure your partners will want to know how much it cost them to allow you the pleasure of getting me off your paranoid and tightly wound ass, and I hope someone will tell them."

"Don't worry, Barrett," said Winston Cray, rising to his feet, his voice suddenly stronger and recovering some of its former timbre. "*I'm* still one of those partners and *I'll* tell them, by God."

Wilmer blanched ivory, his eyes darting now between Cray and Dickson as he too quickly rose to his feet. "Perhaps we've all been . . . too emotional about this issue," he said.

Jamison leapt to his feet as well.

Barrett said, "'*We*'? Do you have a mouse in your pocket, Wilmer?" Then, with a glance at Jamison, Barrett added, "And is somebody playing 'The Star-Spangled Banner,' Todd?"

But Wilmer was already bent at the waist, huddled between Cray and Jamison, his arms draped around each, the Ivy League football captain calling his next play.

By the time his head popped up, Barrett had opened the door and was halfway through it.

"Hold on, Barrett," Wilmer blurted, "please! We've reconsidered. It's a go, after all, okay?"

"Really?" said Barrett with a sardonic eagerness only Mike caught.

"Absolutely. Green light all the way. Just try to keep a low profile in the courtroom, will you? That's really all Ashford and Menghetti have asked you to do."

Barrett shrugged and said, "Isn't that all I'm capable of, Stevie?" He then turned and faced them, filling the doorway, and added, "I appreciate your reconsideration, gentlemen, really I do."

Wilmer smiled his perfect smile.

"But now," said Barrett quietly, "*I* have a problem."

"Yes?" said Wilmer, his smile fading, his guard raised again.

"Yep, now I've got a real problem. You see, first, we've

got young Jamison's distress about those ugly Mafia rumors; then there's your own concern, Wilmer, about the state of my health and well-being. You've both got me thinking now about the—how did you put it, Stevie?—'best interests of the firm.' "

"Okay, Barrett," Wilmer said in the tone of a bank clerk looking into the barrel of a pistol, "what the hell do you want?"

Barrett took a step back into the room; just one.

"Well, let's see. Two things come to mind. Given our mutual concerns, Wilmer, you know, about the 'best interests of the firm,' let's start by cutting those layoffs in half. I like Winnie's idea of finding other places for our good people."

Wilmer stiffened, but nodded.

"Good," continued Barrett. "As for my second modest suggestion—what with Mr. Cray here about to retire—isn't it obvious who should take his place on the executive committee?"

Mike finally saw what the Bear was up to, had probably been up to all along. He held his breath and stole a glance at Wilmer, who now saw the denouement too.

"You want . . ." said Wilmer slowly in a voice as flat as tinfoil, "you want Mike Reasoner . . . to take Winnie's place."

It wasn't a question.

"The term's still five years?" said Barrett.

"Yes," snapped Wilmer.

"Still take ninety percent of the partnership vote to unseat an ExComm member?"

"Yes."

"Good," said Barrett. "I formally nominate Michael A. Reasoner to succeed Winston R. Cray."

Mike felt everyone in the room looking at him. "Bear," he said, "this is too—"

"Hush, nominee Reasoner," said Barrett. "No speeches allowed near the polling place. I must tell you, gentlemen, this is not a negotiable issue."

Winston Cray broke the silence that followed by walking straight up to the presiding partner, placing his hands on the table, and leaning forward to within inches of Wilmer's face. "I second that nomination!" he bellowed in a voice that forced Wilmer's head to recoil. He then walked over to shake hands with Barrett and seated himself on Barrett and Mike's side of the table, beaming with a vitality none of them had seen in years.

Wilmer and Jamison exchanged a look.

"Well, gentlemen?" Barrett said. "A simple show of hands will do. All in favor?"

Cray's hand shot up. Jamison kept an eye on Wilmer, hands still at his sides, balled into fists. Mike watched him too, wondering if Wilmer had one more card to play.

"Have you told us *everything* about the fee arrangement, Barrett?" asked Wilmer, his voice suddenly congenial. Mike didn't like the look on Barrett's face. It was a fair question and he knew Barrett would have to answer. He also knew that Barrett wouldn't lie. Even to Wilmer.

"Full hourly rates . . . plus a $250,000 bonus if the jury acquits or the case is resolved before verdict in a manner satisfactory to the client."

Wilmer smiled. "A *bonus*. Excellent. Okay, Todd and I will go along. For now, Winnie Cray stays on the executive committee and you and Mike stay on as full partners. You win the case and bring home the bonus, then Mike rotates on ExComm in place of Cray and serves till mandatory retirement at sixty-five."

"And if we lose the case?" said Barrett.

"All bets are off. Fair enough?"

"Except for the layoffs of our people?"

"Okay, except for the layoffs."

"Deal," said Barrett. "Put it in the minutes. Now let's see those hands in the air."

Wilmer scribbled in the minute book, then raised his hand, followed quickly by Jamison's. Cray raised his again.

"Good," said Dickson, cheerfully counting—"One, two, and . . . three"—with his index finger.

"With that out of the way," he added, "I go to join the enemy in battle. Have a nice day, gentlemen."

Mike stared at the thoroughly disheveled back of his friend as he strode out the door, knowing where he was really going.

What the hell have we done? Mike asked himself.

14

Grace and Sam Quon entered Field's office for their weekly Monday afternoon status and assignment meeting on the Ashford case. The trial was set to start in exactly two weeks. Field was on the phone but waved them in. He motioned them to sit, then pointed into the receiver and mouthed the word "Money."

They nodded, then engaged in the charade of pretending not to listen as the D.A. charmed a major campaign contributor. Grace mused that Earl Field always kept his priorities straight, and as the minutes passed, she wondered how he would react to her after her blowup in Klegg's office the day before.

When he hung up, he met her eyes directly and said, "Again, Grace, I'm sorry about what happened. Typical defense stunt, that no-torture theory."

So that's it, thought Grace. It was all Dickson's fault.

"It was not pleasant," she said, deciding to let it drop.

"Is Dickson into the booze?" Field asked.

"I don't know," said Grace. "If so, it has neither affected his ability nor curtailed his impertinence."

Sam chuckled.

"He was the best there was," said Field. "What the hell happened to him? Trouble at the firm? Midlife crisis? A woman?"

"Probably all three," said Sam Quon, looking at his notes. "He started downhill when his wife took off with some guy in 1985, leaving their kid behind. She returned two years later married to money and won the boy back, now eleven. That's when Dickson started drinking, ducking cases at the firm, and generally pissing off his partners, who managed to force him into the defense of a white-collar con artist in '93, only weeks after his wife killed herself."

Field stared pensively out a window. "The private wound is deepest," he murmured, then added with a wink at Grace, "Shakespeare."

"And steals all desire," responded Grace, "but for revenge."

"Shakespeare?" said Field.

"No," she said, "Grace Harris. I've already read Sam's report. Ellen's new husband had caught her sleeping with one of his pilots and dumped her in '89. Dickson later found out she'd been dragging the kid all over Europe since then, shacking up with every Tom, Dick, and Pierre. He took Ellen back into court in 1993, and this time he won custody."

Field rubbed his temples. "So did he quit trying cases to baby-sit, or was it because he lost the big fraud case the same year?"

"Probably neither, Chief," said Sam. "His wife killed herself right after Dickson won the custody hearing."

"But now he's back," said Field, rubbing his eyes, "peddling his friendship with John Hernandez. Okay, let's move on. I've got a meeting with the mayor in ten minutes. What do I tell him?"

"Tell him we'll be ready," Grace said.

"Great," Field said. "Is our DNA case solid?"

"Solid, but sleep-inducing."

"What are Dr. Janes's odds up to now?"

"It's one chance in four billion that the blood in the sink, on the towel, and on her fingertips could belong to anyone other than Elliot Ashford."

Field sighed loudly. "Then Menghetti will have to attack the cops at the scene and our crime lab. The old conspiracy-and-contamination crap. How does the lab look?"

"A little like my son's room on a good day," said Grace, "but the procedures seem sound enough."

Field rose and started to leave.

"Earl," said Grace, steeling herself, "one more thing, okay?"

"Shoot."

"Even though we're sure Ashford won't take the stand, I think I should take him on if he does."

Field froze. "What's your thinking, Grace?" he said, turning only his head.

"Just that everybody knows the hard feelings between you and Ashford. The press is already painting this as a grudge fight, which plays into their conspiracy theory. Why make it worse?"

"I'll think about it," he said unpersuasively, and started out the door.

"There are other reasons I should take him on, Earl."

Field exhaled loudly and turned around, but kept an impatient hand on the door.

"Yes?"

"Any minority—Asian, black, women—will see through a token representative twiddling her thumbs at counsel table until final arguments. They'll feel manipulated."

"But you'll be handling all the scientific—"

"I'll be reading technical questions to trained seals wearing glasses thick as Coke bottles. When I'm not doing that, I'll be handing you papers and blowing your nose. They'll smell it a m-mile away, Earl. Let me take Ashford."

Grace met Earl Field's stern gaze with unblinking eyes, saw the skin drawn tight across his cheekbones. Sam disappeared into a wall somewhere, but the room had gone so quiet she could hear him breathing.

"You want to talk about tokenism, Grace? Well, I know a little bit about the subject. I've been the token black on everything from high school golf teams to corporate boards. I'm now a token black in San Francisco government and a damn good one, but I know the way folks out there talk about me in the privacy of their clubs and bedrooms. They don't say I made it in spite of being black, but *because* I'm black! Not that I give a shit what some of them think as long as 50.1 percent of them vote the right away."

Grace felt the color rising in her face, but Field's hard expression suddenly gave way to a half smile. "You guys come down to my office around six and we'll finish up then."

"Whoa," said Sam, gently closing the door behind the D.A. "You touched a nerve."

Grace nodded.

Sam rubbed his eyes, then his neck. "It's not just you, Grace. Earl's brain is writing checks his body can't cash. He's worn out and . . . well, I have to say he's acting a little strange lately."

Grace nodded again. She had never heard Sam utter anything even close to criticism of Earl Field.

"He's never even asked me to trace the chain of possession on the missing evidence," said Sam, frowning and speaking as if to himself.

"Probably assumes you've already done it."

"Of course I have."

"Good. Who was the last person to see the evidence?"

"Her nails were scraped by one of Yang's best men. He marked the plastic bag and set it on the bathroom counter between the two marble basins. He later stored all the physical evidence on the gurney—or at least thought he did—and assumed the scrapings went out with the body like everything else did."

"But it didn't show up with the other stuff at the coroner's office, where the autopsy was performed?"

"Right. It wasn't even missed until it was too late."

"Stay on it, Sam. Why don't you check the crime-scene photos. See if the bag shows up anywhere on them."

"Good idea. They're down in Earl's office. We can check them at our six o'clock meeting."

"Okay. Meanwhile, I want to know everybody who was involved in the transportation of the body, and I want them in here tomorrow."

"Check. One more thing. You didn't give Earl the last and most important reason you should be doing the heavy lifting at trial."

"Which is?"

Sam looked guiltily around the room, then spoke in a self-conscious whisper, as if Earl Field might be lurking under the desk. "That we don't want to lose the case! The chief is rusty, Grace. Heck, who wouldn't get rusty trying to administer this three-ring circus." He paused then, glanced at the door, and added, "But a clear-thinking quarterback knows when it's time to hand off the ball."

Unless, thought Grace, he doesn't really want to win the game. She then set the disquieting thought aside, for it made no sense. Losing would kill him in the gubernatorial election.

She walked over to her single window and gazed out across Bryant Street at two defense lawyers she knew, popping into the Side Bar for an eye-opener. Beyond them to the west, she saw yet another storm heading in from the Pacific. Without turning, she asked Sam a question so casually she might have been talking to herself.

"How could Earl lose the Ashford case and still end up in the governor's mansion?"

Sam gave her a puzzled look. "Is this some Zen parable? You know I don't even like Asian food. Okay, the answer is 'with great difficulty,' unless . . ."

"Unless?"

"Unless he had a damn good spin doctor on his team to make sure the press saw the loss was somebody else's fault."

Grace said nothing. If Ashford did walk, she thought, there was no spin doctor in town more capable than Jack Klegg of laying the blame squarely on the police.

And, if necessary, on Earl Field's co-counsel.

But *why?*

Grace and Sam met again at Earl Field's office at 6:00 P.M. to resume their planning conference. He was not there. She looked at the district attorney's empty chair, resisted a fatuous notion to sit in it. Behind the chair, resting in solitary splendor atop an ebony credenza, a handsomely framed eight-by-ten photograph demonstrated Field's commitment to charitable events and his fine golf swing. In the background of the photo, former majority leader Tip O'Neill and celebrity radio host Frank Dill looked on admiringly.

"You're getting that raccoon look, Grace," said Sam, drawing her attention back to the center of the large southern wing of Field's office.

"It got a little late out last night," she said. "I'll be okay."

Sam gave her a questioning look. "I was here. Didn't see you."

"It's Aaron. One of our little talks that go past midnight and resolve nothing."

"What's the kid up to now?"

"He wants to go to Mexico with one of his friends and enter a motocross race."

"What did you say?"

"I told him no, of course. I said I'd consider going with him next summer if he still wanted to do it."

"You've got to give the boy some freedom, Grace. He's growing up."

"Thanks a lot, Sam, but I want him to keep growing up instead of facedown in a ditch somewhere outside of Cuernavaca. Besides, if anyone gets to go to Mexico, it's me."

Sam shrugged. "Now *that* I approve of. You've got to ease up on yourself, too. This trial is going to be a marathon, not a sprint."

Grace knew she had been looking tired lately. Tired and burdened with a feeling that despite her long hours she was not pleasing anybody lately, certainly not herself. At the office, she was becoming convinced that Earl Field was caught in a game far more risky than politics and that she was getting drawn into it with him without knowing the rules. It had to be something to do with that damn campaign contribution.

Her morose mood was mercifully interrupted by Sam tossing the crime scene photos into her lap.

"Dry hole," he said. "Not a sign of our missing plastic bag anywhere. That's Yang's skinny ass there in that shot of the bathroom counter where his assistant says he last saw the scrapings."

"Why is the coroner's office taking scrapings at the scene instead of at the morgue?"

"Yang's hot idea. Minimize claims of contamination while body's in transit. A onetime experiment. Anyway, that's the assistant coroner's chest there facing Yang, and some other cop's hands and upper legs, but this shot gives you a clear view of the entire counter. Nothing, though the gurney's still there."

"You checked with the assistant coroner who did the autopsy to be sure he didn't take a second set of scrapings at the morgue?"

"Yang told him they had already taken them, then the body was cremated after the autopsy and before the bag showed up missing."

Grace shook her head in dismay. Prosecutors looked for smoking guns to ensure victory; defense lawyers looked for missing evidence, and they wouldn't be disappointed this time. She leafed through the photographs: no plastic bag anywhere, but something did seem out of place.

Earl Field briskly entered his office, seemingly infused with new energy. "Okay, team, where were we?" he said. "How about the defense mock trials, Sam? Tell me they're losing every time."

Sam opened his notebook. "I've interviewed mock jurors from one focus group and two mock trials," he said. "Their expert has an unlimited budget, of course, so he's been recruiting local surrogates who match the predicted demographics of the actual jury that will sit on the case."

"And?"

"The bad guys lost the first two. But on the last one, the actor playing the role of the defense pathologist testified that the abrasions on Ashford's face were consistent with shaving cuts—too regular in configuration to have been caused by a fingernail. They hung six to six."

Field's smile disappeared. "That's ridiculous."

Sam shrugged and extended his hands in a placating gesture to remind the D.A. he was just the messenger. "They seem willing to accept the shaving story to explain Ashford's blood at the scene. At least it raised a reasonable doubt."

Field turned toward Grace. "What will our expert say?"

Grace was studying the photographs.

"Grace," said Field, "would you care to join the party?

"Sorry."

"What does our expert say about Ashford's blood?"

"The scrape on his throat could have been caused by either a razor or a fingernail," said Grace. "The one on his cheek looked too jagged to be done by a blade, but neither cut was fresh enough for a definitive look by the time Ashford was taken into custody."

Field grunted. "Cops."

Grace said, "That means Ashford won't have to take the stand."

"Exactamundo," said Sam. "His expert will say they were clearly razor cuts and that Ashford's blood must have gotten on her fingers from cleaning out the basin—after he left and before she got herself killed by someone else."

"So we won't get a shot at him on cross," Grace said.

Field slammed the flat of a hand on his desk in an uncharacteristic display of anger. "And our splendid police department still hasn't found her fingernail scrapings."

Grace shrugged. Something was still bothering her. Something in the photographs.

Sam held up a hand. "It gets worse. When they build a reasonable-doubt argument around the 'conveniently lost' fingernail scrapings, the voting moved to eight to four, defense."

Field fell into his chair and said, "What kind of mock jurors are they using?"

"The typical San Francisco stew," said Grace. "The defense seems to prefer emotional people who will jump to conclusions—deductive types who will buy the defense picture in opening statement, then selectively filter out evidence that doesn't fit their concept of how the picture is supposed to look. This means we need rational people who will listen to all the evidence—the maid's testimony, the blood evidence, the phony alibi—and allow the full picture to develop."

"The defense has an unlimited war chest," said Field. "Will they use a shadow jury?"

A shadow jury was a group of paid non-lawyers with demographics roughly similar to the actual jury, sitting inconspicuously in the back of the courtroom, listening to the same evidence the true jury hears. Their job was to meet at the end of each day with counsel and offer their impressions: what was clear, what wasn't; how a given witness was perceived; what they would like to hear about the next day; then, at the end of the case, to vote as if they were real jurors. This gave the lawyers a vicarious and often quite accurate peek into the actual jury room, a peek that might motivate them to alter their strategy or even attempt a settlement or plea bargain while the actual jury was still deliberating. It was all legal and often disquietingly effective.

Sam shook his head. "I've checked that with the clerk. They won't be able to use a shadow jury because there won't be spare seats in the back of the courtroom. All but a handful are spoken for. The press lottery gets a dozen, the prosecution and defense get another nine seats each. Then you've got family members, general VIPs, two book writers, and a handful for the general public."

Grace stared at the enhanced crime scene photographs again. What was bothering her? Then it hit her: the shot of the dual basins and the Italian marble countertop; Yang's butt, his assistant's chest, a hand resting on the counter, the half inch of shirt exposed below the cuff of the coat.

And a gold cuff link she had seen before.

"What's the matter, Grace?" said Earl Field. "You've been preoccupied since we started. Are we boring you?"

"I'm far from bored, Earl," she said.

In over ten years of homicide work, Grace had never seen a cop or coroner's office personnel at a crime scene wearing cuff links.

"Earl," she said quietly, "were you there that night?"

"Where?"

"The crime scene."

"Why, yes," Field said, his features unchanged. "Didn't I mention that?"

Grace glanced at Sam, whose expression revealed more surprise than he intended.

"No," Grace said. "You didn't."

"Well, hell, Grace," he said tossing his head to one side, "it was no secret. Every cop there saw me. I picked up the call on my scanner on the way home from the symphony with Terry. She sat in the car while I ran in just to be sure all the bases were covered, then I got out of their way."

Grace studied Field's face. Still calm, smiling.

"Was the body gone when you arrived?"

They were interrupted by the phone, which Field grabbed. Grace turned to say something to Sam, but glanced up and saw a troubled look on Field's face. He was staring straight at her.

"It's Aaron," he said. "He's in trouble. Down at the Youth Guidance Center."

15

Sam drove Grace to the dilapidated center and eased her through the paperwork. Aaron was brought in at 7:40 P.M., head down, holding a battered baseball cap she hadn't seen in a year. Probably worn backward during the big heist. Skip and another friend were still in a holding cell waiting for their parents.

I don't need this right now, Grace thought.

Aaron's pitiful appearance threatened Grace's resolve to be firm, and she subdued an impulse to put her arms around him.

"Tell me what happened, Aaron," she said, her voice as steady as she could make it. He refused to meet her eyes. She bit her lip and added "Aaron?" in a softer tone, realizing that if her son ever needed support, it was now. Punishment would be meted out later, when she was as calm as she was trying to act now.

"Answer me, please."

He glanced up and Grace saw an annoying defiance in his eyes. "Me and Skip . . . we got caught with a bottle of beer in our jackets."

Grace already knew this, but had to start somewhere.

"Where did it happen?" She knew this, too.

"We were leaving this store in the Haight. The clerk sees us and he's all 'What do you kids have in your pockets?' and we go, 'Nothin', man.' Then we get spooked, I guess, and start runnin', but a couple of plainclothes are parked in front."

He glanced at her again, then added a shrug that seemed to suggest she was overreacting to what was obviously a bit of bad luck.

"But *why*, Aaron?" Grace said, the question sounding

naïve even to her ears, but she asked it again anyway. "Why did you do it?"

Aaron gave his head a little jerk to one side that somehow struck Grace as maddeningly arrogant. "I don't know," he said at last, and made that grunting sound in his throat.

"Damn it, Aaron," she said, any impulse to hug the miscreant now thoroughly gone. "Answer me!"

"I guess 'cause they wouldn't sell it to us."

Grace blew air through her lower lip up toward the yellowing fluorescent-lighted ceiling. "Your reason for breaking the law is that *they* wouldn't break the law? *Is this what you're telling me?*"

Sam Quon quietly cleared his throat.

Aaron shrugged. "Jeez, Mom, we *had* the money. I left two bucks in the cooler for mine. So it wasn't exactly *stealing.*"

Grace shook her head in exasperation, as Aaron studied the fake tattoo on the inside of his wrist. "Hey, I'm sorry, Mom, okay? Jeez, such a big fucking deal."

Grace closed her eyes. "Let's get out of here."

Sam said he would go make some "arrangements" and quietly stepped out of the room.

Aaron made the guttural sound again, then, in that sarcastic tone that never failed to drive her crazy, said, "So will you be the assigned prosecutor in my case?"

"I'd be your worst nightmare," she snapped. "Would you like that?"

Aaron glared at his mother with a red-eyed intransigence. Grace knew there was both hurt and fear beneath his arrogance, but she couldn't muster the resolve to deal with such subtleties. She felt dead inside.

"At least," he said, "we'd get to spend some time together if you were."

She stared at him, suddenly unable to speak. Please, God, she thought, it's bad enough he looks like his father; don't let him turn out to be as manipulative, too.

"Don't go there, Aaron," she said finally. "Not a good time."

"When is it ever?" he said, but his voice had lost some of its harshness.

Within an hour they were on their way home in silence, Aaron in the backseat alone.

Sam dropped them off in front of their condominium.

"Thanks, Sam," Grace said. "We owe you one."

"I'm sorry, Inspector Quon," said Aaron. "I mean for screwin' up your evening and stuff. But thanks for helpin' out."

"It's all right, son," said Sam. "We all slip and fall once in a while."

Grace gave Sam a hard look. So much for surrogate-male "tough love."

Aaron stepped out of the car, shuffled up to the front stairs, and waited. Sam Quon leaned closer to Grace. "You're at home now, Grace," he said softly, "not in a courtroom. And he's not the Zodiac Killer, just a good kid going through a bad time."

"I suppose you're right, Sam, but sometimes I feel like I'm drowning and my own kid is handing me an anvil."

"I know," said Sam, smiling. "Just try not to make a federal case out of it, okay? This thing could have been a hell of a lot worse. We all committed some kind of petty theft when we were kids. Most of us didn't get caught. At least he's here instead of in that ditch down in Mexico."

Grace rested her head against the car window. She sighed and stared forlornly toward her son. "I hate it when I become like my father. I tried to be semi-cool back there; even tried to give him a hug when we were leaving. The little twit didn't even respond."

Sam said, "Give him time. He's feeling stupid, scared, and angry."

"Who isn't?" she asked, then added, "Thanks again, Sam." She glanced at Aaron, now seated on the steps leading to the apartment, arms around his knees, head resting on his arms. There he is, she thought, my son the outlaw, awaiting his fate.

Sam's expression turned serious. "I may be out of line here, but is Grace Harris having any fun at all these days?"

Grace managed a wry smile as she gave her head a quick shake. "I'm enduring," she said. "Just enduring. I spend my time prosecuting criminals, raising Aaron, and watching my bonds lose value."

"No men in your life at all, Grace?"

She shook her head. The silent lie came easily, and for the last two weeks at least, it was technically true. "I'm better off with bonds, Sam. They eventually mature."

Sam laughed. "Okay," he said, "but what's so good about being a successful professional in the most romantic city in the world if you come home every night to nothing but a fat-free frozen dinner, a wayward sixteen-year-old, a dying ficus bush, and a television set. Think about it."

"I do, Sam," she said, her eyes misting again. "I think about it every night. Good night, friend."

She watched as Sam drove away, then walked up and unlocked the front door. Without a word, Aaron strode inside and straight up the stairs toward his room.

16

"No," Field told Jack Klegg, "I haven't heard anything more from *L.A. Eye* or, thank God, anyone else."

"Good," said Klegg, his voice deep and imperious. "Has Grace heard anything more from the reporter?"

"No. She would have been all over me if she had."

"Good," repeated Klegg. "It's handled then. With the trial starting soon, that's the end of it."

"Is it?" said Field, knowing Klegg would take the question as rhetorical and would never tell him anything he shouldn't know. Too much knowledge could prove "inconvenient," one of Klegg's favorite words.

"Absolutely," said Klegg. "Next stop, governor's mansion."

The two men were in Klegg's office. The door was closed. Klegg was tilted far back in his chair, staring at the ceiling with his hands clasped behind his head, a portrait of smug arrogance. Field's eyes scanned the chief assistant's desk, pens and pencils aligned in front of him in perfect order; a clean legal pad set at an impeccable ninety-degree angle to a fine leather-bound desk blotter precisely centered on his otherwise bare desk. There was not a file in sight, not even a scrap of paper in his wastebasket.

"But keep an eye on Grace, Earl. She'll do whatever she has to do to become D.A."

"Have you looked in the mirror lately, Jack?"

Klegg sniffed. "I'm just saying our girl scout is ambitious."

"No, Jack," said Field with a croak of laughter, "you and I are ambitious. Grace Harris is a zealot, a true believer. But she'll be your problem come election time, not mine."

Klegg nodded. Field gazed at him, wondering if the chief assistant knew how much he hated him, hated this whole nasty business with Chicago. Klegg was a devious bastard, but he did keep the trains running on time, and had provided a vital advantage to an ambitious black man born in poverty in Hunters Point. Klegg was his leg up, the edge he was damn well entitled to and unfortunately would require if he was going to get where the people of the state of California needed him. It killed Field, of course, to see Elliot Ashford slipping off the hook, but the greater good would have to be served. That was the true test of a man, wasn't it? The willingness to sacrifice personal triumph for the greater good? To forgo short-term gratification in favor of long-term satisfaction? Besides, Governor Earl Field would no doubt find plenty of ways to make life miserable for someone as deserving as Ashford: a little street justice perhaps to compensate for the failure of the judicial system. Plenty of ways.

Klegg tilted forward, removed something from his top drawer, then began filing his nails. Earl Field found himself examining his own fingernails and was glad Klegg was too preoccupied to notice. Maybe Grace had been right. Maybe he should have come out with it at the beginning. It would have been dicey, perhaps disastrous, but whatever he had left would have been his, free and clear. But Grace's advice was the kind that was better never than late, for once he had taken that call from Chicago on his car phone on the way home that night, there had been no time for thinking things through. And once he had stopped at the crime scene and pocketed that little plastic bag, he had mortgaged his own future. And Jack Klegg was now one of the lien holders.

"Isn't it beautiful," said Klegg, tilting back again and showing his perfect teeth, "the way the press is killing the cops?"

"Yes," said Field, distracted from his anguish by the guilty pleasure he took in the police chief's current discomfiture. "They're killing the Mick."

"This is just the beginning, Chief. There'll be the devil to pay when Ashford walks," said Klegg.

The district attorney slowly nodded his head and returned the chief assistant's smile, though his mind and body ached from the weight of a growing despair. It occurred to him that Klegg probably viewed him as just another passenger on the train he kept running on time.

"The devil to pay," Field murmured, repeating Klegg's

words as if to himself. "Yes, Jack, that puts it just about right."

Meanwhile, in Beverly Hills, the Ashford defense team—Menghetti, Dickson, Leviticus Heywood, jury consultant Dr. Eric Tremaine, and two paralegals—sat around an eighteen-foot table in Al Menghetti's spacious offices. Elliot Ashford was listening in on the speakerphone, as the terms of his newly won bail restricted his travel to the county of San Francisco.

"You still pissed off, Elliot?" said Al Menghetti, winking at the others. Although Menghetti had swiftly come up with the bond after the judge ordered Ashford released on bail, the neighboring Alameda County D.A. had put a hold on him for outstanding traffic warrants arising from two unanswered speeding citations and thirty-eight parking tickets. Ashford had to spend another night in jail before Menghetti could straighten things out the next day.

"I'm not happy about it," came the voice.

As Dickson listened, he took in the large room through his red-rimmed eyes and observed that like the rest of Menghetti's penthouse suite, the conference area was decorated in a stark clinical motif, a style seemingly designed to aggravate his nausea. Original Dalí sketches did little to liven the pearl gray walls; even the window mullions and doorjambs were trimmed out in gray, though a high-gloss, slightly paler shade.

There was not a law book in sight.

As far as C&S has fallen, Barrett thought, it still has farther to fall.

The morning sun rose in the room by inches, slicing through slatted shades covering a wall of windows each the size of an upright Cadillac, glowing with the candle power of a Hollywood movie premiere. Barrett longed for his dark glasses, which he must have left at Spago the night before—another drawback to entering a bar during harsh daylight and leaving at closing time. Had he met someone? Not likely.

Maybe, he decided, he'd cut back on his drinking. He had planned on it when he signed on for the trial, but the reality of his subservient position had laid waste to his motivation. What was the use? Menghetti had subtly conveyed the message that he—the top criminal trial lawyer on the West Coast—needed no help from an erstwhile civil litigator on how to win a murder trial.

Menghetti introduced Ashford to Dr. Tremaine over the phone, and explained to Ashford that Tremaine had been in San Francisco running focus groups and mock trials. He would also assist in framing the arguments and in jury selection at trial. Tremaine, in his late forties with gray-streaked reddish hair and the fading remnants of a British accent, was widely acknowledged to be the best in the business.

Introductions completed, Menghetti began to pace, hands clasped behind his back, laying out the facts to Dr. Tremaine as if he were giving an opening statement to a jury. Ashford was uncharacteristically silent at the other end.

Barrett glanced at Tremaine, who seemed to be enjoying himself, taking notes, nodding understanding. Leviticus was taking notes, too, although Barrett suspected his days on the case were numbered. Lev would now be taking his marching orders from Menghetti and wouldn't like it. Barrett felt woozy and slipped out of the room in search of some cold mineral water and the men's room.

Returning to the outer door of the conference room fifteen minutes later, he steadied himself against the partially opened door and listened as Menghetti appeared to be summing up.

"I put it to you, gentlemen," he intoned, "that Earl Field will be able to provide only two explanations for the disappearance of those fingernail scrapings. Either it was the innocent but recklessly culpable negligence of the San Francisco Police Department, or a conspiracy between them and the district attorney's office to convict an innocent man who has worn a political thorn in the paw of this lion who would be king of California."

Barrett winced at Menghetti's overblown rhetoric, but he could see that the others were receiving the message he was taking pains to send: that he was a skilled advocate in complete possession of the facts of his case and damn good at laying them out. The problem, thought Barrett, was that Menghetti had completely missed the point.

"Either way," concluded Menghetti, "the doctrine of reasonable doubt demands an acquittal. That, my friends, is our reality here."

Sound of applause and metallic shouts of "Hear, hear!" came through the speakerphone.

"Impressive," said Tremaine, nodding his head slowly, "quite so."

But Barrett, rubbing his eyes, was nodding his head too, but in the other direction without even knowing it.

"Something on your mind, Dickson?" said Menghetti.

Caught, Barrett offered a pained expression, feeling like a schoolboy reluctant to recite. He jammed his fists into his jacket pocket, shuffled into the room, and quietly slid back into his chair.

"Yes, Barrett," shouted Ashford, his tone echoing Menghetti's condescension, "might as well have your reaction."

"My reaction . . ." Barrett echoed, massaging his temples and noticing through the plastic slab that one of his shoes was untied. "All right," he said, his voice slightly tremulous. "In my opinion, that police-conspiracy approach played well in Simpson only because just about every person important to the case other than Marcia Clark and the judge were African-Americans, including the jury—most of whom harbored understandably negative notions about the police and law enforcement."

Tremaine nodded tentative agreement.

"Our client is not African-American," Dickson added.

"I think," said Menghetti, offering an unreliable smile, "that we all agree our client is white, Dickson."

"I can't jump a foot in the air without a horse under me," said Ashford witlessly. Nobody laughed. Barrett looked pained. Leviticus rose and poured a cup of coffee.

"The majority of your jurors in San Francisco won't be African-American either," said Dickson when no one else spoke.

"That's true," said Tremaine.

"So," said Barrett, shrugging, "there you have it."

"There we have *what?*" said Menghetti.

Barrett cleared his throat. "The police are not viewed the same way by white people in the Bay Area as they are by African-Americans here in L.A. One of the lessons from Simpson is that there are more bad cops than white people think, and fewer bad cops than black people think."

"So?" repeated Menghetti, an edge in his voice.

Leviticus nodded encouragement to Barrett, who shrugged again and said, "So, we should take that fact into account when you talk about a conspiracy theory as a major line of defense."

Menghetti glared at Tremaine as the consultant again nodded agreement.

"I'm not being critical, here, Al," said Dickson, catching the exchange. "I'm just saying most of your jurors in San Francisco will not have had first- or even secondhand experience at having been rousted by bigoted cops and therefore won't be spring-loaded to either believe the worst about them or be motivated by a desire to get even for past abuses. No offense, Al, it's just different up north."

"None taken, Barrett," said Menghetti, though his mouth had dropped at the corners. "But if you're saying I just ignore the missing fingernail evidence, you're dead wrong."

"To the contrary," said Barrett, his voice stronger now, "we make the missing evidence the very core of our defense. But we don't need a complex conspiracy theory; we just say straight out that somewhere in a small plastic bag lies the identity of the real killer, and when the people with the burden of proof provide you with this identity, you will be in a position under our Constitution to provide them with a conviction. *But not one minute before.*"

"*Yes!*" came the voice through the speaker. "Damned clever, Dickson."

"I thought that's pretty much what I was saying," said Menghetti, obviously irritated. "This isn't the actual trial, for Christ's sake."

"I'm sure that's what you were meaning to say," said Barrett agreeably. "My elaboration was unnecessary."

Lev smiled and toasted Barrett with his coffee cup.

"All right," growled Menghetti. "Then let's not get bogged down in detail at this point. Eric? What the hell kind of jury do we want up there?"

Eric Tremaine, part sociologist, part psychologist, seemed relieved to be able to lower the level of tension that had been building in the room. He began by tentatively defining the emotional features of a perfect defense juror, based on his work to date.

"Ideally," he began, "you'd like to find an unevolved

redneck male, preferably divorced, not smart enough to understand or believe in DNA, and harboring an inherent distrust of government and its institutions."

"Sorry," said Barrett, "I'm disqualified from serving on this jury."

Everyone in the room laughed except Menghetti. Barrett noticed Dr. Tremaine glancing thoughtfully at his host, as if wondering how long the ace criminal defense attorney would put up with this iconoclast from San Francisco. He's figured out Menghetti and I have nothing in common, thought Barrett, other than a shared regret that I'm in the case.

"Go back to sleep, Dickson," said Menghetti. "We'll wake you at cocktail hour."

Dickson narrowed his eyes, but let it go. He had caused enough trouble for one morning. The odd thing was that he was actually getting interested in the case. If he were not riding second chair to an egotistical prick wearing a silk suit that cost enough to feed a family in the Congo for a year or two, this might not be such a bad gig after all.

"Hey, hey, Al," came Ashford's cheerful voice. "You be nice to Mr. Dickson. He's known to be one of the truly brilliant West Coast lawyers and we need him."

"Truly brilliant West Coast lawyers?" said Menghetti derisively. Then, glancing at himself in a large mirror near the bentwood coat rack, he added, "That would be a very small group, Elliot."

"I know exactly how many are in the group," said Dickson, unable to resist.

"Yeah?" said Menghetti. "How many?"

"One less than *you* think there are."

Ashford and Leviticus howled. One of Menghetti's paralegals started to laugh, too, but was silenced by a glance from the defense attorney, who sullenly urged everyone's attention back to the agenda.

"Al," said Ashford, "I'd like to hear more from our expert about what kind of jury we're looking for."

"Anything else on that, Eric?" said Menghetti, the trial lawyer already composed and back in charge.

Tremaine nodded. "The juror you want will depend in part on how strong your witnesses are and the kind of story you intend to tell. We'll use a jury questionnaire to help determine whether the juror is a cognitive-type personality or an affective thinker. I think the D.A. will go for the *cognitive* type—the business exec or engineer who will piece together all the circumstantial evidence—and conclude that two plus two equals four.

"The *affective* type we will want is an inductive thinker who decides it's four from the get-go, then starts looking for support to make it all add up. These people tend to have 'selective perception,' that is, they pay most attention to what makes them feel good about the decision they've already made."

Ashford said, "I like it, Al. Has the ring of sound science."

Dickson said, "Some people say that about astrology."

"Ah," said Dr. Tremaine good-naturedly, "a skeptic in our midst?"

"Ignore me," said Dickson. "I didn't think the gas-powered engine had a chance either."

"Have you used a jury consultant, Mr. Dickson?"

"Truth is, Dr. Tremaine," said Barrett, "I haven't even used a jury lately. My concern is not with you but with lawyers who yield control of their case to you."

"No good jury consultant wants control," said Tremaine, "and with lawyers like you and Al Menghetti on the case, I'll be lucky to be able to control my own bladder."

Everyone laughed and Barrett and Tremaine exchanged a look of mutual respect.

"What's next, Al?" said Ashford. "I'm due at the Olympic Club at three o'clock."

"Jesus," said Barrett out loud.

Menghetti shot Barrett a hard look, then said, "Our forensic pathologist is due momentarily."

"What about DNA?" asked Ashford. "Will we be able to find an expert to combat what their DNA chap will say?"

Laughter greeted his question.

"Did I say something funny?"

Menghetti rose and began pacing, tapping his lips with an index finger. "It's a rule of nature, Elliot, that for every man there's a woman. It's a rule of trial forensics that for every expert there's an equal and opposite expert. Show me a guy with a degree, two kids in college, and a mortgage, and I'll show you an expert witness that will say whatever we want to hear."

Ashford's laughter rattled through the conference speaker. "No problem then. You agree, Barrett?"

Barrett sniffed, folded his hands in his lap, and said, "Partly. The trick is finding a qualified, likable, and articulate authority who doesn't have his head up his ass. Al just defined an expert witness as anyone out of town with a briefcase who needs money. But my experience is if you sleep with a whore like that, you wake up with things crawling on you. Nobody can snatch defeat from the jaws of victory faster than a bad expert."

Menghetti gave Barrett another look, but the discussion was interrupted by the arrival of Menghetti's forensic pathologist, Dr. Seybring Lassiter, currently on sabbatical from Stanford Medical, where he headed the department. Barrett exhaled loudly from time to time as the small-boned professor lectured for thirty minutes in a monotone, occasionally smoothing an ill-fitting hairpiece with his right hand, fiddling with his half-glasses, or stroking his pointed chin whiskers.

His impressive professional achievements were interspersed with incomprehensible medical jargon. There were no cuts, there were "evasive lacerations"; there was no sudden drop in blood pressure, there was "vasovagal reaction"; no tiny pinpoint blood spots around the victim's face, rather "petechiae."

"In summary," Dr. Lassiter said, his brow knitted in concentration, "the victim expired as a function of neurogenic cessation resulting from the multiple and invasive infarctions of the carotid artery I have heretofore discussed. Of course, by the time the autopsy transpired, fixed lividity was encroaching—cyanosis having occurred long before, of course—despite which occurrences I am reasonably confident in the validity of my findings."

Menghetti asked several more questions, then smiled and said, "I think that does it for now, Doctor, unless Dr. Tremaine has a question."

"I have one, Al," said Barrett.

"Yes, Dickson," said Menghetti, his tone as flat and colorless as the walls surrounding them.

"Two actually. First, what the hell's this guy been talking

about for the past twenty minutes? And second, why would you want to put him in front of a jury of normal, decent human beings?"

The professor's head jerked around so hard his glasses almost fell off. Recovering his poise, he stood and shoved his notes into a thin leather valise. "I'm sorry, Mr. Menghetti, but I don't think I'll be able to help you on this case."

"Seybring, please," pleaded Menghetti, "Mr. Dickson was just—"

"Mr. Dickson's reputation precedes him," said the professor, still without looking at Barrett, "and I wouldn't care to inadvertently step into a pile of it."

Dickson let out an approving roar. "That's good, Doc. Maybe I misjudged you."

"You aren't in condition to judge a frog-jump contest, Dickson," said Menghetti, but the expert had already strode through the door.

A black silence draped the room. In an ominous tone, Menghetti excused his two paralegals from the room.

More silence.

"Maybe you misjudged *him*, Dickson," said Menghetti at last, "but he damn sure has *you* pegged."

Nobody spoke as Menghetti, the skin drawn tight around his tense jaw, continued to glare at Dickson.

"Sorry, Al, but the more people like him I meet, the more I prefer the company of my goldfish."

" 'Sorry' doesn't cut it, Dickson. With less than two weeks before the biggest trial in San Francisco's history, you just blew off our expert pathologist. Are you out of your fucking mind?"

"Usually," said Barrett. "But sane enough to know you don't want an academic egghead like that talking down to your jury. They'll dislike him and distrust you for vouching for him."

The conference box rattled. "Excuse me, sports, but I'd be damned grateful if you'd both remember it's my life at stake here. Now, I'm not taking sides, Al, but I must say I couldn't understand him either."

Menghetti rubbed his eyes with both hands, then rose to his feet and began to pace. "Okay, Dickson. So much for our strategy of pushing this thing to a quick trial. Now we'll need time to find someone to take Professor Lassiter's place. You'll have to make a social call on your pal the judge—cocktails, golf, or whatever it is the old boys do while the rest of us are working—and get him to delay the trial date."

Feeling Menghetti coming closer, Barrett gazed down at his own hands. "I wouldn't feel comfortable doing that, Al."

"Are you in this case to feel comfortable, Dickson, or to do your goddamn job?"

Barrett looked up and met his cocounsel's fierce gaze. "I don't see overtly subverting the independence of the court anywhere in my job description."

"Then why the hell do you think you were hired?"

Barrett reddened, suppressed a desire to smash that oversize chin, that proud Florentine nose. Menghetti was so close his cologne was reawakening Barrett's nausea.

"Maybe," continued Menghetti, "you should have thought about your precious 'job description' before you sent our key expert packing."

Barrett turned away to hide the anger beginning to blaze in his aching eyes. Deep down, he knew Menghetti was right. So was A. P. Giannini when he said there was no such thing as a free lunch.

"All right," Barrett said bitterly, "I'll talk to him."

Ten minutes later, he was outside, his shirt soaked with perspiration, raging not so much at Menghetti as at Mike Reasoner for asking more of him than loyalty could answer, and at himself for his arrogance in thinking it could. If Mike had been standing there on the sidewalk at that moment, God help the sonofabitch. Barrett's fists clenched at the thought.

Calm down, bozo, he admonished himself, but his swirling thoughts flashed back to a day in 1952, when the country was busy liking Ike and hating North Koreans, and ex-congressman (now murder suspect) Elliot Ashford was probably commencing his second year of primary education at some place like the Menlo School for Boys and young Barrett Dickson was learning his first lesson in the folly of violence.

Barrett was eleven, and growing up under less refined circumstances than Elliot at Saint Anthony's Home for Boys in Topeka, Kansas. His name had been scribbled on a note attached to the box in which he had been delivered to the local fire station shortly after his birth. Then, after two hitches in foster homes, he was sent to Saint Anthony's. He would never know his parents, but most kids there were in the same fix, so it hadn't seemed so bad at the time—until the night he and his best friend, Harlow Flagg, decided to sneak out of Saint Anthony's. They had heard about cockfights that took place Wednesday nights in a barn on the outskirts of town.

"You chicken?" Harlow had challenged.

"Hell no," young Barrett had lied. "I ain't chicken!"

The problem started soon after they had climbed a ladder through the hay-bale opening in the back of the barn, a spot from which they could see the birds already tearing at each other below in an explosion of dust, feathers, and sound. One of the guards spotted the trespassers and signaled them down, setting Barrett's heart racing even faster than the cocks had.

"You two lads come to see blood, did ya?" said a wiry, red-faced little cock-master as he snatched up the winning bird from the previous fight by its blood-and-dirt-caked wings and thrust the bleeding bird close to the boys' faces. Barrett winced from the hot, pungent smell coming off the flapping wings, but even worse from the sight of the bird's white-curtained but unblinking round eye, dull with suffering. Blood splattered across Barrett's face and eyes as onlookers roared with laughter. He fought back tears of fear and rage, then nearly fainted from the putrid stench of blood and grime-stuck feathers mingled with the stale odor of the man who held him from behind.

"How's that for blood, me lads?" shouted the Limey cock-master. "Or is it human blood you've come to see?"

With that, the toughs threw the filthy, blood-smeared boys headlong into the circular dirt pit and ordered them to fight one another. Barrett stared up at the yelling crowd, then at Harlow's pallid face, his features rigid with fear and confusion, his fists extended. Barrett rose, noticed that the right knee of his pants was torn and bloody, and absurdly wondered how he would explain this to Father Dolan. Shouts from the men surrounding the pit reminded him he had a more serious problem.

Both boys tried to fake it at first, but Barrett felt a sharp pain as he was jabbed in the kidneys by something sharp from behind.

"Come on, ye little bastards! *Fight!*"

Any sign of holding back was quickly punished by more sharp jabs to the back from behind, and soon they were at each other. He managed a solid punch to Harlow's nose, but the bigger boy's fists came back at him like raining baseballs, forcing him to the ground. He looked up and the craziness he saw in Harlow's eyes set his heart pounding in his throat so hard he couldn't breathe. He tasted blood. Harlow's? The rooster's? His own?

Then he heard laughter. The men were laughing at him, calling him a sissy and a chicken, goading him. He fought back tears.

"Get up and fight, you little chicken-shit," ordered the cock-master.

Barrett scurried to his feet and began throwing punches at his friend, swinging blindly, frantically, haymakers going nowhere. Then he landed one, then another, and suddenly he was a punishing windmill of flailing fists. The circle of men roared, urging him on. No faking now, both boys lashing out with fists and knees, their fingers gouging and choking. Blood poured from Harlow's nose and his own cut lips.

I ain't chicken, he heard himself shouting, then ran straight into a right cross from Harlow that flattened him again, this time for good.

Harlow was declared the winner and the youths were dumped into the back of a pickup, then delivered to the back door of Saint Anthony's. A week later, their wounds almost healed, they shook hands and forgave each other, but they were never friends again. Worse, a seed of insecurity planted in a loveless birth had now taken root and would later flourish in the heat of a hopeless war into a thoroughly distrustful nature.

He had not wanted to go to Vietnam, but once drafted, he tried to be the good soldier. After his discharge, he was determined to find a nonviolent method of resolving disputes, and three years of law school had nurtured a fragile splinter of idealism that had somehow survived the moral chaos of Vietnam. He graduated with honors, then took a job with Caldwell & Shaw in San Francisco, still wary, but optimistic. He tried cases for over twenty years, achieving an unparalleled success that had masked a growing disillusionment.

But now, the memory of his coerced fight with Harlow Flagg seemed an apt metaphor for what had become of his profession. To Barrett, trial work was nothing now but a buttoned-down, three-piece cockfight and he'd be well out of it.

He took several deep breaths, then walked to the nearest bar and cooled the fire raging in his chest with a double vodka martini.

By three o'clock, he was calm enough to dial the judge's chambers.

17

Twenty-four years before Lara Ashford was murdered, a ten-year-old girl lay on a hard, leather-covered table, knowing that something terrible was about to happen to her. She had been taken at dawn from her bed in the room she shared with nine other females, all much older than she, down to the underground level of the state institution that was now her home.

It was cold down here, even in the middle of a steamy Georgia summer. There were no pictures to look at on the gray-painted cement walls. No windows to break the monotony.

They had wheeled her into the room where she had heard they toasted your brain with electricity. It was no secret what went on down here; in fact, they sometimes made inmates watch it done to others, whether as punishment or as a deterrent they didn't know, but it served both ends.

The two trustees had lifted her off the gurney and onto a leather table with straps along the side. Two other people were already in the room: another trustee she had seen around—a tall, horse-faced man—and a fat nurse with a big nose and red lipstick who always seemed angry at her.

The girl lay waiting for what would happen next, her heart pounding against her rib cage so hard she could feel it in her throat.

"These restraints are for your own good, honey," the nurse told her as she roughly buckled the leather straps around the child's chest, arms, wrists, and ankles. "You don't have these, you might be breakin' your own legs or arms while you're unconscious."

"I done it once myself," said the tall trustee with the long face. "Come to and they done forgot to tie down one

my legs. Done broke it in two places 'cause of all the jum-
pin' and shakin' it did while I was somewheres else."

He came close, smelling of mingled sweat and disinfectant. Then, without warning, he splashed warm water over
her head and sprayed on the foamy stuff her father used
to shave with before he died a few months earlier. Then
he picked up a shiny straight razor in one hand and twisted
her head to one side with the other.

She started to protest as the razor did its work, but nothing came out of her mouth. Then she saw curls of blond
hair floating across her wide-open eye, down past the edge
of the leather pallet and onto the floor. Then the other side.

The horse-faced man then attached metal plates to the
newly exposed areas on both sides of her head, just above
the temples. The tape that held them in place pulled at her
skin and hair if she moved her head. He seemed to be
trying not to hurt her, but the plates were cold and she
knew they would soon turn hot. She struggled, trying to
free one of her tiny wrists.

"Where's the doc at?" she heard the man ask the nurse
as she inspected his work with the plates.

"Out watering his damn petunias," grunted the nurse irritably. "How the hell am I supposed to know where the
doc is? I'm your keeper, not his."

"They'll dock me sure if'n we get behind," he said. "Got
eight more comin' in presently."

"Hell, let's just do it then," said the nurse, who then
snatched up a thing that looked like an ice pick and came
toward the girl. The girl closed her eyes in panic. This was
not the electrical-shock thing she had heard about, she
thought. This was even worse.

The nurse now stood so close the girl caught her acidy
smell now too, almost as revolting as the man's. She dared
to open her eyes and saw the nurse was holding the shiny
thing that looked just like an ice pick inches above her
white chest. Despite her fear, she was transfixed by the tip
of steel poised no more than two or three inches above her
skin. Then she realized it *was* an ice pick! A thin, gleaming
piece of pointed steel with a wooden handle just like the
one they had at home, only this one had some rust deposits
on a chrome band where the pick came out of the wooden
handle, its surface now lost in the pudgy pink fist that

clutched it. Despite her terror, she was aware of a warm liquid spreading under her legs. She hoped the nurse wouldn't torture her for soiling the sheet that covered the pallet.

Before she killed her.

"We don't need Doctor Do-little to handle this little package," the nurse said, and the girl's lids clamped shut in terror. But she felt the nurse unbuckling the chest strap, then opened her eyes again and saw her use the ice pick to jab a new hole in the leather. The girl felt a rush of comprehension, then momentary relief, even though it hurt when the nurse roughly tightened the belt down into the new notch, crushing the child's incipient breasts and yanking her gown aside.

She felt the eyes of the man staring at her from behind the nurse, and when the nurse turned away, he came in so close she could smell him again. His eyes were wet and bulging and he wiped a hand across his mouth and started to reach out toward her, but the nurse shouted at him, then came over and roughly jerked the smock back over the girl's partially exposed chest.

Other straps were similarly modified by the nurse and secured more tightly around the tiny white wrists and ankles by the man. Then the man just stood and stared at her some more.

"Don't you have somethin' to do, George?" said the nurse.

They both walked away then and the girl struggled against the straps, but it did no good. She thought they might even be gone, but then she heard a chair scrape across the wood floor, causing her to stiffen painfully against her bonds. It hurt to move her head, but she turned enough to see that the woman was writing things down in a book and the man was moving around, clicking things on, noisily shoving equipment all over the place as if she weren't even there, as if this had nothing to do with her. Maybe it didn't. Maybe they had forgotten she was there. She tried again to slip a wrist through the leather loop. If she could just free one hand, then she could unbuckle the other straps and run for it. She saw that no one was looking.

She remembered a time when everybody looked at her,

couldn't seem to keep their eyes off her; applauding her, judging her favorably. Her mother was always telling her how lucky she was, but she hadn't believed it. She believed it now.

Suddenly both of them were standing over her again. She clamped her eyelids tight against the bright overhead lights because she knew it was about to start. She felt sick to her stomach, but knew complaining would be useless.

"No shot?" said the sad-faced trustee. "Cain't do it with no shot."

"We can't wait any longer," the nurse said resentfully, glancing at a large clock on the wall behind the girl. "Next one's due here ten minutes from now. I'll give it to her myself."

"I thought only Doc does the antiseptic."

"Anesthesia, you idiot. Barbiturates and muscle relaxants."

"Just that he's the one supposed to—"

"Shut up, George," she said, glancing at the equipment he had wheeled up beside the girl, "unless you want some of this yourself."

As the nurse came toward her with the hypodermic needle, the girl's heart began to thrash even harder against her ribs. She struggled against the straps, but knew that nothing could save her now.

"Calm yourself, pageant princess," came the coarse voice of the nurse as the straps dug into the girl's wrist. "After this you won't feel hardly nothin'."

"Please," the girl heard herself whisper. "A drink of water?"

But the nurse jammed a rubber object into the child's mouth instead, then picked up a hypodermic needle and stuck it roughly into her arm. The pain brought fresh tears to her eyes.

"This is a civilized institution, honey," she said, and within seconds the two voices became blurred. They were still arguing about something, using words she could no longer make out. She knew she would get no water.

Her body began to relax despite her fear. She felt as if she were floating out of the room. She let her eyes close, thinking they might go away if she played possum. It had worked at home sometimes.

"Count to ten for me," ordered the nurse, but the girl didn't answer.

"She's out, George, go ahead."

The little girl wanted to smile because she had tricked them; she wasn't unconscious at all. Then the man said okay, all right then, followed by a strange sound she had never heard. She opened her eyes wide and tried to tell them, stop, she was still awake, but somebody behind her thrust a burning knife blade deep into the crown of her head, splitting it open like a melon, shooting an electric storm through her neck and down into her stomach.

The smiling doctor was watching her when she awoke upstairs in the infirmary. He sat there like he had been watching her for a long time.

"Hello, Amanda," came the incongruously deep voice from the small, balding man who stood between her and a dirty white screen with a scuffed print of green trees and brown animals. He had a perfectly round face with a small, smiling mouth carved into it like a jack-o'-lantern. Amanda had come to distrust this smile; it meant nothing. Just something he wore, like the plaid suspenders with those shiny silver adjustment clips she could see through his parted white smock. Today he wore a ridiculous bow tie that matched the suspenders. Only the stethoscope around his neck, a pair of intelligent brown eyes, and a deep, comforting voice were evocative of a real doctor.

He examined the bruised flesh around her wrists and made a rueful clicking sound with his tongue. "How are we this morning, Amanda?" he said.

Without thinking, she told him she felt fine. She would tell everybody this, hoping they wouldn't burn her brain again.

She would tell everybody this even though it was the truth; even though she really did feel the best she had felt since her father's death.

But mainly she would tell everybody she was fine because that's the only way you got out of a place like this.

"Will you do the bad thing again?" she asked.

"We'll see, Amanda," he said, then made a note on a clipboard. "If we do, I'll be there next time and you won't feel a thing. I promise."

She tried to remember what she had done to deserve what was happening to her and figured it must have something to do with her mother losing her leg or her father dying; that she must be to blame. Her mother had told her that coming here to live was for her own good.

She bit her lower lip, wondering how many more bad things would happen to her for her own good.

Then she decided that if this was for her own good, she would rather be bad.

18

Amanda Keller was awakened by noises from the living room TV. It sounded like the local early morning news feed from CNN. She pulled a pillow over her head, though she realized the alarm was about to go off anyway. She reflected that her disabled mother—with whom she shared the small Noe Valley flat—watched that damned TV all day and most of the night, then had the gall to complain that Amanda's morning *San Francisco Chronicle* was an "unnecessary extravagance."

Amanda Keller put on a robe and tiptoed unnoticed behind Lucinda and into the outer hallway to pick up today's unnecessary extravagance. She liked seeing the newspaper there every morning, always in exactly the same place, folded neatly in quarters with her name on it.

She glanced at the headline:

ASHFORD TRIAL STARTS TOMORROW

She trembled with excitement at seeing written confirmation of what she had seen last night on the *Ten O'Clock News.* Her mother had seen it too, but what Lucinda didn't know was that Amanda had ignored her instructions to "get out of it," and would appear at the Hall of Justice tomorrow morning, probably as a member of the jury pool for the Ashford trial.

Amanda made coffee and carried a cup out to her mother, placing it on top of the front page of the *Chronicle* so her mother couldn't miss it.

"Here's your coffee, Mother," she said, containing her exuberance. "See the headline?"

"I'm crippled, child, but I'm not blind. So it's finally starting, is it?"

"Yes, Mama," said Amanda, planting herself between Lucinda and the TV screen. "The biggest case ever, and guess where your daughter's going tomorrow."

"To work, if she knows what's good for her," said Lucinda, craning her neck forward to get a close look at a plump British teenager accused of murdering a baby. "And while you're there, darlin', find out about why your medical plan hasn't been coverin' my prescriptions this year."

Undaunted, Amanda bent down close to her mother's face, her skin glowing with anticipation. "I've been called for the Ashford trial, Mother! I might even get to sit as a juror! I've checked the astrological signs and the moon is in . . . Mother? Do you want to see the chart?"

Lucinda didn't blink, just stared vacantly at the television screen for several seconds. When she spoke, her voice was oddly devoid of feeling.

"Of all the stupid things you've done, Amanda Keller, this takes the prize."

"*What?*"

"Didn't you hear me tell you to get out of it? Don't you listen when I'm talkin' to you? Now you're going to sit out there and lose a week's work for nothing. Probably won't even get called into the jury box, and even if you do, they'll throw you off for one reason or another."

"But—"

"Congratulations, Amanda. In less than ten years, you've gone from bein' a TV star making $13,000 a week to auditioning for a role as an extra for five bucks a day."

Amanda's shoulders sagged. "I thought you had forgiven me for—"

"Throwin' our dreams away? 'Course I have, child. I'm talkin' about the here and now, meanin' that *here* in this house we can't survive on five bucks a day, so *now* you'd better figure a way to get out of that jury duty."

"But it's a chance to—"

"Join the ranks of the unemployed is what it is," said Lucinda, indicating the subject was closed by raising the volume on the TV.

Amanda straightened slowly, unable to speak and thoroughly confused. Why couldn't her mother see the possibilities? Why had she given up on their hopes for a second chance in Hollywood? It was as if her mother didn't *want* to see the possibilities.

Lucinda had really given up, she realized with a pang of loss. Maybe, thought Amanda, her optimism in retreat, it's time I give up, too.

Amanda reported for work at Ward and Company promptly at 8:30 A.M. and went to her desk in the corner of a fluorescent-illuminated room surrounded by floor-to-ceiling file cabinets housing hundreds of thousands of commercial-leasing documents. She was shocked to see a heavyset Latino woman in her late twenties, hair bristling like the bride of Frankenstein's sitting in her chair, her breakfast spread across Amanda's desk. She was reading a tabloid.

"What can I do for you?" said the woman, looking up through heavy-lidded eyes, as if resenting Amanda's intrusion.

"My name is Amanda Keller. I'm the chief clerk here. That's my desk."

"You're damn lucky to have one," the woman said in a surly tone, continuing to eat fruit and cottage cheese out of a plastic container. "I'll be done with it in just a few."

Amanda felt awkward standing there in front of her own desk, but chose not to make an issue of it, despite the curds of cottage cheese she saw scattered across her desktop.

"Who are you?" Amanda ventured, feeling the first signs of an asthma attack.

"I'm the new file clerk. Didn't nobody tell you? I'm replacing Nick."

Nick was Amanda's right hand in the file department.

"Of course they told me," said Amanda, feeling heat rising in her body. She turned and walked quickly to the women's room. She splashed water on her face, then looked at herself in the mirror.

Why hadn't they told her? she asked herself.

She felt faint and needed to sit down, so she entered a stall, turned the plastic cover down, and sat, head in her hands, realizing she had left her inhaler in the closet of the file room.

Nick had been her savior; she'd be lost without him.

A minute later, the stall door was suddenly thrown open.

Amanda gasped as she looked up. My God, there she was again, the new woman, staring at her in amazement. Amanda's face reddened in embarrassment.

"Christ Almighty!" shouted the intruder, quickly slamming the door shut. "Didn't nobody teach you how to lock a door?"

Amanda quickly latched the door, feeling both stupid and angry as she heard the woman noisily enter the stall next to her. Then she heard giggling.

The woman was laughing at her!

"It's also a hell of a lot neater," came a voice from under the partition, "if you drop your pants first. Didn't they teach you that neither?"

Amanda said nothing, hardly able to breathe. She quickly left the stall and washed her hands, moving her fingers over the scar on her left wrist.

Why am I washing my hands? she asked her reflection in the mirror. It was only 9:00 A.M. and Amanda felt exhausted, slipping toward depression.

She fumed for two hours before summoning the courage to confront office administrator Harold Pierce, a bald, burly man with a shrill voice. He wore floral-design bow ties over striped shirts and always kept a pencil behind his ear. For all of this, he considered himself a ladies' man and resented Amanda's indifference to him.

"Why wasn't I at least . . . consulted?" she managed after brief perfunctory amenities. "Nick has been with me—us— for four years, longer even than George or Amy or me!" Pierce didn't invite her to sit, and she seemed doomed to spend her day standing helplessly in front of people sitting behind desks.

Pierce's small mouth produced a conciliatory smile. "I had my reasons," he said, "and I knew you wouldn't want to do the deed. You should thank me."

"I just don't understand—"

"Marla will be excellent. We're paying her less than Nick, she won't smoke pot in the stairwell like he did— don't act like you didn't know, Amanda—and she happens to be a . . . friend."

A *friend.* So that was it. Amanda took a deep breath, then cautiously reported "Marla's" appropriation of her desk, but Pierce just told her to "deal with it," treating her as if *she* had been the one with the attitude!

She decided she'd better let it drop. He had jumped at her when she'd shown him the jury summons for the following day, acting as if she had asked for time off to get her hair done.

"Well, just get out of it as soon as you can," he snapped, not even looking up at her. "Tell them you're opposed to the death penalty or something. If you're not here, who's going to train Marla?"

As if you haven't already done that, you bastard, she thought, but what she said was, "I'll work with her today and stay in touch by telephone at breaks."

She hurried back to her file room and grabbed the inhaler from her purse in the closet, trying to blot out the image of Pierce and the new woman lying naked in some motel room laughing about the file manager sitting fully clothed on a toilet seat. She pumped her inhaler twice, three times into her mouth.

When her breathing finally returned to normal, she realized she had to try to find another job. But moving to a new company would mean a pay cut, which would further delay her planned escape from Lucinda to her own apartment. She felt like a rabbit caught in a snare, and began counting the minutes until five o'clock. At least she wouldn't have to come in tomorrow.

19

When tomorrow finally came, Amanda stared in wonder at the spectacle awaiting her at the Hall of Justice. Police, several on horseback, struggled to clear the nine steps leading up to the entrance. Sidewalks below and across the street were jammed with curiosity seekers, demonstrators, and peddlers selling "The Ashford Trial—I Was There" buttons; small plaques with tiny pieces of broken glass mounted on black velvet, "guaranteed" to have come from the crime scene; and T-shirts reading "The Real Deal," which is what the San Francisco papers were calling the Ashford case to convey the message that "the City"— as distinguished from its arrogant sister to the south— would show the world how to dispense justice efficiently, competently, and without circus fanfare.

Goggle-eyed citizens who had entered the lottery for the few seats available to the public pushed and shoved to maintain their positions on the steps as they waited to see if their number would be drawn. Other onlookers gazed at the scene from across the street, some clutching the morning *Chronicle* with a headline that blared "The *Real* Trial of the Century!"

At the foot of the main steps and spilling into two traffic lanes, protective police barricades surrounded NOW demonstrators, who carried placards that read "Women for Justice NOW!" and chanted:

> "*When* will the battering stop? *Now,* right *now!*
> *Where* will the battering stop? *Here,* right *here!*"

Amanda shoved through the confusion along with other jury panelists and presented her summons to the deputy at the metal detector. She was sent to the Jury Assembly

Room on the third floor, then to Department 26—a courtroom directly across from the Jury Assembly Room—where she was surprised to see a different kind of bedlam, though more controlled. More than eighty prospective jurors who would normally never have glanced at one another were chattering like old friends, instantly bonded by fate and the hope of achieving their fifteen minutes of fame as a high-profile-case juror.

Amanda, who had never formed a common bond with anyone, fastened her attention not on the audience but on the actors onstage. From her seat in the second row, she had a clear view of the four lawyers inside the rail, chatting together and strolling about like actors before curtain call, occasionally casting an eye across the growing mass of prospective jurors.

Amanda knew about acting from her role as Sharon McPeak and suspected they weren't as calm as they appeared to be. Her lips tightened as she thought about the years of acting lessons she had taken before her exile from Hollywood; before her husband—a powerful agent turned TV producer—started hitting on a sixteen-year-old *Hope's People* cast member who'd supposedly done Mick Jagger one night on somebody's yacht. Amanda had tried to ignore what was going on until the little bitch began rubbing her nose in it in front of the other cast members. She knew then that either she or the Lolita would have to leave the show, but was shattered—along with thousands of fans—when Sharon McPeak suddenly suffered a fatal ski accident at Squaw Valley. The pain that contorted Sharon's face in her final big scene required no acting.

Amanda knew Mark had dumped her from the show as a prelude to dumping her from his life, and within a month he had moved his sixteen-year-old inamorata into his seventeen-room Bel Air mansion. He had moved Amanda into the Beverly Hills Hotel a week before but wouldn't take her calls; nor would any other agents or producers in Hollywood. Such was his power. Only his lawyer called her—the one who had drafted the bulletproof prenuptial agreement.

Out of work and hope, she decided it was time for life to imitate art and she slashed her wrists. She had botched that, too, and after her eventual release from the hospital, she returned to San Francisco and her mother. Although she had no practical experience or education, a woman who recognized her from *Hope's People* offered her a job at Ward and Company.

Sharon McPeak, file girl.

Amanda turned her eyes to the female prosecutor she had seen interviewed once on television, Grace Harris. Nice trim figure, though too modestly concealed by a light gray suit. Probably pretty if she'd take off those large-rimmed glasses orbiting her dark-circled eyes that gave her a slightly owlish look. This woman needed a fashion consultant, thought Amanda, but found herself envying the smaller woman's wide mouth, though it too could have been improved with a darker shade of lipstick.

Despite these shortcomings, Amanda observed, the woman's mouth, delicate features, erect carriage, and lush mane of shiny black hair sliced with silver combined to attract the obvious attention of the huge defense lawyer in the rumpled suit with a face to match. That must be Barrett Dickson, she thought, the washed-up civil trial lawyer she had read about, standing there near the defense table, puffy eyes fixed shamelessly on the back of Grace Harris's head as if expecting a bird to fly out of her hair. When not busy checking out the Harris woman, Dickson walked in small circles without apparent destination, like a person trying on a new pair of shoes.

Then there was the bulldog standing near the big fellow. That would have to be Al Menghetti, she thought, staring straight out at us as if he were on the block at a bachelorette auction. A truly unattractive man with his leering, wide-set dark eyes, loud tie, oversize lapels, and, obviously, an ego to match.

Amanda observed that most of the prospective jurors were stealing looks at defendant Elliot Ashford, cool and dashingly handsome in his dark double-breasted suit. He sat with his back to the gallery, calmly studying his fingernails, looking more like one of the lawyers than a criminal defendant. Though obviously lean and well muscled, he looked harmless enough, even scholarly in appearance with his neatly trimmed, slicked-back blond hair and pale blue eyes behind rimless, half-moon glasses. But when he turned around once to glance at the noisy assembly, something about his expression sent a spasm of apprehension down her spine. Was it the violent act for which he stood accused, or was it his vaguely troubling resemblance to the image of a man her memory wouldn't quite release. Her own father, perhaps?

But of all the actors in the drama about to unfold, Earl Field captured Amanda's real attention. More than that: he commanded it. To Amanda, the others were minor planets orbiting the handsome district attorney. Although not as tall as the other men, he upstaged them with a presence that bespoke confidence without cockiness. Just watching him filled her with a strange excitement as he flashed a perfect smile at Grace Harris standing beside him. Amanda found herself envying the other woman.

Amanda's thoughts were interrupted by doors popping open on both sides of the bench, discharging the court attachés: the court reporter from one side, the clerk from the other. The courtroom clamor dissolved into silence as if prompted by a sign held up in a television studio. The bailiff moved to his chair and table near the holding-cell door, the clerk took her seat behind a cluttered table, and the court reporter straddled her machine. Then, at 10:15 A.M. on October 9, right on schedule, the door leading to chambers was thrown open and Judge John Hernandez powered through it like a halfback. The bailiff cried, "*All rise! The Superior Court in and for the city and county of San Francisco is now in session, the Honorable John Hernandez presiding!*"

Already the judge had taken the bench in eight swift and powerful strides. His message was clear, not just to the gallery and counsel but to the national press as well: *This* high-profile trial will move efficiently, and *this* judge will maintain control of his courtroom.

He raced through the usual greetings and housekeeping matters, occasionally peering down at the prospective jurors over his spectacles. Then he described the nature of the charges against Ashford and instructed them on some of the legal principles involved.

Amanda had read that Judge Hernandez was a judicial anomaly—soft-spoken, yet possessed of a manner that commanded respect whether he was in or out of a black robe. Though he was known to run a tight ship, his harshest sanction never lacked courtesy, and he held no lawyer to a higher standard than he imposed on himself.

A chill of excitement seized her as she realized the importance of what was happening. If only Lucinda could have been here, she thought, she would quickly understand and forgive a daughter's defiance. Amanda prayed she would be chosen.

Next, in a firm voice with just a hint of a Latino accent, John Hernandez ordered the clerk to spin the metal drum holding the names of the summoned panel members and to seat the first prospective jurors in the jury box. The drum contained slips of paper like those found in Chinese fortune cookies. Amanda knew that one of those slips was inscribed with her name, and she squeezed her eyes shut, trying to will the clerk's hand to close on it. A mild touch of asthma and the sound of the wheel combined to make her feel dizzy. She reached inside her purse and touched her inhaler for reassurance.

She opened her eyes as the drum stopped spinning. The clerk reached inside and lifted a slip of paper in her fingers. *Let it be me,* Amanda prayed. Her heart pounded against her ribs as she pictured herself in a posttrial interview providing an eyewitness account of the trial and the underworld secrets revealed during its suspenseful unfolding. Then—who knows?—perhaps there would even be a movie based on a ghostwritten story, with her playing herself in the starring role. Why not? An event like this could at least provide a stepping-stone back into the world of daytime television. She could picture the look on her mother's face, hear the respectful apology: You were right all along, Amanda.

"Juror number thirty-four, Andrea Jackson, J-a-c-k-s-o-n," shouted the clerk, and a large, black woman half ran down the aisle toward the box, her elation unconcealed. Some people behind Amanda tittered, and one of them commented that the woman was behaving as if this were *The Price Is Right.*

The bailiff directed the woman into seat number one, and the clerk, who seemed offensively blasé under the circumstances, set the wheel in motion again. Amanda put her fingers to her throat and furtively glanced at her watch, monitoring her heartbeat, now racing at more than 120 beats per minute, seemingly driven by the *tic-a-tic-a-tic-a* sound of the spinning barrel. She wondered if she could make it to her feet and into the box if her name were called. She again closed her eyes against the dizzying rotation of the cylinder.

They were playing bingo with her life, and by late morning it was clear she was not winning. The jury box· was filled, the so-called six-pack of alternate jurors was seated, and the lawyers had commenced their voir dire questioning. At noon, Judge Hernandez recessed the courtroom for lunch. She had been so sure; why had her name not been called?

After the noon recess, Amanda chose a seat in the rear of the courtroom and watched as the lawyers methodically questioned each prospective juror in the box.

"Ah, Ms. Axelrod is it?" said Al Menghetti in an oily voice. "Would you be able to put your political differences aside and be fair to Mr. Ashford?"

"Oh, yes, absolutely," responded the woman—a bit too quickly, thought Amanda. It was evident to her that many panelists were lying to get on, while an equal number were lying to get off. One juror readily admitted he was put off by what had happened to the jurors in the Simpson case in Los Angeles years before, and the judge interrupted the questioning.

"Please do not worry about being sequestered, ladies and gentlemen," he said. "I don't believe in it. I know what you're thinking: that the only people who did time in that case were the jurors themselves."

The prospective jurors responded with nervous laughter.

"I will only insist," he continued, "that you avoid all forms of media and not discuss the case with anyone. There will be no TV cameras here, and the lawyers will be constrained by what we call a gag order. Only matters that take place in this courtroom—admissible evidence—can be discussed by any of them. In other words, I'm going to sequester the *public,* not the jury. I won't have you walking out of here after your verdict with the public knowing, or even thinking they know, more about the case than you do."

Then it was Earl Field's turn to voir dire the jury and exercise his challenges on those who didn't satisfy him.

After that, the clerk spun the wheel again and Amanda's heart raced with excitement. Oh God, let me be chosen, she thought.

The charismatic district attorney next turned his attention to the juror in seat number six and learned that he had served years before as a member of Elliot Ashford's full-time staff at his Atherton country mansion, with duties that included tending to the motor vehicles, including twin 1936 Bentleys—one black and one white—and "seeing to the ponies," by which he meant the purebred Arabians used in polo matches and an occasional fox hunt. Amanda saw that several of the jurors in the box glared at the defendant, and that Al Menghetti's normal poker face yielded to a pained expression. Amanda judged that not more than one of the sixty-plus remaining panelists had so much as ridden in a Bentley, let alone attended a polo match or abused a hapless fox.

Another juror, a thin-faced little man with an incongruous handlebar mustache that dwarfed his other features, admitted outright concern over rumors that the defendant was somehow connected to the Mafia and that there could be the possibility of intimidation. This remark caused Earl Field and Grace Harris to exchange an amused glance and brought Al Menghetti to his feet, asking the court to instruct the panel to disregard the comment.

"The Mafia is in no way involved in this case," said the judge. "Intimidation of jurors is formula movie fare—not reality. I instruct you all to disregard the juror's comment."

Sure, Judge, thought Amanda, smiling secretly, knowing that not even John Hernandez could un-ring that bell.

Back at the Noe Valley flat that evening after an abbreviated visit to her fitness center, Amanda entered excitedly and saw Lucinda in her usual place on the couch in front of the TV set.

"Mother," she said, "guess what?"

"Shush," said Lucinda, and Amanda realized her mother was watching one of her favorite programs. Amanda restrained herself and prepared dinner, a frozen chicken parmigiana that was Lucinda's favorite. She would share her news over their evening meal together.

"It *is* the Ashford case, Mother!" she said later, eagerly

sitting down next to her mother in front of a TV table. "I was there all day!"

But Lucinda had begun eating, forking hunks of the spicy chicken breast into her mouth while continuing to stare at the television set, which showed a blond woman, long legs crossed at thigh level, reporting to her handsome male co-anchor that a prominent actor Amanda recognized as one of her ex-husband's great "discoveries," who had offered her coke and tried to bed her twice, had checked himself into the Betty Ford Clinic. Amanda watched with disgust as a film clip from the actor's current box-office hit movie played in the background, demonstrating his ability to insert his middle and index fingers deep into an evil assailant's throat, despite the fact that in real life she knew he was probably packing a blood-alcohol level at that very minute a shade under denatured shaving lotion.

"*It's inspiring*," replied the co-anchor, revealing a flawless smile, "*to see that an actor's real-life courage matches what we've seen on the screen.*"

Amanda clicked it off, then remembered it was the only light in the room.

"What the—" said Lucinda, grumbling and reaching for the remote control. By the time Amanda had turned on a lamp, Lucinda had turned the TV back on.

"Mother!" Amanda shouted: "Would you listen to me? I've still got a shot at sitting on the *Ashford* jury!"

Lucinda turned downed the volume, said, "Oh, pish, child," then, turning the volume back up, she added, "it's not even goin' to be televised."

"That doesn't mean it doesn't exist," yelled Amanda over the din of the TV. "The whole world will be following this case. Do you see what that could mean for me? For us?"

"I've already told you exactly what it could mean. Loss of your job and my health plan for one thing. Starvation for another."

"*And rocketing box-office sales!*" said the blond co-anchor, beaming with enthusiasm.

"*True*," responded the perfect smile. "*It's just so darn great when a role model sets an example for the average troubled Joe out there—*"

"You're wrong, Mother! I might have a chance to do

something *important*—and maybe open a door back into television!"

Lucinda grunted disdainfully. "You're a day late and a dollar short for reviving a TV career, kiddo. You're thirty-four years old now, case you've lost count. Besides, haven't you had enough nervous breakdowns for one person? I swear I don't know who'll do your thinkin' when I'm gone."

Amanda paled and looked at her mother in astonishment. "But Hollywood was your dream all along for me. For *us!*"

"Of course it was my dream, *ten, fifteen years ago!* But your mother's practical, thank the good Lord, and time has up and passed us by. Your job may not be much, Amanda, but it does provide the minimum necessaries."

Amanda's knife and fork clattered noisily onto her plate and she sat dumbstruck, staring at her mother, wishing she were able to cry. "But our *dream!*"

"Wake up and smell some reality, child," continued Lucinda, her eyes still fixed on the screen. "And as for this trial, you go off on some fool's errand for two, three months, you've got no job by the time you get back. Face it, Amanda, you're not fit for much and darned lucky Ward wants you."

Amanda looked down at her own clasped hands and rubbed the scar on her left wrist. She felt an asthma attack coming on, but couldn't remember where she had laid her purse.

"Any more of that chicken out there, darlin'?" said Lucinda, but Amanda didn't hear her. She felt her excitement slipping away. Maybe Lucinda was right. With companies downsizing these days, no one was safe.

"Amanda?"

"I'm not even in the jury box, Mama. Don't worry."

"Well, just see you don't get stuck there if they do call you up. Tell 'em you've already made up your mind. I read where that always works. Now how about that chicken?"

"*The worse news for the ladies,*" continued the smile, now the only sound in the room, "*is that the Betty Ford people have told him he's not to date for FOUR MONTHS after his discharge!*"

"*Oh my Lord!*" the woman with endless legs lamented. "*What a waste!*"

Lucinda lowered the volume on the remote. "While you're out there, let's have some of that strawberry frozen yogurt you bought yesterday."

Amanda's incipient asthma choked her voice into silence as she scooped up her mother's empty dishes and escaped into the kitchen. Her head had become a clenched fist of pain and her lungs were starving for air.

She grabbed her purse, rushed straight to her bedroom, and closed the door. She heard a mumbled protest from the living room, but the TV sound rose again and she heard the squeal of her mother's wheelchair heading for the kitchen. Amanda pumped the inhaler twice, three times into her mouth, trying to breathe the precious vapor into her lungs slowly, steadily. She then took a pain pill and three sleeping capsules.

She picked up the paper, but couldn't solve the Jumble and eventually found herself drawn back to the articles on the Ashford case. Soon she was devouring every word. She ran her fingers over the photo of Earl Field.

An hour later, she dropped into a restless sleep full of dreams, including her recurring nightmare in which she is standing at a grave site. Someone close to her, yet unrecognized, is being lowered slowly into the dark earth. She hears a thumping sound inside the casket, but doesn't dare say anything for fear she will be ridiculed.

20

By mid-morning of the second day, it appeared to Amanda that the lawyers had nearly exhausted their challenges. Both Al Menghetti and Earl Field were taking much more time before exercising them. Jurors were being literally cross-examined by both lawyers, each of whom carried thick black binders that supposedly contained vital personal information about the jury pool. Although Amanda worried they might have found out about her medical background, the idea that someone might have gone to the trouble to compile detailed information on her life thrilled her. To hell with Lucinda and Ward, too, thought Amanda. *I want this.*

But as the morning wore on, Amanda's hope faded as the last of the twelve regular jurors was accepted by both sides. Nearly two hours later, her chances as an alternate had dwindled as well, with three already seated. Still, she continued to rehearse her answers to the lawyers' recurring questions, determined to be ready if she got her chance.

Despite all her preparation, when the clerk called out "Amanda Keller!" just before noon, she couldn't respond. What if she had imagined it? What if she stood up and everyone laughed at her? She glanced around her. No one else was getting up.

"*Amanda Keller!* Step forward please!"

She willed herself to rise on unsteady legs and made her way to the front. There, she was directed to alternate seat number four and, in a tremulous voice, began answering questions, first from Judge Hernandez, then from Earl Field. Everything was a blur at first, but after a minute or two, she found her poise and began responding with the unerring skill of an actress reading her lines. She had figured out by now which answers had placed the other prospective jurors in jeopardy.

"Have you read about the case, Ms. Kellah?" said the district attorney.

"Once or twice," she replied. "I'm afraid I'm not much of a reader."

"Seen it on TV?"

"I rarely watch TV news. Sorry."

"Have you formed any opinion as to the guilt or innocence of the defendant?"

"Oh, my, no," she said, sounding a little like her mother. "I wouldn't know how to begin."

And so on.

By four o'clock, all six alternates had been seated and one of the alternates had been challenged. She was still seated. She heard the judge remind each side that they had but two challenges remaining.

Menghetti had been easy, she thought, his appreciation of her beauty obvious, his ego easily stroked. Field had liked her, too. Black men had always liked her. They sensed her goodwill, she thought, remembering how she'd hated her father's attitude toward them when they lived in Moultrie, Georgia. She loved the regal yet melodious way he had pronounced her name: *Ms. Kell-ah.* He had made her feel important.

She worried most about Grace Harris. Amanda had never been drawn to women, particularly attractive women like the deputy prosecutor, and she feared that Harris might have intuited this. She had questioned some of the jurors and had stammered badly when dealing with one of them. Instead of getting embarrassed, she had just asked all of the jurors if her disability would present problems for them, and of course they had all said no. Amanda knew some were lying, wondering why in the world this woman had set out to be a trial lawyer of all things. *Some people's children,* she could hear her mother say.

At 4:30 P.M., the judge recessed court after giving the seated jurors and the rest of the pool the laundry list of admonitions that had already become so familiar that nobody paid the slightest attention to them.

She was still in the box.

Amanda walked—floated, actually—into the fading sunlight and was stunned to find herself blinded by flash cameras and assailed by a barrage of questions from reporters.

"Ever sat before, Ms. Keller? Have you followed the investigation so far? Will it affect your judgment if you're selected?"

As if in a trance, Amanda moved wordlessly through the phalanx of reporters and TV cameras, but her heart was pounding with wild exhilaration. "Over here, Amanda!" she heard as cameras buzzed, flashed, and clicked. "Ms. Keller? Over here!"

She was going to be on the TV news! *Now* Lucinda Keller would sing a different tune.

Amanda bypassed her precious hour at her health club. She couldn't wait.

"Mother!" she shouted, racing into the apartment. "Did you see me on TV?"

Lucinda was at her usual post in front of the television.

"I saw you," she said without enthusiasm, "and your hair looked like your cats had been suckin' on it."

"Then you *know!* My chances are good now!"

"At what? Even if you were selected, you'd just be an alternate."

"I know, but it's *something,*" said Amanda, biting her lower lip.

"A waste of time is what it is; and a fourth alternate at that! TV man was just on, explainin' the whole thing. Alternate jurors can't even join in the jury's deliberations at the end of the trial! Can't even go into the room with the *real* jurors. So get out of it, child, before you end up losing three months' pay for nothin'. Just tell 'em about your asthma."

Amanda stared at her mother. "The judge said it will be a long trial, Mother," she said, her voice quaking. "Anything could happen. That's why they select alternates. You admit you saw me on television. Why did they go to all that trouble if they didn't think it was important?"

"You know the answer to that, child, well as I do. Despite the fact you're no longer the pageant princess or the teen queen, you've still got your looks, which is all the TV men are interested in. Now forget all this foolishness and fetch your mother some dinner. I don't want to talk about it anymore."

They ate dinner in silence, after which Amanda sat for a while with her mother watching *Cybill* on TV. Then she took her sleeping pills, prayed she wouldn't dream, and fell into a deep slumber.

She awoke early the next morning after ten hours of sleep. Her mother was still in bed.

She went to the kitchen and held ice to her puffy eyes— five minutes for each eye—while she made coffee and toast. She then showered and went to work on her hair. After another hour, she was satisfied with what she saw reflected in her mirror: a tall, large-boned but thin woman with good muscle tone; a woman who *Day TV* magazine had once described as "projecting an enigmatic beauty: a full-lipped mouth, crowning a firm chin framed by prominent cheek-bones and deep-set midnight blue eyes that can turn into coals against the contrast of her pale face when a scene calls for anger."

The mirror told her she was still that woman.

She dressed in a glamorous but tasteful kick-pleat skirt that covered the knee and nicely concealed the damage wrought to her thighs by a blundering Hollywood liposuc-tionist when the first signs of cellulite had appeared. An-other one of Lucinda's great ideas.

She touched up her light makeup and concluded she was ready to make the best of things despite Lucinda's de-pressing dismissal of their Hollywood hopes and dreams.

She doesn't want me to leave, thought Amanda as she began brushing her hair again. It's not that *I'm* too old; *she's* too old to let me go now. She's imprisoned in this dump and wants me to die here as her cell mate. That's what she's up to. That's why she's always putting me down, trying to control me.

The force and tempo of the brushstrokes accelerated. Telling me I'm lucky to be a chief file clerk. Telling me my emotions couldn't take the stress of Hollywood.

Amanda stopped brushing, applied hair spray, and took a final approving look at herself in the mirror.

Telling me I'm just an alternate.

*   *   *

She arrived at the courthouse and was recognized by reporters, one of whom asked her if she had been on *Hope's People* years before.

"Sharon McPeak," she said, smiling radiantly.

"That's it!" shouted the reporter, looking around at the others. "Sharon McPeak! I'll be goddamned!"

Cameras blinked all around her until sheriff's deputies arrived and escorted her along with two other seated jurors to the elevator. Though only an alternate, she was being noticed.

Her enthusiasm continued to rebound when, by 10:00 A.M., each side had just one remaining challenge to the six-pack of alternates. She tried to appear reasonably bright but thoroughly uncommitted, totally objective. A sheep, not a leader; a consensus builder, not a maverick. They wouldn't want a strong, overly intelligent woman, she thought. Nobody did.

Amanda watched Earl Field and Grace Harris as they studied the binder between them, but suddenly realized she was being watched by another set of eyes. Irresistibly, she found herself drawn into the gaze of Elliot Ashford.

Embarrassed, she dropped her eyes, but felt compelled to raise them again. The man was not just watching her; he seemed to be reading her mind. Something about his expression made her feel like a child again: a feeling of utter helplessness. She started to hyperventilate but gave him the hint of a smile to mask her feelings, then looked away again. That's exactly what Sharon McPeak would have done, she thought, and she began to feel better.

Judge Hernandez's voice interrupted her thoughts. "The People's last challenge, Mr. Field," he said. She experienced a rush of anxiety. Had the judge been looking at her, too? Reading her apprehension?

Amanda watched as Grace Harris leaned close to Earl Field and whispered something to him. She doesn't like me, thought Amanda. But Field nodded, then rose and announced that the People were "quite satisfied with the jury as it is presently constituted."

Amanda felt her breath leaving her, but didn't dare reach for her inhaler.

"Thank you, Mr. Field," said Judge Hernandez. "The defendant's last challenge, Mr. Menghetti."

"One moment, please, Your Honor," said Menghetti, then leaned close to his client. Amanda noticed that neither one of them paid any attention to Barrett Dickson, who had shifted his gaze toward her and the other alternates, apparently making his own assessment. After another endless minute, Menghetti looked up and boldly surveyed the six of them, one by one. Amanda felt like she was back at a cattle call during her modeling days, where the admen and sponsors did everything but force her jaw open and inspect her teeth.

Now Menghetti's eyes were on her. Ashford's, too. She looked straight ahead, as casually as possible. She wondered if Menghetti saw her as too old for him. He had been hard to read. A tricky one for sure. *Give him just a glance. Don't smile, too obvious. Just a hint, that's it! Perfect.*

He rose to speak and her heart stopped. There was a pain in her stomach and her breath was coming hard now. Her fingers clutched her purse, felt the inhaler there.

Menghetti checked his notes once more, then finally said, "The defense will excuse . . . alternate number six. Thank you, Mr. Sanders."

My God, I'm on! she thought, but a formality remained. Mr. Sanders was replaced, which would give the prosecution another opportunity to challenge not only the replacement but anyone else in the "six-pack" of alternates. Amanda's heart raced as Field and Grace Harris conferred again.

"The People remain satisfied," said Field at last, and it was finished, though she feared she might faint when the clerk instructed them to rise and take the juror's oath. The judge then explained that he had an 8:30 A.M. calendar to attend to and instructed them to return at 10:00 A.M. the following morning.

Walking toward the elevator, she stole two quick pumps from her inhaler, and by the time she was outside, she was ready to smile for the cameras. Not all the reporters who shouted questions at the jurors knew of Amanda's television past, but they knew a good-looking, photogenic woman when they saw one, even if she was only an alternate.

"Give us a smile, Ms. Keller! Over here, Amanda!" She

willingly obliged, just as she had at the premiere of *Hope's People* over a decade—a lifetime—before.

Amanda experienced an unbearable joy as she headed straight for her health club. Now, more than ever, she would need to stay fit. She was bursting with energy, and chills shot up and down her spine as she skipped down the sidewalk like a child on summer vacation.

She was alive again!

PART TWO

THE
TRIAL

*A jury is twelve people who decide who has
the best lawyer.*

—Robert Frost

21

Judge John Hernandez was an unassuming man, but he took justifiable pride in his chambers library. In a high-tech world where law treatises had given way to digitalized versions on computer, Judge Hernandez preferred the feel of a hardbound book. Every available wall space was covered in gleaming oak bookshelves, which he'd paid for himself to avoid even the color of impropriety, and every shelf was crammed with *West's Digest, Bancroft and Whitney,* and the complete *California Reporter,* together with dozens of obscure legal treatises from his days as a practicing lawyer. Two additional freestanding bookcases were devoted to volumes on subjects as varied as world affairs, race relations, sports, and national politics. The only important books missing from the shelves were the U.S. Constitution and the California evidence and criminal codes, which always sat within immediate reach on the bench.

There was little room left for visitors in his cramped chambers, but John Hernandez's calendar left little time for visiting anyway.

Behind his desk hung a plaque from the ACLU and a photograph of himself shaking hands with Governor Jerry Brown on the day of the judge's appointment to the Superior Court bench. Between the plaque and the photo was a corlorful drawing by his seven-year-old daughter depicting her smiling father dispensing justice to a pair of thugs with balls and chains around their ankles. Another creation contained the "Hernandez Ediks," but he kept these in his desk:

"Edik" Number One read:

The sum total of human intelligence among trial lawyers

is constant, whereas the number of trial lawyers is steadily increasing.

"Edik" Number Two read:

If anything can go wrong, it will happen at the worst possible time and in Daddy's courtroom.

John Hernandez was born in 1942, a year to the day after Pearl Harbor, in Watsonville, California. The son of itinerant farm laborers, he grew up at play in fields of the lords of the Central Coast farming aristocracy, watching while his parents and older sister shuffled down endless rows of artichoke fields, bent close to the ground like foraging animals. They earned three dollars a day each. At the age of eight, he began picking alongside his sister during their summer vacations.

In his freshman year at Watsonville High School, he joined a gang and was in and out of both trouble and the public school system until a multilingual counselor named Donald Eggleston took an interest in his case. Eggleston helped the young Latino channel his frustration into constructive change, then later used his connections to get Hernandez academic scholarships to Stanford undergraduate and law schools. In law school, John met a young ex-football player—also on an academic scholarship—whose poverty, ambition, and troubled past seemed to parallel his own. He and Bear Dickson soon became friends.

Now, after twelve years on the bench, he was about to try San Francisco's "Trial of the Century," and it wasn't long before trouble arose, establishing the truth of "Edik" Number Two. A bailiff sent by another judge to help out on the first day had miscounted the number of available courtroom seats, and a second lottery had to be held for those who thought they had secured a treasured seat but hadn't. The five disgruntled losers of the second round of musical chairs then sent a representative to Maggie, Department 26's venerable clerk, demanding they be allowed at least standing room in the rear. Judge Hernandez sat fuming in his chambers after reluctantly sending a message to the jury requesting their patience while he "sorted through a problem."

"Suggestions?" he said, looking at Maggie and Fred, Department 26's young, dark-skinned bailiff.

"They want to see you, Judge," said Fred. "The five citizens."

"The Gang of Five," said Maggie dryly. "That's what the press will call them."

"The press," murmured John Hernandez, pacing, hands on hips. Although most observers regarded the case as a splendid opportunity for the reserved and publicity-shy judge, John Hernandez viewed himself as a man in a cage with a hungry lion, holding nothing but a chair against the flashing incisors of the gathering reporters.

And what will they call *me?* he wondered.

"Who ran this damn lottery?" Maggie said. "I wasn't consulted."

"The P.J.'s clerk handled it," he said.

"That explains everything," said Maggie, looking disgusted.

John Hernandez smiled, though he knew there were archconservatives and even certain senior Democrats among his black-robed brethren who envied his growing popularity and would like to see him fall on his face. Mishandling a high-profile case would derail his ascension to the District Court of Appeal and, perhaps, from there to the Supreme Court.

Hernandez had been galled by the exchange of amused glances between the two Los Angeles newspaper pool reporters when the seating problem first became apparent. The reporters were tired of hearing how much more efficient the San Francisco courts were compared with archrival L.A.'s. Now, before it had even started, the trial had suffered its first delay, and five folding chairs were being arranged along the one side of the center aisle.

A reporter from the *L.A. Times* gleefully scribbled a note that would appear in the next morning's edition:

Perhaps John Hernandez's tacit contempt for "celluloid justice" will now be tempered by his own awakening to the unique exigencies of a high-profile case.

The courtroom was silent as the judge finally instructed Fred to bring in the jury, unable to conceal the frustration in his voice. Before a single word of the testimony had been uttered, he had already lost precious time haggling with the Gang of Five and had violated his commitment to the jury—not to mention the San Francisco fire code.

He watched as the jurors solemnly entered the courtroom. None of them glanced up until each had reached the security of his or her assigned seat. They were the typical San Francisco mix, thought Hernandez, as ethnic and varied as the city's restaurants; a jurisprudential bouillabaisse. Three African-Americans, two Latinos, four whites, and three Asians ranging in age from twenty-three to sixtyseven. Seven women, five men: three housewives, a structural engineer, two secretaries, a retired teacher, a CPA, two unemployeds, and the inevitable retired postal employee. The six alternates were female but for number two, a dark-skinned municipal bus driver of indeterminate ancestry. They were jammed together at the end of the jury box, near the water cooler.

The prosecutors, first Earl Field, then Grace, had taken their seats closest to the jury box, as decreed by custom. The judge had granted Al Menghetti's request to move the defense table at an angle so that he would face the jury, and Barrett Dickson sat farthest from the jury, as decreed by common sense, given his continued expression of constipated misery. The bailiff had heard Al Menghetti urging his cocounsel to "stop looking so damned pissed off at everybody." Barrett had replied in a sardonic tone that he was merely "consumed by solemnity as he reflected on the majesty of the law and his own high calling to its service." John Hernandez had chuckled when Fred reported the exchange. At least, he thought, the Bear had not lost his sense of irony.

Menghetti now leaned against that table, his legs bent at the knees as if awaiting the start of a hundred-meter sprint. Between Menghetti and Dickson sat Elliot Ashford, calmly scrutinizing the jurors, making notes, occasionally whispering to Menghetti.

Judge Hernandez thanked the jurors for their patience and explained the delay, then turned back to the lawyers. "Will counsel state their appearances for the record?" he said.

A competent bunch, he thought. Thank God for that, at

least. Hernandez knew that competent trial lawyers on both
sides of the case always made a judge's job easier. This
would be particularly important in a case to be tried in
the fishbowl of public scrutiny. Still, both Earl Field and
Menghetti would have to be watched. Field's reputation
was impeccable, but his political future was riding on the
outcome of the case, and the judge knew that rational
thinking and civil behavior were often in short supply when
law and politics became intertwined. John Hernandez also
knew that he himself would be tested when the going got
tough, particularly with a bulldog like Al Menghetti
applying constant pressure. His salvation would rest on five
simple words with the proven power to discourage Rambo
behavior in his or any other courtroom:

Not in my *courtroom, counsel!*

The clerk read the indictment and it was time.

"Mr. Field," he said "your opening statement please?"

"Thank you, Your Honor," said the district attorney, and
the "real deal" was under way at last.

"Good morning, members of the jury," he began, so
softly several jurors in the back row had to lean toward
him. "I shall be brief, for when you strip away all the hyperbole and publicity, this is really just another case of
domestic homicide. More brutal to be sure, but still, another all-too-frequent, tragic instance where a warm and
supportive wife has become the helpless victim of a husband's cruel and misplaced wrath."

Field's opening statement was indeed brief. No overblown flood of confusing details such as lawyers in high-
profile cases so often find irresistible. The district attorney
was a politician, but he had once been an effective trial
lawyer, and had read research papers showing that the attention of even the most conscientious juror began to wan-
der after twenty minutes, thirty tops. A bored juror would
quit listening and become a confused juror; a confused
juror would then turn resentful; and a resentful juror would
soon become angry, eager to hear from the other side.

Field also knew that many prosecutors witlessly wooed
the minds of the jurors by papering the walls of the courtroom with mountains of incomprehensible exhibits, while
the defense was winning their hearts with eloquent pleas
for mercy and common sense.

"Another reason I shall be brief," he continued, his eyes moving from one juror to another, "is because the facts before us are so eminently clear.

"Ladies and gentlemen, I have neither the inclination nor the ability to sway you with eloquence, nor to cloud the issues in this case with days and weeks of incomprehensible and cumulative testimony. Instead, the People will place their confidence in clear and irrefutable evidence; not wit, guile or bluster."

He paused, and John Hernandez noticed that three regular jurors had shifted their gaze to Al Menghetti, glaring at him as if they had already found him guilty of wit, guile, and bluster. Then, without a wasted word, Earl Field led the jury up to the night of August 7 and into Lara Ashford's bathroom, quietly building tension that spared no one in the room. The unblinking jurors stared at him as one, transfixed as the district attorney's voice imperceptibly gained in volume and intensity. Then, as he shifted into a no-holds-barred reenactment of the killing itself, his voice began to quake with emotion. His arm slashed the air, demonstrating the assailant's thrusts as he mortally wounded, then tortured his victim before rendering the final and lethal blow. Two jurors in the front row recoiled in their seats.

"What were Lara Ashford's last thoughts?" asked the district attorney, his voice softer now, but no less intense. "What did she think as she watched the man who had promised to love and cherish her extend his hand not in love but in rage; not to caress but to kill? A hand that held not a gift of gratitude but an instrument of horrifying pain and death."

From her seat near the jurors, Grace glanced furtively at some of them, then behind her at Sam Quon, who looked similarly absorbed. When Sam noticed her eyes on him, he blushed at having been caught by Grace so thoroughly enmeshed in the web of Field's melodramatic oratory. Grace had outlined the opening for the D.A., but did not expect him to deliver it with such emotion, forgetting that he would not just be practicing law during this trial; he would be committing politics. Nonetheless, his zealous performance was reassuring.

* * *

In her alternate seat off to the side of the regular jury, Amanda was not merely impressed. She was spellbound, her lips moist and parted as she stared at the district attorney. The tone and authority in his voice nearly overwhelmed her, as did the grace of his movement, the power celebrated in his every gesture. The effect on her was almost unbearable, sexually charged and intoxicating. She could barely watch him and assimilate his words at the same time. She began to succumb to vertigo, and finally had to break his grip on her by looking away. At this point in her life, finally committed to gaining independence from her dominating mother, she could not allow herself to become infatuated with a dominating man.

She forced herself to look over at Al Menghetti, saw that he remained poised like a Brahma bull in a rodeo smarting under the weight of its rider just before the stall door is thrown open. But like the bull, Menghetti could do nothing but wait, for Field, having seized the jury's morbid attention, had begun to tie Ashford to the crime with a litany of facts in support of means, motive, and opportunity: the defendant's expressed jealousy of Senator Dwight Clifton and his frustration at his wife's publicized behavior while they lived in Washington, D.C.; a heated argument overheard by the housekeeper just before the murder, including mention of Clifton's name; the blood in the sink—Lara's blood mixed with an essentially perfect PCA DNA match of the defendant's blood—and more of his blood on a towel used as the weapon's handle; a recently healed cut on Ashford's face which a forensic physician would opine as being "too irregular to have been caused by a razor." Then Dr. Yang's torture testimony and finally, with an understated shrug, the fake movie alibi.

Amanda looked back at Field, still enraptured but more in control of herself. Then she stole a glance at Ashford, not looking so casual now, scribbling notes and shoving them in front of Menghetti. She almost smiled at his sudden agitation but caught herself.

Field next cleverly skirted the edge of prejudice by referring to the Ashford family holding company as Ashford's "Organization." Field would know, thought Amanda, that some of the jurors would have read about Ashford's rumored connection with leading Organization figures. She tried to think of the name of the Mafia don in Chicago rumored to be the defendant's partner in the Ashford family holding company.

She glanced again at Ashford, now whispering in Al Menghetti's ear, hands moving as fast as his lips. Still, Menghetti made few objections and seemed in complete control of himself and his client. Amanda was pleased he did not try more often to interrupt the district attorney. She did not know that objections to an opponent's opening statement are nearly always overruled, serving only to irritate the judge and create the impression of defensiveness in the minds of the jury.

After only forty-three minutes, Field closed, expressing his confidence that the jurors would act on the evidence, obey their oaths, and find the defendant guilty.

The judge declared a ten-minute recess and sent the jurors to the jury room, where they would be protected from the press during breaks in the trial. Twelve minutes later, they were back in the courtroom.

"Mr. Menghetti?" said Judge Hernandez. "Do you wish to make an opening statement at this time?"

"I do indeed, Your Honor."

Strident, cocky, and bellicose from the outset, Menghetti leaned his stocky frame against the barricade of evidence confronting his client. Amanda disliked the way he strutted and railed, devoid of any humility or attempt to ingratiate himself with the jurors. Field's voice had caressed; Menghetti's came at the jury like a series of left-jab, right-cross combinations.

Who, after all, Menghetti snarled rhetorically, had the district attorney been talking about here? Ted Bundy? Richard Allen Davis? Some cruel and depraved lunatic?

"No!" he intoned. "Without a single eyewitness, and on purely cir-cum-stan-tial evidence"—this delivered in the scornful tone of a shock-radio host—"this ambitious self-declared gubernatorial candidate"—an objection sustained here—"this . . . *gov-ern-ment official*"—more scorn—"this known opponent of the defendant, a respected philanthropist and former congressman"—another objection, this one overruled—"has recklessly impugned the integrity of one of the city's most honored and generous citizens"—now a shift in voice tone—"a past member of the city's Police Commission . . . and most important of all"—downcast eyes—"a devoted husband."

Amanda almost laughed out loud, but a glance to her right yielded nothing but a host of raptly attentive regular jurors, seemingly captive to Menghetti's aggressive rhetoric. *What was with these people?* It became clear to Amanda that if she wasn't going to have a vote at the end of the journey, she had better exert some influence over these naïve people along the way.

Although Menghetti's style was mildly repugnant to Grace Harris, she too could not help admiring his skill as he articulated the typical defense themes. The police and the D.A. had rushed to judgment, he said, then tried to make it hang together with the aid of junk science and, worse, the concealment of crucial exculpatory evidence.

A glance at the jury told Grace that they were solemnly caught up in the barrage of words that rushed from the defense lawyer's indignant lips. She saw that Menghetti, like all top defense lawyers, knew that in order to create a reasonable doubt in the jurors' minds, he must provide them with a reason to *want* to find one. In both word and manner, he promised he would supply them that reason, maybe even two or three of them.

This guy was crude, Grace worried, but he didn't look like a bluffer. Did he have an ace up his sleeve?

She didn't have to wait long for her answer. After Menghetti had surgically dissected the state's circumstantial case, striking particularly hard at the police department crime laboratory and the toxicology lab of the San Francisco medical examiner's office, he moved a step closer to the jury and lowered his voice to a conspiratorial whisper.

"Finally, ladies and gentlemen, there is another reason why you must find Mr. Ashford not guilty: Very simply, he could not have committed this murder. It *had* to have been somebody else."

Menghetti took another step toward the wide-eyed jurors.

"Why? I'll tell you why. *Because a woman named Renee Babcock will testify that the defendant was with her at the time of the murder!*"

The courtroom exploded in sound as Grace shot to her

feet to object, nearly struck breathless by Menghetti's outrageous declaration. Then Field was on his feet and both of them were protesting that they had never heard of Renee Babcock or of *any* alibi witness. While the judge pounded his gavel, Grace glared at Menghetti, then at Dickson, from whom she had expected more. She had seen Dickson's head snap up, his eyes suddenly alert as the gallery gasped in surprise.

Renee Babcock?

John Hernandez kept hammering his gavel, but neither he nor the bailiff could silence the pandemonium as reporters raced from the courtroom. When order was finally restored, the judge's voice was resonant with obvious anger as he ordered counsel to side-bar along with the court reporter.

"Who," asked the judge, his voice and facial features again under control, "is Renee Babcock?"

"She's on the list, Your Honor," said Menghetti.

"*What* list?" demanded Grace, looking not at Menghetti but at the judge.

"I gave it to you this morning before court."

"*This?*" said Grace, snatching a list of sixteen witnesses from Menghetti's hand and placing it in front of Judge Hernandez. "Your Honor," she said, "we were handed this less than an hour ago!"

"Explain yourself, Mr. Menghetti," said Judge Hernandez calmly.

"Yes, Your Honor," said the defense lawyer, glancing over his shoulder at his client. "Mr. Ashford told me about her for the first time late last night. He had hoped to protect her identity."

"How gallant," said Grace, noticing that Barrett seemed as angry as she was, and when their eyes met, he gave her a look that said he was also surprised.

Judge Hernandez struggled to contain his frustration as he watched the last of the reporters heading for the hallway. This beast of a case that Hernandez had hoped to keep caged had broken loose.

He slammed his gavel down once more, declared a recess, and ordered all counsel to return to their seats. With the jury gone, the judge turned his blazing eyes on the flushed face of Barrett Dickson.

"Mr. Dickson?"

Barrett rose to his feet and uttered his first words in the trial of People versus Elliot Ashford.

"Your Honor, you and I learned of this witness at precisely the same moment. You have my word on it."

"I accept your word, Mr. Dickson," said Judge Hernandez coldly, "but you *should have* learned of her before I did."

"Yes, Your Honor," said Barrett, casting a hard glance at Menghetti, "I damn well should have."

"Move to p-preclude her testimony," added Grace Harris.

"I'll reserve ruling on that," said the judge, "but meanwhile I order the defense to present Ms. Babcock for examination by the prosecution within the next forty-eight hours, and hereby fine Mr. Menghetti and Mr. Dickson $3,000 each for Mr. Menghetti's allusion to Renee Babcock in opening statement without adequate notice to either the court or to the prosecution."

"Your Honor—" began Menghetti, but the judge silenced him with a raised hand.

"Burying Ms. Babcock's name in a list of sixteen others and turned over to the district attorney only minutes before opening statements is trial by ambush," said the judge, "and telling the jury about her violates our discovery rules, the canons of ethics, and the code of trial conduct of the American College of Trial Lawyers."

Dickson considered saying something more in his own defense, but saw that John Hernandez was not finished.

"You are in a zero-tolerance courtroom," the judge continued. "Understand further that I am not here to referee a mud-wrestling contest. I expect and admire strong advocacy, but I demand *clean* advocacy. Pull another stunt like that, Mr. Menghetti, and you'd better have your toothbrush handy, because you won't be going back to your hotel for thirty days."

"I understand, Your Honor," said Menghetti, "and I apologize. I certainly didn't intend all this confusion."

John Hernandez rose from his chair, towering above them now, biblical in his wrath.

"There is no 'confusion' about what you intended by this tactic, sir," he said through clenched teeth, "but to be sure

there exists no possible 'confusion' on your part concerning my resolve, the fine in your case is hereby increased to $5,000."

Grace cleared her throat as the judge got up to leave the bench. "Your Honor? Might we have the jury instructed?"

Hernandez paused, modulated his tone. "Yes, of course, Ms. Harris. When the jury returns, I intend to instruct them to disregard any mention of Renee Babcock until such time as she actually testifies, *if* she testifies at all. I will also tell them that Mr. Menghetti has violated the law and the rules that govern this trial."

Menghetti wisely said nothing more, and Judge Hernandez left the bench. Barrett fell back into his chair and almost failed to notice that John Hernandez had paused at the door to his chambers and was staring at him with a look of mingled vexation and disappointment.

Meanwhile, in the jury room—a bleak, windowless, yellow-walled place with the cold aura of an army barracks and a long, battered oak table that took up most of the limited space—Amanda turned to the older woman standing next to her, a regular juror named Ruth Salverson.

"Did you see how angry Judge Hernandez was?" she whispered. "I bet Mr. Menghetti is paying right now for that cheap little trick!"

"Well, I don't rightly know," said the tired-looking woman, breaking into an uneasy smile and putting a hand to her blue-tinted white hair. "And I don't think we are supposed to talk about the case."

"We're not to discuss the *evidence*," corrected Amanda. "The judge specifically said the opening statements of counsel are not evidence."

"I suppose you're right," said Ruth Salverson, looking sightly confused.

Amanda engaged her in small talk for a minute: Goodness, you have three grandchildren? You must be proud, and, oh my, another on the way? Do you have any pictures? She then casually shifted gears again. "I guess it's pretty obvious why Menghetti has to take chances like that, Ruth, don't you think?"

Amanda's advocacy had begun.

22

A few minutes later, the defense team huddled in an L-shaped holding cell adjacent to the courtroom, designated by the court for their use during court recesses. The windowless room was normally used for prisoners as they awaited their summons to the adjacent courtroom for pleas, sentencing, or other hearings. The room had two doors: one leading to the courtroom, the other into a hall that led to an elevator to cells on the sixth and seventh floors. A stained and battered combination WC and washbasin stood in a corner, over which someone had Scotch-taped a yellowed calendar—tacks and strings were considered "weapons"—depicting two nineteenth-century Queen's counsel in white wigs, wearing lace shirts bunched at the neck under brocade jackets, both glaring at a hapless-looking witness in the docks. The room smelled of disinfectant.

Barrett sat in an armless oak chair staring at his client across a battered wood table stained with overlapping brown rings. The walls that surrounded them were as barren of decoration as those in the jury room, except for the calendar and graffiti carvings that no one would confuse with the caves of Lascaux. Al Menghetti stood nearest the door, arms folded, just behind his client. Elliot Ashford sat impassively in his chair, legs crossed, meeting Barrett's accusing glare with unswerving eyes that were not only devoid of guilt but also maddeningly affable.

No one spoke.

Barrett listened to the dull hum of the fluorescent lights as he tried to collect his thoughts. He became conscious of an uncomfortable dampness across his back. The roof of his mouth felt cauterized and his throat was a dry shaft. He wished he could have remained standing like Menghetti, but his legs had become unreliable. He felt he had to get away from these men and this case too, consequences be damned.

"First you tell the cops you were at a movie," Barrett said at last, in a voice quavering with anger. "Then you tell me you were with some *guy* whose identity you couldn't reveal! Now it's a *woman,* who you were just 'trying to protect.'"

Ashford smiled without parting his lips, shrugged, then said, "I am a gentleman, Barrett, like yourself."

"Bullshit!"

"Hear me out, Dickson." Ashford removed his glasses and rubbed his eyes. "Renee has a fiancé; a brute who would not hesitate to beat her, perhaps worse. Thus the false movie alibi. I had hoped not to have to reveal my . . . indiscretion, but Al prevailed on me last night."

Barrett's eyes darted up to where Menghetti stood studying the wall calendar.

"*Last night?* Why didn't you—"

"Because, Barrett," said Menghetti, palms extended and turned upward, eyebrows angled submissively, "we simply wanted to protect you, and your relationship with John Hernandez. Besides, you would have insisted we inform the prosecution *before* Field blew his credibility with the jury by telling them Elliot *had* no alibi."

Barrett said, "And now you've blown our credibility with the judge."

"You've got to make choices in our business, Dickson. The legal system is like eating sausage. You don't ask how it got made."

"There's nothing wrong with the way the system was constructed, Menghetti. It's the way people exploit it. Even I can see that. But thanks for reminding me why I'm well out of it."

"You're welcome, Dickson," said Menghetti, missing or ignoring the irony in Barrett's remark. "And don't worry about your buddy Hernandez. He'll calm down. Besides, it's the jury who frees our client or kills him, not the judge. Your problem is you don't have a clue how the criminal defense game is played. When you do, I'll feel free to be more open with you."

Barrett's chair screeched as he rose to his feet. "How's

this for being open?" he said, glaring at the stocky defense lawyer. "Go fuck yourself, Menghetti. You too, Ashford."

Menghetti retreated from the doorway as Barrett stormed toward it, but Ashford jumped to his feet and blocked his way.

"Hold on a minute, old boy. Al is leveling with you now, isn't he? Besides, this is all my fault. I implored Al that if there were any technically legitimate way we could let Field get himself out on a limb, then saw it off—"

"I *know* why you did it," said Barrett, including Menghetti in his withering gaze, "but Johnnie Cochran didn't get away with it in his opening statement in the Simpson case. What made you think you could here?"

A deep staccato laugh issued from Menghetti, now perched on the edge of the table. "You're saying Cochran didn't get away with it? Tell that to O. J. Simpson, if you can find which golf course he's playing these days. As for Johnnie, the judge may have censured him, but our toothless state bar didn't punch his ticket and never will. Get real, Barrett. What's a judge's wrath and a couple thousand bucks' fine compared to what we achieved this morning? Hell, the prosecution can't file an appeal anyway. So what's your problem?"

Barrett knew he was wasting his time talking to these two about legal ethics; debating vultures on the hazards of a meat diet. Ashford was fighting for his life, and Menghetti was the old-style combatant: win at any cost. Dickson reflected that maybe he himself had tilted that way once or twice, before he lost his passion for the game, his instinct for the jugular.

"My 'problem,' " he said, trying to ward off a painful realization that was burrowing toward the surface of his muddled consciousness, "is that you haven't seen the *beginning* of this judge's wrath."

He knew he should simply push Ashford aside and walk out the door. But where would that leave Mike and the others at C&S? Then there was the damn realization, burrowing on, closer now.

"Al knew the risks," said Ashford, whose casually arrogant tone interrupted Barrett's thought, "and remember what Dr. Tremaine's statistics showed us? Seventy to eighty percent of jurors make up their minds during the opening statements and never change them. So we *had* to hit 'em with everything we had."

"And maybe with something you didn't have, Elliot?" said Barrett, his tone laden with disdain.

"What are you getting at, Barrett?" asked Ashford with the innocence of a child.

"Isn't it a tight squeeze getting a cloven foot into those Ferragamos, Elliot? Just how much *did* you pay this Renee Babcock?"

"Stop breathing your own exhaust, Dickson," said Menghetti. "I talked to her last night, and she's legit. No genius, maybe, but credible."

"Don't try that on me, Menghetti. Even if she's 'legit,' which I doubt, it's trial by ambush like the judge said."

"No, Dickson, it's being responsible for the life of *our* client in a capital murder case," said Menghetti, his lips curled in derision. "We're fighting lethal injection here, Dickson, an *execution,* while you stand there pontificating on the Marquess of Queensberry rules!"

Barrett felt Menghetti's disdainful gaze. The defense lawyer was fully on the offensive now, the words flying out of him. "Maybe your pal Hernandez is sore at us right now, Dickson, but *he* at least understands the responsibility a defense lawyer takes on in a death case, which is a hell of a lot more than you do. *He* knows why I don't sleep at night and knows why I can't tolerate some deadheading Montgomery Street fat cat lecturing me on manners in the middle of an alley fight."

Barrett continued to stare at the wall, though it was starting to make him woozy. He wanted to sit down, but Menghetti's relentless tirade continued, his voice ringing even louder now, his words a chain reaction, as if trying to bring Barrett's lifeless eyes back into contact with his own.

"Everybody keeps telling me how brilliant Barrett Dickson was. Well, that's past tense, my friend. You're like the guy who discovered the meaning of life and forgot to write it down. Or wrote it down and forgot where he put it. What I'm trying to do here isn't rocket science, asshole; it's harder! *So just stay the fuck out of my face!*"

Barrett considered shoving the cocky bastard's head through the wall and telling Ashford to find himself another boy, but the same thing stopped him now that had kept him from walking out ten minutes earlier. The painful realization had finally burrowed through.

God help me, he thought, I *want* this case!

He had wanted all along to be argued out of his righteous indignation; was sick and tired of being thought of as a relic and wanted to be at least part of something significant again. Was it to erase the stigma of 1993 and the TDA case? Was it because even though he had grown to hate the courtroom, it was all he could do?

God help me, he repeated to himself as the truth sank in. He lowered himself into the nearest chair, shut his eyes tight, then reopened them. Wanting no more of Menghetti's lecture or Ashford's twisted scowl, he focused on his own clenched fingers.

He then felt someone else's hand squeezing his right shoulder. Menghetti had walked around behind him.

"Enough with the infighting, Barrett," said the defense lawyer, his tone softening. He then dropped his other hand on Barrett's left shoulder and added, "Elliot just wanted to protect Babcock as long as possible and I wanted to protect you. So stop being an asshole, okay? And don't worry about the three large either; I'll pay both fines. Deal?"

"You'll do more than that, Menghetti," said Barrett, looking straight ahead. "For starters, you'll take your hands off me."

Barrett saw Ashford give Menghetti a nod and the defense lawyer removed his hands, then clasped them behind his head, mugging like a captured burglar as he walked around in front of Barrett.

"Okay, Barrett," Menghetti said dryly. "Excuse the hell out of me."

"Maybe. First, tell me if you have any more of these little stunts in mind."

Menghetti smiled. "That's all there is, Barrett, I swear. Look, I'm *sorry,* okay? I was wrong, but I trust your friend the judge will forgive you. Us."

Forgive *us,* thought Barrett. It's "us" now, pirates shackled together in need. He knew then that if he was going to gain any power or influence in this godforsaken case, he'd better seize it now, so he straightened in his chair and gave Menghetti a hard look.

"That brings me to the next thing, which is the three of

us are going to walk back into court now—you'll be on your knees, Rambo; you too, Elliot—and I'll listen while you wrap those fines in an apology that fully exonerates me. *Deal?*"

Manghetti stopped smiling, but nodded. Ashford grinned, then gave each of the lawyers a playful slap on the arm.

"Agreed then, my intrepid champions?" he said. "Is it back to the old struggle for justice?"

"Not yet," said Barrett. "There's one more thing."

"Okay," said Menghetti impatiently, "let's hear it."

"I don't take to being called an asshole, Al, particularly by you. Don't do it again. If you do, I'll hurt you."

"Now wait one fucking minute—"

"I won't tell you again," said Barrett, rising, his huge hands clenched into fists.

Ashford jumped in between them and put a restraining hand on Menghetti's chest.

"Come now, gentlemen, you're supposed to be representing me," he pleaded "This is my *life!*"

The room went silent for several seconds but for the sound of forced breathing.

"Okay, Dickson," said Menghetti at last, jerking his head toward Ashford. "He's right, you know. We've got a case to try."

Barrett felt his strength returning and continued to fix Menghetti with a scalding gaze. Menghetti looked away. Barrett waited, saying nothing.

"And okay, I apologize," Menghetti added, finally averting his eyes, "for the things I said to you a while ago. Everything square? Shake?"

Barrett tried to settle his racing mind. He would talk to John Hernandez after things calmed down, would tell him the truth, and John would believe him. In addition, the testimony of Renee Babcock, assuming she held up, meant they could establish reasonable doubt and undoubtedly win their case. Mike would go on to the executive committee and save himself and maybe even the firm. He, Barrett, would go out a winner, the TDA disaster forgotten by everyone but himself, plus he'd survive the rest of the year at C&S while he prepared for his real estate exams.

And, after all, his client *was* innocent.

"Come on, Barrett," urged Ashford. "Shake hands."

You could rationalize the rape of Poland, Barrett, Ellen had told him after he had won a major jury verdict for a large corporation accused of monopolization and predatory pricing. *Throw in Czechoslovakia and Hungary. The rape of the entire world is not beyond your consummate gift for rationalization.*

Barrett looked at Ashford, then back at Menghetti, feeling the anger leaking out of him. He looked at the clock. Nearly cocktail hour.

Then he watched his arm rise and his hand accept Menghetti's.

23

Grace Harris fumed as Earl Field called Arnold Sun as the prosecution's first witness. The expert he had expected to lead off with had called from Denver the day before, stuck in another trial. This moved a nervous young criminalist with SFPD into the leadoff spot. Grace had prepared Arnold Sun and expected to conduct his direct examination, but Field decided at the last minute to put Sun on himself, telling Grace he had to proclaim his personal commitment to the case from the outset.

The jurors sat quietly with rigid backs and expectant eyes, unaware of any tension between the prosecutors, too focused on meeting the challenge they had embraced. The spectators were also alert now in anticipation of the first testimony, though Grace knew this nervous energy would soon dissipate in the growing heat of the courtroom. Outside, the capricious El Niño had dealt a sudden burst of record-setting high temperatures that blasted the hall's roof, further confounding meteorologists and the city's citizens, who didn't know whether to wear galoshes or sunscreen to work.

"Call your first witness," said John Hernandez, and Earl Field rose to summon Arnold Sun to the stand. The young criminalist licked his lips and approached the witness chair warily, as if it might be booby-trapped. His sallow face was round and unlined, his straight hair coal black and undisciplined. Grace had the uneasy thought that he didn't look much older than Aaron.

The direct examination went well enough as Field led Arnold Sun through Grace's outline, at least until he reached the point in the list of questions where she had written:

Bring out lost fingernail scrapings.

Every experienced trial lawyer knew that any major weakness in a witness's testimony had to be faced head-on and brought out on direct examination before handing the witness over to the opposition. But to Grace's amazement, Field never mentioned the lost evidence; he merely thanked the witness at the end and took his seat.

Grace glanced at Al Menghetti, who looked surprised too, then handed Field a note that read: "Why didn't you remove the stinger?"

Field leaned toward her, plainly irritated. "Never start your case with an apology, Grace," he whispered. "Makes you look weak."

Grace groaned inwardly, fearing that Arnold Sun would soon look not merely weak but deceitful as well.

Menghetti charged through the opening like a fullback.

"Were samples taken from under the victim's fingernails, Mr. Sun?"

"Yes."

"That's important in a homicide case, isn't it?"

"Yes."

"Why do you normally take these samples?"

Sun knew what was coming and stared helplessly toward the prosecution table. Grace looked away. Menghetti quickly took advantage of Sun's mistake.

"Those lawyers over there can't help you, Mr. Sun. It's *your* testimony I want."

The witness glanced nervously at Menghetti, then down at his entwined fingers. "When there has been a struggle," he began, speaking now in a muted voice, "we can sometimes identify an assailant through DNA testing."

"And there *was* evidence of a violent struggle in this case, was there not?"

"Yes."

"I'm having trouble hearing you, sir."

"Yes, there was a struggle."

"Thank you. And these scrapings can be useful in *eliminating* a suspect as well as incriminating an assailant, isn't that correct?"

"Yes," murmured the witness.

"I'm afraid you'll have to speak up, Mr. Sun. We want these good people to hear every single word."

"Yes," said Sun, "the evidence can be used to eliminate a suspect."

"For example, where the DNA from fingernail scrapings doesn't match the suspect's DNA?"

"Yes."

"And you have done that in the past? Actually eliminated a wrongly accused suspect?"

Sun hesitated, then said, "Yes, once or twice."

"But you didn't try to do that in Mr. Ashford's case, did you?"

"Well—"

"Just answer the question, sir."

"No, we couldn't."

"Well, Mr. Sun, the defendant didn't deny you a blood sample, did he?"

"Well . . . no, but—"

"Thank you very much, Mr. Sun," said Menghetti, and sat down.

The annihilation of Arnold Sun had taken less than two minutes.

Grace glanced at Field, saw the veins in his neck pulsing against his collar, but there was no time for conferring.

"Mr. Sun," he said, his tone less composed than before, "*why* didn't you try to eliminate the defendant as a suspect using DNA material from under the victim's fingernails?"

Sun sat up straighter now, raised his head, brushed a lock of hair from his eyes. "The scrapings have been . . . misplaced, Mr. Field."

A stirring rose up from the gallery, drowning out the end of Sun's admission. The gavel came down once. Grace saw a smile replace Menghetti's normally stern expression. The crime lab's dereliction had come out in the worst possible way.

Field said, "Continue, Mr. Sun."

"Somewhere between the crime scene and either our crime lab or the toxicology lab at the medical examiner's office, the scrapings simply disappeared. We searched everywhere."

"So when Mr. Menghetti cut you off a minute ago, what were you trying to tell him?"

Sun looked relieved to finally be fed the straight line he had expected during his direct exam.

"Well, in our opinion, we didn't find the defendant's DNA under the victim's fingernails because we lost the scrapings, not because he didn't commit the murder. In fact, the wounds on Mr. Ashford's face appeared consistent with defensive fingernail scratches."

Grace saw Menghetti start to object during Sun's peroration, then decide against it. She watched Field glance at the jury, then smile at the witness. "Thank you for your testimony, Mr. Sun. That's all I have."

Arnold Sun betrayed his amateur status by starting to leave the witness box.

"Please don't rush off, Mr. Sun," Menghetti said in a caustic tone. "We're just getting to know one another."

Some members of the jury tittered at this, and Grace thought she saw Lani Jefferson, their pick for foreperson, and alternate number four, the Keller woman, glare at those who had.

Menghetti continued. "Your office was criticized in a report by the civil grand jury released on June 6, 1996, isn't that true?"

"I wasn't there then, sir."

"But you know it to be true, don't you." It wasn't a question.

Field rose with a technically correct but ill-conceived objection that caused Grace to cringe inside. "Exceeds the scope of the redirect examination, Your Honor."

"Not so," countered Menghetti in a righteously indignant tone. "Mr. Field elicited from this witness on redirect that they have lost important evidence; conclusive evidence that we claim would have cleared our client. I am now merely showing that this should not surprise anyone, given the crime lab's unenviable record of flagrant incompetence."

Field was still on his feet. "I object also to Mr. Menghetti's gratuitous reference to 'flagrant incompetence' and move to strike it."

"I apologize," said Menghetti with an amused smile, "and withdraw the words 'flagrant incompetence.' Perhaps Mr. Field would prefer I use the only viable alternative to incompetence: *intentional destruction.*"

Field's protest was quick, but the judge was even quicker.

"That's enough, Mr. Menghetti," he snapped, then instructed the jury to disregard the argumentative remark by counsel. "Restrain yourself, sir," he added, glaring at Menghetti, *"or I will."*

Grace stole a glance at the jurors. All were wide-eyed at the exchange, and Lani Jefferson, Martin Chin, and the fourth alternate were all nodding with approval at the judge's stern reprimand.

"Thank you, Your Honor," said Menghetti perfunctorily. "Do you remember the question, Mr. Sun?"

"Yes sir. I agree our equipment was old, but the investigation came about mainly because of the Simpson problem in L.A."

"And the investigation concluded that both San Jose and Oakland had superior equipment to yours in San Francisco?"

"Yes."

"Bigger budgets?"

"Yes."

"Bigger staffs?"

"Yes, but we're in a new facility now."

"That's reassuring. Catching up with the rest of the world, are we, Mr. Sun? Getting the kinks out of a new system?"

Field rose. "Objection: argumentative, compound."

"Sustained."

"Okay, Mr. Sun, let me be clear on this, sir. Are you telling this jury that you have, in fact, *lost* the most crucial evidence in this case?"

"Objection, Your Honor," said Field, and Grace wondered if the jury could hear the anxiety in his voice, the stretched-thin tone.

"Sustained," said John Hernandez, his expression hardening, "and the jury is again instructed to disregard the argument of counsel."

"In fact," continued Menghetti without hesitation, "you conveniently lost the evidence somewhere between the crime scene and one of the two laboratories, am I right?"

"Objection!" said Field. "Argumentative."

"Sustained," said Judge Hernandez. "Will counsel please approach?"

The four lawyers quickly convened at side-bar. "Mr.

Menghetti," said the judge, "the technique of asking improper questions that make your opponent appear fearful of the answer when he or she objects are not permitted in my courtroom. Do you understand?"

"Yes, Your Honor. I apologize for the 'conveniently' part of the question."

John Hernandez's eyes narrowed. "We are only in the first inning of the game, sir, and Babcock was strike one. Be careful."

"Thank you, Your Honor."

The lawyers returned to their places, all looking as if they had achieved a victory except for Dickson, who looked as angry as John Hernandez.

"Mr. Sun," said Menghetti, his voice oozing sincerity, "the evidence is gone, isn't it!"

Sun shifted in his seat. Grace knew he must be feeling the jurors' harsh gaze now. Grace felt her own hands growing cold. This was coming out all wrong. It couldn't be worse if Earl had intended it, she thought, then experienced a deeper chill as she wondered if perhaps he had.

"Yes, well . . ." continued Sun haltingly, "after the coroner's assistant took the scrapings, I assisted in marking the plastic bag. After that, I assumed he had taken it and I guess he assumed that I—"

"Let's just stick with your own erroneous assumptions, Mr. Sun. We'll let the other state's witnesses deal with theirs in turn."

Field started to rise, but Grace put a hand on his arm and he remained seated.

"As I said," continued the witness, "we could not locate—"

"You could not locate evidence that could have eliminated Elliot Ashford as a suspect, *is that not correct*?"

"Well, we . . . could not locate the evidence."

"And that's why you could not eliminate Mr. Ashford as a suspect, right?"

"Well . . ."

"Objection!" shouted Field.

"He can answer," said Judge Hernandez.

"Well, if the scrapings contained the DNA of someone else . . ." said Sun, looking confused again as his voice trailed off.

"You would have eliminated Mr. Ashford," said Menghetti, his barrel chest inflated with righteous indignation,
a hand to his head as if he were learning all this for the
first time along with the jury, "and then gone in search of
that 'someone else,' correct?"

"I suppose so."

"But because the scrapings have vanished, you cannot
now say if they contained the DNA of 'someone else,' or
Mr. Ashford, isn't that a fact?"

"Yes," whispered Sun, whose composure had also vanished. "At least, we can't find the scrapings."

*"Which means you can't find the real murderer either,
right?"*

"OBJECTION!" screamed Field. "Argumentative, assumes facts not in evidence—"

"Sustained," said Judge Hernandez, who turned to the
jury and said, "Members of the jury, I once again instruct
you to disregard that comment and its implication. I'm sure
I speak for Mr. Menghetti when I say this is the last time
I will have to give you this instruction."

He then turned hard eyes on Menghetti. "Strike two,
sir."

"Thank you, Your Honor," said Menghetti in a cloying
voice. "Now, Mr. Sun, would you agree that if the scrapings
had revealed DNA other than that of the defendant, you
would have eliminated Mr. Ashford as a suspect?"

"Perhaps."

"What do you mean '*perhaps*'?" snapped Menghetti in a
sudden, hard-edged tone that caused the witness to jump
in his seat.

"Okay, I suppose you could look at it that way."

Menghetti's eyes narrowed with aversion as he said,
"That's exactly the way I look at it, Mr. Sun."

Grace had never felt so frustrated, for Menghetti had
now achieved the goal of every expert trial lawyer on cross:
total control of the witness. Only John Hernandez's forti-
tude was keeping Menghetti from controlling the entire
courtroom.

Now, without taking his accusing eyes off the hapless
criminalist, Menghetti walked toward the jurors, then
turned to scan their faces as he added:

"And this jury could look at it that way, too, could they not?"

"OBJECT—"

"Withdraw that, Your Honor. Thank you, Mr. Sun," added Menghetti with an acid smile, "you've been most helpful."

Sun, missing the tone of ridicule, dutifully replied, "You're welcome," and stepped down.

Grace gave Sun a quick sympathetic look as he left the witness stand, then glanced down at her notepad and began to scribble purposefully, as if engaged in productive activity. She was still afraid to glance at the jurors, and she didn't want to look at Earl Field. Nor did she want to betray her exasperation.

So, as she often did in moments of overwhelming frustration that she had to conceal from the jury, she scribbled:

lost evidence = <u>hidden</u> evidence = acquittal = cops to blame = political survival?

Her heart was heavy, not only because of what had just happened to their case but because of the realization that her suspicions about Earl Field now seemed more justified. She scribbled again:

L.A. Eye reporter + E.F. at scene + missing evidence = proof of . . . <u>nothing!</u>

She decided that her only recourse at this point was to wait, then make use of whatever opportunities she could seize, despite her limited role, to try to convict Elliot Ashford. Not an easy task, she concluded, now that the armies usually arrayed on opposing sides of the battle line both seemed to be arrayed against her.

She shuddered, and under the second entry added:

<u>Confront E.F.?</u>

But she knew that Earl would hold to his story that he simply did not want to "begin the People's case with an apology." He would say that if he admitted the lost fingernail scrapings, the jury would assume there was much more he *wasn't* admitting. He would also say that he insisted on taking over the examination of the first witness because the public expected it of him.

If she pushed him, he would grow defensive. "It's all the damn cops' fault," he would say. "They lose the evidence, then send us a dope like Arnold Sun who couldn't talk his way out of a fortune cookie."

If she pushed him, he would remind her who had prepared Arnold Sun and maybe even invite her to leave the trial team.

If she pushed him, he would fall back on the trial lawyer's ultimate rationalization: We have to play the hand we're dealt, he would say. I'm a lawyer, not God. I just present the facts; I can't alter the facts of a case.

No, she would think, just the outcome.

From her seat in the jury box, Amanda Keller grimaced as Menghetti swaggered to his seat. *Rude bastard,* she thought, *berating the poor little man that way.* She had known snake-oil salesmen such as Al Menghetti and deceitful charmers like Ashford, too, sitting there looking as virtuous as a priest. *Thinks he'll get away with it,* she thought, reflecting on the cruel hand she had been delivered by fate compared with this silver-spoon pretty boy. Life was unfair, but maybe things were about to change—for both of them. Amanda knew she was supposed to keep an open mind, but she felt more certain than ever that she saw evil behind Ashford's casual and benign facade; his blond hair swept back tight against his aristocratic head, his scholarly spectacles hanging on the bridge of his delicate nose. But did the others see it?

As the trial progressed over the next few days, her frequent sideways glances at the two rows of jurors convinced her that only Martin Chin and Lani Jefferson seemed firmly in the prosecution camp. The blacks other than Lani Jefferson, though not as demonstrative as Jefferson, obviously liked Earl Field and knew a white racist when they saw one. Ditto the two Latinos, which made eight probables, but it would take all twelve to convict and things were not starting well for the prosecution.

Amanda's sympathy for Earl Field grew as he absorbed blow after blow, day after day. Her admiration grew also, which she was now sure was mutual. She hoped the other lawyers wouldn't see the looks they sometimes exchanged. It was more than flirtation, it was foreplay without touching or words. Once when their eyes met, she was shocked to find that she was physically aroused. She squirmed in her seat, embarrassed and mildly uncomfortable, yet wishing she could do something about it, right there as she watched him. She listened without hearing a word he said, for words didn't matter to her anymore. Relying on insights gained in her role as a juror on *Hope's People,* where a guilty man had gone free because the jury was not allowed to hear his earlier confession, and her actress training in body language and tonal inflections, Amanda had concluded that Ashford was guilty. The issue was how to help the district attorney, given her limited position as an alternate. She decided to take inventory, then find a way to become more proactive.

The regulars had already fallen into predictable cliques, governed mainly by race and gender. The three Caucasian jurors constituted a closed society, except for Martin Chin, an Asian who was occasionally welcomed into their midst. The oldest white juror was Ruth Salverson, the drab, pleasant woman whom Amanda had earlier attempted to proselytize. Then there was a bright, thin-faced young structural engineer named Kevin Alston, a bit of a loner who often took a solitary lunch in the basement cafeteria, affectionately dubbed "the House of Toast" by the D.A. staff. He usually sat with his nose in a book, over which he stole an occasional lustful glance at either Amanda or Manon Barnes.

Manon, the third white juror, was a pert, attractive young flight attendant with American Airlines whose sheer energy had established her as a leader of the white trio. That should have been me, thought Amanda.

The two older African-American jurors, a retired postal clerk and a housewife, usually ate lunch alone or together, but they, along with the two younger black jurors, were clearly attentive to anything said by Lani Jefferson, a short, powerfully built schoolteacher.

Amanda was pleased that an obvious leader like Jefferson appeared to be solidly aligned with the prosecution, yet resented the way Earl Field occasionally played to her. She also hated the woman's arrogant manner and the perfume she wore—Sanskrit, a scent worn by Lucinda. According to the newspapers, which Amanda diligently read to keep her scrapbook/journal current despite the court's admonition, veteran courtroom observers had expected to see Jefferson peremptorily challenged by one of the lawyers because she had worked as a paralegal in a San Francisco law firm before earning her teaching credential. But Field had presumably left Jefferson on because of his confidence in bonding with other African-Americans, as well as Grace Harris's ability to bond with other women. The article then speculated that Menghetti has left her on because he was running out of challenges and she fit the profile of a skeptical and ultraliberal juror who would require strong evidence before voting to convict anybody of anything.

That left two Latinos and a long-haired teamster of indeterminate racial background, possibly Native American, who looked to be in his mid-fifties. The teamster, Barney Seagrave, wasn't accepted into the "white regulars" and occasionally associated with the alternates.

But it was Kevin Alston, the lanky, bespectacled engineer, who Amanda signaled out as her next target. She joined him at the coffee table midway through the fifteen-minute morning recess as he was making a cup of instant decaf. Amanda reached for an envelope of regular.

"Cream?" he offered shyly, then added, "Don't tell me you need caffeine on top of all this excitement."

Although indirect, this was the first mention of the case in her presence. Amanda knew he was just making small talk, but it was all the encouragement she needed.

She accepted the cream with a "Thank you, kind sir" that had a familiar, manipulative Southern ring to it. Alston bowed his head awkwardly, and Amanda added, "But if you are referring to the way Mr. Menghetti tries to twist everything anybody says, I think it's more misleading than exciting."

"Oh," he said, startled by her directness. "Well, Mr. Menghetti certainly is a character. Anyways, the name's Kevin Alston. I've . . . seen you around. Well, of course I have. Seen you around, I mean. We can hardly miss seeing each other in such a small . . ."

His voice drifted off in a cloud of confusion and an awkward wave of his hand around the room. Amanda thought he might faint from the exertion of being close to an attractive woman. He pushed his glasses higher on his button nose with a trembling finger. She wanted to laugh at his clumsiness, but she just smiled as she studied him.

About her age, nondescript in appearance behind thick glasses, probably married to a college sweetheart, with 2.3 children and a two-car garage for his Volvo and her Ford station wagon.

"It *is* a small place," she agreed, trying to rescue the brittle juror from his evident awkwardness. "You're an engineer, can't you redesign it?"

He managed a shy smile. "I don't think they'd appreciate it," he said, his eyes like sharp blue particles of light darting nervously behind the bulky glasses, obviously impressed that she must have been listening to his voir dire responses. "How about yourself? What do you do?"

"I'm in charge of a file department for a commercial real estate leasing company," she said, then added offhandedly, "and I work for a boss who's almost as devious as that defense lawyer."

Alston's Adam's apple bobbed, and he seemed to blush slightly. Amanda knew he wanted to retreat from his growing attraction to her, so she reached up and picked a loose thread from his lapel. "Sorry," she added, without clarifying what she was sorry for, then scanned his face with supplicant eyes, waiting for a response.

"Well," he stammered, confused and trying to come up with something neutral, "*all* the lawyers seem quite aggressive."

"Oh, I agree," she said, her full lips curling into a beguiling smile. "Don't get me wrong. I think Mr. Menghetti's a *genius*! I want him in *my* corner if *I'm* ever a Mafia person charged with murder."

Alston now openly recoiled and coughed up a nervous laugh. "I haven't heard any evidence—"

"Oh, my," she interrupted, covering her lips in mock contrition, "I *have* been bad! I forgot we're not supposed to bring outside facts into our deliberations. I guess I *did* need this coffee."

Alston smiled uneasily but stopped retreating.

"So let's talk about you," she continued, trying to ease

the tension. "What kind of engineer are you? A good one I bet."

Alston blushed and looked at his shoes. "Well, thank you. A structural engineer, actually."

"How fascinating," she said, thinking, *Two down, ten to go.* "Bridges and things?"

24

At the end of the third lackluster day for the prosecution, Grace called Sam Quon in to her office. "What have you dug up on Renee Babcock? Earl is going to let me take her on cross."

"Nothing surprising," he said. "Divorced, two kids. Clean neighborhood, nothing fancy. Neighbors regard her as a character, bit of a lush. Ashford has been seen coming and going, but so have plenty of other men. Woman next door says Babcock claims to be engaged to one of them. Nobody remembers seeing anyone around the night of the murder."

"What does she do?"

"Self-described fashion model, but no earned income reported. Lives on money from her 'fiancé,' some child support from her ex, and whatever."

"The 'whatever' being Ashford and others?"

"That's my guess, but neighbors seem to like her despite 'whatever.' She helps out around the neighborhood. A basically decent person and keeps her kids spick-and-span."

"That's it?"

Sam shrugged.

"Terrific, Sam. I'll bring her to her knees by showing she has a cocktail or two between helping out her neighbors and being a model single parent."

"Lighten up, Grace," said Sam, "I'm only the messenger here. It's not easy to prove X wasn't with Y when both X and Y say he was."

"I know," said Grace, drumming a pencil against the palm of her hand as she stared out the window. "I'm sorry, Sam."

Then she turned abruptly and added, "Give me her address."

* * *

"Come sit," said Renee Babcock, surprisingly pleasant and hospitable in the living room of her Cow Hollow apartment. Grace was also impressed with her poise, given the nature of the visit and the fact that she was under siege by a cute little guy who looked to be five or six and his younger sister. A dog cavorted wildly among them, contributing to the benign confusion.

Sam's report, indicating Renee Babcock to be thirty-two, short auburn hair, and "attractive," failed to do justice to her looks and glowing personality. Grace could not help liking her instantly, but after small talk and swapping stories about their kids, Grace eased into her strategy. "Would you tell me a little about Elliot?" she said. "What he's like?"

"Tell me more about your son," she said, kissing her little girl on the cheek.

This is a cool one, thought Grace. "Look, Renee, I'm just trying to learn—"

"You're trying to trip me up, right?" Renee said, her face still glowing with goodwill.

Grace smiled, surprised by the woman's directness. "That's about it," she said. "How are my chances?"

"How are my chances?" repeated the little girl, and both Renee and Grace laughed.

"Sorry, Gracie," said Renee, putting her arms around both children. "You're outnumbered."

Grace picked up her bag. "Well, then, maybe I'd better let you get on with your evening."

Renee Babcock turned serious. "I'm sorry," she said, and Grace made a mental note that Renee was a person who didn't like to disappoint people.

"Look," she continued, "Elliot is no saint, okay? But he didn't kill anybody, no way. And I'm not embarrassed about his bein', you know, an occasional friend."

She added the last with a cautionary glance at her son, then kissed him on the forehead and said, "He sent the three of us to Disney World, didn't he, little guys."

"Elliot's a *nice* man," said the boy. His sister nodded in eager agreement.

"Do you mean, Disneyland?" said Grace.

"Uh-uh. He thought Billy here should see Florida.

Weird, huh? Then up to Virginia; place called Williamsburg. 'Billy's got to get some history about this great country,' he tells me. He was too busy to go, of course, but he had drivers and everythin' wherever me and Billy and little Irene showed up. Hell, Gracie, I'd sleep with Adolf Hitler if he treated my kids the way Elliot does."

Grace smiled. "Are you in love with him, Renee?"

Billy turned and regarded Grace for the first time, making her feel uneasy. But Babcock laughed and shook her head, shaking out her auburn hair. "All's I'm in love with is these guys," she said, then hugged them so exuberantly she nearly hit their heads together.

"Just tell me this, Renee," said Grace. "How are you sure it was the night of August 7 that he was here?"

"You don't forget a night like that."

"Don't you mean morning? Or did he call you later that night after he found his wife's body?"

Babcock clamped her eyes shut for just a second or two and the trial lawyer made another mental note of the guileless mannerism.

"Mornin', sure. Must have been mornin' when I first heard about it. On the news . . ." Her voice trailed off.

Grace said, "I see."

"I'll do better when I testify," she said apologetically.

Grace was touched by Renee Babcock's naïveté. "You realize," she said, "that I'll be cross-examining you?"

"Sure. Of course."

"And that you'll be under oath early tomorrow morning when I take your statement."

"Yes."

"Okay," said Grace. "One last question then: Whose idea was it to go see the movie?"

Renee's face reflected momentary confusion, then clouded for the first time. Grace's eyes were fused to Renee's, hard and unrelenting. Renee looked away.

"I think," she said, the warmth gone from her voice now, "I'd best be gettin' some food into my little animals."

Grace rose quickly. "Of course," she said. "I'm sorry."

"Don't be," Renee said. "It's your job and you're good at it. Tough too, I bet. Oh well."

"I've overstayed my welcome," said Grace. "Really, I am sorry."

Babcock shrugged, and Grace could read her thoughts.

I know what you're really sorry about, Gracie. But it's okay. You're just doin' your job—just like I'm goin' to do mine.

Grace found herself liking Renee Babcock more than she wanted to, despite her growing suspicion that the woman was about to commit perjury for a man who didn't deserve her kindness.

As the day for presentation of the defense case approached, Barrett and Al Menghetti met with Ashford in Menghetti's suite at the Ritz-Carlton. The principal item on their agenda was whether to lead off with their expert DNA testimony or to hit them straightaway with Renee Babcock.

Menghetti sat behind the desk he had rented—almost as garish as the one in his L.A. office—while Barrett slumped in a stuffed chair and the client roamed about the large living room with the sour restraint of a tiger behind invisible bars. Barrett watched his client with growing distaste, then looked away, remembering that for himself, it was just a case, but for Ashford, it was, literally, his life.

"We got a break getting rid of Martin Chin," said Ashford. "The damn Chinaman would have killed me!"

Chin, juror number five, a forty-year-old CPA, had revealed himself during the first week of the trial to be biased toward the prosecution. The judge had dismissed him without explanation after private conferences with two other jurors.

"Thank God he wasn't inscrutable," said Menghetti, winking at Ashford, "but we have the cops to thank for our biggest break."

"The cops?" said Ashford.

"Yeah. Losing the fingernail scrapings. A godsend!"

"A *godsend*? Christ, you idiots keep forgetting I *am* innocent! The scrapings might have shown the presence of a third party—the real murderer, for instance!"

"Point taken, Elliot," said Menghetti, "which might explain why they decided to lose them."

Ashford grunted moodily and continued to pace before large windows overlooking the courtyard below.

"Okay," said Menghetti, "let's talk witnesses. I think we should lead off with Renee Babcock. Any objections?"

"I'll take the stand first," said Ashford. "Those jurors want to hear it from me right up front."

Menghetti and Dickson exchanged a surprised look.

"And don't hand me that 'presumption of innocence' tripe," he added.

"Going with the presumption is the best gamble," said Menghetti.

"Gambling, old chum, is what got me into this mess," said Ashford, "and don't forget: those focus-group people you hired thought I was a superb witness."

"That's true, Elliot, but remember Simpson?" said Menghetti. "He was a professional actor who everyone *knew* would be a superb witness, but he went with the odds and he's a free man today."

Ashford snorted. "You call that *free*? Free to do what? Play golf with strangers in Panama City? Hang out with the coloreds he had spent his life escaping?"

Barrett winced but said nothing.

Menghetti said, "The fact remains, Elliot, Simpson listened to his lawyers in the criminal case and didn't take the stand and he got away with it."

Ashford suddenly advanced on Menghetti's desk so quickly Barrett could not move his feet out of the way fast enough. "Damn you, Al," Ashford shouted, "stop comparing me with Simpson! *I did not kill Lara!*"

As Barrett rubbed his bruised ankle, he observed that Menghetti did not so much as blink. The man is cool, thought Barrett, a guy truly made for the courtroom, a natural trial lawyer—one of those mistakes nature sometimes makes on the way to creating a real person. Unfortunately, Barrett concluded, Menghetti was a man made *only* for the courtroom. When he was not in the presence of a jury, light seemed to leave his eyes and his features turned inward, like a man who had swallowed himself. Was I that way? Barrett wondered.

Menghetti extended placating palms toward Ashford but said nothing more. Ashford's gaze turned toward Barrett.

"Well, how about you, Dickson? Speak up and justify your existence, for God's sake! You saw those focus-group results. You must have some opinion for all the money I'm paying you."

"Sure I have an opinion," said Barrett, "but I don't think you'd like it."

Reading the disdain in Barrett's eyes, Ashford turned back to Menghetti. "Look, Al, you admit I tested well with the mock jurors, and I wasn't even trying. The real jurors will love me!"

"A trial is not a personality contest, Elliot, okay?" said Menghetti.

"For which you should be grateful, Elliot," volunteered Barrett.

Ashford's head snapped around toward Barrett and a vein in the defendant's temple began to dance.

"If that's your opinion, deadhead," he said, "I'm definitely paying you too much!"

Barrett's eyes narrowed, but he realized he had been stupid to open his mouth and said nothing more.

"So it's settled," Ashford said, turning back to Menghetti. "I lead off. Then what?"

Barrett credited Menghetti with restraint and realized he was starting to admire the defense lawyer's cool competence. Ashford was becoming impossible to control, yet Menghetti continued to look as relaxed as a turtle sunning himself on a rock.

"I understand where you're coming from, Elliot," said Menghetti, "but you're forgetting that we've almost won this case without having to put on a single witness. All we really need is Renee and a few well-chosen words in argument about the missing evidence and it's over. Verdict for the defense; the courtroom awash in reasonable doubt. The only way we lose, Elliot, is if the jury learns things—past brushes with the law, unseemly connections, minor indiscretions—things that can come out only if you take the stand, okay?"

"Maybe so," said Ashford, "but those twelve simpletons are waiting to hear me tell them I'm innocent, and whether you pettifogging barristers believe it or not, I *am* innocent!"

"It's not a question of what I believe, Elliot," said Menghetti, finally stirring from his languor. "You're not paying me to *believe* one way or the other. My job is to tell the *jury* what to believe, okay? I don't give a shit one way or the other if you're innocent. You're buying my judgment and my experience, not my nose up your ass."

"That's fine with me, Al, because a nose the size of yours wouldn't fit up an elephant's ass, let alone mine."

This exchange set Ashford to pacing away from the window and behind Barrett, who continued to sit in silence, size twelves now tucked safely under his chair.

Ashford suddenly stopped and Barrett could feel his eyes on him from behind. "Come on, Barrett," he said, "tell our paisano here that an innocent man should be granted the right to declare it publicly."

Barrett unfolded himself into a standing position and winced as he arched his back into a stretch. "I believe Al is right when he says that a man should never take risks when he is winning. I must disagree with Al, however, when he says a trial is not a personality contest. A trial is always a personality contest."

With leaden feet and two sets of resentful eyes following his slow progress, he shuffled toward a French provincial cabinet behind Menghetti's desk and eyed the collection of bottles lined up there.

"That's reason number one why you shouldn't take the stand," he said, "despite the focus groups."

Ashford reddened. "Do you want to explain that remark, Dickson?"

"Sure," said Barrett, turning and seeing that he had managed to irritate both men. "You are not a man tortured by self-doubt, Elliot, and you do not conceal it very well. People don't like that in an alleged murderer."

Barrett paused, noticing that Al Menghetti's scowl had turned into a smile. "Oh, I don't deny that you've got a certain charm, Elliot, but it has a short shelf life."

Ashford struggled to maintain his temper. "You apparently didn't comprehend Eric Tremaine's report, where he says that I—"

"What *you* don't comprehend, Elliot—indeed what very few trial lawyers even understand—is that all we're doing from now to the end of the trial is trying to provide ammunition to the jurors who are already committed to you; evidence they can use to win the hearts of the uncommitted or prosecution voters."

"Well, thank you very much," said Ashford, momentarily

forgetting his anger, "because that's precisely why I want
to take the stand!"

"And that's precisely," countered Barrett, "why you
shouldn't. You'd be giving your advocates on the jury nothing by denying you killed her, because every juror in that
box would lie to save his or her own ass and knows you'd
do the same thing. So what have you accomplished, other
than having your assault felony revealed?"

Barrett felt the resentment in the room slowly disappearing in the wake of his words. He was speaking the
truth, or at least dealing logic, a more desirable commodity
than truth at a time like this.

"So here's what we should do," he continued, pleased to
see that he was commanding the full attention of the room
even without the amber inspiration of the fifteen-year-old
cognac he had spotted on top of the cabinet. "If Babcock
holds up, the case is won and even you will agree you
shouldn't testify. So we put *her* on first, see how she does."

Menghetti was no longer smiling and Barrett could tell
he didn't like the way Ashford was hanging on his words.

"In other words," he concluded, "it's not a decision that
should keep either one of you from getting your rest
tonight."

Barrett reached for his coat and added, "My bedtime,
too. I bid you both a good evening."

"Hold on, Dickson," said Ashford. "I'm not wild about
the way you said it, but I agree with what you say. I'll go
with you on this. We'll lead with Renee, Al."

"I think," said Menghetti, scowling, "that's what I said
ten minutes ago."

"I was just agreeing with you, Al," said Barrett in a
mollifying tone, but Menghetti was clearly upset, reminding
Barrett why he had always tried cases alone.

Menghetti rose from behind the desk and addressed his
co-counsel through tightly compressed lips.

"Since our client seems more inclined to listen to you
than to me, Dickson, why don't you just go ahead and put
Renee on yourself? *You* be the stand-up guy for a change,
and *I'll* be the second-guesser. What the hell, go ahead and
take all three of our witnesses!"

Barrett felt color rising in his face; he knew it was a
challenge, not an offer. He saw that Ashford was grinning,

amused at Menghetti's discomfiture but enjoying his games-manship. He put on a serious face and joined in, saying, "It's quite all right with me, Dickson."

Barrett felt like a character in Sartre's *No Exit,* and re-flected on how swiftly any two members of this unholy triumvirate could gang up on the third.

Menghetti's expression brightened. "See? The client agrees. They're all yours." Then he winked at Ashford.

Barrett saw the wink—was meant to see it—and strug-gled to control his temper.

"I want nothing to do with Babcock, Al," he said. "She's your 'strike one' with the judge, not mine, plus you've al-ready prepped her." Ashford and Menghetti exchanged a knowing look, but Barrett quickly added, "But sure, I'll put on the others. Have your notes typed up, Al, so I can read them. As for closing argument, I'm sure you'll want to split that with me, too. We can work out the details on that later. Sleep well, gentlemen."

He then winked at the two blank-faced men and walked into the night.

What have I done? he asked himself as he waited for his car in front of the hotel. But he couldn't stop smiling.

He overtipped the valet, then spotted two twenties in his wallet. He turned his Ford Mustang toward Stars, humming something that sounded vaguely like "Stardust."

25

Frequent clashes between the lawyers during the next few days tested the mettle of Judge John Hernandez. Amanda liked him. *He* at least didn't seem deceived by Menghetti's tactics.

What worried her was not the judge but the other jurors—mainly the "white regulars"—many of whom seemed unable or unwilling to see through the defense's deceitful tactics. She would enter the jury room seething with frustration after some outrageous defense gambit and they'd be standing around smiling at each other like Stepford wives at a coffee klatch, jabbering, giggling, and rendering such insightful appraisals as "Interesting, isn't it?" (Manon Barnes), "My, they do get upset, don't they?" (Ruth Salverson), and "Wish to hell I wuz fishin' " (Barney Seagrave).

Were they all blind? Could they be part of a conspiracy against Earl Field? Had some or all the regular jurors been threatened or bought off by Ashford's Mafia associates? The mob wouldn't have approached her, of course, because she was only an alternate.

And now time was running out on her. The judge had announced that the two final DNA experts would mark the end of the People's case and that the defense case would take no more than two or three days. Moreover, the alternates would be relegated to "on call" status at the end, to serve only if a regular juror became ill during deliberations. In that unlikely event, the first alternate in line would be called in and the reconstituted panel would begin its deliberations anew.

But only one of the original twelve had been replaced—poor Martin Chin—and there were still two alternates ahead of her with the trial winding down. How could she help Earl Field if she were shut out of deliberations? How would she gain the publicity needed to return her to Hollywood? Hadn't her call to the Ashford jury panel been a sign? The promise of a life-altering experience?

Or had Lucinda been right, as usual?

An outburst of laughter from around the coffee table interrupted her thoughts. Manon Barnes had said something funny to Kevin Alston and Barney Seagrave. Amanda watched as Manon walked away from them, her hips swinging. Alston's and Seagrave's eyes followed her like matched pairs of panting dogs. God, how she hated all of them!

Suddenly the pungent smell of what the jurors called "jailhouse coffee" sent a wave of nausea through her and she wondered if she was coming down with something. Her ears had begun to buzz the day before and today her headache was worse.

She blew her nose, tried to clear her thoughts, to focus on her options now that Renee Babcock would soon cement the final bricks of reasonable doubt into place. She had to help Earl. But how?

If she were a regular juror, she could simply hold out and force a mistrial, giving Earl a second chance. This would have been perfect for her, too, for the media always focused on a hold-out juror and she would get plenty of attention. But with the trial ending, she would have to resort to a different strategy.

She gazed around the room. She turned her eyes on Barney Seagrave, the rough-cut, horny-looking teamster with a ponytail and an earring who had seemed less impressed by Menghetti than the rest and had been eyeing her since the first day. Standing next to him was Kevin Alston, more risky, but still obviously attracted to her. She forced herself to her feet and walked toward them. Her heartbeat increased, but she took a deep breath and threw back her shoulders.

"Well, guys," she said, "looks like we're almost there."

"It's about time," grumbled Seagrave, blatantly staring at her breasts. "I've got a job waiting for me if I can get the hell out of here by week's end."

"Well," said Amanda, "I'll be thinking of you folks sitting here, washing down day-old crullers with this oven cleaner they call coffee."

"Lucky you," said Alston with an appreciative chuckle. He seemed to have grown more self-confident with the passage of time. "Looks like we're in it for the long haul."

"Oh, I don't think it will take you long," said Amanda, willing her hand to be steady as she poured herself a cup of coffee. She glanced up at Seagrave, dutifully holding out cream and sugar. "Other than the Babcock woman—Ashford's most recent version of an alibi—I doubt the defense will have anything and Ashford won't dare take the stand."

Seagrave's eyebrows rose. Alston swallowed and cleared his throat, but Amanda forged ahead. "First the guy goes out to a movie he's already seen, right? That alibi doesn't fly, so now he claims to be with some woman? Give me a break."

Alston turned as gray as his shirt as he looked over Amanda's shoulder. Seagrave's Adam's apple bobbed twice. Amanda knew why without turning, for only one person other than Lucinda wore that god-awful Sanskrit perfume.

"Did I hear you correctly, Ms. Keller?" said Lani Jefferson, in the voice of a schoolteacher dealing with an unruly adolescent. No more than five feet four inches in her schoolmarm medium heels, yet the woman was both intimidating and controlling. Amanda hated her dangling earrings and hair cut short in a Grace Jones look that seemed totally at odds with her somber-colored suits and dresses meant to conceal an ass the size of Alcatraz.

Jefferson's cold eyes now traveled to Seagrave and Alston. Seagrave's reaction was to consider another cup of coffee. Alston nearly dropped his.

"She's done it before," said Alston nervously, unable to meet Amanda's eyes.

"You can't turn her off," said some other juror drawn to the confrontation.

"Oh, but I can," said Jefferson, facing Amanda. "I turned off Martin Chin, didn't I?"

Amanda paled. So that's what had happened to Martin. Her heart raced as she saw the resentment burning in the smaller woman's dark brown eyes. Jefferson was so much smaller, yet she made Amanda feel childlike, eager to please.

"I . . . was just trying to reassure them that—"

Jefferson, hands on hips, cut her off by simply extending the palm of her hand. "Listen, Keller, I get shuckin' and jivin' from my seventh graders every day. I damn sure don't need it from you."

Seagrave started to speak, but apparently thought better of it. Everyone knew the teamster had a family to support and that he'd already turned down two thousand from *American Secret* magazine for just a telephone interview.

Amanda sputtered something about having forgotten the judge's admonition, but Jefferson's accusing eyes prevented her from thinking straight. And under the juror's stern gaze she could hear her mother's voice: *Can't you do anything right?*

"Look, Ms. Keller," Jefferson continued in her exaggerated teacher's diction, drawing out each vowel, "we're trying to be fair jurors here. Do our job, understand? Then along come people like you and Chin who simply won't behave."

Amanda hated this woman; hated the way she was lecturing her as if she were a child, humiliating her in front of the others. Acting and smelling just like her mother. She fought off the urge to slap her hard across her ugly face. She tried to think of something conciliatory to say, but her mind was too confused. Then she became vaguely aware of the ghostly form of a woman now standing behind Lani Jefferson, another juror drawn to the encounter. Juror number two, the widow Ruth Salverson.

Amanda looked toward Seagrave in desperation. Why didn't he say something? He liked her, she knew that. He had probably never had an attractive woman show such interest in him. Wasn't that worth something? Anxiety had turned Amanda's mind into an empty room and she knew that only Seagrave could rescue her now. She let her arm brush against his.

"Was I out of line, Mr. Seagrave?" she asked. "If so, I apologize."

Seagrave considered, then said, "Lani, I think she was trying to make me feel good about gettin' back to work soon and maybe she crossed the line a little. Hell, we all have our notions about what went on that night—not that we should express them or anything—but . . . hell, let's cut her a little slack."

Encouraged, Amanda found words. "Please . . . Lani, he's right. I just slipped. I don't know what I was thinkin'." Her voice had become as soft and gentle as a cultured Southern lady's. "*Please* don't report this. I won't be here long anyway."

"What did she do?" asked Ruth Salverson.

"She commented on the defense's evidence in violation of the judge's admonition," Jefferson said, her eyes still locked on Amanda, "just like Martin Chin did. She should be treated no differently."

Seagrave shifted his feet and extended a knurled hand, palm up. "Chin was a regular juror," he said. "Amanda here is just an alternate. She's just about outta here anyway like she said. Where's the harm? Give her a break."

"She hears the same admonition we all hear, Mr. Seagrave, but your opinion is noted."

Your opinion is noted! Who did this woman think she was! thought Amanda. Then, as if he had read Amanda's thoughts, Barney Seagrave rocked back on his heels and said, "Well, it looks like we already got ourselves a foreman, and self-appointed at that. Or did I just miss the election, Lani?"

Amanda could have kissed him.

"Not at all," demurred Jefferson, "but since you mention it, why not use this as an experiment in group decision-making. We know where you stand, Barney. What's your vote, Kevin?"

Kevin Alston looked uncomfortable, perhaps because of the teamster's suddenly narrowed eyes aimed straight at him. Alston earnestly began to clean his thoroughly clean glasses. "Well, Lani, I suppose that it could be argued, well, you know, technically at least, that . . . well, she didn't exactly comment on the defense evidence."

Jefferson's arms folded themselves into a wall. "How," she asked, "do you figure *that?*"

Alston paled and grinned sheepishly, his eyes clamped shut as he replaced his spectacles. Caught between Jefferson and Seagrave, he suddenly looked more like a defendant than Ashford did. "Well, I don't exactly know, Lani," he mumbled, "but, well, we haven't heard any evidence yet from the defense, so how could she have commented on it?"

Lani Jefferson gave her head an impatient shake of astonishment at the absurdity of his logic, sighed, and turned to the ghostly Ruth Salverson.

"Ruth?"

Ruth Salverson, a woman whose opinion had not been solicited in thirty years, let out a self-conscious cackle as her mind grappled with the issue.

"I wasn't there, I mean here," she said, stumbling over her words. "But it seems like, well, one of those accidents that just happens sometimes." Then her face brightened and she smiled with a wry self-awareness and added, "You know, like overcooking a pot roast?"

Jefferson rolled her eyes, then gave Amanda a last hard look and said, "Okay, Keller, the compassionate majority has spoken. But watch it, because I'll be watching you."

A loud rap on the door signaled the end of the recess and the jurors headed for the courtroom. But Jefferson wasn't finished. She grasped Amanda firmly by the arm, pulled her aside, and spoke in a quiet but intense voice: "You skated this time, Keller, but it won't work again. I know plenty of women just like you, countin' on tits and ass to get your way."

"I don't understand you, Lani," whispered Amanda, more confident now. "It's obvious we're on the same side. You know Ashford's a racist and guilty as sin! I've seen the hatred in your eyes when you look at him."

"That's not the point. You don't hear me talkin' about the case and I better not hear you doin' it again either."

Bitch, thought Amanda, smiling agreement.

That night, after she had cleaned up the remains of Lucinda's microwave dinner, she retreated to her room, stroked her cats, and thought about what might have been. She thumbed through her Ashford trial scrapbook but was without the energy to update it.

Maybe she would at least get to know Earl Field after the trial; that would be something. He was engaged but not married yet, and her efforts to salvage his case would give them a common bond. He had been looking tired lately, she thought, worried too. Little wonder, for losing a case against an obviously guilty murderer would surely hurt his career. Maybe that's what this was all about. A white conspiracy to destroy Earl Field.

She felt terribly alone and inadequate, but she couldn't let it happen. She could not back down now, even if her job, her reputation, her very life were put at risk.

26

The Brazen Head, a little-known but greatly admired neighborhood restaurant in the Marina District, clung to its anonymity by staying out of tourist guidebooks and stubbornly refusing to identify itself with a sign. There were a dozen small tables and an equal number of stools crammed around the shoe-box bar, one of which was regularly occupied between six and seven every evening by Renee Babcock. This pattern had been reported to Grace after Sam Quon had commenced a surveillance the day following Grace's first visit to Renee's apartment.

"Excuse me," said Grace, seated near the door as the witness entered the darkened bar, blinking her eyes. "Renee? Renee Babcock?"

"My God," said the witness in mock horror, "there's just no escapin' the Long Arm."

Grace laughed. "I'm off duty. Just in to see if the pepper steak is as good as it used to be."

"I wouldn't know," said Renee. "I live around the corner on Greenwich and just pop in for a drink or three after I feed the animals. Then I go home and pry their little heads out of the TV set and lock them in their beds."

"So this is the zookeeper's break time?"

Renee flashed her perfect smile. "Well, sometimes I have company after they're asleep," she said guilelessly, "but then you probably know all about that. Elliot told me once I couldn't handle a monogamous relationship. I told him, hell, I can handle several of them at once!"

Grace laughed. Following her first visit with Babcock, Grace had waived her right to a deposition, banking on somehow changing the witness's mind instead of setting her false testimony in stone.

"Have a seat," said Grace. "I'm not allowed to buy you a drink, but company would be nice."

Renee looked longingly at her regular stool at the other end, but then gave a quick shrug and sat. "Okay, Dutch it is," said Renee as the bartender greeted her by name and slid her usual in front of her. A martini with three olives.

During the ensuing forty-five minutes, Renee put down three martinis and nine olives while Grace managed two glasses of Chardonnay. They kept the conversation neutral: kids, fashion, and the high cost of living in San Francisco. Then Renee checked her watch, picked up her purse, and slid off the stool.

"It's been real, Grace. Really. I wish things were . . . more relaxed. You know, different?"

"If I get much more relaxed than I am now, I'll be looking up from the floor," said Grace. "But I know what you mean."

Renee nodded.

Grace touched her lightly on the arm. "I do need to tell you something." •

Renee frowned but hesitated.

"I planned this, Renee."

"That's straight; guess I kind of figured. What do you want to tell me?"

"Just that I'm good at what I do."

"I've figured that, too."

"I mean real good. So if you're lying about that night, I'll get you. That could mean getting hit with perjury. You could go to jail."

"I think," said Renee, her tone cold now, "we covered that the last time you invaded my privacy."

"I'm sorry, but hear me out. Please? Sit for another minute."

Renee slanted her thin body against the bar but remained standing.

"Look, Renee. I don't know what you think you owe this guy, but he's asking way too much of you."

Renee pulled away, put her purse under her arm, and said, "So are you, Grace, and I don't owe you nothin'."

Grace rose and blocked her way. "I know that, but damn it, I know how much those little animals of yours mean to you."

"Leave my kids out of this, *Ms.* District Attorney. I'm going home now."

"That's my *point,* Renee!" said Grace, taking her by the arm. "Home is where your kids need you."

Renee Babcock gave Grace a hurt but angry look through moistening eyes. "I'm sorry I called you tough, Grace," she said. "You're goddamn *ruthless!*"

"Okay," said Grace, "but I'm also concerned about the way Elliot Ashford is using you."

Renee looked away and Grace held on to her arm, more firmly now. "Damn it, Renee, I *like* you! I'm trying to say you don't know what you're getting into!"

Grace felt a shudder pass through Renee. She wanted to put her arms around her. Instead she released her arm and watched her lurch unsteadily out of the Brazen Head.

Barrett listened with unaccustomed attentiveness as Judge Hernandez gaveled the courtroom to order the next day and invited Al Menghetti to call his first witness. An alien feeling had invaded his consciousness. Optimism? Hope? He had briefly interviewed the witnesses he would put on when Menghetti was finished with Babcock and knew they would do well.

There was some anxiety, too, of course, but it was manageable; more an adrenaline rush of excitement than the disabling disillusionment that had crippled him during the 1993 TDA case.

Yes, he thought, things were looking up. Babcock, then his own two experts, followed by arguments, a swift defense verdict, and who knows? Maybe whatever had been dogging him had gone off and begun dogging someone else.

He glanced at Al Menghetti. Menghetti hadn't wanted to share the spotlight, particularly with victory so obviously imminent, but it had been his idea—actually, a joke that had backfired—and Ashford had decided he liked the idea of having a San Francisco lawyer getting on his feet and showing he wasn't just there for local color.

Barrett jumped a little when Menghetti called out Renee Babcock's name and saw every head in the courtroom turn to stare at the woman entering through the large double doors at the rear of the courtroom. The first thing he noticed was that Ms. Babcock possessed an exquisite pair of legs. As she came closer, he saw that she was a full-blown beauty head to toe by any standard. Barrett saw that she also communicated an aura of naïve innocence, regrettably too obscured by makeup to be detected by most jurors, but all in all, she seemed pretty together.

Until she took the oath, when darting eyes and a faltering, high-pitched voice produced a tightening in Barrett's gut—historically an instinctual red light as dependable as a battery-powered bunny beating a drum. He noticed the way she nervously glanced at Ashford, then told the clerk her name in a voice that sounded like she wasn't quite sure. This was not typical witness jitters.

Barrett leaned across Ashford and whispered to Menghetti. "Something's wrong."

"Bullshit," he heard Ashford say to Menghetti, "she's just scared. She'll be fine when she shakes the nerves. The girl loves me."

"She's a character, Dickson," Menghetti whispered to Barrett, "but seemed completely reliable when I prepped her. She'll be okay."

But Barrett's heart was dancing in his chest and a thin line of perspiration had broken across his lip.

Something's wrong, he repeated in an anguished whisper, but no one paid attention.

Menghetti rose to commence his direct examination.

"Have you lived in San Francisco all your life, Ms. Babcock?"

"Not yet," said Renee, and the gallery tittered.

Menghetti smiled. "How long have you known Mr. Ashford, Ms. Babcock."

"We've been friends for four or five years," she said.

"Have you been intimate with him over that period of time?"

"Well, sure, sometimes I tell him stuff," she said.

Oh, shit, Barrett muttered.

"I mean, you've slept together, have you not?"

"No," she said, crossing her long legs, "just sex. I never let him sleep."

A rising tide of laughter from the gallery was quelled by a hard look from the judge, but Barrett wasn't smiling. Something *was* wrong. There was no real playfulness in her manner, no teasing glances at Ashford, and her witty ripostes issued from trembling lips. Renee's slapstick made no sense, unless she was using humor to telegraph a warning. But Menghetti forged onward like a musk ox in an arctic snowstorm, apparently seeing only the path immediately ahead.

"Elliot told me once I suffered from nymphomania," continued Babcock, encouraged by the laughter. "I told him he was wrong, that I enjoyed every single minute of it."

The gavel came down hard on the block but was hardly heard amid the roar from the gallery.

"This is not a comedy club, Ms. Babcock," said Judge Hernandez when order had been restored. "Please restrain yourself."

"Why, of course, Your Honor," said the witness, giving the judge a seductive, closed-mouth smile.

Even some of the jurors were smiling now, but it was clear to Barrett they would give little credence to her testimony. Hadn't Menghetti told her to be serious? Menghetti gave the witness a condescending nod, then turned toward the jury, smiling with them, sharing a joke with them at this ribald woman's expense. Bonding with them. But Barrett could see that Menghetti had recognized a possible problem and was trying to think his way around it.

Barrett then glanced at Grace Harris, whose eyes were locked on Babcock's and whose lips betrayed the trace of a knowing smile. Have you turned her, Grace? he thought, unsuccessfully trying to get the prosecutor to meet his eyes. He looked back at the witness and wondered if Renee Babcock was intentionally playing the fool so the jury wouldn't take her seriously. Maybe she thinks that will soften the impact of the blow she's about to deliver to Ashford.

"Now, calling your attention to the evening of August 7, 1997, were you with Mr. Ashford that night?"

"No," she said. All traces of humor suddenly vanished from her expression, and her voice was uncertain and cracking again. She recrossed her legs, then fixed her eyes on the tip of one of her shoes. Finally, she spoke. "I don't think I was with Elliot that night."

A different kind of reaction went up from the gallery now: a communal gasp of astonishment. Renee Babcock had indeed turned.

"I haven't . . . been with him for two or three months."

Menghetti merely raised an eyebrow and took a step closer to the witness. "Well, it's now October 30, Ms. Babcock," he said nonchalantly, almost indifferently. "August 7 is well within 'two or three months.' "

Jesus, thought Barrett admiringly, was I ever that composed in the face of disaster when I was the one riding the tiger?

The witness shrugged, as if to say so what?

"And you concede you have had many sexual liaisons with Mr. Ashford?" he continued.

"As many as he could handle," she said, winking at Menghetti, renewing her effort to neutralize her testimony even as she gave it. But nobody was laughing now and several of the jurors' foreheads were creased with perplexed disapproval.

Barrett glanced at Ashford, saw veins standing out in his neck, his face crimson with rage, trying to get Babcock to look at him. Menghetti continued to affect calm in the face of the storm and addressed the court as casually as if asking for an exhibit. "Request permission to treat the witness as hostile, Your Honor."

Field started to rise, but the judge motioned him back down. "Granted," he said in a firm voice.

Menghetti walked over to counsel table, snatched up a document, and charged to within three feet of the witness. Not just his expression but his very features seemed to have changed. It was as if that one word from the judge had opened the door to some inner cage, freeing the beast within. His eyes burned into hers until she had to look away. Then his upper lip curled into a menacing snarl as he confronted her with the sworn statement Leviticus Heywood had taken from her.

"Is that or is that not your signature, Ms. Babcock?" he growled.

"Yes, that's my signature," said the witness, more nervous now and running a hand over her hair as if afraid it would take flight. "And I was well paid to give it, as you know, sir, but it wasn't under oath. Now I'm under oath."

"Move to strike everything after the word 'signature,' Your Honor."

"Granted," said Judge Hernandez, maintaining his judicial calm, but with obvious effort.

"You are indeed under oath, Ms. Babcock, and perjury is punishable by—"

"Argumentative, Your Honor," said Grace.

"Sustained," said the judge, eyes fixed on the witness. "Let's get to it, counsel."

Menghetti took three steps toward Renee Babcock. "Did you lie when you gave this statement to Mr. Heywood?"

"Of course I did, and Elliot told me you knew all about the arrangement—"

"Objection," said Menghetti, "and again, I move to strike everything after her admission of deceit."

At the end of counsel table, Dickson fidgeted in his chair, suddenly realizing his hands were clenched into fists.

"Granted," snapped Hernandez, obviously frustrated by what was unfolding in his courtroom—the ship hitting an iceberg on his watch. He knew the press fed on disasters like this. "Just answer the questions, Ms. Babcock."

"What were you promised by Mr. Field to change your story, Ms. Babcock?"

"Nothin'."

"Did the district attorney's office threaten you in any way?"

"Well, yes, in a way."

Menghetti smiled. "Tell the jury what they threatened you with."

The smile was short-lived. "Ms. Harris told me the same as what you just did: that lyin' in court is a crime. Look, mister, I don't think Elliot did it, if that helps you any. Hell, I wouldn't have done what you wanted me to do if I'd thought he was guilty. And God knows I could use the money."

In the ensuing silence, Barrett resisted the urge to glance at the jury. He didn't have to. The woman was the perfect destroyer: ostensibly open, unpretentious, and eminently plausible.

"I see," said Menghetti, affecting an amused curiosity, as if he were assessing the credibility of a talking-dog act. But Barrett knew this dog had Menghetti by the throat. Trial lawyers have to play the hand they are dealt, but if Menghetti had inspected this deck more carefully, he would have seen that the seal was broken.

And now the game was over, just when victory seemed certain.

He glanced over at the prosecution table and saw Grace Harris staring at Renee through moist eyes, an incipient smile softening her face. Field was looking at the witness too, but he appeared anything but pleased, which confused Barrett even more. He was beginning to feel like Alice in Wonderland.

Then he glanced back at Menghetti, and for the first time felt sympathy, as well as respect, for his embattled co-counsel. Babcock was that one-witness-too-many who could cause a lawyer to snatch defeat from the jaws of victory. Menghetti's only hope now was to discredit Babcock before turning her over to Field for a "cross-examination" that would be little more than a perfectly rendered duet.

But Menghetti had an even more serious and highly personal problem, for Babcock's implication had been too clear to ignore.

"Are you suggesting that *I* offered you money to lie, Ms. Babcock?"

"No sir. All's I know is that Elliot said that as far as you were concerned, nobody offered anything to anybody, and there was no way you wanted to be involved in it."

Menghetti looked pointedly at the clock, and though it was ten minutes before time for the afternoon recess, Judge Hernandez took the hint and granted that which the defense lawyer knew would be the last compassionate gesture he could expect.

"We'll stand in recess until tomorrow morning, ladies and gentlemen," he said, and by the time he had given the jury the usual admonitions, the reporters had hit the hallway, cell phones clicking.

Barrett could see the headlines in the morning papers:

Mystery Witness Accuses Defense Counsel in Bizarre Bribery Attempt

Although Barrett would escape direct complicity in the claimed subornation of perjury—thanks, ironically, to his known role as a useless supernumerary in the case—the publicity would kill him at Caldwell & Shaw. Worse, some good people would go down with him: not just Mike Reasoner and old Winston Cray, but many loyal secretaries and associates, possibly even the firm itself without Mike in a governing role. No telling how far this forest would burn now that a match had been set to it.

"I'll see counsel in chambers in fifteen minutes," said John Hernandez, and, with a withering look at Barrett, angrily strode from the bench.

Barrett glanced at Al Menghetti, who sat, head down, eyes closed, arms folded around himself. Gone was the cocky arrogance now, his imperious mien. Barrett tentatively raised a hand, then let it come to rest gently on Menghetti's shoulder. Barrett thought he saw a flutter of the eyelids, but that was all.

27

Elliot Ashford was irritatingly calm just minutes later as he followed Menghetti and Dickson into the holding cell. Barrett stopped just inside the door and rinsed his face with cold water from the small basin. This was between the two of them, he thought. He had been wounded, but Menghetti had been ruined, and it was fitting that he be allowed the first blow.

But Ashford leapt to the offensive. "Okay," he said, "so it backfired. It was stupid of me to trust her."

The muscle working in Menghetti's jaw as Ashford spoke looked like it was about to break through his skin.

"But what I did was perfectly legitimate," continued the defendant. "I simply substituted a false-alibi witness for the real one, who wasn't available. I certainly intended no—"

"Shut up, you fucking imbecile!" Menghetti shouted, his voice seared with mingled anger and despair. "You think this is some goddamn theatrical performance? 'The role of Tony Rizzo will be performed tonight by Renee Babcock'? I almost wish I could be here to see your face when the jury comes in. You'll get the needle for this, you supercilious prick."

Ashford's dark eyes reflected a hint of fear Barrett had not seen before. "Come now, old man," Ashford said, managing a tone both conciliatory and resolute. "Slow down a minute. Perhaps it was an asinine—"

"Asinine?"

"All right. It was stupid of me to—"

Veins popped from Menghetti's neck, and Ashford backed a step away. Barrett moved closer to them, for Menghetti looked like he was ready to ram his clenched fist into Ashford's face.

"You don't need to admit you're stupid, Ashford," Menghetti hissed. "That's now a matter of record. What I want to know is why you set *me* up? Why you told her to say I knew what was going on?"

Menghetti's face had become incandescent, and Ashford's own expression darkened with anger. If it came to blows, Barrett decided, he would just let it happen.

"Watch yourself, sport," said Ashford. "You're getting out of line now. Renee did that on her own. *You* pushed her into that remark. She was probably trying to say you weren't involved and just became confused. She was just a frightened airhead who obviously needs a lesson in loyalty."

Menghetti spun on one heel as if he had been struck, then sat down on one of the built-in prisoner benches, his face buried in his hands. "Oh dear God," he whispered.

"I'll be watching for that lesson," interceded Barrett, his voice steel-edged, "and I won't forget what you just said."

"Your lips are sealed, Dickson. You're a lawyer, remember?"

"I won't be when I blow the whistle on you," said Barrett, advancing on his client but keeping both hands in his pockets. "I'll make it simple for you, Ashford. If anything ever happens to Renee Babcock, I'll personally do the same thing to you, only I'll do it slower."

Ashford met Barrett's gaze, eyes darting, working on what to say next. Then Menghetti raised his head and looked at both of them as if he had forgotten they were there.

"Dickson," he said, slowly rising to his feet, "I want you to witness what I'm about to say."

Barrett nodded, but before Menghetti could speak, Ashford took a step toward him, then reached up and flicked some lint off the stocky lawyer's lapel and whispered, "Come now, old boy. You're supposed to be my lawyer here."

The discipline that had allowed Menghetti to contain his frustration for weeks had all but collapsed. He stepped back, took a deep breath of air, and let it out into his clasped hands as if trying to warm them.

"Try to understand this, Ashford," he said at last. "I will soon no longer be your lawyer. When the state bar finishes with me, I may not even be a lawyer at all. The judge will grant a delay so you can seek out your next victim."

"Now wait just a minute—"

"Shut up and listen!" said Menghetti through clenched teeth. "We're going into chambers soon with the court reporter. I'm going to withdraw as counsel of record and you're going to let me."

Ashford laughed derisively. "Why would I cut my own throat like that?"

Menghetti glanced over his shoulder at a sheriff's deputy, then put his mouth close to Ashford's ear. "Because, *old chum,*" he whispered, his lips drawn tight, his face an ashen mask, "if you leave me in control of your case, I guarantee complete and total failure."

Ashford started to interrupt again, but Menghetti raised a beefy hand and continued: "Then, in the fullness of time, following numerous appellate failures, I will personally walk you to the death chamber. Once there, I will strap you down onto the table. Then I, and I alone, will *push the fucking needle straight into your blue fucking bloodstream!*"

Menghetti then turned and glanced at Barrett. "Lots of luck, Dickson," he said, then straightened his shoulders and strode from the room. "I'll be waiting outside."

Ashford turned to Barrett and raised his hands, palms up in supplication. He smiled thinly and said, "Jesus, what's with Al?"

Barrett stared at the defendant in amazement. *"What's with Al?"*

"You heard me, you stupid ass. Go get him and bring him back in—"

That's as far as he got before Barrett's left hand lashed out and nailed the client squarely on his chin. His right hand was poised for a knockout when the bailiff interceded.

Struggling for self-control, Barrett said, "Al Menghetti just lost a career that took twenty years to build because of you! He's also just fired what might be the last client he'll ever have! And you have the fucking nerve to—"

"Menghetti can't do this to me," said Ashford, slumping on the bench and holding his jaw.

"Oh yes he can, Ashford," said Barrett, shaking out of the bailiff's grasp and heading for the door, "and so can I!"

*   *   *

Barrett grabbed a phone in the hallway and dialed Mike Reasoner. Though his hand was bruised, it was his heart that throbbed with the pain of crushed expectations.

Mike silently digested the news about Renee Babcock's defection and Al Menghetti's exit.

"I'm sorry, Mike," said Barrett, "but I'm out of it too. Ashford may or may not let Menghetti out, but I know he'll fire me."

"Why?"

"His jaw just ran into my fist. Thought you should know."

A long silence followed. Barrett arched his back to ease the pain at his fifth lumbar. He could hear Mike unwrapping a stick of gum.

"Barrett Dickson," Mike said at length, "commission real estate salesman."

"I'll get by. It's you and the firm I'm sorry about, Mike."

"You did your best, partner. I appreciate it."

Barrett hung up and returned to the door leading out of the holding cell from which his client would soon emerge.

You did your best. Mike's words echoed in his head, mocking him.

That was my best?

John Hernandez issued an uncharacteristic growl as he slammed his evidence code on the desk in front of him. "Okay, the record will show all counsel and the defendant are present. Now what the hell is going on here?"

"A search for truth," said Earl Field with a hard look at Al Menghetti, "at least from our side. It seems clear, Your Honor, that Ms. Babcock was offered $50,000 to perjure herself and that Mr. Menghetti knew enough about the arrangement not to want to know more."

"Mr. Menghetti?" said Judge Hernandez.

Menghetti glared at Field and, through clenched teeth, asked that the court reporter be called in.

The judge nodded to the bailiff. "May I ask what you have in mind, counsel?"

"I intend to move my withdrawal as counsel for Mr. Ashford. My client will put his consent on the record, and we will promptly file the appropriate docu—"

"Hold on, Mr. Menghetti," said John Hernandez. "This

isn't Red China. You're presumed innocent of any wrong-doing in this matter until proven otherwise."

"Your confidence is appreciated, Your Honor, but my request stands."

The judge turned to the defendant. "Mr. Ashford? I take it you will oppose Mr. Menghetti's withdrawal?"

Elliot Ashford rose to his feet and, to the judge's and the prosecutors' astonishment, calmly consented to the withdrawal. Barrett could see that John Hernandez was not only surprised but angered. The best and brightest judge on the San Francisco Superior Court was losing control of his case.

"I urge you to reconsider your decision, Mr. Ashford," he said.

"I will not reconsider," said Ashford. "With all due respect, Your Honor, my decision is irrevocable, and I request a two-month continuance for the purpose of obtaining new counsel."

Barrett had never seen the judge so coldly irate. "With equal respect, Mr. Ashford, I deny your request. You still have adequate counsel, sir." He turned to Barrett and added, "Trial will resume tomorrow. I understand you have but two more witnesses—"

"Your Honor," said Ashford, "Mr. Dickson is in the case strictly as . . . a backup."

"Whatever your initial motivation for bringing in Mr. Dickson," said John Hernandez with a knowing glare, "he is an experienced senior trial lawyer thoroughly conversant with the record in this case. You are in capable hands."

"I know just how capable his hands can be, Judge," sneered Ashford, holding his jaw. "He just used them to physically assault me. That's why I've fired him and intend to sue him as well as soon as I can find a real lawyer to represent me."

"Do what you will, Mr. Ashford," said John Hernandez, rising to signal that the conference had ended, "but this trial will resume tomorrow morning."

28

Later that night, Barrett sat silently with Leviticus Heywood in the investigator's office, reflecting on how Julian Gold of all people had convinced Ashford that his long-term interests would be best served by un-firing his only remaining lawyer.

Lev gave him a sideways, quizzical look. "I've been wonderin', Bear. How'd he talk Ashford into keepin' you on?"

"I don't want to know."

"Move to the point, how did he talk *you* into keepin' on?"

"*You* don't want to know."

"I guess it was this sort of openness and communication," said Lev, glowering at his obdurate coffeemaker and giving it a loud whack on one side, "that built Western civilization into what it is today."

"Probably," said Barrett as he bent over and plugged in the coffeemaker. "If you want to know, it was a combination of Gold's inspired art of persuasion and John's threat of thirty days in the pokey for contempt if I didn't say yes."

Lev grunted with satisfaction as the coffeemaker began gasping. "It wasn't either of those things."

Barrett looked out the window. "A sage in our midst."

Lev nodded his head. "Believe it. So how do you feel bein' back on the high wire all by your lonesome?"

"I'm okay. My last two witnesses are wind-up: Shannon Lake, Lara's sister, and Menghetti's DNA guy. I just stay out of their way, hold up cue cards, and keep them talking long enough to dull the edge of Babcock's little bombshell."

"You mean like until hell freezes over?"

"Yeah, about that long. On the other hand, besides watching us shoot ourselves in the foot, the prosecution

hasn't done a hell of a lot and Shannon is going to be great
for us."

"What about having Ashford get up and rebut Babcock's testimony?"

"He wants to, but Gold won't let him take the stand.
Gold figures if the jury doesn't hear about his prior assault
felony and shady contacts, we've still got a hung jury even
with Babcock. They'll settle for that. I'm just praying the
prosecution doesn't put on any rebuttal."

"Because then you'd have to cross-examine somebody?"

Barrett nodded, feeling his pulse quicken at the thought
of it.

Lev laughed. "Look, mom, no net," he said. "Relax,
Bear, how they gonna find another witness this late date?"

Armand "the Weasel" Ligretti was called the Weasel long
before he became a turncoat ex-Mafia soldier, ratting on his
friends. He was called the Weasel quite simply because he
looked and fought like one. Short, thin-shouldered, and
quick, he had once chewed through a rival mobster's jugular after taking two bullets in the chest. Ligretti was a survi-
vor, a convicted hit man who had been granted immunity
from prosecution for that murder and three others on the
East Coast. He had also been given a new identity in the
federal government's witness protection program. Instead
of the gas chamber, the Weasel had elected to live like an
exiled king in federally protected seclusion not even the
Organization could penetrate, occasionally popping out of
his disguise just long enough to pay for his keep by testifying when needed. Armand Ligretti had been a professional murderer. Now he was a professional rat.

He was also Grace Harris's last hope to turn the jury
around. Renee Babcock had been a godsend to the prosecution to be sure, Grace thought, an unexpected windfall.
But a defense witness that backfires rarely satisfies the
state's affirmative burden of proof, and Grace knew they
would have to do more if they were to win all twelve jurors
needed for a conviction.

Her interest in the Weasel began when Sam picked up a
street rumor that Ligretti had attended one or more meetings at which Carmine Rizzo and Elliot Ashford had been
present. The information had raised interesting questions.

Was this just a routine business meeting? Not likely, if a thug like Armand Ligretti was there. And hadn't he already testified *against* the Mafia in a Florida federal court a year or so before? So why would Carmine Rizzo be meeting with him? Was Ligretti involved in some undercover scheme? And if Elliot Ashford wasn't Mafia, what was *he* doing there in the company of a former hit man and the godfather of the Chicago mob? That interested her the most.

On a hunch, Grace called a classmate in the justice department who agreed to forward Grace's work and home telephone numbers to Ligretti's secret location through the Marshal's Service.

It was a long shot, but she had other questions that only he could answer. First, of course, whether the rumor was even true. If it was, might Ashford have mentioned something at one of the meetings that would allow her to establish Ashford's involvement with the Mafia? Grace knew that if she could taint Ashford's reputation as a beneficent ex-public servant by putting him in the company of sinister men like Ligretti and the Rizzos, the jury would begin to see all the evidence in a different light. She knew that jurors see cases as stories, not as disjointed pieces of fact and evidence the way lawyers do. Show them a hero on one side and a villain on the other, and jurors will not only connect the dots in a way that justifies their view of the story, they'll flatly ignore evidence inconsistent with that view.

The classmate said he'd look into it, but Grace frowned as she hung up the phone. Even if Ligretti did have something relevant to say, would the jury believe an acknowledged assassin who had sold his friends down the river to avoid going there himself? And how would *she* be viewed by the jury, vouching for a Mafia rat, a man living off his treachery? As an experienced trial lawyer, Grace also knew that the advocate's most valuable asset was the jury's trust, an asset easily tarnished under their rigid scrutiny.

And even if she could surmount these hurdles, would Ligretti be willing to come out of hiding and testify? Would he even call her back?

All questions, no answers.

*   *   *

Meanwhile, in Lev's tiny office on Market Street, Barrett sat across from Shannon Lake, Lara Ashford's unmarried sister, and took in her handsome features and well-toned body. Her hair was black, cut short with bangs; a twenties look. Her eyes were green and catlike, the kind Barrett imagined one could see in the dark. She was larger than her sister, nearly as tall as Lev in high heels, but well proportioned and possessed of her own unique attractiveness.

"Tell me a little bit about Elliot Ashford," he began as Lev handed her a cup of coffee.

"What can I tell you that you don't already know?" she said. "He's highly intelligent, of course, and quite wealthy. He has been exceedingly thoughtful to Lara and me, particularly since our parents died. He is a good and decent man."

Barrett restrained a smile and nodded encouragement. She sipped her coffee, then put it down in a way that suggested she would not be picking it up again.

"He has enemies, as you also know, I'm sure," she continued. "One of them is prosecuting him at the moment."

"Political enemies."

"Mr. Field is more than just a political enemy, Mr. Dickson. He's a filthy little bastard who made a pass at Lara not long before she died." She paused, then in a throaty whisper added, "It turned into more than a pass."

"How much more?" said Barrett. "Did it go anywhere?"

"I don't know."

"And you think Ashford found out about whatever it was that might have happened between them?"

"Of course he knew."

"So you do know that something happened between them?"

Shannon shot him a warning look of barely restrained acrimony. This, thought Barrett, is a formidable woman.

"Grace Harris is a good lawyer," he said. "I'm just giving you a taste of what to expect."

"Okay, I think she slept with him. Everybody thinks so."

"Lara was not a discreet person?"

Shannon laughed—a surprising outburst, more like a man's laugh—then removed a cigarette from a gold monogrammed case and slipped it between her lips.

Barrett and Lev, momentarily mesmerized by Shannon's

hard beauty, suddenly reacted and began patting their pockets as if putting out a fire instead of trying to light one.

"My sister's indiscretion," she said, accepting a light from Barrett, "was one of the better parts of Elliot's valor. Don't you gentlemen read the papers?"

Shannon Lake radiated a quality of latent power, thought Barrett, as he observed her eyes glowing behind a spiral of smoke. Physical power. She and her sister might not even have been taken as sisters when standing together, for Shannon's was not a fragile beauty like Lara's, nor had she the freedom of spirit that was said to have been reflected in Lara's eyes. There was even something vaguely menacing about her, thought Barrett, as he continued to silently regard her. Still, her face would present sufficient similarities to Lara's morgue shots to evoke the victim's presence in the minds of the jury.

The victim. Barrett closed his eyes tight for a moment, trying to escape the cold description hot-wired into his brain.

Case number 97-5597 . . . a forty-four-year-old Caucasian female with brown eyes and black hair, 64 inches in length and weighing 108 pounds . . .

Yes, he thought, though a larger woman, Shannon would be seen by the jury as Lara, risen from the dead to declare that the petty quarrels she and Elliot had were nothing weighed against their love for one another. Having the victim's own sister take the stand in Ashford's behalf would be dynamite.

Barrett walked over to the window to close out the distracting night sounds of Market Street's beggars, healers, boozers, and dealers: a cacophony of car horns, jackhammers, guitars, a solo saxophone playing a nearly unrecognizable version of "Eleanor Rigby," and a never-ending chorus of dissonant street voices. Lev now sat quietly in a chair next to Shannon, and Barrett realized that both were looking expectantly at him.

"You seem to have a great deal of . . . admiration for Mr. Ashford," said Barrett.

"People misunderstand Elliot," she replied in her

clipped, pedantic tone. "They focus on his negative aspects, dismissing his many fine qualities."

"And I take it," said Barrett, "that loving his wife was one of those qualities?"

Shannon paused, crossed her long legs, crinkled her high forehead, and put a finger to her lips.

"He was incredibly patient," she said at last, "an indispensable quality in anyone involved with my sister."

Barrett glanced at Lev.

"Do you think he loved Lara?"

"Love?" she said, offering them a wry smile. "Elliot is a born politician. Politicians love everybody and nobody."

"Okay," said Barrett, "how about 'like'? Did they get along?"

Shannon turned serious. "I will say they did."

"Did they?"

"Their relationship was symbiotic, quite unique. I am quite prepared to declare that it was . . . thoroughly amicable."

"Amicable," said Barrett.

"You won't be disappointed, Mr. Dickson. I'll do what is necessary."

Barrett stared at her for a moment, then closed his notepad. "We'll keep it brief on direct, Ms. Lake," he said, "but on cross, you'll be asked about the rumors that—"

"And I'll categorically deny them," she said stiffly. "Elliot and I are just friends. I should have sued those gossip-mongering magazines."

"Have you seen Mr. Ashford socially since your sister's death?"

Shannon Lake hesitated a beat, then said, "We've dined together a few times."

"Where?"

Another beat. "At his house."

"Anybody else around on these occasions?"

"Do you mean are there any witnesses to our virtuous comportment?"

"Yes, or the lack of it."

"No," said Shannon, her cat's-eyes narrowing. "No witnesses."

"Did the two of you take any trips together while your sister was still living?"

Shannon paused. "You have nothing to worry about, Mr. Dickson."

So it's true, thought Barrett. Shannon Lake was scorching Ashford's sheets before her sister's body was cold.

"Any gifts? Jewelry? Clothing?"

"He is a generous man, but for our purposes, the answer is no."

Barrett nodded. "I'd better let you get some sleep," he said. "I'll put you on first thing at eight-thirty. Okay?"

Shannon nodded and rose to leave. He watched her pick up her purse, then hesitate as if she needed something more from him. He had often seen this in witnesses who were looking for a level of reassurance neither he nor anyone else could supply them. Especially those who would be skirting the edge of truth.

"I'll pick you up at seven-thirty, Ms. Lake," said Lev, and Barrett walked her downstairs, where a car was waiting for her.

"We'll visit again around eight o'clock," said Barrett. "Thanks for coming in."

"I am glad to be of use," she said, then raised the window as the car sped off down Market.

You're willing to be used is what you mean, thought Barrett, then stood there for a while, listening to the sax man near the door of Lev's building.

"Can you play 'Stardust'?" he said. The big, bearded guy nodded, then flashed a harmonica smile as Barrett peeled off a couple of dollars and walked back upstairs.

"She'll be okay," said Lev when Barrett hit the top of the stairs.

"Sure she will," said Barrett, "as long as it doesn't come out that she hated her sister as much as she loved her brother-in-law."

"You're not thinkin'—"

Barrett shook his head. "I'm a lawyer, not a cop. My job is to get our client off, Lev, not solve his wife's murder. Let's get back to work."

Grace watched helplessly the next morning as the jurors seemed mesmerized by the halting testimony of the tall, dark-clad sister of the victim. Some were moved to tears by her portrayal of the loving marriage, Elliot's devotion to his beloved Lara, and his despondency over her death. Earl had decided to cross-examine her, and got nowhere.

Later that night, as Grace prepared to cross-examine Barrett's DNA expert, she prayed that she would hear from Armand Ligretti. It had been over twenty-four hours now, and Barrett had indicated he would be finished with his case in a day or two. As it now stood, the People would have no rebuttal case but for another sleep-inducing DNA expert.

Her hopes of hearing from Ligretti fading, Grace was falling into a fitful sleep when the phone rang a few minutes after midnight. A voice like sandpaper came through the receiver.

"You wanted to talk to me, lady?"

He didn't offer his name and she didn't have to ask. She sprung into a seated position on the edge of her bed and kept Ligretti talking while she cleared her head. He seemed at ease on the phone and readily answered all her questions. Sure, he had attended a meeting at which both Carmine Rizzo and Elliot Ashford had been present.

"Was the meeting before or after his wife's death?" she asked, fumbling for a ballpoint pen on her beside table. Her elbow hit a lampshade. She found a notepad.

"Both. Two meetings."

"What was the purpose of the meetings?"

"I've been told that wasn't stuff you needed to know about, okay? The U.S. Attorney's got the clamps on."

"Okay. Did Ashford m-mention his wife at either meeting?"

"Nope."

"Say he was unhappy? Mention getting divorced?"

"Nope."

Her head fell back on a pillow. "Did Senator Dwight Clifton's name come up?"

"Nope."

"Was Carmine Rizzo at both meetings?"

"Sure."

Grace stood up, put a hand to her head, tried to collect herself. "Are you sure Ashford never mentioned his wife?" Grace knew the judge would not allow evidence of Ashford's association with Mafia figures unless she could tie it into evidence relevant to the murder charge. "Even after her murder?"

"No. Just indirectly, in the second meeting."

"What do you mean 'indirectly'?"

Ligretti's answer to the question sent an icy vibration up her spine.

"Ashford had this girl with him; a regular knockout, you know, a superfox? Carmine had a little party after the meeting in his suite and she's there with Ashford. After a coupla drinks, I hear him introduce the fox to Tony Rizzo as 'the next Mrs. Ashford.' "

Grace asked, "When you say 'him,' who are you r-referring to?" She held her breath.

"I'm talkin' about Elliot Ashford."

"So this would be soon after his w-wife was—"

"Are you the prosecutor on this case, miss? Have I got the right person here?"

Grace realized she was stammering badly. She took in a breath of air and slowly let it out. "Yes, I'm one of the prosecutors."

Ligretti paused and she was afraid he was going to change his mind. Then she heard a match strike and knew he was just lighting up. "Okay. Sure, it's right after she's been killed. Even I thought it was uncool."

"What was Mr. Ashford's general demeanor? What was his mood?"

"Happy as a pig in shit. Some white-shoe had just got him sprung on bail, so he was on cloud nine. Who could blame him; you shoulda seen the babe!"

My God, she thought. *The missing motive!*

"Did he mention the woman's name?"

"Yeah, two or three times."

"Do you remember it?"

"Not really. That's not the kind of thing I was told to listen for. I think it was Sophia? Sophie, maybe? Something like that."

Her mind was spinning with new hope. If Ligretti would testify, and if he held up . . .

Grace was waiting in Earl Field's office the next morning when he arrived at seven-thirty. He looked surprised to see her.

"Ah," he said, a raised brow over a pair of wary eyes, "Grace, the proverbial early bird."

"You too," she said. "Judy said I could wait for you in here."

He rubbed his hands together, asked Judy for some coffee, then sat down behind his desk and said, "What can I do for you?"

She recognized Earl's cold way of saying "Make it quick," but she wouldn't allow herself to be hurried. It was, after all, the first time they had been alone together for several days. Whenever she showed up for a meeting lately, there was always someone in the room with them, usually Jack Klegg with his close-set, steely little eyes, sitting there silently stroking his burr cut.

"I think we've got something, Earl," Grace said at last, then told him what she had learned. She watched his swollen eyes alternately widen with surprise, narrow with suspicion, then finally harden with barely suppressed irritation by the time she was finished. She also noticed he looked uncharacteristically disheveled. His tie was askew and he needed a haircut.

"Using a rat at the last minute?" he said, shaking his head. "Uh-uh. No way. You should have told me you were considering this, Grace."

"I didn't think there was much hope it would work out. Now it has. Besides, you've been pretty inaccessible since our . . ."

"Recent unpleasantness?" he said, relaxing his face into a sardonic smile.

Grace smiled back, playing the game, then playing her hand. "Earl, look, I don't know what to think. That bail hearing setup by Klegg, the *L.A. Eye* reporter, the missing fingernail evidence—I guess it's all making me a little crazy. But maybe we can still win this thing. Let's give Ligretti a try."

"Forget about it, Grace. I've heard of him. It's too risky. He's got a rap sheet as big as your ambition."

"That was below the belt, Earl."

"Sorry, I meant it as a compliment."

"I'm not here for compliments, or veiled insults either."

"Why are you here, Grace?"

"To try to convince you that we have no choice now but

to take risks! Ligretti can link Ashford to the mob *and* provide the missing motive. It's the bottom of the ninth, Earl, and this may be the home run that could still give us the game."

Field shook his head again, more rapidly this time. "It could be Casey at the bat, too. It's way too dangerous."

"Compared with *what*?" she replied. "Have you watched those jurors? They ate up Shannon Lake and they've tuned us out again. Babcock started the pendulum swinging our way, but now the jury looks like Stonehenge."

"Come off it, Grace. Babcock killed them."

Grace told herself to be patient. "She was terrific, Earl, and bought us insurance against losing. But if we're going to lock up all twelve of them and *win,* we've got to give them a stronger motive. Ligretti can give it to them."

"The feds would never let him testify."

"I spoke with the Marshal's Service in D.C. this morning," said Grace, her voice quiet now. "They're bringing him in."

Field's head snapped up. "Next time you get one of these bright ideas, Grace, please talk to me first before calling the goddamn nation's capital."

Grace started to say something, but he wasn't finished.

"Call 'em off, damn it! We'll go with the odds. You made some good points with their DNA guy, and with Menghetti out of the picture, we'll kill them in final argument."

Grace stood up. She stared down at the D.A.'s luminous black skin, shining in the eerie glow of the single desk lamp, and noticed an uncharacteristic stubble of a beard on his face. Who are you, she wanted to say, and what have you done with my boss?

When she did speak, her voice was trembling, but her words were carefully measured.

"They won't l-let us win, will they, Earl."

It was not a question.

Field didn't flinch; not a muscle moved in his drawn face. "Don't be ridiculous," he said.

Grace held his eyes. "I'm putting Ligretti on the stand tomorrow morning, Earl," she said. "Don't try to stop me."

Then she walked out.

*   *   *

A minute later, a telephone broke the silence in the bedroom of a Nob Hill condominium. A woman snorted and rolled over. Her husband reached for the phone, then spoke in a voice as crisp as someone who had been awake for hours.

"Speak."

The man then propped himself on one elbow as he listened for two minutes without interrupting. Then he swung his legs onto the floor and grabbed a pen and paper. He scribbled a name.

Then he said, "Calm down, Earl, I'll fix it," and hung up.

"Who was that, Jack?"

"Go back to sleep."

Barrett's heart soared an hour later when he heard Grace's voice on the telephone.

"How are you, Barrett?" she asked, giving his stomach a double clutch as his hopes shifted into high gear. Could she possibly be calling to . . . ? No. Not a chance. Grace Harris was all business and he was the enemy. So she was calling to plea-bargain; to spare him the bitter cup of another day with Elliot Ashford. Either way, her voice came at his arid brain like cool water.

"I couldn't be better," he said. "And you?"

"I could always be better," she said.

"I doubt it," he said, trying to strike an ambiguous tone somewhere between cordiality and bald flirtation.

Then she popped the balloon. It was neither of those things; it was the worst possible thing. They had come up with a rebuttal witness and she was putting Barrett on notice as required. He told her thanks and she was gone.

He quickly dialed Lev's office.

"Armand Ligretti?" said Lev, his voice sounding incredulous through the phone. "The rat who testified in Florida?"

"Yeah, that rat," said Barrett. "I need something to work with."

"When's he going on?"

"Tomorrow."

" 'Fraid I can't help you, Bear."

"What?"

"This dude is deep in the witness protection program,

which means *nobody* knows where he is now, and *nobody* can find him, not even the mob."

"You're kidding."

"Not. If the mob knew who he was or what he looks like now and where to find him—we wouldn't be needin' this conversation."

29

D amn it, Jack," said Earl Field the next morning as he
closed the door to his office. "You told me you could
fix this!"

Jack Klegg sat in front of Field's desk. He gazed up at
the ceiling of Field's office and sighed deeply. Jack Klegg
was equally unhappy. The only thing he hated worse than
failing was to be reminded of it.

"I did all I could," he said through tightened lips. "The
fucking Justice Department *wants* Ligretti to testify. They
think it's a *wonderful* idea."

"Now that John Gotti's down," said Field, his fists
clenched on the desk in front of him, "they've probably
targeted Chicago, which means Carmine Rizzo. Nailing
Ashford will be the first shot across Rizzo's bow."

"Bingo."

"Bingo? That's not funny, Jack. If Ligretti nails Ashford,
the mob nails me."

Klegg managed to look contrite. "I said I tried, Earl,
but it's not the end of the world. Just put Ligretti on the
stand yourself."

"Me?"

"Damage control. Minimize his impact."

"Damage control is your specialty, Jack, and you're not
doing a very good job of it."

"The guy's a slug," said Klegg, ignoring the gibe. "Just
make sure it shows."

Field disliked Klegg's imperious tone even more than his
idea. He also didn't like the way the chief assistant kept
looking at him. "Is there something else on your mind,
Jack?"

"Earl," said Klegg at last, "pardon me for saying so, but
you're looking a bit . . . careless lately."

"Careless? What the hell are you talking about?"

"For one thing, you're not a drinking man and you're starting to drink."

"An occasional glass of wine. For God's sake, Jack—"

"I can smell vodka on a man's breath from three feet, so don't think others can't. In addition, your famed haute couture has become casual to the point of shabbiness."

"Christ, Jack, are you a prosecutor or a fucking style consultant?"

"I'm the best friend you have trying to save your political black ass. Have you forgotten that you're being watched every waking minute by the national press?"

Field started to say something, but gave a short nod of his head.

"I know what's eating you, Earl. Just don't let it show. And button down your button-down collar for Christ's sake!"

Grace Harris was pleasantly surprised when Earl Field entered her office ten minutes later to reverse himself regarding Ligretti, but her smile faded when he added, "I'll put him on myself, Grace."

"But—"

"The guy's dangerous, and if he blows up in our face, I've got to absorb the blast."

Grace stiffened. "I thought blast absorption was my role on this team."

"You've done your share, plus you're still cross-examining the defense DNA expert. Dickson's resting his case as soon as you finish and we've got to be ready. I'll meet with Ligretti and the U.S. marshal tonight and put him on myself soon as you're finished."

Grace's thoughts swirled with confused frustration.

"It's your call, of course," she said, reluctantly pulling a thin file out of a pyramid of paper on her desk.

"Yes," he said, holding out his hand. "It's my call."

"Well, his rap sheet is in here—which is probably all Dickson will have—and my outline of questions. I was about to have Sam check out the details of his story, but frankly, there's not a whole lot of time."

"Nobody is more aware of that than I," he said, shooting her a hard look as he snatched the file out of her hand.

*   *   *

When court resumed at nine-thirty, juror number ten, a
young African-American male, was reported hospitalized
with pneumonia. Amanda Keller saw looks of distrust and
apprehension among the regular jurors, already concerned
about the mysterious and still unexplained disappearance
three days earlier of juror number four, the Latino cab-
driver. Both the Latino and number ten had become nearly
as outspoken as Martin Chin had been weeks earlier regarding the guilt of the defendant, particularly after the
Babcock debacle. These forthright comments had temporarily allayed Amanda's fears of a conspiracy against Earl
Field, but the sudden departure of two pro-prosecution jurors now reawakened them.

"Barney Seagrave said maybe Ashford's 'friends' are
sending us a message," Ruth had whispered to Amanda on
the way to the courtroom that morning, then had blushed
with embarrassment.

Amanda tried to look at the positive side of the equation.
First, there was still Jefferson, the jury's obvious leader,
who seemed too hardheaded to be bought or coerced. Second, with these rumors swirling, perhaps the other regulars
who had not already joined the conspiracy would finally
see what kind of man Ashford really was. Last, but far from
least: Amanda was now in the number one alternate seat.

Perhaps there was hope after all, both for Earl and for
herself.

"Does the defense rest, Mr. Dickson?"

"Yes, Your Honor."

"You may call your first rebuttal witness, Mr. Field," said
John Hernandez.

"Yes, Your Honor," said Field. "Call Armand Ligretti."

A gasp went up from the press section, now swelled by
knowledgeable reporters from the *New York Times,* the
Washington Post, and the *Atlanta Constitution.* A minute
later, all eyes were upon the little Mafia soldier as he
walked up the aisle, glancing from side to side through
small, darting eyes, set deep above pitted cheeks and a
rodent nose. Few people noticed the two plain-clothed mar-
shals, one entering casually in front of the Weasel, the
other trailing behind.

Amanda noticed, and wondered what was going on. As

usual, she was also studying Earl Field, who appeared worried. Although he looked more heroic than ever in his fatigue, Earl had lost the cool, dapper look he was so famous for. His mustache was untrimmed and ragged-looking, his suit appeared slept-in, and the confident swagger had been reduced to a shuffle. They were breaking him down, the bastards.

Still, she was relieved to see that he was going to handle the state's last rebuttal witness and prayed he would do something dramatic; something that would shame the uncommitted regular jurors into doing the right thing.

Field went straight to Ligretti's negatives, exposing the Weasel's sordid background in such detail and with such fervor as to make Ligretti redden with anger within minutes.

"You cut a deal with the Justice Department two years ago, is that correct, Mr. Ligretti?"

Ligretti nodded.

"You'll have to speak up, Mr. Ligretti," said Field in a harsh tone that seemed to distance him from the witness.

Amanda noticed that Grace Harris's head snapped up at the district attorney's uncharacteristic gruffness.

"Yeah."

"You were accused of killing people for money? An assassin capable of cold-blooded murder?"

"That's right."

"You were known as the Weasel because of your violent nature?"

Ligretti's features involuntarily transformed themselves into an expression that more than answered Field's question.

"Friends sometimes called me that," he hissed through clenched teeth.

From her seat in the jury box, Amanda began to wonder whether Earl Field had called a hostile witness by mistake. She saw Ligretti glance at Grace Harris from time to time, but the assistant D.A. just glared down at her yellow pad and scribbled.

Amanda was relieved when Field moved into the substance of Ligretti's testimony: tying Elliot Ashford to Tony Rizzo, then into two meetings with mob leaders—including

Carmine Rizzo and one of his top Mafia chieftains—held in Las Vegas and San Francisco.

"Were you in the witness protection program at this time?"

"Yeah, been in for five years now."

"So how did you come to be at these meetings?"

"I was there as part of a sting project for the feds—my latest one—nothin' to do with Ashford."

"Why weren't you recognized?"

"Not a problem. None of the Chicago boys know me, plus which after I left the Florida Organization and entered the program, the government gives me facial surgery. I put on thirty-five pounds. I grow a beard. My own mother wouldn't know me. Also, see, I was a qualified man with the Florida Mafia, so I know how to go about gettin' involved with the mob out here. 'Course I had to watch my p's and q's. Took me a year, hangin' around the Acropolis in Vegas, meetin' people in L.A."

"All right," said Field, glancing at an outline in his hand. "Who is Carmine Rizzo?"

"Don Carmine is head of the Chicago family. Owns the Acropolis and some legit enterprises, like a big piece of the Ashford family holding company."

"Objection and move to strike the reference to Mr. Ashford," said Barrett.

"Sustained and it may go out."

Barrett remained standing. "While I'm up, Your Honor, allow me to point out that when last I checked, we were supposed to be trying a San Francisco murder case, not the Chicago Rizzo family."

"Do you have an objection, counsel?" asked the judge.

"Irrelevant and prejudicial, Your Honor."

"Sustained. Please get to the limited purpose we discussed in chambers, Mr. Field."

Ligretti told of the meeting early in the year when he had first seen Ashford at a meeting with several members of the Rizzo family.

"Did you attend a second meeting with members of the Rizzo family with Mr. Ashford also in attendance?"

"Yeah, in San Francisco."

"Was this *after* the murder of Lara Ashford?"

"Yeah, on September 1. He'd just got out on bail."

"Was Mr. Ashford alone this time?"

"No, he's got a woman with him."

"Can you describe her?"

"A fox. Good-lookin' blond babe and all over him like a wet rag."

Field pursed his lips and nodded.

"Did you hear how Mr. Ashford referred to her?"

"Sure. He introduced her to Carmine as 'the next Mrs. Ashford.' "

Amanda heard a roar go up off to her side.

"Had Lara Ashford recently been found murdered?"

"Yeah, but I never seen a guy so fulla piss and vinegar. Cloud nine."

"Your Honor—"

"Don't bother to get up, Mr. Dickson," said John Hernandez, turning toward the witness. "Limit your answers to what you are asked, sir."

"That's all I have, Your Honor," said Field, and sat down.

Amanda glanced from the witness to Ashford, who sat staring gloomily at his fingernails. She shifted her gaze to Field, then to Grace Harris. For a second, she saw the woman's expression relax into a smile. Amanda fought off one of her own. There it was, she thought, as several reporters headed for the hallway. *The motive.*

But a few minutes later, Amanda's optimism wavered as she saw Dickson's black investigator advance to the rail and hand the defense lawyer a document that caused Dickson's normally stoic expression to unfold into something close to a smile. He slipped the document under his notepad.

The judge looked at Barrett Dickson.

"Cross, Mr. Dickson?"

But Barrett was already on his feet. "I'll not belabor your history as a government stool pigeon, Mr. Ligretti," said Barrett, "except to ask you if you do anything other than testify in behalf of government agencies."

"That's about it, counselor."

"So basically, this is what you do for a living, am I right?"

"You could say that."

"A comfortable living, at taxpayers' expense?"

Amanda wondered why Earl didn't object. She saw

Grace glancing at Field, but he stared straight ahead, inert as a statue.

"You could say that, too, I guess."

"Could I also say that you would lie if you had to? In order to maintain this lifestyle at taxpayers' expense?"

Field shifted, but said nothing for a minute.

"No way would I lie," said the witness at last.

"Then," said Barrett, "tell the jury how you can be so sure the second meeting you claim to have taken place at the Chinatown Holiday Inn in San Francisco was actually on September 1, 1997?"

Ligretti flashed an arrogant smile. "Because it was the first day of the month and a weekday. That's the day I always get my monthly living allowance from the federal Marshal's Service. I also remember getting written instructions for my role in the sting that day along with the check; you know, telling me where to go and what to listen for. I drove up that same night. September 1, a Monday."

Amanda stole a peek at the regular jurors. The witness was the personification of evil, but he was holding up and holding their attention.

"You're positive about the date then?"

"I'd bet my life on it."

"And the credibility of your testimony here today?"

"Damn right."

"Did you wear a wire at either meeting?"

"Me? Hell no. Too risky."

"So we just have your word that these meetings took place?"

"Why would I lie?"

"Didn't we just cover that?" said Barrett.

"Objection," said Grace, drawing a surprised look from Field. "Argumentative."

"Sustained," said John Hernandez.

Barrett was unruffled. "Here's my problem, Mr. Ligretti. You see, you've told us exactly when the meeting occurred and how *you* got to the meeting. What's puzzling me is how *Mr. Ashford* got to the meeting, *given the fact that he wasn't bailed out of his jail cell until Tuesday the second!*"

"OBJECTION, Your Honor," said Field, suddenly alert. "Mr. Dickson misstates the record. Mr. Ashford was freed on bail on the first; it's right in the record."

"You did free Mr. Ashford on Monday the first, Judge," said Barrett, addressing himself now only to John Hernandez, "but Alameda County picked up some traffic warrants on their computer and faxed in a hold on him, which I offer as defendant's next exhibit in order. He spent an extra night in jail. We were unable to get Mr. Ashford out until the second, the day after this meeting Mr. Ligretti just made up."

Amanda felt a sharp pain in her head, just over her eyes, as Barrett Dickson turned and smiled at the black investigator. Then came that damn clicking in her ears she had been experiencing lately as she saw Earl Field lower his head, unable to face them.

"I have," said Barrett Dickson, his eyes scanning the jury as he started toward his seat, "no further questions."

"No questions, Your Honor," said Field, and Amanda nearly gasped out loud. Why didn't Earl do something? she wondered. It's only one day! But as she turned and looked at the other jurors, she could see they needed no further proof that the Weasel was a liar as well as a stool pigeon and a killer.

The judge told them they would be instructed the next morning, then excused them for the day.

There was nothing she could do to save Earl now.

It was over.

Grace felt both anger and sadness as she followed the district attorney out of the courtroom at the noon recess. Anger at Ligretti, at Earl Field, and at herself.

The People versus Elliot Ashford was all but lost now, and so was Earl Field, the ambitious district attorney who had just driven the last nail into a political coffin that would be buried along with the star-crossed case.

And she had helped him do it. She remained convinced that Ligretti was generally telling the truth, but knew how easily an arrogant, unattractive witness such as the Weasel could be thoroughly discredited in the eyes of the jury if caught in the simplest mistake.

Without a recess, it would have been risky—but not impossible—for Earl to have tried to rehabilitate Ligretti. But this was probably what he wanted, though not the way he had intended it to happen. Despite her disappointment with the district attorney, she also felt strangely saddened by her role in the destruction of a man who might well have made a difference in the world. They might have lost the case anyway, of course, but before Ligretti, the police would have been blamed. Her intercession had changed all that. He had nowhere to hide now. She pictured the headlines:

D.A. Busted in Phony Witness Exposé!
Goodbye to State House Dreams of Field!

That night, Amanda tried to escape the pain of depression and her mother's probing questions by retreating to her room and her trial scrapbook. No point in talking to Lucinda, who would just remind her that she had only herself to blame for wasting so much time. She would be right. Amanda had neither resuscitated her TV career nor been able to help Earl Field.

She clipped and pasted with effort, nicked a finger with her scissors. "Shit," she shouted, and threw the book across the room. Then threw the paste jar at the wall next to her bed. Then went into the bathroom and threw up what little food she had eaten for dinner.

She crept back to her bed. She couldn't read, so got up and turned on her thirteen-inch black-and-white television set. She couldn't stay focused on any one program and her set was too old to have a remote unit, so she wearied of jumping up and down to change the channel and snapped it off. The sound of television persisted, though muted, from the living room. She could tell time by the theme songs of Lucinda's favorites: *Hard Copy* at 7:00 P.M., *Entertainment Tonight*, 7:30 P.M., then always *Murder, She Wrote* reruns at 8:00. Amanda took a heavy dose of barbiturates, hoping not to be conscious by the time the themes of *I Love Lucy* and *Bewitched* on cable seeped through the walls at 9:00 P.M. and 9:30 P.M. She turned the lights off and prayed for a respite from depression that only sleep could provide.

But the dubious solace of drug-induced slumber provided no escape tonight, for waiting for her there was her recurring dream, in which some unrecognized person close to her has died and is being buried. Her father? Her mother?

Seems more like a man than a woman, and always the same doll half hanging out of the casket.

Awake again, she knew the loathsome particulars would remain elusive and terrifying, much like her day-to-day existence.

30

Across town, Mike Reasoner and Barrett touched glasses at Postrio near Union Square.

"Well done, Bear, damned well done!" shouted Mike over the din, obviously feeling his drinks. "How the hell did you do it?"

"Lev did it," said Barrett. "The Weasel helped by not knowing that Monday, September 1, was a holiday: Labor Day. His check and instructions probably arrived on Tuesday, the day Ashford was actually released."

"The blindfolded lady works in strange and wonderful ways," said Mike.

Dickson nodded and tried to get the bartender's attention. Not easy in Postrio, still a hot ticket despite Wolfgang Puck's return to L.A. The beautifully appointed bar was jammed at noon with lawyers, stockbrokers, and oil-rich Middle East types talking deals, reeking of cologne and wealth. Barrett noted that the handful of women in the lounge area were not bad for bar fare, particularly those who had come mainly to eat, not to meet a lawyer, stockbroker, or an oil-rich Middle East type. Not bad, but not in a class with Grace Harris.

"Wilmer is going absolutely bat-shit," continued Mike. "He's trying to figure out how to handle your sudden fame. Doesn't know whether to downplay it or try to take credit for it. He's called a partners' meeting for tomorrow."

"A partners' meeting," murmured Barrett with an amused grin. "Does Mr. Excitement still thrill with announcements of new cost-cutting measures? Have we changed from Ticonderoga number three medium-lead pencils to Tinsel-Tint number two? Negotiated a contract with a new copy service perhaps? Discontinued the use of Wite-Out?"

"The man does keep his charisma in check," said Mike.

"Under tight rein."

"Well, here's to you, Bear."

"It was a good day," Barrett said. "Lev came up with Ashford's jail discharge records and the rest was plumbing."

"Bullshit plumbing!" said Mike. "It was surgery. Anyway, Wilmer wants to see you."

"No thanks."

"Why not? Chance to watch him grovel."

"Assure him I don't want our relationship to wither from neglect. Tell him I'll be by soon to bring him a new plastic pocket protector and maybe an AK-47 to aid in his human resources effort."

"Seriously, Bear, you should come by. People there are excited about what you're doing. The place shows signs of new life."

Barrett caught the bartender's eye and signaled him, then turned back to Mike. "Mice," he said. "Mice and elephants."

"Mice and elephants?"

"Focus. Like dealing with witnesses in a trial; assigning priorities. I can't get distracted chasing mice right now. Wilmer's a mouse—rat, actually—in my hierarchy of tasks. Got to deal with the elephants."

"As in?"

"For one thing, I've got to start thinking about my argument. Plus, Ashford still wants to go on the stand and tell his life history."

Mike said, "So what do I tell Wilmer?"

"Tell him I've joined a Hopi tribe and gone to live on mushrooms in the Tree of Immortal Knowledge."

"Reliving your Esalen period?"

The bartender arrived at last with Barrett's Ketel rocks and Mike's single malt. Mike paid, then groaned as Barrett lit a cigarette.

"Jesus, Bear. When did you start that again?"

Barrett took a deep drag. "You're missing a great habit, Mike."

"Seriously, Bear, what do I tell Wilmer?"

"You're a lawyer, Mike. Cite Justice Louis Brandeis on

privacy: The right to be left alone is the right most valued by civilized man."

Mike grunted. "The 'civilized' part lets you out."

"Okay, I'll go join the witness protection program," said Barrett, in the absence of an ashtray jabbing the cigarette butt into his empty glass. "Hang out with the Weasel, where even Wilmer can't find me."

Ten blocks away, at the Hall of Justice, the mood was different. Sam trudged into Grace's office at the hall looking thoroughly dispirited.

"Hi, Sam. What's up?"

"My job for one thing; up for grabs, that is. I told the chief he could lay the Ligretti thing on me if he wanted—you know, 'investigator error'—and he took me up on it. Then he said he might have to put me on suspension to make it look good."

Grace looked at her old friend and realized that no one would escape the wrath of this fiasco. They sat together for a moment of forlorn silence.

"Figured it out yet, Sam?" Grace said at last.

"What's to 'figure out'?"

"You're a detective, for God's sake. I know you've suspected something must be going on."

"I'm listening."

"For starters, Earl's going in the tank on Ashford."

Sam's eyes flashed for a second, but then he fell into a chair in front of her desk and stared at her. "Never took you for a conspiracy nut, Grace."

"He accepted a six-figure favor from the mob, Sam. And now they've called in the debt."

Sam gave her an amused grin. "Do yourself a favor, Grace. Get some sleep. Get off whatever you're taking. Downgrade to Valium."

Grace saw irritation beneath the smile, heard suspicion behind his words. But she couldn't stop now.

"I took a call from a tabloid reporter. That's where it started. Then—"

"What are you trying to do, Grace? Take down the best man to ever run this office and free a wife killer in the process?"

"Just listen—"

"No, damn it, I won't listen! I'm going to work."

Grace was struck by the absurd notion that Sam was somehow a part of it. No, not Sam.

"Okay, Sam. But at least let me answer your question. I'm not going to do anything. Not for the present at least. If I blew the whistle now, Ashford could fall through the gaping crack in Earl's morality. Thanks to Babcock, we've still got a shot at a hung jury. But after that, I'll have to take it to the state attorney general and I'll need your help."

"You'll need help all right, Grace," said Sam coldly, "but you won't get it from me."

"Sam, wait!" But he was out the door.

And Grace was alone.

Barrett left Mike at Postrio and hiked up the hill to the Ritz-Carlton for a meeting with Ashford and Julian Gold, who had flown in from Chicago. Barrett accepted a congratulatory handshake from the *consigliere,* whose bony imprint would haunt him hours later, like the phantom pain he sometimes felt in the tip of his lost finger.

"Well done, Mr. Dickson," said Gold, affecting a reasonably genuine smile, "but we've got a problem. Our Mr. Ashford still wishes to expiate his guilt over the Babcock matter by taking the stand and 'telling the truth.' I've summoned you here to tell him how utterly stupid that would be."

The peach-colored suite was bathed in a dull afternoon glow. Ashford was sprawled across a couch the size of Barrett's '87 Ford Mustang with a wet rag on his forehead, a state of repose much envied by Barrett after a climb up Taylor from which he was still sweating. He fell into a seat near the couch and looked Gold straight in the eye.

"The truth usually works for me, Mr. Gold, and it's his ass on the line, not yours."

Gold stiffened. "I have never liked your attitude, Dickson." He bent so close Barrett could smell his breath freshener and added, "Not at all."

"And I've never liked being 'summoned,' " said Barrett, meeting his gaze. "In fact, if I had known I had been 'summoned,' I wouldn't have come at all."

Gold turned away, skeletal hands clasped together behind him, ignoring his remark. He strolled over to one of the large windows overlooking the courtyard below. A wedding was in progress, and strains of Mozart wafted up from a string quarter. Barrett squinted at the profile of the diaphanous figure framed in the glowing window. In the glare of the sun, Gold's mouth looked like an exit wound.

The wound began to ooze words.

"I'm very disappointed in you, Dickson. After what you did yesterday, I had begun to think there might be something in you worth salvaging."

"But now," said Barrett dryly, "I'll never work in this town again, right?"

"*Wonderful,* Mr. Dickson," said Gold, turning away from the window. "You see, Elliot? Humor in the face of danger. Oh yes, Dickson, there was much I had begun to admire in you, and I've done my homework: orphaned at birth, deprived childhood, football star, top student, wounded war hero, former top trial lawyer in the top firm on the West Coast, now poised to regain his crown. The intrepid trial warrior who never walks away from a fight."

"That's right. Lately I've run. Particularly when I'm asked to represent a creative psychopath who, among his more innocuous pastimes, buys witnesses."

A limp hand moved off the couch, but only adjusted the washrag, then fell back.

"You've no need to run this time," said Gold. "The worse-case scenario now is a hung jury, after which I can assure you that Earl Field will simply walk away from the case, making the usual excuses: budgetary problems, police ineptitude, case load, et cetera, et cetera. There will be no second trial."

"You can't be sure of that, Gold. Nobody can."

Barrett noticed that Gold started to say something, then covered his pause with a malevolent smile. "If I'm somehow wrong about that, Mr. Ashford and I will regroup with new counsel for the retrial, and you can go your own way with an extra $500,000 fee—for you personally, of course—and no hard feelings. But Elliot must *not* take the stand."

The quartet burst into a Bach fugue that merged with Barrett's spinning thoughts to weave a contrapuntal web of confusion in his throbbing head. He eyed the etched-glass decanter across the room, then looked away.

"After the Babcock fiasco," said Barrett, meeting Gold's

dark, sunken eyes, "you may not get your hung jury. Elliot got himself into trouble with the jury because of Babcock, and he's the only one who can get himself out of it. If he wants to get up there and put his word against hers, what are you going to do? Break his kneecaps?"

"Double-dealing little bitch," murmured Ashford through the damp cloth.

Gold glared at both of them.

"We'll also have the element of surprise," continued Barrett. "They'll never expect him to take the stand."

"They wouldn't dream we'd be so stupid," said Gold in a tone of quiet contempt.

"That's why I'm going to put him on first thing tomorrow morning," said Barrett, warming to the idea. "He's going to take those ten steps to the witness stand like he's been wanting to do, put his hand in the air, and tell the jury— and me—that he did not murder Lara Ashford."

"Tell *you*?" said Gold. "Who the hell are *you*? Elliot's guilt or innocence is for the jury to decide, not you or anyone else. Indeed, it's the *last* thing that should concern a defense lawyer!"

"But I'm not a defense lawyer. I'm not much of any kind of a lawyer anymore. You knew that when you retained me."

"Retained you?" Gold said, smiling scornfully, "We didn't retain you, Mr. Dickson, we merely rented you. The lease is up in three days, but until then, you'll do as I say."

Barrett turned to his recumbent client. "You want a hung jury, Elliot?"

Ashford lifted himself up onto his elbows. The cloth fell onto his chest. "Hell, no!" he shouted. "I want my *freedom*! I want to testify and get the whole bloody thing done with."

Barrett turned toward Gold and shrugged. "There you have it straight from the horse's ass, Gold. The man wants to testify and his lawyer agrees he should."

Gold took Barrett's measure, then looked away and demonstrated his resignation by leaving the room. Elliot Ashford reached over and gave Barrett's hand a hearty yank. The string quartet struck up Wagner's wedding processional.

31

Amanda sat alone in the jury room at 9:30 the next morning, studying minute cracks in the plaster that webbed out from the corners above the doorjamb, wondering what Earl Field would want her to do now. He had been trying to signal her, she was sure of that.

She also knew he had to be careful; no telling how wide the conspiratorial net had spread. He wouldn't want to expose her to danger. Not even the judge was above Amanda's suspicion now. Hadn't he kicked Martin Chin off the jury? And the Latino, number four, also an outspoken prosecution juror? And was number ten really in a hospital somewhere? Then there was Grace Harris, now barely concealing her enmity for the embattled district attorney. Had they gotten to her too?

Soon the judge would summon them back into court for closing arguments and instructions on the law. After that, it would be time for the regular jury to begin deliberations and for her and the other alternate to be segregated from the others.

She grimly surveyed the room that had been her home for nearly three weeks. She forced herself to focus, trying to get on a constructive keel. What could she say that would shock these jurors into overcoming their fear or greed or whatever was controlling them?

The answer came to her as if delivered from heaven. It would be a lie, of course, but how else could a conspiracy of lies be exposed except by counterlies? Fire with fire. A lie to reveal a greater truth.

Perhaps this is why her presence on the panel had been foreordained. It would be difficult and even dangerous. But the idea was a revelation she could not disregard. She had no choice now but to act and fulfill her purpose here.

She took a deep breath and started walking toward the group of "white regulars" clustered around Manon Barnes: Ruth Salverson, Barney Seagrave, and Clement Bell, the sixty-two-year-old retired postal worker who had replaced Martin Chin. Amanda picked up a dry cruller she didn't want and smiled at Ruth, who greeted her warmly as always. Barney gave her his usual lusty grin. The others paid her no attention.

"Well, I guess this is about it for me," Amanda said during a lull in the conversation. "I certainly don't envy you guys."

Ruth smiled her motherly smile and said, "It's a frightening responsibility, Amanda."

"And a time-consuming one," said Barney Seagrave. "I for one am goin' to be damn glad to get the hell out of here."

"Not me," said Clem Bell to no one in particular. "This beats TV every which way."

"How about you, Manon?" said Amanda. "Glad it's about over?"

"No way. I've learned loads. I nearly flunked civics, but I think this is the way to really learn stuff about the system."

"But the system doesn't always work," said Amanda, trying to control the tremor in her voice. "That's what bothers me. Look at all the things the jury didn't hear about in the Simpson case. Or like in our own case, Ashford's earlier threat to kill his wife."

"What?" said Manon Barnes and Barney Seagrave in unison. Ruth's creased lips fell open.

"He did *that*?" said Clem Bell.

"It was on TV this morning," said Amanda. "I saw it by mistake when I was helping my mother find a movie channel. I'm sorry, I probably shouldn't have said anything."

"You're *sorry*?" said Manon Barnes, her eyes narrowed and blazing. "It's a little late for '*sorry*,' Amanda."

"My stars," mumbled Clem Bell, still looking stunned as he shuffled away, working an unlighted cigar in his sagging lips.

Manon looked furious. "Lani Jefferson was right about you!"

Amanda looked hurt. "Manon, I apologize. Just forget what I said, okay?"

"Not this time. I'm going to the judge and I'm going right now, before you can do any more damage!"

"Manon, please!" pleaded Amanda. "I could get in real trouble over having done something this stupid. *Please!*"

But Manon was unmoved, and this time, not even Barney Seagrave would meet Amanda's eye.

"Excuse me, Manon," said Ruth Salverson, "but if I heard the judge correctly, Amanda and the other alternate will be separated from us after the jury instructions later today. Isn't that so?"

"Thank God for small favors," said Manon derisively. "So what?"

"Well, goodness me," said Ruth, "she can't cause any more harm then, can she?"

By the end of the recess, Manon had relented, but only after securing Amanda's agreement to isolate herself from all other jurors until the regulars began deliberating. "Not one more word to any of us!" she demanded.

"I won't say another word, Manon. I swear." God, how she hated the frizzy-haired bitch; how she would have loved to put her powerful fingers around that pretty neck. But as she made her exit, acting shaken and contrite, she could barely resist smiling. She saw the troubled looks on each one of their faces.

She would respect her vow of silence, because no more words would be necessary. Her lie was a worm nesting in their brains, restless and immutable.

When the jurors were reseated in the courtroom, the judge informed them that a conflict had arisen on his calendar which he would try to sort out during a brief recess. As they filed back out, Amanda tried to catch Earl Field's eye, to offer him a look of reassurance, but he just sat staring grimly at his hands. He must have known they would be watching the two of them closely now, she thought.

Back in the jury room, Amanda was uneasy. She hadn't figured on this sudden recess; having to sit alone so soon while the others whispered about her. She hid behind a year-old copy of *Better Homes and Gardens,* the momentary elation over her heroic effort fading as she pictured the airhead Manon Barnes, perhaps even Kevin Alston or

Barney Seagrave, getting the magazine interviews, the notoriety, the TV exposure, the book deals.

A peal of laughter went up from the far end of the table where several regulars were huddled, and she caught Manon Barnes looking at her through narrowed, smiling eyes. What had she ever done to her? To any of them? She welcomed her mounting anger as a counterbalance to her depression, but the buzzing had started again and her skin was hot and itching. Fucking Barnes. Fucking Ward and Company. Fucking Lucinda. The world was like a relay team and she was its baton; handled, then passed on to the next tormentor in line.

The bailiff rapped on the door, summoning them back into the courtroom, where the judge apologized and explained that his calendar conflict could not be resolved.

"We'll make up for lost time by resuming at eight-thirty tomorrow morning with the defense's last witness," he said. "I will then instruct you on the law. It is quite possible your deliberations will commence by late afternoon. You are excused."

Amanda felt Manon's eyes on her but didn't care anymore. She had done the right thing, and hadn't she always been taught that you have to break eggs to make an omelette? Well, she thought, even if her sacrifice never came to light, justice at least would be served by her heroism in breaking through the conspiracy and Earl Field would have his career.

Earl, she thought, and a consoling smile crossed her lips despite the pain spreading through her head. Earl would know what she had done because she would tell him.

By the time Amanda reached the flat, she was feeling better, and resolved to share her bold deed with Lucinda, who, friendless and shut-in by choice, was more secure than a lifer in solitary.

"Just look at this place," Lucinda whined as soon as Amanda entered. "It's a mess. Smells like your damn cats!"

"If you'd just let me open some windows—"

"So it's all my fault you're sayin'."

"Nobody's blaming you, Mother," said Amanda. "I'll tidy up in the morning."

Lucinda was watching *Inside Hollywood,* and barely diverted her eyes from the TV screen as she continued to rave. "You *know* I can't keep up with things with you gone all the time."

Amanda looked at her mother staring at the TV, the pinched face, the down-turned mouth. Only Lucinda's pale green eyes, as clear and penetrating as ever, evoked memories of her past beauty. But now even the eyes seemed smaller, slowly disappearing deeper into her head as extraneous flesh closed in around them, like quicksand swallowing emeralds.

Amanda tried to remember when her mother had become so overweight, throwing her once perfectly proportioned body out of whack, shrinking her head so that she looked like a Henry Moore sculpture. It began when she, Amanda, had moved in and Lucinda had rented, then purchased, the wheelchair. That was it, thought Amanda. Any semblance of independence had ended once Lucinda plopped her ass into that damned prison on wheels. *My prison, too.*

"Let's have some dinner," demanded Lucinda. "I'm starved."

Amanda decided she would save the news of her triumph for later, when she had her mother's full attention. She went into the kitchen, methodically unwrapped two packages of diet chicken lasagna from the freezer, poked holes in the plastic tops, and set the microwave for ten minutes. She heard buzzing and thought at first it was the microwave, but realized it was in her ears again. She would have to see a doctor as soon as she got back to work. She felt dizzy and leaned against the counter, then splashed water on her face and rested. When the food was ready, she reentered the living room, placed the dinners on the coffee table next to her mother's wineglass, then sat down.

"Get me some more wine while you're up, child."

Amanda stared at the empty glass thrust under her nose, then at her mother's profile. She got up, returned to the kitchen, and refilled Lucinda's glass. She handed Lucinda her wine and sat down again. Her mother attacked the lasagna, eyes still glued to the TV.

"I've got some really exciting news, Mother."

"Oh really? So do I."

"Okay. You go first, Mother."

"They fired two of your file-room people today," said Lucinda, calmly dabbing her lips with a paper napkin.

"They *what*?"

"Amy and George. Mr. Pierce called, wonderin' when you're comin' back. He says he's appointed some woman named Marla to take charge of your department until you get back. He said somebody had to clean up the mess that's built up while you've been absent."

"Mess? What mess?"

"When the cat's away . . ."

"He can't do that! First Nick, now Amy and George? I can't run the place without them. And *Marla*! She's the bitch I told you about!"

Lucinda smiled. "They can do it and they did it. Didn't your mother tell you what would happen if you went gallivantin' off to that trial? Just let that be a lesson to you, young lady!"

Amanda sunk back into the couch, stunned and confused. The buzzing in her ears intensified, also the clicking now.

Lucinda eyed Amanda's plastic carton of barely touched lasagna.

"You not goin' to eat that?"

Amanda handed the carton to her mother.

"Now," said Lucinda, diving in, "what's *your* news?"

Amanda rose to her feet. "Never mind, Mother. I'm going to bed. I'm not feeling well."

"Hold on a minute. Take these empty cartons with you."

Amanda felt the blood rush out of her face. She sat back down, put her head on her knees, sure she was going to faint.

"Why didn't you tell me when I first came—"

"Shush, child. *Entertainment Tonight* is startin'."

Amanda staggered to her feet and delivered the empty containers to the kitchen, then retreated to her bedroom with her cats. She closed the door behind her, feeling as if she were about to explode, every nerve ending on fire. She grabbed a handful of phenobarb, washed them down with tap water from her sink, and lay down on her bed.

She picked up a book, but the words were confused, jumping around the page with every heartbeat. She would be working for Marla when she got back to Ward. That had been Pierce's plan from the beginning. The bastard. The bitch.

Maybe a hot bath would help, she thought, but that would mean encountering her mother again on the way to the other bathroom.

She listened to the garbled electronic voices blaring from the living room, picturing her mother staring bleakly at some stupid sitcom. She remembered a movie or television scene from years ago where a TV set sucked the viewer inside to a horrible fate. She envisioned the heel and sole of a single shoe as the last thing seen as the body disappeared into the vortex behind the screen.

Her skin was burning up, so she stripped off her clothes. She appraised herself in the mirror over her dresser. Nearly a week without a workout at her club. Her breasts seemed to sag. She ran her right hand down her waist, picturing a headline in the *National Enquirer:* "Woman Trapped in Jury Trial Gains Twenty Pounds on Thighs and Ass!"

She pulled her shoulders back, the breasts rose. She stood erect to narrow her waist.

A man enters her room. He sees she is naked and apologizes. His admiration of her perfect body is clear, but clinical. He is a gentleman and averts his eyes as she slips on a robe. "My name is Steven Spielberg. I've come here to offer you the lead in a major motion picture opposite Tom Cruise. I know this is short notice, but we start shooting next week. . . ."

Fantasy had sustained Amanda all her life, but now even that eluded her. Why was Pierce doing this to her? Had someone informed on her for telling a story to the jurors? Had the conspiracy against Field spread to her own workplace?

She picked up the book again and struggled through three pages, but her eyes stung with fatigue and she set it aside. Sleep eluded her too, partly because of the ubiquitous TV gurglings and the electric hum inside her head, like high-tension lines coiled around her brain. Even the pills failed her. Her mind was in turmoil, a maelstrom of fear and frustration.

32

Grace Harris was not surprised when Field told her she would cross-examine Elliot Ashford. With all hope of a conviction gone, Earl would try to distance himself from the case. Klegg would call it a matter of "political expediency." She understood. It had always been his case to win; her case to lose.

Now, sitting at the kitchen table late at night, she stared glumly at her notes on Ashford and the most recent argument outline she had drafted. Nothing was working.

Focus.

It had all seemed clear at the beginning—Elliot Ashford had obviously killed his wife in a jealous rage. But now, Ashford was but part of a far larger problem. When the verdict was in, her trial would just be beginning. She could not walk away from it, and Earl, supported by Klegg, would fight back. All three of them would be finished in public life by the time the smoke of scandal cleared. She would be seen as complicitous by some, disloyal by others.

She leapt up and slammed the window down as if the unwelcome thoughts had blown in through it.

Focus.

She poured a cup of coffee from the carafe on the kitchen counter.

It would be up to her to strike the right emotional note with the jury at the start, to swing the pendulum of their collective opinion as far as possible to the People's side of the case before Barrett Dickson had his chance to stand and deliver, assuming Barrett Dickson was able to stand when it was time for him to deliver. Despite everything, she caught herself smiling at the thought of him. She could tell he liked her. She wondered what he was like outside the courtroom. . . .

Focus.

Amanda and Manon Barnes passed through the hall's outer courthouse door at the same time the next morning. Manon smiled and fielded questions from the press. No questions were asked of Amanda. No pictures taken.

A strange silence had gripped the jury room, and Amanda sensed a palpable apprehension in the regular jurors as they contemplated the solemn responsibility that would soon be theirs, the power of life and death over another human being.

Members of a firing squad have the consolation of knowing that not all their guns were loaded, but that solace is not available to a jury. At the end, they would be "polled," and if their unanimous decision was death, then each in his or her turn would have to stand and acknowledge that his or her gun was loaded and that they had chosen to pull the trigger.

The bailiff did not appear at eight-thirty sharp, as promised by the judge. Then nine o'clock came and passed with no message. The tension turned into impatience, then irritation.

"This is the shits," said Barney Seagrave, glaring at his watch and irritably flipping his ponytail. His expletive drew a rare critical look from Ruth Salverson, but nods from the others.

"Cheer up, Barney," said Kevin Alston. "At least we haven't been sequestered, or left in here days at a time not knowing what's going on."

"Well," said Manon Barnes, "we don't have to guess what's going on. Lani's late, and you can bet she'll hear about it."

Two loud knocks preceded the bailiff, who extended the court's apology for the delay and beckoned them into the courtroom.

"I regret this delay, ladies and gentlemen," said Judge Hernandez once they were seated. "You have noticed, I'm sure, that one of your number is missing. It is my unhappy duty to inform you that Ms. Lani Jefferson died last night."

The jurors exchanged stunned looks. Even counsel seemed shaken.

"I have been conferring with counsel," continued the

judge, "and, following a moment of silence in honor of her life and service here, we shall proceed without further delay."

Reporters would write in the following morning's *Chronicle* that the first alternate in line nearly fainted when she was instructed to take seat number three. The judge had to repeat her name, twice in fact, before she responded.

33

By the time Amanda had taken seat number three and had regained the powers of observation requisite to the task ahead, she noticed that the lawyers were discussing something with the judge at side-bar. When they began to drift back to their places, Earl Field not only looked straight into her eyes, he *smiled*—a moment she would cherish. The sensitivity and restrained elation in his face wordlessly expressed his feelings: *Yes, Amanda, you are at last where I need you to be.*

Amanda wanted to smile back, but was fearful that Dickson, Ashford, or even another juror might see the feelings passing between them. The real curse of a conspiracy, she realized, was in not knowing how far it extended, who she could trust. So she shifted her gaze to the defense table and saw that Ashford was also smiling at her, but not with his eyes.

The bastard, she thought. Thinks I'm afraid of him. She would have her work cut out for her, but knew she would hold out for conviction no matter what they did to her.

The judge excused them for the morning recess, and Amanda turned to survey the gallery as she stood up. Many eyes were on her now, especially those of the press corps. An electric charge of excitement raced up her spine.

As she turned to leave the courtroom, she stole another glance at Earl Field, but he was talking to Grace Harris. Again, she found herself locked in the gaze of Elliot Ashford. Before she could look away, she was sure she saw a warning look in his cold eyes. Then, just as quickly, he flashed the same malevolent smile she had seen before.

She looked to her left and to her right; surely somebody else must have seen this! The audacity! And this time, damn it, it wasn't her imagination! A shudder passed through her tense body, and she hurried into the security of the jury room.

As the jurors filed out, Barrett slumped in his chair, assailed by mixed feelings: sadness at the passing of Lani Jefferson, relief that she was no longer on the jury, and a sharp pain at L-5. He made two notes on his yellow pad:

Get Lev to look into new juror A. Keller.
Call chiropractor A. Cheng re possible lunchtime appointment.

He felt a hand on his shoulder and turned to see Lev, looking unhappy and thrusting the early edition of the afternoon *Examiner* over the rail in front of Barrett's face. The headline read:

ASHFORD JUROR MURDERED

Jesus, Barrett murmured to himself as he read that Jefferson had been killed in the same manner as Lara Ashford, her carotid artery severed by a thin, stiletto-like object. Someone had entered her apartment and attacked her from behind while she was riding her exercise bicycle.

Barrett shuddered and fought off a familiar sense of dread as he read on. An "informed source" stated that the victim had also sustained multiple puncture wounds to her breasts and genitalia nearly identical to those suffered by Lara Ashford. The county coroner publicly speculated that the murder weapon might have been a shard of glass. The medical examiner said that the wounds would have to be carefully examined for the presence of minute glass particles.

Heat engulfed Barrett's body. He looked up at Lev. "You think it's a mob hit? Maybe just some nut copycat?"

"Neither one, Bear," said Lev, shaking his head. "I think we got ourselves an equal-opportunity killer for a client. Everyone could see Jefferson was pro prosecution, and probably the forelady, too."

"He can't be that stupid," said Barrett, handing the newspaper back to Leviticus. He felt a pain stabbing his stomach.

"You keep sayin' that, and maybe you're right," said Lev, his intelligent brown eyes unrelenting, "though his character could use some work."

Barrett considered Lev's remark. "You really think he did it?"

"I suppose it's possible his Mafia connection didn't figure things were going too well and they were the ones who stepped in."

"Ashford does business with the Mafia," said Barrett, suddenly feeling uncomfortable. "You don't know he's 'connected.'"

"You do business with the Mafia, Bear," said Leviticus with an indulgent smile that made Barrett feel naïve, "you're connected. Joe Kennedy was connected. People you wouldn't believe are connected. Means you give and receive favors. I'm sayin' maybe Carmine felt guilty about benching Tony and decided to send a message to the other jurors that they'd be wise to see things your way."

"My way," said Barrett, putting the paper down and rubbing his temples. "Even if that's true, it doesn't mean Ashford knew what was going down. If Rizzo had Jefferson killed, it was done in his own financial self-interest."

Lev said nothing. Barrett started pacing. He realized that he was being the advocate; that he was unwilling to accept the possibility that his client, growing desperate in the wake of the Renee Babcock disaster, had killed one juror to send a message to the rest. His head throbbed in sympathy with his stomach.

Leviticus Heywood came through the gate and stood beside him near counsel table. "It's called 'insurance,' Bear," he said.

The bailiff reentered the courtroom. "Sorry, gents; got to lock up. Judge just told me to let the jury go for an early lunch."

Barrett managed a nod. "Is the corridor clear yet, Lev?"

"You kiddin'? The vultures are circlin'."

"Fred," said Barrett. "Let us out the back way?"

"Sure," said Fred. "Take a coupla more minutes if you want."

"I disagree, Lev," said Barrett as Fred disappeared into the judge's chambers. "I think it was a copycat. It had to be a copycat. Nothing else makes sense."

Lev leaned closer. "Haven't you been watchin' your own client, Bear? Sure, he's tryin' to charm most of the jurors, but I've seen him givin' some seriously hostile looks to a couple of the others. To most of them, he's sayin', 'I'm too sweet a guy to do such a nasty thing,' but to one or two others, he's sayin', 'Better vote not guilty or you too could wake up with glass up your ass.' Different strokes for different folks."

"That's the basis of your insurance theory?" said Barrett, trying to look bemused.

"Exactly. The man's wearin' a belt *and* suspenders. Makin' sure of at least a hung jury just in case his charm fails him. But you go ahead and think Mafia if it makes you feel better; just forget about all this 'copycat' business."

Barrett got up and leaned against the rail. "Rizzo's not that stupid either," he said. "Not with Gold telling him how well it's going."

"Then we're right back to our boy doin' Jefferson his own self. Maybe Armand Ligretti doesn't follow national holidays, but I do believe his story about Ashford showin' off to the boys in the outfit that first day he got out. Means, opportunity, and now, motive."

Barrett gave Lev a hard look. "Whose side are you on, Lev?"

Lev grinned. "I'm on the side of truth, justice, and beauty, as always."

Barrett didn't smile.

"Open your eyes, Bear. Ashford, or someone actin' on his behalf, has guaranteed you a jittery jury that will either walk him out the door or hang up; if they hang up, he gets a retrial and a fresh start without Renee Babcock."

"And time to find a real lawyer," said Barrett bitterly.

Lev laughed and said, "Sure! Try somethin' different."

Barrett still wasn't smiling. He was asking himself if Lani Jefferson would still be alive if some asshole hadn't come into the case and freed Ashford on bail.

After lunch, with rumors raging throughout the courthouse, Judge Hernandez declared a recess for the balance of the afternoon, "in deference to our deceased juror and the understandable distress we all share."

He then cleared his throat and added: "It has come to

my attention that some of you wish to have a full explanation of the stories circulating around the building concerning the circumstances of Ms. Jefferson's demise. I assume you have done your best to follow my instructions to avoid such information, but I know that our cafeteria line serves both fact and rumor. You are again instructed to avoid all forms of news media, and in return I promise you that when these stories have been either confirmed or repudiated by the police, I will provide you with complete information concerning the exact circumstances of her death."

"We gonna be *see*questered?" said Barney Seagrave, surprising the judge and the other wide-eyed jurors. They had been clearly instructed to communicate with the judge only in writing.

John Hernandez smiled patiently. "I have carefully considered the matter of sequestration . . . Mr. Seagrave, is it? And I have decided against it, at least for now."

The jurors exhaled as one in relief.

"Meanwhile," continued the judge, "I must emphasize the importance of avoiding media reports in any and all forms, particularly now.

"As well as the importance," he added with a wink at Seagrave, "of communicating with me through the bailiff, in writing."

Patches of nervous laughter from the jurors relieved some of the tension in the courtroom. But they looked uneasy as they filed out, except for a grim-faced Clem Bell—bent from too many years toting a mailbag before he was brought inside—who glanced toward Elliot Ashford and mumbled something under his breath that sounded like "murdering bastard." Amanda smiled at this and made a mental note as the jurors gathered their belongings and headed for the elevators.

Amanda timed her exit from the building so that no other juror would be too close to her, giving the photographers a clear shot.

Give us a smile, Amanda! Her shoulder-length blond hair flew toward the camera and came to rest over one shoulder. *Hold it right there, Ms. Keller, okay?*

Her dark blue eyes glistened with an exhilaration not seen since just before Sharon McPeak's fatal ski accident at Squaw Valley.

* * *

Later that afternoon, Barrett sat in Lev's cluttered office drinking day-old coffee and looking sour. They were waiting for their client and a final prep session before his testimony the next day. Lev got up and flipped on the overhead fluorescents, then fell back in his chair.

He gave Barrett a worried look.

"City's gettin' too damn noisy," he said, getting up again and closing a window.

Barrett nodded agreement, shifted his gaze to the north window, toward Montgomery Street. A fierce wind off the Pacific had drawn a curtain of fog against the dwindling daylight and cooled the Financial District fifteen degrees in as many minutes. Commuters raced for cars, buses, and BART rail, collars and lapels held tight against their necks. An occasional break in the white mist allowed the setting sun to ricochet high off the slanted windows of the Bank of America monolith, creating a strobe effect against the backdrop of gray fog.

A chill hit Barrett, too. Hit him square in the heart. He knew where Lev kept his stash of Jack Daniel's and didn't ask permission.

"Sure you want to go there, pard?" said Lev.

"Just trying to improve the taste of this battery acid you call coffee."

"What's eatin' you, Bear?"

Barrett gave him a wry smile. "My client," he said, "and the remote possibility you might be right about him."

The door flew open and Elliot Ashford strode into the room.

"I'm late, gentlemen, so let's get on with it, shall we?"

No one spoke.

"Well?" said Ashford.

"Why don't we start," said Barrett, a sour expression rearranging his features, "with whether you know who killed Lani Jefferson?"

Elliot Ashford gave Barrett a wry smile, then turned his attention to lighting a cigarette. "Don't insult me, old chum. Now, what can I do for you?"

Barrett drained his cup and stared into it for a few seconds.

"It's a simple question, Elliot," Barrett said. "Do you know who killed her? Did *you* have her killed?"

Ashford let out a burst of derisive laughter, then glowered at Barrett. "Listen, you horse's ass," he said, his eyes sparking with anger, "I didn't come here to be asked absurd questions and be accused of murder by my own idiot lawyer. Let's get this over with. I have to get down to Atherton."

Barrett put down his cup and rose to his feet, glaring at Ashford.

"You intending to hit me again, old friend?"

"Maybe. Answer my question. A simple yes or no will do."

Ashford took a deep drag on his cigarette, flicked his ashes on the floor, snatched up his cashmere topcoat, and moved toward the door as he spoke. "No, damn it, I will *not* dignify that question with an answer. You and your lawn jockey here can go to the devil. As for me—"

Ashford seemed unprepared for the speed at which a man Dickson's size could move, and before he could bolt through the door or Lev could come between them, Barrett had crossed the distance between them, lifted the defendant by the lapels, and pinned him up against the wall. He held him there with one hand and snatched the cigarette that was still dangling from his lips with the other, then held the glowing tip of Ashford's cigarette an inch away from his cheek.

"Smoking can be harmful to your health, Elliot," said Barrett through clenched teeth, "as can smart-assing your lawyer. *Do you know who killed that juror?*"

"*No!*" shouted Ashford. "Of course I don't. Now let me go!"

"Put your client down, Bear," said Lev, "like a good lawyer."

Barrett grunted and gave Ashford a shove into Lev's chair.

Ashford quickly collected himself and seemed surprisingly unruffled by the experience.

"No doubt about it," he said to Leviticus as he straightened his lapels. "The man is insane."

"I don't think he likes people smoking in front of him," said Lev, handing Ashford his glasses. "He's tryin' to quit."

Ashford continued to glower at Barrett. "Well, tell him to also quit being so damn crude and physical."

Barrett poured another JD and coffee, then took a seat across the desk from Ashford and continued to stare at his client without speaking.

Ashford looked pleadingly from Barrett to Lev, then back to Barrett and said, "Really, now, Dickson, do you think I'm that stupid? Can't you see somebody out there is trying to set me up?"

Barrett sat sipping his coffee, still silent, wondering what to do next. Had he really expected anything other than a denial? And had he expected that a denial from a liar like Ashford would reassure him? How many alibi witnesses would he have this time? Why even ask? He rose to his feet and reached across the desk toward Ashford, who quickly ducked his head back out of range.

"Steady, 'old chum,'" said Barrett with the hint of a smile. "I just want one of your cigarettes."

Ashford threw the pack on the table. Barrett lit one, inhaled deeply, and said, "All right, let's get to work."

They were finished in two hours and Ashford eagerly rose to leave. "Don't worry about me, Dickson. I'll do my job tomorrow, you just be damn sure to do yours."

Barrett took a sip of his coffee, now cold and bitter. "I'll do the best I can," he said, his tone gritty, "but from this minute forward, I want you to lose all this lord-of-the-manor, 'old chum,' 'old man' crap and do exactly as I say. If I say '*hop,*' you're the Easter Bunny, okay? If I say '*fly,*' you forget the countdown and go airborne. If I say '*scat,*' you're out of here!"

Ashford glanced at Lev as if appealing for intervention, then met Barrett's iron gaze and said, "I'm not paying you to—"

"There's not enough money in Fort Knox," Barrett said, his eyes now burning into Ashford's, "so forget the master-servant bullshit while you're at it. Are we in agreement?"

Ashford broke eye contact, then nodded.

"*Say it!*"

"All right, I *agree,* for God's sake!"

"Good," said Barrett. "Now *scat.*"

34

Amanda headed home from her fitness center in high spirits, still giddy from the renewed attention of photographers, reporters, and courtroom observers. A woman on the bus seemed to recognize her and this added to her excitement. Still, she wouldn't miss the damn Muni bus system one bit. In L.A., everybody had a car.

She got off the bus two blocks early and picked up some Chinese takeout. As she walked the last block from the bus stop, the smell of the kung pao and the warmth of the little cartons against her side added to her resolve to make this a pleasant night. The Chinese food was for Lucinda—her favorite—a celebration of sorts. Amanda could afford to be decent now, with her departure just a matter of a few weeks at most. Her future was now clearly laid out before her. There would be no defense verdict now. They could berate, threaten, and torture; she would hold out. No amount of money could buy her; nothing could coerce her. She would stand firm.

Her heroism in breaking through the conspiracy would return her to Hollywood, unless Earl somehow prevailed upon her to stay. She frowned. There would be difficult choices ahead, but at least she had options now, and maybe she could have both Earl *and* a career. Weren't there several flights between San Francisco and Burbank every day?

She realized she was out of breath and slowed her pace. Had she put on another pound? She had shopped tonight with that possibility in mind and could almost taste the coriander in the small chicken salad she had bought for herself. There would be time for an early morning workout at Dave's Gym.

She twirled in a slightly self-conscious dance step as she entered the flat. Life was good.

*   *   *

"You *know* I shouldn't be eatin' Chinese," Lucinda said, scowling as she greedily studied each carton, her lips drawn tight.

Amanda said nothing.

"It's way too fattenin', and you think I'm overweight already, I *know* you do. So what do you do? Bring me Chinese."

Amanda carried two plates into the living room, then watched as her mother began to shove pot stickers into a mouth that somehow managed to continue dispensing criticism as it gobbled up the little delicacies.

"Why not just feed me steroids like they use to fatten up cattle and chickens?"

"I wasn't sure how you felt about having hair on your chest, Mother."

Lucinda growled, "Oh, she's a comedian now. Don't get too big for your britches, young lady, just because you think you're goin' to be a star again."

Amanda stared at her mother in disgust. She should be out celebrating, she thought, drinking champagne at Stars or Rose Pistola, planning her public relations strategy. But who would she call? No matter. Soon she would have plenty of friends.

She looked around at the cheap wallpaper, peeling at the bottom near the chipped baseboard too warped to keep the cockroaches out. She took in the fake art on the walls as if for the first time, the ceramic trolls and nymphs, the worn plaid nylon upholstery on the time-ravaged chairs and sofa, the East Indian rug that had been her grandmother's, its garish colors unmuted by generations of abuse.

"I've got good news and bad news, Mother," she said, not really expecting her mother to listen to her. "The good news is that we're going to have money again."

Her mother nodded.

"The bad news is I'll be moving back to L.A."

"A star is born," said Lucinda dryly.

Amanda didn't respond, just picked up her plate, dumped everything into the sink, and hurried into the privacy of her room. She picked up her trial journal and began leafing through the pages. Soon her good mood was restored. By tomorrow, there would be a picture of her in the newspaper, maybe a profile. She touched an empty page in her journal where the story and picture would go. She smoothed the page with her hand, picturing her photo, anticipating the story. She loved the grainy feel of the heavy paper. She found a picture of Earl and touched it too, her long fingers caressing his face, his broad shoulders. The thought of masturbation came and went; she was too tired.

It was only nine-thirty. Her skin still felt cool, her well-toned muscles relaxed, the sounds in her head under control. She knew she would sleep tonight, and without pills.

She felt more alive than she could remember.

Barrett Dickson had also reclaimed a semblance of optimism as he sat in his apartment working on his closing argument. The reluctant advocate would do the best he could for his contemptible client, despite Lev's suspicions and the fear that bubbled under the thin skin of his new resolve. Ashford's contrived sincerity would largely neutralize Babcock's buffoonery, and leave the jury with nothing to go on but a failed prosecution case, the Ligretti debacle, and the fact that the most crucial evidence in the case had been either lost or destroyed. It added up to a clear case of reasonable doubt, no matter what the jurors really thought.

Jesus, he thought, I could *win* this case!

Then, as he found himself doing a lot lately, he thought about Grace Harris. So smart, so attractive. A decent person, who would have to bear the burden of the prosecution's defeat. Field would see to that.

He would try make it up to her someday if she would let him.

Across town, in the Hall of Justice, Earl Field and Grace Harris met to coordinate their closing arguments.

"We can't touch the Jefferson thing in argument," said Grace. "Clear grounds for appeal."

Field sat behind his desk, staring at his knuckles. "Yes," he said quietly. "Clear grounds."

"Are you all right, Earl?"

Field managed a halfhearted smile. "Sure. Just a little tired."

"We're not going to win, Earl," she said bitterly. "That's the good news for your friends in Chicago, though it's bad news for the rest of society, particularly the people of the state of California we represent."

Earl Field didn't react.

"On the other hand," she continued, "I don't think we're going to lose, either. The worse-case scenario after I finish with Ashford is a hung jury."

"You're that certain of a hung jury?"

Grace said, "I am now."

"You're referring," said Field, his face still expressionless, "to the solid holdout vote we've just picked up."

"As if you haven't noticed the way the alternate has been staring at you?"

"I've noticed," he said, forcing a tired smile, then stunned her by adding, "but I don't want a hung jury, Grace. I want him found guilty."

Grace wasn't sure she had heard him right. She tilted her head but said nothing.

"He—they—killed Lani Jefferson," he continued, angry now. "I'm sure of it."

"A warning to the others?"

Field considered the question for so long, Grace wasn't sure he had heard it. "Jefferson was probably killed," he said at last, "to warn me as much as the other jurors."

Grace felt a chill. "The 'bingo' crowd?"

Field slowly rose to his feet and stared out at Bryant Street, now bathed in darkness but for a row of streetlights wrapped in fog and glowing like melting popsicles. A car horn sounded in the distance.

"They deny it, of course, but naturally they would." He laughed ironically, pitifully, and added, "After all, I am still the district attorney of San Francisco."

Grace nodded. She didn't know what to say.

"I've got to get him, Grace. I've got to stand up: not only for Lani Jefferson but for the man I was—or thought I was."

Grace felt an electric chill racing up her spine as Field turned toward her with burning eyes. "I can't let that juror's death go for nothing. We've got to bring it home to the jury that they've got to stand up now, too."

Grace nodded, but saw that he wasn't finished.

"You were right, Grace. About all of it. And I know you

knew about the missing evidence, the mob, the works. Thanks for hangin' in."

Grace shrugged to conceal the emotion she was feeling. "I wasn't really sure at first," she said. "Then, when I was, I decided the important thing was to try and salvage the case. After that, Earl, I was going to—"

"I know," he said. "I'd expect nothin' less of you."

Then he cleared his throat, squared his shoulders, and said, "But now I expect more of you than ever before. First, there's got to be a way we can take advantage of what those jurors must be thinking at this point."

Grace tried to clear her head. She wanted to know more but knew she would be better off not knowing the details until later.

"Suppose we move to sequester first thing tomorrow morning," she said. "The word will get back to the jury and confirm that someone is trying to scare them and that we're the good guys trying to protect them."

Field nodded, "I like it," he said, "but we'd also be playing into Ashford's plan by confirming they're at risk."

"But trumping his ace by sequestering."

Field nodded, then smiled broadly and said, "Okay, good. Let's find a way to stop this train wreck, Grace, despite the fact I've pulled up half the tracks."

35

Amanda awoke early the next morning and began counting the minutes until the trial would resume. Her brain reeled with anticipation as she pictured the photographers who would be waiting for her, begging her to look their way as she entered the courtroom today and every day until the verdict of guilty was announced, a verdict she would have achieved despite the forces against her. Amanda was vaguely aware of her penchant for fantasy, but this time her dreams seemed to rest on the bedrock of reality.

At seven, she heard Lucinda in the kitchen, making coffee, taking care of herself again. She smiled, for this was the first indication that her mother believed she was serious about leaving.

Amanda began her preparation. The hair would have to be perfect today. And what to wear? She reached for her best Donna Karan knockoff. It was low-cut but not shocking, and the dress nicely concealed her thighs while revealing her fine knees and calves.

Two hours later, as Amanda entered the Hall of Justice, everything was exactly as she had dreamed it would be: the cameras flashing and whirring, the news reporters pleading for her attention, her name on all their lips.

But again the jurors were delayed in the jury room, and when they were at last called out, a silent alarm went off in Amanda's head. As she and the other jurors filed into the courtroom, the air felt heavy with tension. The judge was already on the bench, which was unusual. Dickson, the big fellow, looked angry, and so did Ashford. That was good, but what was going on?

"Ladies and gentlemen of the jury," Judge Hernandez began, "since excusing you yesterday late morning, I have been in consultation with the police and the county coroner almost continuously, for reasons you can probably deduce. In addition, I have read notes sent by some of you in confidence, and I assure you that in confidence they shall remain.

"That said, it is with great personal regret that for a variety of good and sufficient reasons, I now find the necessity for, and do now therefore declare, a mistrial in the case of People versus Elliot Ashford."

The gallery exploded as one in a mass declaration of shocked denial. The gavel pounded impotently and Ashford slammed fists on the table, drawing anxious looks from Fred and the additional bailiff the judge had ordered in. Most of the onlookers continued to shake their heads in disbelief. Reporters rushed toward the corridor as if storming an enemy beachhead, cell phones drawn. The expressions on the faces of Grace Harris and Earl Field revealed nothing. The jurors looked at one another like shipwreck survivors.

Except for Amanda Keller, who looked straight ahead, her eyes glazed with shock, refusing to believe what she had just heard. Even as Judge Hernandez summoned counsel to chambers—after he had thanked and excused the jurors— she sat frozen in her cherished seat, staring straight ahead. There had to be some mistake.

In chambers, Ashford continued to rage until the judge finally lost patience and threatened to have him removed. Dickson sat pale and expressionless, the scaffolding of his newly constructed hopes collapsing around him. He managed to renew his motions for the record, urging the judge to recall and sequester the jury rather than dismiss them. He then made a feeble double-jeopardy motion to protect the record for appeal.

"Thank you, Barrett," said Judge Hernandez. "That motion is also denied. I now mark and attach as exhibits for the record notes from five jurors indicating their unwillingness to continue on the jury. Some had become good friends with the deceased and simply cannot continue. The record will also show we have only two alternates remaining, not counting Ms. Keller, who became a regular juror yesterday. I must also say, Barrett, that even if there were sufficient willing and able alternates, the tenor of these notes is such that I would be doing your client a serious disservice if I granted your motion and allowed the case to proceed to a verdict."

"They think," said Ashford, roused as if from a trance, "they believe that . . ."

"I'm sorry to say it, and I apologize to you, Mr. Ashford, but this jury, by virtue of their feelings for Ms. Jefferson, is seriously tainted."

"Oh, Jesus, Jesus," murmured Ashford, his anger melting into despair.

"All right, counsel," said the judge, "barring any unforeseen motions, retrial of the case will commerce in two weeks."

Two weeks! thought Barrett. No time to get new counsel and no grounds for extricating himself. The sudden and cold grip of dread in his gut made him forget his sore back; made him forget everything, in fact, except that he was now trapped in the complete retrial of a complicated case that would demand something of him he no longer had to offer.

He glanced over at Grace Harris. She seemed to be reading his melancholy state. He thought he saw her lips part as if to speak to him. She said nothing, of course, yet something was conveyed in the look she gave him in the silence. Something important.

His heart quickened despite his despair.

Thirty minutes later, the skinny bailiff came out to lock up the courtroom and saw a woman still sitting in the jury box, back rigid, hands on knees, eyes fixed in front of her. Juror number three.

"Sorry, ma'am," he said, "but you'll have to leave the courtroom now."

Amanda didn't seem to hear him. All she could hear was the buzzing in her head, the sound of the electric coil as it tightened around her brain. The bailiff repeated himself, then gently put his hand on her arm. Her body jerked as if she had been hit with a cattle prod, and she snarled at him to leave her alone, then pumped an inhaler into her mouth, shook it twice, and dropped the empty container on the floor.

"I have to lock up now, ma'am. Everyone's gone."

"They'll be back," she said, then coughed twice.

"No ma'am, the judge has declared—"

"The judge will change his mind. He has to change his mind!"

"He won't be changin' his mind, Ms. Keller. The trial's over."

But Amanda no longer heard him. "I must be ready," she said, her eyes fixed on the door leading to the judge's chambers.

The bailiff went to his phone at a table just inside the rail and dialed chambers.

"I think we've got a problem out here, Your Honor," he whispered. "Juror number three; you know, the alternate? She won't leave her seat. I think she's a nutcase."

"Nutcases are your department, Ben. Handle it."

Ben handled it by calling for backup, and after token resistance, Amanda finally yielded to the persuasive demand of a sheriff's matron, who escorted the dazed woman from the courtroom.

"Are we in recess?" Amanda said.

"That's right, lady. Recess."

Alone in the corridor, Amanda looked both ways but saw no one. No reporters, no crowds. Everyone was gone. She turned around and tried to reenter the courtroom.

Locked.

She pounded on the door for five minutes, louder and louder, but there was no answer.

In a daze, she finally left the courthouse. She managed to find her bus, though she passed her transfer stop and rode to the end of the line and back. The driver eyed her but said nothing.

Amanda struggled for understanding but couldn't think straight. She tried to remember what she should be doing. Someone had to clear up the confusion at the courthouse and in her head, which sounded like it had been invaded by a swarm of bees. She could feel the buzzing down into her neck now, and rubbed it hard with both hands without result. *Stop it!* she said, and several people turned in their seats to look at her, then quickly looked away.

That night, Barrett sat alone in his apartment, phone off the hook, a bottle of vodka his only companion. He had almost pulled it off, but the death of Lani Jefferson would have consequences reaching far beyond her immediate family: gone now was Mike Reasoner's ascendency to the firm's executive committee, and with it, any hope of saving the firm itself. Gone too was the hope of resuscitating his tattered professional reputation, which somewhere along the way had assumed renewed importance to him. Gone too was Ashford's clear shot at a defense verdict, which Barrett, despite his suspicions, still believed he was entitled to. Leviticus was wrong for once. Ashford neither did it nor had it done. He and his associates would not have risked a possible mistrial on the verge of victory; they would have made it look like an interrupted burglary. Broken a ·window. Raped her. Something. Yes, Lev had been wrong for once. The real murderer or murderers *wanted* Ashford to be blamed for both Lara and Jefferson. That's why they picked a juror obviously leaning toward the prosecution.

But who *had* killed Lara? One of her romantic dalliances? Senator Dwight Clifton? A street lunatic? Someone jealous of her, a sister maybe? The police hadn't tried very hard, but they hadn't turned up any obvious enemies. Ditto Jefferson, who may have simply succumbed to the bent will of a copycat killer.

He decided to change the water in Fred's and Ginger II's bowl. Fred wasn't looking so good.

He poured more vodka into his glass, not noticing or not caring that the last of the ice had melted. He just wanted this night to end, to escape the pain of it.

But sleep would not come, no matter how much he drank. Someone knocked on his door around midnight. Mike's voice. Television was off. Lucky. Stay quiet. Mike's fist against the door, shouting *"I know you're in there!"* That's real original, Mike. Finally, footsteps retreating. Have another drink.

At two-thirty, the misery had blurred into confusion and he staggered into bed. But no comfort awaited him there, and after an indeterminate period of time he gave up, got up, and realized he was still fully clothed. Even his tie was on. Sort of.

He entered the kitchen and found two inches of Ketel left. He'd have to switch to tequila soon if sleep could not be found at the bottom of the vodka bottle.

He found no sleep there, only nausea, then vomiting, on his knees praying to the ceramic goddess, his hands splayed against the cold floor tile. He stumbled out of the bathroom, slipping on the floor as he ripped off his tie, soaking wet—how the hell did that happen—then ducked his head into the kitchen sink and drank from the tap.

"I had it won!" he heard himself say out loud, then to himself: *Sweet Jesus, I had it won.*

For some reason, the notion of DNA popped into his head and the thought of it stabbed at his heart. What did he know about DNA? Absolutely nothing. How could he do this without Menghetti?

How could he do this?

How could he?

How?

Finally, at 4:00 A.M., still slumped in his one comfortable chair, a half-full glass of Patrón tequila fell from his hand. Barrett had finally pulled the shade on the second-worst night of his life.

PART THREE

THE WITNESS

We are all prisoners of our childhood . . .
—Alice Miller

Anybody can kill anybody.
—Lynette "Squeaky" Fromme

36

The participants in the abortive trial had little in common, but the question asked by each of them in the wake of Lani Jefferson's murder was identical.

"Damn it, Julian," demanded Elliot Ashford, irritably pushing his plate aside, *"what the hell do we do now?"*

Although the meal at San Francisco's famed President's Club was winding down, Julian Gold, who never discussed business while eating, refused to be hurried.

"I'd suggest a 1967 Darroze Armagnac, Elliot," he said, dabbing his lips with a napkin, "unless you want dessert first."

Ashford scowled. He was angry at himself for bringing the ugly, unsympathetic *consigliere* to the club for lunch. Elliot Ashford loved his "downtown club," its high-vaulted interiors, the sweeping view of the city, a chef who had trained with Jacques Pépin in Paris, its male waiters, and even the supercilious maître d'. Ashford had promised himself that he would try to put the case aside for an hour or two and let nothing detract from the pleasure of his return to the club, but his patience was exhausted.

"Your humor is inappropriate, old *friend,*" said Ashford in his most sardonic tone, "given the fact that I go back on trial for my life in a matter of days, that I am without competent counsel, and that probably half the country now thinks I'm a double murderer."

Julian Gold sipped from a glass of fine Petite Sirah, then managed a look of mock sympathy as he said, "Come now, poor Elliot, you'll need a sense of humor before this is over."

Ashford angrily snatched up his wineglass, drained it, and slammed it down on the table, drawing surprised looks from nearby members. "I'm fed up with all of it, Julian: the thought of facing another trial, the way people look at me . . ."

Gold glanced up from his veal chop and gave Ashford a look so unreadable it might have passed for either sympathy or disgust. He then pushed his plate away and accepted coffee from the waiter.

"What about trying for a change of venue?" said Ashford. "One of the commentators on CNN mentioned that last night."

"Please pass the cream," said Gold.

It occurred to Ashford that the *consigliere* was intentionally testing his patience, but at last he spoke. "To the extent you've still got a power base, Elliot, it's right here in San Francisco. This story is international now and you won't escape the reach of the press by moving the trial to some cow county in California. And don't forget that Mr. Field is getting his share of bad publicity from his bungling of the first trial."

"All right. But I repeat: What do we do now? What do we do for a lawyer?"

"You have a lawyer."

"I have a walking disaster."

"You also have no choice."

Ashford started to protest, but Gold raised a hand that commanded silence. "The good ones are all too busy or don't want to step in with so little time to prepare. The bad ones you wouldn't want, believe me."

"Christ, Julian, the sonofabitch nearly killed me two nights ago. Practically accused me of murdering that juror. I may be naïve, but isn't a defense lawyer supposed to defend his client, not try to beat him into a confession?"

"Listen, Elliot, for all his faults, Dickson's still smarter than any criminal defense lawyer in town, and he knows the case, plus he remains a friend of the judge, despite the problems with Mr. Menghetti. Even more important, I watched the jury and they liked him. They saw he was nervous, and they liked that, too. Most important of all, the man exudes a certain fundamental ethical quality that trumps his other shortcomings."

Unable to summon up a rejoinder to Gold's litany, Ashford signaled the waiter for another liqueur he didn't want.

Gold hunched forward and spoke in a quiet but intense voice. "Finally, Elliot, you have no viable option. Simply put, you're stuck with the bastard."

Ashford twisted the empty glass in his hand, succumbing to a deepening despair. He felt Gold's eyes on him, assessing him, as always. Then he let out a sigh of resignation and said, "Will he do it? Will he stay on?"

Gold grunted and made a face. "When I asked him, he just stared at me at first and said nothing. So I offered him a personal million-dollar bonus if he won and a quarter million just for trying, over and above what we pay his firm."

Ashford shook his head. "I don't think money's an issue with Barrett Dickson."

"Very insightful, Elliot. I'm impressed. So I also reminded him of how Tony Rizzo had abandoned you, then I insisted you were innocent and told him you merely wanted justice, nothing more, nothing less."

"Good. What did he say?"

"He said: 'Mr. Ashford is to justice as a dog is to a hydrant.' "

"He didn't—"

"He did," said Gold.

"Well, did he agree to do it or not?"

"I suppose he did," said Gold, gazing up Pacific Avenue at some street people at the Columbus intersection, drinking out of paper sacks and arguing.

"How do you know?"

Gold turned back to Ashford. "I believe his exact words were: 'It looks like I'm stuck with the bastard.' "

"What the hell do we do now?" shouted Lucinda, but Amanda said nothing. She had spent the entire weekend sprawled with her cats across the couch in their Noe Valley flat, watching television, struggling to hold together the frayed ribbons of her sanity, and wondering why they had done this to her.

Sometimes the electric current that surged through her body would stop and she would sleep. Often, even her momentary slumber would be tortured by her recurring dream of the man and the doll in the coffin. When she awoke from her naps, she felt as if she had touched a third rail.

At times it seemed her heart was a generator, shooting charged blood through her veins.

She wondered how it had all gone wrong. She had been so sure her jury summons was a sign. She rechecked her astrological charts and everything was in order. Who was to blame for this? The Mafia? Ashford? What had she ever done to them?

On the third morning—Monday—she dressed herself, but she was too shaky to leave the apartment. Lucinda called Harold Pierce to report that her daughter was sick again and seeing a doctor.

"He didn't sound happy, Amanda. And I'm not happy either havin' to spin tales for you."

"Screw him. And screw you too, Mother."

Lucinda put a hand to her chest, too shocked to say anything.

Back in her room, Amanda briefly considered actually seeing a doctor for her pain, maybe going to the emergency room. But what if they kept her?

Like before.

She tried to reassure herself that she would be all right if she could just get some rest. She knew she shouldn't be drinking, but the bourbon seemed to muffle the humming of her veins. If only she could do something to relieve the tight coil of wire in her skull that seemed bent on electrocuting her brain.

She got into Lucinda's stash of cigarettes and started smoking again for the first time in four years, worsening her asthma attacks.

At noon on Monday, Harold Pierce called and she made the mistake of answering the phone. She told him she was on medication but expected to be back to work soon. She couldn't get rid of him. He seemed to be trying to draw her out, and the last thing Amanda wanted right now was to be drawn out.

The phone rang again an hour later. It was the district attorney's office calling to schedule a posttrial juror debriefing and interview, so she took the call. For a moment, the request broke through the walls rising steadily around her, but then she hesitated, realizing she couldn't allow Earl Field to see her looking so unattractive.

"Leave me alone!" she shouted, then slammed the phone down and threw it across the room.

"My Lord!" shouted Lucinda. "Have you gone crazy?"

There was no answer, and during the next few days, Lucinda gave her daughter wide berth. She even began to prepare her own meals. Amanda ate little, caring only for her cats.

Late Monday afternoon, Lucinda cautiously approached Amanda when she was standing at the kitchen sink, wearing nothing but panties. Lucinda was visibly appalled to observe her daughter drinking water direct from the spigot and splashing it on her face, neck, and breasts.

"You've got to get back to work, Amanda," she said. "They called again while you were asleep."

Amanda considered that for a moment. People calling when she was asleep. Talking to her mother.

"You never wanted me on that jury, Lucinda," she said, pointing an accusing finger at her.

"Lucinda?" said her surprised mother. "You've never called me that, child."

"It's your name, isn't it?" said Amanda.

"Why, yes, but—"

"So answer me, Lucinda," said Amanda, eyeing her suspiciously. "Weren't you afraid the jury publicity would lead me back to Hollywood? Away from you and this stinking rathole of an apartment?"

Lucinda's face went totally blank with confusion. Amanda ordered her not to answer the telephone again and returned to her room, now convinced her mother was part of it.

On Tuesday morning, four days after the mistrial, Amanda awoke at 6:00 A.M., her head throbbing. She had finished her mother's bottle of Early Times the night before, and her face was red and swollen. She heard the *Chronicle* thump against the door, allowed time for the delivery boy to clear the hall, then warily opened the door and picked it up.

The dizziness hit her the minute she tried to straighten up, sending her staggering back inside and into the nearest chair. She looked down, not at the paper but at the hands that held it. They didn't seem connected to her. *Is that a liver spot?* She was too young for liver spots, but it was her hand, it had to be. She clenched her fingers to be sure, then violently shook them.

The liver spot was gone.

Reassured, she scanned the paper for news of the case. On page 3, she read that Ashford's retrial had been scheduled to start the day after Thanksgiving. The last paragraph of the article noted that Earl Field would be attending a Democratic fund-raiser at 5:00 that very afternoon at the Hyatt Hotel.

Amanda let the paper slip to the floor.

Earl Field. Why hadn't he called her himself? Was he avoiding her? Was he trying to protect her? She remembered the way he had looked at her during the trial, the wholeness she had felt in his presence. Perhaps he could lead her out of this mess, this state of confusion and pain. Help her fight them.

She decided to attend her first fund-raiser.

"So what the hell do we do now?" asked Earl Field the minute Grace entered his office.

"We try him again, of course," Grace said, noticing that the D.A. looked uncharacteristically haggard. What had happened, she wondered, to his new fierce resolve?

Field didn't respond right away, just stood there in front of her, kneading the palm of one hand with the thumb of the other.

"Of course," he said at last. "But can we win?"

"You'd have trouble finding anyone in town taking bets against us, Earl. The *Examiner* poll shows that most people think the man has now killed two people."

"Do you believe that, Grace?"

"I don't know, but it certainly looks like someone was sending a message to the other jurors."

"Or to us," he said.

"Well," said Grace, "what do you think we should do?"

"I don't know what to think anymore," said Field in a fatigued voice. He started to say something else, then caught Grace looking at his fidgeting hands and shoved them in his pockets.

"Maybe we should consider a deal," he said finally, forcing his eyes to meet hers.

Grace felt her face reddening. "We owe the people of this city more than that, Earl."

Earl Field turned and walked behind his desk, where he fell into his chair, swiveled toward his Bryant Street window, and stared out at the darkening sky.

Grace shook her head and walked out.

As Barrett Dickson drove along Doyle Drive toward the entrance to the Golden Gate Bridge, he said aloud to no one:

"What the hell do I now?"

He had begun to hope—with no great assurance—that the Dickson Curse was dead or that it had just been imagined or that it had simply passed on to somebody else, like the strain of flu currently going around. But a woman was dead, and if Ashford did do it, the demon curse was very much alive.

He flipped the radio on, then remembered the aerial was broken. He turned his thoughts to a trip he would take to New Zealand after the retrial, when he had finished his real estate exams. He pictured himself taking Grace Harris to a movie after he returned, getting to know her. He made a note to call his piano teacher. He tried to take in the beauty of the Bay to his right, the vast ocean to his left.

But a woman was dead.

He tried again to convince himself that nobody had more to lose from a disruption in the first trial than his client. It was true, damn it! Then he thought about seeing Lev and Mike in an hour or so for some laughs and dinner in Mill Valley. Getting away from the city for a few hours. Getting away from it all, if only for a while.

It was only four-thirty, but he had decided to drive on over to Marin County and have a quiet drink or two at the restaurant before his friends arrived. He glanced ahead at the storm clouds now crowning the Marin Headlands, driven in by a hard wind from the direction of the Farallones, slowing traffic to a crawl northward over the Golden Gate. The weather suited his mood.

Entering Marin County, he gazed to the west, where acres of untamed oak still ruled the ridges of the headlands. A few miles north of the tunnel, however, the hillside had been domesticated into rows of condos that erupted like

sores on the face of the saddleback, condos he would soon
be selling to people with two cars, two kids, and nervous,
hopeful smiles.

Freshly paved asphalt roads and rogue patches of surviving forest edged with buckwheat and Scotch broom separated one architectural travesty from another. Adjacent
virgin lands awaited approaching developers with rape on
their minds, while farther north, Mount Tamalpais—fog
spilling down through its ridges like waterfalls—towered
regally beyond their reach.

After their marriage, Barrett and Ellen had hiked up
Mount Tam one spring day and made love near the top,
sprawled and thrashing like animals on dry golden grass
without so much as a blanket. He recalled the raw perfec-
tion of her body and a teasing sensuality that had ruined
him for anyone else. He could still see her tanned face, the
sheen of her long blond hair as it fell toward her small
breasts, brushing the tops of his hands.

Then another face, a woman's face, crowded back into
his mind; the face that had dominated his thoughts for the
past seventy-two hours. Juror number three, Lani Jefferson.

Two dead women with nothing in common but himself.

His heart began to thump against the walls of his chest
as he edged his aging Mustang into the restaurant parking
lot. He turned off the engine and looked in the rearview
mirror. His forehead was beaded with sweat. He was out
of the city now, but the demon cast a long shadow.

He entered Piatti at four in the afternoon and sat alone
under an umbrella on the patio in the rear of the restaurant, watching rain fall on Richardson Bay. A dreary darkness already ruled the day, and by the time Mike arrived
at five-thirty, a state of melancholy ruled Barrett.

"You don't look so good, Bear," said Mike as they
moved inside to the bar.

"I'm fine," said Barrett. "Just a bit ravaged by reality
perhaps."

Mike Reasoner took a quick look into his friend's unfo-
cused eyes. "By vodka is more likely."

"That, too. Allowing myself a drink or two before I resume training for the Big Game. So buy me a drink, old
baldy."

Mike smiled and swung a leg up onto a stool. "Being ravaged by reality hasn't improved your manners."

Barrett lit a cigarette.

"Or your already impaired discipline," added Mike, moving the ashtray as far away as his arm could reach. "When did you start that again?"

"You're missing a great habit," said Barrett, smiling, but he could tell that Mike was studying him, observing the misery in his eyes.

"Good to see you, Bear," said Mike at length. "Sorry about the mistrial. You had it made."

"Good to see you, too, Mike," said Barrett, trying to shake off his depression, "though you're as big as Goat Island. Fall off your diet again?"

"This from a man to whom a six-pack and beef jerky is health food?"

"The temple of my soul is quite fit, thank you."

The bartender served drinks, and the friends sipped in silence for a moment.

"How about the soul itself?" said Mike. "What can I do to cheer you up?"

Barrett forced a smile and changed the subject. "How's Nancy?"

Mike shrugged and looked out a window. "No change, Bear. Not so good."

"Sorry," said Barrett, feeling a funereal silence drifting down on them. He in the jaws of the demon, and Mike dragged down by thoughts of Nancy. He could have kissed Lev's smiling face as he came charging through the outer door into the bar area. They greeted each other warmly and Barrett ordered up a bottle of Lev's favorite beer.

They talked 49er football and laughed about Lev's current problems with his sister-in-law. Barrett asked Lev if he had heard about the cannibal who said to his friend, "I really hate my sister-in-law."

"No," said Lev, "but I'll bite."

"One joke at a time, Lev. Anyway, the other cannibal says, 'Hate your sister-in-law? Try the potatoes.' "

Lev howled and Barrett felt his mood begin to lighten.

"Let's talk about the trial, Bear," said Mike when they had been seated at their table. "What do you see as the main problems and how can I help you?"

Barrett said, "The main problem is Ashford's lawyer, but some things can't be helped. Next, there's the challenge of finding a jury in a city where everyone suspects my client is mob-connected and may have just nailed another victim."

"Let me amend that a bit, Bear," said Leviticus. "They don't suspect; they know. And so would you if you opened your eyes."

Barrett saw Mike's eyebrows shoot up and said, "Mr. Positive Thinker here is convinced, Michael, that our friend Ashford—or someone acting in his behalf—killed one of my jurors in order to send a message to the rest."

Mike shook his head impatiently. "You don't *know* that, Lev," he said, "and damn it, neither one of you should even be speculating about it. That's not your job!"

"It's not speculation, Mike," said Lev. "The guy's a killer. Every time I think I've found something in his favor, it turns out to be a lie. I've seen the police files. I've watched him in court. The man's guilty."

Mike's impatience turned to irritation. "Barrett's an advocate, Lev, committed to a client in an adversary system!"

"Well, I'm not," said Lev, his expression also beginning to betray annoyance. "I'm just an investigator, paid to deal in reality."

"That's bullshit, Lev," said Barrett, finally feeling his drinks. "You never wanted to go up against Earl Field in the first place and you're feeling guilty now that he's looking bad."

Lev gave Barrett a hard look, then spoke so quietly Mike had to lean forward to hear him. "Let's not be gettin' into each other's unconscious motivations, Bear. You got your own special reasons for needin' your client to be innocent of this one. Am I right?"

The truth of Lev's observation irritated Barrett. Lamely, he retorted: "Now he's a shrink, paid to deal in bullshit."

"Jesus, you two," said Mike. "Will you listen to yourselves? A goddamn jury of two, and a hung jury at that."

Barrett let out a sigh and turned toward Lev. "Listen, Lev, you might be right about me, but you're wrong about Ashford. Sure, he's an asshole, but you believed Tony Rizzo when he told you he was with him when Lara was killed, am I right? As for killing Jefferson, trust me on this: Ashford knew he was going to win with this jury. Whoever

killed Jefferson also killed his chances for a sure defense
verdict."

"For the moment anyway," said Mike before Lev could
respond. "His chances aren't killed, Bear, just delayed. You
can win this case, Bear."

Barrett shook his head. "I was coasting on Al Menghetti's handiwork, Mike, reading carefully prepared questions to carefully prepared witnesses. Edgar Bergen."

Another silence.

"What about his blood, Bear?" said Lev, unwilling to
let it go. "And don't tell me you really buy Menghetti's
shaving theory."

"Jesus!" shouted Mike. "Don't you guys ever quit? Let's
eat something."

"Okay, I'll shut up," said Lev. "For now."

"Good," said Barrett, and the table went silent again.

"Listen, Lev," said Barrett in a tone of resignation.
"Let's get the blood issue resolved and see if you and I
can get back on the same page. I can't take on both of you
and Grace Harris."

"Fine with me," said Lev. "How do we do that?"

"Let's try to retain that Nobel laureate Menghetti
couldn't get the first time."

"Sandra Weiss?" said Lev.

Barrett nodded. "She's the top molecular geneticist in
the field, right? We'll get her to do a DNA analysis, both
qualitative *and* quantitative, okay? Put the damn thing to
rest once and for all."

"Sounds good," said Lev.

"Make sense, Mike?" said Barrett.

"Sure," he said, "as long as you're doing it to help your
case; not just to settle an argument that would be irrelevant
if you were real professionals."

"The professor never quits," said Barrett to Lev, and
Lev rewarded him with a smile that said they were still
a team.

"Okay, I'll give up for now, Bear," said Mike, beckoning
for the waiter, "if we can feed that temple you were talking about."

37

The mirror had been unkind to Amanda's dissipated features, but she did the best she could with extra makeup, then hid in the rear of the ballroom of the Hyatt where Earl couldn't possibly see her.

The trip to the hotel had exhausted her, and despite her excitement and the heat under her skin, she almost fell asleep during the brief opening speeches. When Field was finally introduced, Amanda was saddened to hear but a smattering of polite applause. Clearly, the trial had damaged his popularity.

But not his good looks and dynamism. Depleted as she was, Amanda felt the old stirrings, and waited to the end to steal a closer look at him as he left the ballroom. But now he was coming directly toward her, looking in her direction! She feigned a coughing attack and buried her face in a handkerchief. Then she heard his voice—that deep, sonorous voice reminiscent of a time of hope and excitement—and realized he was talking to someone in the row in front of her. She didn't dare steal a look at him, but just hearing his voice was enough to momentarily still the buzzing in her head and fill her with a budding optimism, the possibility of a new purpose.

Perhaps the jury summons was not a false sign after all; perhaps she had simply misread it. The astrological charts had confirmed that her life was about to be dramatically altered, and she had jumped to the conclusion that a return to Hollywood was being foretold. Could it be that the reason she had been summoned to the trial was not to step backward into daytime television, but forward into the arms of this great man. Perhaps the simple act of accepting his love would allow her to fulfill her true destiny.

The voice retreated, and she looked over her shoulder

to see a light-skinned African-American woman take Field's arm at the door. Amanda recognized the woman from television as Terry Morgan, his fiancée. She's attractive, Amanda thought, but far from beautiful.

Amanda's expression hardened as she watched Terry Morgan reach up and straighten his tie, then touch his lips with a finger. Amanda's eyes followed them as they walked off together toward a waiting limousine. She studied the woman's thin legs as she strode beside Field, her skirt provocatively tight.

Who do you think you are? came the voice inside her head.

She left the hotel and took a long walk. It was time to pull herself together, to regain her looks.

The next day, Amanda attacked the machines and weights at her fitness center with a masochistic vengeance. Within days, still claiming sick leave from Ward and Company, she began to feel strong again and could see the puffiness around her face disappearing. She still didn't look good enough to permit Earl Field a close look, but she began to take pleasure in viewing him from a distance; easy to do, for his schedule was a matter of public knowledge. She soon became familiar with his daily routine, close friends, and favorite eating places. After less than a week of this surveillance, she could practically predict which shoes he would wear on a given day.

During the hours when Field was out of her sight, she continued her rigid regimen, and when the full-length mirror told her it was time for the next step, she made an appointment to meet Field in his office. This was also easy, for she had been a juror on the first trial and had "information that might be helpful in the retrial." She chose her words carefully. She could trust no one but Earl now.

Nothing was left to chance in her preparation. She recklessly spent a large part of her dwindling savings on a new dress, a facial, and a massage to compliment her restored figure. Then she had her teeth bleached, her nails manicured, her legs waxed, and her hair coiffed.

She was ready, and none too soon, for it was her last day of sick leave and tomorrow she would have to return to work.

*   *   *

Amanda entered the reception area of the San Francisco
district attorney's office on the third floor of the Thomas
J. Cahill Hall of Justice building. Receptionists peered out
at her from behind two protective windows, speaking
through metal-louvered holes in the plate glass. They reminded Amanda of cashiers in a movie theatre.

Amanda took a seat, and within minutes a secretary
beckoned her through a door and down another hallway,
then past a rabbit warren of cramped offices. She noted the
name "Grace Harris" on one of the few such rooms containing only one desk. At the end of the hall was the D.A.'s
large office. The opulence of Field's office by contrast with
the sparseness of those she had passed was impressive.

"Hello, Ms. Keller," said Earl Field, smiling warmly the
way he had during the trial. He extended his hand and
added, "I appreciate you coming."

Amanda caught her breath as he took her hand in his.
He was even more handsome than she remembered. She
said thank you—which sounded stupid as soon as she had
said it—then smiled back. Her heart was pounding. She
noticed that his hand was warm and felt large for a man
his size. He seemed reluctant to release hers. There could
be no doubt that he still felt the same attraction she did.

Amanda's script called for her to begin by conceding that
his case was in trouble and that the mistrial was a blessing.
Field nodded in apparent agreement with this observation,
but said nothing. She kept talking, but he seemed to be
waiting for something more, more than she was offering
him. She volunteered her impressions of the other lawyers.
She discussed the personalities of some of the other jurors:
what worked with them and what didn't. She reiterated that
most of them seemed to be leaning toward reasonable
doubt.

"Yes," said Field when she had run out of points to
make, "Investigator Quon's interviews with the others generally confirms what you are saying, Ms. Keller. We were
definitely in trouble. I'm afraid that Ms. Jefferson's death,
though regrettable, was not entirely without purpose."

"But you've had so much experience," Amanda cooed,
turning to a positive mode. "Even if there had been no

mistrial, I'm sure you would have turned things around somehow."

"Perhaps," he said, then with a dismissive shrug added, "perhaps not."

This wasn't working. Script change.

"I saw you at the fund-raiser last month," she said. "Your speech was *wonderful.*" Amanda going personal.

"Thank you, Ms. Keller," he said, sounding so business-like! That was all, just *thank you.* Then he added, "My secretary thought you might have some unique suggestions for the second trial."

Amanda flushed. He was supposed to have forgotten about the trial by this point in the scene. Why was he acting so distant? Were they being watched? Her thoughts raced.

"Well," she said haltingly, "I think you should personally handle all the cross-examinations next time. Ms. Harris is a fine lawyer, but, well, she's not you."

He nodded, but somewhat ambiguously. Waiting.

"And . . . let's see. I think you should shorten the confusing DNA testimony."

He nodded perfunctorily.

"Well," she said, feeling perspiration forming at her hairline. "I could tell you where each of the other jurors stood in the first trial."

"We already have their detailed interviews, Ms. Keller."

Nothing she said seemed to interest him. She heard herself talking faster. Her throaty tone had crept up a half octave. He glanced at his watch.

She began making things up; things that the other jurors would never have told an interviewer because they weren't true.

"Most of the jurors would never admit it," she said, "but we believed Armand Ligretti."

He nodded.

"We all hated Mr. Menghetti. Most of us didn't trust him."

He nodded again.

"Dickson seemed to be angry at everyone. If he's still on the case next time, you'll have no trouble."

Field continued nodding politely as she babbled on, attributing her own personal reactions to a majority of the others, but not once did he so much as pick up a pencil.

She told him it seemed a bit warm in the office, and he politely reached behind him and flipped a switch. She kept talking. He swiveled back and forth in his chair. She couldn't seem to connect with him, no matter how many times she flashed her best smile, moistened her lips, or allowed her skirt to hike up well over her knees as she recrossed her fine legs.

Finally, he glanced at his watch again.

"Ms. Keller," he said, "I very much appreciate your effort in coming in to see us. Rest assured that I will consider your remarks quite carefully."

Was he concluding the interview? She felt herself losing focus, just when she needed it the most.

"When," she asked, as if she hadn't just read the answer in the afternoon *Examiner,* "will the retrial begin?"

"Just after Thanksgiving," he said, "and next time, because of good citizens like yourself, I think we'll have something to be thankful for."

Citizens like yourself? He sounded as if he were making a political speech. Her annoyance grew. Didn't he realize the risks she had taken for him? She felt a drop of perspiration skidding down between her breasts. Her face was hot and she wondered if her forehead was shiny. Perhaps she should excuse herself, powder her nose, regroup.

"Ms. Keller," he said, filling the brief silence, "I do thank you for coming in."

My God, he was standing up! She felt her nervousness giving way to anger, but knew she must try to conceal it. There must be a reason he was concealing his feelings for her. She must be patient.

"Please," she said, subduing her frustration, "I wish you'd call me Amanda."

"Amanda," he said simply, and extended his hand.

It was over. He was kicking her out of his office.

Who do you think you are?

As she stormed through the door, Grace Harris was in the hallway, waiting to come in.

"What was that all about?" she asked.

Field shrugged. "That was the alternate," he said, shaking his head. "Keller, I think her name was."

38

Never one to suffer rejection lightly, Amanda surprised herself this time. Instead of resorting to the aid and comfort of pharmacological pacifiers, booze, recreational drugs, or attempted suicide, she returned to her job instead. Between her attendance at trial and a week of sick leave, Amanda had been absent from Ward for more than a month.

Morale at Ward was at an all-time low, and Marla, the new girl, was more impossible than ever. The only thing that kept Amanda going was her new strategy. Having convinced herself that the abortive meeting with Earl had been little more than a "tiff" of her own making, she resolved to be more direct with him. Next time, she wouldn't just sit there like a stone, telling him things he already knew. She would reveal what she had tried to do for him with the regular jurors, the incredible risks she had taken.

She would also be sensitive to his insecurity, remembering something she had read about black men with beautiful white women in *Cosmo* or somewhere. She would tell him he need not be either afraid or resentful, that she understood and accepted his feelings completely.

The minutes dragged on like hours until five o'clock delivered her out of the hated office and into Dave's World Gym. Members at Dave's had always regarded her with admiration, but now her displays of physical strength elicited wonder. The once shy Amanda no longer needed to ask whether she could work in with someone on an exercise machine; it was hers for the glancing. No-necks and pencil-necks alike watched in awe as she directed her frustration with home and office into violent assaults on the welded steel, momentarily pulling and pushing herself out of reach of the languor of depression.

She would look much better for her next meeting with Earl, she thought, curling a fifteen-pound dumbbell at the end of each arm. She wouldn't rush it this time, she promised herself as she completed three sets of a bench press—twelve reps—at 120 pounds.

The morning paper reported that Judge Hernandez had relented and allowed the defense an additional three weeks' delay for the start of the retrial. This would mean that Field would not be locked up in court again until mid-December. She would be ready next time, and on Christmas Day, she, not Terry Morgan, would be showing off his ring on her finger.

On Tuesday, November 18, with less than three weeks before the newly scheduled retrial start date, Grace Harris drove home in high spirits for the first time in weeks. She had just hammered out an arrangement with Earl guaranteeing her an equal role this time.

Trying cases was like other contact sports. Getting into the flow of the game off the bench was difficult, and like other top trial lawyers, Grace liked to establish a rhythm in the courtroom from the moment the panel of prospective jurors filed into the rear of the courtroom. So this time, she and Earl Field would share jury selection, split the opening statement, then alternate witnesses between them during the prosecution's case-in-chief. She would be stuck with the boring blood work again, of course, but would streamline it even more for the retrial. If Ashford were foolish enough to take the stand, she would cross-examine him.

Earl seemed himself again, so they would present a formidable team against a man who had never won a criminal case, representing a man the world believed to be guilty. There was but one problem.

"Jefferson was killed to warn me," Earl had told her, "not the other jurors."

The one problem was that either or both of them might be killed.

Grace was surprised that Aaron was not at the apartment. It was Monday night, their special time together, when, trial or no trial, exams or no exams, they dined at Spenger's across the Bay. He'd drink beer out of her bottle when the waitress wasn't looking, and they would laugh together, sharing more than just bottles of beer.

No note, no message on the machine. She felt panic rising in her. *Jefferson was killed to warn me,* Earl had said.

At eight-twenty the phone rang. It was Otis Gordon, a narcotics inspector who had testified in several of her early cases. All he had to do was identify himself and she knew what was coming.

"Your son has been arrested, Ms. Harris. Want to talk to him?"

"How much?" she asked in a weak voice, half relieved, half angry.

"A quarter of a gram. About four major toots."

"Cocaine?"

"Yeah. Cut with baby powder and juiced with speed."

She felt the air desert her lungs, saw her fingers go white on the phone.

"W-was my son holding?"

"No. Well, not exactly. Patrol found it in the glove compartment of a car driven by a kid named Benson, registered in his father's name."

"Ryan Benson? Shit, Otis, his father's Lowell Benson, the judge in Juvenile."

"Tell me about it. You want Aaron?"

Grace felt dizzy. "I'll b-be right down. What does he say?"

"He admits he chopped down the cherry tree. Knew the stuff was there, but hadn't used it. Told us to check his blood if we didn't believe him. Points for being a stand-up on knowledge. Ryan lied at first, claimed the Phantom must have put it there."

Grace felt her way into a chair as if blind. "Will my son be charged?"

"We're awkward here, Ms. Harris. If both had disclaimed any knowledge, we'd have had to haul in the registered owner of the car. Guess who? The press would have loved that one, so needless to say, the judge is seriously grateful to Aaron for his candor that eventually led to young Ryan comin' across too. Judge came down here, talked to both kids, concluded that Aaron hadn't used, and told me to get him the hell out of here."

"And his son?"

"Judge told me to throw the book at him. So I threw."

"I'll be right down."

Later, Grace and Aaron rode in tense silence over the Bay Bridge toward Spenger's, already adorned in Christmas lights. All six lanes were clogged with late commuters and early shoppers, which made the trip seem endless for both of them. It was probably stupid to have gone ahead with the plan, thought Grace, but she was determined not to allow this or anything else to break their routine. At a time like this, routine seemed important.

Grace had asked him the mandatory questions, throwing in one or two she thought a father might have asked. Aaron's answers were flatly delivered and typically honest: Yes, he knew the cocaine was in the glove compartment. No, he hadn't bought it. Yes, he had tried a little of it the week before to see what it was like, and no, he hadn't volunteered that information to Inspector Gordon.

By the time they hit Yerba Buena Island, Grace was fighting tears of anger, trying to think how best to deal with all this. She could see Aaron's occasional glances her way in the sliced fluorescent lighting of the Bay Bridge's lower deck, but neither said a word, even when they were in the restaurant's waiting area, where the decibel count rendered normal conversation impossible anyway.

Once they were seated at a table and Grace was sipping an uncharacteristic martini, Aaron finally spoke.

"You didn't have to bring me here tonight," he said, making that maddening sound in his throat.

"Force of habit."

The accidental phrase lingered between them.

"I'm not a junkie," he said, "if that's what you're thinking."

"That's good."

"And I'm not goin' out of my way to screw you up. Shit just happens sometimes."

Grace brushed hair back out of her face. "No, Aaron, shit doesn't 'just happen.' People mindlessly *make* it happen, then find some excuse for why it happened to them."

Aaron looked off to the side, though there was nothing there but a wall.

"My skill and training is putting people away for committing crimes. I don't have a clue how to prevent kids like you from committing them in the first place, but I'll be damned if I'll sit here and listen to you try to explain it away by mouthing something you saw on a bumper sticker."

"Geez, you talk like I'm some fucking serial killer. I'm just a kid in the wrong place at the wrong time."

"And I'm just a mom trying to be an adequate set of parents. You don't make it easier by experimenting with illegal substances and then blaming fate!"

Aaron offered his deep-throated grunt. "I was just curious. I'm not doin' crack or smack; just a joint now and then and some beers."

"That you steal if you have to," she said, giving him a hard look. "That was last time. This time it's drugs. Next time, Aaron, you are *on your own!*"

Aaron returned her look with his father's hard eyes. "I'm that way most of the time right now," he said.

Grace stared at her son. A shudder passed through her. She took a deep breath and pushed away her half-full martini.

"I won't leave you on your own, Aaron," she said after a full minute of silence. "And when this trial is over, we'll start over, too."

"That's what you always say, Mom. Sorry, but I don't believe you anymore."

Amanda finished applying her makeup, then gave herself a critical evaluation from various angles, her cobalt blue eyes searching the mirror for the slightest imperfection. She raised one eyebrow. Good. Give him that one. She also liked the half-smile look, with her chin tilted slightly up and to the right. Perfect.

Well, almost. What would she wear? She was nearly broke and would have to make do with what was in her closet. Her spending spree before the first meeting had wiped out all but $1,100 of her savings—barely enough to cover next month's rent. Her Visa card limit would yield another thousand to handle her food, fitness center, and incidentals. She would worry about that tomorrow, after her meeting with Earl. Who knows? A lot could happen in a month. If things went well, she might never have to work again.

Slipping on a bathrobe, Amanda placed a call to the district attorney's office. She took a deep breath and tried to steady herself. He was "in conference," but the secretary dutifully recorded her name and number and assured her he would return the call. Amanda thought she detected a slight hesitation in the secretary's voice on hearing her name, and tried to remember if she had been rude to anyone on her way out last time.

The hours dragged by without a callback. When she could wait no longer, she tried again.

"I'm sorry, Ms. Keller, Mr. Field is still in conference."

With great effort, Amanda assumed her sweetest telephone manner. "Perhaps you can help me then. I was a juror in the—"

"Yes, Ms. Keller, I know who you are."

Bad sign, but Amanda plunged ahead. "I've learned something of great importance to the retrial. Can you schedule an appointment? Perhaps later today?"

There was an instant of silence, then, "I'm sorry, Ms. Keller, Mr. Field is blocked solid with the Ashford retrial starting soon. But I'll certainly tell him you called," said the secretary, then added, "again."

"Thank you," said Amanda, "you do that."

Amanda stroked her temples, tried to relax. *Who does she think she is?* A clicking had started in her ears. *Stop it!* She decided to take a Valium before it turned into that damn electric buzzing sound again. An hour passed, then another, as she paced around the house, drawing irritated glances and occasional remarks from her mother.

"You're determined to wear out the carpet today, Amanda."

"I'm thinking, Mama."

"Thinkin's got you into one mess after another. Why don't you just go make us a nice cup of tea."

"Do it yourself," Amanda said. "I've got to meet Earl Field."

"Earl Field? What does he want with you?"

Amanda turned at her bedroom door, met her mother's challenging gaze, and the words just came out: "It happens, Mother, that I'm seeing Earl."

"You're *what?*"

But Amanda was off to her bedroom. She quickly dressed in the skirt and jacket she had laid out—one she had never worn to court—took a final look in the mirror, and caught a cab to the Hall of Justice.

Twenty-five minutes later, Grace, Sam Quon, and Earl Field were interrupted in the middle of a planning session by Field's secretary.

"Sorry, Chief," came his secretary's voice over the intercom. "It's the Keller woman again, sir. Reception and I are running out of excuses."

Grace gave Field a you-sly-devil look.

Field rolled his eyes and waved her away. "Start over with the old ones. And tell her not to call back."

"But she's here, Mr. Field. In the lobby."

"Have someone else take a statement from her."

Grace covered a smile with her hand. Field turned his back on her.

"She refused."

"Then let her sit," he said coldly, and switched off.

Grace said, "Well, Don Juan, you might have at least offered her a cold shower."

"I think she needs a straitjacket."

"Order one for me. My son was busted last night."

Grace shared her nightmare with Earl and Sam, then told them she had called her parents and they had agreed to take him for a few weeks.

"To Florida?" asked Sam. "What about school?"

"I've made arrangements for home study there," she said. "We need a break from one another."

"It's a wise decision," said Field, giving her a knowing look.

"He's still in conference, Ms. Keller," said the receptionist. "I'm sorry, but are you sure one of the investigators couldn't help you?"

"Thank you, no," said Amanda, wondering if the woman could see the throbbing in her temples and throat. "I'll just wait. Please tell his secretary that it's really quite urgent."

The receptionist shrugged. Amanda sat down again and tried to look relaxed. The receptionist wore tinted lenses and Amanda couldn't see her eyes, but she suspected they were studying her now. Maybe others were watching, too. She scanned the area for a hidden camera lens. The veins under her skin had begun to buzz again. She was reminded of the sound of the high-tension power lines that used to run over her school yard.

At 3:30 P.M., the receptionist made a final attempt to discourage Amanda's vigil, but Amanda remained resolute. Finally, a matronly-looking secretary emerged from a large inner office space.

"I'm afraid Mr. Field had to leave the office, Ms. Keller. There was an emergency in the Family Support Bureau, and he had to run out with his security team. He told me to apologize, and asked me to take down your information."

"He's *gone*? How can that be? I've been waiting right here! Didn't he know I was here?"

"I'm sorry, but . . ."

The woman kept talking, but her words floated toward Amanda like snowflakes and vanished on contact. Amanda tried to rise, but felt cold and dizzy and was aware that her upper body had pitched forward in the chair, her head between her legs. She could also see that the woman looked concerned and was probably saying something to calm her down, but her words didn't register. Amanda felt nauseous and a searing pain shot into her head. She had to get up. The receptionist was saying something, too. Amanda got to her feet but swayed, besieged by vertigo. Suddenly the floor rushed up toward her, then a blast of light. Then darkness.

She heard voices. Was she on the floor? She watched her own hands doing something in front of her, reaching for something. Ah, the umbrella.

I'm going to die right here in his office, she thought, and yet I won't forget my fucking umbrella. Mama will be proud. Your daughter passed away today, Ms. Keller. She's in the city morgue. Really? Did she remember her umbrella? That girl would forget her head if it—

Now someone was holding the umbrella over a casket. Amanda looked inside and it was her father and herself as a child. Whoever held the umbrella kept repeating her name, over and over. She opened her eyes and saw several tense faces looking down at her, then realized she had fainted and was lying on the floor. Someone had put a coat under her head.

"How long . . . what happened?"

"Can you tell us whom to call, Ms. Keller?"

"Do you have a regular physician, ma'am? A family member?"

"Stand back," a man's voice shouted. "Give her some air."

She rose to her elbows, feeling thoroughly humiliated, certain that her skirt was above her thighs, revealing her absolutely worst feature. She gave her head a shake and said, "No, thank you . . . a taxi, please."

As she was helped to the elevator, Earl Field observed the scene from his vantage point in the outer hallway.

39

Amanda dragged herself to work the next day, but despite the persistent buzzing in her head, she could hardly stay awake. She drank cup after cup of coffee and tried to maintain focus, but a single question now dominated her thoughts: Why were they keeping her from Earl? Were they afraid his love for her would somehow hurt him politically?

At lunchtime, Amanda returned to the Hall of Justice and stationed herself at the main entrance in hopes of catching him as he left for lunch. It was no use, and after more than an hour of watching, she was sure someone was watching her. She would have to be more resourceful.

She called in sick again, knowing her pay would be docked this time. No matter. She rented a car, and for the next few days began watching the district attorney again without his knowledge. It was easier this time; she knew his routine. She would follow him from his home in Pacific Heights to his office at 7:00 A.M., then again as he made the rounds of the outlying offices. There would be trips to grocery stores, to clothing stores, to the library—where he once spent thirty minutes without anyone seeming to recognize him—to a golf driving range, to the British Motors service department on Van Ness for servicing of his 1997 Jaguar V8 convertible, to lunches with friends, to a dental appointment.

She longed to feel his arms around her. She sometimes acted as if she could talk to him from a distance, about her feelings for him, her plans for them. She tried to plant things in his head telepathically, and once, during a speech, she willed him to look in her direction and he had.

Her power was growing, but so was the clicking and buzzing in her head.

At night, she would watch real-life dramas on TV with Lucinda. She sometimes felt like a character in the story, and when the drone of the electrical current occasionally thrummed all the way into her brain, she wondered if she was real or merely a figment of someone's imagination.

One night, she came home late from following Earl to a fund-raiser where she had fallen off the wagon and was exhausted. She decided to go straight to her room. Lucinda, absorbed in a rerun of *The Equalizer,* hardly acknowledged her presence. That was good.

Amanda headed straight for the medicine cabinet. She knew that the combination of phenobarbs with alcohol was potentially damaging, but so was her pain. The veins in her throat pulsated as if crawling with vermin.

Lucinda seemed to sense her weakness and grew bolder. Amanda could hear the wheelchair squeaking toward her door. "Amann-dahh," she sang. "You don't have Earl Field in there with you, do you?"

"Shut up, you withered old bitch!"

"Oh, my, please excuse my daughter's language, Mr. Field. Hah!"

Amanda felt the chords in her neck aching from anger and restraint. How she hated that woman.

"And please be gentle, Mr. Field," Lucinda shouted as she wheeled away, issuing a mirthless cackle.

Amanda rose from her bed and took a Demerol. She picked up her trial scrapbook, looked at her own picture taken the day she became a juror, then cursed and threw the book across the room, sending her cats scurrying into hiding and eliciting another sarcastic outburst from the living room that she couldn't hear over the din of the TV.

Sleep did not come, but by eleven-thirty the pain had slackened a bit. She retrieved her scrapbook and looked longingly at the photos of Earl Field. She touched his face, still sure of his love for her. There must be a good reason he was concealing his feelings for her right now, but why hadn't he at least called her? She was being tested, she realized, and would just have to be understanding until it was time for the ultimate truth—her life-altering destiny—to be revealed to her.

The pain was definitely easing now and she was thirsty. She crept out of her room and stealthily entered the kitchen, keeping an eye on the back of her mother's head. She hadn't made a sound, but Lucinda spoke out loudly without even turning her head from the image of Jay Leno in front of her, her voice oozing sarcasm.

"Amanda, why not bring Earl out to sit a spell?"

Amanda said nothing at first, determined not to allow her mother to vex her now that she was finally feeling drowsy. But then she turned and saw the back of Lucinda's small head, the thinning, dyed hair, jiggling from laughter, not at Jay Leno, Amanda knew, but at her.

"It so happens, Mother," she said, stepping out of the kitchen into the living room, "that Earl is very much in love with me. There are reasons we're not together yet, but when we are, don't expect to be invited to live with us."

Lucinda let out a loud, caustic cackle. "Wouldn't want to. Be too crowded with you and his new wife Terry Morgan there with her three kids." Another peal of laughter. "Watch the ten o'clock news once in a while, Amanda. Earl Field's going to be married soon and it ain't goin' to be to the likes of you."

Amanda felt her throat closing up and she knew she would soon be starved for air. "You . . . you'll see . . ." was all she could manage as she raced for her inhaler.

Back in her room, she cursed herself for having thrown away all of Lucinda's cigarettes. She considered walking the three blocks to the corner store, but the thought frightened her. Too dangerous.

An alien feeling was coming over her, as if she were someone else. She caught a glimpse of herself in the mirror on the back of her door and was shocked by what she saw: two burning coals set deep in dark canyons surrounded by ashen skin drawn tight around her skull. Who in the hell is *that*?

She stood frozen in place, horrified. The eyes that stared back at her were not her own. My God, she thought, someone else is inside me! But when she lifted an arm, it moved in the mirror. Good. When she nodded her head, she was relieved to see it move in the mirror too. Unless, of course, someone else had willed her arm to lift. She found a small knife and, after twenty minutes, managed to unscrew the full-length mirror from her door. Nothing behind it.

Get a grip, Amanda, she told herself. You're not crazy. You're not.

She picked up a book but she was too distraught to focus. Goddamn bitch, she thought. She would show Lucinda. She would show them all. She was thirsty again and her skin was burning worse than ever.

She thought she heard a sound at the front door. Had she locked the dead bolt? Her thirst and fear drove her from her room. She peered around the corner, down the short hallway toward the front door, then pulled together the shredded fabric of her courage and made for it. It was still locked, the dead bolt and chain in place! Nothing had changed. Everything where it should be. She walked quickly to the fridge and drank straight from the plastic container. Lucinda was asleep in her room at last, so she tore the kitchen apart looking for any cigarettes she might have missed during the health purge. She grabbed the water and hurried back to her room.

She felt more secure there, but the water did little to cool the blood smoldering just beneath the surface of her skin. She took a cold shower, then another Demerol with two more phenobarbitols. She glanced at her lethargic clock, saw that it had finally moved to nearly four o'clock. In three hours the sun would break through. That always helped. She lay down and pictured herself walking into Stars on the arm of Earl Field.

Screw you, mother!

No, don't even think about her. Don't think about anything!

The next thing she knew, it was one-thirty in the afternoon and Lucinda was calling her name and knocking on the door.

"Amanda? It's Mr. Pierce. He'd like to speak to you."

"Tell him I'm too sick to get up," she groaned. "Tell him I'll be in tomorrow."

Amanda lay on top of her bed in her bathrobe. Her head felt strangely clear, and her body was quiescent but for the mild hum in her veins she now took for granted. She turned her thoughts to her new plan of attack. It was Friday, the day Earl always had dinner with friends at Dino's.

First, an ice pack to reduce the swelling in her eyes. Then some juice and a bagel.

"Mr. Pierce sounded upset, Amanda. You'd better get right down there."

Amanda ignored her. Heard the wheelchair bumping its way toward the kitchen.

"Did you hear me, Amanda? You'd better not get on his wrong side. We have to live, you know."

"Shut up, Mother."

"Don't you do anything to upset him, hear? I'd be dead without that Ward health plan!"

Amanda resisted the opening and returned to her room. Did she still have that rental car? Yes, there are the keys on the bedside table. She quickly dressed and drove to her fitness center for a quick workout, just enough to get some blood circulating in her face. This time she would not fail.

By five o'clock, she was dressed and parked in a metered place just forty feet from where Earl Field's car sat in his reserved spot. At five-twenty, Field climbed into his car and drove to Dino's at the south end of the Embarcadero.

Amanda parked, counted to one hundred, then entered the restaurant and took up a position from which she could watch him without being seen. She allowed herself a second martini for courage, but no more.

She walked to a bank of telephones near the front door, called the restaurant, and asked to be transferred to the bar.

"Sir," said the bartender to Earl Field, "you have a call in the lobby. First booth."

Field groaned. "Must be my secretary," he told the mayor. "No peace with the Ashford retrial starting on Monday."

As Amanda watched Field talking to the bartender, she stared at her reflection in the glass of the phone booth. A moment of doubt assailed her. Maybe she should have waited a day or two. She felt dizzy but shook it off. Not now, Amanda. Be strong. She tilted her head from side to side, raised one arm, then the other. The reflection responded perfectly. She was there all right, though her skin was burning worse than ever. The heat came at her in waves, as if she were being grilled on a rotisserie. She took a precautionary hit from her inhaler and a final look at herself.

Earl Field entered the first phone booth, and when he emerged a minute later, a puzzled look on his face, Amanda was walking past the booth, looking just as puzzled.

"Earl Field!" she said. "My goodness, what a coincidence!"

Field's expression changed from confusion to surprise to suspicion in a matter of seconds.

"Hello, Ms. Keller," he said gruffly. "Goodbye, Ms. Keller."

"Wait, Earl, just a minute. I need to talk to you."

Field took a small step back. "I'm sorry, Ms. Keller, but I'm with people—"

Amanda gave him her most beguiling smile, the one where she tipped her chin slightly up and to the right. "But I'll just be a min—"

"Good-bye, Ms. Keller!" said Field, who had already resumed his swift retreat toward the bar. Not swift enough, however, to shake Amanda, who, taking two steps to his one, had attached herself to him like a barnacle.

Seeing her beside him, Field stopped at the entrance to the bar area and added, "It's a business meeting, Ms. Keller. I can't ask you to join us."

As he turned and again started to walk away, Amanda took him by the arm. Field looked wistfully toward the bar at the backs of his friends. "Earl, stop worrying; no one is watching us. Just tell me why you're ignoring me."

"What?"

"I want to know why you haven't called."

"Ms. Keller, I—"

"You don't have to pretend, Earl. And please call me Amanda when we're alone."

"Ms. Keller, Amanda, I really don't know what to say to you. I'm in the middle of an important—"

"All right," she said, taking him gently by the arm. "Follow me around the corner and give me just two little minutes, or I'll just have to come join you and your stuffy-looking friends."

Field sighed, then hesitantly followed her back out through the lobby area. Amanda walked her model's walk ahead of him, letting him have a good look. She paused on the steps just outside the side entrance to make sure he was following her, then slipped around the corner of the building where they would have relative privacy.

"All right, Amanda," he said gruffly, "let's hear it."

She hadn't counted on his coldness now that they were alone, but managed to stay composed. "It's just that I want you to know I did my best. They turned against us, Earl. I took . . . well, incredible risks to try to turn them around, to guarantee you at least a hung jury."

Field shook his head in exasperation. "I appreciate your past efforts, Ms. Keller, I really do. But . . ."

Field's voice drifted off. He became flushed and, through clenched teeth, said, "Is this why you've been hounding me? To tell me you did your best as a juror?"

Amanda moved closer, her lips now only inches from his, her breasts pressed against him. "Doesn't what I've done mean *anything* to you? Don't *I* mean anything to you, Earl?"

Field's eyes registered anger. He scanned the parking lot and the side door behind him for any potential observers, or worse, people with cameras.

"So that's it!" he said through clenched teeth, taking her by the shoulders and shaking her. "Just how dumb do your people think I am? Okay, Ms. Keller, which hotel room are you supposed to get me into?"

Now it was Amanda's turn to look confused. "It's not that at all, Earl. I'm on your side! They're against both of us. That's why we have to work togeth—"

"Listen up, Ms. Keller," he said, shoving her back against the wall. "You just tell whoever is payin' you that this uppity nigger from Hunters Point is smarter than all of you put together and that *nothin's* gonna keep him out of Sacramento!"

Amanda clamped her eyes shut and twisted her head from side to side in denial. "It's not like that, Earl. I . . . I love you and I know you feel the same!"

At last she understood the reason for his cold rebuffs; for his strange behavior and suspicion despite his obvious love for her. "How could I be part of a conspiracy? I was a *juror,* Earl!"

"Things can be arranged," he said coldly as he hurried off. "I know, I've arranged them."

Amanda fought to regain her focus, despite the pain shooting through her body and the loud hum just behind her eyes. She knew she could convince him if she could just calm him down. She caught up with him and grabbed his shoulder.

"I'm going back into the bar now," he said, shaking her off, "and if you follow me, I swear I'll call the police."

"The *police*?" she gasped. "My God, Earl, everything I've done was for *you*!" Her skin was burning up and her head felt as if it would pop. She glanced at her hand to see if it was on fire, then grabbed his arm again.

"Don't you understand what I did, Earl? What more could you have asked of me?"

Field gave a final look around, then said, "All I ask of you, Ms. Keller, is that you leave me the hell alone!"

He shook out of her grasp again and headed back up the concrete stairs toward the side entrance.

Amanda rubbed the stabbing pain at her temples, then swayed crazily after him, her arms extended, shouting at him.

"Who do you think you are? You stop when I'm speaking to you!"

He didn't look back.

"You *bastard*! You can't just lead me on all those weeks, then humiliate me like this!"

Field glanced back into the eyes of a hysterical and dangerous person and his expression suddenly registered fear. Something like this could escalate, make the papers, kill him at the polls. He looked through the outer window. He was close to the front entry now. A valet was heading toward them, fifty yards away in the parking area, and another thirty yards or so beyond him, a couple who had parked their own car. He had to end this somehow.

Amanda caught up with him, hysterical now, matching him stride for stride.

"I didn't 'lead you on,' Ms. Keller," he said, turning back to her, forcing himself to remain calm. "I don't even know you!"

"Do you deny the way . . . you kept looking at me,

smiling at me?" She was gasping now from the exertion of keeping up with him.

"I always smile at jurors, for God's sake. All of them."

"You looked at me in a certain way. I saw it!"

"I looked at every juror in a 'certain way,' Ms. Keller! So did Menghetti. We're trial lawyers. That's what we do! Do you think verdicts are won based solely on the evidence? Have you been on some other planet?"

Amanda grabbed him hard this time, pulling him off balance. "Are you saying you were just using me?" she snapped. "Is that it?"

"Look, lady. I don't know what to make of you at this point, but you stay away from me or I swear it's 911!"

"You *bastard*!" she shouted again, and lashed out at him with five perfectly manicured nails. He ducked just in time, then backpedaled and turned back toward the lobby. Amanda lunged after him. A shoe came off, but she didn't notice.

"Just who do you think you are, Earl Field? You look at me when I speak to you, hear! You stop it!"

But Field had hurried from the entryway, past the bank of telephones, and was nearing the lobby when he saw the valet closing in from the opposite direction. He had no choice now but to turn back in a final effort to silence his tormentor, clumping along behind him on one medium-heeled shoe. What he saw there was a complete stranger, staring at him through eyes even darker than his own, her irises and pupils undifferentiated in color; a disheveled crazy lady with sprayed hair sticking up like spikes, and the one shoe.

"I've tried everything else, Amanda, so one more word out of you and, so help me, I'll—"

Amanda grasped his coat again with fingers like steel claws. Her eyes fixed on his. "I saved your career, you ungrateful black bastard! And you're going to call the *police* on me?"

Field raised his hand and slapped her, slapped her hard, snapping her neck ninety degrees to the right. The violence of the act stunned them both, and they stood facing each other in sudden silence. A red welt began to spread across Amanda's left cheek.

"I'm . . . I didn't mean," Field stammered. "Oh, Christ!"

Amanda started to speak, but her breath failed her. Field, horrified, watched as her face drained of color and her eyes rolled up into her skull. The restaurant's maître d' came around the corner just as she began to fall and rushed to help catch her as she collapsed at Field's feet, first to her knees, then onto her side. The two men faced each other, and Field could see the questioning expression on the other's face.

"This woman is intoxicated," he said, his trial persona taking control, "perhaps drugs. She seems to be hallucinating."

"Let me take care of this, Mr. Field. The mayor sent me to see what was keeping you."

The valet came up the front steps through the entry door, nearly tripping over Amanda's purse, whose contents had been scattered around the lobby during the melee. The maître d' spotted her inhaler.

"My wife has one of these," he told Field. "Woman's probably had an asthma attack along with too much booze. I'll take care of her."

Recognizing the district attorney, the valet chimed in, "I'll get her car, sir. We'll take care of it. Don't worry yourself."

"I'm terribly sorry about this," added the maître d'.

Field reached into his pocket, handed each of them a C note, along with instructions to expect possible fabrications from "the poor soul." He reentered the bar just as the couple was coming up the steps from the parking lot.

"Hey, Earl," said the mayor, "we're starving here. Must have been important."

"Sorry, Henry. No, it was nothing important," said Field, downing his room-temperature Manhattan. "Nothing at all."

That night Amanda lay rigidly on her bed, still fully dressed. "The bastard," she said to herself over and over, "the paranoid bastard."

She was as convinced as ever that he loved her, but his crazy suspicions had doomed them now. The police! So they were in on it, too. Who else? There was no hope for her now. He should be protecting her; didn't he know they'd get him too?

Lucinda's efforts to learn what had happened went unacknowledged. Still, the old lady sat in Amanda's bedroom doorway in her wheelchair, berating her relentlessly.

"Go ahead, then," shouted her mother, "lay there like some sick cat mumbling to yourself while your mother starves to death."

Nothing.

"Did Mr. Pierce say anything about my health plan? You did go back to work today, didn't you?"

Amanda's only answer was to get up, slam the bedroom door, and prop a chair against the doorknob. Not even Lucinda could be trusted now. Then she closed both windows in her room so she couldn't be seen and so the filthy curtains wouldn't be dancing across her grave when they finished with her. That's what her bed was—or soon would be—a grave, and her blankets were the shrouds she'd be wrapped in after they electrocuted her, then pumped her dry of all fluids.

After an hour of cowering on her bed with her cats, she heard them talking outside, in the living room. Talking about her. Trying to sound like TV voices, they even had music in the background and canned laughter like a regular program.

The cats would be embalmed with her. They would want that. Like in Egypt.

She killed one of them quickly, painlessly, and thanks to the element of complete surprise, almost silently. Just the start of a screech, then the popping sound of his spine, which made no more noise than cracking open a king-crab leg at the Chanticleer. Just grab him by his thin little neck, spin him in a short arc, and no more cat. Got me on the arm, that's not so bad.

Amanda hoped that when they came for her, they would kill her just as quickly and mercifully.

She gave up trying to catch the other one. Siamese were smart. You didn't have to draw them a picture.

The woman outside her door shouted, "What's that noise?" but then went back to conspiring with the others.

Amanda finally fell asleep, but was soon drawn into a variation on her recurring nightmare. The coffin, now containing only her father and the doll, was leaking blood from all four corners. As the box was being lowered, Lucinda reached over and cut the leg off the doll so no one could see her. Amanda tried to scream as the coffin sank into the earth, but nothing came out.

She was just a doll.

Amanda awoke at five-thirty Friday morning after ten hours of troubled sleep and came across the stiffened body of her dead cat near her bathroom door. When she remembered what she had done, she quickly wrapped the dead animal in one of her pillowcases and slipped out of the apartment toward the back stairs. The cat felt like a baby in her arms. She wondered what color her baby with Earl would have been and pictured a perfect golden child.

Amanda feared that the super might hear her walking down the creaky stairs past his room, so she took off her shoes and laid them neatly side by side on the top stair before tiptoeing down into the dark basement. The concrete floor was cold on her feet and she wrinkled her nose against the dank and moldy smell of the place. She shivered as the fingers of her free hand groped for the light switch. There, on the other side of the storage lockers and cleaning equipment, blazed the incinerator. She ducked under a hanging lightbulb and managed to turn the stubborn handle, then pulled hard on the heavy door until it flew open. She recoiled from the blast of the giant oven, said a prayer to the Universal Power, then moved in close again and lovingly cremated her cat.

She returned to her room, quickly dressed, and tiptoed out onto the street. She caught her usual bus into town, but hopped off at Market and Stockton on an impulse and kept walking. She strolled east when she hit Bush Street, toward the Financial District, past once grand Victorians now converted to multiple dwellings for the young-but-upwardly-mobile Montgomery Street hustlers; past a gay theater with ads promising a double bill and "penetrating live action" onstage; then past the two-tiered, green-tiled, schlock-surrounded Grant Avenue entrance to San Francisco's Chinatown, now also surrounded by tourists, frantically posing and snapping each other's pictures.

They didn't even look at her. She was invisible.

The air was leaden in the Financial District and she stopped for a hit off her inhaler. The breeze off the Bay was barely sufficient to rustle her hair. She crossed Sansome, then headed east up Market and saw white light rising north of the Ferry Building behind a copper horizon. By the time she reached the Stuyvesant Building, home of Ward and Company, the sun had risen with the fury of a match dropped in a tray of gasoline. She looked up at the floors occupied by Ward and Company. Lights were coming on already, the early birds pecking for listings in the Financial District's concrete garden, and Muzak would soon start oozing from the ceiling, accompanying the hum of commerce.

She would survive, damn them all! She would endure.

Harold Pierce was up there somewhere, or soon would be.

She looked at her watch. She'd better get up there; she needed this hateful job more than ever now, but she also needed something to clear her head. She stopped at a coffeehouse for a double espresso, then had several.

At 8:45 A.M., Amanda entered the office and hurried to her desk. There was a note from Harold Pierce.

> *I regret to inform you that your services are terminated effective immediately. You will be paid two weeks' severance, but you are instructed to clear your desk and depart immediately.*

It had been written on Wednesday, two days before.

Amanda's gaze began darting crazily around the room and the buzzing in her head became deafening. Something felt loose inside her head. She rummaged frantically in her purse, but her inhaler must have fallen out of it. She read the note again.

"No!" she shouted, rising to her feet and storming into the main secretarial area. Everyone turned around to look at her but she didn't notice. She stormed toward Pierce's office and caught the luckless administrator, finishing a bagel at his desk.

"Are you serious?" she demanded, waving the note in his face.

Pierce froze in mid-bite and stared at the formidable figure looming over him. Without a word, he picked up the phone, dialed building security, and said, "Pierce, second floor. We may have a problem here."

"You bastard! I need this job. I've killed myself here without a word of thanks and damn little pay! Just who the hell—"

Pierce looked genuinely frightened as he jumped to his feet and held both hands up toward the approaching woman.

"Amanda, calm yourself. It's not me, it's the partners. They don't think you're fit to manage a file department right now. Being gone for a month in that trial seemed to change you. Then your absenteeism. A department manager has to set an example."

"So you're going to *make* me an example."

"They took it out of my hands, Amanda. I tried to protect you—"

Pierce never finished his sentence. Amanda was at his face, clawing and slapping at him, overpowering him. The security guard entered the fray and fared little better, sustaining several minor lacerations before the struggling woman was finally subdued by their joint effort.

As she was being driven home in an unmarked gray security vehicle, she experienced an unwelcome return to reality and began piecing together the past twenty-four hours. Earl, the police, her cat, Pierce. She considered her situation. She was nearly broke, she was out of work, and Pierce would make sure she stayed that way. His last words rang in her ears:

"Don't come back. Next time it will be 911."

When she finally arrived home, her nylons streaked, her sleeve torn from her struggle with the security ape, her hair an electric tangle, she realized that she had left her purse in his car.

Lucinda's head snapped around. "What on earth have you been doing, child? Your hair looks like it's been caught in a ceiling fan and your blouse is in shreds."

Amanda didn't seem to hear her.

"Why aren't you at work?"

"I've been fired."

Lucinda stared blankly at her daughter. "You've been *what*?"

Amanda glanced at herself in a mirror over the TV set,

pulled some renegade blond locks of hair into place, and managed to regain her composure.

"You heard me, Mother."

Lucinda slapped her hands against the arms of her wheelchair. "Didn't I tell you what would happen if you took off from work to sit on that thankless jury?"

Amanda said nothing.

"So what are we going to do?" shouted Lucinda over the din of a team of TV surgeons also shouting at one another during a heart operation apparently gone awry.

Dirty dishes were everywhere. Amanda dumped them into the sink. One of the plates broke. She reached down and seized the one that hadn't broken and smashed it, too. Then she swooped an arm across the counter and cleared whatever was left, sending cups, saucers, and glasses shattering into the sink.

Exhausted from resentment and oxygen deprivation, she fell forward against the counter, gasping for air, frantically scanning the area for her purse. The pressure inside her head was building, and she held her head with both hands as if to keep it from exploding. "Get away from here," she gasped. "I've got to . . ."

She looked for her purse, then remembered a spare inhaler in the cabinet where she kept her vitamins. She staggered toward it like an epileptic. *Air! Need air!* Grabbing the inhaler, she tried to relax as she pumped it into her mouth. Once, twice, three times. Men, she thought. All assholes. She collapsed onto a kitchen stool, inhaling deeply, and didn't move a muscle for five minutes. She pumped again, then headed toward her bedroom. She wondered if Field had called the police yet.

40

The next night, Earl Field drove Terry Morgan to the San Francisco International Airport following a triumphant speech to the Association of Business Trial Lawyers at the Sheraton Palace. During the question-and-answer period, he predicted certain victory in the trial about to begin.

Terry had sat by his side at the head table, then he had taken her to KPIX for her 10:00 news show. She was catching a red-eye to the East Coast.

It was a fabulous night outside, an unseasonably high sixties, and in a show of recaptured youthful exuberance, they drove to the airport with the top down and a daring, open bottle of Schramsberg champagne. The occasion was their formal engagement. They had decided to marry on the first Saturday in February.

"We can't count on weather like this," she said. "It will have to be inside."

They agreed on the chapel across from the Alta Mira Hotel in Sausalito.

The plane was late taking off, but after they kissed at the gate, Earl practically skipped back to his car on the deserted fifth floor of the parking garage. God, what a woman! For a while, at least, she had made him forget the frightening days that lay just ahead of him. Tomorrow, he would send the goddamn money back to the Rizzos no matter what Klegg said. Then he would talk to Julian Gold. They would reason together, maybe work things out somehow. Either way, he'd get Elliot Ashford in the retrial, and with Terry Morgan at his side, nothing would keep him out of the governor's mansion.

He saw his car where he had parked on the fifth floor. As he walked toward it, he felt a sudden uneasiness. It was the silence. No planes taking off. No car engines. Nothing.

He laughed at himself as he reached his Jag and hopped in. He closed the car door and inserted the key in the ignition. The car radio came on; Terry's favorite blues song.

It really kills me, the way your smile lights up a room
    when you say hello,
It's heart breakin', the way you whisper in the night so
    sweet and low
But now I know . . .

He smiled, hit the button to raise the convertible top, and was still smiling when the razor-edged piece of glass sliced his carotid artery with the clean precision of a surgeon's scalpel. The only pain he felt was from the hand pulling his hair, yanking his head back over the seat to expose his throat for the fatal thrust. Blood sprayed across the dash and up onto the windshield. Blood everywhere.

You're leavin' me, baby, you turn away from my touch
And it's grievin' me, baby, did I love you too much?

His dying body was roughly pushed across the front seat even as a final protest gurgled from his red-foaming lips. Then his shirt was ripped up and his pants pulled down far enough to allow for punctures into his chest and genitals. A small amount of blood oozed from the wounds, the heart still weakly pumping.

> *You don't love me anymore,*
> *You say my love has smothered the flame,*
> *I've only myself to blame.*
> *And you don't want me anymore,*
> *I'd love you less if I could, if only you would*
> *love me more.*

Amanda flipped off the radio with her gloved fingers. She had been taught how a radio could run down a car battery. Then she opened a large black bag and carefully replaced the glass stiletto, the same shard of glass with which she had killed Lani Jefferson.

41

Earl Field was given a hero's farewell by a bereaved city as both political foes and critics of his erratic performance at the Ashford trial granted him in death a restrained respect he had rarely enjoyed in life. Grace Harris joined the chorus of silence, for though it would have been to her political advantage to expose Jack Klegg for brokering the "bingo" deal with the Mafia, she resolved, for now at least, to let Earl's involvement with Chicago be buried with him.

At a last-minute meeting, the mayor and the Board of Supervisors had reluctantly acknowledged that Glide Memorial Church, everybody's first choice for the memorial service, was simply not large enough to accommodate the expected crowd. Someone volunteered that Earl Field had been an Episcopalian, and following hurried consultations, the service was rescheduled.

Grace Cathedral, the jewel of Nob Hill, was fitting for the occasion. In medieval times, various factions within a community would unite to build a throne worthy of its bishop, a monument that would bring respect and renown to the city. Grace Cathedral, with its 170-foot soaring towers, housing six-ton bells seven feet in diameter and flanked by stained glass worthy of Rome, had surely achieved this purpose.

The seemingly endless serpentine of people entering the church was as colorful and varied as Joseph's coat of many colors. The more conservative parishioners in attendance glumly watched the stream of multiracial mourners pouring through every door in a bizarre cacophony as they alternately sang, moaned, rejoiced, and clutched each other. The clamor was accompanied by the sound of congos, bongos, harmonicas, trumpets, clarinets, and clapping hands. A

North Beach contingent earnestly squeezed their concertinas as if to quell any notion that the murder had been Mafia-inspired, and a smaller group of women arrived from the Haight-Ashbury wearing Birkenstocks and sad faces, playing haunting melodies on flutes and recorders.

Terry Morgan sat on one side of the aisle in the second row, her anchorwoman's poise now thoroughly unraveled by uncontrollable sobbing. On the other side, seated just behind the decedent's survivors—two sons and a daughter by the first Mrs. Field—sat a tall woman, dressed entirely in black, her face veiled. Amanda wore the veil not out of fear of detection but as an imagined entitlement. Grandiosity, not trepidation, now inspired her, for had he not loved her despite his foolish suspicions and transparent efforts to conceal it? Had she not held him against her breast at the end, comforting him in her arms? Was she not the last to look into his perplexed eyes as the light slowly drained from them? And had she not kissed those full lips, tasted the still-warm blood there? Could she not taste it even now?

Who, then, could lay superior claim to the black veil of mourning in honoring this man's life than she, who, in ending it, had killed a part of herself as well. She wished she could weep tears of closure the way others did, and cursed the stupidity that had necessitated his death. If she could but somehow take back her foolish admissions that last day, uttered in a daze of fear and anger; crazed, rambling boasts concerning the lengths to which she had gone to save the case and his career. Had she mentioned Jefferson by name? She couldn't even remember, but Earl Field was far too brilliant not to have deduced that it was she, not Ashford, who had murdered Lani Jefferson. And though she had saved his case and his career, he would then have had no choice but to tell the police. Earl Field was a man who placed duty over love, even over his own happiness.

But she had forgiven him, and surprisingly had found happiness, too. Killing Jefferson and Field had brought about an epiphany in which she now recognized no law higher than her own need, and no need greater than her own. She was a whole person at last.

On the other side of the church, two rows behind Terry Morgan, Grace Harris sat with Aaron, whom she had flown back for the occasion. From her position, she could see

Jack Klegg, seated with the honored few who would soon deliver eulogies, a group that included the mayor and the lieutenant governor. Klegg's burr-cut head was on a swivel, nodding at acquaintances from his place of honor, then tilting toward the mayor's ear and whispering with the subdued animation of someone watching a tennis match.

Unnoticed in the rear of the great cathedral, two burly men shifted uncomfortably, coping with the confined leg space afforded by the narrow pews. Barrett Dickson had been reluctant to come, but Lev had insisted. He could feel Lev's worried eyes upon him now as he fought the urge to run outside.

And to keep on running.

Beyond the hallowed windows and festooned walls of the cathedral, and continuing for the next several days, speculation raged concerning the identity of Field's murderer, and the news media's finger of guilt again pointed directly at Elliot Ashford.

Dr. Thomas Yang, whose reputation for accuracy was exceeded only by his need for the world to be aware of it, fueled the fires of suspicion by opining that the jagged entry wounds in Field's throat were identical to those found on the throat of Lani Jefferson and consistent with wounds inflicted by a weapon similar to that which had killed Lara Ashford. When he also disclosed that the most recent victim, like the previous two, had been tattooed with the same ritual-sexual markings, newspaper and talk show polls ran four to one that it was Elliot Ashford who had killed the antagonist who had humiliated him at the inaugural ball that night, had repeatedly called him a white supremacist, and had dared to summon him to the bar of justice.

San Francisco papers screamed for an arrest, and the surrounding county periodicals—the *Marin Independent,* the *San Jose Mercury News,* the *Oakland Tribune*—decried the ineptitude of a police department that could not even protect its top law enforcer. Racial issues lurked at the fringes of the growing unrest, for, after all, this was America.

Barrett slept poorly that night as usual, and as usual, he rose at 1:00 A.M. and stumbled bleary-eyed into the bath-

room, milked his stubborn bladder, cursed his swollen pros-
tate, then fell back into his loveless bed with the grace of
a coal barge charging through canal locks.

After that, he knew it would be anybody's guess whether
he'd sleep again, but if he could carve out another two or
three hours before the first light signaled amnesty from his
nocturnal prison, he would be grateful. He tried to turn his
mind to something soothing, but images of Ellen appeared
as they always did about now: she young and gorgeous; he
once again that crazed, reasonably handsome young idealist
with the steady stream, the priapic penis, and, as sports
commentators insisted on saying, "his future all ahead of
him." But in his half sleep, her image would fade and he
would be alone again with the beast—the demon curse—
and would toss back his blanket, hot with despair and
frustration.

Was Elliot innocent? Could he, Barrett, be right, and the
rest of the country, including Leviticus Heywood, be
wrong? Nothing in law school or his years of practice had
prepared him to deal with people like Ashford and Julian
Gold.

He groaned as he remembered his scheduled meeting
with the *consigliere* and the defendant later in the day. His
skin was suddenly ice-cold and clammy, and he tried to pull
a blanket back over his massive shoulders.

He visualized himself studying texts on DNA, only
slightly less baffling to him than Joyce's *Finnegans Wake*
or particle physics; reading thick files of documents, having
to memorize many of them; long days and endless nights
of desolate privation. When he imagined himself approaching the first prosecution witness, a pang of fear
stabbed at his gut.

He dozed from time to time, but at 7:00 A.M., tired of
wrestling with his squandered past and dubious future, he
gave up trying for another hour's respite and got up and
dressed himself. His stomach was raging against the coming
of the light, so he skipped his usual breakfast of toast and
coffee in favor of a morning walk.

He headed down Green Street from his Telegraph Hill
apartment into the heart of North Beach, then took a left
on Grant Avenue and headed for the Caffè Trieste, where

three smiling generations of Gianni women greeted him and served him espresso.

Papa Gianni had come from Trieste, Italy, to San Francisco in 1957 and opened the city's first European coffeehouse just in time to supply high-octane caffeine to regulars like Michael McClure, Allen Ginsberg, Lawrence Ferlinghetti, and lesser Beat poets of the era. Papa Gianni must have had doubts too, thought Barrett, crossing the endless sea to a foreign land where he barely spoke the language. What had given him the confidence to carry on despite the fear and uncertainties that must have assailed him?

He paid his check, then, outside again, moodily retraced the steps of Jack Kerouac past the original site of the City Lights Bookstore and the also departed Mooney's Irish Pub; past the Savoy Tivoli, past other restaurants and coffeehouses now crowded with men and women in gray suits reading the *Wall Street Journal.* Where have you gone, Joe DiMaggio? Kenneth Rexroth? William Burroughs?

Barrett wandered down Filbert to Washington Square and found an empty bench. He considered a bloody Mary, wondered what time Moose's opened, but then rose and cut over to Mama's instead and ordered an omelette.

He saw a father watching his seven-year-old son attack a strawberry waffle, and a stab of poignancy overcame him. Daddy's day with the kid. He wished he knew where Jared was now.

He wondered what kind of kid Grace had raised. How old he was. Probably about ten years younger than Jared. He caught himself wondering how he might get along with Grace's boy. Despite his current confusion, he realized he had been thinking a lot about Grace Harris lately. Her image momentarily cooled his fevered mind, before his thoughts turned back to his imminent chat with Julian Gold and Elliot Ashford, then beyond that to the retrial.

He tried to picture himself cross-examining Arnold Sun, who would be well prepared this time. In fact, they'd probably dump him and bring in a grown-up for the retrial. He pictured Thomas Yang and at least a half dozen other forensic scientists, Chief Investigator Sam Quon and the SFPD officers. Every one of them would be tougher this time as a result of the working-over Menghetti had given them before, ready for him. Retrials were the hardest thing for trial lawyers. Too much of the battle plan had been revealed to the enemy.

To pull it off, he'd have to be fully committed, and to Barrett, this meant a total belief in his client's innocence. He knew this wasn't the way criminal defense lawyers were supposed to think in an adversary system, but he wasn't a criminal defense lawyer and he no longer valued the adversary system.

The kid finished his waffle, caught Barrett looking at him, and smiled. Barrett smiled back and looked away.

It would be painful to try a case again. But wasn't pain a reminder that the body was still alive?

The waitress placed the omelette in front of him. He stared at it, then picked up a knife, buttered a piece of toast, and wondered if fate might be throwing him a second chance: one last shot at digging out of whatever it was he had fallen into. Might he somehow find a way to will his bearlike carcass up that rickety ladder, one flimsy rung at a time, toward something a little better than what he had become?

Maybe, he concluded, we were more like sharks than we realized. We keep moving forward or we die. Perhaps that was the truth he would have to find a way to live with.

He stopped eating. The fork dangled from his fingers. *Truth!* Of course!

He broke into a smile, pushed his cup away, left money for the check, and headed back to his apartment. He knew exactly what he had to do now. If he was going to give Ashford his best in this case, Ashford would have to give him something first.

Something more important than money.

42

After comfortably settling himself in Earl Field's office, Acting District Attorney Jack Klegg's first order of business was to call a press conference in which he spent the first five minutes laying out his strategy for "carrying out the vision of my predecessor," then the next twenty talking about his plans for straightening out the mess he had found. His euphoria lasted only until the Q-and-A period, during which the gathered press displayed far more interest in what Grace Harris was planning to do on the Ashford case than in what he was going to do about rehiring the competent career prosecutors Earl Field had fired, and cutting furniture costs.

Deflated, he returned to his corner office on the third floor of the Hall of Justice to consider the possibilities. He had to be careful; this was his career now, not Earl's. He couldn't afford mistakes.

Ten minutes later, the possibilities were sharply narrowed by the call he had been dreading.

"Yes . . . yes, of course, no problem," he said into the phone. "I'll do it right away, Julian."

He rubbed his eyes and summoned Grace Harris for a meeting to "discuss handling of the Ashford matter."

As she walked down the hallway toward her confrontation with Klegg, Grace was also considering the possibilities. She expected that Klegg intended to either take Earl's place on the trial team or, worse, take over the prosecution by himself. She knew that either option would be seen by insiders as grandstanding, but by the general public as an heroic gesture. "I owe it to Earl," he would say, than tacitly blame the first trial team for the adverse verdict he would inevitably suffer.

As she entered, she noticed the daily trial transcripts meticulously stacked on his desk and a copy of the bound volume containing the posttrial jury interviews.

"I've completed a review of the first trial and the jury postmortems," he said. "Although some of them thought Ashford might be guilty, they were going to walk him out on reasonable doubt—even before Jefferson was killed."

Uninvited, Grace took a seat, wondering how much second-guessing and mindless critiquing she would have to endure before he dropped whatever bomb his devious mind had formulated.

"I know all this, Jack. What do you want? I'm very busy right now preparing for the retrial."

Klegg raised an eyebrow, but then tilted back in his chair and turned his gaze to the south window as they had both so often seen Earl do. "The pure and simple fact, Grace, is that the case is unwinnable. We cannot justify putting the city and county to the expense of another fool's errand."

"You're going to *dismiss* the case?" she said.

"No, Grace. *You're* going to dismiss the case."

Grace shook her head in both amazement and dismay. "I don't think so, Jack, and I think you're smart enough to know that the buck for that decision wouldn't stop with me. There would be nothing left but bones by the time the press finished with you. You wouldn't be recognizable, let alone electable."

Klegg snorted with derision. "I'll simply take responsibility for mistakes that have been made by others in the past, Grace. I think the press will come to understand that Earl was using the power of his office to wage a personal vendetta against a hated personal and political enemy."

"You'd destroy Earl's reputation to advance your own petty ambitions? That's hard to believe, Jack, even coming from you."

"Come now, Ms. Righteous," Klegg said, unruffled. "Your protector is dust in the wind and I'm in charge now, for which you should be grateful. I'm trying to save your job *and* your life."

"I'm touched, Jack, but—"

"Damn it, Grace, just play along with me."

"Play with yourself, Jack," said Grace, rising. "I'll close the door so no one will see you."

"Hold it, Grace!" Klegg bellowed. "Doesn't Earl's murder tell you anything? You or I could be next on their list for God's sake!"

"This isn't about us n-now, Jack; this is about who's running the criminal justice system in this country."

"Oh, spare me that sanctimonious bullshit," Klegg bellowed, throwing both arms in the air. "What about your son? Are you willing to put him at risk?"

Grace barely raised her voice. "I'm banking on your friends selecting you next, Jack. After all, you made the deal with them and you're next in line under Earl. Besides, I've sent Aaron away. He's safe."

Klegg stared at her, momentarily silenced by his frustration. "Damn it, Grace," he spit out at last, "I'm running this place now and I'm ordering you to dismiss the damn charges."

"Forget it, Jack. I won't do it, and you won't either."

"The hell I won't," Klegg shouted, coming out of his chair. "And then I'll dismiss you. Consider that a done deal, pure and simple. Now get the hell out of my office."

Grace didn't move. Then she spoke. "It won't be your office for long if the press learns about your dealings with the Mafia."

Klegg met her gaze, then gave his head a quick shake. "But they won't," he said. "You wouldn't do that to Earl, Grace. I know you too well."

"I do a lot of things I don't like. Standing here talking with you for one."

Grace paused just long enough to catch the look of comprehension on Klegg's face. She had hit a nerve.

"I'm going to retry this case, Jack, and I'm going to win. Consider that a 'done deal.' "

She turned and walked out, leaving his door open.

The next day, Julian Gold and Elliot Ashford waited for Barrett to arrive at Gold's room at the Ritz-Carlton. The room was charged with tension, for Gold had broken to Elliot the bad news about Grace Harris's refusal to dismiss.

"Calm yourself, Elliott," he said. "Maybe Klegg will be able to dismiss it later. In any event, I have a backup strategy."

"I can hardly wait."

"I'm going to see that you're indicted," he said with a hint of a rare smile, "for the additional murders of both Jefferson and Field."

Ashford glowered at him. "I'm not in the mood, Julian. And as for those murders, you can tell your friends in Chicago they've caused me nothing but trouble. Tell them that as much as I hated the black bastard, they were insane to kill him."

"Don't be absurd, Elliot. I've had to convince Carmine that *you* didn't kill those people. Why would he have ordered something like that when victory was within your grasp?"

"I don't know, but somebody did."

Gold shook his head impatiently. "Whoever it was, we'll find him and deal with him. Meanwhile, we've still got to deal with Grace Harris and your retrial."

Ashford walked to the bar and mixed himself a weak scotch and soda. "All right, tell me your strategy."

"I just told you. You're going to be indicted for the new murders."

"Oh, Christ."

"Hear me out, Elliot. Klegg is going to get Grace Harris to indict you on the new killings, even though there's not a shred of evidence connecting you to them other than the similarities with the first one—"

"Which I also didn't do, may I remind you."

"Of course you didn't, Elliot, but do you want to hear the payoff or not?"

"I'm listening," said Ashford, folding his arms and pushing his glasses up on his nose, "though your logic so far might make more sense if I stood on my head."

Gold ignored him. "Soon after the retrial commences, Klegg will 'realize' that Harris has overindicted, publicly accuse her of an irrational attempt to carry out Earl Field's vendetta, and order her to dismiss the new indictments. She will look ridiculous and the jury will see that the overzealous prosecution has sailed completely out of control."

"If Klegg couldn't get her to dismiss the present charge, how do we know he'll be able to dismiss the new ones?"

"Fair question. He has good reasons for not dismissing you now, but when the press figures out she has no evidence, she'll be pressured to do it herself. Besides, even if she doesn't, the new unsupported indictments would drag down her case on Lara. You win either way, once she indicts you on the new murders."

"It sounds too good to be true."

"It's perfect, though I must confess that there will be certain . . . inconveniences for a while."

"Inconveniences?"

A knock on the door announced that Barrett Dickson had arrived at the top floor. "Nothing about this to Dickson," said Gold, raising a warning finger as he advanced toward the door.

"Hello, Mr. Gold," said Barrett, glancing inside the huge suite.

"Come in, Mr. Dickson," said Gold, attempting a smile.

Up close and in the morning light, Julian Gold looked even more ghostly than usual to Barrett. With the exception of his lips, his face was entirely colorless, even his eyes. The skin on his face was withered—not from the sun, Barrett knew, because he shunned it like a vampire, but by a lifetime of guile and resentment that had given him exactly the face he deserved.

"Come have a seat," Gold said. "Take off your coat."

"To what do we owe the honor, Barrett?" said Ashford. "No more accusations, I trust."

Barrett shook his head. "I can't blame you for being upset, Elliot. I've not been involved in many criminal cases, as you know."

"We don't want you merely 'involved' in this one, Dickson," said Gold. "We want you 'committed.' "

"I don't blame you for that, either," said Barrett, "and to me they're one and the same."

"No, sir," said Gold. "In a bacon and egg breakfast, the chicken is *involved;* the pig is *committed.*"

"Fair enough," said Barrett, "and I think I've come up with a way I can be."

"Excellent," said Gold, rubbing his hands together. Ashford reached for his glass. "What do you have in mind?"

"I want Elliot to take a polygraph."

"You *what?*" said Ashford, his cocktail glass suspended just short of his lips. "Who the hell . . . what kind of idiot are you?"

"The kind you've retained and the kind who wants you to take a polygraph. Pass it and you'll have the very best I can do."

Ashford spun around, ran a hand through his blond hair, then spun around again. "Jesus, Julian. Talk some sense into this man."

But Gold looked mildly amused by the confrontation and just shrugged. "It wouldn't be admissible even if you failed it, Elliot," he said, "so where's the harm?"

Ashford sputtered, but before he could speak, Gold added, "And you *are* innocent, Elliot." He fixed his cold eyes on Ashford in a way that surprised Barrett. "Are you not?"

Ashford slowly walked over to a window overlooking the courtyard, one hand holding his drink, the other thrust into the pocket of his blue blazer. Barrett waited, aware that his hands were perspiring. A breeze drifted in from an open window and settled uncomfortably across his damp back.

"All right, you bastard," said Ashford to Barrett, "I'll take the damn thing."

"Good," said Barrett. "I've made arrangements with Astin Testing in Marin. Clay Astin's an independent guy. Retired FBI. Respected by every agency in the state. Here's his card. 10:30 A.M. tomorrow. Be on time."

As Barrett walked out, he glanced back at Ashford, staring at the card in his hand as if it were in a foreign language.

At 11:20 A.M. the next day, Clayton Astin called Barrett.

"Your Mr. Ashford just left, Bear."

"Was he alone?"

"No. He was with some cast member from *The Night of the Living Dead.*"

"I know the gentleman."

"Anyway, I ran Ashford through the whole process, Barrett. Twice in fact."

"And?"

"He's clean."

"You're sure?"

"Hell, Barrett, we get fooled once in a while, but I think this guy's telling the truth."

"All three victims?"

"A little shaky on the wife, but that's typical given the emotional component: you know, guilt from years of previous misdeeds of one sort or another—"

"How about whether he enlisted someone else to do Jefferson and Field for him?"

"Exactly the same readings with the same minor reservation. In answer to your next question, I'll bet you dinner at Wendy's he not only didn't have those people killed but doesn't have a clue who did. I hope this makes your client feel better."

"I don't know about him," said Barrett, a smile breaking across his face, "but you've damn sure made my day."

Barrett hung up the phone, swept up in a torrent of well-being, a feeling he had almost forgotten.

"He's innocent!" he said aloud to Fred and Ginger II. "The sonofabitch is *innocent*!"

43

So," said Mike Reasoner, entering Lev's office on Market Street, "your boy passed with flying colors?"

Barrett turned away from the window, smiled broadly, and gave Mike a thumbs-up. Lev sat behind his desk, his brow still furrowed with skepticism.

"Lev?" said Mike. "What's the problem?"

Barrett touched a finger to his lips. "Good news can ruin Lev's day, Mike," he said in a stage whisper. "Particularly when it reveals him to be a stubborn-ass cynic."

Lev looked at Mike and tilted his head in Barrett's direction. "Should we break the news to Pollyanna that the reason lie detectors ain't admissible in court is because they fail the test of scientific reliability? Because they sometimes lie?"

"Come on, Lev," said Barrett, planting an affectionate hand on his friend's shoulder, "we're not talking about palmistry or studying the entrails of a hawk here. You know that Clay's the best in the business."

Mike smiled and said, "I agree, Lev. Don't wreck the moment. Let him go win his case now without fear of setting off a plague of locusts or an 8.5 earthquake. Maybe even do a little justice in the process."

" 'Maybe,' " said Lev, "is definitely the operative word here."

Mike shook his head. "I'm with Pollyanna on this one, Lev. You don't fool Clay Astin very often. What's it going to take to convince you that you're on the side of the angels?"

Lev slid a ten-page bio across his desk. "This little lady right here."

"You got Sandra Weiss?"

"She's on board, and she *does* deal in scientific reliability."

"Let's hope we like her answers."

Barrett said, "Speaking of answers, Mike, have you come up with any?"

"A few," said Mike, opening his briefcase and handing a research memo to Barrett. "You look good on everything but the state's DNA evidence. We can't hope to exclude it."

Barrett scanned the memos. "This is good work, Mike. I'd prefer you not tell Wilmer you're helping with this."

"Don't you tell him either. I'm strictly moonlighting in this dog and pony show and I'll need deniability with Wilmer if you lose the case."

"Leviticus," said Barrett, "do you hear a cock crowing?"

Mike smiled and closed his briefcase.

"Okay," said Barrett. "If we can't keep their DNA evidence out, we've got to deal with it better this time."

"Which is where Sandra Weiss comes in," said Mike.

Barrett glanced at his watch. "Lev and I are meeting with her in an hour."

"Terrific," said Mike. "Let's hope she says that the small quantity of Ashford's blood supports your shaving theory; better yet, that it might not be his blood anyway."

Lev made a face. "How can Bear claim Ashford cut himself shaving to explain his blood, then turn around and argue it wasn't his blood in the first place? That's completely inconsistent."

"Simple," said Barrett, winking at Mike. "I'm a lawyer."

Mike gave Barrett a disgusted look, then said, "We're allowed to argue in the alternative, Lev. We've got to have a backup if the jury decides there's a bit too much of that type AB blood to have come from shaving."

"A bit too much?" said Lev. "Place looked like Sweeney Todd with a chain saw."

Mike wasn't amused. "Could you guys pretend to be half serious about this capital murder case you're about to try?"

Barrett nodded his head gravely to show how serious he could pretend to be.

Dr. Sandra Weiss, head of the National Genetics Institute located in Palm Desert, California, and one of the leading molecular geneticists in the world, entered Lev's office fifty-five minutes later. Barrett liked what he saw. Her resonant voice and firm handshake instantly proclaimed her confidence, and a helmet of salt-and-pepper hair worn short gave her an aura of authority beyond her forty-eight years. Her tall, wiry body radiated a marathoner's energy, and an undeniable intelligence lay behind clear, penetrating blue eyes. Although she was otherwise plain-featured—arguably homely—Sandra Weiss's smile briefly illuminated Lev's bleak office as she greeted Barrett. He made a mental note to be sure to draw that smile out when she was on the stand. The successful forensic witnesses were not just smart with an impressive pedigree; they were likable as well.

After only an hour of talking with the doctor, Barrett was convinced she would be invincible in her account of the shortcomings of the San Francisco Police Department's handling of the evidence, the police and coroner's office's questionable record in matching DNA probes, and the problems inherent in any DNA-matching situation. In the next two hours, Dr. Weiss provided Barrett with the basic tools to understand DNA and an outline for cross-examining the prosecution's lead DNA expert. They scheduled another meeting the following evening to discuss her preliminary findings on the DNA samples they had provided her.

"She'll be dynamite," said Lev when she had left.

"Nitro," said Barrett.

"Then why the look?"

Barrett was tired, but his instincts were flashing caution. There was an occasional reticence in the woman, he explained to Lev, as if she were holding something back. Lev said maybe she'd just been locked up in an ivory tower too long for normal socializing, and Barrett was ready to write it off to general pre-trial paranoia—until she called him at his apartment two hours later.

"I hope I haven't awakened you, Mr. Dickson."

"Trial lawyers don't sleep much this close to trial, Doctor. What's on your mind."

"Well, an ethical problem actually. It's been bothering me terribly. I didn't want to bring it up earlier in the presence of Mr. Heywood, but there is something I feel you must know."

* * *

Barrett found Sandra Weiss waiting for him at a table in the lobby bar of the Stanford Court hotel, sipping a port.

"Thanks for coming," she said. "I know you don't need another problem right now, but I had no choice."

Barrett ordered a Calistoga water with lemon and invited her to begin.

Not one to mince words, Sandra Weiss came to the point. "I've found something else in Ashford's blood samples I didn't pick up at first, an alteration in his gene pattern. He has incipient Huntington's chorea, a disorder of the basal ganglia."

"English, please, Doctor?" said Barrett. "I'm a bit tired."

"Sorry. The brain shrinks. The cerebral cortex, to be more precise."

"Doc," said Barrett wearily, "I don't mean to appear ungrateful, but my own cerebral cortex is on overload right now. What's this got to do with anything?"

The geneticist explained that although the presence of the defective genes leading to Huntington's disease can be diagnosed even at birth from a single cell sample, the onset of symptoms is usually delayed until the early fifties.

"How old," she asked, "is your client?"

"Fifty-two," Barrett said. "So what are the symptoms?"

"Swift and complete mental deterioration," she said, "then, mercifully—unlike Alzheimer's—death follows quickly. If he's fifty-two now, I wouldn't give him many more years."

Barrett lit a cigarette and glanced around him.

"I'll give you an overview of the medical aspects of the problem," she continued, "then I'll stop for any questions you might have."

"I already have one," said Barrett. "Why the hell are you telling me all this?"

Dr. Weiss said, "I'll get to that in a moment. First, you need to know that medicine and ethics have become inextricably bound, particularly now that we're on the verge of mapping every gene in the human body.

"A single microscopic cell can tell us things about a patient's future he or she might never want to know. Did you know, for example, that at least ten percent of male parents are not the true fathers of their children and don't even know it?"

Barrett thought of Jared, whose uncanny resemblance to himself had provided him a measure of confidence after he had learned of Ellen's betrayals.

"How do you usually deal with that kind of information?" he asked.

"A medical geneticist who stumbles onto this kind of finding will rarely disclose it. But Huntington's presents a more difficult issue. A person who knows he has a limited, indeed targeted, life span may be shattered by the knowledge, but at least he will have the chance to make the most of the years—or months—he has left. Would *you* want to know?"

"So the ethical issue is whether you tell him."

There was a moment of silence. He watched Dr. Weiss's furrowed brow and pursed lips, her slightly hunched posture.

"More precisely," she said, "the issue is whether you tell him, Mr. Dickson."

Barrett rubbed his eyes as his fatigued mind raced in circles.

"I've struggled with this for several days now," she continued. "I am a total stranger to the man, and given the fact that his wife is dead, well . . . I decided, after meeting you this evening, that you, as Mr. Ashford's legal representative—"

"Would be the most logical person to tell him he's been given a death warrant with no possibility of appeal," said Barrett, an edge creeping into his voice.

"Yes," she said.

Barrett's frustration yielded to his trial lawyer's perspicacity.

"Doctor, I'm a bit weary, and I know you must be too. But I must ask you a related question with serious legal ramifications. Would a person with Huntington's disease be competent to know the nature and quality of his acts; to distinguish right from wrong?"

A barely audible chuckle issued from Dr. Weiss's small mouth. "I know what you're getting at, Mr. Dickson," she said, "but that's a game for you lawyers and psychiatrists to play. But if I had to guess—assuming he's a typical case—I'd say he's had numerous blackouts by now and is mentally unreliable."

Barrett was sitting up straight for the first time in hours. "I take it you'd be willing to testify to that much at least?"

"Yes, I could testify to that, although I would want to examine him first and take a history."

Barrett put his glass down and eyed the table next to him on which rested what appeared to be a double vodka or gin on the rocks. His tongue swept across dry lips.

She said, "You're considering it?"

"A drink?"

"An insanity defense."

"I don't know," said Barrett, grinning sheepishly. "My client's innocent, but if he wants to pick up an additional margin of safety with the jury, I'll arrange an examination."

He saw that Dr. Weiss was studying him, whether with sympathy or medical concern he wasn't sure.

"Science can be a curse or a blessing," she said,

Barrett looked at his watch. "Well, thank you, Doctor. I think. We'll talk tomorrow then about your findings on the blood at the scene?"

The sympathetic look again. "Yes, and I *am* sorry about burdening you with all this."

They shook hands awkwardly and bid each other good night.

As Barrett drove back to his apartment, his earlier good mood having evaporated into the humid air, he considered his situation. Might Ashford have killed Lara and not remember? The others, too? Did Ashford know he had Huntington's? Did Carmine Rizzo know? Might Rizzo consider it unsafe to have a mentally unreliable head-case roaming loose with insider knowledge in his head? And wouldn't Ashford know this and consider it unsafe to have a mentally unreliable lawyer roaming loose with knowledge of his condition?

Ashford may or may not be a murderer, thought Barrett, but he would damn sure know where to find one and wouldn't hesitate to drop the dime to save his own scalp. Barrett's hands tightened on the steering wheel as he realized that Sandra Weiss had not only signed Ashford's death warrant with her discovery but, if Barrett wasn't careful, perhaps his own as well.

A traffic light turned yellow, then red, but he kept on going, and as he glanced in the rearview mirror, his anger at Dr. Weiss grew. If a doctor didn't know how to deal with something like this, how the hell was he supposed to know? Playing God was a doctor's game, he thought, or maybe a judge's. Trial lawyers are often seen as the devil, but never God. What the hell am I supposed to do? Walk up and say, "Excuse me, Elliot, good news! Losing doesn't matter anymore; you'll be dead in a year or so either way."

Would Ashford even believe him? If he did believe him or if he already knew about it, what then? A call to some scumbag with a silencer who knew how to silence people? He slammed the steering wheel with both palms.

Maybe it was time to float a plea bargain. He knew there was no reason to hope Grace would take a deal or that Ashford would go for it even if she did. But at least he might learn something. If Grace was open to a deal, he'd learn she wasn't as confident as he had assumed. And if Ashford was open to it, he'd learn his client wasn't as innocent as he had hoped.

Anyway, the game had changed now and he needed a way out of it.

The next day, Grace Harris and Barrett appeared in John Hernandez's courtroom to argue two defense motions *in limine* designed to keep the prosecution from mentioning either the Mafia or Renee Babcock in the presence of the jury. Predictably, Grace lost the first and won the second and would be allowed to read parts of Babcock's testimony to the jury. Afterward, she was pleasantly surprised when Barrett came over and sat on the edge of her counsel table. She was even more surprised when he floated the possibility of a plea bargain.

She managed an inscrutable expression. "What do you have in mind, Barrett?"

"I haven't discussed this with my client yet," he said, "but I'm thinking voluntary manslaughter, you strike the prior base term of three years."

She gave him a quizzical look and said, "Heat of passion?"

"Whatever," he said. "Maybe imperfect self-defense."

She raised an eyebrow at that. "What did she threaten him with? Her exposed throat?"

Barrett winced. "You don't have to pull that crap with

me, Grace. You know I don't think my client killed anybody."

"That's what you're paid the big bucks to believe, counselor, even if you're wrong. Look, I know you were ahead of the game when the courtroom went dark before, but things are going to be different this time."

"You mean because the quality of your opposition has plummeted?"

Grace felt herself reddening. "Not at all. In truth, I'd rather face Menghetti if you must know. But you won't put on Renee Babcock this time around and I won't put on Armand Ligretti. You'll lose, Barrett."

"Look, Grace. I had doubts about Ashford, too. So I sent him to Astin Testing and Clay Astin himself gave him a clean bill, not only as to Lara but the other two as well. Here's his report."

Grace perused it quickly, feeling Barrett's tired eyes on her, wishing she looked a little less tired herself.

"Let's get rid of this thing, Grace," she heard him say.

Grace met his unwavering eyes, then said, "I'll take it up with Klegg. You must know I can't recommend it."

"Fair enough. You alone in this now, Grace?"

"Looks that way. You?"

"Looks that way," said Barrett with a smile. "May the best man win."

Grace gave him a bemused grin. "You don't have to pull that crap with me, you know."

Later that same afternoon, Grace met with Jack Klegg and Sam Quon, who, like Grace, looked like he had aged five years since the death of Earl Field. Grace, sitting next to Sam and facing Klegg behind his desk, proposed they counter Dickson's laughable voluntary manslaughter suggestion with murder two and fifteen to life.

"What happened to Judge Dredd?" said Klegg, obviously savoring this new development. "The ironhearted Amazon? I thought it was always a battle to the death for you, Grace, no quarter asked or given."

It galled Grace to subject herself to Klegg's predictable ridicule, particularly knowing how much he wanted to be rid of the case. But she forced herself to stay calm, letting him have his fun.

"May I ask," he continued, "who or what has caused you to finally recognize the folly of putting the public to the expense of another trial?"

"Clay Astin. He gave Ashford a clean bill."

Klegg's eyes widened. Grace knew he had relied on Astin many times himself. "I've seen his report," she added.

Klegg said nothing.

"You made the point yourself, Jack," she said. "We would have lost the first one. It's even remotely conceivable the guy's innocent. Astin is as good as they come."

Sam made a face and looked out the window.

Klegg said, "What's your take, Sam?"

"Astin's wrong this time," said Sam.

Grace was surprised and showed it. Sam looked at her and shrugged.

"I agree," said Klegg. "It's not a perfect science, and even Clay makes a mistake occasionally."

"I think we should go back to Barrett with something," said Grace, "given all the factors."

"It's 'Barrett' now, is it?" said Klegg with a wry grin that Grace ignored with great effort.

"I would agree," Klegg continued, "if Menghetti were still on the other side."

"But he's not," said Sam. "And you'll run all over that burnout, Grace."

Grace said, "That 'burnout' has won nearly every pretrial motion he's filed so far, Sam. He even looks different, and he's got Mike Reasoner helping him on the briefs."

"But he'll be all alone when there's a jury sitting there," said Klegg, "and he'll fold under pressure. He's afraid to try this case and will take any deal he can sell to his client. We just need to soften him up a little more. The pure and simple fact is he'll eventually wimp out and take murder one and life. Maybe I'll take it, too. Stonewall him, Grace."

Although Klegg was disagreeing with her, Grace was pleasantly surprised to see him taking a hard line. Was he ready to defy the mob as Earl had finally done? Not likely. Had he worked something out with Rizzo? More likely.

"All right, Jack," she said. "I'll tell Dickson."

"We're playing hardball here, Grace. Tell him also you're going to convene the grand jury and charge his client with the additional murders of Earl Field and Lani Jefferson."

Grace felt her stomach double-clutch. She looked from Klegg to Sam, then back to Klegg. "Are you serious, Jack?"

"Damn straight I'm serious. If we indict him on the others, his bail will be revoked. Special circumstances, pure and simple. The press will see we're keeping him from doing it to somebody else, maybe save a life."

"I'm all for saving lives, but what do we do for proof?"

"That's up to Sam and the police. My job is to give the public what it wants, and the public wants us to be tough with this guy. Every poll in the country says that Ashford killed all three of them, and some of them are saying we're dragging our feet."

"So our charging policy is now being dictated by popular polls?"

Klegg interrupted her. "It happens, Grace, that polls reflect attitudes of people. It also happens that we represent the people."

She felt it slipping away and looked to Sam for support. But he gave a little shrug that seemed to say he thought Klegg was right for once.

She persisted. "Indicting Ashford with the additional murders based only on their modus operandi will taint Lara's case on which we at least have credible evidence! The jury will conclude we're overreaching on all three murders."

Klegg rose from behind his desk, then said, "Are you saying you don't think Ashford's guilty?"

"Which murder are we talking about now, Jack? Lara Ashford? Lani Jefferson? JFK? The Grand Archduke Ferdinand?"

Klegg's face reddened; he started to speak but restrained himself. Grace glanced at Sam, but disregarded the warning in his eyes.

"Look, Jack," she said. "He probably did murder Lara, despite Clay Astin, but he's simply too damn smart to have done the others exactly the same way. As for Lara, I'm just saying we've got to face realities here. I'm not sure I can even get a conviction on that one based on what we saw in the first trial."

"Let me get this straight," Klegg replied coldly. "You think he did it, but you need an insurance policy guaranteeing you'll win your case. Listen to yourself, Grace."

Grace was too angry now to speak. Sam didn't move. Why didn't he see through Klegg's idiocy?

"Look, Grace," said Klegg in a more conciliatory tone, "I admit we are weak on Lara—all the more reason to bring in the other two murders to strengthen our hand with the jury."

That did it for Grace. "Brilliant, Jack. We strengthen a weak case by taking on the additional burden of proving two cases that are even weaker."

She now saw why Klegg wouldn't plea-bargain. He had found a way to both deal with the Chicago problem and enhance his political prospects. The prosecution case would eventually unravel now, giving Ashford his freedom and making a fool out of one of his potential opponents in the June election.

"You're a bastard, Jack," she added. "This city deserves better."

Klegg's head snapped around and the skin on his elongated face was suddenly drawn taut across his checks. "Your fellow deputies are lined up outside my office," he said quietly, "all wanting a shot at this retrial. Just say the word and you're off the case."

Grace met his glowering eyes. He'd like me to quit, she thought. Then all his problems go away.

"I'm going back to work," she said, and walked toward the door.

"Grace?" said Klegg as she reached the doorway. "Please have those proposed grand jury indictments on my desk by day's end."

Grace walked out. This time she slammed the door.

Three days later, Barrett heard a noise from far off, a stubborn ringing that sounded like an unanswered telephone. He opened an eye, then rotated his head in the direction of the sound. It was coming from an unanswered telephone. Next to the telephone was a clock that read 6:26 A.M.

"Dickson," he grunted.

"Barrett, for God's sake, they've *arrested* me."

"Elliot? What do you mean they've arrested you?"

"I mean they've arrested me! Get down here."

As Barrett drove to the hall, he considered Grace's betrayal and his own naíveté in trusting her. Judge Lucy Kelly McCabe, one of the brightest stars on the Superior Court bench, had once told him that she preferred the criminal department over civil because the criminal lawyers didn't play games like Barrett was used to in commercial practice. Grace apparently hadn't heard the news.

Barrett arrived at the seventh floor of the Hall of Justice where no-bail detainees are held and found his client nearly hysterical. Barrett explained that there was no way to get bail set now because he was charged with multiple murders, then began to count the minutes until he could gracefully signal the guard that he was finished. He returned to his apartment and caught Grace Harris by phone just as she was leaving for the office.

"Hello?"

"Is this the Amazing Grace Harris?"

"Who's this?"

"Dickson. I want to commend you on your amazing guile. Within forty-eight hours of asking you for a deal on manslaughter, you've charged my client with two additional first-degree murders. Do you vacation at the gardens of Gethsemane by any chance?"

"I don't b-blame you for being—"

"Remind me not to ask for another deal. Next time, you might respond by indicting Ashford for the slaughter of six million Jews."

"Listen to me, Barrett—"

"Never again," he said. "I'd heard that you were tough, Grace, but trustworthy. I know better now."

"If you're implying I've done something unethical, Barrett—"

"I'd heard that criminal lawyers were more civil than civil lawyers," he said, "but I guess it was just another lawyer joke, and a bad one at that."

Barrett stood for a moment staring at the dead telephone, then poured himself an unwanted cup of coffee. It was clear to him that what little he thought he had understood about women had been wrong. He had just been wrong about Grace Harris. Why had he begun to trust her?

He fed Fred and Ginger II, then struggled through a five-finger exercise on the piano. He got up and poured his coffee into the sink.

What the hell was going on with her? he wondered. It bothered him that it was bothering him so much. The hell with her. She had probably been playing with his head; throwing him off-balance like trial lawyers always try to do to one another. But she wasn't just another trial lawyer. She had become important to him.

But to hell with her.

As he stared into a sink full of dishes, another reality intruded. There would be no plea bargain, and he would have to tell Ashford what he knew.

He decided to allow himself one glass of wine. It would be another long night.

44

The next morning, Barrett forced himself awake at seven o'clock. His head was fuzzy from the bottle of wine—the first glass hadn't done the trick—and from tossing and turning while he tried to think of a nice way to tell someone he was about to die.

"What the hell are you saying?" screamed Ashford an hour later as he slammed his hand down on the scarred wooden table. "There's nothing wrong with my head!"

Barrett patiently explained what Dr. Weiss had told him about Huntington's disease, carefully watching his client's face for any hint that he already knew about it. But Ashford just kept fuming and shaking his head. When Barrett shrugged to indicate he was finished, Ashford leaned across the table and grabbed his arm.

"Listen, Dickson. Lara was pregnant eight years ago, but my son died in childbirth. Now she's dead and I have no heir."

Barrett waited. Ashford leaned back and rubbed his face with both hands, then stared at the ceiling as if he were trying to make up his mind about something.

"I'm sorry," said Barrett, feeling he should say something.

"I've met someone," he said softly, but Barrett noticed that his client's fingers were trembling against his lips as he dragged on his cigarette. "I'm going to marry her as soon as I get out of here."

Barrett felt a stab of pain in his stomach that shot through to his lower back. Then he felt Ashford's eyes appraising him, awaiting his response. His response was to stare over Ashford's head at the door with the chicken-wired window, wanting nothing so much as to walk through it and never look back.

"She will give me my heir, Barrett," said Ashford, gripping Barrett's arm tighter.

Barrett met his client's eyes for a second or two, then looked away to conceal the anger that was driving out the feelings of compassion he had borne into the room just minutes before.

"But not if I'm some kind of mutant monster, damn it! I *can't* plead insanity!"

Barrett said nothing, but pulled his arm away.

"Attorney-client communication," Ashford added.

Barrett stood, then leaned against his chair. "Now listen to me, Elliot. I've believed in your innocence. I don't know what to think now, but what I do know is that you're out of choices. You've painted yourself into a corner with those phony alibis."

"I can explain all that—"

"The hell you can. The minute you take the stand they've got you. You'll be clobbered with your prior violent assault felony, your hatred of Earl Field, and God knows what else. You'll lose more than you'll gain."

"What about my polygraph?"

"It's inadmissible. Look, Elliot, you never know what's going to happen in a jury trial, and as a gambler, you must know there's a time to walk away from the table. Whether you believe Dr. Weiss or not, her testimony along with a forensic shrink could not only keep you off death row but maybe allow you to duck prison altogether."

"How?"

"Even if the jury finds you did it, you'd go off to a cushy sanatorium for a few months—maybe a year—establish that you've 'regained your sanity,' and walk out the—"

But Ashford cut him off. "No sanatorium, no temporary insanity," he said, the pitch of his voice rising. "I could lose everything."

"Elliot, you could lose your *life*! Have you heard a word I've said?"

"I heard you," he said at last. "I heard every word. I have my reasons. I want to be alone now."

"Elliot, please . . ."

Barrett realized that tears were streaming down his client's cheeks. He watched in silence as the prisoner slowly rose to his feet and pressed his cheek against the chicken-wired glass window, his fingers splayed flat against the cold walls surrounding the door into the rear corridor.

"Okay," said Barrett softly. "I'll be back in a day or two. Take some time to think it over. We'll decide then, okay?"

Ashford didn't answer.

"You look tired, Grace," said Sam, entering her office a week after their meeting with Klegg.

"My turn at the clinic last night."

"You'd better let that go for a while," said Sam, looking like he wanted to talk. "Let some other do-gooders out there have a shot at saving the world."

"Most of us there settle for just making a difference," said Grace.

"Well, it's good the new indictments kicked the trial over into January. Ashford won't get his Christmas verdict, and you'll be able to get some rest."

"And you'll have more time not to find any evidence connecting Ashford to Jefferson and Field."

"I guess I deserve that," said Sam, smiling. "Look, Grace, I know you feel Jack and I ganged up on you. I want you to know that despite Clay Astin's reputation, I'm still sure Ashford did all three of them."

"I'm sure you're sure, Sam."

"I'm trying to apologize, Grace. I guess you haven't seen today's *Chronicle*?"

Grace took the proffered paper and felt her heart quicken. After ten days of screaming for Ashford's arrest, the *Chronicle* now speculated that "Grace's Amazing Ambition" had overcome her good judgment in seeking the new indictments. The reporter had interviewed three top criminal defense lawyers and an assistant D.A. from Los Angeles, all of whom agreed that she had jeopardized the original case by bringing in the two additional murders. The article also lamented "Ms. Harris's refusal to justify the decision by revealing even a hint of the evidence she had presented to the grand jury and would soon present at trial."

"I won't say what I'm thinking," she said.

"That you told us so?" said Sam. "That you're the one now taking the heat? That it was a bad idea?"

"Keep going," Grace said absently as she scanned the article. "They've definitely portrayed me as the architect of the strategy. There's only one thing to do now."

Sam looked alarmed. "You're not going to do anything extreme, are you?"

"I'm afraid so, Sam, given the state of my bank account," said Grace, grabbing her coat. "I'm going Christmas shopping. After that, I'm going to treat myself to a very expensive lunch."

At 1:00 P.M., Barrett and Mike took seats at the bar at Stars.

"Your usual, counselor?" said the bartender to Barrett, after taking Mike's order of a McCallum's single malt.

"No, Ken," said Barrett, and ordered a bottle of Perrier.

"I'm impressed," said Mike.

"I'm modestly curious about what it might be like to try a case with a functioning brain."

"I'll drink to that. That is, if it won't bother you."

"No more than everything else you do."

When they were seated in the club area for lunch, Mike spotted Grace Harris seated across the room with a woman friend.

"Yeah, she looks good in civies," said Barrett, squinting to view her profile and the sheen of her black hair as it curved around her pale throat. "Too bad her heart's gone colder than a well-digger's ass."

"I thought you'd gone sweet on her, Bear. But you're right about the Iron Maiden. You don't win thirty first-degree murder cases without the milk of human kindness going sour."

"Not to mention the cream of her integrity," said Barrett. "Still, I sure like the way she looks, and she's smart. Witty, too."

Mike grunted. "I'll bet she's as witty as a Mylar blanket—with considerably less warmth." He sipped his single malt, then added, "You like her, that's the problem. Just because she's smart and pretty, you think she could save you from drowning."

"Save me from drowning? Hell, she's the one with her foot on my head."

As Grace suddenly turned toward him in recognition, her

expression friendly, Barrett felt an almost forgotten stirring. He self-consciously held up a hand—the one with a complete set of fingers—like someone taking an oath.

She responded to Barrett's ambiguous greeting with a friendly wave and he found himself impulsively moving toward her on unreliable legs, walking stiff-legged from the ass, not the ankles, like a kid on stilts or Karloff doing his monster. Yet he couldn't stop his legs from moving him closer to her, or an uncertain smile from breaking out, causing crow's-feet to fan out across his ruddy cheekbones.

"Hello, Barrett," she said, putting her glass down and offering her hand. "Nice to see you. This is my friend, Jillian Jacobs."

"Pleased, ma'am," Barrett said, awkwardly extending his hand and already regretting his impetuous invasion.

"Sit with us?" Grace said.

Barrett composed himself, gave her the most casual smile he could muster. "I'd like to," he said, "but I just remembered we're not on speaking terms."

"Oh, my," said Grace. "Jillian, please tell Mr. Dickson I said, 'Oh, my.' "

"Oh, my," said Jillian, looking with mock sadness at Barrett.

"Jillian," said Barrett, "would you tell Ms. Harris that jailing my client in response to my good-faith-settlement overture was an interesting approach to building a foundation of trust."

Grace's lips parted in a beguiling smile. "Jillian, would you explain to Mr. Dickson that although I'm the one looking really stupid over the recent indictments, I don't really run the district attorney's office?"

Barrett smiled and concluded that it would be less awkward for him to sit down for a moment than to continue looming over the two women, feeling like a poorly designed building.

A waiter placed his half-filled glass on the table to his right. "Your Perrier, sir."

"Jillian," he said, feeling playfully exuberant in the glow of Grace's presence, "tell your friend I'm not one to hold grudges, and that if that was an apology, I accept."

Jillian Jacobs, sitting between the lawyers, said, "Who communicates between you two in court, the judge?"

"In court," said Grace, "lawyers speak either to the judge or to the witnesses, rarely to each other, except to disrupt. As we're not in court at the moment, Jillian, would you suggest to Mr. Dickson that we break precedent?"

Dickson reached for his glass to propose a witty riposte, but knocked it over instead, spilling some of the contents on the sleeve of his coat, and the rest on the table. He then turned the color of his crimson tie as he reached for a napkin.

"That will come out with a little Perrier water," ventured Grace sympathetically. Jillian laughed. Barrett managed a smile.

"They make these tables too small," he said, trying to rise to his feet without inflicting further damage. "Nice meeting you, Jillian, and my apologies to you both. I just came over to practice my disruption skills."

"Actually," said Jillian, obviously enjoying the spectacle, "we were quite bored until your disruption. Stay a while, please."

"That's gracious, Jillian," Barrett said, too embarrassed now to look at Grace, "but having destroyed your table, I'll now return to my stool and set the bar on fire."

Barrett rejoined Mike and asked Ken to send them drinks and a towel.

"What a klutz," Barrett mumbled.

"It could have been worse," said Mike unconvincingly.

"Not without the aid of explosives," said Barrett.

Back at Grace's table, Jillian Jacobs leaned conspiratorially toward her friend. "He likes you, Grace," she said. "And he's very handsome in a roughcut sort of way."

"If you like that sort of way."

"I wonder," said Jillian, raising a suggestive eyebrow, "what he's like beneath those Perrier-drenched clothes. I'm referring to his mind, of course."

"Of course," said Grace, swirling the red wine in her glass. "He was once the best there was. He's currently staging a comeback of sorts."

"What else? Is he married?"

Grace gave her friend a sideways look. "Widowed. Don't tell me you're interested? You *are* married, remember?"

"How could I forget," said Jillian, frowning. "But you're not."

Grace rolled her eyes and let out a laugh. "Don't be s-silly."

But Jillian Jacobs just stared at her with a knowing smile.

45

Earl Field's death had dramatically altered many lives, but none more than Amanda Keller's. The buzzing and clicking in her ears were gone. Over two weeks of blessed peace since Earl Field's death. It was like an exorcism. Every day was pretty much the same now. She would awake feeling strangely detached from all that had happened. All sense of time and space seemed to abandon her in these first moments of wakefulness. Then it would not be a question of remembering what she had done so much as endowing the recollection of it with the substance of reality. My God, she would think with both pride and regret, I did that!

She would read and reread every account of the murders she could find, interrupted only by Lucinda's complaining, the only lingering irritant in Amanda's new life.

"Quiet!" Amanda would say in a new, authoritative voice, and Lucinda would be quiet, at least for a few hours. Lucinda obviously had no idea how to deal with this calm yet aggressive behavior other than to stay out of Amanda's way. The new Amanda came and went at her whim and simply ignored most of Lucinda's questions. When asked how they were to survive, however, Amanda had said she was back on unemployment. She was civil, even pleasant at times, but always distant. She paid the rent, provided adequate food, and even granted a modest allowance for Lucinda's wine and cigarettes.

Amanda liked seeing the confusion in Lucinda's eyes as her mother watched and waited for things to get back to what had passed for normal in their relationship.

But Amanda knew she would never again occupy the skin of that other lifeless, frightened person, that slavish piece of crap she had been. Though she still yearned for

Earl Field, she felt grounded for the first time, finding joy in the experience of things that had previously gone unnoticed: her surviving cat's beauty when sleeping, a cappuccino on Union Street, a flower defying the December winds, a breeze as it lifted off the Bay and set palm fronds on the Embarcadero rattling like a giant mobile.

She kept her scrapbooks up-to-date and sometimes clipped out pictures of the late district attorney and juxtaposed them with snapshots of herself. Her favorite was a photo of all twelve jurors coming down the courthouse steps the day she became a regular juror. Earl Field stood in the background giving an impromptu news conference and she was looking over her shoulder at him. Little did anyone suspect that he was already in love with her even then, and sadly, no one ever would.

She resumed her workouts, but with less weight now and more reps. It was a regimen designed to achieve tone rather than bulk, an apt metaphor for Amanda's new life. Although she was content in her new persona, it became clear to her that she still longed to return to Hollywood. She still wanted stardom and the perquisites of fame and wealth that accompanied it. She daydreamed of spotlights and limos, martinis and furs.

But there was an important difference now. For the first time in her life, she wasn't responding to the needs and desires of her mother, her employer, her producer, her ex-husband, or anyone else. She wanted it for herself.

And one clear, brisk morning, while sipping a cappuccino at Starbucks on Union Street, it came to her how she would get it.

Barrett arrived on the seventh floor and found an entirely different Elliot Ashford waiting for him than the one he had left in tears of confusion two days earlier. Cool and arrogant again, Elliot knew exactly what he wanted.

"There'll be no temporary insanity defense, Dickson. In the first place, I didn't kill her."

"I'm not saying you killed her; it's a plea in the alternative."

"Legal gibberish! You're asking me to admit to a crime I didn't commit, then makes excuses for it."

"That's not the—"

"And Julian must not be told any of this, Barrett! Understand?"

Barrett nodded.

"I know things, okay?"

"And you're afraid they might—"

"You never know with these bloody fools, but I'll not take the risk. And I must tell you, Dickson, that if this absurd story about me being crazy does get out, I'll know where it came from and I guarantee I'll get you before they get me."

"You don't have to threaten me, Ashford. I couldn't tell anyone if I wanted to. It's privileged information."

"Good. Then maybe we'll both be privileged to live long lives—assuming your doctor friend is wrong and you're as good in court as they say you used to be."

The telephone was on its fifth ring by the time Grace came through the door and snatched it off the hook. It was Aaron calling from Florida.

"How are you, pumpkin?"

To her surprise, Aaron was having a terrific time. He was enjoying himself so much, in fact, that Grace began to feel an unreasoning pang of jealousy. He missed her, of course, and his friends, too, but not school; he was too busy enjoying trips to historical sites with his grandfather.

"Are you keeping up with your other studies?"

"Sure, Grandpapa helps me. He's taught me all kinds of stuff about the Old Country and things about our roots I never heard about. How come you never told me anything?"

Another black mark for mom, Grace thought. "I didn't know you were interested."

"I'm going to be a better kid when I get back, Mom. I'm studying to be bar mitzvahed. I'm even learning some Hebrew!"

Grace was beginning to fear that her son was coming too much under her father's influence, but then tossed it off as motherly possessiveness. Besides, she had survived it, hadn't she?

They talked about the case, then Aaron asked if she was still going to Emeryville on Wednesday nights.

"I've been too busy lately," she said uneasily. Had her

trial lawyer's instincts picked up a judgmental tone in the question?

"Maybe it's for the best," he said. Then it all came out. Aaron had wanted to see her perform, but she only sang on Wednesdays, a school night, and she wouldn't allow it. So he got Skip Hodges to borrow his brother's car one night and they had trailed her to Emeryville.

"It was just something to do, Mom. We were sort of playing detective and Skip had never even heard you sing. I didn't plan on telling you about it ever, but Grandpapa has taught me that concealment is the same as a direct lie."

"My God," said Grace, her hand tightening on the receiver. "Did they l-let you into the bar?"

"We acted like we were there for dinner, then walked right into the cocktail lounge and just stood there. Everyone was watching you, so they didn't pay any attention to us for a long time. You were great, Mom. Not a single—"

"Stammer," she finished for him, trying to regain her composure. Relax, she told herself, just two kids having an adventure. "It's common, Mel Tillis the most famous example. Many of us don't stammer when we sing. So we sing in public to try to . . ."

Her voice trailed off and there was an awkward silence. She was afraid to ask what else he had seen. Had he stayed? Seen her leave?

"I must tell you, Aaron, that I f-feel you and Skip were invading my privacy. I'm n-not happy about this whole situation."

"Well, that makes two of us, and like I said, maybe it's better you're too busy these days."

My God, she thought, he *had* seen her—them—walking across the parking lot. Toward her brief interlude at the motel next door.

"Don't worry," Aaron said, confirming her worst fear, "I don't need to tell Grandpapa the rest. He's upset enough about you as it is."

Grace fell onto a kitchen stool, overwhelmed by frustration. She could hear her father's judgment in Aaron's tone. Could she be losing him?

"Don't you want to say hello to him?" Aaron continued.

"No," she said. "Not tonight."

Grace rang off sadly, wondering if she should bring her

son back before her father turned him into a knight of the righteous. She dropped her head into her hands, wishing she had time to cry.

Barrett, Klegg, now Aaron, all down on her. She might win her trial, and the election too, but at what cost? She vaguely remembered a parable about a man who had gained the world at the cost of his soul, but couldn't remember if it was Old or New Testament. Did it really matter? And couldn't worse things happen to her son than becoming religious?

Like becoming dead?

So she would not bring him home. What she would do is end this case as fast as she could, consistent with her duty to the people, then take him to Maui for a week before putting him back in school. She would reprogram her son with her own set of weapons: walks on the beach together, snorkeling, movies, the great water slide at the Hyatt, sundown dinners.

She rose to her feet and looked around her, glad at least that Aaron couldn't see the mess she had allowed to build up in his absence. She started to pick things up, but felt too tired to do anything but collapse in bed.

Then she would take the time to cry.

She rose the next morning without the new energy she had hoped for, but with a firm resolve to take whatever they threw at her and give it back with all the strength and skill she could muster. She had overslept, so she skipped breakfast and raced to the Hall of Justice for the weekly 8:00 A.M. "planning conference" with Jack Klegg. She had come to dread these demeaning exercises as a waste of time.

Today's meeting would not be a mere waste of time, for Klegg was not alone.

"You know Barrett Dickson, Grace."

Grace nodded, feeling heat flooding her face. Barrett nodded back.

Why hadn't Klegg warned her? She involuntarily ran the fingers of one hand through her hair, knowing it looked a mess.

"As you might have surmised, Grace, Mr. Dickson and I have been discussing the Ashford matter."

"I surmised that it must be something important," said Grace, "to warrant getting Mr. Dickson out of bed this early in the day."

She was pleased with the ostensibly calm but deliberately edged tone in her voice. She prayed she would not stammer.

Barrett was unruffled, even gave her a smile. Was he mocking her or was there sympathy in that smile? She didn't like either possibility.

Klegg scowled. Then, to the apparent surprise of Barrett Dickson, Klegg said, "As you know, Grace, the new indictments you obtained on the Jefferson and Field killings are causing us hell in the press. I've asked counsel here to be candid if he knows of any evidence connecting Ashford to these crimes other than the similar m.o., and I accept his word he knows of none. As we've found none either, I'd like you to dismiss the indictments."

Grace said nothing. The enormity of Klegg's declaration rendered her speechless. Of all the indignities he had perpetrated and all the dirty tricks he had ever pulled off in the ten years she had known him, this was the Super Bowl, the Grand Slam, and the Triple Crown of outrageous duplicity. It didn't get any worse than this, she thought as she glowered in disbelief at the acting D.A.

Then it got worse.

"Mr. Dickson and I," said Klegg in his perfected sycophantic tone, "have also been discussing the original case against his client."

Grace looked from Klegg to Barrett, then back to Klegg again. "Either my watch has stopped, Jack," she said dryly, "or my invitation to your earlier meeting got lost in the mail."

But Klegg forged ahead as inexorably as a landing craft bound for Normandy beach, indifferent to any obstacle Grace might be about to lay in his path.

"Mr. Dickson has been quite persuasive in arguing that the second trial will only be a reprise of the first. The pure and simple fact is that the best we can hope for is a hung jury, another mistrial."

Grace could stand no more and knew her face was revealing her anger and humiliation. "Don't you think, Jack, that we should discuss this matter privately?"

Barrett responded by starting to rise from one of Klegg's large leather chairs. "No problem, Grace," he said, but by the time he reached an upright state, Klegg had assumed a standing position as well and was motioning Barrett to be seated.

"Look, Grace, there is no need for games here. The pure and simple fact is that our posttrial debriefing interviews with the jurors came out the same as the defense's. We were going to lose, and face it, there *was* reasonable doubt."

Grace rose to her feet also and gave Klegg a hard look, but his expression was unyielding. She said, "But that was because—"

"Grace," said Klegg, "just hear me out."

"I w-won't hear you out, Jack," said Grace, "and I again urge you not to say another—"

"Please, Mr. Klegg," interjected Barrett, "I'd prefer to step outside for a moment."

"Stay right where you are, sir," said Klegg. "Let's all sit back down and discuss this like professionals."

Barrett shrugged but seemed to be waiting for a cue from Grace before descending back into the beckoning leather chair. But Grace was moving toward Klegg at a speed that suggested she might vault over his desk. Instead, she planted herself in front of it, solid as a fence post.

"Let me give it to you as 'pure and simple' as I can, Jack," she said. "I will not be a party to whatever little scheme you've cooked up with Mr. Dickson here. Nor will I dismiss Lara's case."

Klegg said nothing. So Grace turned toward the door and added, "Do it yourself."

Klegg circled his desk and blocked her path. "Are you blind to what's been going on here, Grace? It was Earl! We *never* had a solid case against Ashford. Earl's ambition blinded him to what every juror could clearly see. Sure, maybe Ashford did it, but we've never been in a position to prove it and we never will be!"

Grace stood her ground. "And where were you, Jack, when the original decision was made to indict Ashford? Standing right next to him as I recall."

Klegg tilted his head toward Barrett and said in a tone

that only Klegg could pull off—at once soothing, threatening, and, as always, patronizing—"Grace, we're not alone."

Grace could not help smiling at the irony. "You soon will be, Jack. Trust me."

Barrett loudly cleared his throat and walked over to a window.

Grace turned and started through the doorway. Klegg's voice rose, saying, "You might also consider your future here, Grace! Prosecuting is a tough job calling for tough decisions. Not suited for everyone."

Grace turned and said, "Thank you, Jack, for not adding that 'prosecuting is man's work.'"

She stormed down the hall to her office and flipped on her computer, but not to draft a dismissal.

MEMORANDUM
To: Interim District Attorney Jack M. Klegg
From: Interim Chief Deputy Grace Harris
Date: 12-7-97
   Please accept my resignation from the Office of the District Attorney, City and County of San Francisco, effective immediately.

Grace hit shift-F7, then walked over and picked her memo out of the printer. She signed it, then folded it in thirds, and sealed it in an envelope with Klegg's name on the outside. She made two extra copies for herself and began cleaning out her desk, then slammed a drawer shut.

Screw it, she thought, I've had enough for one day. She gave Klegg's copy of the resignation to Bertha, a pool secretary, then went back for her coat. It would be cold outside.

She heard her phone ring but ignored it and headed down the hall toward the elevator lobby.

"Oh, my God, Grace, there you are!" said Pam, her regular secretary, in a low but nearly hysterical voice. "I've been trying to reach you. There's a person in reception who insists on seeing you; said it had something to do with the Ashford case."

Grace started to explain that there wasn't going to be a case. Instead she just shook her head and kept walking down the hall. But Pam was insistent.

"Grace! This witness overheard Ashford personally threaten Lani Jefferson . . . the day she was murdered!"

Grace's head spun around, and she saw that Pam was serious. Her heart started dancing in her chest. "What?"

"Really! She also has evidence connecting Ashford to Earl's death!"

Grace raced into the reception area.

There, looking up at her with innocent impassivity, was the alternate, Amanda Keller.

46

Grace called for Sam Quon, then escorted Amanda into her office. When Sam arrived, Grace offered her some coffee, then listened, hardly breathing, while Amanda told her story. When she was finished, Grace called in a steno and took her through it all again, hitting her this time with everything but her swivel chair in an effort to shake a story that, if true, would give her the ammunition she needed to send Elliot Ashford to death row and to checkmate Klegg's most recent move.

"It was the same day Lani Jefferson was murdered," said Amanda. "I had left the courtroom after the others and Lani was still waiting at the elevator."

"Anyone else there?"

"There was another woman who appeared to be a county employee."

"Did Ms. Jefferson appear unusually nervous that day?"

"No. Lani was always poised, always dressed beautifully," Amanda said, her eyes softening. "I envied her, but I admired her even more. She was a beautiful person."

Grace studied the woman in front of her, remembering the way she had stormed out of Earl Field's office that day, obviously upset. What had that been about?

"Can you tell me again for the record, Ms. Keller, how Ms. Jefferson was dressed that day?"

"Yes. She had on a mauve blouse with large black buttons under a gray jacket and a cream skirt."

Grace was astonished by the woman's keen memory for detail and apparent credibility. "Please continue."

"Well, the other lady—the one who seemed to work there—got off at the second floor, and just as the elevator doors were about to close, *he* came in!"

"He?"

"Ashford. Elliot Ashford. There we were, in an elevator with an accused murderer. I should think jurors would be protected from that!"

Grace shrugged and said, "They used to not even have a jury room. Jurors sat in the hallway during every recess alongside accused murderers."

"Well, I was terrified because of what he had said to me earlier, but Lani seemed calm. Mr. Ashford smiled at both of us and said, 'Ladies?'—just like that—then stepped to the rear so that now he was behind us."

"Can you describe this other woman? The one who got off when he got on?"

Amanda's brow knitted briefly, whether in concentration or annoyance Grace couldn't tell.

"Medium height, dark hair, fortyish, I'd say."

"Would you know her if you saw her again?"

"I honestly don't know."

"Okay, then what happened?"

"As soon as the doors closed, Mr. Ashford started talking in a low, sort of monotone voice, like he was having a conversation with somebody. But nobody else was in there but us. I know that makes no sense but that's how it hit me."

"Don't worry," Grace said. "Just tell it like you remember it. What was he saying? The exact words if you can remember them."

"I'll never forget them. He said, 'Ms. Keller, you're only an alternate and about to be excused, so consider this your lucky day. Ms. Jefferson, on the other hand, is someone who is going to vote to acquit—or she's sitting on her last jury.' "

"Did either of you respond to this?"

"Not me. I was too petrified. But I'll never forget Lani just turning around and looking him straight in the eye and saying, 'I'll see you in chambers tomorrow morning, Mr. Ashford.' "

"What did you take that to mean?"

"That she was going to tell the judge about the threat."

"What did he say then?"

Amanda shivered in her chair and put her head down, staring at her tightly clasped hands. She seemed on the brink of tears.

"He . . . told her . . . he'd see her in hell first."

"Those were his exact words?"

"Yes, 'I'll see you in hell first.' "

"What happened next?"

"Nothing. When we got to the ground floor, we tried to be casual but got out as fast as we could. That's the last time . . . the last time I ever saw Lani."

"And the second threat involved Mr. Field?"

"Yes. That was after the mistrial. I was picking up some forms for my mother at City Hall during my lunch hour and I walked into this little restaurant called Pat's Seafood Grill, I think. I didn't see him at first and he didn't see me either because I sat at a table closest to the door with my back to his back. But then I recognized his voice."

"As Mr. Ashford's?"

"Yes. I couldn't believe it at first and I wasn't trying to listen, but I was sure it was him."

"What made you sure?"

"Two things. First, I heard him tell his friend across from him that he was going to have it out once and for all with that—I won't say the word he used."

"It's all right. Tell me exactly what he said."

"He said . . . 'that nigger D.A.' "

"What was the second thing?"

"That was when his friend was leaving a few minutes later. Mr. Ashford got up and told him good-bye and I got a good look at him. I decided I'd better leave, too, but the problem was he glanced around as he started to sit back down and recognized me, too."

"How do you know that?"

"Because he leaned right down and said, 'Well, well, if it isn't the alternate,' or something like that."

"What happened then?"

"He sat back down at his table. I asked for my check and I heard him ask for his, too."

"Did he say anything else to you?"

"Yes, but not just then. He got up after the waitress had delivered our checks, then he picked mine up and went to the cashier and paid both of them. I didn't know what to say. Then he came back and dropped two dollars in front of me. 'That's a tip for your waitress,' he says, then he says,

'Now here's a tip for you: Keep your pretty mouth shut if you don't want to end up like your friend.' "

"Meaning Lani Jefferson?"

"That must have been who he meant. Then he said, 'Have a nice day,' and gave me that mean little smile of his and just walked out. I never saw him again."

Grace took the witness through another thirty minutes of interrogation, forcing her back over her story a third time, looking for the slightest inconsistencies. There were none. She then readied her final question. If the witness could provide a credible answer to it, no juror could doubt her.

"Why is it that you've only just come forward with this information."

"I was afraid, Ms. Harris. I knew Mr. Ashford had killed Lani and that he could kill me just as easy!"

Perfect, thought Grace, one of those answers trial lawyers liked to bait a trap with. She knew if she didn't ask the question on direct, Barrett would have to ask it on cross. He would have the answer stricken, of course, but the jury would never forget it.

"Did you tell anyone at all?"

"I tried to tell Mr. Field, but he accused me of lying. He almost threw me out of his office!"

So that was it, thought Grace, remembering the day she saw Amanda charging out of Earl's office. Grace's last trace of lawyer's skepticism evaporated.

"I even came back," Amanda added with a hurt look, "but he refused to see me."

Grace remembered that, too.

"Did you consider going to the police?" Grace continued. "Didn't you know you would have been protected?"

Amanda inhaled sharply, then slowly dropped her flawlessly coifed head. A well-manicured hand went to her ample chest, just below the sternum, as if something were stuck in her throat. Grace could read the pain on her face.

"Don't you think I *wanted to?*" she said, her voice breaking, then asked for a drink of water.

"Of course," said Grace, pouring from a Calistoga bottle she kept on the credenza behind her desk. "Would you like to stop for a while?"

Amanda gulped the water, holding the glass in both

hands. "No," she said. "It's just that if I hadn't been such a coward, Mr. Field might be alive today. But I figured that if he didn't believe me, the police wouldn't either. Now I wish I'd at least tried."

Grace continued to scan the witness with her lawyer's penetrating gaze. She missed no movement of Amanda's hands, no flicker of the dark blue eyes, no trembling of the dark red lips. She studied every inch, every pore, of the witness's face, looking for any sign of deceit or hyperbole. She saw only anxiety and guilt.

"Would you like some fresh coffee, Ms. Keller?"

Amanda was biting her lip and again seemed about to cry, but she took a deep breath and shook her head.

"I've been terrified. I'm going to be even more afraid now that I've come forward!"

Perfect, thought Grace. She's afraid of Ashford and the jury will see it.

"You did the right thing, Ms. Keller," Grace said. "I think that's enough for one day. Oh, wait . . . I guess the steno caught it, but I got behind in my notes on something here. Would you tell me again what Ms. Jefferson was wearing in the elevator that day?"

"Certainly. She had on a dark gray jacket over a mauve blouse. Her skirt was a cream color; so were her purse and shoes. Did I mention that?"

"I don't think so," said Grace, again amazed at the witness's consistency and attention to detail. "Not the purse and shoes."

Amanda laughed self-consciously. "I notice things like that," she said. "I was in entertainment for a while."

"I know," said Grace. "I read that in one of the papers."

"Really? Someone told me that I was mentioned."

"Are you still at the same address?"

"Yes."

"I'll be in touch, and thank you for coming in, Ms. Keller."

"I'm glad I did. I feel relieved. Please call me Amanda. And may I call you Grace?"

"Of course," said Grace, glancing at her watch and nodding toward the stenographer. "Time 3:47. Off the record."

As soon as she had escorted Amanda to the lobby, she returned to the pool secretary's desk and was relieved to see the envelope containing her resignation right where she had left it. She retrieved it, took it back to her office, and tore it into pieces.

At her meeting with an astonished Jack Klegg early the next morning, Grace ended it by saying she would try the case alone. Klegg could come up with no defensible reason for denying her request. Barrett had already declared to the judge that he would be trying the case himself, and Grace knew that saddling herself with a co-counsel would play into Barrett's solo underdog role, "pitifully outnumbered against the unlimited resources of the government."

He'll be outnumbered, she resolved, but only by me.

As she put a copy of Keller's transcribed sworn statement in her briefcase, she realized that Earl might have still been under the mob's control when Amanda tried to talk to him. Either that or he simply didn't have the patience to hear information that could have saved his life. Either way, Grace now understood why Keller had seemed so upset when she left that day and why she had been so persistent the day he refused to see her at all.

Poor Earl. Headstrong and flamboyant, egotistical and manipulative, yet she missed him. Missed his dash and good humor. As was said a dozen times at his funeral: The man had style.

She took a cup of coffee to her office and glanced at the morning *Chronicle*. She nearly dropped her coffee, for there on the front page was a headline that blared:

MYSTERY WITNESS HEARS D.A. MURDER THREAT

She felt heat flooding her body. She had told only Klegg and Sam Quon about the witness. Who had they told?

Nothing was secure anymore, she thought, and no one would be safe once Ashford read the article, especially Amanda Keller. Would her witness still be willing to testify now that her cover had been blown so quickly? Keller would know that Ashford's connections reached well beyond prison walls.

Grace decided she would call her key witness and offer police protection as soon as she talked to Jack Klegg. She misdialed twice before connecting with him.

"I didn't tell a soul," said Klegg. "I swear it. Look,

Grace, this place has more leaks than the office of the President. Who was your steno?"

Grace hung up. She doubted that it was the steno, and knew it wasn't Sam. It never occurred to her that Amanda Keller had retained a public relations consultant who had just taken the first step in choreographing his new client's triumphant return to Hollywood.

47

A week later, Amanda Keller gave her face and hair a final touch-up as she anxiously awaited her third conference with Grace Harris. She knew this one might be difficult.

A secretary appeared in the reception area at 8:00 A.M. and led Amanda to Grace Harris's office without a word, then quickly stepped out of the line of fire as soon as Amanda stepped through the door. Amanda was now certain Grace had seen the article in *California Confidential* that had appeared five days after the *Chronicle* story.

Magazines had lined up for an interview with "the mystery witness" along with every supermarket tabloid in the country. Amanda and her new public relations agent had chosen *California Confidential* based on a weighted formula that pointed to *Confidential* as the leading zookeeper feeding the public's ravenous appetite for salacious gossip seasoned with a touch of reality. *Confidential* also seemed to have the best linkage to the Hollywood star machine.

The terms of the deal were simple: in return for an exclusive interview, Amanda received a modest—but urgently needed—check for $20,000, plus final approval on photo selection and republication of selected favorable reviews of her work on *Hope's People*.

"I take it you've seen the article," said Amanda, her deep-set eyes lowered contritely.

Grace stood behind her desk, hands on hips. "I've seen it."

Amanda had been concerned about Grace Harris's reaction, but her agent convinced her that her status as the prosecution's key witness now entitled her, like the proverbial eight-hundred-pound gorilla, to sit any damn place she pleased. But the agent didn't have to face the diminutive

Grace Harris, staring at Amanda with an intensity that would have made any gorilla blink.

"I can't believe you d-did this!" Grace said, pointing the folded tabloid at Amanda like a pistol. "Then there was the *Chronicle* story that came out right after our first meeting. Was that you also?"

Amanda looked down. She had decided to gain credibility with the prosecutor by telling the truth on subsidiary issues.

"I'm sorry, Grace. I was just—"

"Didn't we agree you were not to talk to anyone?"

Christ, thought Amanda, this woman was beginning to sound like her mother. But she concealed her irritation and stared at her hands, saying nothing.

"What were you thinking of, Amanda? Don't you see you've thoroughly compromised your credibility as a w-witness?"

A chill of concern passed through Amanda. Had she gone too far? Was she being dismissed? This would have to be good. She slowly raised her head, eyebrows slanted into a picture of contrition.

"I . . . I'm so sorry, Ms. Harris. It's just that . . . well, I have no job now, and . . ."

Amanda reached into her purse at this point, removing a wrinkled tissue, wishing for the millionth time she could cry real tears.

". . . and I had to have the money for my mother. She's an invalid, you see. The reporter promised me I'd get to review the story before it was published, and I planned to run it past you too, but then—"

"They did," interrupted Grace, "what they always do."

"I suppose so," Amanda said, dabbing at her dry eyes with a Kleenex, a catch in her voice, a sudden sobbing sound. That's it, she thought: Us against the rotten tabloids. She plucked an inhaler from her purse, not even sure she needed it except as an additional prop. "I feel so stupid, and I swear I didn't even say most of those things."

She saw Grace's features soften. Amanda pumped the inhaler twice into her mouth.

"Asthma."

"Oh," said Grace, the thread of her anger unraveling.

"What will you say when Mr. Dickson accuses you of making up the entire story just so you could sell it?"

"I'll tell him and the jury the absolute truth, just as I've told you," said Amanda, knowing Grace was smart enough to read the subtext: *And I'll break down for them, just as I'm doing for you now.*

"You realize you have created two problems for yourself. In addition to the money motive, Dickson also now has an advance copy of your 'testimony' in writing. He'll be well prepared for you."

"But, I told you, I didn't even say many of those things."

"That just makes it worse. He may subpoena the *Confidential* reporter to contradict you. Either way, you'll now start out on the defensive, denying and apologizing."

Amanda looked up pitifully. "Just as I'm doing now."

The assistant D.A. did not seem moved. "Exactly. This is how cases get bogged down and start going sideways."

Amanda decided to trust her agent's assessment of her new importance and take a chance.

"Would you be better off without me, Grace? I don't want to do anything to jeopardize your case against this terrible person."

The offer seemed to irritate the assistant district attorney even more. "Of course not," she snapped. "It's just going to be tougher now."

The agent was right! thought Amanda. I am an eight-hundred-pound gorilla. She moved toward Grace and touched her lightly on the arm. "Then I'll need your help. I'm so stupid in these matters. But if you'll stand by me, I know I can get through it. I'm telling you the truth, Grace, and the jury will see it."

Grace glanced up into the contrite face of the taller woman, then fixed her with a scrutiny that was difficult for the witness to endure. This girl's tough, thought Amanda. To break the tension building inside her, she looked away and added, "I'm still so afraid, Grace."

"You'll be all right," said Grace, granting Amanda an unenthusiastic smile. "I'll arrange some protection for you."

"Thank you. I was embarrassed to ask before. Do you think my stupidity has made things even more dangerous for me?"

"Let's sit down," said Grace as if she hadn't heard her, "and get to work. We don't have much time now."

"I'm ready," said the witness.

•

"So what about this Amanda Keller, guys?" said Mike Reasoner, holding a copy of *California Confidential* in his hand. "What does Ashford say about her claims?"

Lev said, "Gee, Mike, take a wild guess."

"He doesn't know the woman," said Barrett, "other than having a vague recollection that she was an alternate juror."

The trio sat in Lev's office, practically yelling at each other over the noise of the morning commute. Lev rose and slammed a window shut.

"Okay," said Mike, "but this means Ashford will have to take the stand."

Barrett nodded. "I know."

Mike said, "Have you contacted Keller, Lev?"

"She won't talk to me. Us. You'll have to get help from the judge, Bear."

"Or start publishing a tabloid," said Mike.

"I'll take it to the judge," said Barrett, "but meanwhile we need to find something on her."

"I'm on it," said Lev. "Got me a guy working the angle in Hollywood. Got to be lotsa dirt in Hollywood."

"What about the *Confidential* reporter?" said Mike. "Didn't you tell me she gave him some bullshit about being in an intimate relationship with Field? That sounds like a fertile field."

"That's what my guy down south heard," said Lev. "I'm talkin' to the reporter face-to-face day after tomorrow. I'll come up with somethin'."

Barrett sighed and refilled his coffee cup. "I hope so, Lev. The trial starts in three days, and I'm sitting here wondering how to cross-examine an attractive woman who supports an invalid mother and whose devotion to the cause of justice has compelled her to put her very life in jeopardy."

Lev grunted and gave Mike a rueful grin. "The Bear's got himself a tiger by the tail."

Mike nodded. The three men sat in silence for a minute.

"Motive," said Barrett at last. "Maybe that's our angle."

"Motive?" said Lev. "Isn't that what the cops try to prove?"

"Not Ashford's motive. Keller's. Why did she come forward? And why now?"

"Maybe she got religion," said Mike in mock solemnity. "A longing for truth, justice, and instant fame."

"Her fifteen minutes," said Lev.

"Or," said Barrett, furrowing his large brow, "maybe it's another one of Ashford's con jobs."

"Con jobs?" said Lev.

"Yeah. Maybe our friend Mr. Ashford has created another Renee Babcock masterpiece, this time with a *Witness for the Prosecution* twist. Remember Marlene Dietrich?"

"Tyrone Power and Charles Laughton," said Lev reverently. "Man, they sure knew how to make a movie without explosives in those days."

"Think about it," said Barrett. "The Keller girl testifies she heard Ashford threaten everybody but the Pope, then breaks down under my withering cross and admits she's a queen from another planet who played harpsichord for Lawrence Welk. The jury is so pissed at the prosecution they walk Ashford out the door."

"Maybe I missed something," said Leviticus, "but isn't that good for us, assuming it works?"

"That kind of game isn't good for anybody, *especially* if it works," Mike said. "Besides demeaning the justice system, it makes fools out of all of us."

"That may be a touch sanctimonious, Mike," Barrett said, "but after Babcock I'm on guard. You know what they say: 'Fool me once, shame on you; fool me twice, pay the price.' "

"The man's a god," said Lev in mock wonderment.

Mike groaned and said, "Let's go have some breakfast."

PART FOUR

THE RETRIAL

If at first you don't succeed . . .   —*Anonymous*

Attempt the end, and never stand in doubt;
Nothing's so hard but search will find it out.
    —Richard Lovelace, "Seek and Find"

48

The second trial got off the ground quickly and efficiently. Everyone knew their lines now, understood their roles. The press knew their assigned seats and the lucky lottery seat-holders knew how to behave, thanks to a stern lecture from the bailiff, who now knew how much confusion could be generated in a high-profile case on opening day. Judge Hernandez had only to reach for his gavel to cow the courtroom into abject silence.

Barrett felt the usual first-day panic that all trial lawyers suffer, knowing that a crucial fact or witness might have been overlooked and that at any minute something could, and probably would, go terribly wrong. There was never enough time to prepare for all the inevitable contingencies of a major trial.

Barrett glanced at Ashford, typically calm in appearance but no longer tanned from his usual winter weekends in Palm Desert or skiing at Aspen. Still, the jailhouse pallor had not completely eradicated the righteous indignation reflected in his pale blue eyes and the upward tilt of his aristocratic chin.

Barrett looked to his right. There was Grace, efficient, smart, and scary. Scary, because she was too small for him to bully and too smart for him to fool. He turned his head further around and vaguely smiled in the direction of the panel from whom he would soon select a jury. Mike Reasoner was out of town on a case for C&S, and although his legal research on the case was finished now, it would have been comforting to see him in the courtroom. Lev was there, thank God, right behind him and apparently as serene as the Buddha, though Barrett knew he must be suffering inside, having failed to dig up anything negative on the state's new star witness. Three rows behind Lev sat

Julian Gold, staring at Grace Harris as she perused her documents, immobile except when an occasional cough shook his skeletal frame.

Back in the fifth row on the side closest to the jury, and looking as inconspicuous as possible, sat Dr. Eric Tremaine. Tremaine usually sat next to counsel during jury selection, but Barrett always worked alone, so a simple plan was devised. Tremaine would touch his right ear if he liked the juror; his nose if he didn't. A cough meant Tremaine had no strong feelings, in which case Barrett would rely on his trial lawyer's instincts and the background information Tremaine had already pulled together on each juror on the panel. If Tremaine removed a white handkerchief from his pocket, Barrett was advised to accept all the jurors then seated even if he had challenges remaining. This white flag of surrender meant that the jurors in the wings were no better or potentially worse for the defense than those already seated.

The jury was selected in three hours, considerably quicker than at the first trial, mainly because Tremaine had removed his handkerchief from his jacket pocket after Barrett had used just four of his challenges. Barrett had hoped for either yuppie country-clubbers or anti-government left-wingers, bookends bracketing the cultural continuum whose "preexisting cognitive constructs," according to Tremaine, might make them more sympathetic to the defendant. There were a few of these strange bedfellows, but Grace sent them packing.

"We're perfectly satisfied with the jury as it sits, Your Honor," said Barrett, concealing his disappointment.

Grace accepted Barrett's capitulation and was soon on her feet, making an opening statement that within twenty minutes had Barrett perspiring, Ashford scribbling notes, and the jury staring at Ashford with overt disdain.

"Now we turn to the defendant's third victim," she intoned, an unfeigned catch in her voice. "Earl Field. It is in Mr. Field's brutal murder that the defendant's arrogance is best revealed.

"Yes, members of the jury," she said, taking a backward step in the direction of the defendant, "arrogance. For killing his w-wife was not enough; the defendant brutally tortured her as well. And threatening jurors was not enough;

he had to murder one, and in the identical way he had slaughtered his wife. And even that did not satisfy his need for revenge for having been brought to the b-bar of justice like a common criminal. He had to kill the man who had dared to charge him with murder."

Barrett's usually inscrutable expression was giving way to exasperation as Grace Harris now planted herself squarely in front of the defendant and stared directly into his face.

"Yes, ladies and gentlemen, arrogance. Elliot Ashford is not some deranged multiple killer who buries his victims in a basement or shoots people from a tower. He is not a disgruntled ex-employee who snaps one day and wreaks vengeance on unknown citizens of the community. He is an educated man, born to great wealth, a powerful man whose brutality in committing these acts was equaled only by the diabolical skill he employed in an attempt to deflect suspicion from himself."

Grace paused and turned back toward the jury. "How did he do this? By a means so absurdly simple, yet so incredibly brilliant, it might well have worked."

Grace's voice rose now, both in volume and intensity. "The evidence will show that Elliot Ashford staged the death of his last two victims in the identical manner as his first, a strategy calculated to make it appear that no one as smart, as rich, as powerful as he is could possibly have done such a stupid and obvious thing; that the killings must be the work of a copycat, or perhaps someone trying to frame him."

She moved closer to the jurors, lowered her voice, and looked into each of their eyes as she continued speaking.

"But the p-police were not fooled, ladies and gentlemen. The prosecution was not fooled. And I am confident that when you have heard the evidence"—Grace paused here to make sure every eye was upon her—"you will not be fooled either."

Barrett Dickson rose to his feet almost apologetically. "Your Honor, I have been reluctant to interrupt counsel's stirring argument, but—"

"Say no more, counsel," said John Hernandez. "I was about to do it myself if you didn't. Turn it down a notch or two, please, Ms. Harris. Argument comes at the end of the trial, not now, as you well know."

Barrett's restraint had paid off. By allowing her to cross the line into argument, he had won the first skirmish of the trial.

"Thank you, Your Honor," said Grace, then proceeded methodically to outline her proofs as to each victim, focusing on motive, means, and opportunity. She stammered only a few times as she artfully exploited Ashford's initial lie about attending a movie when the murder occurred, his second failed alibi attempt in the first trial involving Renee Babcock, the defendant's angry shouting at his wife overheard just before the murder, his blood mixed with the victim's at the first crime scene, and the fact that only one person had a motive to kill all three victims.

"Members of the jury, that person is Elliot Winston Ashford."

Then, at last, Grace opened the bomb-bay doors.

"But can you be certain?" she asked rhetorically. "Certain beyond a reasonable doubt that the murders of Ms. Jefferson and Mr. Field were also the handiwork of the defendant? Yes, ladies and gentlemen, you can, because the People will present a witness who was an alternate juror during the first trial and who has had the courage to come forward and who will tell you from her own lips what she heard the defendant say from his; who heard Elliot Ashford threaten the lives of both of these victims! *Who heard him threaten to do exactly what he later did!*"

This was what everyone in the courtroom had been waiting for: The clincher.

The key witness.

49

"Your opening statement was terrific, Bear," said Leviticus later that evening as they ate takeout in his office. "Really."

Barrett knew that his friend was really just acknowledging the fact that he had been able to rise to his feet on cue and even managed to articulate a few complete sentences as he swam against a prosecutorial tidal wave without drowning.

"Well, hardly terrific," Barrett said, lifting a hot pot sticker with his fingers, "but at least nobody laughed out loud."

"And I only saw two or three of 'em givin' you the finger when you finished," said Lev.

Barrett dropped the pot sticker back on his paper plate. "Was one of them Grace Harris?"

"Naw," said Lev. "You had already put her to sleep, along with most of the spectators."

"Thanks for helping me through this problem I've got these days with overconfidence."

"You're welcome. I just thought an eight-year absence from the winner's circle might have gone to your head."

"Black humor from a black man. Just what I need in my hour of dark desperation."

"Okay, seriously, Shylock," Lev said, stabbing ineptly at cartons of kung pao chicken and chow fun with uncooperative chopsticks, "you were good."

"Just good?"

Lev dropped a chopstick. "I say 'terrific,' you don't believe me. Then I say 'good,' and that ain't enough! Jesus, Bear, you're one hard dude to please."

"You could have put a little more feeling in it."

Barrett sipped from a glass of iced tea in silence for a

minute, then stood and stretched, trying to coax some color back into his face. He knew his opening statement had been flat and lacking in energy. His unsupported allegations that the People's key witness was motivated not by the courageous pursuit of truth but by fame and fortune had sounded hollow and contrived, even to him. He tried to think of how he might have done it better; maybe mention Kato Kaelin by name? Maybe point out that nobody else had heard any such threats?

"Why didn't you mention the *Confidential* journalist?" asked Lev. "I told you his notes are full of Earl-this-and-Earl-that and how much he loved her and all kinds of bullshit."

Barrett grunted. "You—or somebody looking as big and ugly as you—told me he won't come up here and testify. 'Protecting his source.'"

"He might change his mind."

"And he might not," said Barrett. "What you're really asking is why didn't I pull a Johnnie Cochran and just tell the jury about it anyway?"

Lev looked out the window. "Eric Tremaine says eighty percent of jurors make up their minds during opening statements and don't change them."

"I know, and yes, I was tempted."

"You're just too virtuous, my man," said Lev with a wink.

"I'm just too chicken-shit. I don't have Cochran's balls."

"Seriously, Bear, I think your openin' swung them back to where they'll at least take a hard look at Keller. I'm sorry I've come up dry so far. Not even a speedin' ticket."

"There must be something," said Barrett irritably. Discussing Keller always triggered a rush of anxiety. "She was in *Hollywood,* for Christ's sake."

Lev shrugged. "There ain't nothin', Bear. What can I tell you?"

"What can you tell me?" said Barrett, jabbing his chopsticks toward Lev. "You can tell me how I explain to our client that the best investigator in San Francisco, operating with an unlimited budget, cannot find one piece of trash in the world's biggest trash heap."

"Oh, now that's different," said Lev. "I found a heap of trash; it's just that none of it helps. I talked to her ex-husband, for instance, a guy who gives sleaze a bad name. Five minutes with him made me feel sorry for the woman. The worst thing anybody says about Amanda Keller is she's a little weird, like half the people you'll have on your jury. Like you're bein' right now."

Barrett rubbed his red-rimmed eyes. "Sorry. All this damned tea is making me cranky. How about any past contacts with Ashford?"

"None. Forget your notion that she's an Ashford plant ready to take a dive on cross. Fact is, she's probably telling the truth about the bastard."

"Let's not get into that again, okay? Just keep looking."

"I've looked everywhere, Bear."

"Well, look everywhere again. I need dirt on her; I need dirt on the cops, the crime lab, the medical examiner, the acting D.A., the D.A.'s janitorial service. I need dirt on Amanda Keller's dentist and her goddamn gardener if she's got one! I need dirt on anybody and everybody they're going to throw at us!"

Lev smiled and nodded his head. "Now you're beginning to sound like a criminal defense lawyer. As for the D.A.'s office, forget it. I've checked again with several lawyers with an ax to grind. Nothin'."

Barrett shrugged his massive shoulders. "All right, but don't give up, okay? Especially with Keller."

"I'm back to L.A. tonight."

"Sorry, but it's necessary."

Leviticus shrugged and said, "Don't be sorry. This trip saved me from goin' home tonight to meet my sister-in-law's first interracial boyfriend."

"Guess who's coming to dinner?"

"Exactly. The man is said to be of the white persuasion."

Barrett smiled and chucked his plastic container in the wastebasket.

"Thanks for doin' your own dishes," said Lev.

Barrett looked down at his friend as he stood near the door, but he wasn't smiling now.

"If we don't get to Amanda Keller, Lev, Ashford goes down."

Leviticus's face suddenly betrayed fatigue, even discouragement. "I'll keep tryin', Bear, but you best get some

sleep. Big day tomorrow. Sounds like Harris is leadin' off
with Amanda Keller."

"Yeah," said Barrett, "big day."

In her Russian Hill apartment across town, Grace sat
with Amanda and Sam Quon at the kitchen table, finishing
a second pot of coffee.

"Let's go through it once more," said Grace.

Amanda shook her head. "I'm exhausted, Grace. I'll look
a mess tomorrow if I don't get some sleep."

Sam nodded in agreement. Grace knew she was being
obsessive, even more so than usual, so she decided to call
it a night.

"Just promise me, Amanda, that you won't take the bait
when he hits you with the *Confidential* story. Tell it straight,
just like you told us tonight, okay? And don't look for me
to object no matter how hard he hits you. I don't want to
appear overly protective on this issue, so you'll be flying
solo. Just don't panic."

"I think you've hit me harder than Dickson ever could."

"And you've handled everything I threw at you. But if
you think of *anything* the defense might have—so much as
a DUI or spitting on the sidewalk—call me here anytime.
Remember, there's nothing we can't handle, as long as
we're the ones who handle it first."

"There are no skeletons," said Amanda, with a coquettish smile that had even charmed the virtuous Sam Quon.
"I know I must sound terribly boring, but I've been a
good girl."

"Okay," said Grace, "and I've been an obsessive nut
who's just as tired as the two of you. So Sam will take you
home now and pick you up tomorrow at seventy-thirty
sharp. No more showing up in a limousine, okay?"

The flat seemed eerily silent after Amanda and Sam had
left, and Grace wished she could call Aaron to hear his
voice and tell him how much she loved him, but it was
after 2:00 A.M. on the East Coast. She hadn't realized how
much she needed him. She had never felt so alone.

She picked up her Keller testimony outline, wondering
why she was feeling uneasy. The opening statements had
gone better than she could have hoped, and Amanda Keller
seemed untouchable. What was gnawing at her?

She knew what Earl Field would say in this situation: *The bride is too beautiful.*

"Your first witness, Ms. Harris?" said John Hernandez at nine sharp the next morning.

"Call Amanda Keller, Your Honor."

The bailiff signaled the deputy at the door, who quickly disappeared into the corridor. Witnesses had been excluded from the courtroom, so Amanda was waiting outside. As the rear courtroom door opened again, people turned around as if they were wedding guests hearing the first strains of the processional. Grace all but expected people to stand up as she came walking down the aisle, radiantly beautiful despite the most toned-down dress Grace could find in her wardrobe. Her face was relaxed and glowing with health, her body as well toned as a gymnast's, with long, firm legs set off by medium heels and taupe-colored stockings. She elicited a communal gasp from the gallery as she strode forward. The courtroom artists might have been at a Paris fashion show. Even John Hernandez seemed momentarily transfixed.

Grace would muse later that with her entire professional career riding on the outcome of the next sixty minutes, she had somehow managed in that moment to be painfully conscious of her own relative plainness.

It was all over in less than an hour. Grace's concise direct examination of Amanda Keller had come off without a hitch as the witness recounted Ashford's threats with startling realism. Barrett sighed as he saw two of the jurors scowling at his client without even being aware of it. He knew they were seeing themselves in Amanda's situation, sitting as a juror.

On cross, Amanda immediately burned Barrett by flawlessly reiterating her earlier testimony and volunteering things she hadn't even mentioned on her direct examination—the trial lawyer's worst nightmare. Asking the most simple yes-or-no question invariably provoked further lurid descriptions of Ashford's menacing looks and warning gestures. Every time Barrett touched the stove, he got his fingers burned.

Let her go, he told himself, yet this was the witness that had to be broken. He had to keep trying.

"You didn't tell the judge about any of this during the first trial, did you?"

"No. Like I said, I was terrified."

"If you were so terrified—as you have told us fourteen times now by my count—why didn't you seek the protection of the judge, the bailiff, or even the police?"

Amanda sat quietly for a moment and Barrett thought he had her. "I considered it," she said, a tremor in her voice, "but how could I be sure they could protect me from the Mafia?"

A murmur rose from the gallery. The bailiff rose.

"Move to strike, Your Honor," said Barrett quietly. He was beginning to feel weak and shaky, as if in the grip of low blood sugar. There was suddenly not a sound in the courtroom, just his own breathing. He felt every juror's eye on him.

How deep can I dig myself? wondered Barrett. I should be on the prosecution payroll.

"The answer may go out," said the judge, "and the jury is instructed to disregard it."

Sure they will, thought Barrett.

"It is true, Ms. Keller, is it not," he said, "that you at no time told anyone any of this until only a few days ago."

"Mr. Dickson," said Amanda, adopting the patient tone of someone addressing a child, "I've been afraid to even tell the invalid mother I live with."

Oh, Christ, he thought, another land mine. Not that he needed any help burying himself deeper. He figured he'd stop when he got to six feet. Everything was backfiring on him. Still, he stumbled forward, bobbing and weaving, his bloodied face absorbing her left-right combos, still looking for an opening.

"Now about this elevator incident. Were there any other witnesses to that?"

The witness straightened up, refocusing. "Just the lady I described in my direct examination."

"The average-height lady with average dark hair and average looks?"

"Yes," said Amanda, apparently missing his sarcasm. "And Lani, of course."

"How about in the café, when you say you heard him tell some man he intended to settle a score with Mr. Field. Anyone else hear that?"

"I don't think so," said the witness.

Barrett glanced at his notes. "And you say the man he was eating lunch with in the café was medium height, dark hair, average build, and fortyish?"

"That's correct."

"He sounds like the twin brother of the lady in the elevator and half the people in America. Can you be a little more specific?"

"Objection, argumentative."

"Sustained."

"Okay, so this average-looking gentleman was seated and facing you, right?"

"No. He was facing my back. When I heard what sounded like Mr. Ashford's voice, I turned around and saw the back of Mr. Ashford's head and that's when I glanced at the other man."

"He was seated, facing Mr. Ashford?"

"Yes."

"Then can you tell the members of the jury how, if he was seated, you know he was a man of medium height?"

The witness hesitated, then said, "I suppose I estimated his height based on what I could see of him."

"So he might have been a long-waisted short man or a short-waisted tall man?"

"No, I remember now. I glanced at him again when he got up to pay the check and leave."

"I see. That's when you saw that he was actually a normal-waisted man of normal height with an average build, normal-looking hair, and—"

"Objection!"

"Sustained! No more of that, please, Mr. Dickson."

"Yes, Your Honor. Now tell us again what Mr. Ashford said to you after this other man left?"

"That's when he turned around and recognized me. He asked me if I had gotten an earful, and I said no, I hadn't heard anything."

"That was a lie, wasn't it?"

Amanda bristled. "Yes, it was a lie, but what would you have done under the circumstances?"

Barrett shrugged. "I guess I'd hope to be as good at lying as you are."

"Your Honor!" shouted Grace.

"Next question, Mr. Dickson."

"Yes, Your Honor. Please continue, Ms. Keller. What did he say then?"

"That's when he told me to forget I ever knew him unless I wanted to die on a LifeSpin like Lani Jefferson."

"Would that be the exercise bike Lani was riding in her living room when she was killed?"

"Yes."

"And let's be clear on this, Ms. Keller. Because of the fact that Ms. Jefferson is dead, and you can't identify the man he was with in the café, or the woman you and Jefferson were with in the elevator, we have only your word that any of this even happened, am I right?"

Barrett saw Amanda start to glance at Grace, then stop herself. He thought he saw her lips tighten. She didn't like having her honesty questioned.

"Just your word, Ms. Keller," he repeated. "Am I right?"

"Well, there might have been someone—"

"Objection," said Grace. "Argumentative."

"Overruled."

"You were saying, Ms. Keller, there might have been someone else?"

"I don't know, maybe the waitress. I'm telling you the truth, Mr. Dickson, really I am."

Woman, thought Barrett, thou art beginning to protest too much. He had also seen Grace's head snap up and Amanda's eyes flicker in her direction. Even a blind hog, thought Barrett, sometimes comes up with an acorn.

"And if the waitress did overhear something, Ms. Keller, what part would she have heard, the part about Mr. Field or the threat to you."

"*Objection!* Hypothetical, argumentative, and assuming facts not in evidence."

"This is cross-examination, Your Honor," said Barrett, puzzled that a seasoned trial lawyer like Grace Harris would be making such technical and doomed objections. "Not a very effective one, I'll concede," he added, "but cross-examination all the same."

"Overruled. Answer the question, Ms. Keller."

The witness paused as if to think. "I guess it would have been when she came to give me my check, after the other man had left."

"Can you give us a description of this waitress, Ms. Keller? Was she, by any chance, average height, dark hair, normal—"

"Your Honor!"

"That's enough, Mr. Dickson," said John Hernandez.

"I apologize, Your Honor. Can you describe the waitress that may have overheard this threat?"

"I'm sorry, Mr. Dickson. I was quite upset by what had been said to me. She might have had blond hair, I think, but I don't even know for sure she heard anything."

Barrett paused, wishing that Lev were here instead of down in L.A. He'd be heading out the door on his way to Pat's Seafood Grill. Keller seemed to be uneasy now, but in the jury's eyes, Barrett knew he had only made himself look like a bully and the witness appear more sympathetic. He figured he had done Grace enough favors for one cross-examination and would let loose with his closing zinger and sit down.

"Isn't it a fact, Ms. Keller, that you received $20,000 for the story you sold to *Confidential*?"

"No, sir."

Now he had her. "You weren't paid by *Confidential*?"

"Oh, yes, but it was $20,575. They wanted me to come to Los Angeles for photographs, and I made them pay my mother's expenses so that she wouldn't be left alone. That's my mother sitting in the back in the wheelchair."

Barrett could only watch helplessly as the jurors' heads turned as one to glance at Lucinda Keller, looking pathetic in the rear of the courtroom. He hoped no one noticed as he flicked a finger across his sweat-beaded forehead.

"But the fact is, Ms. Keller, you did fly down there and tell them a story that was different from the one you've told here. Correct?"

"Maybe different in some small part," she said. "They made up some things, like I guess they always do." She paused for a moment as if about to cry, then added, "You must understand, sir, that I would do almost anything for my mother—and God knows we desperately needed the

money we got from that terrible magazine—but I would
never lie under oath. Not for her, not for anyone."

Another backfire. Barrett almost laughed at the absurdity
of his situation. The woman was ready for anything he
could throw at her.

"That's all I have for now, Your Honor," he said in as
confident a tone as he could muster, and took his seat,
feeling the cold wetness of his shirt against the back of his
chair, unable to meet the scowling eyes of his client.

"Redirect, Ms. Harris?" said John Hernandez.

Grace Harris quietly replied that she had no questions
on redirect—the supreme insult to an opponent's cross-
examination—and called her next witness, a DNA expert,
whose anticlimactic pedagogy would lull the jury to sleep
even before Amanda could complete her press conference
in the marbled first-floor lobby.

At the lunchtime recess, Sam Quon shot through the rail,
grabbed Grace's hand, and pumped it enthusiastically.

"We've got him, Grace! You might as well rest your case
right now and let the jury do its job. Well done, champ!"

But Grace looked preoccupied, even worried. "Champ?"
she said. "Or chump."

"What are you worried about? The jury loved her. She
was unbelievable!"

Grace looked at Sam with worried eyes. "That's exactly
what I'm worried about."

50

That night, still at the office, Grace finished prepping her DNA expert for his cross at nine o'clock the next morning, then entered the small conference room to which Sam had delivered Amanda Keller. Sam Quon looked uncomfortable, and Grace could see that Keller was not happy.

"Hello, Amanda," said Grace, "thanks for coming down."

"I'm not sure I had a choice, Grace, what with Charlie Chan showing up unannounced at my apartment and all but arresting me. Would you mind telling me why I'm here? I thought I was finished. I had important commitments tonight."

"I'm sure you did, Ms. Keller, but this is important too. Let's begin with an apology to Mr. Quon. I don't permit racial slurs in my office."

Amanda flushed and turned to Sam Quon. "Of course," she said. "My remark was stupid and insensitive, Sam. I guess I was trying to make light of the fact that I was upset by the way you approached me. I felt like a criminal."

"Apology accepted," said Sam, "and as soon as you and Grace are finished, I'll take you wherever you're supposed to be."

Amanda bowed her head slightly. "Thank you. Now, Grace, what can I do for you?"

"You can begin by explaining why you changed your testimony on the stand today."

If Amanda was caught off guard, she didn't show it.

"I don't understand," she said, her eyes questioning.

Grace opened her trial notebook. "You'd like examples? Why is it you suddenly have seen the elevator lady around the courthouse and think she's an employee. We went over this several times and you had never seen her before."

"Did I say that? Well, I was nervous up there, Grace. It's not important, is it?"

"It's important that you tell us the truth, Amanda, and the truth is a constant. It doesn't change from day to day, even if you're nervous. Now who was this lady?"

Amanda frowned. "I haven't the slightest, Grace, really. Maybe I had seen her around, I simply don't know."

"And what was all that about a waitress possibly overhearing Ashford threaten you in the café? How could you have failed to tell us about that?"

Amanda coughed, then coughed again. "May the accused have a drink of water?" she asked. "Sam, would you be a gentleman?"

Grace reached for her Calistoga and poured a Styrofoam cup half-full and handed it to her. Amanda sipped from the cup as if she were holding a very dry martini in a stem glass at the Four Seasons.

"He was making me look stupid," said Amanda finally. "He might as well have accused me of being a liar!"

"So are you saying you became one?" said Grace.

"No, there *was* a waitress and she *may* have heard it. I didn't testify I was sure she had heard it, did I, Sam?"

Sam shook his head.

"Good," said Amanda, "and besides, I think I did tell you about the waitress. Look at your notes, Grace. Didn't I say that, Sam?"

Sam shrugged and said, "If you had, I would have gone there to interview all the waitresses."

"Well, given Dickson's insulting behavior, I thought I handled that question very well."

"You always handle yourself well, Amanda," said Grace. "Maybe that's what's troubling me."

Amanda rose to her feet and leaned against Grace's desk. "Do you want to explain that remark?"

Grace shrugged. "I think you follow me; indeed, I'm beginning to think you're always a step ahead of me."

Amanda's dark eyes lashed Grace's face. "Well, I'll tell you what's troubling me, Ms. District Attorney," she said in a tone Grace had never heard from the soft-spoken woman. "I've come forward like a good citizen and put myself in jeopardy, given you hours of preparation time, then spent the worst sixty minutes of my life on the witness stand winning your damn case for you—and this is the way you show appreciation?"

She snatched up her purse and added, "This meeting is over, Ms. Harris. If you'll be so good as to call me a cab, Sam, I'll be waiting in front of the courthouse."

"Hold on a minute, Amanda," said Grace, "I have an obligation to—"

But the door slammed behind the prosecution's key witness and she was gone.

Grace and Sam sat in silence for a moment, then Grace said, "Go pick her up out front, Sam. Take her to her damn party or whatever."

"Sure," said Sam, then added in a gentle voice, "I guess you know you were pretty rough on her, Grace."

Grace doodled on a pad in front of her. "I'm worried, Sam. I'm having serious doubts about her."

"Easy, Grace, you're talking about our star witness."

"That's what's bugging me, Sam. I think our Ms. Keller is a bit too good to be true."

"And you're a bit too much of an obsessive worrier. I can't remember all the times I've heard you say that about other witnesses."

Grace shook her head. "This isn't just another witness, Sam. Amanda Keller represents the only evidence tying Ashford to Jefferson or Earl and the sole reason I'm still a member of this office, prosecuting this case."

Sam shrugged and said, "That shouldn't raise the bar for her. Anyway, what's done is done, and we've got nothing to be ashamed of. Besides, I happen to think she's telling the truth. She was just nervous and confused, like she said. Who wouldn't be?"

"I hope you're right, Sam, but how does a witness forget to mention during the course of three lengthy prep sessions something as important as having a death threat possibly overheard by a third party."

"Okay, but why would she stick her neck out in a case where people are dying like flies?"

"I haven't a clue. Publicity? She's getting plenty."

Sam threw his arms in the air. "I haven't a clue either, Grace, but her credibility is for the jury to determine, not us."

"Our job is to present the truth, Sam, you know that.

We've got a different burden than defense lawyers do. I also have a moral dilemma if I think she's lying."

Sam frowned, and Grace could see that he was losing patience. "Well, I hope you can find a way to deal privately with your private 'dilemmas.' "

Grace reddened. "As a public servant, Sam, I don't have the luxury of private dilemmas."

"That's exactly my point!" said Sam. "You've got a slam dunk with the jury now, Grace, *and* with the voters in the June special election. Stop worrying so much."

Grace turned away from him, from further escalation.

"Excuse me now," said Sam, "while I go try to salvage our witness."

The breeze from the slammed door ruffled the pages of her trial notebook, while out in front of the Thomas J. Cahill Hall of Justice, the subject of their argument waited for the unmarked county vehicle she knew Grace would eventually send to pick her up.

Sleep for Barrett Dickson that night was even more elusive than usual. The spirit was willing, the flesh was weak, but the mind was racing like a linear accelerator.

If he had managed in the past by extreme means to assure himself that his client was innocent, Amanda Keller's testimony had begun to convince him otherwise. And now Sandra Weiss's revelation had put him in a trap. Who said that knowledge is power? he reflected. Too much knowledge could kill a person.

Whether innocent or guilty, Huntington's would kill Ashford, but Barrett was a lawyer, not a doctor, and he knew he was sitting on a blackout defense that could win Ashford a defense verdict. He owed Ashford that much at least, particularly after his showing against Amanda Keller; his dazed, sleepless state had not dulled the residual pain from his failed encounter with the state's key witness. Even as a child, Barrett had suffered an emotional afterburn from stupid mistakes, an angst that persisted even after the specifics of the stupid mistake had long been forgotten. The adult Dickson had held such anxieties in check by becoming a workaholic, by simply obsessing most stupid mistakes out of his life. Except for Ellen, of course, after whose departure he had almost traded down from workaholicism to alcoholism.

He rolled over on his right side. Got up, went to the bathroom. Got back in bed. Tried the left side.

Armed to the teeth with ammunition provided by Dr. Weiss, he would do better with the state's DNA expert tomorrow, then maybe try another plea bargain with Grace. Weiss had been able to review the expert's first trial testimony and had driven a tank through the holes she found. The bad news was that though she had concluded the shaving theory was plausible, it was more likely Ashford's blood at the scene than anyone else's. Still, he would kill Grace's expert tomorrow the way Keller had killed him today.

What a business.

Barrett's anxiety would have been somewhat allayed had he known that Grace was thinking along the same lines.

Maybe the best way out for everyone was a plea bargain, she realized, though she hated the idea and hardly ever engaged in what she called "backdoor" deals.

Meanwhile, however, despite her doubts, it was time for her to call and make peace with her key witness. Sam had been right. She had been unfairly rough with Amanda. Grace had seen witnesses so jittery they couldn't even state their names after taking the oath. Amanda was at least entitled to the benefit of the doubt. She picked up the phone.

Amanda graciously accepted the proffered apology and Grace hung up feeling reassured by the conversation. She was so relieved, in fact, that she didn't notice the expression of despair on Sam's face as he entered her office and slowly approached her desk, dripping wet from yet another storm raging outside.

"I just spoke with Amanda, Sam," she said, rising and glancing up at him. "I apologized and she accepted, so we're back on track."

Sam wiped residual drops of rain off his face. "No, Grace," he said quietly. "We're completely off the rails."

"What?"

"I couldn't find the waitress Amanda told us about at Pat's Seafood Grill."

"So?" said Grace, looking puzzled. "It was a long shot, Sam. It's not the end of the world."

"The reason I couldn't find her is because Pat doesn't hire waitresses. Which is why, incidentally, he's being sued under Title VII. There has never been a female waitperson at Pat's Seafood Grill. Never."

Sam's words registered first in Grace's head, then in her stomach. She fell back into her chair, then leaned her head against her steepled fingers.

"Shit," said Grace.

"Yeah," said Sam. "Shit."

51

As predicted, Barrett dismantled Axel Janes, the prosecution's pontifical DNA expert, in front of a gratifyingly attentive jury. Ashford smiled and shook Barrett's hand at the end of the day, and Grace gave him a weary nod that conceded he had done well. Barrett then stalled after the bailiff had taken Ashford away, systematically moving papers in and out of his trial bag until Grace prepared to leave.

"Cup of coffee?" he asked, and she nodded yes.

They walked down the street to the Cafe Roma, Barrett feeling awkward at first, slouching along with his trail bags banging at his sides. They found a back table and engaged in small talk for twenty minutes or so, finding they had more in common than they thought. They discussed wayward sons and single life, and Grace found herself telling him about growing up in New York and how she missed the shows, the shopping, the museums. When he asked why she had left, she told him it was his turn and asked about his early days as a trial lawyer.

He smiled, warmed by her interest and by the memory of it. "Opposing counsel in civil cases used to meet in an Italian restaurant called Rocca's," he began. "The place was so dark you couldn't read the menu at lunch. It's now called Stars."

"You're kidding," she said, pointing to the cream.

He automatically put the cup in his right hand down on the table, then passed the cream to her with the same hand. His left hand stayed in his lap whenever possible, a habit born of vanity. The ugly stub there was a grotesque reminder of the limitations of battlefield medicine. Also an occasional reminder that he could never do again what his blind youthful exuberance had compelled him to do that

day: bravely, mindlessly charging into the spurting barrel
of a Viet Cong rifle.

He shuddered. What had Mike said about him in
Moose's that day? That it wasn't just losing he was afraid
of?

That had rankled at the time, but now Barrett realized
he was indeed afraid of just about everything: losing, winning, even standing in front of those twelve ordinary citizens who could somehow goad him into places he no longer
wanted to go. Like the way crowds he had seen in Spain
seemed to push the matador closer to the horns of the bull.

Like the way bullies could taunt an eleven-year-old boy
lying facedown in blood-caked dirt.

I ain't chicken.

"Thank you," came Grace's welcome voice as she passed
the cream back to him. "I never would have guessed."

Barrett blinked.

"About Stars," she said.

He smiled. "Yeah, we'd fight like hell all morning, then
go to Rocca's and drink too much at lunch, then go back
and fight all afternoon. But we settled cases when we could,
fought hard when we couldn't, and were friends again at
the end of the day."

"Back at Rocca's?"

"I'm afraid so."

"Sounds like the good ol' days, with the good ol' boys,"
Grace said, offering a wry smile.

"We thought so," he said, sipping his coffee. "But that
was a long time ago. I don't know how or when trial lawyers lost their civility toward one another, but it's taken
the satisfaction and joy out of trial work."

"I know what you mean."

"So this is it for me," he said. "My last trial. I'm going
into real estate."

Grace looked surprised, though not as surprised as he
was that he had told her.

"I can't believe you would leave . . . I mean—"

"I've got my reasons," he said, rescuing her and changing
the subject. "Look, Grace, we got off on the wrong foot
somehow. I'd like to see our gloves come off when the bell
rings at the end of the day."

She held up her hands. No gloves.

"I'm serious, Grace. These 'frigid purgatorial fires' between us aren't helping me sleep any better at night."

Grace glanced up from her coffee cup. "Dylan Thomas?"

Barrett smiled. "I'm not sure. T. S. Eliot, I think. Anyway, you said you're sorry about those indictments and I was wrong to think you were the architect."

He then paused to see if she would say anything, but she just sat there looking beautiful, waiting him out.

"So," he said, "let's get civil, okay?"

"I'd like nothing better," she said.

He allowed a moment of silence between them, then decided on a little more conversation before he tried his pitch. "Are you going to be our next district attorney after you finish me off?"

A smile crept up into her eyes. "Not if Jack Klegg's ambition or my own good judgment prevails."

"I wouldn't bet a nickel on either of those things stopping you."

"Well, there's also the good judgment of the voters to consider. No, Barrett, I think I'm safe."

Barrett watched her as she pensively stirred her coffee. She wore no ring. He knew that, but wondered if she was in a relationship. "Your folks still alive?"

"Yes. My father's a rabbi. Forbade me to become a lawyer, actually. 'A woman's place' . . . well, you know."

"So you had to make it on your own?"

"Thanks to a student loan. Columbia Law."

"What brought you out here?" he asked.

"Long story. My interviews for a litigation job at the best firms on Wall Street did not go well. I'd make it almost to the end before my first stammer, at which time I'd get some enthusiastic advice on the merits of a career in estate planning."

"Not what you had in mind," said Barrett, smiling.

"I figured anyone could write a will or form a corporation. I wanted to be a trial lawyer."

"This woman's place," said Barrett smiling, "was in the courtroom."

"Exactly. The place where people go for justice."

Barrett was touched by her ingenuous and unembarrassed declaration. He guessed that the courtroom was also a place where a mark could be made, a father proven wrong, his grudging approval ultimately won.

"Anyway, I decided to take a break and visit an old boyfriend, an NYU undergrad classmate named Harris who was living in San Francisco. He got me an interview with Wilson & Lively, a small local firm. They offered me a job, and on an impulse, I took it."

"I think I can figure out what came next. Harris offered you marriage, and you were seized by another impulse."

She nodded. "The only two impulsive acts of my entire life. Two years later, I wound up here and he wound up somewhere else. No regrets."

"I suspect that a third impulsive act will wind you up in the corner office on the third floor someday."

"Two impulsive acts in one lifetime is enough for me." She laughed, a soft, low sound that captivated Barrett. "Besides, I'd be a crummy administrator," she said.

"You could assign yourself to try all the tough cases. You're damn good at it."

"I appreciate that, particularly coming from you. I saw you in court when I was just starting out."

Barrett looked into his cup. Her remark had made him suddenly feel old. Was that intentional? What the hell, time to get on with it.

"I do have an agenda in asking you out to this elegant place." He knew he was sounding flirtatious but couldn't help himself.

"I suspected as much, which is why I didn't wear my dancing shoes."

Maybe there's hope, he thought, and smiled at her.

"I want to propose a plea bargain," he said. "This thing has cost our taxpayers enough. You've got a weak case on Lara which, no thanks to me, you would have lost the first time out but for the intervention of fate. Clay Astin says my client's telling the truth and didn't kill anybody and you know Clay is good. You've got no case at all on Jefferson and Field, except for a truck named Amanda Keller that ran over me yesterday. Of course, I don't expect you to agree with anything I've said so far."

Grace's brown eyes glowed. "But I do, Barrett. The part about Amanda Keller running over you."

Barrett smiled again. "Okay, and I ran over your expert today. Let's end this thing."

"Why would I want to? We've been there, Barrett. I'm opposed to plea-bargaining in general, particularly in a case where my own boss was the victim. Besides, the last time I checked, I was ahead by about three touchdowns."

"It's only the first quarter, and I scored today. Win or lose, there'll be a costly appeal, then maybe a third trial. Somewhere along the way, the taxpayers will insist on a deal. Why not make it now?"

Grace raised an eyebrow. "What kind of deal did you have in mind? Time already served and a heartfelt commitment from Mr. Ashford to stop sticking glass into people's throats?"

"Much tougher," said Barrett, granting a smile, then he threw out his opening gambit: "Voluntary manslaughter on Lara. Six years."

Grace rolled her eyes. "And maybe out in three? Where do you dream up these ideas?"

"Will you communicate it to Klegg?" said Barrett.

Grace's expression darkened. "You know I have to," she said.

"There's more I could tell you, Grace, but for my own personal reasons I can't."

"Why should that surprise me? We're adversaries, Barrett, remember? Although I confess I'm intrigued by your 'personal reasons.'"

The curiosity in her wide, dark eyes cut to Barrett's soul, and he wanted desperately to tell her about Ashford's illness. But since he couldn't in good conscience bare his client's soul, he decided to bare his own.

"I don't want anything in this crazy contest to get in the way of getting to know you better after this is all behind us."

Grace surprised Barrett by tilting her head in a playful manner and allowing her full lips to part into a coquettish smile. "Well, Mr. Dickson, I do believe you are coming on to me."

"You could say that."

"I believe I did say that. Are you?"

"Yes."

"Good, but also unwise."

"I know it."

"At least premature."

"I know it. Another reason to settle now."

Grace raised an eyebrow in what he hoped was mock disapproval.

"I was kidding," he said. "Bad timing. Bad taste."

"Your specialty, I hear."

"I'm changing."

"That's good. As for the kidding, at what point did you start with the kidding?"

"Just the last part. The part about the case, not about you."

"Okay."

Barrett's intuition told him she would like to recommend the deal, but that she would not be shaken from her principles. He decided not to press it further. He got them both refills at the counter and they returned to small talk. When they had drained their cups, she rose and they walked outside. They shook hands, and he found it hard to let go of hers.

They headed in different directions toward their cars, and Barrett kept watching her as she walked away, hoping she would look back.

Barrett drove home with the windows open to the December air and his radio turned up. He sniffed at the back of his hand where she had touched it and smiled as foolishly as a boy in love.

Grace unloaded her dishwasher at home, heard herself singing for the first time in weeks. But beneath the stirring in her heart, she knew that to allow feelings of affection for one's adversary in the pitch of battle was not just unprofessional, it was dangerous.

Early the next morning, Grace and Sam Quon met for a hastily scheduled meeting with Jack Klegg. She had called this one in order to comply with her obligation to inform Klegg of Barrett's indicated plea offer. She smiled as she thought about Dickson, pictured him lumbering toward her the day before with his typical unstudied languor. There was something in that walk that belied Barrett Dickson's legendary reputation as a courtroom killer. She could tell a lot about a man by the way he moved, and only a man essentially decent and pure of heart could walk in such an ungainly manner.

What was she thinking? What she should be thinking about is what she would tell Klegg, who was ready to jump at almost any offer. She had low-keyed her doubts about Amanda when she called Klegg, deciding she should give her witness an opportunity to explain the Pat's Grill problem before writing her off completely. Besides, Klegg already had enough leverage in his crusade to end the case.

Grace rubbed her red-rimmed eyes as she waited for Klegg, and for just a moment the thought of ending the case was like a calming warm bath. She briefly surrendered to thoughts of seeing Aaron home again and not having to deal with Amanda Keller anymore. She thought about how Keller had eaten Dickson alive. She was smart. But was she honest?

Klegg walked in, listened to Barrett's floated plea offer, and without hesitation said, "Take it, Grace."

Before Grace could respond, Sam objected, even more strongly than before.

"Your objection is noted, Sam," Klegg said in a patronizing tone, "but Grace's instincts are nearly infallible and she's told me about your lying key witness."

"I didn't say she was lying, Jack," protested Grace. "There are just—"

"I know what you said, but it's time we end this damn thing."

Sam stood and faced Klegg, as erect as she had ever seen him. "I realize I have no vote," he said, "but I have served here longer than anyone in this office. We have a clear murder one case, Jack, and the public will know something is fishy if we cave now."

"Why would they think that?"

"Because," said Sam, "I'll tell them what it is that's fishy."

Grace wondered if she had heard Sam correctly. Klegg narrowed his eyes but remained calmly curious. "And just what will you tell them, Sam?"

"I'll start with the fact that someone at your office extension has been making and receiving calls from a number listed to a Julian Gold in Chicago and another number at the Acropolis hotel in Las Vegas."

Grace could have kissed him.

"How do you know that?" said Klegg, his jaw muscles starting to work.

"I'm an investigator, remember?" said Sam, who then smiled wryly and added, "I knew you'd want to know about someone using your telephone."

"Maybe you'll soon be a *private* investigator, Sam," said Klegg, and stormed past them out the door.

"My God, Sam," Grace said, "when did you suspect Klegg?"

"Probably about a hundred years after you knew all about him. Am I right?"

Grace nodded. "For what it's worth, Earl—just before he was killed—had decided to take them all on."

Sam nodded. "Anyway, I think you can tell Mr. Dickson that Mr. Klegg declines his kind offer. And now you'd damn well better win."

"Don't worry, Sam. I think we've got Mr. Ashford where we want him now."

"I'm talking about the election!" said Sam. "I need this job."

At nine o'clock that night, Julian Gold paid Barrett Dickson a surprise visit at his apartment.

"I'd offer you something to drink, Julian," said Barrett, "but I don't like you."

Gold smiled. "Ever the comedian, Dickson. Your remarkably droll sense of humor justifies my trip from Chicago just to see you."

"I assume you've heard about my masterful cross of Keller and have come to relieve me of my engagement? You could have fired me by phone, Julian."

"I've not only heard about it, I've already perused the daily transcript. She took you apart, Dickson. Embarrassing, was it? A woman with no formal college education thoroughly dismembering a man once regarded as one of the finest cross-examiners in America."

"I could hardly have done worse. It will get better."

"Really? That would be very disappointing."

"Pardon me?"

"I think you might do considerably worse if you applied yourself. Indeed, Mr. Dickson, we're counting on it."

"You want me to throw him to the wolves. Is that it?"

Gold laughed, the first time Barrett had ever heard him laugh out loud. "Dickson, the things you don't know about criminal law astonish me."

"And amuse you as well, I see. What's your point?"

"My point is that with Keller in the picture, Ashford can't win. So we want to alter our strategy now to ensure the success of his appeal."

Barrett felt a sharp pain in his stomach. So that was it. The appeal would be based on inadequacy of counsel, a ground currently in vogue and often as successful in winning a new trial for the convicted defendant as it was in destroying the reputation of the incriminated trial counsel.

"No," he said firmly, "I couldn't do that."

"Of course you could. Just go through the motions and finish it out. Keep screwing up. Keep your money. Everybody parts friends. Agreed?"

"I mean I *won't* do that."

Gold cocked his head, seemingly unperturbed by his reaction. "With all respect, Mr. Dickson, your current reputation as a trial lawyer could hardly be further damaged. We're only asking that you continue to do what you are obviously well suited to do, which, of course, is nothing. No objections unless they are ill founded, nothing but a token cross of the state's witnesses. Then put on little or no case of your own. After the appeal, I can assure you there will not be a third trial and your client will be a free man."

Barrett met the *consigliere*'s cold eyes. "I think this is the point in the movies where they say, 'And if I don't go along?' "

Gold laughed again, but it was his little ventriloquist laugh, the one where his lips neither opened nor moved; the laugh that never left his throat.

"Come now, Mr. Dickson. This is real life. Your health and well-being are not in jeopardy. We're just talking lawyer to lawyer about how to salvage a disastrous situation for our mutual friend and client."

"I'm not recording this conversation, Mr. Gold. You don't have to sugarcoat it."

More silence. He's waiting me out, thought Barrett. Okay.

"You mentioned my health and well-being, Gold," Barrett added. "What, may I ask, is the state of my client's health and well-being?"

"Never better. What's your point?"

Barrett told himself to be careful. Either Gold was being typically cool or he didn't know about Ashford's Huntington's. "Nothing specific," he said, "but I've been thinking that the best way for Elliot to be sure of ducking death row would be to assert temporary insanity."

"On what possible grounds?"

"The argument goes like this: A person like Elliot Ashford could not have committed such a savage piece of butchery *unless* he was temporarily insane. We buy a pair of shrinks who are opposed to the death penalty and they'll weave a spell on the jury. I just thought I'd throw it out there since you seem to have sworn off optimistic thinking."

"I haven't lost my optimism, Mr. Dickson. Indeed, I've just outlined the way Elliot is most likely to escape death row. My way."

Barrett rubbed his chin. At least he had learned something. Gold didn't know about the Huntington's.

"Well?" said Gold.

"Well, what?"

"I'm waiting for your answer."

Barrett took a deep breath. "I'll continue to conduct myself the way I have, which, according to your assessment of my competency, is exactly what you have in mind."

"Don't play word games with me, Mr. Dickson. You know exactly what Carmine and I want, in addition to which I now want a straight answer."

Barrett tried to rotate the tightness out of his shoulders. He realized he had stopped breathing and took a deep one before delivering his answer. "Okay, Mr. Gold, here's your answer: You can all go fuck yourselves."

Gold winced, but only for a second, then shrugged. "Life still has many pleasures, sir," he said casually as he turned toward the door, "but at my age and state of health, fucking is no longer one of them." Then he paused in the doorway and added with a malicious grin, "All things considered, however, I have preferred growing old to the only known alternative. Wouldn't you, Mr. Dickson?"

Gold then disappeared down the hallway, not waiting for a response.

Barrett closed the door and walked slowly to the kitchen. He microwaved some day-old coffee and was pouring it unsteadily into a cup when the phone rang, sending both cup and coffee flying, scalding the back of his hand. He grabbed the phone, then stretched the cord to the sink so he could douse his hand with cold water. It was Grace.

"I'm sorry to bother you at home, Barrett."

"It's no bother at all," said Barrett, the burn forgotten.

"I thought I should t-tell you that . . . well, there won't be any plea bargain."

"Oh."

"So . . . see you tomorrow then?"

"Sure. Tomorrow."

"Thanks for the coffee yesterday. I enjoyed talking with you."

"Me too. With you."

She added a good-bye and hung up. Barrett had forgotten his hand but now realized that a large blister was forming.

And that the pain was about to increase.

Grace had rarely felt sorry for an opponent, nor had she expected anyone to feel sorry for her. Trial advocacy was dog-eat-dog in the service of the Greater Good of Justice. You won some, you lost some, but the judicial system generally emerged victorious and that was what was important. She would win this one, she thought, as she threaded her way through heavy traffic toward home at 8:20 P.M., but it would be a bittersweet victory over someone she had grown to care about.

She parked her car in the basement garage, then stopped at the first floor to check her mail. Sam Quon had stuffed an envelope in her box. She stuck her purse under her arm and opened it immediately. Sam had scribbled a short note on an article from *Entertainment Weekly,* then put a red circle around a piece on page 3:

Hollywood UPI. *Emory Goldsmith, CEO of Reprise Productions, today announced the signing of Amanda Keller to star in the screen adaptation of David Heller's* Thursday's Wife, *currently in preproduction. Keller won critical acclaim for her TV role in* Hope's People, *then disappeared from sight, surfacing last week in San Francisco Superior Court as the prosecution's star witness in the Elliot Ashford triple-murder trial.*

Asked to compare her real-life role in the Ashford case with her acting role in Thursday's Wife, *Keller said, "Acting* is *real life. It's good to be back."*

The note from Sam said, "Don't tell me you told me so, okay?"

52

Monday's session was unremarkable and would have been outright boring but for frequent and impassioned skirmishes between counsel that had Mike Reasoner and Leviticus Heywood exchanging perplexed looks as they observed their friend's strange and aggressive conduct.

Barrett Dickson was behaving like a man possessed, objecting and waving his arms like a man under attack by stinging bees. His contentious manner throughout the day inspired a cartoon on the editorial page the next day depicting Grace Harris armed with a whip and chair, fending off a growling bear in a cage.

On the witness stand, Thomas Yang, the coroner and chief pathologist, droned on despite Barrett's constant interruptions about how carefully he had supervised the autopsy and how diligently he had followed the standard approved procedures for preserving evidence in a murder trial.

Judge John Hernandez sat as upright as he could on the bench, his eyes hooded with mingled boredom and curiosity, wondering what the hell Barrett was up to, fighting each and every point with such uncommon fury. Yang didn't seem important enough to warrant the torrent of objections and constant requests for voir dire examinations that Barrett was making during the coroner's direct examination.

When it was Barrett's turn to cross-examine the coroner, he fired questions so fast the court reporter frequently had to appeal to the judge to urge Dickson to slow down.

"You never saw it, Dr. Yang? The evidence bag?"

"Just at the scene."

"So the scrapings *were* taken."

"Yes."

"By you?"

"Yes."

"Because?"

"Pardon me?"

"Why did you take scrapings from under the victim's fingernails?"

"Isn't that obvious, sir? To assist in identifying the perpetrator."

"Of course it's obvious, Doctor. What isn't so obvious is why you lost or disposed of them."

"Objection!"

"Withdrawn. Let me put it this way. Were the scrapings lost or intentionally disposed of, do you know?"

"Lost, of course."

"Not disposed of?"

"Lost."

"Who lost them?"

"I don't know."

"If you don't know who lost them, then how do you know they were lost, not disposed of?"

And so on for the entire afternoon until, despite Grace's skillful efforts to intercede, Coroner Yang's calm arrogance progressed from petulant defensiveness to quarrelsome invective, then abject surrender.

"So can we sum up, sir, by saying you don't have a shred of forensic evidence connecting Elliot Ashford to the murders of either Jefferson or Field?"

"That's generally true."

"It's specifically true as well, is it not?"

"Well, it is my opinion that Jefferson and Field were killed with the same weapon that killed Lara Ashford, so if the defendant killed Lara—"

"No, Dr. Yang!" said Barrett, grabbing People's Exhibit 1 and thrusting it so close to Yang's face he involuntarily recoiled. "This was the weapon that killed Lara Ashford, according to your testimony in the first trial."

Yang shrugged. "I meant to say they were killed by the same type of weapon."

"You *meant* to say. This is a capital case, Doctor Yang, and you have been offered by the People as an authority, so I urge you from now on to say only what you mean and mean only what you say."

"Objection," said Grace, "he's arguing again, Your Honor."

"Sustained. Don't lecture the witness, Mr. Dickson."

"It's true, isn't it," continued Barrett, seemingly oblivious to the interruptions, "that you think Elliot Ashford killed Jefferson and Field because you think he's the one who killed Lara Ashford?"

"Yes."

"You mean that, sir, or are you just saying it?"

Grace started to rise again, but let it go.

"I believe it to be true."

"But it's also true, isn't it, that if you had the lost or disposed-of fingernail scrapings, we wouldn't have to 'believe' anything, would we? We'd know the true identity of Lara's murderer, wouldn't we?"

"In all probability, we would, assuming we could tie them to a specific person's DNA."

"Not 'in all probability,' sir. If we could do that, we'd know beyond a reasonable doubt who murdered Lara Ashford, wouldn't we?"

"Yes, you are correct."

"And then, in your view, isn't it a fact that we'd also know beyond a reasonable doubt who killed the others?"

"Yes."

"Because you believe the same person killed all three."

"I have said that many times."

"But we don't have the scrapings, do we?"

"No."

"So we can't specifically tie them to anyone, can we?"

"No."

"So you can't say, and we can't know beyond a reasonable doubt, who really killed Lara Ashford, can we, Doctor! Or either of the others!"

"Objection," said Grace, though she also seemed drained by Barrett's tireless campaign, "invading the province of the jury and calling for a legal conclusion."

But Yang was already slowly shaking his head in the negative and everybody in the courtroom saw it.

"What the hell was that all about?" asked Mike an hour later as he took a seat next to Barrett at Bix, located in an alley called Gold Street, an informal border marking the end of the Financial District and the beginning of North Beach. It was only five o'clock, but the bar was already lined with upwardly mobile stockbrokers, lawyers, and other yuppie life forms, all of whom, Barrett had noticed, were considerably younger and prettier than himself. But the food was good and it was a long way from the courthouse.

"Not that you weren't terrific, Bear," Mike added, "just a little over the top."

Barrett sighed and drank straight from his bottle of Clausthaler. "I've got a problem, Mike."

"No shit? Stop the presses."

"No, something new. I've been instructed to take a dive, play the deadhead."

Mike expelled a stream of air from puffed cheeks. "Inadequate counsel," he said, slowly nodding. "Grounds for appeal. Smart. Might even work in your case. 'Counsel had hardly any criminal experience, tried only one in his career.' "

" 'And lost that one,' " Barrett added.

" 'Inherently unreliable.' "

"Don't forget 'occasional lush.' "

"It'll play," said Mike. "They'll get a new trial after he's convicted, then find a way to disappear Amanda Keller."

"Or the D.A. will be justified in throwing in the towel."

Mike reached for his single malt scotch and said, "Ironic, huh? We pressured you into this case at the outset and you agreed on condition you wouldn't have to do anything but deadhead. Now you're alone in the case, sober, regaining your legendary skills, and suddenly *they* want you to deadhead."

Barrett shrugged.

"But now the Bear is back, and the taste of possible victory is like honey in his mouth."

"Poetic, Mike," said Barrett, "but they're going to hurt me if I don't roll over."

Mike's drink stopped short of his lips. "You've been threatened?"

"Gold's meaning was pretty clear, even to me."

"So that's what you were up to today: sending Gold a message."

"I wanted him to know I won't roll over for anybody."

"You're an idiot," said Mike, then said nothing for a minute other than to order another scotch.

"Stipulated," said Barrett.

"What are you going to do?" Mike said at last.

"I thought I'd ask you, Mike. I'm a little too close to all this now."

Mike looked into his drink.

"So what do I do?"

"Jesus," said Mike, surveying the ceiling as if wisdom might be lurking there. "Jesus, Mary, and Joseph."

"Yeah, well, thanks for your wise counsel, Mike. I knew you'd come up with something."

The maître d' interrupted Mike's dazed distress to take them to their table, where Mike rendered his carefully thought-out answer. "I don't have the slightest fucking idea what I'd do, Bear."

"Yeah, well . . ."

"Maybe it's time to see the judge."

"I've got no evidence. Gold would just deny it."

Mike nodded, sipped his drink, then bobbed his head from side to side and said, "Look, Bear, you do think Ashford's innocent. Maybe you should go along, just skate a little."

"This from the country's greatest proponent of the adversary system."

"You're my best friend, Bear. To hell with it."

"Aren't you forgetting the victim in all this?" said Barrett.

"Not for a minute. Ashford will win his appeal and he'll be free."

"I wasn't talking about Ashford. Who saves my reputation, Mike? Who exhumes the rotting remains of my professional status in this town if I tank this case?"

Mike looked up in surprise. "I didn't know you gave a rat's ass anymore."

"I give a rat's ass."

"Okay, how about another shot at plea-bargaining."

"No hope. She's rejected two offers already and came back with nothing."

Mike rattled the ice in his glass.

"Drinking for two now, Mike?"

"The reformed pot calling the kettle black?"

Barrett chuckled and said, "Touché. I'll join you for a toddy or two as soon as this nightmare is over and I'm out of this fucking business."

"Selling real estate," said Mike in a tone of disgust.

"It's not a crime, for Christ's sake."

"In your case," said Mike through tight lips, "it should be a felony."

"What the hell are you pissed about?" Barrett said.

"Don't ask," said Mike, his eyes suddenly hot and intense.

"I'm asking."

"All right, here it is: I've been pissed for a long time, and watching you today in court just dug it all up again."

Mike paused to signal the waiter. "I don't know if you know this, Bear, but I'm not really a great trial lawyer."

"The hell you're—"

"Let me finish. I know what I am. I've had my share of honors and I've won more than my share of cases, some of them big ones. I'm a damn good trial lawyer, okay?"

"I think that's what I was trying to say, Mike."

"But I'm not a *great* trial lawyer, and what *I'm* trying to say is that I'd give anything . . . *anything,* you asshole . . . to have in my possession for just one year the gifts . . . the natural ability you seem so goddamn determined to throw away."

Barrett solemnly regarded his friend, then shook his head slowly and stared down at his hands.

"Look at me, Bear, damn you! I meant what I said about you being my best friend, but I've also hated your guts at times, did you know that? Partly because I've always envied you, but mainly because the thing I envied most means nothing to you. Nothing!"

Barrett couldn't help smiling.

"Grin, you prick! Think it's funny, do you?"

"No, Mike, it's just another irony. You see, all I've ever wanted . . ."

Barrett felt his throat tightening. He took in a breath, then a sip of his nonalcoholic beer. Then he took in another breath and let it out. "All I've really wanted is to have what you have, Mike—a home and a wife and kid to talk to. Hell, I'd settle for just a home."

Mike's shoulders relaxed and he reached out, put a hand

on Barrett's arm. "You have a home at C&S, Bear. I know it's not the same and that you've been a runaway. But the door's still open, and it may be the only home you'll ever know. Don't throw that away, too."

Barrett shook his head again. "It's over, Mike. Even if I did try to come back, I know I'd find a stranger sleeping in my bed."

" 'Said the Papa Bear,' " Mike murmured through a forced smile. "So we're back to Steve Wilmer again. Or is it the bond salesman who ran off with Ellen? Or the son who ran off by himself? Or are we all the way back to some scared teenage girl leaving a cardboard box at the fire station with a baby in it?" Mike was no longer smiling, getting angry again. "Jesus, Bear, it's time to let it all go, okay? Stop feeling sorry for yourself and do something about it."

Barrett said nothing. He wasn't smiling either.

"Oh, fuck it!" Mike said, breaking the tense silence. "I think I liked you better when you were drinking."

Barrett threw two twenties on the table and rose to his feet, saying, "I think I liked you better when I was drinking, too."

"Fine, so where the hell do you think you're going?"

Barrett didn't answer at first, but then turned and met his friend's angry, anxious eyes. "I'm going," he said quietly, "to do something about it."

PART FIVE

THE JUDGMENT

My soul is a broken field, plowed by pain.
                    —Sara Teasdale

53

"Try the linguine carbonara," suggested Julian Gold to his pallid-faced and perspiring dinner companion. "I'm told it's quite excellent here."

"Here" was a tiny restaurant named Ciao Bella, hidden deep in the Santa Cruz mountains north of Monterey in a rain-swept village called Ben Lomond.

Passing through the large open doors five minutes earlier, Jack Klegg had been startled, for the inside of the place was as garish and astonishing as the outside was understated and inconspicuous. He felt he had entered a time warp. "Twist and Shout" blared from concealed speakers, and every square inch of wall space was covered with entertainment and sports memorabilia. The memory of Marilyn Monroe was clearly held in reverence. Record album covers picturing Pat Boone, Chubby Checker, and Elvis, plus glossies of Mickey Mantle, Willie Mays, and Vida Blue covered the walls and ceilings.

The spectacle of icons from another time and the insistent beat assaulting Klegg's eardrums as he passed through the bar momentarily silenced the fear that had been stalking him throughout the day.

Why had he been summoned by Julian Gold? And why to this place? Should he have even come? Klegg knew that Santa Cruz had been branded three decades before as "the murder capital of the world," and it occurred to him that a body buried in these mountains might well lie undiscovered for at least another three decades.

"I'm . . . not that hungry, Mr. Gold," said Klegg later as a waiter hovered. He wondered why they couldn't open a damn window somewhere. "Late lunch," he added. "Maybe I'll just have a glass of Chianti and a Caesar salad."

"You don't look well, Jack," Gold said. "The drive over the hill must not have agreed with you. I'm told they average one killing a month on that winding fourteen-mile-long butcher shop they call Highway 17."

Klegg nodded, loosened his tie. This was his first face-to-face meeting with the notorious *consigliere* and it had taken him less than a minute to mention the word "killing."

"I want to thank you, Jack, for meeting me at this rather out-of-the-way spot," said Gold, his voice as soothing as its raspy quality would permit. "I hear the food is marvelous and I don't expect that the mountain folk around us will recognize you. Of course, after you're district attorney of San Francisco, you'll find privacy more difficult to come by."

Klegg's wary eyes softened with relief. "I could live with that," he said.

"Assuming all goes well, I think you could live with that a very long time," said Gold, his mouth offering what Klegg took to be a smile. "So, let's get our business out of the way, shall we?"

For the next five minutes, Klegg listened in amazement as the *consigliere* outlined a dramatic reversal in strategy.

"We would like, Jack, for you and Ms. Harris to press Mr. Ashford to the wall. To that end, we expect you to leave no stone unturned and spare no cost in terms of forensic experts and technical support."

"You want Ashford *convicted*?"

"No, but that's something even we can't control. What we want now is for Elliot to plead insanity—and soon. You see, Jack, with this new witness in the picture, it appears our friend will indeed be convicted. Our prior plan, as we have discussed, was to appeal and secure a reversal based on inadequacy of counsel. You then, without fear of great criticism, would dismiss the case rather than burden the taxpayers with a third trial."

"Of course," said Klegg, "so why the full-court press now?"

"Patience, Jack," said Gold as a waiter retreated. "Mr. Dickson recently suggested to me the possibility of an insanity plea. Although Elliot has refused, it occurred to me that it would be very much to Mr. Rizzo's advantage if he were to enter such a plea."

"Because he might win on such a defense? I doubt it."

"Of course not. But Mr. Rizzo has decided to take advantage of the corporate dissolution provisions under California law in order to secure the return of his $60 million investment. A recent inventory revealed that the tangible assets—heavy equipment and the like—are sufficiently valuable after liquidation to assure the return of our investment and then some."

"And you would be able to do this if Ashford admits insanity?"

"He'd not only be admitting it, Jack, he'd be asserting it, and California law permits a shareholder with more than thirty-three percent of the stock to sue for dissolution in a closely held corporation where such action is 'reasonably necessary' to protect his investment."

Gold then extended his hands, palms up, and added, "One can't expect a multimillion-dollar company to be run by a lunatic, can one?"

"Hell, Mr. Gold," said Klegg, his appetite returning, "I'm not a commercial lawyer, but isn't that option already available to you? He's a defendant in a multiple-murder trial, for God's sake."

"Yes and no," said Gold sipping a decent local red, a '92 Ahlgren Cabernet. "Yes, you are definitely not a commercial lawyer, and no, it's not available to us now. He is innocent until proven guilty under the Constitution, and by the time his appeals are exhausted and final judgment is rendered, he will have been in absentia from the company for more than one year, triggering an automatic reversion of all Resource International stock to the family charitable foundation."

Klegg issued a low whistle, which he noticed seemed to irritate the *consigliere*. "A foundation?"

"For cancer research," said Gold, "which is what Ashford's old man was dying of. Anyway, with your able assistance, Jack, we anticipate a rather different beneficiary of the assets of Resource International."

The next day, Grace Harris, aware of the disastrous fate of her Los Angeles counterparts in the Simpson case, continued to move the state's case forward swiftly and without fanfare, refusing to be seduced by her growing celebrity into overtrying her case. Although the Ashford trial was not being televised, publicity about the triple murder and its social and political connections had mounted to a fever pitch, and Grace had become nearly as famous and recognizable as L.A. prosecutor Marcia Clark. Nearly everybody wanted a piece of her, and although she steadfastly refused to be interviewed, she found herself on the cover of *Newsweek* and hounded by the press and TV talk shows.

Barrett, though less in demand, also shunned publicity, and contributed to the streamlining of the prosecution's case with a unique—some called it "bizarre"—manner of cross-examining the prosecution's lineup of criminologists, lab technicians, and DNA experts. Each time Grace finished the direct examination of an expert witness, Dickson asked but two questions: *"Hypothetically, Doctor, could the traces of blood on the victim's fingers you claim to be Mr. Ashford's have gotten there as a result of Mrs. Ashford rinsing out the basin after he had cut himself shaving and before she was murdered?"*

After extracting grudging but inevitable concurrence with this question, Barrett would then ask whether the blood on the towel could also have been placed there by Ashford after shaving, and before the murder. Another pause, followed by reluctant agreement.

Barrett would then turn to the jury, shrug, and sit down. The brevity of the cross appealed to Julian Gold, who though highly capable, was no trial lawyer, and therefore mistook Barrett's sudden succinctness as belated capitulation to his demand for a rollover. But Grace saw through the strategy and reduced questions to her forensic experts by half and tentatively canceled two of them altogether.

"May I ask, Grace," said Klegg outside the courtroom at a recess, "what the hell you two are doing in there?"

"He's playing chess, Jack, and I have no choice but to check him," she said. "He knows he can't beat our experts on cross, so he's trying to make us look foolish for wasting so much of the jury's time. But the real genius in his approach is that it focuses their attention on the only facts that tend to support his case. I've got to avoid playing into his hands."

Klegg took her firmly by the arm and guided her out of earshot of a crowd milling around in the hallway.

"I'm reluctant to second-guess you, Grace, but I don't like it. We need to give this case everything we've got, and what we've got are some damn good expert witnesses."

Grace was both stunned and gratified by Klegg's apparent change of attitude. "I agree, Jack, but with Amanda Keller's testimony the only way we can lose now is if we overtry our case like they did in Simpson."

"Okay, streamline the expert witnesses' testimony if you think it's best, but at least put them all on the stand. I want Ashford pressed to the wall, and I damn sure don't want it said that we held anything back. I want pressure on this guy."

Grace gave Klegg another questioning look, but he didn't blink. "All right, Jack," she said, too busy to try to figure out the latest turn of this particular worm. "I'll keep on pressing."

"Good," said Klegg. "And if Dickson comes sniffing around again looking for a deal, tell him to go to hell. We're going all the way on this one, Grace."

The afternoon session went well, and with Klegg having flip-flopped, Grace thought she saw a bright light at the end of the tunnel.

Until five o'clock that afternoon, when Sam Quon walked into her office and, without comment, handed her a handwritten and undated letter that drained the blood from her face and told her the light was from an oncoming locomotive.

"Where did you get this, Sam?"

"It was in Earl's personal files. I was assigned the project of putting his stuff in order before turning everything over to his daughter. I just now finished going through them."

The letter was postmarked December 6, 1997, a week before Field's death, was addressed to Earl Field, and purported to be from Amanda Keller. The third paragraph read:

> Like you, I hate people of Ashford's ilk, bigoted, pretty-boy brats born wealthy, going though life sneering at the rest of us.

The paragraph went on to say that her involvement in the first trial had been "foretold," then professed her gift of special insight into people's thoughts and her "absolute certainty" of Ashford's guilt. The letter closed by saying she would do anything to help him "convict this animal and put him where he belongs."

Grace stared at the words until the witness's misspelled prose began to blur on the scented, apricot-colored paper.

Worst of all, the letter, though postmarked after the claimed threats by Elliot Ashford, bore no mention of any such threats.

She handed it back to Sam and said, almost to herself, "We're dead."

Sam nodded slowly. "Giving this to you instead of to the shredder was the hardest thing I've ever done."

"Does Klegg know?"

"I wanted you to see it first. He would have used it to make you go for a plea bargain."

Grace shook her head. "He's swung a hundred and eighty degrees now. Claims he wants to convict. But let's confront her before we talk to him."

"Why do you suppose Earl never mentioned it?" asked Sam.

"He thought she was a crackpot. I saw her leave in a rage one day after he had given her the shoe."

"He might have been right about her being a crackpot."

"That 'crackpot,' old friend, has outsmarted all of us."

Sam winced. "When do you want her in here?"

"Yesterday, okay? I've put it off too long as it is. Ms. Hollywood and I have to have a chat. And no warning of the agenda. I want to see her face when I confront her regarding the 'waitress' at Pat's and this little literary gem. Dickson's got a standing subpoena to recall her as a witness; just tell her we think he might do it and we want to prep her."

"I'll do it, Grace," said Sam, his brow creased with concern, "but let's keep an open mind, okay? She might have a perfectly good explanation."

"I'm sure she will, Sam," said Grace, her voice quaking with anger. "She always does."

* * *

That night, Grace reluctantly entered her empty flat, wishing more than ever that Aaron was there.

She shed her coat and walked to the kitchen. She poured herself a glass of wine and sat at the breakfast table, looking out at the empty, darkened street, the streetlights barely visible in the heavy fog. Dishes from breakfast, rinsed but unwashed, were scattered on the kitchen counter where she had hurriedly left them. An unread morning paper lay in front of her.

She wondered how things had gotten so out of hand. After talking to Amanda, she would have to show the letter to Klegg and the worm would turn yet again. She pictured his statement to the press:

Ms. Harris, who has been under severe emotional pressure since the death of Earl Field, simply misread the quality of the People's evidence. Once her error came to light, I had no choice but to dismiss the case.

She would be offered up to satisfy the media's need for a scapegoat. Ashford would walk. Klegg would be elected D.A.

Her father would have been right.

The sound of the telephone jarred her out of her thoughts. She picked up the receiver, hoping it was Aaron.

"Hello, Grace," came a familiar voice that was definitely not Aaron's. "It's Barrett Dickson."

"Yes?"

"I need to talk to you about a couple of things."

"All right."

"I mean privately."

"Isn't that what we're doing now?"

"On the phone? One never knows these days. May I swing by your place?"

Grace said nothing. It would be the worst possible time to see him. He might see through her despair.

"It's not phonefare, Grace."

"All right," she said at last, and gave him her address.

Twenty minutes later, Grace—her hair brushed out and a light blush applied—was looking into Barrett Dickson's red-rimmed eyes.

They engaged in small talk for a few minutes, during which Grace, despite her own travails, felt a growing sym-

pathy for him. His face was pale and his clothes had begun
to hang shapelessly on him. She offered him coffee and a
piece of a boysenberry pie she had bought on a whim,
thinking of Aaron. He accepted, and she led him into the
kitchen, where he tore into the pie as if he hadn't eaten in
days. Then he stared thoughtfully at the empty plate. "Did
you make this?"

"I'm a lawyer," she said, sitting across from him at the
dinette table, "not a ceramic artist."

Barrett smiled. "I figured you could do pretty much anything, Grace. Bake pies, convict killers, make plates."

Grace laughed and shook her head. "My culinary ambitions went into remission years ago. I leave that to Marie
Callender now. I just try to be a decent mother and a
decent lawyer. That's enough for me."

"Is it really?" said Barrett, holding her gaze. She knew
what he meant.

She finally broke the tension with a smile to let him know
she had caught his meaning. "For now, yes."

"May I ask how long you've been a single mom?"

"Aaron's father left before he was one year old. That
was in 1982."

"I admire you, all you've done."

Grace shrugged off the compliment, though it warmed
her pleasantly.

They then stirred awkwardly and silently in their seats,
and Grace, not knowing what to say, offered him more
coffee and pie. He declined.

"So," she said at last, "now that your hunger is taken
care of, might there be something else on your agenda
tonight?"

"All right," said Barrett, pushing the plate aside. "First,
I want to explain why I've been a bit . . . blustery lately.
I've been told to go in the tank. The Attila routine was my
little way of telling them no."

"Your people are already planning their grounds for appeal," she said. "Or should I say, 'planting'?"

He nodded.

"Amanda was that good, was she?"

"You know she was," said Barrett. "If I were in better
shape, I'd take off my shirt and show you the tire tracks
on my back."

"Well, thanks for telling me. I wondered what was going on."

"I saw the look on your face and needed you to know."

"Is my opinion so important or were you suddenly obsessing for boysenberry pie?"

"Both, I guess." He smiled and took a breath. "What you think has become very important to me."

Grace felt a stirring that was hard to suppress. She wanted to reach out to him, to touch his weary face, to tell him she was glad he felt that way. But years of discipline contained her feelings, and she kept her hands on her empty cup.

"I'm glad you t-told me," she said ambiguously, a sudden shyness overcoming her. She was afraid to meet his eyes and decided to keep the conversation on safe ground. "But if you plan to lead the Huns into court again tomorrow, perhaps I'd better eat a raw animal for breakfast."

Barrett laughed easily but said nothing. He was going to let her set the tone now.

She looked at him and said, "What else?"

"What else?"

"Did you want to tell me. You said there were a couple of things."

"I was going to try another shot at a plea bargain, but I already know your answer, so forget about that. Maybe I just needed to see you."

Grace felt her pulse pleasantly quicken again. It hurt her to see him sitting there looking so utterly defeated, completely unaware that the state's key witness might be a perjurer.

"Oh," she said.

As if encouraged by her hesitation, Barrett leaned forward across the table and kissed her on the cheek. She didn't move, partly out of surprise. Barrett didn't move either, except to kiss her again, this time on the corner of her mouth.

Now she moved, meeting him halfway across the table, their lips joining in a kiss that somehow must have survived Barrett's maneuvering around the table, for he was now pulling her up out of her seat and enveloping her in his arms. For a moment, her thoughts were scattered by a dizzying passion, but she managed to pull her lips from his and bury her head in his chest.

She could feel his heart pounding, felt it like a drumbeat that was leading her emotions deeper into conflict with sound judgment. This was insane, she realized, but she heard him saying her name over and over and felt his gentle touch on her hair, her neck, and she allowed herself another twenty heartbeats, then another twenty. She felt his need for her and she realized she wanted him too. Now. Right now.

This was beyond insane, but she granted herself another ten heartbeats, then somehow found the will to pull herself back from him. "Please, Barrett," she heard the voice of reason say. "No more. Not now."

He smiled self-consciously as he let her go. "I think this is where I say I'm sorry, but obviously I'm not. I . . ."

"Please," she repeated, embarrassed by the breathless sound of her own voice, "please go now."

Barrett held up his hands in mock surrender and collected himself. "This trial can't last forever, Grace, and when it's over—"

Grace shook her head quickly, resolutely. "But it's not, Barrett, it's far from over."

"All right, but when the trial is finished, Grace, I hope we'll be just starting. Can we at least talk about that?"

She met his eyes, relieved that her emotions were back under control. "Look, Barrett, a couple of lawyers having a cup of coffee and discussing a possible plea is one thing, but adversaries making out over boysenberry pie in the middle of a murder trial is something not contemplated by the rules of professional conduct and you know it."

"The pie was your idea."

She didn't smile. "It shouldn't have happened, Barrett. It didn't happen."

"Okay then," said Barrett, his smile erased, "let's be a couple of lawyers discussing a possible plea. The problem is you've already indicated that the plea-bargain part of my agenda is as doomed to futility as the part just completed."

She could see she had hurt him. "I'm sorry, Barrett, about all of it. But yes, I'm afraid this is a c-case that will have to be decided by a jury."

"You don't need to be sorry for anything. I was out of

line a minute ago. As for dealing this case, I really can't blame you for saying no to that either. You hold all the cards."

Including, she thought, feeling ashamed, a joker that's wild.

Grace shrugged, feeling worse by the minute.

"Thanks for the coffee and pie," Barrett said, attempting a congenial tone. As he turned toward the door, he gave her a weary smile that stabbed her heart.

Why, she wondered, did I let him come here?

But she said nothing as he took himself out the door and headed down the hallway. Grace watched him for a few seconds, fascinated as usual by the way he walked, the unstudied languor in his stride.

She closed the door before he could look back, then turned and leaned against it. It would be a long night.

54

Grace greeted her key witness during the noon recess the next day, trying to muster a tone of cordiality she did not feel. Sam had warned Grace that Amanda was furious about being summoned from Los Angeles, where she had taken up temporary residence at the Hotel Bel-Air. He had endured a blistering verbal assault all the way in from the airport. Waiting for fifteen minutes in Grace's cramped office while the morning session spilled over into the noon hour had done little to improve her mood.

"Give me one good reason, Grace, why Dickson would call me back as a witness?" she demanded. "Didn't I hurt his client enough last time?"

"It's standard procedure," said Grace. "He has you on twenty-four-hour recall, but he may never exercise the option. Still, it's best for us to be ready, just in case."

"I hope you realize you could hardly have picked a worse time for this," she said, her voice still crackling with annoyance. "I was supposed to have finished a photo shoot this morning, the script for *Thursday's Child* was just delivered to me, and I had to put off a lunch date with the film's director today!"

"We'll get you back to Los Angeles on the two-thirty flight, Ms. Keller, and we do appreciate your coming."

"And do you have any idea what flying does to my skin?" she demanded rhetorically as she checked her makeup in a compact from her purse, then smoothed out the folds in her beige Chanel jacket—an original. No more knockoffs for Amanda Keller.

Grace realized the woman was not listening, so she stopped talking.

"Well," continued Amanda haughtily, "I'm parched.

Sam, would you be a gentleman and get me some Evian water?"

Grace poured water into a cup and handed it to her.

"Don't you still want to see Ashford convicted?" Grace asked as Amanda took a sip.

"Of course I'd like to see justice done," said Amanda, uncrossing and recrossing her long legs, "but life moves on, don't you know? I'm in a world now beyond anything you could imagine, Grace. Do you know who I dined with last night at Spago?"

"We'll not take much of your time, Ms. Keller," said Grace, her patience exhausted.

"Good. I can't imagine what Dickson thinks he could get from me that would help his case one bit."

Grace poured Sam and herself some water, then looked straight into Amanda's eyes and said, "Suppose he knew of a letter you wrote to Earl Field. A letter in which you say you'd do anything to convict the defendant, but a letter that makes no mention of the threats you've testified to."

Amanda blinked, then blinked again. Her lips tightened slightly, but that was all.

The witness was listening now.

Grace could hear the clock ticking behind her. Sam coughed. No one moved.

"A letter?" said Amanda, laughing nervously.

"A letter bearing your signature."

Grace felt a grudging admiration for the woman. She was obviously buying time with the pretext of trying to remember, too smart to rush into the trap of a quick denial. Grace continued to study her, the deep-set dark eyes, no longer flinching, the long and lustrous blond hair that age had not yet coarsened with brittle streaks of gray like her own, the large rectangular designer gold ring she now wore, the fine navy blue skirt and jacket that had traveled from L.A. without succumbing to a single crease.

"Yes," she said, meeting Grace's eyes, "I believe I did write him."

"Did you write him more than once?"

"Just once," said Amanda, rubbing her ring with the thumb of her right hand. "I believe it was just once."

"Do you recall what you said in the letter?"

"I presume you have the letter, Grace," Amanda said coolly, "and that you know exactly what's in it."

Grace said, "I just want to be sure you do, Amanda. In case you're asked."

"And just how would Dickson know to ask? Does he have the letter?"

"No," said Grace, "but that's n-not the point."

"Then what is the point? In the first place, Dickson apparently knows nothing about this so-called letter. In the second place, what's wrong with a concerned citizen writing to an elected public official?"

"It depends," said Grace, "on whether the author of the letter is a key witness for the prosecution in a murder case and whether the letter betrays overt hostility toward the defendant and a willingness to do anything to convict him."

"Because I called Ashford a beast or whatever I called him? All the jurors felt that way about him."

Amanda's voice began to take on a tone of righteous indignation. "Because I said I would do anything to help convict him? That just meant I was willing to risk my own life to see justice done!"

Amanda leaned forward and her voice took on a conciliatory tone. "Don't you see, Grace, I had to make the letter strong to try to get his attention. The truth is, he had . . . not taken me very seriously. If only he had . . ."

"Then why didn't you mention the threats that were the basis of your testimony in this trial?"

"I don't know. I guess it was because you don't put something like that in a letter. You don't know who's going to open the mail for someone as important as Earl Field. But that's what I wanted to tell him, face-to-face. But he didn't respond. Then he was killed and I was afraid to speak out."

Grace was beginning to feel like a straight man in a surreal comedy act. The witness had an answer for everything and was not only unembarrassed by the letter, she was proud of it. One more try.

"Do you have special powers, Amanda?"

"What?"

"You say in your letter that you have a gift of special insight into people's thoughts."

Amanda gave a self-deprecating laugh and said, "Did I

say that? I just meant I have a woman's intuition. I was, after all, writing to a man."

Grace didn't smile. "Are you a religious person, Amanda?"

Grace saw the witness's face darken. "Not really," she said. "I would say spiritual, hardly religious. Isn't this getting awfully personal, Grace?"

"Not nearly as personal as Mr. Dickson might get if he calls you back to the stand. Do you believe in ESP or parapsychology?"

"No," snapped Amanda, obviously fed up with the interrogation, "but I often locate water with one of those magic wands when I'm not busy practicing voodoo and worshiping Satan. Satisfied?"

"Amanda, this is necessary—"

"If you feel I'm some kind of kook, Grace, then the hell with you. I'm finished with this case anyway!"

"Maybe," said Grace, "maybe not. Please just tell me what you meant when you said your involvement in the first trial was 'foretold.' Do you believe in tarot cards, Amanda? Astrology? The I Ching?"

"All of the above, like plenty of other people," Amanda snarled. "So what?"

"Do you believe you were put on the first trial jury for a purpose? Is that what you meant by your presence being 'foretold'?"

Amanda suddenly seemed tired. Her voice now took on the bored tone of a teacher lecturing a child. "Are you aware that water covers seventy percent of the earth's surface and makes up ninety-seven percent of your body weight?"

"I've heard that, yes."

"And are you familiar with the effect of the moon on ocean tides?"

"Yes."

"Then can you doubt that the movement of celestial bodies such as the moon and the stars can influence our own tiny, insignificant bodies? Or that the positions of the planets in the zodiac at the time of birth can provide a perfectly logical basis for determining events? Yes, damn it, I do feel that my call to jury duty was a sign, and you should be grateful I was there and stop treating me like a nutcase!"

Grace glanced at Sam, who only raised his eyebrows slightly as if to say, Now what? She walked over, opened a window, and decided to follow her intuition.

"I have serious doubts about what you said in court, Amanda," she said in a quiet voice that belied her growing apprehension.

"That's quite clear," snarled Amanda, "even to a nutcase like me."

"Chief Investigator Quon checked out your story regarding Pat's Seafood Grill. They don't hire waitresses at Pat's."

"Oh, Christ," said Amanda, springing to her feet, "that does it! Waitress? Waiter? How am I supposed to remember such details? Am I a witness in this case or a defendant?"

"It depends, Amanda. Perjury is a crime in this state."

Amanda Keller's face was flushed with anger, and Grace guessed she wasn't acting. Sam apparently didn't think so either, for as Amanda advanced on Grace's desk, Sam rose and moved in closer.

"*Just who do you think you are?* The jury? The judge of my character? Well, fortunately for me and the people of this state, you're neither one. Whether I told the truth—which I did—is up to them to decide, not you!"

Grace knew she was right, and that if Barrett did call her back to the stand, she would fly up from L.A., beat him up again, then fly right back and resume the launching of her movie career. This was a formidable woman, a frightening woman.

"Open any newspaper in America, Ms. Harris," continued the glowering witness, now pacing theatrically in front of Grace's desk, "and you'll find your horoscope. Any day of the week! People all over the world believe in astrology and predestination, and I won't stand here for another minute and be humiliated by your witch-hunt!"

Grace glanced at Sam and he shot her a look that told her to back off. She collected herself, not easy with an enraged and well-muscled, nearly six-foot figure looming over her. The blue of the witness's eyes had turned as dark as night.

"Ms. Keller," interposed Sam Quon, "I think there might be a misunderstanding here. We have a duty to check and double-check everything and everyone, particularly witnesses we have vouched for. Please sit down and let me get you more water. I'm sure we can work this out."

Bless you, Sam, thought Grace, though I still think you're wrong about this one. Grace decided that her own horoscope from this morning's *Chronicle* should have read, "Don't take on any major problems today."

Amanda stood now as if frozen in front of Grace's desk, taking in Sam's words without detaching her dark gaze from Grace's eyes.

A horn blared from Bryant Street, followed by a shouting match three floors below them. Amanda suddenly shivered, turned, and walked over to the window, arms clasped around her.

Now what? thought Grace.

As she broke the silence, Amanda's voice seemed to come from another place, another person.

"If there has been a misunderstanding here," she said, sauntering back and resuming her seat, "I'm sorry for my part in it. I hardly ever notice clerks or people waiting on me. So maybe it was a waiter at the restaurant, not a waitress. Let's face it, one can't always tell the difference here in San Francisco."

No one laughed.

"As for the letter, I was just trying to help out. I had been treated rudely by Mr. Field a few days before when I went to him directly. Perhaps I overstated things in an effort to get his attention, but my only regret is that I failed."

Grace took in Amanda's contrite expression, the angled eyebrows, the innocence conveyed by the awkwardly clasped hands. She again recalled the irate Amanda leaving Earl's office that day weeks ago, a recollection that did tend to corroborate her account. She watched Amanda now as she removed her inhaler from her handbag. She didn't use it, but closed her eyes and rubbed her neck with her free hand.

Grace's neck was aching now too. What if she really was telling the truth?

"Well?" said Amanda, absently rearranging some errant strands of hair that had fallen across her eye. Then the hint of a smile as she said, "Now what? Take me away in irons?"

Now it was Grace buying time. She had never been in the presence of a person at once so suspect and yet so maddeningly convincing.

"You do believe me, don't you, Grace? Sam?"

"I honestly don't know, Amanda, but as you've pointed out, I'm not the jury. I'm going to leave it to them."

Amanda rose quickly to her feet again, her momentarily calm features giving way to the flush of anger again. "Well, thank you for that inspiring vote of confidence. May I leave now?"

Grace rose too. "Chief Quon will take you to your mother's apartment."

Amanda snatched up her purse and glared at Grace. "That won't be necessary. Just call me a cab, please."

Sam called her a cab and saw her out, then returned to Grace's office. "Well?" he said.

Silence.

"You don't trust Amanda," said Sam.

"Do you trust her?"

"She's our witness, Grace, and she's right about one thing."

"And that is?"

"You're starting to look at this case more like you were a juror than the meanest prosecutor west of the Mississippi."

"Just because I'm distrustful of a woman who keeps lying to us?"

"Damn it, Grace, you've never liked her. Admit it. I'm as cynical as you are, but I think her explanations have been plausible."

Grace knew that on the rare occasions Sam resorted to an expletive—even in its most benign form—it meant he was getting very angry.

"May I ask," he said, "just how you intend to 'level the playing field'?"

Grace shrugged. "I really don't know, Sam, but it doesn't feel right the way it is."

Sam unbuttoned his jacket and jammed his hands in his pockets. "Look, Grace, I don't trust Keller completely either and I don't like her at all, okay? But Ashford's guilty as sin, and if we don't win this case, any respect for our criminal justice system that somehow survived the Simpson debacle will go right down the toilet. Can't you hear it, Grace? 'Another guy with money, so he beat the system.' "

"But what if she's lying, Sam, and an innocent man takes the needle based solely on her testimony? Have you thought about that?"

"That's good thinking, Grace," said Sam, throwing up his hands and heading for the door, "for a defense lawyer!"

Sam's words resonated in Grace's head long after he had left, and as much as she hated the thought, she knew she could not delay taking the matter to Klegg as acting D.A. She found him reading a copy of the *Wall Street Journal.*

"Hello, Grace. Take a load off."

She laid the story out quickly for him, then watched as he read the letter.

"Interesting," he said, folding the letter back up.

"I think Earl considered her a flake, Jack. I saw her leaving the office one day in a rage after he had given her the shoe. I think we've got a real problem here with our star witness."

Jack Klegg gave his head a quick shake. "From what you've told me, Grace, she has a logical explanation for everything in this letter. What does Sam think?"

Grace had hoped he wouldn't ask that question, but she answered it honestly, then said, "I respect Sam's opinions, Jack, but my instincts scream out that she's lying to us and that we should get out of this case."

"Obviously the defense hasn't seen this, right?"

"They haven't seen it."

"It's clearly not so exculpatory that we have an obligation to reveal it to them, right?"

"I suppose you're right—interpreting the law technically."

"No one," said Klegg, his close-set eyes fixed on her as he slid the letter back toward her, "has ever accused Amazing Grace Harris of doing otherwise."

55

Barrett parked in front of his apartment, depressed and dog-tired from a failed final attempt to persuade Ashford to plead temporary insanity. Ashford had refused to even discuss the matter, but Barrett resolved to try again before court the next morning.

He had pressed Ashford, pressed him harder than a defense lawyer should ever press a client. But Ashford's admission that he was seeing another woman had triggered a renewed suspicion in Barrett that his client had fooled everyone—except for Lev, of course—and that Armand Ligretti had indeed been telling the truth.

If so, then Ashford had indeed introduced a young woman to the Rizzos at a Mafia meeting as "the next Mrs. Ashford."

If so, Barrett had used his skill and experience to destroy the credibility of a truthful witness, a major step in helping a possible murderer escape justice.

If so, the old Dickson Curse was alive and well.

He opened the door to his apartment and entered the small living room. The place smelled musty, rank. He remembered he hadn't emptied the garbage in days. On his way back out the door with a bulging plastic bag, he noticed the light blinking on his answering machine. He set the garbage down in the hallway, then walked back and pressed "Play." The last message was from Grace Harris. "Call me" was all it said. No name or number. He needed neither. His heart pounded as he dialed her flat.

She picked it up on the first ring, and spoke quickly, mechanically, like a person who has made a decision and wants to act on it before she changes her mind.

"I need to speak with you," she said, "as soon as possible."

"Ten minutes," he said, then hung up and raced out the door, almost tripping over a bag of garbage that would have to be dealt with later.

"Don't say anything, Barrett, just listen. I have . . . I'm beginning to have concerns . . . oh, God, this is too damned difficult!"

Barrett glanced around the silent living room. "What's the problem, Grace?"

"I asked you not to say anything, okay?"

"Well, somebody around here has to try to complete a full sentence."

Barrett could see she was deeply troubled. The skin on her face was pale and stretched thin over her prominent cheekbones. The hollows under her eyes were darker than ever and, to Barrett, gave her face a gaunt beauty he found irresistible. He had seen traces of gentleness in Grace, but never vulnerability. He saw it now, and had to fight the urge to take her in his arms.

"All right," she said at last, "I'll p-put it to you straight: I'm having concerns about the credibility of Amanda Keller."

Barrett put up a restraining hand, but she continued, the words coming even faster than before. "It started with the mystery waitress you questioned her at length about. It turns out Pat's Seafood Grill hires only male waiters."

Barrett stared at her in such stunned silence she averted her eyes. He had never seen her looking so troubled, even during the Ligretti catastrophe. He decided not to tell her he had sent Lev to Sam's and that Pat's illegal policy was what had prompted him to recall Keller as a witness.

"Any questions so far?" she said.

"Yes. Do you have any of that berry pie left?"

"You're just trying to ease the situation."

"Yes, plus I missed dinner tonight."

She smiled as she shook her head in resignation and led him into the kitchen. The pie had been thrown out, but she made tea and toast and he made small talk and she seemed to relax somewhat, but her expression remained serious. They sat in the kitchen and the memory of his last experience there aroused him. He noticed that the morning paper lay on top of the table again, still folded and bound with a rubber band.

"Why are you telling me this, Grace?" he said. "I represent the bad guy, remember?"

"Because there's more at stake here now than the guilt or innocence of Elliot Ashford."

"Like what?"

"Like convicting a man on possibly perjured testimony. Like the integrity of our little piece of the American system of justice."

Barrett chuckled. "When the American system dispenses justice, it's by accident."

Grace wasn't amused. "You wouldn't be in this case if you really believed that."

"Thanks, Grace, but I'm in this case strictly as a favor to a friend—and I don't mean Elliot Ashford."

"It doesn't matter why you're in the case. I need your help."

"That's a good one, Grace. Like the Chicago Bulls asking the Warriors to spot them points."

"I need you to recall Amanda Keller as a witness."

"Funny you should say that. My subpoena was served today."

"Good. I'm going to give you a letter she wrote to Earl Field a week before the murder and you're going to cross-examine her on it."

She pushed the letter toward him.

Barrett exhaled, his amorous longings abruptly forgotten. He said, "Are you disclosing exculpatory evidence to an adversary pursuant to a legal obligation to do so?" Christ, he thought, I sound like a real lawyer.

"No, but I feel I have a moral obligation to give you an opportunity to deal with it."

Barrett cocked his head to one side, raised one eyebrow, and said, "Hypothetically, let me see if I have this straight. You're asking me to help you discredit your star witness?"

"By George, I think you've got it."

Barrett shook his head. "What's going on here, Grace?" he said. "Has your Prozac prescription run out? Your oath as a representative of the people in an adversary system means nothing to me, nor does your treasured justice system, but I know it means everything to you. Hold a gun to your head if that's what you want to do, but don't expect me to pull the trigger."

Grace gave her head an impatient shake. "Just let me tell you what—"

"No, damn it, I won't let you! Maybe it's just slipped your mind, so I'll say it again: You're the D.A., Grace; I'm the slimy defense lawyer."

"What's your guess," she said, pointing her spoon at him, "as to the probable outcome of this case?"

"I make it Bulls 120, Warriors 30."

"Then I suggest you do as I say."

Barrett started to rise. "Sorry, Grace. I may not be keen on the justice system, but I know that you don't make it better by breaking the rules."

"Okay, I'll put it in basketball terms: I've played by the rules because I believe the sport would be in chaos without them. But maybe a game has to be lost once in a while to keep the sport clean."

"Do you know what they do in basketball to players who shave points?"

"I don't even know what that means, but I'm ready to take the risk, whatever it is."

Barrett leaned across the table and looked into her tired eyes. "Well, I'm not. For a person so enamored of the system, you've apparently forgotten how it works. Number one: If I rip your key witness apart, your whole case could go down, including Lara's murder counts, even though Keller has no connection with that one."

"I know how it works, Barrett."

"Number two: If you provide me with a document that could only have come from your files and I use it to win the game, you won't just lose the game, you'll be banned from the sport for life. Follow me?"

Grace said nothing. Barrett reached over and covered her hand with his. It felt cold. "Listen, Grace. There's a lot you don't know about me and my track record when I try to 'help' people. Let's just say that I care too much about you to be a part of what would happen if I did what you want me to."

Grace's eyes met his, taking in the implication.

"That's right," he said, brushing strands of hair back off her tired face, "you must have figured out by now how I feel about you, Grace. I guess I've loved you since the day of that crazy bail hearing. I just didn't trust it. I've got a little problem with trust, which is another thing you don't know about me. Anyway, the bottom line is that I won't sacrifice someone I care about for a system I no longer care about or for a guy like Elliot Ashford."

"He's your *client,* Barrett."

"As if I could forget it."

Grace got up and poured them both another cup of tea. Barrett watched her, wondering if she was thinking about his impetuous declaration of love or Elliot Ashford. She put the cups down, then took his hand.

"Barrett, you do realize the timing couldn't be worse? For us, I mean."

Barrett sighed. He knew she was right. "And timing is everything," he said, forcing a smile.

"Well, n-not quite . . . everything."

"I see," he said, though he didn't really see and didn't want to see what else—or who else—was standing in their way. He felt his face reddening with embarrassment and wished he could take back his foolish words. God knows he could come up with plenty of good reasons she might have for not wanting to involve herself with a burned-out guy driving a burned-out Ford Mustang, carrying a brief-case full of multiple listings instead of high-profile cases. He should have known.

"I don't think you do see," said Grace, interrupting his emotional self-immolation. So Barrett waited, hardly breathing, while she sat staring into her empty cup again as if looking for just the right way to let him down.

"Okay," she continued, "it's partly your obvious disdain for the justice system that I'm a part of. It bothers me, Barrett. It bothers me a lot."

"Jesus, Grace," he said, "according to the polls, a majority of the country feels the same as I do."

"But they're not trial lawyers. All they see are the high-profile cases that bring out the worst in all of us. They see Judge Ito unable to control Cochran in Simpson, Judge Weisberg unable to control Abramson in the first Menendez trial, but they don't see thousands of *competent* judges and *decent* lawyers trying murder cases to a just conclusion every hour of every day of the year."

"That's true, but—"

"So you know better, Barrett, yet you wear your contempt for the system as if it were a badge of honor. I see it as a chip on your shoulder and it bothers me."

Barrett sat silently for a minute, then said, "Like I said, Grace, there are things you don't understand about me: about me, my past, and the system."

"All right, but you don't seem to understand that when you belittle the system, you belittle me too. You may think of me as naïve or a dupe or whatever, but I believe in the criminal justice system, and I honor it too."

Barrett reached for his tea but said nothing. Grace looked a little embarrassed by her high-minded declaration. "It's like what Churchill said about democracy, Barrett: 'It's the worst system in the world—' "

" '—except for all the others that have been tried,' " said Barrett. "I know, I know. But like democracy, it can be exploited, Grace. I know, because I've done it, and good people are dead now because I did."

Grace looked perplexed but undeterred. "Would you want to add your client to the list? See him on death row because of your failure to expose a lying prosecution witness? I may or may not win on the Lara murder, Barrett, but Keller is all I have on Jefferson and Field."

Barrett said nothing.

"You were one of the great trial lawyers, Barrett, and I care about your reputation, whether you do or not. You can help me and also help a reputation that doesn't need another loss right now."

Barrett felt a chill pass through his body and slowly withdrew his hand from hers. A terrible sadness suddenly came out of nowhere and engulfed him. He couldn't stop it. He thought of Tim Hardin and his hit from the fifties.

If I were a carpenter, and you were a lady
Would you marry me anyway
Would you have my baby

So, thought Barrett, I wasn't wrong about the beat-up guy in his beat-up car.

Her voice broke through his thoughts again. "So will you help me, Barrett?"

Angry now, he said, "Like I said, Grace, you don't fix a failed system by breaking its rules. You get out of the system."

"That's the easy way," said Grace.

"The coward's way?"

"I didn't say that."

"You haven't said a lot of things," said Barrett with obvious annoyance, and reached for his coat, "but I can read between the lines. I won't help you destroy yourself, Grace, even if it would make me someone you could be proud of."

Grace looked puzzled.

"I would never want to be an embarrassment to you, Grace, but I'm finished with the law. I'm . . . not what I was, okay? Nobody knows that better than me. So the hell with it."

He slid the letter back across the table and got up to leave, but Grace jumped to her feet also and grabbed him by the arm with a force that surprised him.

"They call you Bear," she said, angry now, "but you're nothing but a stubborn mule! I'm doing this for the justice system and your goddamn client, not you! Don't you see that your obstinance is depriving me of my moral options? Your macho paternalism won't allow anything bad to happen to me or anything good to happen to you!"

Barrett pulled his eyes away from the heat in hers.

"Forget about me for a minute," she continued, "and forget about the brilliant lawyer hiding somewhere in that baggy suit, *but don't deny your client a shot at a fair trial!*"

Barrett picked up his coat and headed for the door. "This conversation never happened, Grace. Thanks for the tea and misplaced sympathy. I'll see you in court."

56

Barrett could see that Elliot Ashford was seething the next morning. He stormed out of the holding cell into the courtroom like a Brahma bull with spurs sunk in his side.

"What the hell did you tell Julian Gold, Dickson?"

"About what?"

"Did you or did you not tell him about your expert's bullshit diagnosis."

"I didn't tell him about Huntington's if that's what you mean. Why?"

"He's insisting I plead insanity; says it's my only hope. Says you suggested it."

"I did tell him that an insanity plea is your only hope," said Barrett, "and he obviously agrees it would be in your best interest. But I didn't mention Huntington's. You have my word on it."

Ashford began pacing with such truculence as to draw a concerned look from the bailiff.

"Sit down, Elliot, and let's resolve this issue calmly once and for all."

"There's nothing to resolve, Barrett," said Ashford. "I'll spell it out for you. Number one: There won't be an insanity defense, because I'm not insane. Number two: I want you to fire Dr. Weiss and stop trespassing in my bloodstream! Am I going too fast for you?"

"Yes, Elliot, and in the wrong direction. We've got to have an expert wit—"

"And I've got to have some privacy! My blood is my business. So is my bloodline. You think my future wife is going to give me a son after you get me out of this if she thinks I'm some kind of genetic monster?"

Barrett glanced to his left at the bailiff, who averted his

eyes. "Hold it down, Elliot! I don't have to tell you the consequences of an affair with another woman coming out at this
point, particularly one that preexisted Lara's murder."

"And I don't have to repeat the consequences to both
of us, Dickson, if Carmine hears that a man walking around
with names, dates, places, and certain events in his head
may sometimes be *out* of his head!"

Barrett ignored the tacit threat. "He doesn't know, okay?
Now listen closely, Elliot. The one thing the prosecution
has lacked up to now is a clear motive for killing Lara.
Does anyone else know about this woman?"

"Tony. Nobody else."

"How about at the party Ligretti described?"

"Don't be ridiculous. Do you think I'd take Linda into
that den of vipers? She wasn't there. Sure, I've had girls—
one-nighters—but Linda doesn't even know that I'm
connected!"

"All right," continued Barrett, "but the fact remains that
if we don't plead insanity or at least put on a DNA expert,
your hotly desired procreation efforts will be limited to
Lady Palm and her five daughters while you await your
turn on death row."

Ashford gave Barrett his most malevolent smile. "Joke,
you Neanderthal. At least I'll still be alive. Will you?"

After court, Grace grimly awaited the arrival of Amanda
Keller. She had rested her case midway in the afternoon
and Barrett had earlier informed the court that he would
recall Amanda Keller as his first witness the next day.
When Sam had informed Amanda of this, she had reacted
with obvious apprehension and insisted on meeting with
Grace.

"What is he going to ask me, Grace?" asked Amanda,
obviously nervous as Sam escorted her through the door.
"Does he have the letter?"

"No, he doesn't have the letter."

Grace could see instant relief spread across the witness's
face. "Why did you want to see me?" Grace asked.

"Aren't you going to prepare me for my testimony
tomorrow?"

"I prepared you thoroughly the first time," said Grace.
"I'm sure you'll do fine."

Sam's normally inexpressive face registered as much surprise as Amanda's, and Grace knew what he was thinking. Hadn't Grace joined herself at the hip with Amanda during three arduous prep sessions before the key witness's first appearance on the stand? Hour after hour of tough mock cross, preparing her for anything Dickson might throw at her?

Grace turned her eyes from Sam and back toward Amanda, watching her reaction. She remembered that there had hardly been a trace of uneasiness in Amanda during those earlier meetings, or even when she was on the stand. But now, the witness's fingers trembled slightly as she touched her bloodless face.

"That's it?" she said. "You're not going to give me any preparation at all?"

Grace resumed her seat behind her desk, then held Amanda's eyes hostage to her own. "Here's your preparation, Amanda," she said. "Tell the truth."

"So you're going to hang her out to dry?" said Sam after he had returned Amanda to the Ritz-Carlton. "Just like that?"

Grace tapped the end of a pencil against the top of her desk. She turned slowly in her chair and stared out the window.

"Earth to Grace," said Sam. "Jesus, this is becoming a habit. Come in, Grace."

"She needs no preparation," she said quietly. "Dickson doesn't have enough to hurt her, and she'll chew him up and spit him out. Again."

"So?" said Sam, a wide smile breaking across his face. "Is that so bad? The good guys win one? Faith in the criminal justice system restored? Crime doesn't pay and all that?"

Grace turned back toward him and Sam was surprised to see the despair in her face. She said, "I'm no longer so sure what's supposed to happen, Sam."

Across town on Telegraph Hill, Barrett Dickson sat at his kitchen table, trying to decide how best to examine the state's key witness. The Pat's Seafood Grill story would hurt Keller, but he knew he'd need more to destroy her credibility. He called Lev.

"I'm cross-examining Amanda Keller tomorrow. Anything new?"

"You callin' her back to the stand?"

"Yes."

"Even a dumb cat don't jump up on a hot stove twice, Bear."

"Thank you, Uncle Remus. Does that mean you haven't found anything on her?"

"I'm afraid not," said Lev. "You want me to call that *California Confidential* reporter? Take another try at gettin' him to come up and testify to his notes?"

"Could you go down there tonight? You know calling won't work."

"Check your watch, Bear. 'Tonight' ain't that far off from bein' tomorrow."

Barrett knew he didn't have to tell Lev that there were plenty of night flights to L.A. or that he wouldn't be asking unless he was desperate.

"I'll call you later if I can get in the door," came a tired voice through the phone. "I'll call from L.A. in the mornin' either way."

"Thanks, Lev."

"If I don't find him, it won't be for lack of tryin'."

"I owe you, Lev."

"A thousand dollars plus expenses to be exact."

Barrett said goodbye and inventoried his meager arsenal. The waiter-waitress thing—she might be ready for that—and possibly the claimed romance with Earl Field, too. But together, they'd at least put a dent in her credibility even if they didn't smash it.

Which is what it would take now to turn this thing around.

57

"You've already been sworn, Ms. Keller," said John Hernandez, "but I will remind you that you are still under oath."

"I understand, Your Honor," said Amanda, radiant in a navy Calvin Klein blazer, a white silk Valentino blouse and mid-length skirt.

It was 9:00 A.M., and as Barrett slowly rose to his feet to begin his examination, he felt wired and light-headed. He wished he had skipped that fourth cup of coffee. His mouth felt as dry as the carpet he stood on.

Lev had called at 7:30 A.M., having bushwhacked the hapless *Confidential* journalist earlier as he came out on the front lawn of his Brentwood home for his morning paper. When the reporter threatened to call the police, then tried to hit the private investigator with his rolled-up newspaper, Lev knew his trip had been in vain.

Judge Hernandez looked down at Barrett, waiting for him to say something. Barrett glanced at Grace, whose expression betrayed nothing and whose eyes avoided his. Mike was back in the courtroom for moral support, and Julian Gold sat in the rear row, monitoring his performance as usual.

"Mr. Dickson?" said the judge, his tone concealing any impatience Barrett knew he must be feeling.

"Yes, Your Honor," said Barrett, and cleared his throat as he sauntered out from behind the security of counsel table. "Ms. Keller, we talked at great length about the threats you say my client made against two of the victims in your presence, do you recall that?"

"Yes."

"I'd like to pick up where we left off. You told us you

heard Mr. Ashford say something about Mr. Field in Pat's Seafood Grill. Do you recall that?"

"Yes."

"Would you refresh our memories as to what you claim Mr. Ashford said?"

"He said something about having it out with that—then he used the N word—'once and for all.' "

Barrett concealed his disappointment at the response: word for word what she had said the last time. Grace must have prepared her well.

"And you told us a waitress might have overheard some of it, do you recall that?"

Amanda cocked her head and gave Barrett a bemused and knowing look that did not bode well for the home team.

"Oh, did I say waitress?" she said winsomely. "It could have been a waiter. I was pretty shaken by Mr. Ashford's threat. It could have been either one. In fact, now that I think of it—"

"It was probably a waiter, right?" said Barrett, returning her shrewd look. At least he would let her know he knew she was lying. Control was always the issue in cross-examination, and he had to start somewhere.

"Why yes, I think it was. He was."

Barrett snatched up a bound volume and said, "I believe you also told us this waitress who is now a waiter had long blond hair, do you remember that?"

"Many men have long hair these days, Mr. Dickson," Keller said, smiling amiably.

"Tell me, Ms. Keller," asked Barrett, feeling frustrated and deciding to abandon the scapel in favor of a meat ax. "When did you find out that Pat's Seafood Grill doesn't hire waitresses? Was it after you realized you had lied to the jury last week?"

Whispering rose from the gallery. Amanda's left eyebrow shot up and she again looked over at Grace. Barrett followed her gaze and saw that Grace's eyes were on her notepad, on which she was calmly scribbling. He then glanced up at the judge, who was also staring expectantly at Grace, but still no objection came.

"I didn't lie, sir, I told you I was just confused."

"I see," said Barrett, noticing offended looks from two of the jurors who were probably viewing him now as a desperate bully, which is exactly what he was feeling like. Terrific, he told himself. Grace is making herself look bad by not objecting and I'm getting nowhere anyway.

"You're not entirely free of bias in this case, are you, Ms. Keller?"

Amanda gave Grace a worried look, and Barrett wondered if she was afraid Grace had given him the letter. Good, let her think it.

"I believe I am completely unbiased, sir."

Dickson leaned against a corner of the defense table, fingering a cassette tape he had removed from his pocket. Amanda's eyes flicked at it, then darkened.

"Isn't it a fact that you were in a . . . personal relationship with one of this defendant's alleged victims?"

"Absolutely not."

Grace's head popped up for the first time, then she casually turned and glanced at Sam Quon seated behind her. Sam shrugged to say he didn't know what was up. Dickson softly clicked the cassette twice on the table, then pocketed it again and fished a tabloid out of his briefcase.

"You were interviewed by *California Confidential* magazine, were you not?"

"Yes, I believe I was."

"On or about January 17?"

Amanda shifted in her seat, but her voice and expression were unwavering. "That sounds about right."

"By a Mr. Damone?"

"Yes."

"And that interview was taped, was it not?"

"I don't remember," she said, and Barrett saw the first glimmer of hope. "I've given dozens of interviews in connection with my new film project. I suppose it might have been."

Barrett patted the pocket into which he had just slipped the tape and said, "Yes, Ms. Keller," then proceeded to recite a litany of statements in the article, all of which the witness calmly admitted were both true and accurate.

"Now, did you also tell Mr. Damone some things that did not appear in the article?"

"Of course. They never print everything."

"All right. Now, if you told Mr. Damone during that

interview that you were in a romantic relationship with Earl Field, would that also be true and accurate?"

"But I didn't tell him that. I hardly knew the gentleman. Mr. Field, that is."

"So you admit that everything in Mr. Damone's story is true, but you deny now, under oath, that you told him you were romantically involved with Mr. Field?"

Amanda shifted in her seat and her eyes grew even darker. The imperious smirk was gone now.

"I can't imagine why I would have said anything like that."

Out of the corner of his eye, Dickson caught a hunched figure quietly rising to his feet in the rear of the courtroom. Dickson's absurdly charged brain registered the notion that Julian Gold was preparing to shoot him, but the *consigliere* was just reaching for his cellular phone as he headed for the hallway. Calling Carmine Rizzo, thought Dickson.

"Can you think of any reason why Mr. Damone might think you *did* tell him that?"

Still no objection.

"No, I can't, other than to say those tabloid writers are all a bunch of jackals."

Dickson moved closer to her and spoke in a quieter, almost sympathetic voice.

"I don't fault your characterization, Ms. Keller, but just suppose that Mr. Damone had made a tape of that interview, and you were to hear your own voice describe a personal relationship with Mr. Field. Would that refresh your memory as to whether you told Mr. Damone that you had an affair with Mr. Field?"

Several people in the gallery audibly gasped. Sam Quon's foot jiggled wildly, but Grace sat silent as a stone.

John Hernandez cleared his throat in Grace's direction. Twice. Suddenly, utter silence prevailed in the courtroom. The air was so packed with tension Barrett felt that if he so much as snapped his fingers, the room would explode.

Amanda openly glared at Grace now—how could the jury miss it?—but the assistant district attorney seemed preoccupied again, this time with something on her fingernail. The witness's eyes then returned to the pocket into which Barrett had dropped the tape. Her face was pale where she touched it with the back of her trembling hand, her eyes pleading as she turned toward the judge, who continued to stare at Grace.

When she could delay no longer, Amanda spoke in a voice bereft of its earlier authority.

"Well . . ." Her voice trailed off and she asked for a drink of water, quickly provided by the bailiff. "It's possible," she said at last. "I don't recall everything I said to every interviewer."

Barrett decided to go for the end zone. "Ms. Keller, isn't it a fact that you were in an intimate relationship with Mr. Field, but intentionally failed to disclose it when you testified two weeks ago?"

Amanda Keller was flushed now, whether with fear or anger Dickson could not say, even after she replied in a voice shaking with emotion. "That, Mr. Dickson, is a rude and provocative question, and you are not a gentleman."

"Stipulated, ma'am. Now answer my question."

"Is it so wrong to protect the memory and reputation of a dead man?"

"The jury will decide that, Ms. Keller, and I will assume from your answer that you were intimate with Mr. Field and that you concealed that fact when you testified during your first appearance here and lied when I asked you about it a few minutes ago. Are my assumptions correct?"

After yet another awkward silence, Amanda nodded her head in the affirmative and uttered a soft "Well, yes, but for the perfectly good reason I just told you."

"Because you were fearful you would appear biased toward anyone charged with his murder?"

All eyes but the judge's were on the witness. The judge's eyes were locked on Grace, questioning, reproachful eyes. Then, before Amanda could answer the next question, John Hernandez beckoned counsel to the bench but waved off the court reporter.

"You both know I rarely meddle with trial counsel's approach to a case," he said softly when both were leaning toward him, "but I must say, Grace, you're letting Barrett get away with murder, and maybe his client, too. I'd like an explanation before I start making objections myself."

Grace paused for a moment as the clerk handed the judge a note, then glanced at Barrett and said, "I can't stop the court from making any objections the court might believe to be required by the rules."

Hernandez glanced at the note, then gave Grace an even more puzzled look. "Well, you may not have noticed, Grace, but the acting D.A. is in the rear of the courtroom having apoplexy. He doesn't seem to understand your approach either. I've got to take a quick phone call off the bench, but I'm holding the jury right here. Take a minute to sort out your intentions, Grace. If you won't start objecting when we resume, I will."

Barrett cleared his throat and said, "It's moot, John, I'm finished with my cross."

Grace shot Barrett an annoyed look as John Hernandez nodded and informed the jury he was being called to chambers for sixty seconds. He told them to remain seated, then moved swiftly off the bench, leaving Grace and Barrett standing at side-bar.

"Good job, counsel," Grace whispered, "given the limited material you've chosen to work with. Where did you get the cassette, Tower Records?"

Barrett shrugged noncommittally.

"Oldest trick in the book," she said, almost smiling. "Now listen up, you bullheaded genius: the letter is undated but addressed to Earl. She calls Ashford an 'animal' and claims she can read people's thoughts. She's a nut, Barrett, and a pathological liar."

Barrett gave his head a quick shake and spun away from her. She followed him down from the bench and cornered him as he took his seat at counsel table.

"Nowhere to hide, big guy," she whispered, bending over, her lips close to his ear. Despite his frustration, he was aware that her scent was evocative of a spring garden, a bouquet of jasmine and boxwood.

"The letter makes no mention of any of the threats, Barrett. Not a word. *She's made it all up!*"

"Damn it, Grace," he snapped back at her, "we've been through this. I'm sorry about the way I handled things the other night, but I haven't changed my mind. My cross-examination is finished."

"But you haven't finished *her*! You've only wounded her, Barrett, but you do have her scared now. Look at the way she's watching us. She's sure I've given you the letter, and you can probably bluff her into admitting the contents even if you won't take the letter itself!"

Barrett shook his head. "Klegg would know my information had to come from the letter or from your own lips. Either way, he'd blow you right out of the office, maybe out of the law altogether. Now please get the hell away from my counsel table."

Grace leaned in closer. To anyone watching, they were two adversaries having an argument over an evidentiary ruling.

"You're a rookie at reading criminal juries, Barrett Dickson. I tell you your client's still ticketed for death row. You'll never forgive yourself if that happens and I won't either. You've got to finish her off if you want to level the playing field. I'm right about this, trust me."

Everyone was watching them now, including Ashford, who was straining unsuccessfully to hear what they were whispering to each other. No one would doubt that the lawyers were angry now, and the jurors stirred uneasily.

Barrett forced himself to relax. "I've always been trust-impaired, Grace, but that's not the point. Hell, I know what you're trying to do and it's commendable, but I still won't be a party to it. And despite the fact that my client may be guilty, I think I've done damned well by him. If I take the next step and use what you've told me, you could end up selling real estate and that would be very embarrassing to me."

"Oh, God! Are you still on that?"

"I'm being funny now."

"There's nothing funny about senseless martyrdom, Barrett, and as for my future that you seem determined to control, I considered the risks before I called you two nights ago. Don't underestimate me. I'm not quitting, just making it a fair fight."

"Grace, I really think—"

"*I, I, I!* Just where did you get the ego to presume that everything bad that happens to people you care about is your doing? You're good, Barrett, but you're not God! My son told me once that shit happens and I got mad at him. Well, maybe we both need to understand that sometimes it just does, and that you might want to take a close look at why you need to think otherwise!"

Barrett turned crimson. "Thank you, Doctor, now get the hell—"

"You represent a client in a capital case, counselor! *Now represent him!*"

"Like you're representing the people? We're both screwing our clients, Grace, and we both have our reasons. But I won't let you destroy yourself, so get the hell away from me!"

Grace suddenly smiled at him. "Well, I won't let you *not* let me. Do you remember what you said to me at the bail hearing that first time we were opposed, just before you cleaned my clock?"

"No."

"You said, '*Watch this.*' "

John Hernandez returned to the bench, and Grace sauntered back to her chair even as Barrett reached out to stop her.

"Any further questions, Mr. Dickson?"

"No, Your Honor, I'm finished."

"Thank you, Mr. Dickson. May the witness be excused then?"

"Yes, Your Honor," said Barrett.

"*No,* Your Honor!" said Grace, rising to her feet and approaching Amanda amid surprised looks from everyone in the courtroom.

"Ms. Keller," said Grace. "Just three quick matters. First, you've been accused by Mr. Dickson of bias. Are you biased against Mr. Ashford?"

"Not at all," said Amanda, looking relieved.

"You have no personal animosity toward him, do you?"

"None."

"You've never referred to him in any kind of derogatory fashion," Grace said, "have you?"

Amanda's eyes narrowed. "I don't . . . no."

"Good," said Grace, turning and staring directly at Barrett. "And I assume you've testified here based on what you heard, not speculation or guesswork."

"That's correct."

"You don't claim any secret sources of information, special powers, or other such abilities, do you?"

Amanda's eyes narrowed slightly, but she managed to appear puzzled by the question. "Of course not," she answered.

"Excellent. Finally, then, Ms. Keller, you have candidly

admitted a romantic relationship and your understandable reason for concealing it—"

"Objection, Your Honor," said Barrett quietly.

"Sustained," said John Hernandez. "It will be up to you, members of the jury, to decide whether the witness's reasons were 'understandable' or not. You will disregard counsel's characterization."

"Of course," said Grace in a tone of exaggerated repentance, "and I apologize both to you and the members of the jury."

Judge Hernandez, looking almost as confused by now as the witness, nodded politely. Now she's even suckered John into her game, thought Barrett.

"What I was getting to, Ms. Keller, is that to protect Mr. Field's reputation, you were concealing your relationship with him before he was killed as well as after. Correct?"

"Absolutely."

"You didn't tell friends?"

"No, Ms. Harris, no one."

"Didn't reveal letters he had written to you or you had written to him?"

"No."

"And that was to protect his reputation?"

"Yes."

"Very well, then," said Grace casually, and turned to Barrett. "Your witness, counsel."

Barrett looked at Grace, saw the hint of a smile, then turned away, slowly shaking his head. To outward appearances, she had merely performed a routine rehabilitation of her witness. But revealing the letter had bounced the ball back into his court and he had no choice but to catch it. He was being tricked and cajoled into trying to win his own damn case!

"Mr. Dickson?" said John Hernandez.

Barrett felt every eye in the courtroom on him. But most of all he felt his client's hand gripping his arm and his client's breath in his ear.

"Barrett," whispered Ashford, "Keller's lying. I swear on my mother's grave, I threatened no one. She's lying!"

Barrett stared into his clenched hands, then, without turning his head, said, "I know she's lying, damn it, now shut up!"

The harshness of his words caused Ashford to pull his hand back.

"Sorry," said Barrett, "I'm trying to think, okay?" The problem was how to prove that the letter was written *after* the threats, and that Amanda had made no reference to them at the time she wrote it—letter that he—Barrett—wasn't supposed to even know about. The bigger problem was that Grace had said the letter was undated and Keller would probably remember that.

The biggest problem of all was to somehow expose Amanda without also exposing Grace.

His head raced with questions without answers as the specter of old fears and failures plagued his efforts to think clearly. How did he let himself get into this situation? His heart was pounding so hard against his ribs he imagined the lapel of his suit coat jumping with each beat.

"Mr. Dickson?" repeated the judge.

Barrett rose slowly, then walked stiff-legged toward the witness. "Just a couple, Your Honor.

"First, Ms. Keller, at the risk of sounding like Perry Mason, I want to remind you that you are still under oath."

"Yes."

"I'm back to this issue of possible bias, Ms. Keller. In response to Ms. Harris's question, you said you've never referred to the defendant in a derogatory manner. Do you recall that?"

Barrett was somewhat encouraged by the sound of his surprisingly resonant voice. Maybe this could work.

"Yes."

"As I recall, you used the word 'jackal' in reference to tabloid reporters earlier today. Do you consider that a derogatory comparison?"

"Yes, I suppose it is."

"So here's my question. Have you ever compared my client to a jackal, or to any other kind of animal?"

Barrett watched Amanda's eyes narrow again and dart accusingly between Grace and himself. A cornered jackal came to mind.

"I don't remember," she said finally, and a juror raised her eyebrows in surprise. "I suppose it's possible, given the things he had said to me."

"You might have called him an animal, for instance?"

"It's possible."

"And it's true that you have wanted this 'animal' convicted of these crimes, haven't you?"

"Of course, but who wouldn't, Mr. Dickson, having overheard the threats he made."

"I'll come back to that in a minute, Ms. Keller. Now, other than hearing those threats, you've just told Ms. Harris you possessed no other inside information or 'special powers.' Do you remember that?"

Amanda's face was suddenly flushed with barely contained anger. Barrett was sure every juror saw it and must be wondering what was going on.

"Can you tell where I'm going with this line of questions, Ms. Keller? Can you . . . *read my thoughts*?"

Amanda started to speak, but stopped herself and again stared angrily at Grace Harris. Barrett noticed that Keller's breath was fast and shallow. She seemed short of breath, nearly gasping for air. She's scared, thought Barrett. This just might work. She knows I've got the letter now, or thinks I've got it, which is just as good.

"I really . . . don't have the slightest idea . . . what you mean, Mr. Dickson."

Bullshit, thought Barrett. Stay cool, he told himself, remembering the denouement must not implicate Grace. He had to make Klegg think he knew less than he knew, while making Keller think he knew more.

"My last few questions have to do with the letters you mentioned to Ms. Harris. First, how many were there?"

Keller's expression hardened. "Just one."

"Did you write it or did he?"

"I wrote it."

"He didn't write you?"

"No."

"All right. How long before Mr. Field's murder was your letter written?"

"I have no idea. I didn't date the letter and haven't seen it since I wrote it."

"I assume that one of the purposes of your letter was to inform Mr. Field that you'd be willing to testify against the defendant?"

"Yes."

"And still you say you weren't biased?"

"I was a concerned citizen."

"It sounds to me like what you were concerned about was convicting Mr. Ashford!"

As Amanda shook her head in denial, Barrett, the hook now baited, strode toward her and added in a louder voice, "Do you really expect this jury to regard someone who volunteers to help the prosecution convict an 'animal,' then does so, to be an *unbiased* witness?"

Amanda recoiled from his approach. She put a hand to her chest and her breath began to come in quick gasps. Barrett knew he was being seen by the jurors as a bully, by others as just plain stupid, but he held his position, staring into her eyes from but two feet away. She would either take the bait now or back away.

She smiled then, a confident and radiant smile, "Well, I'm afraid you don't know much about human nature, Mr. Dickson, plus you've forgotten what I said just a few minutes ago."

Yes! thought Barrett. It might work.

"Oh?" he said.

"How can you say I was biased about saying those things when I had heard *that* man saying worse things! Making those vicious threats! Using the N word! Anyone hearing what I heard would have said what I said and would have called him what I called him!"

Bingo! thought Barrett, though probably neither Keller nor the jurors yet understood that the prosecution's star witness had just handed Elliot Ashford the keys to his freedom.

"Now, getting back to this letter you sent, you didn't mention the threats you claim to have overheard, did you?"

"I don't know," said Amanda, "probably not."

"Didn't you think them important—as a concerned citizen?"

Amanda's eyes darted toward Grace, then over at the papers on his desk.

"Well, I'm sure I would have mentioned them *if* they had already occurred."

Perfect, thought Barrett. She's counting on the fact that the letter is undated.

"And since you can't remember the date, you assume

you wrote it before hearing the threats? Is that where the matter stands?"

"Exactly, sir," said Amanda, her features relaxing.

"Well, ma'am, I've got a problem with that. You see, you told me just a minute ago that your justification for calling Mr. Ashford an 'animal' in the letter was not because of any bias against Mr. Ashford *but because of the 'vicious' threats you had already heard him make*!"

A quiet murmur from the gallery rippled through the courtroom, silenced not by the gavel but by Barrett's own raised hand. Such was his sudden control now that it extended to everyone in the courtroom.

Amanda appeared to have had the wind knocked out of her.

"So the letter had to have been written *after* the threats, Ms. Keller, and we're left with the real reason you didn't mention these so-called threats to the D.A. in that letter, are we not?"

Amanda said nothing as he moved up to within inches of her face.

"There simply weren't any threats, were there, Ms. Keller." There was no upward inflection of Barrett's voice at the end of his sentence.

Amanda stared at Barrett with unconcealed hatred and the shallow breathing started again. Several of the jurors leaned forward in their seats, and it seemed that at least a minute passed before Amanda looked up at the judge and said, "Must I answer these impertinent questions about my private letter, Judge? Is nothin' sacred anymore?"

Barrett wondered where the Southern accent had come from.

"In the absence of any objection, Ms. Keller," said the judge, glancing at Grace, "you must answer the question if you can."

Amanda started to answer, but then glared again at the judge. "Is this how you treat a concerned citizen who risks her life to put that . . . yes, damn it, that *animal* where he belongs?"

An eerie silence had fallen on the courtroom as Amanda turned her gaze of unrestrained hatred on Barrett.

"And just who do you think you are, sir?" she snapped.

"I'm a *lady*! I'm a respected actress! I'm not the one on trial here."

"You are at the moment, Ms. Keller," said Barrett softly, "and I sentence you to return to Hollywood, where your acting skills might be better received than they were here today."

Amanda sat silently, her lips in a tight line, her face pale even through her makeup. Barrett then returned to his seat amid a renewed babble of sound from the gallery, only partially silenced by successive blows of the gavel.

"Any further questions, Ms. Harris?"

"None, Your Honor."

"You are free to go, Ms. Keller," John Hernandez said, then added ominously, "for now."

Grace looked up as Amanda stepped down from the witness stand. Although the witness appeared to be in need of CPR, she managed one final wrathful glare toward her as she passed. But Grace hardly noticed, for she had just seen her career pass before her eyes. Although Barrett had done a masterful job of concealing the source of the knowledge she had provided him, she knew it wouldn't fool Klegg. It would be over for her now.

She glanced over at Barrett, whose expression reflected not victory but despair; the reluctant warrior she had forced into the kill.

Then she looked at the jurors as they filed out of the courtroom. They were glowing with excitement. They had seen it all now, at least so they thought. But among the things they didn't notice as they left the courtroom were the following:

Judge Hernandez's lingering look of confusion
Sam Quon's raised eyebrows as he stared at Grace
Mike's unconcealed thumbs-up to Barrett
Barrett's rejection of Ashford's attempted embrace
Grace's barely perceptible nod to Barrett
Julian Gold's murderous gaze at Jack Klegg
Jack Klegg's murderous gaze at Grace Harris
Barrett's hand returning an Eric Clapton cassette to his
    trial bag

58

John Hernandez sat alone in his chambers during the lunch hour, wondering if his trial had just careened out of control. What was going on with this Keller woman? And what had Grace Harris been up to? Why hadn't she objected to the verbal annihilation of her own witness? Should he have jumped in sooner? Should he have stopped the fight, thrown in the towel when it became evident that Grace would not?

He couldn't resist switching on the *Noon News* and they were already all over it, of course. When something went wrong in a courtroom, the media were as predictable as line dancers. The late edition of the *Examiner* would have a hurriedly sketched cartoon in the editorial section captioned "Amanda's Last Dance," picturing the key witness as the beautiful Salome, bearing the head of Elliot Ashford on a platter—but about to step on a banana peel.

Thank God he had at least kept the prying eye of the TV camera out of the courtroom. It could have been worse. Still, he felt like a man walking a tightrope without a safety net. And the day wasn't even over.

But a boring calm blanketed the courtroom during the afternoon session, and Judge Hernandez once again leaned back in his swivel chair. The highly anticipated appearance of Nobel Prize winner Sandra Weiss had been canceled at the insistence of the defendant, leaving Barrett Dickson to rely on Menghetti's expert from the first trial. John Hernandez observed two of the jurors snoozing as the balding, overweight defense toxicologist launched a tedious two-hour, three-pronged assault—"corruption, contamination, and conspiracy"—against the crime scene officers and the city labs. Maybe, he thought, his expression once again serene, the ship of justice was drifting back on course.

In the rear of the courtroom, Jack Klegg also looked relaxed for the first time all day. The morning session had outraged him and filled him with grim forebodings, but a lunchtime call from Julian Gold had put him at ease. When he hung up, in fact, he realized the scenario couldn't have played out better if he had written it himself. Gold had adjusted to the new development, having abandoned his insanity-plea notion now that it seemed obvious that Ashford would soon be free to return to the helm of Resource International.

Even his political fortunes would be improved, Klegg realized, for Grace Harris's bizarre abandonment of her star witness would focus all blame for the inevitable loss on her alone, thus eliminating his most credible opponent in the upcoming special election.

But nonetheless, members of the press, he would say, looking solemnly into a camera's lens, *I hold myself responsible. After Earl Field's untimely death, I should have taken over the Ashford retrial rather than entrusted it to Grace Harris.*

Things had a way of working out.

No such consolation awaited Amanda Keller, who seethed as she lay in wait on the third floor near the offices of the district attorney. When Grace finally emerged into the public corridor just before 7:00 P.M., Amanda fell into step beside her.

"I thought we had become friends, Grace," said Amanda. She appeared calm to Grace, almost cordial, though her manner seemed even more staged than usual.

"And I thought you someone worthy of trust," said Grace, not breaking her stride toward the elevator. "We were both wrong."

"Well, *you're* wrong if you think you can just brush me off now after ruining my name and reputation. I won't have it."

Grace said nothing, as she could see that her former witness was deeply troubled. Just keep moving, she told herself.

"I trusted you, Grace, and damn it, you lied to me. You gave him the letter, then sat there like Rip Van Winkle and let him make a fool of me."

Grace kept walking. The elevator seemed a hundred miles away.

"Here's the afternoon *Examiner,* Grace. Have you seen it?"

Grace shook her head.

Amanda thrust the front page in front of her. In the center, Grace could see a large photo of "the state's key witness" descending the steps of the Hall of Justice over a blaring caption that asked:

Actress or Bad Actor?

"The article implies I'm some kind of crackpot who made up a story just to get publicity!" Amanda snarled, slapping the paper against her hip. Two Asian city employees turned to look at her. Grace's apprehension rose, but they had reached the elevator at last.

"Don't you see, Grace," she said, hands balled into fists at her side, "what happened this morning could ruin me in Hollywood."

"If it's any consolation, Ms. Keller," said Grace, turning her back on Amanda and punching the down button next to the elevator, "your machinations have ruined me too, right here in San Francisco."

Amanda's features stiffened as she moved in front of Grace. "Then you'd better figure a way out of this for both of us."

"There is no way out, Amanda," said Grace, meeting Amanda's eyes for the first time, "for either of us."

"Of course there is. Just put me back on the stand and we'll put things back together."

"Humpty-Dumpty would be easier—"

"*Stop it!*" snapped Amanda, her tone now menacing. "You listen to me when I speak to you. Hear? You do what I tell you right now or I swear you'll regret it."

"Are you threatening me, Amanda?" said Grace.

"That's exactly what I'm doin'," Amanda said in that same chilling Southern accent. Grace's fatigue was turning to apprehension, but she knew she must not let Amanda see it.

"I've had enough of you, Ms. Keller. Why don't we go right down to the Southern Station on the first floor and talk to the duty officer about whatever it is you're going to do to me."

Amanda's dark eyes blinked and she shook her head wildly. "Don't be silly, Grace. I just meant . . . I just meant that I might . . . consult my Los Angeles lawyers about my rights in this matter. That's all."

"Fine," said Grace, stepping around Amanda, who was trying to block her passage into the opening elevator, "you'll need lawyers if I decide to charge you."

Amanda's eyes widened. "Charge me? That's insanity!"

"No, Amanda. 'Insanity' is putting up with you even one more minute. Now please get out of my way and stay out of my life."

Grace was relieved to see that the elevator was full of people as she stepped in. But just as the doors were closing, Amanda got on too, her expression suddenly contrite.

"Please, Grace," Amanda whispered pleadingly, "I can explain everything if you'll just listen."

The elevator started its descent, which, to Grace, had never seemed more sluggish. When the doors finally opened at the ground floor, she headed for the rear of the building, hoping Amanda would turn toward the main entrance. "Even the newspapers say you failed to protect me."

"You could easily have protected yourself by simply telling the truth." Grace knew she was being drawn in, but the remark annoyed her. "That's t-r-u-t-h, Amanda. Means not to lie. About yourself, about Earl, about what you've done—"

Amanda suddenly reached out and took Grace by the arm. "About what I've *done?* How did you . . . what did you mean by that?"

"Let go of me, Amanda, or damn it, I'll have you arrested right here and now!"

Amanda stiffened as if in a seizure. She stared at Grace, her lips pressed together, her features frozen except for her eyes, which had again turned dark with fury. But Grace saw something else, too. Fear.

"How could you do that to me, Grace? I thought we were friends! Can't you see that I need your friendship more than ever now?"

Grace shook free of her grasp and walked away. She was

relieved to see Amanda's reflection in the glass window, hurrying off toward the main doors.

As Grace entered Klegg's office with Sam Quon the next morning, she saw several newspapers spread across his large conference table.

"Congratulations, Grace," Klegg said. "My first case as D.A. and the press is clobbering us."

Each paper had put its own spin of ridicule on the previous day's proceedings: "The Unreal Deal" (the *San Jose Mercury News*); "The Jurisprudential Equivalent of Mad Cow Disease—Tragic, Yet Inescapably Humorous" (the *San Francisco Chronicle*); and "The Trial of the Century or the Guile of the Century?" (the *Marin Independent*).

"Acting D.A., Jack."

"What?"

"Unless I somehow missed the election, you're still *acting* D.A."

Klegg offered his lips-only smile. "You gave him the letter, didn't you."

"No," said Grace truthfully, though she knew he wouldn't believe her. "Why would I do a thing like that?"

"That's what I'm trying to find out. You damn sure didn't protect Keller. You served her up and Dickson ate her for lunch."

"You're right," she said. Ironic, she thought, that after she had struggled so long to convict Ashford, she had to stand here and be reprimanded by a man who had probably wanted him freed all along.

Klegg exhaled loudly through pursed lips to make sure she knew how stupid he thought she had been. "So how will you handle all this in your opening argument?" he said. "I've told the press we'll work together from now on, so it better be good."

"I won't."

"You won't what?"

"I won't 'work together' with you and I won't 'handle' it in my opening. Amanda Keller is a liar who had everybody fooled until yesterday. I don't like it any better than you do, Jack, but my apology—our apology—to the jury for having vouched for her as our witness will be to ignore her in opening argument."

Klegg ran a hand over his burr head, fixed her with his close-set eyes. His eyes darted over to Sam.

"She's putting me on, right?"

"I don't think so," said Sam.

"Don't act so damn stricken, Jack," said Grace. "I'll make a great argument anyway and you'll take complete credit for it. Ashford will probably still walk, so you won't have to wake up in the morning next to a horse's head. I'll get blamed for the loss and you'll be elected D.A. You're getting everything you've wanted."

Klegg couldn't hold back a grin that never failed to irritate her. "Okay. Just promise me you'll at least say something to explain her in opening. Otherwise, we both look bad."

Grace smiled wryly. "Afraid the voters might pick up a new broom in June, Jack? Sweep the whole place clean?"

"Just do it, Grace. That's an order. Explain Keller and show some contrition in your opening argument for not protecting her or I'll hang you out to dry the minute you leave the courtroom."

"I've already hung myself out to dry, Jack," said Grace, "and if you think you can make it hurt more than it already does, go for it."

"Don't tempt me, Grace. You do what I say or I'll confirm to the press that you tanked. I'll tell them you betrayed the People's case by turning evidence over to your adversary."

"Oh, God, Jack," Grace said, sighing deeply, "how I'll miss you when I'm gone."

"And don't tell me you didn't give him the goddamn letter; I know better. I'll get your ticket pulled and maybe Dickson's, too. So forget that crap about refusing to mention Keller in your opening."

"Listen, Jack," said Grace, dropping her shoulders. "I was just kidding, okay?"

"That's better."

"The truth is, I won't miss you a bit."

59

"M r. Dickson," came a voice from behind Barrett he had grown to dread, "there's a man here who wants to meet you."

Barrett spun around impatiently, for the judge would be entering the courtroom any minute now. There stood Julian Gold beside a stout, vigorous-looking man in his mid-sixties with a still-smoldering cigar jammed deep into one cheek. Though no more than five feet eight in height, power issued from every inch of his robust body. His head was perfectly round and his hair was thick and ash gray, the same color as his eyes. He smiled at Barrett like a man who knew he needed no introduction, and his handshake was firm and friendly.

"Mr. Rizzo, I presume," said Barrett, freeing his hand from the enthusiastic pumping.

"I'm pleased to make your acquaintance at last, Mr. Dickson," said Rizzo in an incongruously high-pitched voice. "I know you are busy at the moment, but I wanted to pay my respects. You've done a wonderful job for my dear friend Elliot, and I wanted you to know I am in your debt."

"I wish I could say it's been a pleasure."

Ashford glowered at him.

"I know, I know," said Rizzo, squinting with delight, leaning close to Barrett in a conspiratorial manner and speaking in a stage whisper. "The man can be a giant pain in the behind, eh? But you see, I'm the one to blame. Elliot wouldn't be in this situation if I had let my idiot son come out here and simply tell the truth for once in his wasted life. Do you have a son, Mr. Dickson?"

"Yes."

"Then perhaps you can forgive an old man the weakness

of fatherly love and understand why I am so grateful to you, eh? If an innocent man had been convicted, it would have been on the head of Carmine Rizzo."

Barrett cocked his head. "Tony was really in Napa that night?"

"Oh yeah, he was there, the little shit. I've seen the pilot's log and the dated documents signed by Elliot. Tony and Elliot were definitely together that night."

Rizzo then extended his hand again. "But you are busy. I'll let you—"

"Mr. Rizzo," said Barrett. "Tell me about Armand Ligretti. I'm sure Mr. Gold described his testimony."

Rizzo's features compressed as if in pain. "That weasel! He fooled us all for months, but he didn't fool you, thank God. Oh, sure Elliot had a girl; what the hell, we all did! I had two of 'em myself that night! But the remark about 'the next Mrs. Ashford'? Hell, I heard it, too, but it was Tony who said it, not Elliot. Tony brings in Elliot's 'escort' for the evening and says, 'Here she is, boys, the next Mrs. Ashford.' A joke, for Christ's sake! But that's what the little rat must have heard."

Before Barrett could decide what to say next, Rizzo was pumping his hand again, then spinning and disappearing into the protective custody of Gold and two bodyguards.

Barrett turned and met the accusing eyes of his client. "You didn't believe me," said Ashford quietly. He actually looked hurt, the one emotion Barrett had never observed in Ashford.

"I had my doubts," Barrett said, "but it didn't affect my efforts, did it? So what do you care?"

Elliot Ashford rested a hand on Barrett's arm, so gently he could barely feel it. "I care," he said.

"All rise," shouted the bailiff, and the judge entered the packed courtroom for what promised to be the last day of trial. Lev and Mike sat in the first row, just behind Barrett. Glancing to the rear of the courtroom, Barrett scanned the SRO crowd and spotted two judges, the speaker of the California State Assembly, a local TV star filming a cop series in San Francisco, Jack Klegg, Julian Gold, Carmine Rizzo, and Amanda Keller, sitting next to an immaculately groomed gentleman Barrett figured to be her publicist or agent. A full house.

"Does the defense have any further witnesses, Mr. Dickson?" asked John Hernandez.

Barrett said he didn't and bounced the ball once more back into Grace's court. She said she did, and Barrett was impressed with her brief but hard-hitting rebuttal case: first, Dr. Theodore Benton, a toxicologist, who shored up the DNA proof that the blood at the scene had to be Ashford's; then Dr. Paul Jankowitz, who established that the amount of Ashford's blood found at the scene was unlikely to be the product of a shaving cut.

The jury paid little attention to either one, or to Grace for that matter. They were ready to do their work and go home. But Barrett knew that even when the jury proclaimed Ashford not guilty, it would be Grace's victory, not his, and his face burned with shame. There was anger, too, for he was still smarting from the things she had said that had goaded him into complicity with her professional-suicide attempt; implying that his demon curse was merely a cynical mask he wore to hide from reality, wallowing in the sanctimony of an imagined victimhood. Bullshit! What was the payoff in that? What the hell, he thought, it was nearly finished now, and in defeat, Grace would suffer a bitter victory; in victory, he would suffer an equally bitter defeat. He just wanted it over with.

Grace stood and rested her case, and it was time for argument. She rose without hesitation, her carriage erect and confident as she strode toward the waiting jurors and began her opening argument.

He had never seen her more passionate and articulate. She relentlessly hammered on the defendant's blood at the scene, his lies, and his attempted subornation of perjury involving Renee Babcock in the first trial. When she had finished milking every detail of the People's evidence, she walked to the clerk's table, picked up People's Exhibit 1, and moved back toward the jury.

"Finally, I suggest to you members of the jury that neither the defendant's great wealth nor his ability to buy testimony nor his past political notoriety"—the litany gathered speed and volume now—"nor his powerful connections nor his lawyer's eloquence nor anything else can alter the fact that on August 7, 1997, shortly after a violent argument with his wife Lara"—she paused, turned, and stared straight into the eyes of the defendant—"Elliot Ashford tortured, then murdered her."

Ashford stared back, unblinking, and an uncomfortable silence momentarily dominated the room.

Grace then turned back toward the jury. She slowly raised the gleaming shard of glass over her head so that it was pointed toward the jurors, then swung the object in a slow horizontal arc across their faces, brandishing it in such a way that no one could fail to observe its cruel and lethal potential as a weapon.

"He plunged this very shard of glass into her small, helpless body," she said, her arm suddenly slashing the air between herself and the wide-eyed jurors, "again and again, mutilating her body—her skin, her flesh, her organs—as her life slowly drained away."

Barrett, wide-eyed himself, noticed that juror Lloyd seemed about to cry and several others had gone pale. Grace, her voice quaking with emotion, then demanded a verdict of guilty of first-degree murder and took her seat.

It occurred to Barrett only after a quick scan of his notes that there had been not one mention of Amanda Keller.

Christ, Barrett thought, could she possibly have turned them around? Not likely, but whatever the pundits might have written about her yesterday, it was obvious that Amazing Grace Harris was back today. Barrett was amazed at her spirit and humbled by her resiliency. At the same time, he felt a new, gut-gnawing uneasiness. She had done what she felt she had to do concerning Amanda, and was now a prosecutor again. She would give him no quarter in this final round.

Hernandez was making some notes and, in a minute, would call on him.

It was her goddamn argument that was making him uneasy. It had been pure emotional hokum, of course—a manipulation of the irrational part of the jurors' minds—but it had been damned effective. Her words hung in the air around him still, charging the atmosphere with density that weighed him down in his chair.

"Mr. Dickson?"

The judge's voice cut through Barrett's distraction, and

he glanced at the jury and willed his shoulders to relax as he took a minute to gather himself. He looked over at Grace, who even now refused to meet his eyes. Why was that? he wondered. Was it because he had helped her wreck her own career? Or had she figured out he was no longer the man who had inspired her ten years ago? Hell, he could have told her that, he thought, and besides, I'm the one who should be pissed-off here, considering all the things she had said to him.

"Your argument, Mr. Dickson?"

He rose and faced the jury, all eyes upon him now, waiting for magic.

Waiting.

He had almost forgotten how insatiable jurors could be in their silent hunger for words that would sway them, words that would disturb and excite them. In that passive silence, they demanded more attention than a division of West Point generals. And given enough opportunities over enough years, Barrett knew those twelve silent citizens could suck trial lawyers dry and turn them into barren husks.

They had done it to him.

Then it hit him, the thing Grace had somehow intuited when she had accused him of needing to feel responsible for "everything bad that happened to people you care about." Why, he had asked, would any one want to do that?

There it was. The payoff. In ascribing blame to himself for Ellen's suicide—playing God—he had found an excuse to escape the ravenous gaze of jurors, the outrageous demands of clients, the possibility of losing, the need to prove himself week after week.

I ain't chicken.

Grace hadn't needed great skill to get him to sink her key witness, just enough persistence so that he wouldn't look like a total heel. Not that he wanted to hurt her—that part was sincere—but in the end he just couldn't face losing again. He had quit caring about winning, but he couldn't live with his fear of losing.

When had it started? With Harlow Flagg in that dirt pit stained with the blood of roosters forty years ago? He'd never know for sure, but somewhere along the way, he had, in fact, become "chicken." After he'd given all he had to juries and to clients, Ellen's death had given him all he needed to give it up.

"Mr. Dickson?"

So now what? He looked at Grace again and this time she met his eyes. He couldn't read them. He didn't need to. It was all up to him now.

He silently mouthed two words to her that only she would understand.

"Watch this."

No hesitation now, by God; no sympathy for his beloved adversary. Nothing now but himself and the jury and the doing of that which he had once done so well. Any seed of irrational doubt his opponent had planted would soon be revealed for the emotional humbuggery it was—a seed planted on rock. Then he would plant his own seed of *reasonable* doubt into the fertile opening she had chosen to leave him.

At Grace's table, she had indeed read his words and knew she was lost. It made her angry, for she had begun to think there was hope for a guilty verdict, at least as to Lara. She knew she could not blame Barrett for using the weapon she had forced into his unwilling hand. Still, his accepting of it, then his aggressive wielding of it, had hurt her deeply. Maybe this is the way she should have expected to feel after abandoning the rigid code that had held her life together for forty years. Had she expected it to feel good?

"I'll be brief, members of the jury."

Grace heard his baritone voice—typically deep, but not yet fully resonant—and saw that the jurors were watching him carefully for any trace of weakness in his demeanor; any clue to what he really believed beneath his advocate's words.

"I'll start with the question that is on every one of your minds: What became of the state's key witness?"

Already, she saw two jurors in the back row nodding. What was more fickle, more capricious, she thought, than a jury. And what was more mercurial than the pendulum's swing during closing arguments. She looked at Barrett now and could almost feel the sense of challenge surging up his spine, the adrenaline surfing his bloodstream straight to his brain.

"Yes, ladies and gentlemen, you must be wondering why the prosecutor eloquently commented on every witness except one: *the one witness on whom all three of her murder charges rise or fall.* Yes, folks, I said all three.

"You see, the prosecution wants you to believe that Elliot Ashford committed the first murder because the modus operandi in the last two murders—the glass, the torture, the wounds—were nearly identical to Lara's. The prosecution also wants you to believe he committed the last two murders because the state's key witness allegedly overheard him threaten the victims.

"Get it? You're supposed to believe so much in the testimony of their key witness regarding the Jefferson-Field murders that you forget about the frailty of their proof surrounding Lara's death!"

Grace winced as she saw juror number eight, Mary Lloyd, an obvious leading candidate for foreperson, nod slightly at this. Seeing that movement of her head was like watching a lover flirting publicly with another woman.

He was on a roll now, demanding the confidence of these people, their trust; yes, he would want their trust most of all. And she could only sit by helplessly as they gave it to him. At that moment, she hated him.

"I give Ms. Harris credit for creativity. I'm reminded of a Hollywood set. A dazzling set, complete with a lovely leading lady, Amanda Keller. Have you ever seen one of those sets? They consist of a facade so realistic you'd swear it was real. You'd be wrong, though, because if you went behind it, you'd see there's nothing there.

"This facade of a prosecution case might have succeeded in convicting an innocent man but for the fact that the leading lady—currently the hottest and probably the highest-paid interview in Hollywood—forgot her lines." Grace saw him turn toward her as he added, "And was exposed as a liar.

"Yes, members of the jury, a liar. An 'intimate friend' of Earl Field, Ms. Keller was so starved for vengeance she came in here determined to do as a witness what she had been unable to do as a juror: convict Elliot Ashford. Then, so that you would think her testimony was objective—

therefore truthful—she tried to conceal her relationship with Field. And so you would think the defendant was guilty, she made up threats, unmentioned, of course, in a letter written to the very object of the supposed threats, unmentioned because they never happened.

"But Ms. Keller had another motive for making up her stories about Elliot Ashford. The oldest and most seductive of them all: fame and fortune. In this, she has succeeded, though her talents might lie even more in creating fiction than in acting it out. Fortunately, in this drama at least, she finally slipped up and was upstaged by the truth—at least all we need of it.

"Judge Hernandez is going to tell you that you cannot convict Elliot Ashford if you entertain a reasonable doubt concerning the charges that have been brought against him. But the defense does not have to rely on the concept of reasonable doubt, for are you not *certain* that Amanda Keller was lying to you? Or how about their other star witness, Armand 'the Weasel' Ligretti from the first trial. Remember his sterling testimony I read to you last week? Are you not *certain* he was lying?"

Barrett was at the rail now, on top of them, not letting one of them escape the righteous indignation of his words, the demands of his eyes. "I understand why the prosecution did not mention Ms. Keller. I won't dwell on her either, except to say she would have gone after anybody charged with her lover's murder if it would get her to Hollywood. When you see her on the screen, folks, you can say, 'I knew her when; I knew her when she used the witness chair instead of a casting couch as her path to stardom.'

"Amanda Keller is not worth one more minute of our attention, but when you go into that jury room to decide Elliot's fate, ask yourself why the prosecution would vouch for patently false and treacherous witnesses—unless they realized, as we all do now, that their case was so weak they had no choice."

God, thought Grace, he's calling him "Elliot" now.

"So, there's not just a reasonable doubt about the prosecution's failure to shoulder that burden, ladies and gentleman, there's a reasonable *certainty!*

"You may wonder," he continued, his tone suddenly relaxed and conversational, "what is the reality here? Who *did* kill these people?

"I submit that nobody knows. That reality is up to the police now, though their bungling loss or intentional destruction of Lara's fingernail scrapings will surely hamper their quest. That reality is beyond us; it's not up to you or me to discover the true killer. It's only up to me to point out that it was not Elliot Ashford. And it's only up to you to know a liar when you see one.

"The only person Elliot cut, members of the jury, was himself—while shaving."

Grace saw two of the jurors nod in agreement. She realized they believed him; they were with him now. No reasonable doubt about that. Hell hath no fury, she thought, like a juror deceived, and Ligretti and Keller had been revealed as the king and the queen of deception.

How could she get them now to consider even the *valid* evidence against Ashford? How could she even get to her feet for her closing argument? Was there a small opening in Barrett's "reality" argument? Maybe.

Barrett finished up with a quick review of his best evidence and another attack on the police department and crime lab, then walked up close to the jury and rested his hands on the rail, connecting with them.

"Ladies and gentlemen, this is not a movie. This is a courtroom. We are not playing roles here. Oh, it's true that like actors, you and I will go home after our jobs here are finished. We will go to dinner or watch television or go dancing.

"But if you find Elliot guilty of murder as charged, he goes to a real prison with real bars or to a very real death.

"But I know that's not going to happen. The case against him is like a bad movie built around a rotten actress. Ladies and gentlemen, give it the reviews it deserves. I urge you to send a message to people who would exploit our criminal justice system for publicity, fame, and fortune. I urge you to find Elliot Ashford not guilty!"

There was not a sound in the courtroom. Grace had heard silences like that before—she called it a Gettysburg silence—and she knew what it signified.

"Your closing argument, Ms. Harris?" said John Hernandez, and all eyes fell on the assistant district attorney.

*   *   *

Barrett barely heard John Hernandez's words. Ashford was whispering things into his ear and he didn't hear them either, though he could feel Ashford's hand closing around his wrist like a claw, squeezing hard with gratitude.

He didn't want to hear or feel anything outside himself until he had to. He wanted to drink it in, drink it all in. He had forgotten how good it could be, how spine-tingling, intoxicatingly fucking *grand* it could be!

The claw increased its pressure and Barrett turned to acknowledge his client's appreciation. He then glanced over at Grace, who seemed preoccupied with a pad of paper in front of her. She scribbled something there, then crossed out what she had written and wrote something else.

"Ms. Harris?"

Then she crossed that out, too, and threw the pad into her trial bag on the floor. Get up, Grace! thought Barrett.

She got up, then walked past the lectern and took up a position directly in front of Barrett.

"First, I'd like to address counsel's preoccupation with my failure to mention Ms. Keller in opening argument. I mention her now because he talked about Ms. Keller and me in his argument more than he talked about his own client. Mr. Dickson would have you believe that the witness was on trial here, and perhaps me as well.

"He seems particularly concerned about Ms. Keller's credibility, and why I didn't prolong this trial in my opening remarks by dwelling on her relationship with Mr. Field. I'll deal with this concern now, not because Mr. Dickson is troubled but rather because some of you might be."

She strolled back toward the jury, as casually as if she were in her own living room entertaining friends. "Remember when Mr. Dickson asked you 'What is the reality here? Who *did* kill these people?' Remember what he said then? He said you should let the police take care of that. In effect, you shouldn't care about reality. Well, let me tell you, members of the jury, that caring about 'reality' is precisely why you are here! That's why His Honor is here. That's why we're all here. To find the reality; to find the truth.

"Even if we ignore reality elsewhere in our lives, we must not do it in a courtroom, ladies and gentlemen, for if we do that, we are lost as a democracy. At the very heart of a democracy is respect for the justice system, and the foundation of our justice system is a search for the truth: the 'reality' Mr. Dickson tells you not to concern yourself with.''

Barrett squirmed uncomfortably. Unfair, he thought, but clever: twisting his words about catching the real killer into a polemic on patriotism and casting him in the role of Benedict Arnold. Grace may have ended up being the director of a bad film, but people were watching it. He looked up at the clock, wishing it were tomorrow. Wishing she'd get on to something else.

"So despite Mr. Dickson's request, let's *do* face reality here, members of the jury. Yes, Amanda Keller came across as a hopelessly muddled witness. Why? I submit her confusion on cross-examination was a reflection of her despondency. Amanda Keller was tragically and secretly in love with Earl Field, a highly visible public figure engaged to another woman. So yes, she concealed her love, from you and from the rest of the world. Then, in her grief at his death, she resolved to do nothing that might sully his fine reputation. So she kept her secret. Was that so evil?''

Barrett saw a juror involuntarily shake her head in the negative. Well done, kid, thought Barrett, kicking himself again for giving her that "reality" opening. But how will you explain the unmentioned threats? And the waiter/waitress problem? And Keller's blowup at me?

"But the real reason I didn't waste time on her testimony in my opening," continued Grace, "is because the other evidence we have presented to you is more than sufficient to eliminate any reasonable doubt as to the defendant's guilt.''

Smart, thought Barrett. Do the best you can with a disaster like Keller, then get the hell out of town. What else could she do? But Grace's problem is that jurors aren't stupid. They'll know—at least some will, and they will point it out to the others—that she sidestepped the real issues with Keller.

"So how do we know from the evidence before us," continued Grace, "that the defendant is guilty of Lara's death? Members of the jury, let me count the ways.

"First, the defendant's blood is everywhere. The bathroom that became her chamber of horrors was awash with blood, ladies and gentlemen, hers *and* his! Does the defense really expect you to believe you can bleed that much from a shaving cut that was healing and barely noticeable three hours later?

"I think not, ladies and gentlemen of the jury, but 'reality' is for you to decide."

"Second, this was a domestic-rage killing with sexual revenge written all over Lara Ashford's tortured body. You heard the maid's testimony: Senator Dwight Clifton's name was mentioned during the loud argument she overheard between them just hours before her death. Was she preparing to see the senator? He denied it, of course, in his deposition that Mr. Dickson read to you, though he had to admit he was in town for a fund-raiser. Senator Clifton was in town and the maid heard them fighting about him. Just a coincidence?

"I think not, members of the jury, but 'reality' is your province, not the judge's, not mine, and certainly not Mr. Dickson's."

The old Jesse Jackson repetitive-theme routine, thought Barrett. Effective too, given the material she's got to work with, but not enough. They get in the jury room and somebody says, "Yeah, that was stirring, but where's the beef?"

"Mr. Dickson mentioned the first trial," Grace continued. "I'd like you to bear in mind the transcripts I read to you and ask you to answer this question as soon as you reach the jury room: Does a truly innocent man claim that he was at a movie, then, when that is proven to be a total fabrication, offer to pay someone $50,000 to provide him with a phony alibi?

"I don't think so . . . but 'reality' is for you to decide.

"I suggest that Elliot Ashford murdered his wife in a jealous rage, ladies and gentlemen, then belatedly went about the business of deceiving the police so that they, and you, would think he was innocent. Did it work?

"I don't think so, *but 'reality' is for you to decide.*

"Yes, the defendant committed Lara's murder, and probably the other two identical murders as well: Jefferson's, to send a message to the other jurors; Field's, to settle a long-standing personal and political score, his enmity further aroused when the district attorney dared to bring him to the bar of justice.

"But let me be most clear on this: If you do have a reasonable doubt concerning the murders of Field and Jefferson, *you must not let it affect your judgment on the evidence in Lara's case.*"

Brilliant, thought Barrett. She's punting on both murders supported by Keller and going all out for a conviction on Lara. Hoping for Solomonic justice, the baby cut in half. They give me Jefferson and Field and give her Lara. Shit.

He began to feel uncomfortable again and a glance told him Ashford was worried now too. Christ, could he possibly lose this case despite all the help she had given him? He was astonished to realize how much he wanted—needed—to win it now. He had lost any possibility of a relationship with Grace—along with a large measure of his own self-respect—but must he now lose the case too? He swung around just enough to catch Mike's eye. He looked worried, too.

Grace picked up the shard of glass again. She walked toward them again, but her arm hung freely from her side, and this time her voice was soft and unthreatening, pulling the jurors closer to her.

"Can we begin to imagine the pain Lara Ashford suffered at the hands of this man before death finally liberated her? Can you hear her screams of anguish?"

Barrett glanced at the distressed looks on the jurors' faces, none more distressed than the look on his own.

"Now, from that place of final peace, Lara Ashford screams out once more. She screams out for justice, ladies and gentlemen of the jury. She screams out to you, for no one can give it to her but you. You must not let these crimes of unimaginable cruelty go unpunished."

"I urge you to find the defendant guilty of first-degree murder."

Grace took her seat and John Hernandez broke the silent tension by excusing the jury for the mid-afternoon recess.

That was strong, thought Barrett, despite his concern. Damn good, but probably not enough to blast through the barrier of reasonable doubt the judge would soon instruct them on.

He wondered if she was aware that she had delivered her entire closing argument without a single stammer.

After the jurors had been instructed by the judge and locked in the jury room to begin their deliberation, the clerk told counsel the judge wished to see them in chambers. As Grace stood at counsel table packing her trial bag, she turned and met Barrett's eyes. A look of despairing acceptance passed across the gulf that now separated them.

A familiar voice from behind startled her from her thoughts.

"Hello, Grace," said Amanda Keller, leaning against the rail.

"Hello, Ms. Keller," said Grace. "Sorry, I can't speak with you now."

"I just want to know one thing," said Amanda, running fingers through her lush blond hair. "Where did I slip up?"

Grace tossed the last of her papers into her trial bag, stuffing them in now so that she could get the top closed and reach the privacy of chambers. "It doesn't matter anymore, Amanda."

"Well, damn it, it matters to me! At least turn around and look at me! I'll lose everything now! Look at me, Grace! It matters to you, too!"

"Only three things matter to me right now, Amanda. A hot bath, seeing my son soon, and never seeing you again."

She turned and walked toward the door to the judge's chambers, trying to shake off a nagging sense of menace.

John Hernandez offered both lawyers a drink from a decanter he removed from an oak credenza. Barrett declined with thanks, though he would have liked nothing better. He felt numb from the sheer craziness of it all and thought it best to stay that way. He'd buy himself a beer or two later to cry in when no one was around.

"I'm sure my worthy adversary could use one," he said, "after the tongue-lashing she just got from her star witness."

Grace offered them a wan smile. "She's looking at me as the one who ruined her comeback in Hollywood."

Barrett nodded. "If looks could kill, John, Grace would not be drinking your fine brandy now."

"I'm sure she'll salvage her career somehow," said Grace. "She's smart."

"Almost too smart," said Barrett.

Grace took a seat across from John Hernandez, then accepted the glass he held out to her. Barrett remained standing beside her, feeling awkward but too nervous to sit down.

Hernandez toasted them both. "Now that our work is finished and it's in the hands of the jury, Grace, would you like to tell me what's been going on with her?"

Grace sipped her drink, and Barrett saw her take a deep breath as color slowly ebbed back into her face.

"I'm still working through it, Judge. She was lying, of course, and now she's demanding to know how she 'slipped up.' "

"Sounds like she's now admitting she was conning us all along," said John Hernandez.

Grace nodded.

"You handled her well in argument," said Hernandez, "but I'm afraid she killed you with the jury."

"Grace," said Barrett, "I hope you understand that—"

"Of course I do, counsel," she said, looking up at him. "You had no choice but to draw and quarter me in your closing argument. I would have done the same thing to you if the situations were reversed—though with considerably more finesse."

He smiled. They were the first words she had said to him about Amanda Keller's testimony, and her attempt at humor in the face of disaster touched him.

He said, "I've never once—in all my years in this tough business—had a tougher opponent."

"Well, come on!" said Judge Hernandez. "You needn't *both* look so glum. Christ, Barrett, you look even more dejected than Grace, and unless I misread this jury, you're probably going to win! You destroyed Keller on cross!"

Barrett forced a smile, avoiding Grace's eyes.

John Hernandez's prediction was correct, for in less than three hours of deliberation, with the courtroom still jammed, the jury returned with its verdict.

"We the jury, in the above-entitled case of People versus

Elliot Ashford," read the clerk in a loud voice, "find the defendant not guilty on all counts."

The courtroom was surprisingly silent as the judge thanked and excused the jury. Grace accepted condolences from Sam Quon and consoling looks from two of the jurors. She wouldn't look at Klegg and didn't want to look at Barrett. In the tradition of adversaries, however, he approached her now, hand outstretched.

"I'm sorry, Grace," he said, taking her hand. "Sorry about all of it. For whatever small consolation it might be, I really believe he's innocent and that you did the right thing."

"I have no regrets," she said, "but forgive me if I'm not able to be more gracious in defeat. I had hoped the jury would give me Lara."

Barrett pulled her closer.

"Ashford had an alibi he couldn't use and wouldn't let us use, Grace. So he got inventive. I still think he's innocent."

Barrett could see she wasn't in the mood for consolation.

She picked up her bag and headed for the preplanned escape route through the judge's chambers. "I guess the best man won after all," she said.

"No," he said. "I think we were both beaten by a woman."

The judge had ordered an expedited property release so that citizen Ashford could also be swiftly spirited away through chambers and avoid the nearly 150 reporters and photographers gathered on the front steps of the Hall of Justice.

The prosecutor, defense attorney, ex-defendant, and escort of sheriff's deputies slipped out through the side door of the judge's chambers. They took an elevator to the basement, then walked quickly and without speaking through the bowels of the hall. Eventually, they broke into the pale daylight, where Sam Quon's city vehicle and Carmine Rizzo's gray limousine sat double-parked on Harriet Street. A handful of reporters and photographers who had foreseen the stratagem were across the street under umbrellas, held at bay by a phalanx of raincoated police.

Sam was waiting with an umbrella for Grace and she was almost into his car when she heard Barrett's voice.

"Grace," he shouted, obviously winded from the sprint through the catacombs, "are you going to be okay?"

She was touched by his look of concern and weariness. She considered just saying "Okay, yes, I'll be okay" and moving on, but she decided to be straight with him.

"I've decided to resign from the office, Barrett. I'll pick up Aaron in Florida, then go job hunting back in New York. I've passed the bar there and should have no trouble getting work now."

She saw the look of astonishment on his face as she entered the car and signaled Sam to drive off. When they made a turn at the end of Harriet Street, she could see that he was still standing where she had left him; alone, pelted by rain, and as stark and motionless as the tree next to him.

Barrett was stirred from his dazed state by the sound of Ashford shouting at him. "Dickson! For Christ's sake, have you gone deaf on me? It's payday, you incredible hulk. Come up to my hotel in an hour and I'll have a check ready for you."

Barrett looked toward the sound. A tinted electric window descended in the stretch limo, revealing Julian Gold's head, with Rizzo's profile barely visible on the other side of him. Gold turned his face to him. Barrett thought of a death's-head, a memento mori. The head, though, gave a quick nod reassuring Barrett that, barring an act of God, he would now outlive his client.

"All right," he said as Ashford hopped inside.

He would take the money, but what he really wanted—now that Ashford was free and could never be tried again—was to know the truth once and for all.

60

"Come in, counselor," said Elliot Ashford with a theatrical sweep of his arm, and Barrett entered the spacious living room of his client's suite in the St. Francis hotel. "We'll have to make this quick," he said. "Victory party down on the peninsula."

"No problem," said Barrett, watching Ashford's hand as it reached into a pocket of his robe and withdrew a check. Barrett had never seen a client's check. Checks always went straight to the firm's accounting department. Reddening, he quickly slipped it into his trouser pocket without looking at it.

"I'd like you to stay in touch, old chap," Ashford said, pouring himself a drink that he raised in tribute. "Well done and thank you. By the way, the firm's been paid, and that check's for one million dollars. Personal bonus."

Ashford sipped from the glass, then, getting no response from Barrett, clicked on one of the several television sets Barrett knew must be scattered throughout the suite and began surfing channels. Barrett felt mildly disappointed not to have been offered a drink. It would have been cold comfort to have turned down a victory drink from this supercilious bastard.

But he was not surprised. He knew from long experience that defendants quickly distanced themselves from their lawyers following a favorable verdict, choosing to attribute the victory to the inexorable hand of justice rather than to the skill of a resourceful lawyer. To credit the lawyer was to tacitly concede merit to the charge. "Of course I won," the client would say over cocktails with a casual shrug. "The facts were all on my side."

"I might want to retain you as my local *consigliere*," Ashford tossed over his shoulder.

"*Consigliere?*" Barrett said. "I had just about persuaded myself you were not really a member of the family, Elliot; just connected."

"I was just kidding about the *consigliere.* I'm only important to Carmine because he owns a big piece of me. But after what's been said during this trial, every one will be sure I'm thick with the mob no matter what the hell I say. Hell, old friend, you know how it is. Lie down with dogs, and all that."

Barrett wandered toward the window. He was feeling the itch of a flea himself.

"But I'm quite serious about working with you again," said Ashford, still switching channels, ignoring news bulletins about his victory and release.

"No thanks."

"Why not?"

Barrett shrugged and forced a smile. "Hell, old friend, you know how it is. Lie down with dogs."

Ashford smiled wryly, sipped his drink. "Well, we'll see. You took my money once. You'll take it next time."

"There won't be a next time, Elliot."

"What's your problem, old boy?" Ashford turned around to look at him, showing mild interest for the first time. "You've just won this month's 'Trial of the Century,' scored a quick million for yourself, and locked in a place on *Larry King Live* and the *Today* show. New York publishers will besiege you, old man. Your phone will be ringing off the hook."

Barrett thought about how little he would miss his client's sardonic smile, the reflection from his tinted glasses, the posture that spoke of the invincibility of wealth. He looked through the window overlooking Union Square. A field of umbrellas bloomed like black flowers in the rain.

Barrett wished he could be like so many of his brethren at the bar: "Don't ask, don't tell." Do your job, take the money and run. But he lingered. He had to know.

Ashford stared vacantly at the screen as he cruised the channels, stopping for a few seconds on an old *Rumpole* rerun.

"You'll work for me," he murmured, as if to himself.

"I don't think so," Barrett said, succumbing to a mean anger for which he reproached himself even as he uttered the words. "Working with you has no future. You'll soon be more in need of a skillful mortician than a flea-infested lawyer."

The arc of Ashford's glass to his lips froze in midair and the room went totally silent. His eyes drained of their usual disdain, he turned toward Barrett.

"I know, counselor," he said. "I know all too well."

Jesus, thought Barrett, there it is. Part of it anyway. He had never wanted a drink so much. He took a step toward the door, but only a step, for years of unconvincing protestations by lying clients, posttrial purges of wrongdoing, and other metaphoric deathbed confessions held him there. He had to know the rest.

"You've had blackouts, haven't you." It wasn't a question.

Ashford drank deeply. "Several," he said, then held his empty glass out to Barrett, as in a toast. "One of them at the worst possible time."

"For Lara," said Barrett, rubbing his suddenly throbbing temples. "Still, you managed to make it up to Napa afterward—"

"Strange how things work out, isn't it? I didn't kill Field. I hated the bastard, but I didn't kill him. The Jefferson woman either. I still don't have a clue who killed them or why. Someone wanted them added to my docket, I suppose. Ironic, isn't it? If they hadn't, I might not be here in these reasonably decent rooms, a free, if dying, man, doing the postgame locker-room interview with my victorious attorney."

Barrett stared at the back of Ashford's head, waiting for more, waiting for the rest. The how. The why.

Waiting.

But Elliot Ashford just turned his back to Barrett and the volume up on the TV.

Amanda Keller checked out of the Ritz, hounded by the press, demanding that she respond to the defense's attack on her character that had gone unanswered by the prosecution.

"Were you really in love with Earl Field?" one reporter yelled as she leapt into the backseat of a waiting limo. "Why did Grace Harris throw you to the wolves?" shouted another. "Do you expect Harris to instigate perjury charges against you?" demanded a third.

She collapsed in the rear seat, her chest too tight to allow air passage into her lungs. She pumped from her inhaler, but without relief. She felt her heart racing faster and louder. She closed her eyes against flecks of light that pierced her vision like steel splinters. Bright lights flickering from without and within.

She took refuge at her mother's apartment and was amazed at how quickly Lucinda, who had been glued to local Channel 2, began to regain the upper hand.

"Congratulations, dear. You've managed to make yourself more unpopular than Mark Fuhrman. I'm embarrassed to leave the apartment."

"As if," sneered Amanda, hating the woman even more than usual.

"As if what?"

"As if you ever leave the apartment anyway and as if anybody would give a shit if you did. As if there was somewhere for you to go and someone to recognize you if you went there."

Lucinda shifted in her wheelchair. "That's cruel, Amanda, even for you. But I've got to know what happened with Grace Harris."

"Nothing happened. She just sat there and let Dickson maul me."

The phone rang. *"Don't answer it, Mother!"*

The last call Amanda had taken at the Ritz was from Emory Goldsmith. Not one of Goldsmith's secretaries, not his assistant director, not one of the production assistants. Emory Goldsmith himself.

What the hell's doing? he had demanded. The media is killing you down here! They're saying you're not only a liar but probably nuts! He told her his money people were "waffling."

What happened to "just spell my name right"? she had said, but he hadn't laughed, just told her that being a little kooky was still okay, but they don't buy undependable or uninsurable. He told her the L.A. papers were saying there might even be perjury charges filed. It was a new industry now, run by bean counters, he had told her, and she had damn well better straighten things out fast and call him the minute she had.

The problem was things would never be straightened out

now, and a voice was screaming at her from somewhere
deep inside:

Can't you do anything right?

Nausea flooded her body and she started for the bathroom, but dizziness sent her reeling back to the couch. Her
head was throbbing and the light show was back, playing
across her eyes, whether open or shut, accompanying the
voice.

Who do you think you are?

"I'm Amanda Keller, damn it!"

Lucinda looked at her daughter. "Who are you talkin'
to, child?"

"You asked me who I was, you withered bitch, and I
told you. Who the hell are *you?*"

"I know," said Lucinda, each word sounding like a foot-
step in gravel, "*exactly* who I am. I am a maimed woman
who endures day after day without knowing why! A woman
who bore a cruel and ungrateful daughter who's apparently
ready for the rubber room again! *That's* who I am."

Amanda stared blankly into her mother's calm face.

"You heard me, the institution! So just *stop it* if you
don't want to get more of that electroshock like when you
were a kid."

Amanda continued staring, her face contorted by memories she had long since given up trying to hide from herself.
Why had they never talked about it? A détente of silence
for more than twenty years.

"Why did you send me away, Mother?" she said finally.

"For your own good," she said, a harsh edge to her voice.

"I remember seeing my name in the paper," said
Amanda, her voice suddenly a pained monotone. "I was
the one who found him, the gun barrel still in his mouth."

"Of course you were the one, child," said Amanda, a
sinister grin on her face. "That was not so surprisin', was
it, since you were the one who put it there?"

A grim smile crossed Amanda's face. "Well, well," she
said, "the wise old witch has known all along?"

"Of course. It's been just another burden I've had to
bear."

"A girl has to protect herself," said Amanda, "when her
mother won't."

"I didn't know what he was doin'."

"You didn't want to know. You just ignored what he was doing to me, then you ignored what I did to him. Other than to send me off to the institution."

Lucinda bristled. "You can't blame me for sendin' you there. I could have had you put in some reform school! You murdered him in cold blood!"

"And I'm sure you grieved a full ten or fifteen minutes for that dear husband of yours who couldn't seem to keep himself off his little beauty pageant queen. I should have done you while I was at it. My head's still full of the electricity you let them pump into me."

Lucinda looked uneasy now as she raised herself up into her walker and scuttled like a crab toward her room, furtively glancing back at Amanda.

Amanda groaned and let her head tilt back, felt her eyelids flutter, and allowed her mind to escape the walls of time and space surrounding her, just as she used to do as a child in the institution.

She let the delicious memory play across the screen of her consciousness, allowing the nostalgia to cool the fire in her head.

The man sleeps a deep and drunken sleep and doesn't hear the door open. Doesn't see the shiny black barrel of his .12 gauge shotgun inches from his face. Doesn't smell the metal or feel the steel against his lips. Not until it's jammed against his teeth, and even that pain won't have time to register in his alcohol-drugged brain before it splatters against the headboard.

61

Barrett Dickson sat in his office at Caldwell & Shaw, caressing an Anchor Steam from a six-pack he had picked up from the grocery store on the corner, wishing it were a Ketel kamikaze or three fingers of Patron tequila. He was in the mood to taper on.

Grace was leaving, getting as far as she could from the scene of their crime. That fucking Ashford. Should he tell her he was the one who killed Lara? That would be the frosting for sure.

With nowhere else to go, he had decided to get a start on cleaning out his desk at the firm. He had grabbed a newspaper from the reception area on the way in, wondering what they'd say about him. What *could* they say about him? That he could sing on key? Knew all the words to the *Sergeant Pepper* album and a dozen Dylan songs plus Hoagy Carmichael's "Stardust"? That he had a kind disposition outside the courtroom (where he now intended to spend roughly 100 percent of his time), and that he had just collected a million bucks for sending a wife butcher back onto the street? And that he had needed help from his opponent to even accomplish that worthy feat?

Jesus.

Should he tell her? Maybe he should. Maybe not.

He reread the part of the article that reported on how Lani Jefferson was "apparently seized by the hair from behind while exercising on her stationary bicycle, then stabbed to death in almost precisely the same manner as Lara Ashford."

He reread the sentence again. Something other than its macabre tone was bothering him, nagging at him.

Stationary bicycle.

No, he thought, it couldn't be. Yet he felt the hair stand

on his neck, his scalp tingling like it did when he used to see something no one else had.

No, no, it couldn't be, but he read the paragraph again, then reached for the phone and called Stars, where he was supposed to be celebrating with Lev and Mike. He asked Ken the bartender to find Leviticus Heywood.

"Lev? It's Barrett. You work out all the time. How many kinds of exercise bikes are there?"

"Bear? You said you was goin' straight to bed, not to a crack house."

"I'm serious."

"Hell, I don't know. Twenty or more, I'd guess."

"That's what I figure. You still have your cop buddy working swing?"

"Far's I know."

"Do me a favor. Call him and have him check the investigation report on Jefferson's death. I want to know what kind of bike she was on when she got killed."

"Okay, Bear, now listen. You wait right there, 'cause I'm gonna send him to pick you up instead. And don't operate any heavy machinery in the meanwhile, okay?"

"Just do it, Lev. Is Mike still there?"

"Yep."

"Good. I'm at C&S. While you're talking to your buddy at SFPD, tell Mike to get over here pronto and get on his computer. Tell him to—"

"Whoa, Bear-man, slow down. You best tell him your own self, you know, given the fact you're makin' no sense whatsoever."

"Okay, put him on."

Barrett tapped his fingers on the desk, waiting . . .

"Barrett? Terrific! Are you coming to join the party?"

"I'm at the office, Mike. I need you to get over here right away. Get into your computer and Lexis, Nexis, Texas, or whatever the hell you people do with computers to see if any news story since November 5, 1997, mentioned the kind of exercise bike Jefferson was on when she was killed."

"What?"

"Mike, don't argue, okay? It's important. I've seen something in today's *Examiner* that's got me thinking."

"Barrett? It happens I'm holding that very same paper in my very own hands. Now, I want you to turn to page

one of that very same paper and look carefully at the headline thereon. I think you'll see not only that the trial is
over, but that you actually won! So get over here and I'll
buy you a soda pop."

"It's not over, Mike."

"Then I'd better call the *Chronicle* so they don't make
the shame mistake. Same mishtake. Fuck it. Anyway, Bear,
why should I have to leave the good company of our mutual friend, the Right Honorable Leviticus Heywood, and
go to the office when you're already there?"

"Two reasons, Mike. One, I don't know how to even
start a computer. Two, I'm heading over to Lev's office to
start going through trial transcripts. I'm serious about this,
Mike. I think I'm onto something important. Call me at
Lev's the minute you have the answer and tell Lev to do
the same after he's talked to his cop friend."

Mike groaned, "Give me a break, Bear—"

"It's *important!* Have Ken pour you some coffee to go
and take a cab. Leave your car right where it is."

Barrett hung up, jammed the article in his coat pocket,
and ran for the elevator.

Amanda was back in her room, the brief euphoria vanished, huddled against the headboard of her bed with a
chair lodged against the door. She could not stop trembling.
She sat like that for a half hour, swaying back and forth,
arms hugging her knees, her head bombarded by swirling,
painful scraps of data—mistakes, regrets, illnesses, disasters,
humiliations, frustrations, penetrations—Christ Almighty, a
lifetime of experiences, nearly all of them bad, jarring her
brain.

"I won't go back," she screamed. She went into her
closet and pulled down a shoe box from the top shelf, too
high for Lucinda to reach. All these years and not even
Lucinda knew she still had the gun the studio had arranged
for her eleven years before. She had never had a use for it.

"I won't go back," she repeated, more softly this time.

She paced around her bed for a few minutes, trying to
focus, occasionally glancing out the window, the loaded gun
in her hand.

Then she put the gun down and studied herself in the
dresser mirror. She lifted an arm. Her image in the mirror

raised an arm too. Okay, she wasn't crazy, but she looked awful. Still, she was a lot prettier than Grace Harris, the little bitch. Harris!

No fancy law degree like Harris, but she was just as smart! Had her fooled for ages. Yet the little bitch had the upper hand now. No doubt about it.

I think you're protecting yourself, Amanda, she says to me. Accuses me of lying about Earl, *about what you've done,* she says.

"Something will have to be done about Grace Harris," Amanda said out loud. "For my own good."

Barrett let himself into Lev's office at 7:15 P.M. and went straight to the answering machine. Lev had already scored. The message said the bike was a LifeSpin, manufactured by a company called Health-Ease, and sold direct to consumers via TV infomercials.

Barrett went from file cabinet to cabinet, yanking each one open until he located the box of trial transcripts he was looking for. Lev called to make sure he was all right and Barrett told him to go on home.

Thirty minutes later, Mike called. He still sounded high, but clear-headed. He also sounded disappointed.

"Not one mention of the type of bike Jefferson had, Bear. Sorry. I've checked everything, including the local-newspaper morgues."

"Okay," said Barrett. "Perfect! Thanks, Mike."

"That's a *good* thing?" said Mike. "Then would you mind telling me what the hell I've been doing this for?"

"Don't have time. Call you at home later. I think I'm on to something . . . *sonofabitch!*"

"Well, thanks a lot—"

"Not you, Mike. I love you. Goodbye."

There it was, right in front of him, where it had always been.

Amanda had no idea how long she'd been lying on her bed before the harsh ring of the telephone caused her head to snap up.

The phone kept ringing, over and over again. Good, let it ring. But the next time it rang, she heard her mother pick up the phone, heard her say hello to someone.

"Amanda!" she whispered from her bedroom doorway a minute later. "It's Emory Goldsmith! He knows you're here and insists that you talk to him."

Amanda cocked her head to one side. Words registering. Familiar.

Goldsmith. Hollywood. Hollywood Goldsmith.

Hollywood.

"Calm yourself, Amanda," said her mother. "Take a deep breath."

Then it all came back to her; came back with painful force. She remembered everything. The trial, the cross-examination, Harris figuring out what she had done, threatening to have her arrested on the spot, Goldsmith calling to tell her she was nothing but shit in Hollywood unless she could "straighten things out."

And all because of Grace Harris, the bitch who'd sold her out.

I think you're protecting yourself, Amanda.

"Amanda!" shouted Lucinda. "Did you hear me? The man won't hold on forever!"

"Tell him I'll call back in an hour."

Amanda's bedroom door slammed shut again. When she emerged ten minutes later, she carried a workout bag Lucinda had never seen before.

"Amanda!"

But Amanda had gone to straighten things out.

Barrett's heart was pounding in his throat and his hands shook as he held page 973 of the daily trial transcript for Wednesday, February 11, 1998. It was all there, just as the nagging voice inside had told him it might be.

He had been examining Keller on the threat she claimed to have overheard in Pat's Seafood Grill. She had testified that Ashford had then asked her if she had "gotten an earful" and she had said no, she hadn't heard anything.

Barrett read the passage once more to be sure.

Question (by Mr. Dickson): "Please continue, Ms. Keller. What did he say then?"

Answer (by Ms. Keller): "That's when he told me to forget I ever knew him unless I wanted to die on a LifeSpin like Lani Jefferson."

Question: "Would that be the exercise bike Lani was riding in her living room when she was killed?"

Answer: "Yes."

My God, thought Barrett, it all made sense. Not one mention of the brand name anywhere in the press. Only an admitted exercise freak like Amanda would have noticed something like that in the middle of killing someone. But why Jefferson? Had she killed Jefferson to get on the jury to ensure that the "animal" would be convicted? Or was it to gain publicity as a regular juror? Or both?

But then the mistrial had thwarted her ambitions and had required a new strategy.

Amanda Keller had become the key prosecution witness to a murder she had committed herself!

Had she killed Field, too, making the killings look like the "animal" had done it, then devising the threats to confirm it?

Then something else hit him, hit him harder than a defensive cornerback at full throttle: the image of Amanda's face when he was walking into chambers after the verdict. The "tongue-lashing" he had overheard and mentioned to the judge in chambers. The look he had seen on Keller's face when she was barking at Grace about her lost Hollywood career.

If looks could kill, he had said to John Hernandez. Shit!

He called Grace, got her answering machine. Was she out? Was the phone unplugged? Should he leave a message? He hung up and tried again. Was she all right? Was he being crazy? He was sweating now, the dizziness gone but his head throbbing.

He slammed the phone into its cradle and raced down the stairs.

As Barrett encouraged his Mustang up Market toward Seventh, then up Leavenworth toward Russian Hill, Amanda casually walked up from the sidewalk in front of Grace's apartment building and fell into step with an elderly gentleman walking up the stairs to the outside door. She had been waiting for someone to show up for nearly an hour.

"Allow me," said the old man.

"Well thank you, kind sir," she said, and preceded him

through the security door. She knew he would use the elevator, so she took the stairs, and within minutes she was standing in the deserted fourth-floor hallway, ringing the doorbell to 4B.

She tried to compose herself as she rehearsed in her mind every movement she would make once inside. She knew where everything was from the prep session they had done here. She prayed Grace would be alone so she wouldn't have to fire the gun. That would attract attention. She wished the gun had a silencer like they always had in the movies.

Grace was surprised to hear her doorbell ring. No one had buzzed from below. She looked through her peephole and groaned. Oh Christ, she thought, of all people! And just when I thought my day couldn't get any worse.

She opened the door, but kept the night chain latched.

"Hello, Grace," said Amanda, smiling. "I hope you don't mind. I was in the area and thought if you had a minute, well . . . I'd like to clear the air about Earl and me."

"I'm sorry, Amanda, but I'm very tired—"

"I understand, and I know how you must feel about me personally, but I'm feeling so stupid about all that's happened, the ridiculous things I've said to you."

"How did you get in?"

"Just as I was about to ring your apartment, a gentleman came along and we entered together. I'm sorry if I've been impolite barging in like this, but I'm returning to L.A. tonight and knew I wouldn't sleep a wink if I didn't explain what happened in court today."

"I'm simply not able to see you now, Amanda. Come by the office the next time you're in town."

"Please, Grace, let me come in, just for a minute. What I have to tell you will make sense out of all this mess I've caused. I know how you must feel about the way I've behaved, but you've become important to me and I can't go back to L.A. without your forgiveness; at least your understanding. There's something Earl wanted you to know, too. And it's rather drafty out here in the hallway."

Grace took in the woman's contrite face and almost felt sorry for her. She also had to admit a certain curiosity about Earl.

"Please," Amanda added. "I'm deeply troubled by all this."

Troubled is right, thought Grace, which is why I'm not letting you inside.

"Grace, I'm begging you. Just two minutes."

"I'll give you one minute," said Grace.

Grace released the night chain, but instead of inviting Amanda inside, she quickly stepped into the hallway and blocked the door. She had smelled Randy and Krys's dinner cooking in the apartment next door, only a shout away.

"All right, Grace, I'll be brief. But what I have to tell you about Earl is extremely confidential, so perhaps we could get out of this draft?"

"No," said Grace, "we can't. Whatever you have to say can be said out here."

Amanda's features suddenly contorted with anger. "I don't think so," she said, opening her handbag and removing the .38 snub-nose.

Grace gasped, not just at the gun now pointed at her heart but at the other object she had seen in the oversize handbag: a shard of glass with a patch of leather attached to the thick end.

"Not so much as a peep, Grace! Now let's go inside."

"My God!" murmured Grace. *"You?"*

At the main entryway downstairs, Barrett pushed the buzzer to apartment 4B, "G. Harris."

No answer. He pushed it again. And again. She was probably not home yet or maybe in the shower. He suddenly felt ridiculous standing there: Knight-errant Dickson to the rescue without a distressed maiden in sight. He started back toward his car, then shook his head in frustration and began pushing buttons up and down the brass plate.

"Now what?" said Grace in a tone that belied her fear.

"I really did come to tell you something, Grace," said Amanda, the gun leveled at the smaller woman. "First, you'll be happy to know that your cruelty has cost me my role in *Thursday's Child—*"

Grace smiled despite the circumstances.

"You think that's *funny?*"

"No, I think it's absurd," said Grace. "You stand there

whining about Hollywood after testifying against a man charged with murders *you* committed?"

"That brings up the second reason I came up here. Let's move inside, Grace. It's time for Elliot Ashford to take revenge on another prosecutor who tried to put him on death row."

Grace didn't move. "Nobody will believe you this time, Amanda. Let me get you some help."

Amanda let out a humorless laugh. "*You* get *me* some help? That's good, but the last time I checked, I was the one with the gun here. Now get inside!"

"It won't work," said Grace.

"Why not?" said Amanda.

"Ashford's modus operandi," said Grace, eyeing the gun. "He doesn't shoot people, right?"

"The gun was just to make sure I got inside," said Amanda, smiling again. "Mr. Ashford's standard weapon of choice is right here in my handbag."

"Well," said Grace, silently pulling the door shut behind her. "Mr. Ashford's going to have to do it right out here in the hallway. Forgive my lack of hospitality, Amanda, but I seem to have locked us out."

Grace thought she heard a buzzer, or was it coming from next door?

Amanda's calm expression vanished. Her lips tightened against her bared teeth.

"Open it, you little bitch!" she whispered, and hit Grace hard across the face with the pistol. "And no more talk. You are irritating me. STOP IT!"

Grace sagged against the door, holding her jaw. She started to speak, but was hardly able to breathe. She knew she had to keep talking somehow.

"I'm sorry, Amanda," she gasped. "Calm down, okay? I'll stop. What do you want me to stop?"

Grace knew she was babbling, but she had no protection now but words.

"Open the door, damn it!" snapped Amanda. "Now!"

"I have no key, Amanda," said Grace, opening her bathrobe pockets. "But listen to me . . . it's not too late, let me help you . . ."

"Help me?" Amanda sneered. "I think we've been through that."

Grace tried to control her fear, but the pain in her jaw and Amanda's rage was engulfing her.

"Amanda, please . . ."

"*Stop it!*" Amanda snapped in a hushed but intense tone. "You want it right out here then, Gracie? Okay, why not?"

As Amanda spoke, she lowered the handbag to the floor. Neither her eyes nor the point of the gun left Grace's face. Then, dropping into a crouch, she deftly grabbed the make-shift leather handle at the thick end of the glass shard with her free hand.

Grace tried to slide sideways, but Amanda quickly rose and jammed the barrel of the .38 into Grace's throat, hard up under her chin. She placed the glass fragment between her teeth, then ripped Grace's robe open, exposing her bare breasts.

"First, the ritual torture to those nice little tits. Ashford's trademark, right?"

Grace instinctively covered her breasts and felt a sharp pain as the point of the shard pierced the skin on one of her hands.

"Drop your goddamn hands, child," whispered Amanda, "or I swear I'll pull the trigger! And remember, one scream, even a peep, and a bullet goes right into your brain!"

Grace obeyed, vaguely aware of blood drenching her white robe. The shard must have struck a vein in the back of her hand.

Though her chin was thrust upward by the cold barrel of the .38, Grace helplessly watched Amanda's hand as she guided the glass lance toward her left breast. Then came the searing pain as one, then another wound was opened by Amanda's shallow, piercing thrusts. Grace's scream of agony was cut off by the hard point of the gun jammed deep into her throat.

"Please don't do this, Amanda," she gasped, fighting to remain conscious from the blow to her head and the pain from the punctures. It was her only hope now. "We can . . . work this out."

But Amanda wasn't listening. "I didn't get to do this to Jefferson while she was conscious. Had to nail her right away. Same with Earl. This is interesting."

Grace felt as if the gun jammed into her neck was the

only thing keeping her on her feet now, for her legs had gone limp under her.

"Enough with the foreplay," said Amanda, and through half-closed eyes, Grace saw the point of the deadly icicle of glass launched toward her throat.

"Amanda, no—"

"*Grace!*" Barrett shouted as he hit the top of the stairs at the end of the hall and began racing toward the two women. He saw Amanda look toward him and saw Grace grab for the gun as she deflected the glass shard.

But Amanda was too powerful and pinned her to the wall with her left forearm, then calmly steadied her right hand on that same forearm and said: "Hold it right there, big boy—this gun is loaded."

But Barrett barely hesitated before continuing his suicidal charge down the hall.

The shot rang out and Barrett felt the first bullet hit him in the shoulder, but he staggered forward, zigzagging like they had taught him in the army. Less than twenty-five feet separated them now as he saw Grace bobbing and weaving under the red-tinted piece of glass.

And Amanda, leveling the gun straight at him again.

She fired off two more rounds and Barrett felt the first as it shattered his sternum. The force of it knocked him off balance for a step or two and he heard himself howl in pain as he resumed his charge, bellowing maniacally now, arms wildly flailing the air, as a fifth shot buried itself somewhere in his stomach. That leaves only one left in the chamber, he thought, but only ten feet separated them and the barrel, looking as big as a cannon now, was pointed directly at his face.

But Amanda never got the last shot off. He was on her now and all three of them hit the floor with Amanda on the bottom. He pinned her arms and saw that Grace had struggled to her knees. He was amazed at Amanda's strength, and was relieved to see Grace chopping at Amanda's arm and wrist with the side of her hand. The shard finally fell from Amanda's fingers, aided by a head butt from Barrett that KO'd Amanda—and nearly himself as well.

Krys peeked out cautiously from next door and curious neighbors from other floors were peering out of the stairwell. Police Communications on the fifth floor of the Hall of Justice received three 911 calls in the next five minutes.

After Amanda had been taken away, Barrett lay back on the floor, woozy, his head cradled in Grace's lap, a police attendant standing anxiously nearby.

"You okay?" he said.

"I'm fine," she said. "Just be quiet now. An ambulance is on the way."

"This . . . cinches it," he said. "I'm . . . getting into another line of work."

"Don't talk, big guy."

"Guess Amanda didn't appreciate my cross-examination."

"I could have shot you myself during that cross-examination."

"That good, huh?"

"That good. Now relax. The medics are on the way."

"Churchill . . . summed it up pretty well."

"About democracy?"

"No," gasped Barrett, "when he said . . . there is nothing more exhilarating . . . than being shot at without result."

Grace shook her head and held him closer. "It was not entirely without result, dear Barrett," she whispered. "You are hurt. Badly."

"You should talk. You're bleeding all over my blood."

"Hush."

"He did it, Grace," Barrett whispered. "That's one of the things I came up to tell you."

"Churchill? I doubt it," Grace said. "He would have used the navy."

"Seriously. Ashford did it."

"No, dear, Amanda did it. She admitted it to me."

"Field and Jefferson. But it was Ashford . . . Ashford killed Lara."

Grace clamped her eyes shut against the words and Barrett felt a shudder pass through her.

"I'm sorry, Grace. Look, we're not mind readers; just lawyers doing our job."

"Did we 'do our job,' Barrett?" said Grace, looking down at him with eyes so anguished Barrett had to look away. "Did we really? If I had done my job, a murderer would be behind bars now."

Barrett tried to find the right words, but all he could think about was his stupidity in telling her about Ashford, particularly at this particular moment.

"Listen, Grace, based on what we knew . . . hell, we thought we were doing the right thing. Sometimes . . . maybe you just have to do the best you can . . . then accept the consequences."

Disconsolate, Grace shook her head and said nothing.

"You did do the right thing, Grace; even I can see that now. And for whatever consolation it is . . . Ashford will probably be dead from Huntington's sooner than he would have been executed by the state. Besides, I'm the one to blame—"

Barrett grimaced and arched his back as the burning ache in his stomach merged with the pain from his shattered sternum.

"Hush, Barrett."

"I was . . . completely taken in by the bastard, Grace."

"And I by the bitch," said Grace, trying to smile. "So now be quiet while I think of how to thank you for saving my life."

"That one's easy. Just stay right here in San Francisco. The city needs you. I . . . need you, too."

Grace managed to smile and said, "Now please, dear Barrett, be quiet for once in your life."

He felt Grace's hand on his clammy forehead, was vaguely aware that her hand was red with blood, whose he could not tell. He heard someone trying to get her to lie down. Felt darkness crowding in on him.

"There was another thing I came up here to tell you . . ."

He heard the distant wail of a siren, the closer sound of a dog responding. His voice had trailed off into a dream in which he was back in Vietnam, heading a patrol near Pleiku, looking through the stubble of burnt grass for a lost finger.

And this time he found it.

62

A faint trace of color had crept into Barrett Dickson's face as he lay confined for a second day in Ralph K. Davies Medical Center's intensive care unit following surgery for repair of his sternum and removal of a bullet that had barely missed his liver. A third bullet had passed through the flesh of his shoulder.

His color improved even more as he realized that Grace Harris, a bandage on her head from the pistol-whipping, was at his side, holding his hand, and that Leviticus Heywood was pushing his way into the ward.

"Jesus, Bear, can't I go home for an hour or two without you getting your ass shot up? Oh, excuse me, Ms. Harris."

Barrett smiled weakly at his friend. "Fortunately, it was nothing so important as my ass," he whispered, then turned to Grace. "Lev knows that's where I keep my head buried most the time."

Before Grace could formally introduce herself, a nurse with a young intern in tow caught up with Lev and insisted upon his immediate departure.

"Come back tomorrow," the irate nurse told him. "I'm throwing him out of my ward at 8:00 A.M. He'll be somebody else's problem then and you'll be welcome to him."

"Don't get Nurse Ratched pissed off, Lev," said Barrett weakly. "I've got to live with her one more night after you've reached the safety of the streets."

The nurse offered Barrett a good-natured raised fist and motioned again for Lev to follow her out.

"Okay," said Leviticus, his hands raised in surrender. "I'm gone. Sorry I wasn't there to protect you, Bear." He then glanced at the nurse and added, "And can't stay to protect you now that you really need it."

After Lev had allowed himself to be escorted out of the

ward, Grace told him that Caldwell & Shaw had arranged
for him to be moved into a large private room tomorrow.
Mike Reasoner had tried to get in to tell him that Winston
Cray had stepped aside early so that Mike could be elected
to join the executive committee without delay. On a motion
made by Cray to the full partnership, Mike had also been
elected as the firm's presiding partner. Mike told her that
Wilmer would remain on the committee to serve out his
term, but a change back to the professionalism and civility
of the past was, according to Mike, "blowing in the wind."

Barrett grunted with satisfaction. "Good for Mike," he
said.

"Good for you, Barrett," said Grace. "Mike also wanted
me to tell you that the doctors have given Nancy at least
ten more years, to match the extension you've won for
him."

"Now *that's* good news," said Barrett.

"There's more. A corner office is ready for you as soon
as you're able to return to C&S."

Barrett laughed, then grimaced in pain. "Don't make me
laugh," he told her.

"It's no joke. They want you back."

"In their dreams."

"Me too."

"They want you, too?"

"*I* want *you* back," she said. "On your feet." Then she
gave him an enigmatic, half-lidded, seductive look that excited him despite the effects of the morphine dripping into
his right arm, and added, "Or off your feet for that matter."

"Talk like that makes for a swift recovery," he said, taking her hand again. "Now say you're not leaving San
Francisco."

"Okay. You're not leaving San Francisco."

"Please, it really hurts to laugh."

"I'm not going anywhere, Bear."

"Good. There's somebody I want you to meet. His name
is Jared Dickson."

"Your son?"

Barrett smiled. "I hired Leviticus to find him. He's flying
in from New Zealand and will be here tomorrow. He thinks
I'm hurt, so play along."

"That's wonderful, Barrett! When can I meet him?"

"Soon. He and I have some catching up to do first. Some fence-mending."

Grace paused a beat. "I hope ours is in good repair."

"I hope ours no longer exists."

Grace looked at her clasped hands. "I've been a bit withdrawn since the verdict. I guess flouting all the rules doesn't come easy to a rabbi's daughter, especially when it results in the bad guy getting off. Anyway, thinking about how easily one or both of us could have been killed that night somehow put things in perspective. Forgive me, Bear?"

"Your request is under submission, counselor. Which reminds me, I never finished telling you the other thing."

"What other thing?"

Barrett yawned. "The other thing I wanted to tell you that night."

"Before you passed out on me."

"Yeah . . . well . . . it wasn't out of boredom," he said, then closed his eyes and fell asleep.

As the facts emerged during the following week, Grace, her relatively superficial cuts bandaged and healing, was besieged by requests to run in the special June election to fill Earl Field's office. Her bravery during the attack by Keller was portrayed in the press as "heroic" and "beyond courage." The *National Law Journal* described her as the "new paradigm of prosecutors—tough but temperate, fearless but flexible." Grace mused at the irony. She had conspired with a defense lawyer to set his guilty client free and for that had become everybody's choice for D.A. Everybody's but her own. She couldn't convince herself she deserved it.

Still, there was no stopping it now. What had started as a quiet women's movement had become a tidal wave of national support, fed by newspaper and magazine articles that trumpeted her track record of courtroom victories and community commitment. *People* magazine picked up on rumors of a romantic angle involving her trial opponent, a man who had helped her trap, then vanquish the murderess Keller. The Bar Association wanted to run a plebiscite on the candidates for D.A. but could find no one of repute willing to run against her.

Grace tried not to take it too seriously, but when her

mother called to say she was proud of her baby, Grace burst into tears despite herself. "Your father is praying for you, dear," her mother added, then whispered, "I heard him tell a friend on the phone that you were going to be the Attorney General of San Francisco."

"Tell him . . ." said Grace, laughing and choking back more tears, "tell him I'm proud of him, too."

Jack Klegg, sensitive as always to the direction of the wind of public opinion—and to the skeleton in his own closet—shocked Grace by announcing his support for her candidacy.

Wednesday night, as the groundswell continued, Grace drove across the Bay Bridge to Spenger's with Aaron to renew their traditional weekly dinner together.

"I know you've felt gypped by having no father and a working mother," she told him after they had shared a beer. "I need to know how you would feel if I ran for the D.A. job. If I won, it would demand even more of my time, and I won't run if I don't have your support."

Aaron stared pensively into her eyes, then reached over and took a swig from Grace's beer glass. "You've already got a ton of support, Mom, and I can't even vote."

"You know what I mean. Can you put up with being ignored even more than you have been?"

Aaron sat erect, then reached across and covered her hand with his. She was amazed at how large his hand was, how mature he seemed. "If you can keep putting up with a brat of a son who's violated every law of the Torah," he said, meeting her gaze with steady eyes that reminded her more of her father's than of his.

She nodded, and was relieved when he smiled and added, "And who's been a full-blown pain in the ass for the past three years."

63

Grace sat outside at Sam's in Tiburon, warming her hands with an Irish coffee and watching a handful of sailboats bravely venturing out of the San Francisco yacht club, the norwesterly wind at their backs. Barrett came lumbering up to her table, late as usual and carrying a dozen rosebuds.

"For you, madame," he said with an awkward flourish.

"They're beautiful, Bear, and they're just opening up."

Barrett nodded. "I noticed," he said, and sat down beside her.

"What inspired this romantic gesture?"

He smiled libidinously. "I enjoyed last night."

"Oh, that," she said, blushing. "The third impulsive act of my life."

"Don't forget the fourth," he said.

She slapped him playfully on the arm.

"Have you thought about what we talked about earlier last night?" Grace asked.

"About me accepting Doug Young's offer of partnership?"

She nodded. "He's good and he's ethical and has a solid criminal defense practice. Undeserved though it may be, the whole world also seems to be pounding on your door again. You'd be good together."

"I don't know," said Barrett, rubbing the back of his neck. "I'm not sure. I was thinking of applying for a job as your campaign manager instead. But I don't think you even need one."

"I think we were talking about your career, not mine."

"I love the *National Law Journal* story," he said, ignoring her remark. "Called you 'fearless but flexible.' "

"You know better."

"Words like flexibility could kill your Iron Maiden reputation."

"And also my stammer by the way. At least for now."

"I've noticed that, too."

"So are you going in with Doug?"

"I want to, but there's one thing I'm not quite sure about."

"Are we back to the God complex? The fallibility of the justice system? The grandeur and mystique of peddling real estate?"

Barrett smiled and shook his head. "Nah. The Dickson Curse is dead and my problem with the justice system was that I expected it to be perfect. That's too heavy a burden to put on anything that involves imperfect people."

Grace put a hand on her hip. "Excuse me?"

Barrett smiled and said, "Except for you, of course, dear. Any system that produces someone like you can't be all bad."

"Then what's the thing you're not sure about?"

Barrett reached over and took her hand.

"I'm not sure it's a good idea to have two lawyers in one family."

Grace looked up and saw the confirmation in his eyes. She took his hand in hers and kissed it.

"If that was a proposal, Barrett Dickson," she said, "I accept."

He said, "You realize we're talking about a life sentence here?"

She felt the tears coming then, couldn't stop them. "It's the only deal I'll make with you, counselor," she said. "Now, let's get out of here."

EPILOGUE

As Amanda Keller was transported under heavy guard to the van that would return her to the Fontera Prison for Women the day after her sentencing to life without the possibility of parole, she heard it—softly at first, then louder as she approached the van.

It was a crowd numbering in the hundreds, many of them shouting, "Aman-da, Aman-da, Aman-da!"

Someone had breached security and the press was all over the place. She tried to wave to them as she heard the van's rear steel door swing open with a squeal and mounted the first step leading up into the van. As she reached the second step, she shielded her eyes from the afternoon sun and saw them then, saw all of them, heard them chanting her name. Some carried "Free Amanda" signs; others carried placards that decried child abuse. Most were women. Cameras everywhere.

Newspapers from around the world had covered the sentencing hearing the previous day and many had quoted Amanda on their front pages.

"I'm not insane," she had insisted to the judge. "In fact, I've never felt better. Really. It *is* too bad about those people who died, but in a way you could say it was self-defense."

"Self-defense?" the judge had said.

"Killing them saved my life, Judge. *Gave* me life, actually, empowered me. Made me into a whole person. The irony is now that I'm finally a whole person, you might have to kill me. Makes perfect sense, doesn't it?"

At this point, the judge had again urged the defendant to cooperate with counsel, accept further testing, and plead insanity, but Amanda had looked offended and said, "I'm quite all right, Judge. For the first time in my life I have total clarity, though I'll admit there's a hazy ring around it sometimes, like the moon in winter."

While spectators had exchanged glances over this, the judge asked her if she was ready to be sentenced. She shrugged and asked him what he could do to her that would be worse than having a father who had stolen her innocence, a husband who had stolen her career, and a mother who had stolen her mind before it was old enough to discover itself.

Before the judge could manage a response, she added that if he had decided to sentence her to death, she'd just have to live with it—then broke out in raucous laughter.

But no one was laughing today as Amanda ascended the top step of the van that would return her to Fontera. A crescendo of solemn enthusiasm greeted her, the signs held high, the voices shouting her name as one, louder than ever.

"Aman-*da*, Aman-*da*, Aman-*da!*"

Amanda looked out at them, a quizzical half smile on her pale face. She glanced around quickly and suddenly realized how poor the lighting would be for the photographers. *Oh, well . . .*

She wet her lips and gave the whirring cameras her best look, the perfect tilt of her head, chin up, kid. Chin up.

"Aman-da, Aman-da!" they shouted.

She waved again as best she could with the damned manacles on, and reveled in the warmth, the enthusiasm of the crowd; the fame that could never be taken from her now. Tomorrow, she would read in the *Chronicle* that she had, for a third time, been a participant in a high-profile murder case. But this time, not just as an alternate juror, not even as a key witness. Both important, but only featured roles.

This time she had unmistakably been the *star*.

As guards beckoned her to enter the van, she gave the cameras and on-lookers what she knew they had come for: her extraordinary smile.

Then she gave them something else, something nobody had ever seen: tears, real tears, euphoric tears streaming down radiant cheeks. Amanda smiled again and raised her manacled hands high above her head, one fist clenched in the power salute, the other showing two extended fingers.

Victory.